JESSIE FORD

Her millions of devoted fans already know her from her bestselling novel *Love, Remember Me.*

Now, in A DIFFERENT BREED, author Jessie Ford proves, once again, her talents for depicting another time and place, for reaching into the souls of men and women, for probing the hearts and minds of those who love, who survive, who show great courage in unknown times....

Please turn the page to meet the people who dared to be

A DIFFERENT BREED

HONEY GREER RADCLIFFE. Her husband dead, her money gone, her beloved plantation gone to ruins, she is eager to leave North Carolina and forge a new life out West as a healer, as a yet unheard of woman doctor....

CAMERON WOLFE. An able trail guide hired to guide Honey out West, he is in constant struggle between his Apache upbringing and the civilized world he has returned to. Though he and Honey are immediately attracted to one another, they are equally repelled by their different ways of life....

SHAHAR. A beautiful African woman with strong psychic powers, she is Honey's former slave and confidante. She accompanies Honey on her long trek west, insisting as the journey continues that Honey and Cameron are soulmates....

COYOTE. A fierce Apache warrior, he is filled with hatred for Cameron Wolfe. Intent on revenge, he will not rest until he has brought Cameron to his knees....

NOLLIE. As Shahar's daughter, she has grown up with Honey on the family plantation. She too accompanies Honey on the trail, determined to make a new life of freedom for herself out West—at any price....

NATHAN RADCLIFFE. He was Honey's husband in long ago times, when belles were Southern and soft-spoken—and men who were arrogant and reckless were thought to be merely charming....

Also by Jessie Ford
Published by Ballantine Books:

BURNING WOMAN
SEARCHING
LOVE REMEMBER ME

A DIFFERENT BREED

Jessie Ford

BALLANTINE BOOKS • NEW YORK

Grateful acknowledgment is made to The University of Arizona Press for permission to reprint excerpts from the book IN THE DAYS OF VICTORIO: RECOLLECTIONS OF A WARM SPRINGS APACHE by Eve Ball. Copyright © 1970.

Library of Congress Catalog Card Number: 87-91383

ISBN 0-345-33170-2

Printed in Canada

First Edition: April 1988

*To my sons Greg and Chris,
who have the spirit.*

ACKNOWLEDGMENTS

On more than one occasion I've heard it said that writing is the loneliest profession in the world; a fact that is made less so for me by my agent Diane Cleaver, who has believed in me from the start; by my editor, mentor, and friend Cheryl Woodruff; by Nancy Holder and my husband Ted, who often listen and support me. And when, as we say in our house, "the really world" has intruded on my work, there have been veritable angels: Sharon and Rob Batcher, Gary Smalley, Kasey Papera, and Gayle Baker. To you all, my gratitude.

Nothing worth doing is completed in our lifetime; therefore, we must be saved by hope. Nothing true or beautiful or good makes sense in any immediate context of history; therefore, we must be saved by faith. Nothing we do, however virtuous, can be accomplished alone; therefore, we are saved by love. No virtuous act is quite as virtuous from the standpoint of our friend or foe as from our standpoint. Therefore, we must be saved by the final form of love which is forgiveness.

Reinhold Niebuhr—
The Irony of American History

PROLOGUE

A baby in each slender arm, Mammy Shahar settled on the summer swing in the gallery outside the nursery. Fed, bathed, and tired, both girls were crooning for their lullaby. Olivia rubbed an eye with a plump fist and put her head on her mother's shoulder as Honey pitched her body softly against Mammy's hip, urging her to begin. Without this ritual, the warm night air filled with heartrending wails no one within earshot could ignore. If separated before they were sound asleep, the girls created an equal cacophony. Every evening, Mammy's gentle song, in time with the slowly moving swing, ushered in the nighttime for listeners and believers alike.

> *Lord be watchin'*
> *Girls a' fussin';*
> *Babies close they eyes.*
>
> *Night be callin',*
> *Stars be fallin';*
> *Babies close they eyes.*
>
> *Souls be nearin';*
> *No need fearin';*
> *Babies close they eyes.*
>
> *Heartbeats hummin';*
> *Dreams be comin';*
> *Babies close they eyes.*
>
> *No use fleein'*
> *What I seein';*
> *Babies close they eyes.*
>
>
> *Blood be spillin';*
> *Hate be villain;*
> *Babies close they eyes.*

1

Dead be brothers;
Heartbroken mothers;
Babies close they eyes.

All that hatin'
Pleasin' Satan;
Babies close they eyes.

Mammy's seein'
Love be freein';
Babies close they eyes.

To much danger
We be strangers;
Babies close they eyes.

World be needin'
Diff'ren' breedin';
Babies close they eyes.

Han's together;
Hearts together;
Babies close they eyes.

Love be only
One kine color;
Babies close they eyes.

Truth go beggin';
Hate be reignin';
Babies close they eyes.

Love's forgivin'
All that's killin';
Babies close they eyes.

Souls returnin',
Past be churnin';
Babies close they eyes.

Man be comin',
No use runnin';
Babies close they eyes.

No more glances;
No more chances;
Babies close they eyes.

Can't be stallin',
Lord be callin';
Babies close they eyes.

Tell you, fleein'
won' be freein';
Babies close they eyes.

But, Lord knows,
Seein's not believin',
When peoples close they eyes.

"Jus' nonsense," Shahar said when pressed about the meaning of her song. "Jus' loose words rattlin' in my head at day's end. Babies' soothed by it, and tha's what matters." Her answer usually satisfied, but if one heard Mammy's song often, the verses varying according to mood, or got to know her better, one began to wonder if it was simply "jus' nonsense" as she insisted.

PART ONE

Dreams

I have spread my dreams under your feet;
Tread softly because you tread on my dreams.

William Butler Yeats—"Cloths of Heaven"

CHAPTER ONE

Arizona Territory
March 1865

Cameron Wolfe collected Trevor Jefferson's letter shortly after arriving in the broad desert valley of Tucson but didn't bother reading it until he was neck deep in steaming water in one of Hattie Mullins's bathtubs.

He had been on the trail for several days, and the warm Arizona Territory sun was a welcome balm after the weeks of cold rain he had encountered traveling down the center of California and east through the mountains. Ringed by rolling foothills and mountains in the distance, Tucson was a place where Cameron felt truly comfortable. He loved the usually dry landscape of green cacti and bushy greasewood shrubs, even more after it rained, when it was dotted with yellow, white, and blue flowers.

During the War between the States, Tucson had been almost abandoned. But with the Southern defeat in sight, Cameron imagined Tucson would once again become a thriving watering hole for a multitude of outcasts, most of whom were on their way somewhere else.

Hattie provided Cameron with her largest tub and the bathing enclosure with the most privacy. At first Cameron lay back leisurely in the hot water and let the heat soothe taut muscles as he smoked one of the fine cigars Hattie said she kept expressly for his pleasure. Cameron did not believe her but relished the aromatic smoke anyway. Enjoying himself, he closed his eyes and relaxed, content with the world—and with himself for the moment.

He could easily have fallen asleep in the soothing water, but his reverie was broken by Hattie, who came up quietly behind him and began kneading his shoulders and neck with the skill of an experienced masseuse. He groaned with pleasure as her fingers relieved muscles that were tight with tension, and leaned forward to let her continue her artful stroking down the length of his lean, muscular back. "I've missed you, Mrs. Mullins."

"Well, I confess I've not been pinin' much for you," Hattie teased, wanting him to be clear on how it actually stood between

7

them. Although quite immune to gossip, Hattie was not eager to
have another lover's jealousy provoke a second murder, even
though the first incident had seemed only to enhance her reputation in Tucson.

"But I suppose I'm glad enough you've come back," she admitted, then kissed him on the jaw just below his right ear. She
had never known a more heroic figure of a man than Cameron
Wolfe. He was tall, impressively muscled, perfectly made; by
contrast, most men seemed pale imitations. His chiseled features
would make him handsome by anyone's reckoning, Hattie
thought; his clear, vividly blue eyes were a test to a good
woman's virtue. His prowess and daring were at least as impressive as his physical appearance.

Her eyes dancing, Hattie dried her hands and forearms on her
apron and faced Cameron with a grin, then bent to receive his full
and hungry kiss. When she stood up again, Hattie ran her fingers
through her thick mane of auburn hair, arranged her curls with an
air of propriety, and tried to ignore how easily he aroused her.
"What's your letter say? And who's to know you'd be passin' this
way and be familiar with me?" she snapped at Cameron saucily.

"Hattie's baths are known worldwide."

"Then I should be a rich woman."

"You could make your fortune in Sacramento or San Francisco
any time."

It was a tempting suggestion and Cameron Wolfe was an appealing devil of a man, but Hattie thrived in Tucson's dry air. "I
won't ever leave the desert, and you know it. Not even for yourself," she said, staring into those intense blue eyes.

"You won't have a better offer all day."

"We'll see, dearie," she said before hurrying to disappear
around the partition. "There's a whiskey beside you," she called
over her shoulder.

Grateful, Cameron reached for the drink and then studied the
weighty envelope's audacious decorative script. He sipped his
whiskey slowly and opened the letter, pausing to reflect on both
the sender and the startling amount of paper money enclosed.
Cameron estimated that there was easily two thousand dollars in
the envelope. Trevor Jefferson was never one to be overgenerous,
and with great curiosity he read the letter drafted on heavy bond.
Whatever Trevor wanted had to be, at least in his mind, urgent
and something of a risk.

3rd of February, 1865

My Dear Mr. Wolfe,

As I am certain you will at some time arrive at Mrs. Mullins's, I am taking the liberty of posting my correspondence to you through her. I regret to inform you that I am unable to meet you in Independence as originally planned. Nor can I afford at this time to wait any longer to travel to that city with my niece. Therefore, I make an urgent appeal for you to come at once to Greerfield, North Carolina. I have enclosed an amount of money which should, I hope, adequately recompense you for any inconvenience the added distance and duties may cause.

As you already are aware, I journeyed to North Carolina with the hope of persuading my niece, Honey Jefferson Greer, to return with me to California, where she can begin a new life away from a land ravaged by war. However, upon my arrival at Greerfield, I learned that only days before I arrived, she had married Lt. Col. Nathan Radcliffe, CSA, a man of excellent reputation, whose family I have known a good many years.

I, of course, then offered refuge to both my niece and her husband, but a few days following, we were informed of Colonel Radcliffe's death in the aftermath of the siege of Ft. Fisher of January fifteenth. This news rendered the young widow very ill, which you can appreciate. When I felt it seemly, I tendered my offer of refuge again, and Mrs. Radcliffe accepted gratefully, but, due to the delicate state of her emotions, shall not be fit to make the journey West on the schedule originally planned.

Wanting to be of solace to my dear niece, I have remained at Greerfield far longer than I intended, and now, with very pressing matters to conclude, I am forced to leave North Carolina. I cannot predict exactly when my business will be at an end, nor can Mrs. Radcliffe promise precisely when her health will permit her to undertake the journey West. I must return to Sacramento when my affairs in Richmond are settled, and expect to be at home in California before your party embarks westward.

Certainly, I imagine, by early spring, Mrs. Radcliffe shall be in a better frame of mind and ready to travel. Mrs. Radcliffe will be accompanied by two of the family's negroes, Shahar Daniels and her daughter Olivia, without whose company, my niece would not attempt the journey. Anticipating your able assistance, Mr. Wolfe, I shall expect your party to be on the road West before May.

In the event you are in need of more money to make the journey comfortable for my niece, do not hesitate to contact me in Sacramento. Additional funds will be available at my bankers in St. Louis *should you need them. Telegraph me in Richmond, Virginia, of your agreement to the task.*

Confident that you shall be able to provide this additional assistance to my lovely and gracious niece, who has suffered more than her due in this long and unfortunate war, I remain indebted to you.

Trevor Meade Jefferson

Cameron refolded the letter and returned it to its envelope, which he laid carefully on the dry rug next to the bathtub. He found Trevor's request as extraordinary as his apparent confidence that Cameron would comply with whatever he requested provided that the sum of money involved was large enough. Trevor's arrogance in assuming that any man could be bought for a price enraged Cameron. The attitude assumed that all men were without honor.

Fortunately, complying with Trevor Jefferson's latest request would not involve Cameron's honor but merely require a reordering of his plans; however, he did have sudden reservations about the basic wisdom of Trevor's niece journeying west. Cameron imagined Mrs. Radcliffe to be far too fragile for the rigors of the Santa Fe Trail, the hazards of which he was particularly familiar with.

For a period of years the Apache had maintained an agreed-on peaceful coexistence with the white eyes, but since the execution of Mangas Colorado in 1863, a treacherous act committed when the great Apache leader had come in under a flag of truce, the Apache were dedicated to revenging themselves for the numerous acts of betrayal by white eyes. The Apache had no reason to trust white eyes to live in Apacheria as honorable neighbors to the indian; therefore, all travel within their territory was risky. The route through Apacheria was, however, the route with which Cameron was most familiar, and certainly no routes west were without peril.

Originally, in planning to meet Trevor and his niece in Saint Louis and guide them west, Cameron had intended to provide them with as luxurious travel accommodations as could be obtained, but even with the most comfortable conveyances available, the journey would be a difficult endeavor at best.

Cameron had seen a photograph of Honey Greer taken the year before. In every other photograph he had ever seen, the subjects looked stern and forbidding, and while Honey Greer had obviously been ordered to square her shoulders and look sober, at first Cameron thought he detected the light of mischief in her eyes and the notion of a smile at the corners of her mouth. But in studying the photograph, he had realized he was mistaken. Undoubtedly, Honey Greer was irritatingly spoiled, passionless, and dull—as useless as all women of her class, her whims anticipated by a legion of slaves, admirers, or relatives eager to please her.

Cameron couldn't deny Mrs. Radcliffe's beauty—even for a white eyes. In the photograph, her light-colored hair and pale skin contrasted dramatically with a gown of some shimmering dark fabric; a delicate jeweled locket her only adornment. The hair pulled severely but becomingly from her face revealed regular features; the reasonable expanse of forehead suggested intelligence, and her brows were shapely and dark. Her lips were pleasantly full, indeed, sensuous; the ears were close to the head and delicately formed.

On viewing her photograph, Cameron wondered why she remained unmarried. At twenty-one years of age, she was elderly from the standpoint of a suitor. Perhaps an unpleasant temper... but, Cameron admitted to himself reluctantly, the daguerreotype belied such a possibility.

From Trevor's earlier descriptions of his niece, Cameron envisioned Honeysuckle Jefferson Greer as being as fragile as the flower for which she was named and hadn't relished shepherding such a woman safely across the continent even with her uncle accompanying her. Cameron had expected Trevor to bear the major burden of indulging Mrs. Radcliffe's whims on the long journey and did not for a moment relish the prospect of taking his place. He frowned at the prospect of the journey ahead, especially on the trail, where everyone was expected to pull his own weight. Cameron variously was a cowman, drover, rancher, and trail guide—*not* a wet nurse.

More to Cameron's liking would have been a robust and uniquely independent creature like Hattie Mullins. In his opinion, Hattie was the only type of woman who could be expected to thrive on the frontier. Certainly it was unlikely that Mrs. Honeysuckle Radcliffe enjoyed herself or indulged her passions as frankly as Hattie did.

The more Cameron dwelled on the prospect of assuming the role of Mrs. Radcliffe's guide and protector, the more Trevor's imperial attitude nettled him. Trevor's request sounded more a command than an entreaty, and while he owed Trevor at least a few favors, fulfilling this request exceeded all legitimate obligations.

Cameron and Trevor were not quite friends but were partners in a number of enterprises that had furthered Trevor's interests and been instrumental in Cameron's success in California. Trevor had been fair in their dealings but had always maintained an air of superiority that at times grated on Cameron's pride. As one of Trevor Jefferson's *vaqueros*, Cameron expected nothing more. But later, as headman and drover and then as an independent rancher himself, and a man of means by most people's standards, Cameron expected more equal favor from the Southern gentleman who traded on his aristocratic origins for social and political gain.

Cameron decided to mull over his prospects a while longer. In fact, it would be a good idea to sleep on Trevor's proposal. He put his empty whiskey glass down, then sank beneath the surface of the water. When he emerged, he soaped his hair, then stood and lathered his body, aware only of how good it felt to remove the dust and sweat of the trail from his skin. The thought of not having to sleep on the ground at night but in a bed released a somewhat surprising revelation. "I'm more white eyes than Chiricahua now," Cameron muttered, uncertain exactly how that fact made him feel.

He toweled himself dry, remembering how not so long ago, much to the shock of his Saint Louis relatives, he had not been able to bring himself to sleep in a bed. Even now the mattress he slept on in his house near Sacramento lay on the floor, an oddity but a concession to living in the so-called civilized world.

Finally, dressed in the clean clothes Hattie kept on hand for him, Cameron felt his hunger acutely and successfully repressed all thoughts of the past. But full of Hattie's baked chicken, tamales, and coffee; sated by lovemaking; and subdued by the country's habit of a siesta in the midday heat, Cameron dozed and, as he did often, dreamed of another life; a life lived as an Apache, a life as relentlessly hard as the searching Arizona Territory sun. By comparison, he thought, every experience before or since had not been much of a hardship.

Long ago, his family murdered before his eyes on the trail to California, young Cameron Wolfe had expected to die, too. Instead, the nine-year-old from Saint Louis, who fought as fiercely as any indian warrior, had been bound and dragged away from the soul-searing scene of death. At first a slave of the Chiricahua Apache, Cameron had understood nothing of his captors. He knew only unreasoning grief and hatred. He never cried and swore to die before being disgraced, enduring all punishment inflicted for defiance with a bold, fixed countenance.

The Chiricahua acknowledged Cameron's bravery, indeed sparing his life when at nine years of age he was older than most male captives. Slowly, Cameron's need to survive replaced the need to defy, and he was educated in the ways of the fabled nomadic Chiricahua. He lived like an Apache, eventually thought like an Apache, and, except for his brown hair and blue eyes, appeared to be an Apache. His Apache name, which was never spoken aloud, meant "Fierce Enemy," and at eleven years of age, he was adopted by the band's chosen leader, Acha. All memory of a previous life, the one spent as a white boy, seemed to vanish.

Seven years later, when he was a man of eighteen, in a period of relative peace between white eyes and Apache, in circumstances impossible to foresee, Fierce Enemy tried to shed his Apache skin and return to the white eyes' world, only to discover himself a man caught between two worlds. He eventually carved out a life for himself on the western cattle trails among other men who were usually, one way or another, also exiles. A man of fierce pride, he grew used to his loneliness, in fact preferred it, allowing no one to diminish him with notions of superiority, to make him feel less than he was. Yet burning deep within him was the desire to fit in, to become an ordinary man.

But Cameron Wolfe was an extraordinary man, and after he left Saint Louis for the second time, all who met him sensed it—sometimes before they knew it for a fact.

CHAPTER TWO

"I give you my word you'll find Cameron Wolfe all one could desire in a guide across the continent, my dear," Trevor Jefferson had insisted more than once. "He's long on experience, short on palaver."

Honey conjured a vision of a coarse, trail-hardened ruffian, something straight from lurid newspaper accounts. Trevor promised that Cameron Wolfe was "difficult to know but without peer in the wide open spaces. On more than one occasion, I've seen his good sense avert disaster on the trail. Once, in a stampede, without thought to his own safety, I saw him go after an injured cowboy at a full gallop and, at the precise moment, lean out of the saddle and lift the fallen man from the ground. A simply amazing feat! Wolfe has the strength and stamina of three ordinary men."

Still, she was not soothed.

"Now, Honeysuckle, you just have to put your trust in your Uncle Trevor. Don't fret for even a second. We don't want any furrows on that beautiful young forehead of yours. Let me and Mammy and Mr. Wolfe handle everything. You just sit back and fan yourself like a proper Southern lady. Don't fill that pretty head of yours with any unnecessary thoughts."

Not comforted, Honey liked even less having Trevor speak to her so condescendingly, as if she were feeble-minded. The situation proved disconcerting enough to drive her to approach Shahar for the kind of help only she could provide.

Honey found Shahar in the dining room lighting the lamps before serving the evening meal. With supplies pitifully low, Shahar lit only one of six lamps on the carved rosewood sideboard and only two of twelve at the table. Honey fussed with the frayed lace at the cuff of her sleeve as she sought the slender dark negro woman's steady gaze with her own uncertain one. "I'm very ill at ease in spite of Uncle Trevor's oft-repeated assurances. I wish you'd apply to your Spirits for some sort of message about the wisdom of our venture."

Lighting the last lamp on the table, Shahar looked down at Honey serenely without any trace of the smile to which she was entitled at Honey's plea. She replied to Honey's anxious request with a slight nod, which Honey knew would be all she could expect for the time being.

"I do appreciate all Uncle Trevor is doing for us, but I'm very upset by the way he often speaks to me," Honey went on to complain. "You've heard how he talks—as though I weren't issued my fair ration of brains, or worse, as if I were too helpless to feed myself. I'm not used to having my concerns dismissed as if I were a nervous, tittering female. Father never treated me so badly—Dr. Greer was never one for treating females as if they were mentally inferior."

Shahar laughed. "You just make sure you remember the dead as they were. It's easy to recall only the good things when someone's passed on. Your memory's gettin' rusty."

"Why, Mammy, are you speaking ill of my daddy?"

"Never, child. Only you need to remember things clearer sometimes."

"Why, if my uncle has painted me badly to the man he's sent for, I'll be forced to ride all the way to California in an ambulance."

"Let the man get a good look at you, Honey Radcliffe. He might even have you pull the wagon."

"All right, Shahar, you've had your fun. Just don't you forget the favor I asked."

"No, ma'am. Not in a million years."

Shahar's remarks to Honey about her memory of her father stayed with Honey until she paused in her daily rush of duties. Thoughts of her father coupled with those of leaving Greerfield forever made Honey very melancholy. Honey remembered and revered her father, she believed, as he deserved: for being an exceptionally honorable, decent, and intelligent man, a worthy citizen of the state of North Carolina, a man sought after for his advice not only as the region's only physician but on matters of business pertaining to the efficient and economical use of one's properties—land and people. In the long run, one did not succeed if either was poorly managed.

Honey thought of herself as Dr. Greer's favorite child. She had had three older brothers of whom the doctor had reason to be proud, but only she had collected their father's widest smiles and fondest words. Not easily swayed in matters that disputed her opinion, Honey knew she often tried the doctor's patience. But with sound reason and charming wiles, Honey often won her father over to her point of view. But as Shahar had pointed out, Honey did not always have her way with Dr. Greer, and in truth had failed to triumph in the matter most dear to her.

Honey and her father had spent years in regular debate on the subject, yet Honey staunchly believed her victory was inevitable. Ultimately, Phillip Greer would be convinced that his only daughter should follow in his footsteps and become a doctor. In the end, she was shocked to learn Dr. Greer had never seriously considered such an outcome.

Truly bred gentlemen did not practice medicine; certainly, no female of any delicacy became a doctor. Nevertheless, Honey argued her case whenever she could. Her final defeat was painful and her memory of it, as Shahar had reminded her today, was covered with cobwebs. Honey now recalled her defeat as being as bitter as she thought Atlanta's fall to General Sherman must have been. In her last battle with her father on the subject, when she was sixteen, Honey had pulled out all the stops.

"Why are my needs so unimportant to you, Father? If I were Clay, or James, or Billy, you'd move mountains to see my request granted."

"But the very point is you are, my dear, my daughter, not a son."

This point of his argument had brought Honey close to tears, but she had bitten them back. "I'm surely as worthy as any of them."

"Dearest child, it is *not* a question of worth, and well you know it."

"But . . ."

"Don't interrupt me," Dr. Greer warned in the sternest voice he ever used with Honey. "You may not care again to hear what I have to say—and this is absolutely the *last* conversation we shall ever have on the subject—but the truth is, Honey, you are not fit to be a doctor: You are a female. You have no choice in the course you must take. A woman has a God-given destiny she cannot deny."

Honey's scowl was as stubborn and fierce as she could summon. "Father, I do not deny my destiny as a female. I only want to be a doctor also."

"You have already promised yourself to Nathan Radcliffe—and quite willingly, I thought."

Honey sighed. "Yes, *willingly*."

"No woman of true refinement aspires to be a doctor. Certainly, I can't see Nathan permitting himself to be the husband of a female doctor. Can you?"

Truthfully, she could not. Nathan Radcliffe was as desirable a husband as a woman could find but even more conventional in his thinking than her father. If he had known the extent to which she for years had helped in her father's surgery, he would have been horrified—and, Honey was sad to realize, possibly would consider her unfit to marry. Her own father had permitted her in his surgery reluctantly, only in situations of grave emergency, favoring her presence until he had begun to rely on his daughter as a nurse.

"If you were a doctor, who would be your patients? All considerations of delicacy aside, who would trust a woman?"

"Your patients trust me well enough as your nurse."

"You believe, therefore, that these same patients would accept you for their doctor?"

"Why wouldn't they?"

"Your reasoning fails to acknowledge elementary human nature."

"And?"

"Even common understanding holds all women inferior to men. They are weaker by their nature, more subject to emotion over reason. Who, then, sensibly, would submit his life to the judgment of a woman?"

"I am *not* inferior because I'm female!"

"My dear child, you cannot argue God's law."

Honey burned with fury for the unfairness of God, for the stupidity of men—even those whom she loved dearly. But she realized at last that on this subject at least Phillip Greer was immovable. No amount of logic or charm would move him.

She felt hot, well aware that her face was glowing a brilliant and unbecoming red. Behind her eyes, bitter tears of defeat ached to be released—the very proof of her inferior female emotions, she knew—and she would die before she gave her father the satisfaction of a demonstration of her woman's weakness. With the indestructible will she was famous for, Honey sat dry-eyed.

"You are a fine, intelligent girl, my darling child, soon to be the loveliest woman I know, as fine a specimen of womanhood as can be found on earth. You will honor Nathan Radcliffe as his wife. But you must learn your place in the scheme of things, as we all must. Your duty in life is decided. One day you will be the loving and obedient wife of the heir to one of North Carolina's most distinguished and wealthy planter families. As the Radcliffe heir, Nathan will be able to provide you with more than adequate support and a secure position in society. You might argue with me now, but as you mature to your fullest, you will forget all of this nonsense about becoming a doctor.

"I've discouraged you in this notion from the start, Honey. I only recently realized that you were serious." Phillip Greer smiled at himself. "I suppose I should have known it was more than a youthful fancy, given your sometimes willful inclinations for divergent thought and practice. I suppose a wiser father would have known you would not be so easily dissuaded."

Honey forced herself not to squirm under his upbraiding and

he continued almost as if he were amused. "I had hoped you
would grow to be more docile—for your own good, of course. It
does not serve a woman well to be too strong-natured. I don't
believe Nathan Radcliffe has in mind a willful wife. Do you?"

Honey took a deep breath, able to reply only with a shake of
her head.

"Above all else you will wish to please your husband. You
will honor your mother's memory by being a good wife to
Nathan. Blood will tell, Honey Greer. Learn to bend with grace
to me as you must with your husband." Phillip Greer finished
with a frown. "I wish no mistaking on your part, daughter. I will
entertain no further utterances from you on the subject of your
becoming a doctor. Otherwise, in the time you have left until you
go to the female college, I shall forbid you to continue to assist
me in my practice."

Honey's eyes widened. He had chosen her punishment well.

"And may you understand that I will *not* be cajoled. If you
defy me in this, there will not be one opportunity of appeal."

Honey felt her father's words as if they were blows. Under
duress, she blushed crimson, but her tears were gone. Like the
vanquished in a battle valiantly fought, she bore her defeat sto-
ically. "Yes, sir," she answered firmly.

He had won.

For days after her plea for help from Shahar's Spirits, Honey
watched Shahar withdraw little by little from the everyday world.
From years of experience, Honey knew exactly what the nearly
imperceptible changes in Shahar meant, while others, if they noticed the alteration of Mammy's behavior at all, would have said
that she was simply distracted. And heaven knew, there was
plenty to distract one these days!

Less attentive to the everyday world, Shahar was listening,
alert to signs and visions no one but those who were particularly
attuned could see. Chosen young, Shahar had an ability to divine
dreams and signs that had not waned but had intensified with the
years. Little by little, Shahar would be less with the visible world
and more and more in the hazy world beyond. Then, summoned,
she would not sleep but sit in her bed with her eyes open in a
trance or pass beyond sleep into a state where she was unreachable by means ordinary or extraordinary.

When she woke from these states, Shahar did not always share
her insights, but on this occasion she informed Honey straight-

away. The fact that it was the middle of the night did not faze her. She went directly to Honey's room and sat beside her on the bed. For a few minutes Shahar watched Phillip Greer's only remaining heir breathe easily and, for once in a long while, sleep peacefully. "Sleep soundly while you may, Honey Radcliffe," Shahar whispered, "for you're about to lose many a good night's sleep.

"The one I sang of all those years is about to show himself at your door." Shahar hummed a little of the so familiar lullaby. "Remember, Honey, what I said—'no use runnin' '—and you'll want to!" she whispered.

All these years I've been troubled. Now I see why. Mr. Nathan was never meant for you. That's why I never could be easy with him—even with your papa's determination for you children to wed. Shahar smiled down on Honey and stroked the graceful pale arm that lay outside the covers. Honey stirred in her sleep but did not wake. *Yes, yes, he'll be here shortly. I saw him plain as day, riding up to the gate with a string of dusty horses in tow. He looks to be maybe a little dangerous—a man you might not open the door to if you weren't expecting him. But this man will shine his blue eyes on you and take your will away—even though he's scowling. Yes, child, brooding as if he'd like to murder you. With as much to learn as you have, as much pain to pass through.*

The next day Shahar again seemed her usual alert, strong self. "I'm relieved this was only a brief excursion!" Honey said, but was annoyed by the anxiety Shahar's state had caused her, even though the woman's journey had been made at her specific request. "Thank the Lord, this time there wasn't much rattling and rumbling in empty rooms. I don't have patience to put up with such goings-on these days."

Yet when Shahar began to pronounce her visions, Honey cut her short. "Don't give me *every* detail," she snapped in a tone she used with other negroes but never with Shahar, whose essence she perceived as neither black nor white. "I only want to know, regardless of Trevor's instructions, whether I should allow Mr. Wolfe to set foot in my house."

"You've no choice. You must let him in."

"*Must?*" Honey said, but refrained from making any further comment that might display her skepticism. She had, after all—albeit in a moment of weakness—requested the communication. "Thank you, Shahar. That's all I care to know," she answered more civilly to the woman she regarded as mother, friend, and ally.

A part of Honey Radcliffe wanted to trust implicitly this message from beyond, but she had been weaned early from Mammy's lullabies and darky superstitions. Once Honey, the last Greer child, had left the nursery, Mammy was cautious not to indulge her "pagan instincts." At a certain age, Dr. Greer, the children's father and Shahar's master, could simply not tolerate such lapses for the sake of the children. But until he had made a point of eliminating the heretical from all conversations of religion, Honey's upbringing had been seasoned with spirits and a sense of other worlds mingled with the purely physical.

When Cameron Wolfe arrived, however, Honey regretted not having demanded all the details of Shahar's vision, and as she looked down from her window one morning on a man on horseback at the gate, dressed in buckskin and trailing a string of several horses, she could only imagine her fate in his hands to be a wretched one.

Cameron Wolfe sat erect and confident in the saddle and dismounted with an easy, fluid motion. When almost immediately he looked up in the direction of her window, she sensed that he saw her, although in the morning light it was impossible. As she gazed at him and as he seemed to gaze at her, Honey felt something disturbing and dark in the air that stood between them. She shivered yet boldly forced herself to go directly down to meet him.

At the second-floor landing, Honey encountered Shahar, her usual cool grace curiously ruffled, which intensified Honey's own alarm.

"He's arrived at last," Shahar announced, ecstatic.

"Yes, I saw him from my window." Honey touched the locket at her throat in a gesture of nervousness.

"It was exactly as I saw it." Shahar hugged Honey fiercely.

"One would think you didn't trust your visions," Honey accused as Shahar all but dragged her before the man who would be their guide on the journey west.

"Mr. Cameron Wolfe, just as promised," Shahar announced, and immediately retreated from the room, leaving Honey alone with him.

In that instant of first meeting, Honey felt as if her heart had suddenly expanded in her chest, and a lightness of being gave her the sense that her body was being lifted above the floor by an unseen pair of hands. Cameron Wolfe was at once strange and familiar—unsettling as no one else had ever been on first meeting. *Shahar! Shahar!* Honey's mind cried silently. *You have corrupted me.* But she forced herself to appear utterly calm. "Please sit down, Mr. Wolfe," she said coolly, receiving him in the library.

He turned slightly to face her more directly, and she was unable not to stare almost in rapture as a shaft of sunlight wafting in from high windows seemed to collect in his vibrant blue eyes, his deeply tanned face causing his eyes to seem especially clear and intriguing.

"We've been expecting you, of course," Honey said finally, then was all at once at a loss for words. He had a few days' growth of beard and was, she guessed, a little weary, an observation that gave her needed inspiration. "Perhaps you'd care for something to eat before we begin a discussion of our plans for travel."

"I would, thank you."

He had instantly recognized the stunning, fair Honey Greer from Trevor's photograph. Nevertheless, Cameron Wolfe was startled by the color of her pale eyes, eyes that he had expected to be blue but that were instead an arresting golden shade of brown. He was caught off guard, unexpectedly drawn to her beauty, a fact he would have vehemently denied. *Too long in the saddle*, he noted mentally, dismissing his piercing but purely physical response.

"Has traveling been difficult with the conclusion of the war?" Honey wondered as she pulled a bell to summon Nollie Daniels, who would fix him a late breakfast.

"Hasn't been easy."

"The Yankees did all they could to devastate us," Honey answered accusingly, "although the roads are difficult at best." Rarely made ill at ease by the gaze of a man, Honey felt her cheeks turn red under his bold scrutiny. "I've tried to prepare myself for your arrival," she hurried on, "but I'm afraid a myriad of details remain. Since it's already April, I can only hope I shall be ready to travel in early May, according to my uncle's plans."

"I plan for us to leave before April is up."

Honey frowned. Clearly, Cameron Wolfe intended to be in charge. "I see you are direct, Mr. Wolfe."

"No point not to be."

"I agree."

As though by that reply she had given him permission, Cameron Wolfe now let his eyes wander more slowly over Honey Radcliffe. His insolence offended her, but, not daring yet to challenge him, she lowered her eyes and toyed with Nathan's locket.

Instinctively, she knew Cameron Wolfe disapproved of what he saw. In fact, in Cameron's eyes Honey Radcliffe was too perfect. A doll of china bisque, and all too breakable. Dressed in black as was appropriate to her mourning, she was the picture of vulnerable womanhood, which both fascinated and repelled him.

He wondered what had possessed Trevor Jefferson to consider a long journey by land for such an obviously fragile creature, and although their arrival in California would be considerably delayed, Cameron began to calculate the easiest methods and all possible alternative routes for travel than the one already planned.

There was a soft knock at the door, and when it opened, Nollie Daniels entered the room. "You wanted something?" she said, interrupting without waiting to be addressed first. Honey blushed, which Nollie noticed, amused by her reaction.

"Mr. Wolfe, this is Nollie Daniels. She and her mother, who met you at the door, will accompany me to California. I believe my uncle has already informed you."

"Yes, ma'am," Cameron replied, and while Honey turned her attention to Nollie, he gave the comely young mulatto better than a glance. She wore an unusually bright yellow dress covered by a long blue bibbed apron. Instead of the head scarf Cameron was used to seeing on bondswomen, Nollie's hair was not covered but braided in a multitude of long narrow braids whose ends were bound with colorful ribbons. She had an air of independence Cameron was not used to observing in a slave woman.

"Please prepare Mr. Wolfe something to eat, Nollie—something hearty."

"Won't be long, sir," Nollie said, politely but without a sign of deference, and left Cameron and Honey alone again.

"I wonder, Mrs. Radcliffe," he said as he resumed their conversation, "if you're recovered enough to embark on this journey your uncle's set out for you."

"What makes you believe I've been ill?"

"I understood that your health's been too poorly to travel."

"I understand your misconceptions, Mr. Wolfe," she said, feeling compelled to explain, "but I was not unwell in the usual sense. I have suffered the death of my husband but am now

sufficiently recovered to embark on our journey. You need have
no special worries concerning me."

Cameron remained unconvinced. "I'm sorry about your husband, Mrs. Radcliffe," he said, well enough acquainted with
grief himself to sound sincere.

"Thank you," Honey replied, surprised by his convincing tone
but not wishing to suffer additional words of condolence. "May I
show you to your quarters, Mr. Wolfe, and afterwards Nollie will
have prepared something for you to eat."

When she led him to the kitchen, Honey found that, as usual,
Nollie had produced a miracle with meager resources: a generous
omelet, a bowl of hominy, cornbread with two choices of preserves, sweet potatoes, boiled chicken flavored with thyme and
with stewed apples on the side, and a pot of lavender tea. However, it was a meager table compared with what would have been
provided before the war. But Honey expected that Cameron
Wolfe, whom she decided was the crude cowboy of her most
anxious conjuring, would never know the difference.

"When you finish, perhaps we should begin to consider the
journey in detail," she said, and when he nodded, she hurried
from the room to seek Shahar.

Honey found Shahar in the pantry behind the kitchen. "Tell
me what your impression is," Honey demanded in a whisper.

Crouched to retrieve a jar of apple butter from a low shelf,
Shahar stood up and stared thoughtfully at Honey. "It's what you
think that's on your mind," she said in a normal volume.

"Shhhh," Honey cautioned anxiously. As usual, the truth had
not slipped by Shahar, and Honey made an effort to put her feelings into words, still hushing her voice. "I find him . . .
disturbing."

Shahar's delight with Honey's reply bathed her thin, dark face
with gentle amusement. "I can see that plainly. You've not had
such high color for weeks."

Honey gave Shahar a reproachful look. "If I'd not already
made a commitment to this journey, not taken steps I can't retreat
from, not had *your* promise that we should trust him . . . I
wouldn't set one foot from my door with that . . . man. He positively reeks of danger."

Shahar chuckled softly. "Now, I wouldn't have put it quite that
way . . . but the man 'positively' has an air about him."

Honey grimaced. "Perhaps a bath would cure that—and put

me a little more at ease. Do you think he'd be offended, or worse, angered, if we suggested he bathe?"

"Maybe he doesn't believe cleanliness is next to godliness."

"Oh, Shahar!" Honey groaned softly. "Surely Uncle Trevor wouldn't send us an utter savage. He led me to believe the man was at least a little acquainted with civilized ways."

Her mistress's despair made Shahar laugh aloud. Honey's re-action to Cameron Wolfe pleased her and served to confirm her own premonitions as well as her perceptions on the instant of meeting him. No one her mistress had ever known, Shahar was privileged to know, had stirred up Honey Greer in quite the way this man had. Indeed, he was the man for whom Honey was destined; Shahar was not the least surprised that Honey had ob-jected strongly to him at the outset.

Shahar had never forthrightly stated to Honey her unhappiness with Honey's proposed union with Nathan Radcliffe, an alliance that everyone of true influence in Honey's life had applauded. She had grumbled quietly, as one without real power could only do. Her opinions were ignored, of course, but Shahar knew in her heart of hearts that Honey agreed. Her adamant wish to be a doctor, which grew stronger after her betrothal, was not a subter-fuge but had only concealed the truth: Nathan Radcliffe, hand-some, privileged, self-assured, domineering heir to a fortune, was merely the man Honey had been tutored to bend toward. Shahar had seen the match as ruinous to Honey, a premonition that had brought her the closest she had ever been to falling from favor with Honey's father, Dr. Phillip Greer.

Shahar smiled in bittersweet remembrance. Indeed, Honey Greer was as much her child as Phillip's.

No.

More.

Phillip Greer was Honey's parent by accident of blood, as he was Nollie's father also. *Honey was always more my child than his*, Shahar asserted silently. By toil. By pain. By love.

"You'll have to *do something*, Shahar," Honey interrupted, used to relying on Shahar's innate resourcefulness.

Brought back to the present moment by Honey's strident urg-ing, Shahar only chuckled more.

"Well?" Honey sounded desperate.

"When I show Mr. Wolfe his room, I'll give him a little shove into the bathtub. I've already ordered water drawn."

"I've shown him to his room already."

"I'll pretend I didn't know."

"You love to bait me, don't you!" Honey said, but smiled at last.

"Now get on with your work, Mrs. Radcliffe, or we'll all still be standing here come June."

Honey returned to the library and reluctantly began again to pore over household diaries and ledgers. Before she could leave for California, much of her property would have to be sold and taxes would have to be paid. She wondered who would buy her war-devalued land and what was left of her possessions. She would have to almost give away even the best of her real assets to secure the payment of taxes. She had already lost a fortune in goods and slaves, and she stood to lose nearly everything of value, certainly that which was most dear! It grieved her deeply that for this end, her husband, father, and three brothers had died.

The figures needing to be tallied in her account books blurred before Honey's eyes, and slowly, in her mind's eye, the figure of Cameron Wolfe sprang up.

Honey saw him clearly and knew there would be no leniency in him, knew he would be unfeeling in his assessment of her needs. She saw him stare at her with his intense blue gaze and sensed that he would not permit her to carry west all the items she considered essential to her well-being.

Cameron Wolfe would not be a man to travel with a long train of her personal keepsakes and possessions behind him. It would be easier to leave some items behind now, Honey acknowledged, than to deposit dear articles of furniture and mementoes along the trail. Many immigrants to the far West were forced to do so whenever the trail became increasingly difficult. Better to make the decision now, Honey realized with a frown, than have Mr. Wolfe toss her things willy-nilly onto the road.

Cameron's presence, his cold blue eyes, stern visage, and posture akin to a strict military bearing, caused Honey to imagine herself obeying his commands like any good soldier, with a stiff salute.

More tears sprang to her eyes. Truly, she was not ready to leave her home and, especially, take her leave in the company of Cameron Wolfe. Miserable, Honey covered her eyes with clenched fists and propped her elbows on the desk.

When she looked up, Cameron Wolfe stood before her in the flesh. Startled, Honey protested. "I didn't hear your knock!" she cried, more quick to rebuke him than might be wise, she sensed immediately.

Cameron was undaunted; his harsh gaze held hers. "Have you a list of what you want to take with you?"

"Of course." Honey handed him a ledger.

Without invitation, Cameron seated himself across the wide desk in front of her and perused the list in silence.

Honey awaited his judgment anxiously and, as he read the journal, took further stock of him. He seemed at ease, but she realized there was nothing in his countenance to give her even one clue to what was going through his mind.

From the moment he had set foot in the Greer house, Cameron's expectations had been confirmed. The house was filled with expensive furniture, paintings, sculpture, and, to his mind, frippery and frills the wealthy considered items of necessity. Almost from the moment he had agreed to lead Trevor's niece across the continent, he had anticipated paring down the list of items she wished to take with her. Yet the only surprise he found in the ledger was the boldness of her otherwise elegant script.

Cameron could not help but recall other women who had made the hard journey west and the items they personally had mourned. Sometimes an item of seemingly little value might have kept a woman in balance a little longer in the face of the relentless hardship of the frontier. The loss of a set of china cups, a piano, a table, or a bedstead sometimes seemed to make a great difference to a woman. He was surprised at his inclination to sympathize with Mrs. Radcliffe, for certainly, beyond her remarkable beauty, there was nothing especially endearing about her. She more than fulfilled his expectations of her as a person of little significance.

Cameron spent several minutes going over the four-page list. "I'm afraid you've little concept of the rigors of the journey you face, Mrs. Radcliffe. Please pare your list by half."

His gentle approach, his allowing her to trim the list herself, left Honey speechless.

He misunderstood her silence. "Maybe you prefer that I do the whittling?"

"No!" Honey came to her senses and to her feet. She put out her hand for the ledger and almost snatched it from Cameron's hand when he extended it to her. Holding it safely in her hand again, Honey turned crimson, curious to know if she had just seen the shadow of a smile cross his face. Embarrassed by the intensity of her response, she lowered her gaze from his and sat down again.

"Then I'll see that my horses have been properly looked after before I take that bath your slave has troubled herself to arrange."

"A very good idea. However, Mr. Wolfe," Honey said firmly, "before you go, I should like to point out that Shahar Daniels is not my slave. She was manumitted by my father's hand—before Mr. Lincoln's proclamation. In any case, the war has ended slavery. Furthermore, I suggest that in this house you refrain from assuming much of anything."

Cameron touched his forehead in a mocking salute. His tone held the same sort of mockery. "Whatever you 'suggest,' Mrs. Radcliffe," he replied, not waiting for her permission to withdraw.

CHAPTER THREE

Cameron Wolfe insisted on seeing the Greerfield Plantation for himself, property that lay a few miles north of the town of Greerfield. "Your uncle'll hold me accountable for whatever decision you make about your property," Cameron said by way of argument. Because he knew the Greer fortune was based on slave and tobacco land holdings, before arriving at Greerfield he had assumed that the Greer family lived on a plantation, which all Southerners did in the imaginations of those basically unacquainted with the South.

"Obviously you've been subjected to the lying Yankee press," Honey told him.

Cameron was surprised to learn that Phillip Greer had been a lifelong practicing physician and had always lived in town, not on one of his three plantations. "My father acquired most of his land through his marriage to my mother," Honey explained, revealing nothing more than was common knowledge. "When Daddy married my mother, he owned some five hundred acres and ten slaves, a respectable amount of property. My mother was a widow and, through her husband's death, had acquired a fair and prosperous plantation, which, of course, became my father's when they married. Then, at my grandfather Jefferson's death,

Mother inherited the Jefferson holdings. She, rather than her brother Trevor, inherited because Grandfather disowned Uncle Trevor when he left North Carolina vowing never to return. Grandfather felt his son had walked away from his duty." Honey paused. "I believe you already know a little of my Uncle Trevor's history."

Cameron nodded. He had met Trevor in Texas, and both men had gone to California at about the same time. He knew that whatever fortune Trevor had, he had acquired on his own.

"With the death of my three brothers in the war," Honey continued, "I've inherited, in addition to the house in town, a cotton plantation in Alabama, a rice plantation in South Carolina, and a little way down the road from here, Greerfield Plantation, which constitutes the primary portion of the estate. Of course, the plantations are managed by overseers, two of whom, since the beginning of the war, are negro."

Honey studied the seemingly impassive man who sat across from her in the parlor, his blue eyes as bright as glass and as clear. Bathed and dressed in clean clothes, Cameron Wolfe might have passed as a gentleman, except for the contagious air of restlessness he emanated even while he sat perfectly still. Alert and watchful, he listened to and comprehended her every word. And while he appeared interested in all she said, Honey had the disquieting notion of being stalked—an animal surveyed by a cunning bird of prey.

Honey suppressed a shiver and continued. "With the defeat of the Confederacy, what's left of my property is nearly worthless on the market. Many of our negroes are already gone. Soon there may be no one left to work the land. Those that remain have promised to stay, but who can predict what will happen tomorrow?"

Honey took a deep breath. "If the remaining free negroes continue to work the land and, in exchange for their labor, receive sustenance from the plantation, the situation will be hardly different than it was before the war. One has to wonder what has changed to the negro's advantage. What in truth does it mean to the negro to be free? Regardless of Mr. Lincoln's order and the outcome of the war, there's precious little money for anything, certainly not for wages. When one considers the amount of destruction and bloodshed, it's hard for me to see that there has been a change for the good, and much for the worse."

To Cameron, freedom was not an insignificant gain. "Obviously, Mrs. Radcliffe, there's a world of difference between being a freed man and a slave, if only to the Spirit. Have you never thought about what it would mean to be a slave?"

Honey stared pensively at Cameron Wolfe. "As I am a woman and, therefore, subject to the decree and whims of men—father, husband, brother—I believe I understand perfectly."

"There is no comparison, I promise you, between being a white lady and a black slave."

"Yes," she said. Acknowledging his point but not caring to engage in a philosophical debate, she immediately returned to the subject of her problems with her remaining property. "There are any number of foul speculators about—and already I've been approached by one—willing to take Greerfield off my hands for next to nothing." Honey's voice began to shake with rage. "You have to understand, Mr. Wolfe. Greerfield has some of the richest tobacco land in the South. Why, the man is little more than a thief wanting my property virtually for free. He should be shot!"

Cameron smiled, imagining Honey Radcliffe trying to accomplish such a feat, but he understood perfectly her fury over someone wanting her valuable property for nothing.

His smile made Honey uncomfortable. "The truth is," she added quickly, "I shall barely be able to pay the levied taxes. I shall have to use nearly all the gold Trevor left me for the journey ahead."

"In that case, I insist on seeing Greerfield for myself," he said, covering his surprise at her mention of gold, which was forbidden specie.

"I'll be glad to show you . . . but I must warn you, the plantation hardly shines the way it used to. The war's made it impossible to keep things going in the way we were accustomed." A model of both economy and prosperity for owner and, to a lesser degree, for slave alike, Greerfield had been diminished greatly by the collapse of the Southern way of life.

"I preferred to live in town—to be near my father and assist him—but you should have seen Greerfield before the war, Mr. Wolfe. We had some two thousand acres of tobacco planted, and ten acres of vegetables, plus orchards, and a formal garden filled with hundreds of flowers—roses, violets, gardenias. The main house was flanked by cottages for slaves; stables, barns, and storage rooms; carpenter, blacksmith, and other shops; a smokehouse and the dairy—why, we once had a nice herd of English cattle. Sometimes we had twenty house servants in addition to a head cook, a pastry cook, ten seamstresses, and the same number to do the laundry. The brass gleamed; you couldn't find a speck of dust anywhere by half past eight in the morning."

Honey's eyes suddenly glittered with tears. "It could have been a century ago, for what's left now," she whispered, then was silent.

Caught up in her emotion, Cameron gazed fixedly at her. He was touched by her beauty and sensed the depth of her disappointment, although he had trouble understanding the desire to live the kind of existence that she had described. He was drawn to a freer way of life. To be encumbered with possessions of the kind she had mentioned seemed more a burden than a blessing.

"We sometimes spent long stretches at the plantation, where life was entirely different from our life in town. Out there, almost everything we needed was grown or manufactured on the property. Very little had to be brought in from the outside. That wasn't true of every plantation. In fact, Greerfield supplied all our needs in town," she explained.

"We worked so *hard*. Our people worked so hard, and now it's all in ruin." Honey seemed ready to lapse into nostalgia once more but held herself in check. "You said you wanted to see Greerfield, Mr. Wolfe. When did you have in mind?"

"As soon as my horse is saddled."

"I'll go with you."

"Are you sure you should be venturing out on such a threatening day?" he said, surprising her with his concern.

"Mr. Wolfe, when are you going to disabuse yourself of the notion I'm an invalid?" she said as she stood up. He also rose to his feet. "Truly, I can hardly remember when I was last sick. A scarf, a hooded cloak, gloves and boots, and you'll have trouble keeping up with me," Honey insisted. "Mr. Wolfe, I truly wonder about the women to whom you are accustomed. They must all be ethereal creatures, given to constant vapors."

Cameron not only smiled but laughed aloud, an act of which she had doubted him capable.

Honey laughed too. "I'm so relieved that you can laugh," she teased with genuine merriment, and, as she might a brother or a close family friend, touched his arm in a gesture of warm familiarity. Then, shocked by her boldness with this man, truly a stranger and socially her inferior, Honey pulled away as if she had been burned. "I beg your pardon, Mr. Wolfe," she said. "I can't imagine what came over me."

At her last response, Cameron's expression grew dark. He reached for her soft hand, holding it firmly in his, stroking the long tapered fingers and short sculptured nails with his thumb. Neither could help but notice the contrast of the whiteness of her skin with his darkness. He waited to speak until Honey's large golden eyes stared directly into his. "I am *not* a leper, Mrs. Radcliffe," he informed her caustically. "You may safely touch me," he said, then immediately let go.

Honey's golden gaze locked on his hard blue one. She debated arguing the propriety of her gesture, then declined. Slowly she let out her breath, which unconsciously she had been holding, and, trembling inside, breathed deeply again. "I shall be ready to ride, Mr. Wolfe, in a matter of minutes," she said. Then, as if he had made no impression on her, she swept grandly past him, leaving the door to the parlor wide open for him to follow.

In the saddle Cameron discovered Honey to be an expert horsewoman. Familiar with the terrain, she led him at a sometimes daring pace over level ground to Greerfield Plantation. For the first time, Cameron considered that he might have underestimated her.

Above the west bank of the river, through stands of pine and oak, they raced down a narrow, sandy road. The air was brisk, and by the time they reached the first lush, green overgrown field, both riders and horses were winded. Honey slowed her horse to a walk. "We're here," she announced. "What would you like to see?"

"Everything."

"As you wish." She smiled and led him on horseback from field to field, some full of black laborers toiling with hoes to prepare the ground for planting. "In the past, all this was devoted to tobacco," she said of the open acres beyond the woods they had just left, an expanse that stretched as far as the eye could see, here and there dotted by log tobacco barns where the green tobacco leaves were dried after harvesting. "Now most of what's tilled is put to table crops—sweet potatoes and corn, mainly. We're hungry in these parts—but not as hungry as many other folks. Again, more area than usual will be put to perishable kitchen crops as soon as the weather turns warm."

As they rode on, Honey gestured to fields that had been left untended. "Closer to the river some of the land will revert to swamps if uncared for," she explained.

They approached the cluster of slave cottages. It was apparent that many were completely abandoned. Many needed their pine siding painted. "As I told you, some of our people left us." The structures were small and not especially well kept, but neither were the hovels unfit for human habitation like many of the slave quarters on other properties he had seen.

In a short while they reentered the main road and turned with it toward the river. Soon they came to a broad drive lined with large azalea shrubs that were not yet in bloom. "You should see this road later in the year," Honey said as they entered the drive. "In summer we're overcome with blossoms."

When the drive straightened, suddenly they faced a majestic mansion. Usually not one to be impressed by such things, Cameron was awed by the elegant design of the structure, which seemed to grace rather than intrude on the lush, verdant landscape.

Although the house also now needed a coat of paint, with three stories and broad, pillared galleries on every floor winding about it, there was no doubt the inhabitants had lived grandly. On a cool summer evening one could have a table and chairs brought into the night air and sit with a refreshment as long as one liked.

"Most of the house is closed, of course," Honey explained as they advanced. The house was shaded on three sides by ancient gnarled oak trees and enormous pines. Now many of the windows were boarded up. "You're welcome to wander inside to your heart's content. I'll get a lamp, but I warn you, the house is quite vacant—empty of its life.

"Out of necessity, I sold much of the furniture for pathetic amounts," Honey added softly. "So much is gone, it's difficult even to recall the spirit that once was here. And when I consider how ridiculous the sums were, I rebuke myself. Yet there's no avoiding that even that little money was needed."

Only the rear portion of the first floor of the house was now in use, occupied by the black plantation overseer and his family. To conserve resources, the kitchen was used for the benefit of all plantation hands. After enjoying a pot of herb tea prepared for them by the overseer's wife to chase the chill, Honey took a lamp and guided Cameron through the house silently except for an occasional explanation of the purpose of a room. "We came here often for celebrations of one kind or another, the grandest, of course, at Christmastime. And we came here in summer to try to keep cool."

Cameron had never been inside a house of such grand proportions. True, the spacious rooms of the three-story structure were nearly bare of furniture and the empty walls were scarred by impressions of paintings that were no longer there, and in rooms upstairs discarded toys were left from a bygone day. But in the vaulted ceilings that graced many of the rooms, in the sculptured facades of doorways and marble fireplaces, in the rise of arched windows and the curve of balustrades, Cameron had the imagination to sense that those who had lived here for generations were different from others who only aspired to the wealth and grandeur of such a place.

When Cameron and Honey emerged into daylight from the house, he advised her with conviction, "Don't sell. I've money enough to see you west. Pay the taxes. If necessary, let the land lie fallow. Don't let speculators steal it. One day it will again be worth something to you."

Honey almost broke down and cried. "Thank you," she whispered. "My uncle didn't seem to care, and for the first time I think I understood why Grandfather disinherited him. Trevor urged me to take anything I could get. Thank you, Mr. Wolfe."

Her smile of gratitude seemed to caress Cameron's face. He nodded in acknowledgment. "Trevor Jefferson has his sights aimed on other things," he said, and for several moments gazed thoughtfully at Honey Radcliffe, drawn into the sudden intimacy and trust she now extended to him.

Quickly, Cameron reclaimed his senses. "We'd best get you home, Mrs. Radcliffe," he said abruptly. "Unless I'm mistaken, we're in for a downpour."

Honey looked beyond Cameron into the threatening sky. "More likely a deluge, Mr. Wolfe." They hurried their horses. With Cameron's help, she mounted sidesaddle, then pulled the hood of her cloak over her hair. "I fear we'll be soaked through before we get home."

"I've been wet to the skin before," Cameron answered, grinning, "and so have you, I'm sure."

They urged the horses to a lively pace, and before long the rain began, assaulting them as if the heavens had opened the floodgates of a damn. With the fury of the wind against them, the road grew treacherous and slow. As she had predicted, they soon were soaking wet. "Where did this come from?" Honey demanded when they were forced to stop and then pick their way around a fallen tree. "I'd never have ventured out if I'd been the least aware of weather like this brewing."

They could have taken shelter in one of the abandoned tobacco barns, but wet as they were, they preferred to continue home. Later, with her hood blown from her head, Honey considered their choice an error.

Shortly after entering a broader section of road, Honey abruptly reined in her horse. "I hear something," she said, closing her eyes and hoping to hear better. "Cries of distress." But in the howling storm, she failed to place the sound.

"I hear it, too," Cameron said, and they rode on as quickly as they could on the frequently boggy road until they came to where they should have encountered a narrow bridge. But the crossing had been washed away, and on the opposite bank where the bridge should have touched land again lay a man wedged firmly beneath his wagon in the streambed.

"It's Howie Allston," Honey shouted to Cameron over the roar of wind and rain. He was either unconscious or dead.

Allston's horse, wedged amid debris from the bridge and struggling to keep his head above the rising water, was the source of the desperate cries they had heard, his terror communicated now to Cameron and Honey's animals, making them restive. They were forced to ride some distance before finding a safe place to ford the swiftly flowing stream; hours seemed to pass before they reached the washed-out bridge again. By then the water had risen several inches.

"I'll see if he's still alive," Cameron called to Honey as he dismounted.

"No. I can do that," Honey said, already on the ground. "You free the horse."

Unaccustomed to taking orders from a woman, and with strong misgivings about the wisdom of allowing Mrs. Radcliffe to go down the bank with the water level rising so fast, Cameron nevertheless took a length of rope from his saddle and slid quickly down the muddy bank, unmindful of the danger to himself.

For her part, Honey was terrified, grateful for her sure sense that Cameron Wolfe would successfully do whatever needed doing to free the frantic animal. If there was nothing else about him, Honey realized, shivering in the midst of the excitement, there was an unmistakable aura of power about this man Uncle Trevor had seen fit to send her.

Cameron spent a few moments trying to soothe the frightened animal, which at any instant could have turned the incident into a disaster for the three people now involved. With an unlucky plunge, the horse might dislodge the wagon and cause all concerned to be swept downstream.

Cameron took his knife from its sheath on his belt and swiftly cut the trace reins from the wagon, then forced his back against the stream bank. Summoning all his strength, he used his body as a lever to force away debris that the current had pinned against the horse's right foreleg.

The animal pulled free, then stumbled and, terrified, brayed and thrashed wildly. Honey held her breath as Cameron gained a firm grip on the bridle, and almost unbelievably Cameron swung himself onto the horse's back. At once Cameron took control and the animal staggered up the slippery bank to safety.

Immediately Honey discarded her rain-sodden cloak, reefed up her skirts, and eased herself halfway down the bank until she could just reach below Howie Allston's ear and feel the artery in his neck. The pulse was slow but steady. "He's alive," she shouted, but Cameron didn't hear her.

The wagon covered Howie Allston to midchest, but he seemed to breathe without much effort, and Honey assumed the wagon must not be weighing heavily on his midsection. Carefully, she eased herself farther down the bank and into the water where, barely able to keep her head above water, Honey discovered she could slip her hand under the wagon to the middle of the injured man's thigh.

With the current against her, the wagon did not budge when she tried to force it to move. Desperate, knowing she was helpless alone, Honey abandoned the effort and crawled slowly back up the bank until Cameron reached her.

"He's alive," she shouted as the rain continued to fall heavily, "but the wagon won't budge. Not for me, anyway."

Cameron nodded and swiftly cut the trace reins from the harness of the horse he had just rescued before bringing his and Honey's horses to the edge of the bank. "Hold them here," he said as he knotted the horses' reins and the severed trace reins together. "I'm going down again. When I shout at you, lead the horses upstream, then keep an eye out for me. When you see me on the bank again, tie the horses down and come give me a hand." He disappeared down the bank and secured the leather to the wagon axle.

Honey did exactly as Cameron had said and waited anxiously for his signal. The risk he was taking was enormous. If the horses should slip, if the wagon should slide, not only Howie Allston but Cameron Wolfe could be crushed against the bank and drowned.

Cameron acted as if by instinct, quickly tying a doubled portion of rope he had taken from his saddle around the man's chest and under his arms. Allowing a considerable length between them, Cameron then looped a double length of rope over one shoulder and across his own chest and dug the heels of his boots into the muddy bank, positioning himself above and behind the injured man. He then raised an ululating cry that sliced through the noise of the continuing downpour and sent the horses on the bank in motion with little urging from Honey. Her hair rose on end at Cameron's cry as she vigorously slapped the horses' flanks with her riding crop. The animals strained against the fast-moving current to the full degree of their strength.

The instant the wagon shifted, freeing the injured man, Cameron tugged on Allston's dead weight and then brought him swiftly up the bank. Once on the bank, Howie Allston appeared to rally to consciousness but, focused on his pain, moaned incessantly, unaware of Honey's or Cameron's presence.

"Your knife, please," Honey demanded, forgetting all about the chilling cry that had pierced her body moments before.

Cameron gave her the knife, only afterward surprised at the ease with which he responded to her command. She used the knife to slit open Allston's pants legs. It was obvious that both legs were broken, but no bones protruded from the flesh, and blood issued only from superficial scrapes of the skin.

Cameron was amazed by Honey's utter calm and apparent expertise as she felt the man's fractured legs. He would have predicted she would be squeamish, an unreliable assistant in almost any emergency, and would not have been at all surprised to see her faint.

"I think the only thing to be done, Mr. Wolfe, is for you to go for a wagon while I remain here to give any comfort I can."

Cameron hesitated only a moment before doing exactly as Honey had said, at length returning with a wagon and two other men to help.

Soon Honey was in the wagon bed next to Howie and, with Cameron's assistance, ignoring Allston's screams, had carefully reduced and set the fractured bones. Grateful that the cold had minimized the swelling, Honey applied splints to immobilize the fractures. When the patient was amply covered with blankets to overcome shock, she ordered the wagon put on the road.

The rain had stopped, but the road was miserable. Only great effort by Cameron and the men he had brought with him from town, who cut logs to fill otherwise impassable sections of the road so that the wagon could move, brought them safely to Greerfield.

Howie Allston was awake for the ride. "I remember falling in and thinking I'd be drowned," he said to Honey, "but nothin' more—until you set the legs, that is. Gawd-awful painful."

Honey nodded sympathetically. "You're alive, and with Lilly looking after you, you'll mend."

"Thanks to you coming along in time."

When they got him home at the far end of town, Honey reinforced the splints before turning her patient over to his wife. "Keep him warm. I don't think you'll have trouble keeping him down. But to repair, the bones must be kept at perfect rest and the splints kept on until the bones heal. A little brandy, perhaps, will stimulate and soothe. I'll call back on you soon."

"We're so grateful, Dr. Greer."

Honey smiled, by now used to the appellation "Doctor." She had tried to dissuade the local people from addressing her as Doctor, but since her father's death she had not been successful in discouraging that form of address.

"Dr. Greer?" Cameron inquired as he drove the wagon home, curious. Perhaps there was more to Mrs. Radcliffe than met the eye.

"It's a long story, Mr. Wolfe, which I'm too exhausted to discuss at present." She shivered violently with cold and kept shivering until she had stood for quite a while in front of the fire in her own kitchen.

Having watched for them since Cameron had returned for the wagon, Shahar let them in the door immediately and clucked with worry. "You're tempting fate, you two," she said as she hurried them to stand before the fireplace, which was wide enough for eight-foot logs and tall enough for grown men to stand in.

"I can't r-r-remember being s-so c-cold," Honey said, her teeth chattering rapidly.

Shahar didn't allow her to stand before the fire long. "Take this candle and get into the pantry and off with those wet things," Shahar ordered Honey, giving her a pile of clothes that she had already collected and pushing her in the direction of the pantry door. "Don't dillydally. Get dressed, then wind this old blanket around you and come back to the fire."

With the pantry door shut behind Honey, Shahar turned to Cameron. As tall as he was, Shahar looked him directly in the eye and, with an air of authority, said, "I can't say I've seen much to give me any comfort that you're the man taking us half-way 'cross the world."

"I can't promise you won't get wet. Maybe even drown."

Shahar gave Cameron a good once-over and handed him a blanket also. "At least you're honest, Mr. Wolfe, but you should have brought Mrs. Radcliffe with you for a change of clothes the first time you came in."

"I doubt I could've convinced her to leave her patient."

Shahar gave Cameron a knowing *harrumph*, then dismissed him. "You can shuck your clothes in there," she said, pointing to a large broom closet. "Then wrap up in that blanket and warm yourself by the fire while I get you something dry to put on."

From years of experience denying hardship of all kinds, including extremes of weather, Cameron did not let the cold penetrate his consciousness the way it had eventually pierced Honey's, but he did as Shahar bade and hurriedly stripped naked, then wound a large wool blanket around himself.

As he stood again before the fire, Honey joined him, not dressed but huddled in her blanket, still shivering and reluctant to leave the warmth of the fire and go back to the cold pantry for the few minutes it would take to don dry clothes. "I c-couldn't wait," she sputtered, her face filling with color at the awkwardness of the situation. She found it impossible to look him in the eye. "Why aren't your t-t-teeth chatt-ttering, Mr. W-Wolfe?" she wondered as she turned away from his surprised stare.

"Getting soaked is nothing new to me," he said.

"Please don't stare."

"I'm sorry," Cameron said, and faced the fire directly.

But Honey could not keep from gaping and stared at Cameron's broad, deeply tanned shoulders and the well-defined muscles of his bare arms. He was lean and tough. When she finally caught herself and turned her gaze to the fire, she said, "My uncle tells me you're an unusual m-man. You m-must be to be subjected as we were to the elements and not f-feel ch-chilled to the v-very bone."

"And maybe you've taken a chill, Mrs. Radcliffe," Shahar

interrupted, hastily handing Cameron a stack of dry clothes. Then she took Honey roughly by the elbow and hurried her back into the pantry. "Now, wouldn't it just spoil everything if you were to take a chill! Why aren't you dressed?"

"The reason I'm not dressed is that I felt it more important to get warm, Shahar, and I m-must protest your intensifying Mr. Wolfe's impression that I'm s-something fragile."

"He'd best understand he's taking charge of people, not just another herd of cows," Shahar answered. "It's not a bit encouraging he's not blue with cold himself."

A few minutes later Shahar served hot soup, toasted corn-bread, and steaming tea to the freshly dressed pair as they sat before the fire. "Now that's sensible," Shahar said when Cameron agreed to a second serving.

Cameron watched Honey drink her tea. "In spite of the excitement, I'm afraid it's time, Mrs. Radcliffe, to talk about your ledger," he said. "Earlier, I went over your list of necessities and marked what can best be sent by ship—that includes almost everything. A little clothing, food, and cooking gear is about all you need take with you. We'll take only one wagon, several pack mules, and our saddle mounts to begin with. Once we reach the Ohio, we'll go downriver and then to Saint Louis by steamer. I'll provision for the trail there and in Independence."

"I suppose I need only acquiesce," Honey said, annoyed. "If I'm to send everything by ship, why did I have to pare down my list in the first place."

"I wanted you to decide what things you could live without."

"I shall now take the liberty of enlarging *your* list, Mr. Wolfe. I see no reason not to."

"If you wish."

"I do." Honey resented Cameron for so completely taking charge but silently agreed that her original list had been longer than necessary. Still, she felt that his demand that she pare it to the bone was unfair. "I suppose you'll want a list of the clothing and jewelry I intend to carry with me."

"No, just don't overdo it."

"I wouldn't think of it," Honey snapped. "Have you asked Shahar and Nollie for their lists?"

"No."

"I suppose you didn't think they'd have possessions."

"The slaves I've known have never had anything but the clothes on their backs and, maybe, a blanket."

"Again, you assume too much."

"I'll look over their lists at once. Also, we should begin packing and crating *today*."

"Yes, sir." Honey frowned and looked away from Cameron. She stared into the fire. Fatigued by the events of the morning, she seriously thought of begging for time, even another day. For weeks she had waited in dread of this very moment. In reality, until now all talk of going west had remained an abstraction, a fantasy. But once the packing had begun, each step taken hastened the hour of departure.

With the war's end and with the great changes likely to come, if she remained in North Carolina, at least there would be something of the old way of life and remaining friends to comfort her. In California, save for Nollie and Shahar, who, thank the Lord, had promised to go with her, and Uncle Trevor, of course, everyone and everything would be strange and new. Honey therefore was determined to increase the list of items to send by ship around Cape Horn. Yet, she realized sadly, those things she would add to her list were only objects from home, not home itself.

When she and Nathan Radcliffe had dared speak of the notion that the Confederate States might be defeated, they had talked as if little would change. It had been their dream that once the scars of war had healed, life would return to normal. She had tried to believe they would live their life together in a gay and splendid way and soon forget the miseries of war. They would go to Europe and spend whatever time they could there, traveling from one capital and spa to another before their first child was born. Instead, it would be her furniture and other possessions that would be going on an excursion by sea, and not to Europe but to the American West, a place Honey still envisioned as a wild and hostile country.

Honey fought the tears that threatened to fill her eyes. She must never allow Cameron Wolfe to see her cry—never confirm for him the weak woman he seemed to want her to be.

Honey clenched her teeth together firmly in her jaw. Why should she expect something more from this man than the rest, when every man she'd ever known, including her father and her husband, seemed to demand her dependence? It fit their dream of her, she realized.

But not her own.

Perhaps her desire to be a doctor was outlandish, but in truth,

Honeysuckle Jefferson Greer Radcliffe, declared brilliant by her teachers and even her father, was barred from her dream only because she lacked the all-important male appendage—a fact she discovered only due to her exceptional medical experience. Her mental abilities often exceeded those of the young male doctors she had met during the war, so it followed that only a few inches of anatomy had kept her from following in her father's footsteps.

Blessed—or was it cursed?—with a thoroughly female form, Honey Radcliffe didn't want to be a man, only a doctor. In her father's practice and in the late misbegotten war, she had performed almost every procedure to which she had been exposed, eventually as competently as any of the men she stood beside, who called her nurse. No less bloodied, and often more caring, which was in itself damning. Emotion was forbidden in medicine; sympathy and caring was for women, mothers, *nurses*. By contrast, this weakness made the men she stood next to appear strong, if not invincible.

Honey turned back to Cameron Wolfe and gazed at him thoughtfully. She was about to turn herself over to another man! First her father, then her husband, and in a short while an uncle. But for a brief time at least there would be an interlude when she would be in Cameron Wolfe's charge. And what did he want from her but weakness? Proof she was a docile, submissive female!

What else? He was a man.

Honey glared fiercely at Cameron Wolfe but a moment later softened her gaze. Cameron was not to be held responsible, she realized, for all that had happened to her—for all her withered, unfulfilled dreams.

To compensate for what she knew must have seemed a hateful stare, Honey smiled at Cameron with unusual warmth. "I see no useful purpose in further delay, Mr. Wolfe," she said at last. "I'll begin packing at once."

But a warning of delay came later that night when, after several hours of crating furniture with the assistance of two black carpenters and their helpers, the work was halted for the night and Honey noticed a fine sheen of sweat on Cameron's face. She granted that with the work he had been doing, he had earned the right to sweat, but with experience in observing such signs, she knew he should not be in more of a lather than the rest of the men.

Honey handed Cameron a towel. "For your brow," she offered

casually. "I'll get you some water." He didn't refuse and drank gratefully while Honey looked purposefully into his eyes. They were moist and bright. Too bright, she knew. "Mr. Wolfe, you've a fever."

Cameron shrugged, but Honey's cool hand came quickly to his forehead, then his cheek. "You're sizzling! Why didn't you say something? You should be down in bed."

"I'm not in the habit of giving in to fever. I'll sleep it off," he said, relishing the coolness of her soft hand lying gently on his burning skin.

"I hope so," she answered doubtfully as she lowered her hand. Concerned with the sudden onset and the degree of Cameron's fever, Honey worried especially about deadly yellow jack, which less than a year ago had taken her father's life. A common plague, yellow fever, she was relieved to note, was unusual this early in the year.

But in the morning, when Cameron didn't appear as usual for breakfast, Honey inquired after him, then went straight to his door and knocked. When there was no response, she knocked more loudly and then opened the door.

He seemed to be asleep, but when she touched his bare shoulder and tried to rouse him, he only opened his eyes and squinted at the light. He tried to focus on the figure standing beside his bed, then gave up and, resting an arm over his eyes, immediately fell back asleep.

Honey touched Cameron's cheek and then his throat with her hand. She felt the throbbing pulse of the artery and was alarmed by the rate. "I'm afraid you didn't sleep the fever off, Mr. Wolfe," she said. "You should know ignoring something doesn't necessarily make it go away."

He didn't stir, and she left him and fetched a basin of witch hazel. Shahar followed with a pot of tea.

"I don't think he'll be drinking any tea soon," Honey said with obvious concern. "He's in a very deep slumber." She placed the basin of witch hazel on the bedside table, then sat next to Cameron on the bed. His sun-darkened skin glowed red with fever. "At least it's not a yellow cast," Honey said.

"That's some comfort," Shahar answered.

Honey gently lowered Cameron's arm from across his eyes so that she might more easily apply cool compresses to his forehead. She, Nollie, and Shahar took turns and spent much of the next two days bathing him and urging him to drink tea and broth.

From time to time when he slept he muttered fragments of unintelligible words.

"I can't make out for the life of me what he wants," Shahar related to Honey, perplexed. "He just babbles."

As she sat beside him, Honey grew increasingly curious. She remembered the hair-raising cry he had given to set the horses in motion when they had rescued Howie Allston. Familiar with Latin, fluent in French, she became convinced that what she had first assumed were fragments of English in fact were words of a foreign tongue. Perhaps Spanish? she wondered, which she didn't speak. She stared at Cameron Wolfe and wondered about his origins. His surname was Teutonic, yet his manner seemed almost too exotic for that origin. He was mysterious and, she confessed, in some ways fascinating.

After one of her sessions with him Nollie confided, "If you can ignore his dreadful jabbering, he's wickedly handsome. Look at him a spell—it's enough to make a lady give up her vow of chastity."

"He looks rather ordinary to me," Honey replied.

"You'd be lying if you said you wouldn't like to get better acquainted. He has a pure sweetness in his face."

"Most men look like angels when they're sleeping. Even the worst of them," Honey replied knowingly, but when she was again alone with him and lowered the covers to his waist to bathe him, the near perfection of Cameron's body at last assailed her senses. He slept naked, and his skin burning with the heat of fever quickly warmed the cool cloth she used to sponge him. Honey could hardly avoid an urge to touch him, to apply the witch hazel with her hands, but quickly denied herself that pleasure.

A few deep scars marred Cameron's smooth dark skin. Perhaps, Honey speculated, his scars were from knife wounds, a possibility she conveniently used to cement her earlier image of him as someone dangerous.

As her father's helper and as a nurse in the war, Honey had viewed hundreds of men and thought herself immune to any sensuous impression of a man's physique, yet even with his scars, she had to admit Cameron Wolfe had one of the most magnificent bodies of any man she had ever seen. He was perfectly made: hard-muscled, long-limbed, wonderfully proportioned.

Honey stared at Cameron's face, now passive in fever-induced sleep. If she were to mold a face in clay, she would wish to make one so clearly masculine yet beautiful. His dark brown hair was thick and full. The eyes were set just wide enough apart and enhanced with thick, black lashes; the brows were pleasantly heavy, dark, and arched; the nose was straight. His mouth had a firm set in the jaw and the lips full, even sensual, Honey mused.

Purposefully, Honey bathed Cameron's face and from time to time dipped another cloth into the tea, letting a few drops accumulate on his lips in hopes that he would instinctively lick the moisture away and thereby receive some internal relief. She worried alternately over his fever and his taking more chill. When he was chilled, she covered him with blankets.

Often he was restless, and when he opened his eyes, Honey saw in them the mark of fever and a lack of recognition. He gazed at her, seeming not to see her, and implored her with words she did not comprehend but in compelling tones she could not truthfully mistake. Uncomfortable, she nevertheless remained to soothe the muscles of his chest and arms with repeated applications of cool witch hazel. She spoke to him softly, hoping to ease his apparent distress, glad he was not a soldier and it was not wartime, and for once she had the time to lavish care on her patient. Her ministrations might be of no value in the end, but at least if he should die, she would not be haunted by the feeling that she had failed for lack of sufficient time to attend to him.

Once when she bathed his face and pressed the cool cloth against his burning eyelids, he freed her hand and laid it against his cheek, then brought it to his lips and kissed her open palm.

Quickly but gently, Honey drew away her hand, ignoring the alarm that surged through her veins at his touch. Once more she dipped the cloth into the basin and laid the cool compress on his closed eyes. Then, reasoning that direct massage would benefit him more, she began to apply witch hazel directly to his body with her hands, only vaguely aware of how fair she was in contrast his dark skin. Briskly, she stroked his arms, chest, and to just below his waist.

She alternated massage and feeding him cups of herb tea or chicken broth. "I wish it were beef tea," Honey apologized, believing that dedoction to be of greater benefit, but at last Cameron's fever came down a notch.

She urged him turn onto his stomach and spent what to her seemed hours applying the distillate to the burning muscles of his back. When he pulled away the covers completely, she gave the same attention to the tight muscles of his buttocks and legs.

The solution evaporated quickly from his fevered skin, but, exhausted, Honey finally had to stop. "Try to sleep," she urged him, and covered him lightly with only a sheet.

Restless, Cameron turned on his side. He looked at Honey, recognition now obvious in his eyes. "Please." He reached for her hand. "Stay."

Startled, Honey nevertheless sat beside him on the narrow bed.

"You'll cure me yet, 'Dr. Greer,'" he said.

She smiled, but her weariness did not escape him. "I'll do my best. We're counting on you to take us safely to California."

"So selfish motives spur the doctor on."

"A little self-interest many times outweighs the noble, Mr. Wolfe—which it's best to remember."

"Is that what kept you going in the war—self-interest?"

Honey looked deeply into Cameron's eyes. "War hospitals are nothing less than perfect hell, Mr. Wolfe."

Cameron brought Honey's hand to his lips again. "And yet you've still the power to heal."

Tears came to Honey's eyes. Only weariness, she thought, instantly aware of her desire to yield to his tenderness but rescued by the armor that she used to defend herself against intimacy. Nearly overcome by a dreadful need to be comforted herself, she trembled. "I'll send someone else to sit with you. You must try to sleep," she said, quickly overcoming her emotion—her dreadful weakness—and hurried away.

Finally, in the late afternoon, Cameron fell asleep and slept soundly through the night. Honey resumed the vigil early in the morning, and when she covered his forehead with her hand, she found his fever gone. "At last," she sighed.

Cameron woke and stared at her, obviously confused.

"You've had a frightfully high fever," Honey explained, offering him tea. "Try to drink this."

Silent, he rolled on his side and raised himself shakily on an elbow. He felt weak and drank the liquid slowly.

When he finally drained the cup, Honey poured more.

"How long have you been here?"

"Don't you recall?"

Cameron lay back and closed his eyes. He felt light-headed and remembered nothing. "I'll be on my feet in a moment."

"I think not."

He opened his eyes and trained them on Honey defiantly. "I never lie in bed."

"You will now," Honey informed him. Her tone was commanding, demanding his compliance. "I'll go for some broth," she said, and left the room.

When she returned, he lay propped in bed, unwilling to admit that against her advice he had tried to get up and nearly blacked out.

"This will give you strength," Honey urged, spooning broth into his mouth. "Perhaps even restore your memory." She smiled.

When he could take no more, he thanked her. "I don't remember anyone ever looking after me like this."

"Not even when you were wounded?"

He looked puzzled.

"The scars on your chest must have caused you some disability."

Cameron stared at Honey. "They were ignored."

"Surely you mean endured."

"Maybe."

In the silence that followed, they gazed at each other until Cameron finally smiled and then, with weariness, closed his eyes. For over an hour Honey continued to sit by him, simply, she told herself, because her presence comforted him.

When in his sleep, Cameron eventually turned, facing away from her, Honey pulled the blankets over his shoulders and tucked him in. He remained very much a stranger, Honey realized, but as she looked down on him, she admitted to herself that she wanted to know more about this man, her appointed guardian—much more than she ever would have dreamed.

CHAPTER FOUR

As the items Honey required to be packed and crated accumulated, Cameron's temper alternated between irritable and sullen. Even the things she left behind seemed to offend him. In his opinion, a woman requiring the trappings Honey did in order to be happy was more trouble than she was worth. By contrast, Cameron needed very little to be content.

When he came upon Nollie, Shahar, and Honey packing trunks of Honey's clothes, his mouth gaped. The piles of gowns, fancy and plain; chemises, petticoats, corsets, and such; hats, slippers, boots, and shoes seemed to equal a small mountain. Cameron watched briefly but left without comment, his face red with irritation, not embarrassment, as the women supposed. They couldn't help but laugh at him when he exited the room.

Cameron had been careful to make plain to Honey that she could carry only a small amount of clothing with her on the journey. "I shall be reasonable," Honey had promised, but when he saw the woman packing, he was doubtful. "I hope Shahar and Nollie will be more reasonable."

Cameron explained the proposed route of the journey to the women and told them that they would be accompanied by three men of his acquaintance and a woman, all of whom were to meet at Greerfield shortly before the departure from North Carolina. Then he got down to the task of actually preparing the three Greerfield women for the journey west.

He felt certain he could teach Honey Radcliffe what she needed to know. Even in the short time he had been at Greerfield, he had seen her set broken bones, excise carbuncles, surgically remove a tumor, treat burns, and deliver a baby. If she could wield a surgeon's knife, surely she could learn to shoot. But Nollie Daniels, who could cook perhaps better than anyone he had ever known, and her mother, Shahar, who he could easily see had made herself irreplaceable in the household, seemed to him less likely to be comfortable with firearms.

Cameron spent some time trying to decide just what the relationship of the three women was. He could hardly forget Mrs. Radcliffe's pointed advice that Shahar and Nollie were not slaves. But clearly, there was something more between the three than the obligation of a former mistress to her slaves. If he had not known better, Cameron would have assumed some sort of blood relationship.

Often, he realized, Nollie spoke to Mrs. Radcliffe as if she were her equal, and, what was even more astonishing, Mrs. Radcliffe would answer without the batting of an eye in a tone that implied the two *were* equals. Occasionally they bantered back and forth as if they were sisters. They were close in age. Perhaps, Cameron reasoned, the explanation simply was that they had been reared together. Even so, it seemed to him, pointed deference on Nollie's part should have been in evidence. Nollie was too often downright saucy.

As for Shahar, Cameron knew that she had mothered Honey even while Honey's own mother had been alive, which explained the obvious affection between the two but not the depth of the attachment or the deference Mrs. Radcliffe sometimes clearly exhibited toward the slender black woman.

Cameron noted a resemblance between Mrs. Radcliffe and Nollie, which Nollie's multitude of long, slender braids only concealed from a less astute observer, and was driven to speculate further. Aware that bondswomen were available to their masters for more than hard labor in the fields or house, Cameron studied Shahar Daniels with care. She had raised the three Greer boys to be men; perhaps she had provided considerably more than the usual looking after.

Now middle-aged, Shahar was an indisputably handsome woman but a far cry from the kind slave traders reserved for "special consideration" by prospective masters. He thought of the fancy light-skinned negro women he had seen. The images he conjured did not begin to fit Shahar, whose skin was especially dark. Unusually tall, her regal bearing and narrow, even features were crowned by full sensuous lips, which gave her a decidedly exotic appeal. She radiated a remarkable vitality that alone might well draw any man to her side.

He imagined Shahar young again and in his mind's eye saw her quite seductive, but he found it hard to believe her the promiscuous negro woman that all black women were reputed to be. She had a dignity, a rarely bestowed and beautiful smile, an inner strength that reminded Cameron how easily a man's desires could overwhelm the truth of a woman's real nature. Most white men believed indian women to be nothing but whores, yet the Apache women he knew were as chaste as any on earth. Perhaps negro women suffered from a similar unjust reputation, and a plentiful number of white men ready and able to promote the notion. It was likely, also, Cameron thought, for the Greer boys to have done their share to increase the Greerfield slave stock.

More naturally appealing to Cameron than Shahar was Nollie, with her lighter skin and lithe youthfulness—and her curious resemblance to Mrs. Radcliffe. Of average height, Nollie was straight and trim, with very pleasant features, beautiful dark smoky gray eyes, and a sway in her walk sometimes that quickened his pulse. Nollie easily could have been put on the block by a master for a high price. But smiling at his own salacious fantasies, Cameron admitted he had no intention of propositioning any female who could wield a butcher knife as adroitly as Nollie Daniels could.

Instead Cameron forced himself to concentrate on the considerable task before him: training the three Greerfield women to shoot—straight.

"What do you know about guns?" he asked, anticipating their answers.

"More than I care to know of the damage they do," Honey replied instantly.

"Nothing at all," Shahar and Nollie chorused, the answer he had expected.

"You have to learn to protect yourselves."

The women looked at one another in alarm. Honey spoke for them. "We expected to be under *your* protection."

"If it comes to your needing defense, Mrs. Radcliffe, I'll likely need help."

"What about the men you said would be with us?" Nollie demanded.

"If we're attacked by Apaches, I promise you, you'll need to be armed and able."

The women accepted Cameron's logic, and a more sober group of students there never was. Yet in the next weeks the women resisted, sometimes shrieking in their discomfort with the action, noise, and purpose of the rifles and handguns. It seemed a brutal business learning to shoot, especially the notion of killing another human being.

Stymied by their obvious repugnance, stubborn resistance, and slow progress, Cameron eventually felt forced to urge them. "Think of the enemy as nothing more than savages—not human. Hope to be killed rather than captured," he warned.

"Please, don't say any more," Nollie begged, both she and Shahar instantly reconsidering their decision to go west.

Honey threw her Henry carbine at Cameron's feet. "I've spent the last four years of my life trying to heal too many bodies wounded by this kind of weapon. If I'm in serious danger, I believe I'd prefer you shoot me." Honey had read of women captured by savages and thought she knew what to expect.

Cameron let his hard blue gaze settle on Honey Radcliffe. In spite of his considerable exasperation, a feeling of admiration for her welled up within him. He lifted the rifle from the ground. "Treat this gun with more respect, Mrs. Radcliffe. It may someday save your life." He extended the weapon to Honey, but she refused to accept it. "I admire your not fearing death but I'd hoped you also had the courage to live."

As Cameron spoke to Honey, a breeze came up and stirred the leaves of the oak trees around them. She felt his gaze bore into her and in the silence of the moments before she accepted the rifle felt isolated and alone with him, as if they were captured together in amber. She understood the heroism of choosing to live over death. She felt also a sense of recognition—the odd sense that she had met this man sometime before.

"I don't know about you," Nollie said when Honey finally took back the rifle, "but I intend to get to California *alive.*" Then Nollie fired the carbine and hit the target squarely.

Shahar laughed at her daughter. "Give the girl a rifle and a knife and the indians best stay hidden."

Honey laughed too and later even struck the target herself. Within the week, all three could clean, load, and accurately fire the Henry and a variety of handguns.

"The ability to shoot straight gives me an odd feeling of power," Honey confessed to Cameron.

"Don't let it go to your head," Cameron urged her. "Always imagine the enemy ferocious, more experienced, and cunning."

"You speak as if you've encountered the Apache firsthand."

"Often."

"And?"

"And what?"

"What should we expect?"

Cameron gazed at Honey and knew she would not like his advice. "Save one bullet for yourself."

"First you urge me to live; then you suggest I kill myself."

"The Apache have no reason to be lenient with white men."

Honey heard no sympathy for his own race in Cameron's reply. "And even less compassion for white women, I suppose."

"The Apache, Mrs. Radcliffe, have little experience with compassion, either in nature or man."

"They are purposefully cruel, then."

"*Hardened*, not cruel. And no more vicious than the white man," Cameron answered, and in the moments that followed before he left her staring after him, Cameron Wolfe drew Honey shivering into the silence that surrounded him.

CHAPTER FIVE

If Shahar needed to stay within the margins of the everyday world, she could manage for a time to foil the Spirits. But now, amidst the hurly-burly of their preparations for travel west across the continent, if there was an urgency, it was to grasp the tendrils of her dreams and allow herself to be pulled away by them. Shahar opened the pores of her soul and waited to be summoned.

At first the darkness proved a void.

Experience told her to be patient.

She knew that the discordant hum she but no one else sometimes heard when Honey and Cameron Wolfe were in the same room together had an explanation. When the time was right, Shahar knew she would have it. Therefore, she kept her own counsel.

Then, one morning, Nollie burst into Honey's room with no announcement. "It's Mammy!" she cried, shaking Honey awake. "I can't rouse her."

Honey bounded out of bed in the dawn, not bothering to pull any sort of wrap around her shoulders or find something for her feet, and rushed to Shahar's room on the second floor.

Fast on Honey's heels, Nollie lit the bedside lamp, which Honey lifted above Shahar, who seemed not to be breathing, her skin unusually cool to Honey's touch. Had Honey not witnessed the state before, she surely would have thought Mammy dead.

Honey took a silver hand mirror from a bureau and placed the glass beneath Shahar's nose. She waited for the mirror under the nostrils to fog over.

Nothing happened.

Nollie began to cry. "She isn't breathing—is she?"

"I won't say that, not yet," Honey replied, and thrust the lamp into Nollie's hands. She sat beside Shahar then and felt for a pulse, her own heart pounding wildly. After several fearful seconds, Honey finally felt a faint response against her fingertips.

Nollie began to sob.

"Shhhhhhhhh!" Honey ordered, and gritting her teeth, with every nerve alert, watched and waited for a sign. Ten minutes of agonizing silence later, there occurred several seconds of clear movement beneath Shahar's closed eyelids. After another long pause, there was more eye movement beneath the lids.

Honey breathed a deep sigh. To her knowledge, it had been years since Shahar had experienced this kind of state. Honey shuddered as she realized that many an army doctor in the war would have declared Shahar dead without a moment's hesitation and ordered the body removed for burial. But Shahar was not dead, merely "traveling," as she described it.

Feeling a wildly churning mixture of anger and ecstatic relief, Honey rose from the edge of Shahar's bed. "She wouldn't *dare* pass on at this moment," Honey insisted, pale with anxiety and clearly much the worse for wear. Then she hugged Nollie, whose tears were now in gratitude, and sighed. "I can barely remember the last time this happened. You know, there's nothing to do but wait her out."

"How could she?" Nollie sobbed, relieved yet horrified, humiliated that her mother had resumed the practice of communing with her Spirit Beings. "I thought she'd been cured. How could Mammy do this—especially now?"

Honey released Nollie from her embrace. "It's probably my fault," she mumbled.

"Your fault?"

Honey headed for the door. "A few weeks ago I asked her to consult her Spirits."

"You didn't!"

"You needn't carry on, Nollie. I already regret it," Honey said, hoping to stave off Nollie's wrath as she hurried back to her own room. But Nollie was a step behind her.

"It's a disgrace! It's heathen!" Nollie cried. She held herself above other negroes who believed rather openly in Spirits. "Your daddy ought to have put an end to her conjuring once and for all."

"You know he only had limited power where Shahar was concerned," Honey reminded Nollie. "When she wanted something, Shahar usually had my father where *she* wanted."

"Damnation, girl. She's stirred up good. And it's all *your* fault." Nollie stewed, remembering the usual goings-on when

Shahar was "traveling." "Now she'll be dragging her spooks with us the whole way to California."

"Maybe we can persuade her to leave them somewhere along the trail," Honey suggested wistfully.

"Just *what* did you ask Mammy to do?"

"Nothing important," Honey said firmly, then splashed water on her face from a basin on a bureau.

"Tell me, or I'll make trouble."

Honey laughed at Nollie's lapse to a threat from their childhood. *Tell me or I'll make trouble for you with your daddy.* Honey began to brush her hair. "All I did was ask her to consult the Spirits about Mr. Wolfe."

" '*All*'?" With a loud groan, Nollie flopped down on Honey's bed. "That's *all* she'd ever need to sashay into limbo and bring back every last one of her Spirits."

Honey pulled off her nightgown and put on a thin chemise and petticoat. "I've said I was sorry."

"You haven't even begun to be sorry. A flat-out invitation is what she's been waiting for . . . and what with Mr. Wolfe, she has fresh fat for the fire."

"You know I had to be in a state myself to ask for help."

Honey opened the wardrobe, and Nollie seemed to revive. "You've not worn the challis this week," she said, getting up from the bed. She pulled the dress out for Honey's inspection. Honey nodded her approval, and Nollie helped her into it.

Then Nollie took down another dress, a brown silk taffeta trimmed with black velvet, from the wardrobe. "You taking this with you?"

"I may have occasion to wear it. We will, after all, be aboard a steamboat, and in Saint Louis for a time."

"Aren't you giving up mourning a little soon?"

"My best mourning dress is worn thin from so much use."

"Mmmmm." Nollie held the shimmering taffeta against herself and gazed thoughtfully into a long mirror, then laid the dress on the bed and removed her apron and work dress. Throughout their childhood, Nollie had felt free to try on Honey's dresses, which she continued to do long after her mother forbade it. *Dressing up only puts foolish ideas in a colored girl's head. What's more, no colored lady wears that kind of dress.*

Nollie still longed for the kind of clothes that had filled Honey's several highly polished walnut wardrobes to overflowing before the war. Often she tried to deny her resentment over the disparity of their stations in life, and this moment was one of them as Nollie enjoyed the dream of possessing such a magnificent dress—and having a respectable place to wear it.

Nollie was a head shorter and more delicately boned than Honey, and the tafetta gown fit her loosely even without the requisite boned corset Honey would have worn.

Honey pulled in the waist at Nollie's back so that the dress appeared to fit, except in the bust, where Nollie lacked Honey's abundance. "That's a perfect color on you. And a good thing your mother's unconscious." Both young women laughed, then began to giggle uncontrollably. Later, when they went downstairs, Honey stood beside Nollie in the kitchen and did her best to fill in for Shahar, which wasn't easy.

Before the war, Shahar's fate as a bondswoman had not been the common one of unremitting toil and exhaustion. She had rarely performed strictly menial tasks, but as other negro servants slowly disappeared from the Greerfield house, choosing, as did many slaves throughout the South, to strike out on their own, it had been necessary for Shahar to assume duties she had never had before. By the time the South had surrendered and only a half dozen servants remained in Greerfield, the situation had demanded that even Honey acquire a number of domestic skills— far more than she cared to.

This morning Nollie and Honey worked silently side by side, with Honey earnestly trying to help more than she got in the way. Nollie was demandingly finicky about what went on in her kitchen, and Honey obediently gave her all to kneading bread dough.

Of all the times to choose, Honey thought to herself, a light sheen of perspiration coming to her brow, *why did Shahar have to hie off with her Spirits now? What was so damned urgent?* Their fate had been decided. No message from the netherworld could possibly alter their course at this point in time. "At least not mine," Honey muttered to herself, but she worried anxiously that Shahar might change her mind about making the journey west.

Honey remembered a bit too clearly that Shahar had not been wildly enthusiastic about the journey in the first place.

"Uncle Trevor wants me to return with him to California." Honey had told Shahar nervously.

"So I hear." Shahar laced Honey's corset as she helped Honey dress for dinner with her uncle. Honey had revived the formality of dressing for dinner when Trevor Jefferson arrived from California.

"Well?"

"Well, what?" Shahar chuckled softly. "You don't want *me* to decide for you, do you?"

"I wish you would," Honey sighed, lifting a petticoat over her head.

"So you can blame me if you get to being unhappy?"

"Shahar, *please*. This is no time to remind me of my failings."

"Who else would dare?"

"You've changed the subject. Now, please, consider my proposal seriously."

"I have. California's a mighty long way to go. And dangerous."

"Can you promise there'll be no more danger here?"

"I suppose not—not with General Sherman heading this way." Both women fell silent and, as Shahar fastened the long panel of buttons down Honey's slim back, fearfully envisioned Sherman's troops marauding over their beloved land.

"I can't go west without you. Or Nollie. I simply couldn't."

"You recall, of course, that I'm now a free woman. And Olivia, also."

Honey stiffened at Shahar's reminder. "Of course I remember." Honey pulled away from Shahar and moved to the uncovered window. Unable to face Shahar eye to eye, she kept her back to her. "When have I ever treated you like a slave? I think of Nollie more as a, well, my sister. I always have. When I look at either of you, I don't think of you as 'negro.'" Honey's voice wavered. "I can't leave you behind; I love you; you and Nollie are all that's left of my family." Honey clenched her jaw and bit back tears. "Surely you know."

"Still, it needs to be said," Shahar answered gently, for the moment choosing not to enter into a discussion of the accuracy of Honey's memory regarding her behavior as mistress of Greerfield.

Honey turned slowly to face Shahar again. "Then if I go, you'll come with me?"

For several moments Shahar stood silent and gazed reflectively at Honey. "I am getting old," she said.

"As I am—and before my time! That's not an answer."

"I can't speak for Olivia."

"But for yourself?"

"If Olivia will go . . . I will, also."

"I *cannot* go without you," Honey repeated, and reached for Shahar's comforting embrace.

Shahar had sighed from deep within her soul. "Then we three shall have to go together," she said, a promise Honey remembered clearly as, covered with a paste of sweat and flour, she fumed. *Damn Shahar's Spirits. They'd best not interfere!*

From time to time throughout the day Honey looked in on Shahar, who might be "gone" a few hours or days, but in the past never more than two days running.

"Shahar is unwell this morning," Honey explained to Cameron as she laid the table for his breakfast herself. "Our dwindling fortunes leave us but six people in town. So I'm doctor one day, servant the next—a white woman reduced to the level of a slave." She favored Cameron with a smile. "Be assured, I've learned a good many things during the war. By far, I prefer to be waited on hand and foot and would rather do surgery than scrub pots, thank you." Cameron was deceived by Honey's gaiety, but not Nollie, as both women waited on Shahar's recovery.

The next morning, much to their relief, Shahar regained consciousness, but she did not appear downstairs. Instead, she sat in her room for the whole day. From experience Nollie and Honey knew Shahar would not be her old self for several days. She needed time to gather her thoughts, to sift through the prophecies and symbols she had been subjected to before she revealed anything to anyone, if she shared anything at all.

A strong current of excitement ran through Shahar's veins, tempered by flashes of terror. She was not infallible. She saw others' destinies more clearly than her own; sometimes her deciphering was off. Foresight was at best a mixed blessing, one's powers limited, one's ability to intercede minute, one's right to interfere open to argument. A sign might appear more ominous than it was. Or less. Occasionally she was completely baffled, but Shahar usually saw clearly, just as she had seen Cameron Wolfe that first time.

This time, with the exception of the frequent mention of Nathan Radcliffe's name, Shahar was entirely satisfied with her travels, certain that she clearly perceived what had been laid out before her. In life, many circumstances needed to be changed, but according to the will of God, not the whim of man, who was frequently deaf and ruled by self-interest. God, Shahar believed, was often misquoted.

It did not please Shahar to have knowledge of the pain that Honey would suffer in the months ahead, although she believed sincerely in the justice of karma and the transmigration of souls as well as the necessity of tribulation for the maturing of the soul and its ultimate purification. In her own case certainly, Shahar had borne many severe trials, the road to salvation having been a hard one.

Greerfield's other house slaves had all been overtly Christian converts whose heritage of animistic beliefs was subdued in the presence of the master and his family. The others viewed Shahar's philosophy as a curious aberration explained by her journey from Africa to Egypt and India and, finally, America. Exotic at least, her obvious rank and favor in Dr. Greer's household lent credence to her mystical bent. Shahar was thought to be a seeress and was held in respect.

Now Shahar surrendered to a violent shiver and pulled her favorite shawl over her narrow shoulders. She knew her intuition about Nathan Radcliffe had been correct; she was more convinced than ever that as Honey's husband he would have been Honey's undoing.

Where a good man would have had proper influence on Honey, weaning her away from willful ambition by the weight of reason, as Phillip Greer originally had tried to do, Nathan's first choice would have been to force Honey's submission by asserting his rights as a husband and *master*. Honey, who loved nothing better than a challenge, would have taken up the gauntlet, wise or not.

Shahar had seen in Nathan cruelty, a streak of meanness, even a need to destroy that no one else seemed to notice and that a spirited woman, a wife especially, would attract in him. The Greer and Radcliffe families' influence aside, Nathan had pursued Honey Greer for the worst reasons: She was spirited, and he had wanted to break her.

Shahar well had known men like that herself. Her own mother had been owned by such a man, an Englishman in Africa, where Shahar had been handed over to a Frenchman at an early age for a handsome price. From Africa through Egypt to another Englishman in India, then to the New World, and at last to Phillip Greer for the settlement of a gambling debt, her punishment for being barren.

Shahar had learned to make use of a smoldering elusiveness, which in reality was unexpressed rage as much as pride, and cultivated her sensuality to secure better treatment, the desperate choice of a slave who was hungry and powerless, whose whippings had erotic implications. Uprooted, tutored, subjugated and used, Shahar had nothing of her own but the Spirits, cures, and rituals of Africa to comfort her, which from land to land underwent metamorphoses. Beyond a vivid desire, she had no real dream of ever being free, but even in bondage her soul was freer than the air.

At first Shahar had believed life was like a vine that climbed a tree trunk, each new leaf causing the vine to spiral ever higher up the trunk as, at death, one's soul passed from one body to another in a continuous spiral of life. Shahar's African name meant "Grandmother Has Returned." She believed the sense of God to be innate to all born human. In Egypt, she had encountered the teachings of Mohammed; in India, the concept of karma and a different view of life after life; elsewhere, varieties of Christianity, always with the emphasis on obedience and the reward of final peace after death for the good slave.

In Dr. Greer's household, she was exposed to daily reading of the Holy Scripture, which Margaret Greer had instituted for the benefit of her family and the house slaves. Jesus spoke to Sharhar; she saw in the Redeemer the love of God. And privately, she still held fast to the notion of rebirth.

When the children had been little, she had told them stories that were an amalgam of her experiences and were used to prick the conscience of the wayward rather than apply the rod. "Once there was a Princess. She was very beautiful and lazy and, most of all, wicked. She knew how to behave. To please Allah, she must keep her temper, do right by her people, and above all praise Allah. Instead, she was willful. She became drunk; she woke the palace with the screaming of her slaves when she beat them. She forgot God's name. When she died, Allah turned the Princess into a flea. Now she would endure a thousand lives if ever she would please Allah."

"A flea?" Honey and Nollie had protested, both resolving to be forever righteous.

When Honey was no longer a child to be unduly influenced, Shahar had argued her position openly. "More than once in the Bible, Jesus himself says John the Baptist was the Prophet Elijah come back to life, and 'born of woman,' not returned in a 'chariot of fire' in a whirlwind. 'He that hath ears to hear, let him hear.'"

"Say the Lord resurrected Elijah," Honey countered, "surely one doesn't take that to mean *everyone* will be resurrected time after time as you insist. Furthermore, the Bible says John came only with the 'spirit and power' of Elijah. Not as Elijah himself."

Shahar shook her head. "Jesus said John *was* Elijah. The spirit means the soul: John had Elijah's soul in his body."

Honey scoured her Bible for the texts on which they disagreed. She found them and read them aloud. She conceded how Shahar might have come to her conclusions but thought Shahar's interpretation much too simple. "You're being too literal."

"'He that hath ears to hear, let him hear,'" Shahar repeated, not impressed. "Do you deny the Lord performs miracles?"

"It will indeed be a miracle if some day you convert me."

Shahar smiled triumphantly. "I don't need do any such thing. You'll convert your own self."

Until she had come to Phillip Greer at the age of twenty-four, Shahar had vowed never to give life to a child for the slave master's gain and with herbs had poisoned each new life within her, setting those souls free for yet another evolution. She came to Phillip Greer under the taunt "He'll tire of you and send you to the fields where you belong" as nurse to Phillip's children, and for his wife, who held no suspicion about Shahar having stolen her husband's affections until she saw that Shahar loved the infant Honey almost as dearly as her own Olivia, who had been born the year before.

To Shahar, Olivia was a miracle, the cultivated flower of unexpected passion, gauze for raw wounds, and Honey, her lover's daughter also, a twin. Margaret recognized that Shahar's affection for Honey was not the ruse of a cunning servant but adoration for a child who might have been her own.

Margaret Greer, who from the advent of her third son was unfit to bear more children, watched her husband slowly withdraw, with her rival beneath her very nose, unseen. Like so many other white Southern women, Margaret was blind to the truth in her own household yet cognizant of the sin that gnawed voraciously at the foundation of slave-owning society: the licentious use of negro women by white men.

Margaret simply could not imagine Shahar, who was "appallingly" thin by the day's standards and a head taller than Dr. Greer, with her "purely black skin and purely negro features," would ever appeal to the Doctor in spite of her indisputable grace and appealing tenderness and, when offered, radiant smile. In addition, Shahar had a slave husband abroad, Lin-Davey, who worked on a plantation a day's ride away. Margaret did not know it was a marriage of convenience arranged by Phillip Greer to better conceal his liaison with the handsome and elegant Shahar.

Unlike his wife, Phillip Greer saw beyond the polished shade of Shahar's black skin. That which was distasteful to his wife was appreciated by him. He saw the aristocratic length of her nose, perceived her mouth as full and sensual, her "bramble for hair" as a frothy dark halo.

Ignorant of what was going on around her, Margaret spoke freely to Shahar of the distressing influence wayward husbands had on their impressionable young sons. "Why it only encourages them to behave abominably. And if she's a bondswoman, they breed those treacherous mongrels." Shahar, silent, was furious yet sympathetic toward her mistress's aching jealousy. It pained Shahar to watch the woman suffer——a woman who at heart was tender and romantic, a woman who had named her baby Honey-suckle because of the fragrance wafting in the windows the morn-ing of Honey's birth. In reality, Phillip was as much his wife's master as he was Shahar's.

Margaret Greer never confronted either Shahar or Phillip with her suspicions of their venery, which was a secret to no one save the youngest children. The three principal actors played out the tragedy as if they were blind. Wooing her husband away from his black wench, whom she too late knew to be Shahar, and saving his soul became Margaret Greer's *raison d'être* but was, finally, her *raison de mourir*: Margaret died in childbed, delivering a stillborn baby she had conceived in a desperate effort to win back her husband's affection. "The truth is," Shahar had sighed to herself at her mistress's grave, "all women's no better than slaves."

To Phillip Greer, at first, Shahar was only a slave mistress who embodied the image of the naturally promiscuous negro woman, a reputation suggested to him by Shahar's former master, which, as a man who was avoiding a wife's bed, Phillip was willing to encourage. He felt an instantaneous attraction to Sha-har, but his passion was not to remain simply sexual. Over time, Phillip's relationship with Shahar evolved to one of deep love. The miracle was that Shahar could love Phillip, too.

In the beginning, to survive and preserve her sanity, the slave told herself the good master would free the good slave and did whatever Master Greer required, while, without risk of rejection, Phillip, a man who needed more from a woman than mere sexual service, had shared all of himself—good and bad. Shahar's salvation had been that underneath the cruelty of the system of slavery, at heart Phillip Greer was a decent man. The more of himself he shared with her, the more Shahar found she could trust him.

As Shahar gave herself up to Phillip gradually, his seduction all the more complete, they grew entwined, more enmeshed as daily Shahar assumed more responsibility and became the surrogate mistress of Greerfield, the keeper of the keys. The inconsistencies, the biting omissions, she knew were karma: this but one life.

Phillip discovered that Shahar was witty, intelligent, and often shrewd. Once she had released her conviction that she could not love a white man, there arose within her an untapped wellspring of love that overflowed and filled up his soul. Within their bond of affection, both lovers were liberated.

In her time, Margaret Greer herself never had more authority, and Shahar reigned for years as the unspoken mistress of Greerfield. Fortunately, Dr. Greer had been forward-looking enough to make arrangements for Shahar's freedom and a small legacy in the event of his death. But at his death, during the late War between the States, all Shahar had received was her freedom and the promise Honey had made to her father:

"Promise me you'll make it your *duty* to look after Shahar."

"I will, of course," Honey promised, never having intended otherwise.

"All this has not turned out exactly as I'd have it."

"Not as any of us would, Father."

He then asked for time alone with Shahar. A convert under her influence, he believed they were soul mates. "We will meet again," he promised before he died in her arms.

Without him, alone, Shahar wondered, *What woman is ever free?* Even a proper white lady, a woman of delicacy as Phillip had insisted Honey become, was expected to be a perpetual child, passively dependent on her master—father, husband, or brother—some male, for a lifetime. The idea of freedom did not apply to women, black or white.

What was it about the female that made men crave to have her under their thumbs? Was it something in *women* or something fearfully lacking in them? Were women naturally weak or naturally *too* strong?

Free or not, Shahar felt tied to Greerfield, at least while Honey was there. The truth was, as Margaret Greer had known, if not flesh of her flesh or bone of her bone, Honey was Shahar's daughter in spirit. The truth had become blurred long ago.

In that debate about going west, Shahar had faced the most difficult dilemma of her life—which daughter to choose—and Nollie had put her mother through proper hell.

"I'm *not* going!" she had insisted, warming up if necessary for a scene of high drama.

"And just what will you do with yourself?"

"I'll stay behind and keep the house in order."

"There's far more to be in charge of than you realize. Besides, the house is to be closed up tight."

"If I stay behind, she won't have to board it up."

"You're a freed woman now. She has no duty toward you anymore."

"She can't sell me off, either. And you don't have to continue to jump when she gets a notion in her head. You're a freed woman, too."

Shahar scowled at her obstinate daughter. "Of course, with so many run away, you could take up the hoe and earn your keep. . . ."

"I could stay with China and Jotham."

And go hungry? Shahar had wanted to say. Instead she offered, "Put it under your pillow, daughter. We'll talk again tomorrow."

"I'm *not* going. That's final."

Shahar let Nollie stew in her own juices for a few days, but when Shahar did not bring the subject up, Nollie decided she still had a few more things to say.

"My right eye if California will be a fresh start for *me*. Why should I go a million miles so *she* can imagine nothing is changed? In her mind we're still slaves. In California, she'll be the lady again. She won't have to lift a finger, but you and I—we'll *still* be doing laundry and wringing chicken necks. We'll always have to say, 'Yes, ma'am.'"

"That's not fair."

"You're taking *her* side *again*! She's *not* your mistress anymore! When are you ever going to see my side?"

Shahar would not be baited. "There's nothing left for you here, girl. Here, you're just one more dark face in an ocean of dark faces."

Nollie ran from the room, but when the storm passed, she reluctantly conceded. "I'll go with you, if only to see if the streets are really paved with gold."

"If you had a husband, you could stay behind."

"Hell can freeze over, I'm not getting married, and that *is* final!"

Gracefully, Shahar had let Nollie have the last word.

CHAPTER SIX

In Honey Radcliffe's opinion, the three men who arrived at Greerfield to join the party going west were ordinary sorts. Wilton Ramsey, Timothy Watts, and Roarke Murray had traveled from California with her uncle, Trevor Jefferson, earlier in the year. While Trevor had visited Honey, they had gone on to Richmond and waited for him there but had not returned with him to California. The woman who accompanied the men, Ruth Blocher, a Confederate widow and a refugee of burned-out Richmond, was Roarke Murray's sister, and she hoped to make a new life for herself in California. She seemed already to have an eye on Wilton Ramsey as a potential new husband, Honey noted, but also, very early after meeting Cameron Wolfe, Ruth seemed to take an avid interest in him, almost immediately inquiring whether he was a married man.

Ruth was a plain but pleasant-looking woman with a natural grace, and Honey could understand readily a man's interest in her. Cordial and warm, she seemed always to be smiling. She looked a man directly in the eye when she spoke to him, making him feel the center of the world, a gesture that Honey knew was a salve to any man's vanity.

This evaluation aside, Honey took an instant dislike to Mrs. Blocher and in private found fault with the woman's appearance —the drab brown color of her hair, the narrow set of her blue eyes, her lack of tasteful clothes—unforgiving of the fact that Ruth had been one of the many to flee Richmond with little more than the clothes on their backs.

"You'd think the poor woman had the evil eye," Shahar remarked to Nollie.

"Well, Mammy, Mrs. Blocher's not the sort Honey would usually take up with."

Shahar paused to consider her daughter's assessment. Although seemingly a pleasant woman, Mrs. Blocher was cut of too common cloth to establish anything but a distant rapport with Honey Radcliffe. "Still, she mustn't forget her manners. She's just short of rude to the lady."

"Maybe you should scold her," Nollie offered.

"I'll do that," Shahar promised, but hesitated, believing there was more than the gap in social standing to make Honey rebuff Mrs. Blocher. Perhaps her response was simply foreboding on Honey's part, for Shahar had been forewarned of grave trouble between the women who would travel on this journey.

"What do you mean impolite," Honey demanded when Shahar challenged her attitude with Ruth Blocher. "I've been nothing but civil to her."

Shahar nodded. "Exactly. Even Nollie sees it. I'm sure even Mr. Wolfe notices. You're like the cat stalking a bird—pretending to look away but at any moment ready to pounce and pull its throat out."

Honey looked at Shahar as coolly as she did Ruth Blocher.

"I know you thrive on trouble, Honey Greer, but it's a mighty long distance to California. Besides, child, I'm absolutely certain when all is said and done, you've nothing to worry over. The man is helpless to avoid you."

Honey's eyes narrowed as she strained to comprehend the shift in conversation. "What, exactly, is that supposed to mean?"

"Mr. Wolfe."

"Mr. Wolfe?" Honey shook her head as if to clear it and focus better on Shahar's meaning.

"He's come for you."

"I see," Honey said, growing very ill at ease. "Shahar . . . what are you saying?"

"I thought you knew," Shahar said, clearly shocked by Honey's apparent innocence. "At least there've been times I've seen you two together and thought, 'Honey knows.'"

"Knows what, Shahar?" Honey's eyes narrowed.

"I've seen clear as day, Cameron Wolfe is the man you've been waiting for."

"Waiting for? Truly, Shahar, I . . ."

"There'll be many trials and tribulations, even grief. But you'll lay down your life for him, if need be."

Honey was struck dumb.

Shahar paused before continuing; she knew Honey needed time to absorb the idea of having any sort of personal attachment to their guide. "Or, perhaps, it's only that you shall be reborn."

"How can you consider such a thing! Even if you do, I recall your strict standards about men who dared court me away from Nathan. There was a time, Shahar Daniels, when you'd have never allowed Mr. Wolfe even to set foot in this house." Honey laughed aloud at the very idea of Cameron Wolfe coming to court her. "Now just imagine it, please, Shahar, Mr. Wolfe arriving at my door in well-worn buckskin to escort me somewhere—why, every woolly-headed darky in the county would have collapsed in astonishment." Her eyes sparkled with amusement, but, truly outraged by the idea, she felt very near tears.

"There's more to the man than meets the eye. You've shared many lifetimes together."

Honey waved her hands as if to clear the air. "Stop this nonsense at once! I *won't* hear another word! I can see I'll repent my begging you to call on your Spirits to my dying day."

"My silence will change nothing," Shahar said with absolute calm. "You've been waiting all this life for Mr. Cameron."

"You're mad!" Honey said angrily. "If ever I waited for anyone, I waited for Colonel Radcliffe! And you see what came of it."

"I know now more surely than ever, Mr. Nathan was not for you."

"How can you say that? We were meant for each other. Everyone said so." Tears glittered in Honey's eyes. "My father insisted!"

"Dr. Greer surely was wrongheaded in the matter. The truth is, Mr. Nathan was poison for you—and he was even denied the opportunity to make you truly his wife."

"By heaven, I suppose—a fact which, of course, the whole world knows." Honey glared at Shahar. "You're usually so reasonable, not a lunatic at all. If you were a common wide-eyed darky taken to tossing babies over graves, I'd better understand your inclination to this preposterous bent."

"I cannot ignore the Spirits, nor can I deny my memory of the past," Shahar replied. "And you, Honey Greer, can't go calling on me to seek the advice of my spirit guides, then be denying them 'cause you don't like their advice. You'd do remember,

Jesus said John be Elijah born again—and what Jesus say be good enough fo' this darky."

Honey covered her ears. "Shahar, *please!*" she begged, refusing to be called into a debate. "How could you think that man and I . . ." Honey's words stuck in her throat. With humiliation she recalled her brief yet intense attraction to Cameron Wolfe.

"I know it's true; in your soul, so do you."

Honey straightened her posture and steadied her voice. "I warn you, Shahar, don't ever bring this subject up again!"

"You cannot avoid the truth forever, Honey Greer."

Flushed with color, Honey gave Shahar a scathing look. "Radcliffe!" she corrected, and rushed from her room.

CHAPTER SEVEN

All was in readiness for the traveling party to leave Greerfield the next morning. The Greerfield house was boarded up, and the last planks to seal the front door were standing in wait. Arrangements for the other Greer properties had been made also. Yet, in spite of three cups of strong valerian root tea, Shahar's favorite "soothative," that Honey drank to ease Shahar as much as to calm her own nerves, Honey still was not the least drowsy. The tea usually worked wonders by inducing drowsiness, although sometimes it also inspired vivid dreams. But not this time, and when all of the others seemed to be asleep in their beds, Honey, dressed in a white batiste nightgown and pink silk wrapper, silently prowled the Greerfield house like a cat surveying the night landscape.

Using a small lamp to light her way in the warm late April night, Honey slowly roamed from one unoccupied room to another, upstairs and down. Everything had been checked and rechecked for readiness, yet Honey seemed to search the three-story house as if she feared some vital detail had been overlooked.

The possibility existed that she might return to Greerfield, and furniture to be left behind was covered with sheeting as protection from dust. Honey found it hard to believe that she would *never* come back to North Carolina, yet she faced that probability. In the next few years the prospects for the South were grim. How could they not be with a generation of Southern men obliterated, a way of life destroyed, and the survivors demoralized?

Slowly, Honey walked from room to room, touching objects she would leave behind in a poignant ceremony of farewell. Downstairs, still restless, she knew it was useless to go to bed. In the dining room she pulled the dust cover off the long rosewood table and sat down at its head perhaps, she realized, for the last time. Honey listened for the familiar creaks and whispers of wooden beams as tears welled in her eyes. "Good-bye," she whispered to the house that from birth had sheltered her.

She folded her arms on the table, laid her head down, and cried, but in a short while regained her composure and relaxed into the ample comfort of the armchair. She extinguished the lamp. Soon dreamy from the rhythm of her own breathing, Honey would have slept but for a sudden sense of the presence of someone in the room.

Cautiously, Honey looked about her but could detect no one in the almost total darkness. She strained her hearing to the slightest wisp of air. "Who's there?" she wondered aloud, not so much frightened as curious.

"I am," came the answer from somewhere across the table.

Still unable to see him, a chill ran up Honey's spine. Heart pounding, she had not fully expected a response. From his daring proximity, she would not have been more startled if a specter had materialized before her eyes. She lit the lamp again to find him standing in the doorway to her right.

"I heard some rustling and decided to take a look," Cameron said as he approached the table.

"In this household, Mr. Wolfe, a 'rustling' doesn't necessarily mean you'll discover anyone," Honey remarked coolly. She felt she should appreciate his sense of responsibility and concern for the welfare of the household but instead was annoyed by his intrusion upon her privacy, his having spied on her. "How long have you been there?"

"I found you on the third floor."

Astonished that she had only just become aware of him, Honey stared at Cameron Wolfe. "And only now informed me of your presence?" She thought his insolence outrageous and paused for his response. When there was none, she made an observation of her own. "You're as silent as a cat or, perhaps, a savage indian, Mr. Wolfe." Honey wondered where he had acquired traits that allowed him to follow her unobserved and utterly silent; or perhaps he was by nature secretive and cunning. Again, Honey sensed the dark and mysterious about him.

"Nothing sly about you, Mrs. Radcliffe. You're easy to track."

A silence followed during which Honey felt herself physically drawn to Cameron Wolfe, possessed again by a desire to know much more about him: who he was and where he had come from. She thought of Shahar and her opinion of his presence, of her belief in their past lives and their destiny together in this one. How utterly preposterous! Honey thought as she gazed now at Cameron Wolfe, yet her curiosity remained, and as she sat before him, consciously opened her mind and heart, and tried to fathom the essence of the man to whom, tomorrow, she would entrust her person—the man who would lead her from civilization into the wilderness and across the wide expanse of the American continent.

In the four past weeks Honey had learned to admire Cameron Wolfe. Her natural discretion and ingrained polite regard for privacy had kept her from direct inquiry into his background, but voluntarily he had informed her of his little formal education, which surprised Honey greatly since she had judged from his ability to read and his confident manner and speech that he had had a fair amount of schooling. Regardless, she had concluded, Cameron Wolfe had an excellent mind. Furthermore, he had intuitive powers, more than any other man she had known. He also possessed a wealth of common sense. Thus far, he had been able to perform any task required of him and seemed widely experienced, more than Honey expected of a man who said he had been "a drifter, cowboy, drover, and rancher."

She was no longer afraid of him, in fact, now discovered herself inclined to him in a very unsettling and fundamental way. Instinctively, Honey knew, if Cameron Wolfe were to breach the few feet between them now, she would pull him tightly against her and revel in their contact. She would, she admitted, invite his kiss and respond passionately.

Honey inhaled deeply, only halfheartedly wanting this strange yet wonderful tension to ease and disappear.

When Cameron did exactly what she yearned for him to do, Honey rose to embrace him, yielding her open mouth to his. Passion leapt from her, ignited by the flames she felt escaping from him. She returned Cameron's fierce kisses, his strong arms encircling her more tightly. When he called her name tenderly, all conscience, all sense of propriety vanished. His mouth on hers, her body cleaving to his, felt absolutely right.

His heart beat wildly against her breast, and as he moved deliberately against her, his hunger, his longing sounded a responsive chord within her. Honey wanted only to give him whatever he required and never, even for a moment, considered that she ought escape him.

Her own heart leaping in her breast, Honey felt light-headed, faint. The pale glow of light surrounding them seemed to shimmer. The universe began to spin. Honey closed her eyes. Pressed against him, aching deliciously, she lost all sense of time and place.

Drained of all connection with the present world, she had a sense of knowing, of embracing the familiar. His scent, his taste, the man himself, she recognized. She felt she had never not known him. Each intoxicating kiss, each daring caress magnified this perception. He seemed to seek her very soul.

For a moment Honey feared she would swoon under the duress of her heightened emotions, but when she opened her eyes, she saw as clearly as any woman enraptured by a man. At first she was only aware of his shining blue eyes as he smiled down on her, but when she focused on his beautiful face, she saw details out of the corners of her eyes that mystified her.

The light of candles flickering made the scene especially dim. There were fresh rushes on a bare stone floor. She inhaled deeply the fragrance of rosemary and lavender and realized that the man in whose arms she was wore a many-tiered high collar of elaborate lace, a deep rust-colored, quilted wool doublet and breeches, and sleeves also edged with ruffs of lace. A short black velvet cape covered his shoulders; a heavy sword was at his hip. By startling contrast, she wore a gown of dark brown homespun tied at her slender waist with a thin leather cord, her long hair pulled back at the nape of her neck and fastened with the same kind of crude tie. Although what she saw perplexed her, she could not fathom why and so dismissed it, preferring instead to dwell on the perfect man who held her in his arms.

"I thought my wait never to end," she purred as he lowered his hand from her waist and pulled her even more closely to himself, then thrust against her in a way there was no mistaking.

"I come a vast distance. 'Twas not a trifling quest."

"Yea, sir. Still, I am exceeding curious—with needs full bold as yours, what took thee?" She kissed him deeply and teased him mercilessly with vigorous motions of her body against his rigid shaft.

"Alas, I tarry but a moment, then need be away."

"'Tis ever thus." She sighed and raised his hands to her breasts. "Hast thou not yearned for me?"

"Just so!" he cried, affected deeply by her gesture.

She kissed him repeatedly; her hands traveled to his impressive erection. "Then, sir, thou shall this while make good thine oath to stay with me till the bright light of the morrow!"

"Aye, lass, I dream of the occasion, but not this eve," he pleaded.

"So what I prayed rumor is truth!" She tried to pull away from him. "Thou hast wed the lady Edwina!"

"Never! Unless the Queen Herself commands." Forcefully, he held her in his arms and, with thoroughness, seduced her with his passion. She replied to his urgent groans with quick provocative movements against him as she both surrendered and pursued.

"Let me carry you to your bed, or come with me to mine," Cameron strained to whisper when, finally, he pulled his mouth from hers.

Forced to make such a choice was a jolting interruption and enough to bring Honey abruptly to her senses. Frozen in his arms, her fingers laid on him indecently, she stared in horror at Cameron Wolfe, all too aware of the degree of his excitement. Desperately, she struggled to regain control of her whirling emotions and a grip on reality. Not many moments before this, Honey Radcliffe would have sworn that she was innocent of the seductive dance they did, but the sudden descent of spiraling sensations left her aching miserably and made that argument unsupportable.

His blue eyes blazing with sexual heat, the memory of her touching him, Honey stared at Cameron, both of them still burning from her bold caresses. "Please, forgive me!" Honey stammered as she forced herself from Cameron's viselike embrace. "I can't begin to explain!"

Stunned by her behavior, Honey questioned her sanity. What on earth had possessed her? How could she have behaved in so lewd a fashion? *Never, not even with Nathan—especially not Nathan!*

In pure dismay, Honey put her head in her hands, quite close to giving way to a barrage of hysterical tears. Reason had always been her ally, but the wild sense she had of knowing him, the stirring of her blood, and the familiar pleasure of his touch were things she felt she could never account for rationally. How could she, who lacked any carnal experience with men, have responded as if they had often made love?

Perhaps it was simply that she had experienced some sort of vision. *In this house, such events cannot be said to be unheard of!* Certainly she had every reason not to be herself. With the war. With her losses. With her witness to so much misery and death. . . .

Honey was frightened: Was she suddenly deranged? With that suggestion Honey lost her composure completely and began to cry. Then, abruptly, her eyes dry and her expression reflecting her bewilderment, she decided to test him. "Did we speak of Edwina?" she inquired calmly.

"I don't call one woman's name when I'm with another," he said bluntly.

Honey forced herself to look Cameron in the eye. "You must think me at the very least a loose and wretched woman."

Cameron glared at Honey harshly. "Does it matter, Mrs. Radcliffe, what I think?"

"Of course it matters," Honey replied, tears flooding her eyes again. "Before this awful episode, I thought we, at least, held one another in high regard. And now..." Despising herself, Honey's tears again rushed unrestrained.

Cameron took a deep breath. "Maybe this journey is too much for you, after all," he suggested to her firmly but with surprising gentleness.

"There is *not* a thing wrong with me!" Honey shouted.

Cameron laughed at her vehemence.

"How dare you laugh?"

"How dare *you* plead innocence, Mrs. Radcliffe!" Brusquely, Cameron lifted Honey off her feet and into his arms. "I'm taking you to your room."

"Put me down. I'm perfectly capable of seeing myself to my room." When it became obvious he had no intention of putting her down, Honey added in as decisive a tone as she could manage, "I hope there shall be no unfortunate misunderstanding this time. I intend to go to bed."

Again Cameron laughed.

"Alone!"

Smiling broadly, Cameron secured Honey more tightly in his arms. "Yes, ma'am."

This promise, given without any note of rancor in his voice, soothed Honey noticeably. "I shouldn't blame you if you thought me at least a little mad."

"Not mad, Mrs. Radcliffe, but, like your kind, accustomed to leading men on for sport."

Honey bristled. "I am not *that sort* of woman."

"No?" Cameron answered as they arrived at her door and he put her down. "Then give me an *honest* answer this time." Cameron drew Honey forcefully against him and seized her mouth with passion, instantly renewing a perilous level of excitement in himself and her.

At first Honey struggled, astonished by the seeming depth of his emotion and by her own furious desire to submit to him. But just as she was about to surrender to the wild sparks that shot through her every fiber, Cameron released her from his impassioned grip. "My apologies, Mrs. Radcliffe," he said with remarkable detachment. "I was wrong."

Forced by a tremendous weakness in her limbs to support herself by leaning against her door, Honey gasped for air. "How dare you? How dare you?" she sputtered as he walked away. An impotent response, it was all she could muster while reaching behind her for the doorknob and, trembling, retreating to the safety of her room.

Shaking not from anger but from the effect of Cameron's kisses, Honey ran to her bed and burrowed underneath the covers. She wished she could hide away forever. Her feelings and her thoughts in shambles, she recalled with astonishing clarity their fevered exchange of kisses and caresses and ached desperately from his incandescent touch.

Honey thought long and hard about the moments she had spent in Cameron's arms, reviewing as best she could what had happened, convinced she had not purposely led him on. Instead, believing devoutly in rational explanations for all experience, she chose to believe she had been subjected to some sort of vision. "Damn you, Shahar, for filling my head with wicked ideas!" Honey cried, acutely feeling the need to assign blame to someone besides herself. Surely, if Shahar had not suggested that Cameron Wolfe was the man she was destined for and spoken eerily of their past together, a suggestion to which she was vulnerable by reason of . . . exhaustion . . . insanity . . . this embarrassing experience might never have happened.

In Honey's distressed condition as a widow, as a survivor of the recent devastating war, Shahar had been able to put notions into her head that, although absurd, had acted on her imagination like yeast on flour. Shahar's supposed gleanings from the Spirits, her revelation that Honey and Cameron had shared other lifetimes together, had only been the catalyst. *But wouldn't only a lunatic hear a conversation which, clearly, could have only come from another time and place?* If she had been in her right mind instead of responding like a harlot to Cameron Wolfe's efforts to make love to her, she would have put him in his place!

Honey considered herself a complete skeptic about reincarnation and had argued her position with Shahar often, yet something deep within her soul wanted to believe Shahar's pronouncements, and something deep within her was compelled by the logic and philosophy that promised another chance at life, a chance to redeem mistakes.

For hours Honey kept herself awake countering her sudden instinct to believe with logic. That learned men whom her father had read and admired, Ralph Waldo Emerson, for one, accepted reincarnation as a fact did little to sway Honey's opinion. Even déjà vu, the sense of having been someplace before although it is in fact the first occasion of one's visit, which Honey freely admitted experiencing, was not convincing enough evidence for her. Shahar believed that sense of knowing was a bit of memory from a past life. "If it were true we live over and over again, why wouldn't we remember *everything*, not just bits and pieces, so that we might benefit from past errors in our present life?"

"I've not all the answers."

"You ask me to accept the notion of rebirth only on faith?"

"Seems sometimes faith is needed to believe in God at all."

"Mammy, you blaspheme!"

"Only your faith, Honey Greer, makes it so!"

In the case at hand, Honey believed it was quite illogical to argue, as Shahar did, that she was destined to be united with Cameron Wolfe when he in every respect was so obviously beneath her regard. His apparent competence at whatever he did, his perfection as a vigorous, masculine man, as well as his mysterious appeal, could not overcome the fact that he was quite a common sort, without real breeding, social position, or education. Yet neither was Honey prepared to accept her responses to

Cameron Wolfe this night as natural. Certainly she had no experience whatever to claim them so. What Shahar had suggested was impossible, Honey insisted, and yet she could not explain her behavior logically.

On the last night she would spend in Greerfield, tormented, confused, afraid she might never again be free to be a complete skeptic about Shahar's philosophy, Honey Radcliffe lay in her bed and groaned aloud for her humiliating responses to Cameron Wolfe's lascivious advances and, exhausted, prayed fervently for sound, sweet dreamless sleep.

CHAPTER EIGHT

Both were naked, their skin glistening with a thin moisture from the joyous effort of making love. Breathing heavily, he now held himself quietly above her. There was no mistaking his adoration, which cast a tenderness over his strong, manly features. In the candle glow, his was the figure of a golden statue worthy of worship in a pagan rite. He smiled down at her and reached for several stems of lavender that lay beside her pillow, then drew the soft, fragrant blossoms gently across her cheek and down to the throbbing pulse at her throat. He tantalized her as with feathers, descending along the curve of her neck to describe each love-tender breast, each taut nipple.

She inhaled deeply of the delicate scent of lavender, which mingled elusively with the bolder strewn herbs, rosemary, and thyme. She feared she might expire from the effect of too intense sensation.

He knew she was at the precipice of release, and he was merciless, taunting her by lightly inscribing circles on her silky abdomen. He listened with pleasure to her soft moans until she cried out wildly beneath him, then, meeting her starry gaze, gathered her into his arms to be enveloped by the same delirious frenzy as she was. Afterward, tears and laughter and words were smothered by kisses, their passion the greedy hunger of oft-separated lovers.

Later, she lay silent and watched him dress, filling her sight with his impression, which would have to last until she could hold him in her arms once more.

In the next breath, fully clothed, she bathed at the edge of a bubbling stream, the heat of the summer sun driving her far downstream into the shade of overhanging trees. Usually such heat was only mildly oppressive, but pregnant, she felt she was being roasted alive. Waist deep in the gently flowing water, she knelt until the water came to her chin. Bathing threatened her health, but the risk meant nothing to her.

She had walked for days, her only goal to reach him. She was gaunt, but her still small belly was prominent. As some women did, she suffered greatly, but her misery was not simply physical. He didn't know of her condition yet, but word of his marriage had reached her ears. No doubt he would expect her to bear his child gladly: Bastards were as common as sparrows. In spite of everything, she still believed his whispered vows of love but felt the fool to have thought his promise to make her his wife a true one. She felt ruined by his betrayal, too late understanding that the only kind of woman he would take as a bride would be a favorite at court, and a virgin.

The next instant, concealed by trees, she stood next to the final steep approach to the castle. Certain she saw her lover standing at the casemate above the bridge, she waited until a quarter of his mounted horsemen passed before her, then ran into their midst. In the melee of startled horses and men, in spite of the attempt to avoid her, she was trampled several times.

Still conscious, she heard the snorting and nickering of horses and the searing oaths of men. She felt broken and tasted dirt and blood on her tongue. Then she felt a hand on her shoulder as a man turned her over in the road, his angry face at some time replaced by one contorted with grief. Tears streamed from the man's eyes. She knew him. "Gavin," she murmured.

"But why?" he demanded.

"I thought myself your lady."

She felt his hand on her high round belly. "Oh, my love." He pulled her against him tightly. "My only love," he cried.

A heartbeat later, she was gone.

Honey bolted upright in her bed, panting, sweating, certain the taste in her mouth was a noxious mixture of mud and blood. The clock downstairs began its musical announcement of the hour, then began to chime. One. Two.

Honey waited, then fell back on her pillows. Only two A.M.! Without a doubt, this would be the longest night of her life. Purposefully, she tried to avoid the vivid recollection of her dream and the vivid recognition of the man she had just seen in her nightmare—the same figure of a man she had held in her arms earlier in the evening when she so wantonly...

I've surely gone mad. What else was there to conclude about the events of the evening? It wasn't unheard of for the mind of a woman of a certain age to give way. She knew personally of women who kept to themselves for reasons of inconstant mental health, some merely eccentric, others fitful.

But, Honey reasoned, she could not justly use the excuses of being "a certain age" or being feeble-minded. There was no history of lunatics in her family, with the exception of Lucinda, who was a cousin by reason of a second marriage and whose condition was perhaps assignable to the blood of the second spouse.

Honey sighed in frustration. The night was interminable! She needed restful sleep, not sleep tormented by vivid, unsettling dreams. In the morning she needed to be refreshed, ready for the commencement of a long journey, not exhausted and with heavy eyelids.

The experience of her dream was as if the events were actually occurring, each sensation, every emotion real and deeply felt. There was no distortion of events, as was often the case with nightmares, which she suffered very infrequently. Surely the upsetting realities of her life were to blame—and how weary she was of that excuse, which conveniently covered every recent mishap!

Honey shivered violently.

Even now, with eyes closed, she seemed to have the memory of the taste of every kiss, a sense of every caress. She remembered the fragrance of lavender—and seemed to breathe it still! She felt not only his presence but his weight upon her body, her union with him.

Impossible! Honey's rational mind insisted.

The left side of Honey's face and body ached, the hand especially; her head throbbed.

In her dream, the most injured side of the woman's body had been the left.

Honey's right hand moved to her flat abdomen; she sensed it swollen—high and round.

Honey's eyes filled with tears, her heart as full of lonely grief as the bathing woman's in the dream had been. Had that weakness she had felt on first meeting Cameron Wolfe been recognition? Had it been *déjà vu*? If so, what explained her adamant unwillingness to meet her fate with him this time? Was she fated to love him, perhaps die because of him again? "Reason enough to be wary, Shahar, to be unwilling to believe," Honey whispered.

She could hear Shahar's reply: *"There is nothing to fear. One life leads to another; your duty only to learn."* Honey surrendered then, and let her emotions flow freely, without questioning or striving further for explanations, whispering "Gavin" the instant before she finally fell asleep.

CHAPTER NINE

In the morning, after a cold breakfast, everyone but Honey abandoned the house. Throughout the meal she had not been able to look Cameron in the eye, but when he finally reentered the house, she summoned the courage to meet his direct blue gaze.

"My apologies, Mrs. Radcliffe, for last night. I assure you, nothing like that will happen again."

"And I assure *you*, Mr. Wolfe, should you dare take another such liberty, I shall not respond in any misleading fashion." Honey's face was a deep shade of red by the conclusion of her threat.

Cameron smiled, a light of unconcerned amusement boldly showing in his eyes. "I understand perfectly. Now, if you'll come with me, we're set to leave." Cameron extended his arm to Honey. For a moment she hesitated, then accepted.

He led her to a wagon loaded high with baggage and helped her settle into the high seat. Without another word, Cameron turned away and supervised the final closing of the Greerfield house. Items to be transported west but not carried on the trail were crated and stored at the port of Wilmington for shipment by sea at the first opportunity. These possessions would probably arrive in Sacramento a short time after she did.

Honey felt calm, quite beyond tears, yet she could not bring herself to look back at the house as the final sturdy planks of pine were sealed over the front entry. She wanted to remember the house open and full of life.

They had not far to go to the Greerfield wharf, where they would board a steamer for Fayetteville. A number of people, black and white, came to see Honey, Shahar, and Nollie off, and none of the three escaped tears. Honey had expected to see some of Nathan's people, but they disappointed her.

"Mrs. Radcliffe's ailing," Shahar reminded her.

Although she had not long been a member of the Radcliffe family and perhaps had never been a recognized member under law, she had thought the ties between the Greer and Radcliffe families were sufficiently close to warant a farewell the day of her departure, perhaps for good.

Standing at the rail next to Honey when the paddle wheeler *Mary Beth* finally pulled away from the dock, Mrs. Blocher offered her sympathy. "I know how hard it is to leave friends and family," she said.

"Thank you," Honey answered in acknowledgment of the kind remark.

"But I didn't have anything or anybody left in Richmond to stay for. You, at least, had your house and beautiful things still standin'. In your place, I think I'da stayed put."

Honey stiffened her back but held her tongue.

Shahar patted Honey's arm. "It will be easier once we're on the road," she whispered as encouragement.

"Will it? Or will it only be so dreadful an experience, I won't recall this pain?"

Shahar shrugged her shoulders, and everyone in their party except for Cameron and Roarke Murray, who elected to remain with the wagon and the dozen horses and half-dozen mules on the cargo deck, seemed to settle into his or her own private thoughts. They sat inside an enclosed passenger deck on wide, high-backed wooden benches. Foremost in everyone's mind was the hope of bearing up under the hardship of the long journey ahead. In such a party, it was to be expected that at least one person would fall by the wayside, and each one hoped he would not be that casualty.

If in spite of the last weeks of frantic preparation Honey truly felt the whole episode of planning a bit surreal, boarding the steamer bound for Fayetteville made the event entirely real. Not accommodated in a luxurious private cabin for the long day's journey, Honey sat next to Nollie and faced Shahar, both of whom, in spite of the emotional farewell at the dock, now seemed surprisingly at ease.

There was no turning back, Honey realized, but she could not think of a time when she had been more terrified or lonely in her life—*Only in my dream did I feel so miserable . . .*

Shahar put her hand on Honey's tightly folded gloved hand. "You're color's gone pale, and we've not even left Greerfield wharf."

Honey's heart was pounding so wildly, she couldn't speak.

"Maybe you should go outside for some fresh air."

Honey shook her head slowly. "I don't suffer seasickness," she replied, but would be eternally grateful Cameron Wolfe could not see her. It would only renew his concern for her health. "I'm fine," she lied.

"You look to me very much like you're about to . . ." Nollie said, but caught a furious look from Shahar and did not finish. "I'll go out with you if you want."

Honey declined and after a few moments of unbearable restlessness closed her eyes. Breathing deeply several times, she tried to empty her mind of every thought and slowly relaxed. She began to daydream as an odd mixture of familiar images began to drift through her brain. She thought of the afternoons of croquet with friends on shaded summer lawns and glasses of lemonade flavored with long sprigs of sharp tangy mint, then of scenes from her years at Mrs. Isabel's Boarding School for Young Ladies in Columbia. Next she remembered her brief sojourn to a female college some years later where she continued to study music, French, and the decorative arts, where the mornings were spent contemplating the virtues and writing essays on morality and the value to society of passionless womanhood. She recalled how she had been bored to tears with such occupation, and rather than a failure, had returned home unmatriculated to "practice" medicine with her father. Memories of nursing Confederate wounded for days at a stretch assailed her—of often doing little more than listening to last wishes and the names of family to notify, if that. In her head there rose a series of hideous scenes of blood and pain and the unforgettable stench of death; the dreams put aside; the loved ones committed to the earth; a husband she had never really known.

Then, with weariness from the unpleasant night just passed, Honey drifted readily into that twilight stage of consciousness before falling asleep, at times still aware of what went on around

her, at others oblivious. In this state, the image of a man in
Elizabethan dress mingled with images from the present day, a
jumble of fragments. His face was indistinct, but she recognized
the man, felt drawn to him and enormously sad. Beginning to
cry, she woke with a jolt.

Tears blurred her vision for a moment, and she dabbed her
eyes with a handkerchief she pulled from the wrist of her un-
adorned black traveling dress. She stared at Shahar, who was
obviously lost in her own thoughts. Only Nollie looked her way.

"I don't know why you're taking on," Nollie said, conveniently forgetting her earlier refusal to set foot from Greerfield.
"There's nothing important left. All the people and things that
matter, they're gone. Might as well start fresh."

"Did my eyes deceive me, or didn't I just see you crying at the
dock?" Shahar said, then turned her gaze on Honey, who reached
for her and Nollie's hands.

"Till death do us part, ladies," Honey said.

"You mustn't say that," Nollie insisted, and pulled her hand
away. "In spite of what I said, my heart is just about pounding
right out my chest. Besides, you can't fairly argue there was
something to stay on for," she persisted.

"I'm happy to hear you say so, but I'm more interested in
what you imagine lies ahead," Shahar challenged the young
women.

Nollie huffed. "As if you hadn't already peeped into your
crystal ball, Mammy! I'm positive you already have everything
all laid out." She shot Honey a troubled glance.

"I wish *I* could interpret dreams," Honey suddenly blurted
out, wishing she had the courage to confide her recent visions to
Shahar.

Nollie rolled her eyes. "Oh, Lordy. This is going to be a *long*
trip."

Desperate to avoid the images that still tugged at her, Honey
squeezed Nollie's hand and forced gaiety into her voice. "Come,
Nollie, let's indulge in a game we haven't played for years: telling the future."

Nollie heard the false note in Honey's voice and withheld the
abrasive reply that was already forming on her tongue. Instead,
she nodded agreeably and, putting curiosity at the back of her
mind, fell into a contemplative pose.

With hands joined, the three women stared in silence at one
another, participating in a game often played when Honey and

Nollie were children. After several moments of concentration, Nollie volunteered, "I'm scared."

"Not permitted," Honey insisted.

More silence.

"This shall be the adventure of our lives."

"You better hope none of us loses her scalp."

"Nollie!" Honey and Shahar chimed together.

"No fears, just pretty dreams?"

The two other women nodded.

"Mmmmm." Nollie let her mind wander some more, liking the game less and less as the moments passed. Finally, she offered, "I'm going to have a house of my own, a trunk full of silk gowns, and hats, and a carriage with horses, and a *gentleman*."

"You'll marry him, of course," her mother insisted.

"Absolutely not."

Shahar scowled at Nollie.

Nollie ignored her mother. "Your turn," she said to Honey.

Honey took a deep breath. Should she speak her heart's wish or suggest a more likely course?

Her heart! This, after all, was only for amusement—to keep her mind off other, more disturbing turns of mind. "In California, there will be such lack and need, I shall be allowed to be a doctor. I'll become famous. Other female doctors will be welcomed after me."

Nollie laughed. "You mean to say you'll be *infamous*. A lady doesn't have her name before the public."

Honey frowned. "This is *my* dream, remember?" She turned to Shahar. "We'll be daring and give you a turn." Honey hoped Shahar could not read her mind or visualize events that had occurred as recently as the night before.

"The rule is, you can only make predictions about yourself, remember?" Nollie prompted her mother.

After several moments of reflection, Shahar said, "The strongest image coming to mind concerns Honey, not me."

Immediately, Honey regretted having invited Shahar into the game. "You heard what Nollie said. Think only of yourself."

Shahar stared intently at Honey. "I see chaos."

"Glory be!" Nollie grumbled. "We could've stayed home for that. You wonder why we never allowed you much say?"

"But we did," Honey reminded Nollie, "when we were brave enough."

"Make her stop," Nollie implored. "I'm already nerved up enough." She pulled her hand out of Honey's and her mother's grasp.

"Come, Shahar, something pleasant," Honey implored.

"And a lie?"

"If necessary," Honey said, and stretched out her hand to Nollie, who again linked hers with the other two.

"In the end, I see myself happy and satisfied," Shahar admitted.

"Lord God be praised, and that's enough," Nollie said, quickly breaking their chain of hands again. "Now, I'd like to read a little, or maybe enjoy the sights out the window. I haven't been this way in a long, long while."

"You can't see anything out that filthy glass."

"I'm just happy not to be the one to scrub it clean!" Nollie said, and gave her mother something of a smirk.

Honey smiled at Nollie, who always preferred to cook rather than to clean, and hoped Nollie would be able to have at least that wish fulfilled in her new life. Honey looked then to Shahar, who had already closed her eyes to rest. She was much darker than her daughter, and taller; Honey thought Shahar looked regal in repose, a slender African queen. For her serenity alone, Honey understood her father's fondness for the woman.

Honey knew her father had acquired Shahar in a game of cards from a doctor with whom he'd studied in Paris at the École de Medicine. Shahar had come to him well after the law had forbidden the importation of slaves, her exchange settling the friend's debt, which Honey knew had been in excess of a thousand dollars, making Shahar a bargain since she was young and healthy, a good woman to breed more slaves to add to the profit of the Greer enterprises. Honey did not know that the prominent reason for Shahar's sale had been her failure to bear children or that Nollie was her father's child. Shahar, after all, had a husband, whom Honey had known.

By the time Honey was old enough to question her father's deep regard for Shahar, it was easier not to delve too deeply, not to probe. Honey loved Shahar. Her brothers did also. Her father's affection made perfect sense to the child, as did Shahar's loyalty to him. Since Dr. Greer was a Christian and a law-abiding citizen, it also followed that his affection had respectable boundaries, limits that forbade intimacy outside of marriage as well as the mixing of the races. Dr. Greer never spoke to Honey of holding any opinion contrary to the common one regarding whites who impregnated black women, spawning inferior mongrels.

Shahar was as exotic as she was beautiful in Honey's eyes. She refused to eat any meat—flesh—of any kind; had held the children's rapt attention with Hindu or African fables, and often entertained them with predictions of the future.

"Some would say you're a witch, Mammy. Lucky you didn't live in old Salem," Honey's brother Clayton had said once when one of Shahar's projections had turned out to be amazingly accurate.

"What makes you think I didn't?"

The children's hair had stood on end.

Never one to mince words, Honey demanded, "What makes you think you *did*?"

"You'd have burned at the stake!" Billy said.

"No. Been hanged or, maybe, pressed to death," Shahar corrected. "In fact, I was hanged."

"Oh!" the four Greer children exclaimed in unison. Then, afraid to inquire further, they quickly changed the subject.

Shahar's Hindu-African belief in reincarnation had always troubled Honey. Shahar had been baptized in the slaves' Baptist church, which was strongly in favor of submitting to authority, of doing one's duty to one's master, and which, on the subject of life after life, was as conservative as the Episcopalian, Honey's affiliation, which asserted that the faithful waited until the end of time for resurrection from death. Shahar's long trances, when Honey became aware of them, were infrequent, as were the apparitions that came accompanied by cold drafts, sometimes in the dead heat of summer, and were put down to childish "imaginating," the tinkling of voices to mere musical wisps of wind.

Uneasily still, Honey admitted that part of her longed to believe in the salvation offered by rebirth—the chance to redeem one's mistakes, to evolve into a higher state of being—but logic continued to work against her. "Wishful thinking," Honey sighed. Loving Shahar, she tried to be patient with the woman's fast but un-Christian beliefs, but her patience sometimes wore thin. She lamented having been in such a weakened state as to cause her to beg Shahar to stir up the Spirits.

Daring to reflect on the incident with Cameron Wolfe the night before, which she wished to blame on Shahar, Honey blushed crimson, grateful that for the moment Shahar's eyes were closed! She wondered how Shahar would interpret her lewd behavior with Cameron Wolfe and the images that had taken her over and caused her to act obscenely, that tormented her sleep and now even threatened her daydreams.

Would Shahar's explanations be more appealing than the one of *insanity*?

Perhaps, Honey allowed, but in the bright light of day she was convinced nothing good could come from interpreting her responses to Cameron Wolfe as linked in any way to a past life—a wholly absurd notion.

Would her intimation that bodily harm would come to him should he think of daring any future advances cow him—or her dreams? Would it diminish his appeal, which, if honest, she could not deny?

How convenient it would be to take no responsibility at all for her behavior! To blame the pull she felt toward the man on a connection to a romantic past! Yet considering other plausible excuses, this one by far had the most appeal!

How unfortunate I know it to be a bald-faced lie! She also instinctively understood that whatever her conviction regarding the more spiritual side of life, Cameron Wolfe was a considerable force to be reckoned with—*a living, breathing, virile man*—and any future they had significantly more urgent than anything in the past.

CHAPTER TEN

The steamer *Mary Beth* arrived in Fayetteville very late in the afternoon and was met at the dock by Samuel Hadley and his daughter, Rebecca. Honey had known Becca at the female college before the war. The young women embraced each other joyfully. "The war is over for good, at last. We all can start up our lives again and begin seeing our dear friends. I only wish the end could've come a little earlier for your sake. I'm heartbroken about Colonel Radcliffe," Becca said to Honey, and hugged her friend tightly a second time.

"I am glad you've come this way—and disgraced to show you what has befallen us," Becca confessed as they settled in a wagon her father had borrowed to bring them to what was left of the Hadley Plantation for the night.

Soon after hearing accounts of Sherman's march through South Carolina, with the Union Army then sweeping north through Fayetteville to Goldsboro, Honey had written her friend, wanting to know how she had fared. With Becca's letter, Honey learned a good deal about the shocking destruction of the Hadley property, yet she was unprepared for the actual devastation both of their plantation and of Fayetteville in general. Buildings had been leveled and burned to the ground, the countryside was ravaged, and large woods had been destroyed by fire, all in the name of foraging but truthfully for revenge—which, of course, was denied.

"As you can see, we lost nearly everything," Becca pointed out on the short ride to the Hadley Plantation. "Sherman's dogs —and they smelled worse than the worst kind of dirty dog—scavenged everything. What they considered unusable was broken and burned. They hacked up Mama's piano with my daddy's own ax. We only managed to save what we could carry and what we'd hastily buried in a secret underground cellar.

"Union rats rolled up carpets, took tools, bedding, clothes, and food, of course, caring not at all that we were left homeless, to starve. The animals they didn't carry off they killed, leaving the carcasses to rot. They even set the house on fire. Fortunately, rain, the bane of our last war efforts, doused the flames. That's the only reason we have part of a roof over our heads now. We hid from the enemy in the woods, forced to wallow like hogs in mud. The supposed saviors of the black man even stole from our negroes. You just can't imagine, Honey, what it was like."

"No, I can't," Honey answered, with a chill recalling newspaper accounts of Sherman's march north that had filled her with terror, struck dumb by what she now saw of the effects of that army's punishing movement. Only a miracle had kept Greerfield property on the high west bank of the Cape Fear River from a similar fate. Now, seeing for herself what easily could have happened to her own home, Honey felt only rage.

"What did your mammy foresee of all this? Did you have any warning?" Becca wondered. "We surely could have used a little prophesying in these parts."

"Mammy kept a good deal to herself about the family, not wanting to break our hearts," Honey answered. "But she named in order the boys in Greerfield who would die on the battlefield until my brother Clayton died. We didn't have the courage to ask if she'd known about him. We were afraid to ask anything about the other boys.

"I'm sure she knew about my father also. But not Nathan. Nathan's death surely did surprise her."

"I say it's a curse to see what lies ahead," Becca reflected. "It was best not to know a thing about our misery in advance. I'm sure if we'd been told, we would have simply refused to believe it possible, the Lord being on our side." Becca sighed, feeling at least a hundred years old, then went on cheerfully. "Surprisingly, we're already quite comfortable, and thrilled that you can spend at least one night with us."

Comfort, Honey realized, was relative as the party prepared for a modest meal. "'Sherman's dogs' is an apt description, Mr. Wolfe," Honey observed to Cameron as they strolled on the ravaged Hadley grounds. Despite the upheaval, the remnants of dogwood trees and azalea bushes had begun to bloom. "You should have seen this ordered, immaculate land before its defilement. What sort of creatures would ravage the country this way?"

"Where we're headed, total destruction is the usual result of warfare."

"Then we're headed to the end of the civilized world."

Cameron appraised Honey without revealing any emotion. "What do you think white men do when they come up against indians? How much do you guess is left of indian camps after an attack?"

"Why do the savages murder innocent men, women, and children?" Honey demanded indignantly.

"They have their reasons."

"But where does it end, Mr. Wolfe?" Honey wondered.

"It doesn't. Not in our lifetimes. Not until the indian is murdered to a man."

Honey was not shocked by Cameron's grizzly evaluation. The question in most minds was whether the red man was actually a "man" at all and not some inferior being; extermination was the policy if pacification failed.

After supper, Honey bade her hosts and the company good night and retired to a tester bed that had been rescued after an attempt by the enemy to reduce it to firewood. Patched in many places, the bed also lacked its canopy drape and stood as a stark reminder of the war, a skeleton.

Exhausted as Honey was after the first day of travel, the emotional departure from Greerfield, and the unsettling encounter with Cameron the night before, the reunion with Becca drained her strength completely. The war had touched Greerfield in significant ways, and in reality Honey had lost almost everything dear to her, but at least she had been spared witnessing the physical ruin of her property.

Surely, Honey believed, the destruction of her home in Greerfield would have been the final blow. How the Hadleys and so many others had survived beyond that insult was a marvel to her. She at least had not had the horror of seeing Greerfield put to the torch before her own eyes or of seeing everything most familiar to her in ruins. She might at least still think her home, if not her life, intact.

Honey believed sincerely that she had never done anything to deserve what had befallen her as a result of the war. She deserved entirely, she felt, the life promised her, the one she and Nathan had dreamed of. She had done nothing so wicked as to merit widowhood or to be reduced to relying on her only remaining relative for sustenance. Marriage to Nathan had meant assuming the responsibilities of womanhood, of sharing her husband's life, putting his wishes ahead of all others, even her own. Obediently, she had put to rest all those inclinations deemed childish fantasy. She had begun to look forward to motherhood, if not the other duties required of the wife of a Southern gentleman. In essence, Honey had exchanged her dreams for those that more precisely belonged to others, and with their loss also, felt her very soul in shreds.

She felt enormous anger and hatred for the Yankees who now overran the South. Even if she might try to dismiss them, the invaders or their leavings were everywhere. At least, she comforted herself, the farther they went west, the less likely she would be to see the enemy. California, Honey had conveniently forgotten, was pro-Union. Surely Trevor Jefferson's state could not be Yankee at heart!

Sleepless, Honey tried to imagine the world she was about to enter; the contrasts of view that came to mind made her uncomfortable. While Uncle Trevor painted one scene, Cameron Wolfe drew another. Cameron's description of his property near Sacramento was pleasant enough, however; the overall landscape of the West from his perspective seemed more barren and cruel than Honey cared to contemplate. If she listened solely to him, far from an escape from the unpleasant aftermath of war, the journey west seemed something of a journey into the lower depths of hell.

When Honey was tired, everything seemed more bleak than it actually was, and in the morning, rested, she still felt eager to get on the road and leave the destruction of Fayetteville and the reminders of war behind them. Ready at daybreak, the party set out for Solemn Grove, some forty miles west of Fayetteville, the mules and the horses that Cameron and the other men had brought with them from the west and the wagon packed to the limit.

At best, North Carolina roads always were poor, and war had done nothing to improve them. Traveling was slow; ten miles a day was good. As they moved westward across the rolling sand hills region covered with longleaf pines to Albemarle, on a crest of the low-lying Uwharrie Mountains, they passed Solemn Grove and ancient Creek indian ruins. After Mount Gilead, they ferried Lake Tillery and began to move north through Concord and to Salisbury, where in passing through the party could not help but gape at the burned-out Confederate stockade of some twenty acres, a site that had been a cotton factory but during the war had served as a prison for thousands of captured Union soldiers, loyalists, and native criminals. The journey's first 140 miles on land took thirteen days of effort and for the most part was uneventful.

At night the party lodged at inns or farms when possible or simply pulled off the road and pitched a tent. At an inn, eager to get some sleep in preparation for the next day's journey, grateful though they were that they were freed from setting up camp, the travelers usually did not linger long over the evening meal. Only rarely did Honey and Cameron remain at the table together after the others departed, but on one occasion they breached the silence that had existed between them the whole of the journey. "I'm surprised to find your endurance equal or better than the others'," Cameron said.

"You overlook the fact that I've spent a fair portion of the last four years nursing wounded twenty hours a day," Honey reminded him defensively, while she blushed furiously at the discomfort of being completely alone with him for the first time since her lapse of sanity. "I may not have toiled in the fields with my negroes," she continued nervously, "but my stamina is equal to many a man's."

"Looking at you, it's hard to imagine you working in a war hospital," Cameron confessed.

"You've forgotten the long hours I sat by you."

Cameron shook his head.

It was a pleasure to sit with you, a voice inside Honey whispered at the memory of Cameron lying naked while she bathed his fevered body with cool witch hazel. Honey blushed at her vision. "I'd be a doctor now myself, if . . . well . . . if I'd had my way," she stated emphatically.

Cameron smiled at the heat of Honey's announcement. "Grateful as your patients would be, doctoring still seems an unfit calling for a lady."

"Then I'd prefer not to be a lady." Honey frowned. "I've as worthy a brain in my head and as stout a heart as any man."

"I don't doubt it," he said, but did doubt she would ever jeopardize her standing in society as a lady. It was one thing for her to assist her father and later take his place at home in the emergency of war, and another for Honey Radcliffe to do what was required to be a full-fledged physician and surgeon. Otherwise, this able woman would no doubt already be a doctor, Cameron guessed.

Honey warmed to her subject as she remembered her debates with her doctor father, which had brought her into years-long serious conflict with the person she loved most in the world. *I don't deny my ultimate destiny as a woman, Father, I only wish to be a doctor also!* On this subject and many others, on occasions too numerous to count, Honey had put his love and devotion to her to the acid test. In a family whose tradition it was not to teach girls to read but to teach them a few useful domestic skills—music, needlework, fluency in French and, perhaps, Italian—that would be an advantage when traveling abroad, Honey demanded to be tutored just as her brothers were. She also made a slave her best friend, taught her to read—and both girls were formidably unrepentant when the fact came to light. *I had no choice but to teach her. Nollie wanted to read*, she had said, only one tear escaping her eyes after she had received the only whipping of her life. *The color of Nollie's skin, her fortune in life, shouldn't be the test of her ability to learn as much as she can*, Honey had argued with both her father and Shahar, who was equally upset with her master's daughter. *You give her too much to hope on*, Shahar said, who was far more severe with Nollie than she ever was with Honey. But Honey had the last word, *Nollie deserves to read*, she had insisted, just as Honey later insisted she *deserved* to be a doctor even if no female of any delicacy ever entertained such a notion.

As she looked into Cameron Wolfe's intelligent face, Honey deplored how useless logic seemed to be on the subject of being female. The prevailing notion about the place of women in the natural order of the universe left them little to do but breed offspring and heirs. Honey stared at Cameron and thought how futile it was to continue their conversation. If she had failed to impress her father, who well knew her abilities, what hope did she have of making her arguments before Cameron Wolfe, a much simpler man—and surely a man convinced of a woman's inferior status in the scheme of things?

But Honey had been forced to keep still on the subject of her heart's desire for too long to remain silent at this opportunity to speak out. With fervor she regaled Cameron Wolfe with every reasonable argument in her favor that she had ever used with Dr. Greer. She shared with Cameron some of her experiences during the war without regard for his discomfort or possible embarrassment over the things she candidly revealed of the work she had done.

"I might lack the physical strength to do some of the amputations I saw performed, but I don't lack for general ability in any other area I can think of."

"I've no reason to argue with you."

"But then," Honey sighed, "neither do you have any say in who and who will not become a doctor." She had shared the most important, even intimate, of her thoughts with him, and, unexpectedly, felt very close to him. She smiled at Cameron tenderly. "I fear I've subjected you to an unfair diatribe, Mr. Wolfe, but you aroused my most passionate side and, it appears, caused me to keep us both from a good night's sleep." She rose from her chair.

Keenly subject to Honey's charms, Cameron stood when she did. He extended his arm to her. "I'll take you to your door."

Honey hesitated, reluctant to touch him, recalling with embarrassing ease how she had behaved with him before.

With their quarters upstairs, they were required to climb a narrow staircase, which should have caused Honey to precede him. However, when they reached the staircase, Cameron put his arm around Honey's waist and drew her closely against him.

The contact made Honey feel weak. "I'm more tired than I realized," she said to explain the near buckling of her knees. At her door, conscious again of the outrageous desire to have Cameron pull her into his arms and kiss her, Honey could hardly find the voice to say good night.

Inside the room, Honey leaned against the closed door to catch her breath. In the dark, one of her companions snored, and Honey smiled as she focused her attention on something other than her trembling body. "Fatigue," she whispered to excuse her weakness, but in her heart she knew that diagnosis to be nothing more than a self-serving lie. In truth, Cameron Wolfe affected her senses in fundamental and wonderful ways.

In the last year of the war, the numbers of Confederate deserters in North Carolina had multiplied greatly. By 1865, the specter of ultimate defeat and the advance of Sherman's troops on unprotected Southern families and farms had caused even more unauthorized absences from the ranks. Most men who deserted the field returned home to defend their loved ones and what was left of their property, but a small number turned on the very people they had sworn to defend, attacking and robbing any likely target, and for some a new life began.

When farther west through Morganton, then to Asheville, a town divided by two rivers and surrounded by the Great Smoky and Blue Ridge mountains, the road became more treacherous, Cameron and his charges seemed cognizant of possible danger. As they crossed the Blue Ridge Mountains, a palpable tension, a wariness, sprang up among the travelers, who now watched everyone they encountered on the road with suspicion. Rumors of robberies in the region were rampant. Even Governor Vance, in his statement at the end of the war asking for the cooperation of all North Carolinians, had alluded to the state's problem with persons who were nothing less than highwaymen. However, most of those whom the party from Greerfield passed by in a small but steady stream were seeking only what they were seeking: refuge and perhaps escape from the past and its memories.

In the hazy mountains, which from a distance were truly blue in cast, and amid wildflowers whose crimson-purple blooms were beginning to unfold, Honey lost any sense she had had of their travels being something of a great adventure. Mention of the Cherokee indians whose ancestral grounds they now traversed, while no threat, nonetheless brought to her mind disturbing images of the savages they might well encounter much farther west.

The men of the Greerfield party alternated driving, and the women took turns riding in the wagon, which was a blessed relief as the number of days on the road accumulated. Discomfort and inconvenience became the rule; if tempers didn't flare, neither did they rise much above the cheerless. The wagon mired more often in the road now, and once a wheel broke, forcing the men to unload the wagon for repairs. It was not an unexpected event and might be repeated a score of times in the trek across country. The knowledge did nothing to raise Honey's spirits and pushed her very close to regretting entirely her decision to go west.

As the party neared the North Carolina and Tennessee border, Honey sat in the wagon next to Cameron in silence, afraid to speak her mind for fear of demanding they abandon the journey at once and turn back to Greerfield. His ever alert manner and avid attention to the road and their surroundings did nothing to relieve Honey's anxiety.

"This is perfect country for an ambush," he told her. "Nothing but climbing from low to high ground." The road was hardly two wagons wide.

Honey wanted to cover her ears but reminded herself that today they'd only seen several deer, some possums, and two black bears at a distance and heard myriad bird calls. To bolster her courage she recalled that the party was armed to the teeth, with repeating rifles and handguns at the ready. Wasn't Cameron Wolfe reputed to be, in her uncle's words, "the best possible guide"? She had nothing to be concerned about; weary, she eventually nodded to sleep.

Unknowingly, Honey leaned against Cameron's arm comfortably, when, suddenly, he grabbed her, pulling her with him as he jumped from the wagon. Coming awake again in the midst of chaos, Honey heard sounds of gunfire and screaming.

When they landed, Cameron seized two rifles from behind the wagon seat and tossed one at Honey. "Use it. Your life depends on it!" he ordered, and began firing in front of them, using the wagon mules for cover. Shots came at them from the turn in the road they were about to make, but Honey saw no one.

The other members of the Greerfield party had heard Cameron's shout to get off the road and had scattered into the trees, the women screaming, the men returning fire. Cameron had become aware of an unnatural silence as they had entered the curve of the road when the calling of birds had stopped abruptly. Instinctively, he had known they were about to be ambushed.

Her heart in her throat, Honey fired her weapon without hesitation. Then, distracted by a woman's moan of pain, she turned to see Shahar, who had been riding immediately behind the wagon, lying on the ground, obviously wounded. Honey began to move in Shahar's direction, but a bullet slamming into the wagon just above her head forced her back and to the ground.

"Stay put, damn you, till I tell you to move," Cameron growled. Cameron moved forward, forcing the mules to block the road with the wagon, then took cover in the trees, taking Honey with him and leaving Shahar behind.

The ambushers had positioned themselves perfectly so that they held the high ground under cover of enormous boulders and trees. With opportunity, they could easily pick off travelers as they advanced up the road.

"We can't leave Shahar out there in the open!" Honey protested. Shahar's horse had deserted her, and she lay very exposed. Her right side was bleeding, and she was semiconscious, perhaps from the fall from her horse. Shahar's moans made Honey feel desperate.

"Yes, we can. Don't you move from this spot unless I tell you! She took a shot probably meant for me. But we can't help her now." His look made Honey as afraid of him as of their attackers. Cameron knew their only chance to survive was for at least one of their party to get to higher ground behind their assailants.

His move into the trees brought two of the outlaws partially into the open, one in a tattered Confederate uniform. Cameron immediately felled the ununiformed man, then, crouching, ran back toward the wagon, which as he approached it lurched suddenly forward.

He ran alongside the wagon as it moved, while another of the outlaws swung from around the bend, his sights drawn on Cameron. As the outlaw fired, at least two other shots rang out, Honey's one of them, wounding the outlaw and forcing him to retreat, but when Honey looked to Cameron again, he had disappeared. A sick feeling of fear came over her.

Roarke Murray ran toward her. "Wolfe says for you to get back with the other females," he called as he ran to her side. "They're back a bit."

"I'm not leaving Shahar."

"Suit yourself," Roarke grumbled, and took off down the road, keeping under cover as best he could, dodging behind trees, shots ringing after him. Then he crossed the road and disappeared. He had left behind a loaded revolver and more ammunition for Honey's carbine.

All at once there was silence, and for a moment Honey thought she might be alone on her side of the road. She couldn't get to Shahar, she agonized, without being a target herself.

Then Wilton Ramsey appeared to her left, his freckles standing out prominently against his paler than usual white skin. "There's at least three more still behind those rocks," he shouted. "He and Murray are trying to get 'round 'em. You best get back with the other ladies."

Suddenly, across the road, a great number of rounds were fired, but no shots seemed to come their way. Instantly, carrying her rifle with her, Honey sprang at Shahar. Wilton Ramsey followed, and together they dragged Shahar into the trees. Wilton then hoisted Shahar over his shoulder and ran back with her to where Ruth and Nollie waited, frightened but in relative safety.

When she saw her mother carried so unceremoniously, Nollie began wailing, and when Wilton laid Shahar on the ground, Nollie kneeled next to her, "Where's Honey?" she cried, and frantically began to look after Shahar's wound.

Honey had paused to pick up the extra weapons Roarke Murray had left her when she noticed the silence that had abruptly fallen over the scene. Then she heard Cameron's voice. "Hold your fire," he cried, and soon after appeared in the road with Roarke Murray. "Two more dead. Two others in retreat. Seems there were only five of them."

As Cameron approached, Honey dropped the weapons and rushed forward. "Thank God you're all right," she cried, and threw her arms around him.

"I think you must've given God a hand," Cameron said, glad to return Honey's fierce embrace.

"If I did, it was a miracle."

"I'm glad I forced you to learn to shoot."

"So am I!" Honey said, and hugged him tightly. "So am I!" Then she seemed suddenly fully aware not only of the tone of what she had said but of the fact that she was holding Cameron fiercely and familiarly. Blushing deeply, Honey backed away from him. "I must look after Shahar," she said, turned, and ran.

Not offended this time by her abruptness, Cameron caught the smiles of the three other men and smiled broadly himself.

Honey found Nollie bent over her mother. "It's not as bad as it looks," Nollie said. She had split open the sleeve of Shahar's dress to uncover the wound and applied pressure to quell the bleeding.

With a worried look, Honey knelt next to Shahar and examined the wound. "I guess it's not much, but it hurts like the devil," Shahar whispered to Honey. Ruth Blocher had already made bandages from Shahar's petticoat and now offered Honey fresh ones.

"The bullet seems to have passed through the fleshy part of your arm, missing the bone, thank God," Honey said, refusing the fresh cotton for the moment. "I need carbolic from my doctor's bag in the wagon."

"I'll get it for you," Ruth said, rising. "We surely haven't got very far before getting into a peck of trouble," she observed before leaving. When she returned, she watched Honey quickly and expertly clean and bandage Shahar's arm.

"It could've been so much worse," Honey said when she was done. She gently kissed the hand of Shahar's affected arm, then pressed it against her cheek. "Did you foresee this?" she wondered, trying to make light of what was too frightening to consider—the loss of Shahar.

"If I had, I'd have stayed put at home."

Cameron brought Shahar a shot of a strange alcoholic brew that was too pale to be whiskey. "Your turn to ride in the wagon," he said as he offered her the cup.

"I won't argue, Mr. Wolfe," Shahar said, wincing at the bite of the liquor. "I don't know which is worse, the pain or this awful stuff."

Cameron smiled. "Mescal. A little cure-all I brought from Apache country with me," he said, and helped Shahar to her feet.

"Someone ought to shoot the distiller."

"Probably someone has."

"Surely you're going to pursue those other men," Honey demanded. "Why, they may be lying in wait for us in the road ahead right now."

"More likely we've seen the last of them. They were no match for us when there were five of them. Obviously, they're not Apache used to taking on regiments."

"But Shahar could have been killed—any of us could have been killed!"

"That's a fact, and you're *not* to forget." Cameron spoke not just to Honey but to everyone in the Greerfield party, especially the women.

"But you *can't* just let them get away!" Honey argued.

"Seems odd to hear you cry for blood, Mrs. Radcliffe, when I could hardly get you to pick up a gun not long ago," Cameron observed.

"I take this personally."

"We've got to get moving again. Stay alert, ready to defend yourselves. It may be like this all the way to California. Maybe we'll catch up with them. If we do, ladies, do your damnedest not to scream. Scares the horses and keeps me from hearing what I need to." His gaze fell hard on Nollie, whose screams had been the most shrill.

"Yes, sir," Nollie said meekly, terrified to think that such an event might occur again.

With his sister, Ruth, close to tears at the same thought, Roarke Murray tried to soothe the obviously frightened women. "Don't you fret none, ladies. If it happens again, we'll just dispatch the bastards like we did this time. Mr. Wolfe's deadly—you shoulda seen him in action over there across the road. Snuck up on his man, cut his throat, and gutted him as silent and quick as you please. I shot another, and we scared off the other two." He had thought to reassure them but succeeded only in horrifying the women, Ruth Blocher immediately succumbing to tears.

After collecting the wagon, which had moved forward several hundred yards, and the strings of horses and mules, which fortunately, had dispersed no farther than nearby grazing, and with little ceremony burying the dead, the party got under way again. When they reached another stretch of particularly steep roadway and crested it without incident, they breathed a collective sigh of gratitude, and Cameron entertained the hope of stopping that night at a tavern where he had earlier enjoyed very decent mountain hospitality. On particular guard, he often rode next to Honey but sometimes dropped back and watched her at least as carefully as he did the road and surroundings.

Seated sidesaddle on her mount in their procession, which for the main appeared like it was, a collection of refugees from the war-ravaged South, Honey managed to manifest an elegant and regal attitude. Easily, she could have been a lady of a Renaissance court traveling in a caravan Cameron had read about when still a child in Saint Louis.

Cameron smiled at this vision of Honey.

In many ways this was exactly how he wanted to think of her: a helpless damsel used to being fawned over and unable to do much of anything for herself, a delicate ornament. But the reality of Honey Radcliffe was something quite different, Cameron had discovered. Beneath the fragile demeanor was a strength of character, sometimes a fierceness, and an intelligence that seemed more like a man's. Cameron smiled to himself at this comparison, for if there was anything Honey Radcliffe was not, it was masculine. Increasingly, he was plagued by his physical attraction to her, responding to her purely female essence, a fact that at first annoyed him immensely.

In the beginning, Cameron had viewed Honey as totally unlike the women who usually appealed to him and very different from his Apache wife, whose memory he revered. When he discovered Honey to be far more complex and able than he had allowed, his dilemma became how to regard a woman as bold and as different as she.

And then there was the overpowering effect she at times had on his senses. Wildly attracted to her on the night he had drawn her forcibly into his arms, Cameron had behaved rashly yet experienced the impossible—a feeling of previous and passionate intimacy. When she had responded, he had instantly lost all of the little regard he had for propriety. All he had been aware of was the lightning that crackled between them, the fire he could not deny. In spite of her shamefaced protests afterward, Cameron believed Honey must have experienced something similar, for he would never forget the bold way she had handled him. No man would.

This afternoon, when Honey put her arms around him, he had again been aroused in a manner impossible to ignore. This time, however, although his blood raced in his veins, with great effort Cameron had been light with her. Even now his heart pounded and his body responded to think of her clinging embrace.

Cameron breathed deeply, exhaling slowly, hoping to ease his tension. He was eager to return to the tavern and inn he had visited at Panther Pass several weeks before where perhaps the proprietor's serving girl would be as accommodating as she had been on his earlier stay. Yet Cameron knew images of Honey Radcliffe would not soon leave him at his ease.

The trail they followed crossed the Old Wilderness Road and carried the party west and north into even more steep-ridged passes, the mountains covered with numberless pine, oak, spruce, beech, and ash trees. Interspersed among them were dense pockets of flame azalea and mountain laurel and myriad delicate wildflowers, in some places wide, tangled thickets of pink rhododendron in full bloom. At Honey's urging, Cameron allowed them to stop briefly while the women, with the exception of Shahar, gathered sweet blackberries from the edge of a stream.

Her fingers stained with juice, Honey offered, one by one,

each of the men a brimming handful of berries. When she gave Cameron his allotment, she offered him several extra berries, which he ate from her hand. "Up you go now," he said reluctantly, giving her her horse's reins. "You've distracted us long enough." He smiled on her gently. On the move again, it was hard to keep his mind off her, until the smoky haze of the mountains they had grown accustomed to suddenly turned acrid and dense.

No flames were seen, but soon everyone was choking, with tears streaming from their eyes. Surrounded, at first Cameron tried vainly to turn the party back, but the wind shifted and engulfed them in terrifying smoke. On a ridge, with steep forest above and below them, it was difficult for even the hardened men of the party to obey Cameron's harsh order to stay calm. As they rode single file, one person could hardly see another; the animals were more terrified than their riders and were difficult to control. Wild animals crossed the trail in both directions, trying to find safety; then the wind shifted again, and the smoke seemed to clear.

They hurried on, but after only a few dozen yards flames leapt into their immediate path, forcing the party back again. In the event the wagon would have to be abandoned, Shahar had mounted a horse, and even Cameron, who was the calmest among them, could not conceal his concern. He led them as rapidly as possible from one burned-out section of trail to another. It was obvious the fire had been carefully set.

"Perhaps those men set the fire," Honey shouted, voicing the concern of all. Cameron did not answer but led them up the side of the mountain where it was clear, only to have gunshots ring out at them again. In the already perilous situation, they were forced to defend themselves. Among the women only Nollie lost control and screamed, which proved disastrous as her horse took off as if he had been whipped, wildly dodging trees, with Nollie screaming even louder.

Instantly, Honey set after her, her first thought that Nollie, a fairly inexperienced horsewoman, would probably be killed. Nollie's horse plunged madly but some distance forward broke past the smoke and darted onto the road. Honey knew the animal would probably run until completely winded. If only Nollie could hang on!

As she pursued it, it seemed to Honey that Nollie had the

best horse in the pack. But at last Honey overtook her, and with her help, Nollie reined in the beast.

Honey dismounted, helped Nollie down, and embraced her. "I can't stop shaking," Nollie complained, and they began to laugh. "Do you think he'll beat me for screaming?"

"Just let him try!"

They became aware again of gunfire, and unexpectedly, a man they didn't know came flying at them on horseback, gun drawn. "Get on them horses," he demanded.

When Nollie began screaming, he hit her, giving her a sharp, glancing blow on the side of the head that knocked her to the ground.

Honey went to her knees, crying, "You bastard!" Nollie was out cold, and before Honey could do anything to help her, she was yanked to her feet by her hair. Nearly raised from the ground, Honey grabbed for the man's punishing hand with her own.

"Get on your horse or you'll get worse than your nigra." Honey, compelled by the man's strength alone to do as she was bidden, mounted her horse, to have the reins snatched away from her. Then her abductor forced the horses to gallop and, very shortly, veered off the trail and rode into an invisible hollow.

CHAPTER ELEVEN

Cameron found Nollie as she was walking back down the road in hope of finding her mother and the rest of the Greerfield party. She had a swollen, bloodied wound on the side of her head and began to cry the moment she sighted their guide. "I'm sorry I screamed. I couldn't help myself. Now I can't find Honey or my damned horse," she choked between sobs.

Cameron lifted her with him onto his horse as she explained what she remembered. When they returned to the others, Shahar tried to comfort her, but she could do little.

The fire had burned itself out while Cameron and the others had defended themselves against six men, two of whom they recognized from the earlier attack. Their leader appeared to be the same man in the bedraggled Confederate uniform. "Must be a

Yankee with a stolen uniform," Ruth later insisted of the scoundrel.

Again the Greerfield party killed two of the outlaws, and this time Roarke Murray was hit in the right hand, which prevented him from being much help to the others. Before setting out in search of Honey, Cameron sent Roarke with the women and the wagon in Timothy Watts's charge down the road. He hoped they would reach the inn at Panther Pass before nightfall.

Not until well after dark did Cameron and Wilton Ramsey reach the inn themselves. Grim-faced, they were met with anxious inquiries. "Nothing. We tracked them a while but lost the trail before it got dark."

"It's happened before," the innkeeper cautioned. "Not takin' no women, but attacks on the road. People's des'prit these days." He brought coffee, a large bowl of thick ham-flavored bean soup, and large slabs of dark heavy bread for Cameron and Wilton. "My boy'll give you a hand in the mornin'. It's the best we kin do. Other folks might come outa the hollers t' give a look if 'n I send word."

In the morning, however, as they were saddling the horses for the search, two men came in off the road. One, dressed in an especially filthy long gray Confederate overcoat, asked for Cameron by name. "Got somethin' I 'spect you want."

"Know this man?" Cameron asked the innkeeper's son.

"Seen him."

"Where's he from?"

"Camps down in a holler a ways back. Never find it less'n y' know th' country fer yars."

Cameron turned back to the outlaw. "What could you have that I'd want?"

"Got me a lost lady."

"And being a gentleman you're offering to bring her to us, now you've found us." Cameron smiled as if he believed what he had said.

"Not exactly. Ya see, I figured she's worth somethin' fer all the trouble we had with y'all." Not wanting to appear anxious, Cameron didn't respond. He waited to hear the man's proposition. During the pause, the negotiator lifted his hat and scratched his head, which was covered with filthy blond curls. "Ya see, if 'n I don't get back in reas'nerble time an' a fair sum in my pocket, I've a friend who ain't had a female in a whole lot of days run t'gither—longer than I care to think on—an' never a lady. He's been talkin' mosta the night about what he's set to do, givin' the rest of us all kinda idears." He smiled at the listening men, his lewd pleasure apparent. "Don't think th' lady got much shut-eye for all his jawin'." He began to laugh, but before he could finish the first round of laughter, Cameron put two bullets from a .45 no one saw him draw through the man's head and had the man's companion in his sights before anyone had a chance to react.

"I'll give you a much slower, painful death unless you lead me to the lady and I'm satisfied she's all right."

Astonished with the turn of events, the outlaw choked on his wad of tobacco. "I'll lead ya wherever ya think ya wanna go," he sputtered.

Cameron relieved the man of his rifle, two revolvers, a long butcher knife, and his boots; let him mount up; tied his arms painfully so that his hands were barely free enough to manage his horse awkwardly; then stuffed his mouth with rags to keep him silent. Then, with a rifle in the man's back, Cameron urged him on.

Well armed, Cameron, Timothy Watts, Wilton Ramsey, and the innkeeper's son, Matthew, followed the outlaw for nearly an hour deep into a hollow the men from Greerfield might never have found. As they approached the outlaws' camp with its miserable shack for a shelter, there was a thin wisp of smoke rising from the chimney. A shallow stream rushed several yards behind the shack. Hidden by trees, they dismounted a good distance away. While Timothy lashed the outlaw to a tree, Cameron concealing himself carefully behind rocks, shrubs, and trees, scouted the camp on foot.

When he returned, Cameron spoke to the outlaw. "I'm sending you out to your friends. If you make one false move, I promise I'll wound you, not kill you. And I promise if that comes to pass, you'll be begging me to kill you for days. I lived with Apaches. If you think you've lived a long time up till now, the next three days'll seem longer. Understand?"

The outlaw nodded solemnly, his memory of his companion's demise a great spur to keeping his word.

"When you get halfway to the door, stop and call your friends. Say you've come for the lady. Your partner stayed behind as a surety. You've seen the money—in fact, her ransom is gold."

The outlaw's interest immediately intensified. "As soon as the lady's left safely at a spot you've arranged, your partner's to be released with the gold. Say we're nervous, and you better hurry, or you're sure the deal'll be off. Promise it's all working perfectly. Tell them how anxious we are to get the lady back."

Cameron untied the outlaw. "Before you think of a double cross, consider your brains roasting slowly over a fire while you're dangling just above the flames so you stay alive much longer than you want to." Cameron pulled the rags from the man's mouth.

"Glad to help you out," the man rasped, and did exactly as he was told, feigning glee for the way their plans were working out so agreeably. "Bring her out and let me get going. Coulda got even more out of 'em if Caswell'd brought the nigger girl along. Maybe next time." He laughed.

"Want one of us to go w' ye?"

"Best not. Things're going perfect to plan."

Cameron watched anxiously for Honey, angered greatly when he saw that one of her eyes was purple and swollen shut. She was sullen, dirty, and drawn-looking, but otherwise she appeared unharmed. Her hands, which had been tied behind her, were untied when she was put on her own horse. She followed the mounted outlaw docilely, in silence.

They moved quickly into the trees, and when he was completely concealed from the shack, Cameron revealed himself, signaling Honey to remain silent.

Still terrified and exhausted, at first Honey thought she might only be having some strange sort of vision and refused to trust her eyes. While Timothy Watts held a rifle on the outlaw, she could only stare vacantly at Cameron, who carefully lifted her from her horse and into his arms. When he felt her against him, it was as though he had been dead and his life had suddenly been given back to him.

While he tended her eye with a cool cloth dampened with water from the stream, Cameron confirmed that there were only two men in the shack. "Did they hurt you?" he demanded almost gruffly as they sat above the stream's edge.

"No," she answered in barely a whisper, carefully shaking her aching head. "Not beyond this." She touched her face just below the swollen eye.

Cameron hoped she was telling the truth.

"Now we're even."

Cameron smiled. "I suppose so." He took her in his arms.

Honey clung to Cameron, glad for the comfort of his tight embrace, but the terror-filled hours she had spent with her abductors, who had spelled out in crude graphic detail what her fate would be if they for some reason failed to ransom her, took their toll, and she wept freely.

When she was done, Cameron asked, "You'd tell me if they hurt you?"

"Yes. I'm all right," she promised.

Reluctantly, Cameron entrusted Honey to the innkeeper's son to lead her to safety; then, with the other men, he prepared to commence a showdown with her abductors. A prearranged signal from Cameron would set the avengers in motion. There would, Cameron knew be no justice rendered for the men's crimes unless he arranged it personally.

During the wait, Cameron strategically stationed himself, Wilton, and Timothy in the trees surrounding the shack and tied up the cooperative outlaw near where he was stationing himself. He hoped the two men in the shack would show themselves; if not, he would use their companion to draw them into the open.

As he had hoped, one man, the man in the Confederate uniform, ambled out to the stream. As he squatted to fill a bucket with water, he was struck forcefully in the chest with a knife Cameron had thrown with deadly accuracy. With the force of the blow, the Confederate outlaw sat down in the shallows. The instant he looked up, he saw Cameron on the other bank of the stream, then was struck in the forehead with a rock Cameron had launched from a sling. The outlaw slumped forward, having made no attempt to defend himself.

Unwilling to assume the man dead, gun drawn, Cameron swiftly waded the ice-cold stream and, shoving the outlaw onto his back, pulled the knife from his chest. Then, without a second thought, he cut the man's throat. Now he had only to wait for the man in the shack to get curious about his friend's failure to return.

The moment that man stepped from the cabin, Cameron dispatched him and then, with no mercy, put his gun in the ear of the outlaw still tied to a tree. "You've earned yourself a quick death," he told the man, and fired two shots.

CHAPTER TWELVE

After a tearful reunion, Honey gratefully put herself into Shahar's care. "Aren't the three of us a sight! Shot at. Beat up. Only Mrs. Blocher escaped harm."

"And she's the one been cryin' since the first ambush," Nollie complained.

"Even at the worst moments I knew you'd be all right, though. I felt sure Mr. Wolfe would never let you die this time."

Honey stared at Shahar.

"Don't you look at me like you don't know what I mean."

Honey sighed. "Mammy, I've not the strength for your prophesying just now," she said. After having something to eat and taking a hot bath, which took some doing, Honey went to bed, although it was only midday. She slept fitfully at first, then slumbered deeply, then began to dream of their ordeal on the road and the horrid sleepless night she had spent with her captors. Later, Honey dreamed again of her death before the lover named Gavin and awoke thrashing in her bed, her pulse racing, sweating and terrified.

In the dark, she realized Nollie and Shahar lay sleeping on pallets beside her and, carefully, so that she did not disturb them, abandoned her uncomfortable bed. Through the thin common wall, she heard voices from the inn's public room, certain she recognized Roarke's deep baritone and Cameron's, then Ruth's soprano voice. "I hope she's not too la-di-da to be properly grateful for being rescued. It's only thanks to you, Mr. Wolfe, she's alive."

"La-di-da?" Honey sniffed. " 'La-di-da?' " She burned with irritation.

"I'm sure, if it'd been me you'd saved, I'd show proper gratitude. I'd find some way, Mr. Wolfe. You can be sure."

Cameron made a reply she could not distinguish. Hearty laughter followed, and then Honey realized there were no more voices she recognized. Mad with curiosity, certain she knew exactly how Mrs. Blocher would have shown her gratitude, Honey dressed and reentered the common room, only to find it empty of all but the innkeeper.

"You feelin' better?"

"Yes, thank you."

"Would you be wanting somethin'?"

"No, thank you . . . yes, a cup of tea," she stammered. "Have you seen Mr. Wolfe?"

"Think he's gone out."

"Alone?"

"Far as I know."

When a mug of tea was set before her at a table next to the blazing pinewood fire, Honey scalded her tongue with an impatient sip. *Why should I care whether he's alone or not? If Mrs. Blocher should capture his fancy, why should I feel slighted?*

"I shouldn't," Honey muttered.

"You want something?" the innkeeper said from across the room.

"I said nothing," Honey replied, certain she had not spoken aloud.

The man responded with a grunt.

Several minutes later, the tavern door opened and in walked Cameron Wolfe with Ruth Blocher on his arm. The instant Cameron's eyes met Honey's he disengaged his arm from Mrs. Blocher's. "Good night, ma'am," he said to Ruth, and went directly to Honey's table near the fireplace. "Why aren't you still sleeping?"

"Voices out here woke me."

"Sorry." Cameron smiled. "Do you object if I sit with you and have a drink?"

"I've no objection, of course," Honey said, glad to see Ruth Blocher ascending the stairs as Cameron got a bottle of whiskey from the proprietor then sat on the bench next to Honey. He poured himself a drink but before lifting the glass took Honey's chin in his hand and raised her face more to the firelight. Gently he brushed his fingers over her bruises. "Thank God this is all they did to you."

"Yes, thank God," Honey whispered. "What have you done about those men?"

"They're waiting Judgment Day."

"You mean they're all dead?"

Cameron nodded.

She shivered. "Which is nothing less than they deserve. I hope Mrs. Blocher's right in thinking they were Yankees."

"I don't think they were men to have any cause but their own."

"I want you to know how grateful I am for your rescue. I'm not as 'la-di-da' as some think."

Cameron shrugged and drank some of his whiskey. "What does the opinion of other people matter to you?"

Honey stared into Cameron's incredibly clear, intense blue eyes. "I'm not as free as you are, perhaps, Mr. Wolfe, to ignore the opinion of others. Especially now that all I have left is my reputation and my honor."

"Then you are no freer than the slaves you once owned."

"Perhaps," Honey admitted, and realized again there was more to Cameron Wolfe than met the eye. As she gazed at him, Honey's mind filled with a strong desire to again have his arms around her. Then, suddenly embarrassed, shocked by the ease with which she seemed to fall under his spell, Honey stood up abruptly and bumped Cameron's arm, causing him to spill his whiskey.

"Pardon me, please," she said, and hastily pulled a handkerchief from her skirt pocket. She tried to blot the spill from the table, the front of his shirt, and then his lap—which had a very noticeable effect on Cameron. Realizing too late where her hands had flown, Honey turned to flee.

But Cameron stood and seized her. Merriment danced in his eyes. "You always seem to be running away, Mrs. Radcliffe," he observed with none of the anger he had displayed on the first occasion when she had pulled away after touching him. "What are you afraid of? Maybe yourself?"

Honey could not look Cameron in the eye and bit her lower lip in answer to his question. She felt the errant foolish child as she stood before him with eyes downcast, but as Cameron drew her close and kissed her, she did not respond as a child or suffer any illusion. She succumbed to him exactly as a passionate woman would, leaving no doubt in either of their minds about the effect that her touching and arousing him had had on her—or from whom she had tried vainly to flee.

Shahar stirred on the uncomfortable pallet, waking slowly; fragments of distorted dreams made her coming alert more difficult than usual. At first conscious only of the pain of her wound, she focused on her discomfort and for several minutes stared into the darkness. When she realized Honey was neither in her bed nor in the room, Shahar sat up and lit a candle on the small table next to her bed. She listened for sounds she might recognize, then, rising, pulled a wool shawl around her narrow shoulders.

Shahar opened the room door and peered into the drafty, unlit hallway, where light from the fireplace in the common room provided scant illumination. She move silently to the entryway of the public room in time to see Honey and Cameron embracing. For a moment a voyeur, she felt the intimate scene confirm her deepest intuition, the color of the aura vibrating around the couple verifying the purity and felicity of their contact.

She saw Honey succumb, then struggle to pull away from Cameron's tight embrace, but from so far away she could only wonder about what they were saying to each other.

"What do you want from me?" Honey gasped, still trembling from Cameron's kiss.

"More than this." He forced his mouth on hers again. "Much more."

Honey felt close to tears. "You want more than I can possibly give!"

He smiled and caressed her face with his kiss. "I need you."

At last Honey succeeded in pulling free from Cameron. "Please," she begged. "I won't be able to continue my journey if you don't leave me alone. I'll have to go back."

Cameron watched Honey's eyes fill with tears. "There's no going back, Mrs. Radcliffe, not for either of us," he confided. "The past is behind us, and this is a new life. All I want from you is what you are free to give."

As Honey stared at Cameron, drawn to him in a desperate and alarming way, tears began to spill from her eyes. With Nathan there had been a hopeless inevitability about their union, yet she had felt oddly, perhaps unreasonably, in control. But with Cameron Wolfe, Honey felt pulled by invisible lines of frighteningly tenacious strength. Shahar's pronouncements echoed in her head, but Honey insisted she would not be owned by other people's dreams and purposefully resisted the feeling of being inevitably drawn to Cameron. She recalled pieces of her own dreams then but struggled to divorce herself from a union she equated with mysterious spells.

Honey's tears subsided then, and she took a deep breath, able at last to look at Cameron clearly. But instead of stepping back and retreating to the safety of her quarters, she reached out to

Cameron, touched him gently, and drew him slowly to her, moving gracefully into his arms. With her head against his chest, she reveled in his warmth, in the nearly overwhelming sense of being where she belonged, seeking tenderness, not passion.

Honey tipped her head back then and, with a look, bade Cameron kiss her, giving in that kiss more of herself than she had ever given anyone before.

CHAPTER THIRTEEN

Honey knew without a doubt that only circumstances had again preserved her virtue, if in truth she had any virtue left. For did not the inclination of one's heart make one guilty whether or not the act had been committed? Certainly, Honey realized, had the night been spent in Greerfield, she would have gone with Cameron to his bed or welcomed him in hers. Even milder weather would have conspired against morality, for if it had been a warm summer's night, she and Cameron would have slipped from the inn to seek a lover's nest in some secluded bower—with no wild vision on which to blame untoward behavior.

As the days went by, Honey continued to marvel at her eagerness of that night and more at the persistence of her yearnings.

Why, Honey wondered, had she never experienced this nearly overwhelming urge to submit herself to Nathan? Could there be any truth to what Shahar insisted was fact? In his remark that the past was behind them and this a new life, had Cameron Wolfe meant more than the obvious? Could she have known and loved him before? Honey shivered at the prospect—and at the violence of her recent dreams.

Honey thought also of the book by Emerson that her father had kept by his bedside since he had received it from a friend just before the war. After the death of his sons, and in his last illness, Dr. Greer seemed to take special comfort in one essay in particular: "Nominalist and Realist." One passage that she had read to him again and again before he died stayed with her: "It is the secret of the world that all things subsist and do not die, but only retire a little from sight and afterwards return again." Perhaps her father had come under Shahar's influence too.

Honey pondered her fate in life thus far. Why did she never dream of Nathan, who had been a man far more suited to her by shared experience and upbringing than Cameron Wolfe? Perhaps if she had been more responsive to Nathan, these last few years might have been more tolerable and the prospect for her future as Nathan's wife more consistent with the vision of others and less a condemnation. If she had longed for Nathan in the manner she seemed to lust after Cameron Wolfe, Honey reasoned, probably her consuming interest in medicine would have dwindled into nothing as her father and others had insisted it should.

Perhaps.

Disturbed deeply by her responses to Cameron Wolfe, Honey chose to act indifferently toward him and resolved to conquer the base instincts he had aroused in her. She refused to weaken or to fall prey to foolish fantasy, which was how she now judged Shahar's view of the cycle of souls. Honey excused her behavior on the night before they had left North Carolina and entered Tennessee as an aberration, the result of an exceptionally trying day, and as the party traveled onward she was wary of their guide. But in spite of her resolve, as the journey grew more arduous and the party climbed the road toward Newport, then veered off a western course and proceeded north to Greenville, Cameron continued to kindle within Honey yearnings she could hardly ignore.

Still in the forest primeval, Honey wondered about men who had been destined to carve out trails that at first led nowhere. What dissatisfactions and longings had driven her uncle Trevor, her brother Clayton, and scores of others ever westward? Dreams of fertile land? Of a better life? Of gold? Dreams of what, it hardly mattered. And had women followed only with reluctance?

What dreams had set Cameron Wolfe on the trail? What motivated him to wander still? He had built a home near Sacramento, Honey knew, yet Trevor had said that Cameron still could be found on the trail more often than at home. Trevor had said Cameron no longer needed to be on the trail to earn his living—he chose to be.

Honey watched Cameron out of the corner of her eye, and day in and day out, traveling truly did not seem to tax him as it did the others. She suspected he sometimes quit a day's journey earlier than he would have liked only in consideration for the wounded and less trailworthy members of the party. He was so much at one with whatever beast he rode, it was easy for Honey to imagine Cameron a centaur from Greek mythology, a man rising from the shoulders of a horse.

She sometimes forgot her resolve of purer thoughts and let her imagination roam free. She remembered him half-covered in his bed, felt the rippling muscles and his smooth skin beneath her cool, sensitive hands. She closed her eyes and indulged her memory of his kisses and his responses to her touch. She felt his arms around her, his eager body pressed tightly against hers. . . .

"Wake up or for certain you'll be falling off that horse!"

Honey snapped alert and glared at Nollie.

"Don't give me a nasty look, girl. You'd be mighty furious if you landed face first in a horse pattie, and me not saying a word to warn you."

Honey laughed. "Indeed, I would."

"We'll stop soon for something to eat. Maybe you can nab yourself a few winks," Nollie suggested, "though I can't understand why you don't sleep better at night. You're looking better, but still you're forever jostling me with your tossing and turning. I'm always ready to drop as soon as we get off the road at night. What on earth keeps you in such a stir?"

Honey shook her head.

"You know, you got dark circles under your eyes. If you don't start sleeping better, Mammy'll give you one of her physics."

"Just the thought should cure me." And perhaps the idea had helped, Honey acknowledged some days later when she had slept soundly several nights in a row. Not a doctor but a wily woman with her roots and herbs, if Dr. Greer's medicines did not produce miraculous results, Shahar could concoct something sweetened with honey to cure what ailed you—occasionally also making your hair fall out in handfuls. Trickery or spitting out the potion when Shahar turned her back only meant a double dose.

"I hope you've noticed I've been sleeping better lately," Honey said to Shahar a few days later.

"Mmmmmm," Shahar considered Honey's coloring. "You could do with some sunshine."

"If we ever get out of this eternal forest." Honey agreed with Shahar that she was looking a little pale. She longed for the sun and the flat, open land of her home. And while Honey adored riding horseback, she was quite ready for a change. The riverboat they would sail from Louisville, Kentucky, down the Ohio and up the Mississippi River to Saint Louis, Missouri, loomed as an extravagant luxury to the saddle-weary.

Honey dreamed about the landau carriage her family had owned before it was confiscated in the war. Lined in red Moroccan leather, pulled by four perfectly matched bays, it had been a gracious way to travel. The gigantic and serviceable wagon they had with them on the trail and took turns riding in did not in any way provide comfort, only a brief respite from the saddle.

Honey tried not to dwell on the many miles the party had yet to travel before reaching California. Since the shared danger of the ambushes, the members of the Greerfield party felt very close to one another. For a while Honey felt Ruth Blocher continued to resent her, but now that Honey was so obviously ignoring Cameron, even Mrs. Blocher seemed friendly. Honey watched the woman flirt with Cameron and wondered at Wilton Ramsey's patience but concluded the man was blind to what was going on. He was perhaps as young and as innocent as he looked.

When Honey rode with him in the wagon, Wilton engaged her in conversation about her uncle, inquiring what she knew of him but informing her of more than he gleaned. He made it clear and seemed proud that he had been hired by Trevor Jefferson for the journey south, and he had plenty to say. "You watch, Mrs. Radcliffe, your uncle'll be governor of California, and soon. He knows everybody to know in Sacramento, San Jose, and San Francisco. And south, too. His house is always full to burstin' with people from all over. You'll feel right at home there."

Honey tried to imagine Trevor as the governor of California. Somehow the vision eluded her. She pictured the state with its vast territory as a wilderness or at least as something on the order of a vast mining camp. She knew that many people had already settled there, and at this date very few were mining gold. Yet she could not quite conceive of the West being settled in the same sense that cities in the South were. She imagined nothing as grand as Columbia or Richmond, not with indians on the warpath. As was common, the West and its territories and states— Texas, New Mexico, Arizona, and California—were one in her imagination.

With many rivers and mountain slopes yet to cross, the Greerfield party bent westward again across the Tennessee border through Bull's Gap, Beans' Station, and Tazewell and funneled through the Cumberland Gap into Kentucky, much like hundreds of thousands of others who dreamed of settling somewhere in the

West. Slowly they descended into high tablelands, encountering
widely dispersed settlements and farms. The flowering of mountain laurel and rhododendrons followed them the entire distance,
while the trees gave way somewhat to grasses in fertile valleys.

Through Richmond to Lexington, the Greerfield party became
restive as the end of the first leg of the journey neared. As the
terrain leveled out, a sense of urgency took them over one by
one, and tired as they were, there was no dragging of feet.
Sunrise found the party eager to get on the road and almost unwilling to see the day end.

At Frankfort they were mere days away from the Ohio River
and the commencement of another sort of journey, a respite from
the arduous road and a time to prepare mentally for perhaps the
most hazardous leg of the whole journey: the Santa Fe Trail.

On the steamboat, Cameron would arrange third-class accommodations for the other men and for Ruth Blocher. He, Honey,
Shahar, and Nollie would have berths in first class. "Even if
we're put in steerage with the horses and mules," Ruth Blocher
said, "I'll be grateful. Just not to have to *sit* on a horse will be
heaven on earth—and all I ask of heaven itself!"

Of the same mind, Honey smiled broadly. "And a bath—with
hot water in a tub!" The women all sighed at once, then laughed,
the men with them.

"And maybe a few swigs of *good* whiskey—pardon me,
ladies," Roarke Murray said. "After a bath, of course."

"Of course!"

When the Greerfield party at last reached the Ohio River and
boarded the *Lady Mildred*, a magnificent paddle wheeler, Honey
realized that as difficult as the last weeks seemed, the truly civilized world was about to vanish from view. At last she understood the terror of ancient sailors who embarked on a long
voyage imagining the world was flat. Under that restriction, a
ship blown off course might face a dreadful end. Yet knowing the
world was indeed round gave Honey no comfort as they sailed
from the bustling port of Louisville.

CHAPTER FOURTEEN

From Cameron's point of view, the first leg of the journey had gone remarkably well. Every member of the party had proved to be fit for the trail, including Mrs. Radcliffe. He had misjudged Honey as a hopeless Southern belle, only to discover that she was indeed a paradox: strong, resourceful, quick-witted, and yet one of the most alluringly feminine women he had ever known.

Cameron's purely physical attraction to Honey held no mystery for him: She was perfection to the eye in that regard. Usually he pursued a woman for no more than the gratification of very elemental needs; that he would want more from a woman had not often occurred to him. He rarely paid a woman for her company, and beyond the rudimentary, a woman's status mattered little to him.

It surprised Cameron that he could be so patient with Honey. So much about her tempted him, yet she had eluded his bed, and while this fact did not make him glad, neither did it make him angry. If he had not known her as well, he would have been tempted to believe that she often played the temptress and then withdrew to tease and torment a man beyond endurance. Not long ago he had believed just that, but truly, the assumption no longer seemed to fit. He had tasted her kisses and was fully aware of the passion simmering beneath her usual polite, controlled surface, yet he also understood that propriety mattered to her kind of woman. In spite of his great attraction to her but without fully understanding why, Cameron knew he would wait for Honey Radcliffe, however long that would be.

Still, Cameron was troubled by how Honey had managed to avoid him since the party had left the inn at Panther Pass. Many times he had looked in her direction only to see her purposely turn away. Her abduction surely had marred her, yet at her rescue she had been almost eager for his comfort.

The gaze of her golden eyes, which like fool's gold might promise much more than it could deliver, haunted him, and he hoped the weeks aboard the *Lady Mildred*, a superior class of steamer, would give him an opportunity to approach Honey Radcliffe and resolve whatever kept them from the intimacy he craved and, he knew instinctively, she desired also.

Cameron had courted only one other woman, his Apache wife, yet so strong was Honey's appeal, he forced himself to disregard his almost boyish nervousness. Instead, he focused on the pleasure of this particular river trip. It had been six years since he had been aboard a steamer of the *Lady Mildred* class, and at that time he had been a lowly roustabout, not a passenger with a private cabin in first class. Privately he relished the experience of strolling the Texas deck as a paying passenger.

As a roustabout, he had been dirty and poorly clothed, laboring long and hard sawing pine to keep the steamer's boiler going and the steam wet enough to prevent an explosion that would sink the boat. He had been an odd white man among the free negro deckhands yet as removed from the white man's world as any black man. Feeling more indian than white at the time, Cameron had become a roustabout to escape Saint Louis when he finally acknowledged that he would never gain the acceptance of his white relatives or, at least in Saint Louis, ever be more than an outcast in the white man's world.

He found life aboard river steamers a world of its own, if not tolerant of a man's race at least accepting of a man who did his share of the back-breaking labor, the life forming a bridge from his past to his future. While on the river, Cameron took his first job as a cowboy with a drover who had come aboard to carouse and gamble.

At first Cameron trailed cows from Texas to Saint Louis, a more natural occupation than steamboating for the daring Apache horseman who lived very near the surface of Cameron's white man's skin. Bitter toward the previously loving family of uncles, aunts, and cousins who had rejected him as an eighteen-year-old man who had survived nine years with the Apache, he found life on the lonely trail more palatable than the abhorrence he had seen in his blood relatives' eyes.

To his remaining family in Saint Louis, Cameron's survival among the Apache made him nothing more than a dirty savage. As such, they feared him guilty of any of a number of heinous crimes of which white men knew every indian to be capable. He had often heard men mutter "Savage devil" at him, under their breath but just loud enough to be heard. Women hurried out of his path, and children hurled stones at him, then, thinking better of it, fled for their lives. For the most part Cameron's relatives had been too polite to mention their fears or to question him openly about his experiences, but the expressions on their faces, the suspicion in their eyes, their failure to aid him even when his life was at stake, were things he would never forget or be able to forgive.

An Apache never forgives.

If nothing else, Cameron had expected his return from the dead to be a shock to his relatives. He had been prepared for this; he realized that on finding a man dressed in an Apache buckskin shirt, breechclout, and long-legged moccasins at the door, not many white men would be unflappable. Cautious, therefore, Cameron went to the back door of his uncle William's house. When the servant who came to answer recovered her composure, she summoned her obviously nervous mistress, Cameron's Aunt Rosamund, who, when she learned Cameron's identity, was so overcome by shock that her husband, William Wolfe, had to be called home from Wolfe and Steinhart's Emporium.

While Aunt Rosa was being fanned and revived with the help of an elixir to which strong spirits were added and his uncle William was in transit, Cameron was left to stand awkwardly in the entryway, much like a piece of forgotten furniture. When William arrived, it took him a few moments to recover; then, temporarily ignoring Cameron's need for a good scrubbing, he took his nephew's hand and pumped it vigorously. "There can be no doubt." The young savage had the remarkable blazing, unusually vibrant blue eyes of all the Wolfe men. Unbelievably, beneath the sun-darkened skin and the dirt was living, breathing blood kin. "We had no idea anyone survived."

"I am the only one."

"And now, at last, you've managed to escape the savage brutes."

Outsmarting the cunning, diabolical indian was something to congratulate a man for. "Except for the filth, you appear hearty." Indeed, robust, if especially lean and undernourished—which was ample cause for suspicion. How could his nephew have existed all these years without consorting with the savage devils who had captured him? The idea of this boy, now a man, embracing the indians' way of life rather than death filled William with repugnance, which Cameron, weary and secretly emotional, did not immediately sense.

As time passed, the shock of Cameron's return never seemed

to wear off completely, and he experienced only fleeting moments of joy in the reunion with his family. At first the true sentiments of his relatives were cloaked in the excitement of his return, but gradually he sensed their disappointment, which caused the already taciturn Apache to withdraw even further into himself.

In the beginning his relatives failed to say what was really on their minds, or they assumed the worst, and Cameron, remembering the narrow rules the Wolfe family lived by, was reluctant to bring up more than a few details, which seemed to shock them unreasonably.

A first cousin, Katherine Wolfe, William's daughter, was the only family member in whom Cameron could even begin to confide. He remembered her lovingly from his childhood for her devoted care for him, his brother, and his sister during his mother's frequent long periods of illness. Remarkably, for he was a warrior and she a mere woman, Cameron shared his story with his cousin. Katherine listened and heard his pain, his horror, his grief. She knew the degradation of his enslavement and admired his courage, applauded his survival and his rebirth as an Apache.

"When a Chiricahua dies, all his belongings are put to earth with him or burned. We Apaches are afraid of the dead man's ghost and purify ourselves with smoke to keep the dead one's ghost away. For the same reason, we cut our hair to disguise ourselves. The camp is moved, the grave never visited. We mourn, we cry, but the dead one is never mentioned and is supposed to be forgotten. Otherwise, sorrow or sickness takes over the ones left behind.

"I observed these customs when my wife died, but shortly after her death, Welcome Brook's ghost came to me in dreams, not for evil, which is usually what the presence of a ghost signifies, but to comfort me. I didn't use ghost medicine to keep her away because I wanted to keep her near me as long as possible, and because she was a good woman, I knew she would have to leave me soon to go to the other life underground. She reawakened in me a strong memory of my true mother and father. I could not force them from my mind."

Katherine tried to comfort him. "Truly, you're more Apache now than one of us," she observed, not unkindly. "I wonder if you can ever comfortably live among us again." She acknowledged Cameron's love for his Apache wife, his terrible loss at her death. Katherine also understood his need to return to Saint Louis.

Soon, however, it was clear that in the sight of his other relatives, there was something disgraceful, even dishonorable, in his having survived the bloody incident in which the Apache had murdered his mother, father, brother, and sister. His adoption by the Apache as one of their own and, later, his marriage to and apparent loving regard for an indian woman were inconceivable to them. He knew only that he had offended them and was not even vaguely aware of the grudging admiration on the part of those few aside from Katherine who sensed what it had cost him emotionally to survive.

He had returned to his white family in mourning for a young wife and baby, not expecting them to understand his broken heart yet hoping to be welcomed back into the loving family that had adored him as a child. Although he was confident of himself as a man and reasonable in his pride, their rejection nonetheless tore at him, rending his heart, the place where at the moment he was most vulnerable. He spoke from painful experience when he told Honey Radcliffe that neither of them could go back to the past.

His silences were misinterpreted by his relatives, causing them to imagine him the archetypal cunning, brutal savage. His refusal to trim his hair or to sleep in a bed, rather than on the floor, his lack of ease in constricting white men's clothing, and his restlessness indoors were viewed anxiously. Aunt Rosamund spoke for the others. "We were warned not to take you back!" Her overwrought statement jolted Cameron into remembering that captives were believed to be lost souls, forever contaminated by their association with the barbaric red man.

Much of civilization seemed alien to Cameron. He had more difficulty than he had expected adjusting to his old way of life. Privately, he acknowledged that his relatives were correct: In his soul at least, he was more indian than white.

The white man lived to plunder and possess the earth; the Apache lived *with* the earth. The indian believed God to be approachable and everywhere, revealed through dreams and visions and seen in many forms. The indian knew of the spirit in all things in the natural world. Ussen loved the Apache and lent them his power for their good. The white man's god, Cameron was reminded forcefully by men who thought they imitated Him, was a distant, formal, unmerciful being.

The deeper Cameron's sense of his family's rejection, the

greater his reluctance to conform; as far as he was concerned, an incident of hazing by drunken ruffians was the final act of rejection. On that occasion, as on others, Cameron tried to avoid a physical encounter with the bullies who taunted him as a "dirty redskin." At the time, he still wore his hair long and had kept his Apache shirt and moccasins. He realized that his dress was odd but had not in his transition from Apache to white eyes yet been able to shed everything indian.

Forced to defend himself against five hooligans, the feat accomplished in spite of a nasty knife wound, Cameron looked up into the crowd of onlookers to see his Uncle William and two other adult male cousins, none of whom made a move to aid him. He was not bitter that strangers failed to enter the fray. But to have his family ignore his need, an unthinkable act to an Apache, wounded him more deeply than the knife.

Finally, Cameron turned away from his Saint Louis kin and went in search of a place for himself somewhere between the white and indian worlds, wanting as rapidly as possible to cast out his pain. Without bitterness, he denied his need for acceptance and his desire to be loved.

Cameron now accepted the attraction he felt for Honey Radcliffe by simply acknowledging the utterly female essence that compelled his attention, having overcome his initial impression. But beyond this concession, Cameron was only vaguely aware of what caused him to be drawn to her. That gaining Honey's acceptance might heal wounds of rejection and aid him in surmounting losses he had suffered—that she could make him whole again— were feelings Cameron Wolfe could not articulate. He knew only that for reasons he could not readily justify, Honey Radcliffe was more than a woman for conquest. She was a woman for him to love.

CHAPTER FIFTEEN

During the last days on the trail before the party reached Louisville, the thing uppermost in Honey's mind had been a bath—not a mere splash of cold water from a stream or a camp bath from a basin while shivering in the tent or a quick sudsing in the privacy of her steamboat cabin, but at least an hour's soak in a large, comfortable tub with hot water added as the temperature of the water cooled. That others might be waiting for the same luxury would not trouble her at all. As the Greerfield party neared the Ohio River, Honey believed she would gladly kill for the privilege of an hour's soak.

At last alone in that dreamed-of bath, a warm wet cloth draped over her eyes, Honey let her thoughts drift aimlessly. From the past, faces, scenes, conversations, and moods sifted into her consciousness until, chilled, she was forced to rise, drain some cold water, and add more hot. Completely at ease, she then lay back and closed her eyes again. The additional hot water made her tingle, then feel soporific.

As beads of water from the steam collected on the wall of the small bathing enclosure, Honey's aching, saddle-sore muscles seemed to uncoil. Too easily, Honey imagined, she could lie back, nod off, and drown. Repeatedly she added hot water to the bath, treating herself just as she had promised.

Eventually, however, there was a timid knock at the door. "Miz Radcliffe, I's lettin' y' know yo' time's almos' gone."

Honey made no reply to the maid, whose tone was plainly urgent.

"Yo' should know, others'r waitin' an' they be not so patient."

Honey didn't care to know any such thing.

"Miz Radcliffe?"

Resentfully, Honey sat up and began to bathe. "I shall be out in a moment," she announced.

"If not, I'll come and get you!"

Startled, Honey recognized Cameron's voice, but not quickly enough to avoid instinctively crouching in the water to conceal herself from the eyes of a potential intruder. Then, furious, she stood up. "You wouldn't dare!" she cried without thinking, instantly to realize her stupidity as the door came open and Cameron strode in.

Honey lunged awkwardly back into the water and, as she drew her knees against her chest and her arms around her legs, slipped and banged her head against the edge of the tub. She realized the floor was swamped and Cameron was splashed with bathwater, but what followed was a blur, not to be recalled later when she opened her eyes and discovered herself in bed in her cabin. She was warm but stiff, and Lord, how her head ached!

Honey rolled onto her side. It was almost completely dark in the cabin, but she recognized Shahar's seated form in a chair across the cabin.

"Shahar?" Honey whispered, not wanting to wake her if she was asleep.

When she received no response, Honey lay back and stared into the dark. Alert, she became aware of the motion of the boat and heard the familiar rumbling sound of a steamer's enormous churning paddle wheel. She heard music and laughter, too, and from time to time the muffled voices of those promenading on the deck outside her cabin.

Realizing she was both hungry and thirsty, Honey sat up on the side of the bed. Dizzy, nonetheless she gripped the headboard and stood up. "Shahar!" she cried as her knees gave way.

"Coming!" Shahar answered, leaping to Honey's side. She helped Honey stand, then sit down, forcing her to bend at the waist and put her head between her knees.

Shahar then lit the lamp. "You must go easy, child. You've been in bed over a day now."

"More than a day? No wonder I'm hungry."

Shahar helped Honey sit in the chair where she herself had just been sitting. "You sit still and I'll get you something to eat." She put a shawl around Honey's shoulders and a quilt over her lap. "Don't you move," she ordered as she went out the door.

"I wouldn't think of it," Honey whispered, but sat up so that she was better able to see herself in the dressing table mirror. She took up her hairbrush to try to put some order to her disheveled mass of curls. A comb and patience were required, and although weak, Honey was determined to undo as many knots as possible before Shahar returned. When she finally was finished, she stared into the mirror, unhappy with the results. "At least it's clean," she remarked aloud, remembering that she had washed her hair the very first thing in her bath.

The memory of Cameron's interruption of her bath confused her, and she put her head in her hands for a moment. Could she be recalling the event correctly? Could he possibly be that brazen?

Indeed he could, she decided, as she looked up into the mirror again and found him standing not more than a foot behind her.

"You must be a damned indian, the way you sneak up on a body!" Honey complained, but this time she did not move. Nor did she smile.

"If I'd knocked at the door and asked permission, would you have let me in?"

Honey was silent.

"Shahar came to tell me you're awake."

"Why should she do that?"

"She knew I've been worried."

"You deserve to be."

Cameron watched Honey in the mirror, glad to see the sparkle of life in her eyes—even if she was angry with him. "I've come to say I'm sorry. You tempted me, and I could not resist."

"I see," Honey answered slowly. "Which makes me your accomplice?"

Silent, Cameron rested his gaze on Honey's golden-brown eyes.

She stared back at him.

"I'm sorry you got hurt. I meant only to devil you."

In her heart Honey knew Cameron was speaking the truth. "I suppose your reasoning is only an example of male logic," she sighed, resigned. "I had three brothers, and I've often been victim of such reasoning." She smiled at Cameron then, and the tension between them evaporated.

Cameron laid his hand gently on the top of Honey's head. He stroked her hair and laid his hand on her cheek. "I'm glad you're all right."

"I will be as soon as I've something to eat."

Cameron smiled at last.

"I'm thirsty, too," she added.

Cameron poured her a glass of water from the pitcher on a nearby table and as she drank sat near her on the bench in front of the dressing table.

"I've a terrible headache."

"That will go away."

Honey squinted at him. "I hope so."

"And so will the buzzing."

"That complaint, fortunately, I don't have."

They heard Shahar at the door, and Cameron stood to answer, but before he did, he turned back to Honey. "When you're on your feet, Mrs. Radcliffe, you must have dinner with me in the salon."

Honey did not reply.

"If you say no, I'll come for you anyway."

Honey looked up at Cameron, obviously considering a retort. "Have I a choice?"

Smiling, Cameron leaned over Honey. He touched her cheek and lifted her chin. "None," he whispered, and kissed her gently on the mouth.

CHAPTER SIXTEEN

Nollie laced Honey's corset and cinched it especially tight. "Dr. Greer'd skin you if he was alive. You know it. Making eyes at our guide, for heaven's sake."

"He never took a whip to anyone. Let alone me."

"You know what I'm saying." Nollie's outrage boiled over. "Don't pretend you don't."

"Loosen my waist, please!"

"You weren't unconscious the last hundred miles on the road, were you, Mrs. Radcliffe? Mr. Wolfe's been courting Mrs. Blocher under your very nose. That man's a tomcat."

"Nollie . . . Nollie, calm yourself. And, before I expire, loosen my waist!"

"You're getting fat as a pig," Nollie said as she hastened to ease Honey's corset.

"I am *not*!" Honey answered as soon as she had taken a deep breath.

"By rights you should still be in mourning. No lady in mourning should wear *this* dress." Nollie fanned out the skirt of the gown Honey would wear over a hooped and flounced petticoat at dinner with Cameron: a shimmering dark brown silk taffeta with short, very bouffant sleeves to offset the severe V of a neckline that plunged nearly to the waist. An inset of tucked black velvet inserted in the lower part of the V shielded the breasts, and a wide sash of the same fabric nipped the waist. Fourteen tiny round black velvet buttons descended the bodice back to a little below the waist. A thin black velvet ribbon tied at her throat and Nathan's locket perched just above the swelling of her breasts would constitute the only ornamentation of her ensemble.

"You'll be immodest, if not indecent."

"You never objected to the dress on any other occasion. Why

are you in such a state tonight?" Honey demanded impatiently. "Would it be you're sweet on Mr. Wolfe yourself?"

Nollie blushed but said nothing.

"You are! And you're jealous!"

Nollie threw Honey's dress on the bed and went to the dressing table. She grabbed Honey's brush and began to clean it furiously with the comb. "In recent days, many things have changed, Honey Greer," Nollie said angrily, "but not everything."

Bewildered by Nollie's inflexible demand that she adhere to the strict codes of class and rigid decorum, Honey nevertheless resisted Nollie's obvious attempt to make her feel guilty.

"*I* at least know a man that suits me," Nollie added, hoping to have the final word.

Honey smiled. "So do I, Nollie," she said firmly. *So do I.*

Had she been near, Nollie would have been beside herself to watch Honey and Cameron together in the elegant dining salon of the *Lady Mildred*. There was an unmistakable current of affection between them that would have outraged Nollie's keen sense of propriety, especially as it applied to her former mistress.

The salon, exclusive to first-class passengers, was lavishly furnished with dark wine velvet draperies, cushioned chairs covered with the same fabric, sparkling chandeliers, and polished wood decking covered with large costly Asian rugs. Heavy, elaborate linen covered individual tables set with fragile crystal and china and baroque silver. In this setting, among other glittering passengers, it was easy to sense oneself in a pleasant and fanciful dream. It was easy also to forget the dangers of such travel. Only the month before, 1,700 people had died when the steamer *Sultana* exploded on the Mississippi River. The *Lady Mildred* sailed the Ohio, and Honey, at least, was certain they were surely protected by heaven from harm.

Dressed in a dignified frock coat, Cameron helped Honey remove her satiny black lamb's cape. He looked uncomfortable but very handsome. His blue eyes shining and his hair carefully combed, he seemed boyish and innocent, and Honey smiled at him for sheer joy.

"A good steamer," Cameron said after the steward had poured them sherry and disappeared, "will have food to make any trip worthwhile."

"Have you often traveled by steamboat, Mr. Wolfe?" Honey wondered, wanting to know everything about him.

"Not traveled, Mrs. Radcliffe, *worked*."

"Oh?"

Her voice showed her surprise and somewhat apprehensively at first, Cameron told her a little about the year he had spent on the Mississippi River as a roustabout.

She could imagine him doing the hard, dirty labor of a roustabout, yet it did not detract from his appeal. In fact, although she had been raised with the notion that no respectable white man performed physical labor of any kind, the image of Cameron doing such work made him all the more attractive to her. She had seen him on the trail, bare-chested, felling trees to be laid down in boggy stretches of the road, straining to move a wagon and horses that would just as soon sink from exhaustion. In that image, there was nothing demeaning as far as Honey was concerned.

"I'd still be on the river, maybe, if I hadn't gone to trailing cows."

"But not a roustabout forever, surely?"

"Maybe not," he speculated. "But there's a seductive way about river life. Many a man has been lured from a respectable life."

"You among them?"

Cameron laughed. "Not hardly."

From the far end of the large dining room, violins, flutes, and a piano began to play familiar and romantic tunes.

"Promise me we shall dance later." Honey smiled at Cameron. "I haven't danced for much too long a time."

Cameron was grateful to have the waiter and his entourage of stewards arrive before he could answer.

The waiter unfurled Honey's and Cameron's napkins and laid them with ceremony in their laps. Then, one after another, six plain but ample courses were served: a julienne of fish, a wedge of melon with sliced lemon impaled on a fork on the side, tenderloin of beef and mushrooms, veal larded with vegetables and green peas, sliced sweet cucumbers, and tomatoes à vinaigrette. Throughout, French champagne was poured.

Cameron did justice to the full portions; Honey, to smaller amounts, grateful she had missed luncheon to wash and arrange her hair. Finally, they had bowls of fresh peaches and cream, a decanter of brandy, and coffee.

"Isn't it wonderful to be able to drink real coffee again?"

"I didn't go without until I came south," Cameron answered

as he decanted brandy. "But it's far easier to live without coffee than food."

"Yes. Thank the Lord, we weren't truly in want, as many others were."

"You should have to forage off the land sometime."

"I cannot even conceive of living in such a fashion."

"Men do."

"They can be little better than brutes."

"They are men, like we are."

Honey contemplated Cameron over a brilliant crystal brandy snifter half-filled with the rich amber liqueur. The room was dim but a small lamp on the table illuminated his face. He was still, pensive, looking at her as if from a portrait, and again she wondered what kind of a man he truly was, just as she might if she had been gazing into an unknown face in a painting in a gallery.

"You're forever saying unexpected things," Honey said before a sip of brandy momentarily stole her voice. She was aware of feeling a trifle light-headed yet deliciously at ease. "First you force me to learn to use a gun, primarily for the purpose of slaying savages on the warpath, then you remind me they are human creatures like ourselves."

"Your country has only just ceased a bloody war with brother against brother."

"My country, Mr. Wolfe? Is it not your country also?"

"Until I arrived in the South, indeed the rebellion seemed to be taking place in another country."

Honey drank more of her brandy while she gave some thought to Cameron's point of view. It almost seemed impossible that anyone who lived in a state that was a member of the Union could not be consumed by the war as she and everyone she knew had been in one way or another in the last four years. "It sounds as if you live in a different world entirely from the rest of us. I know my uncle was well aware of the war."

Cameron acknowledged her observation about Trevor with a nod and poured her more brandy.

"I should have more coffee instead," she protested, but drank the brandy. "And now we must dance, Mr. Wolfe. I cannot resist the music, and you must not deny my wish. There are few things I enjoy more than dancing—if I were anyone other than who I am, and greatly more daring, I should go west and be one of those saloon girls that dance all night and day."

Cameron laughed. "I would like to see that," he said, but

made no move to escort Honey to the dance floor.

Slightly bemused by his ignoring her request, Honey rose from the table and extended her hand to Cameron. "Come now, Mr. Wolfe, don't be bashful."

After another deep swallow of brandy, Cameron rose from his chair. "I don't know how to dance."

Honey looked at him incredulously. "How can anyone not dance?" she said lightly, then took his hand. "I shall show you how," she said, and led him to the ballroom floor, which lay behind an open double door adjacent to the dining salon. A few other couples waltzed gaily.

Taking Honey into his arms seemed natural enough to Cameron, although the distance she held him apart from her seemed quite unnatural. She smiled into his eyes and at first forcefully led him about the dance floor, sometimes unable not to giggle at his awkward resistance.

He felt rather like a mule, and foolish, but Honey was as charmingly determined as he was ungainly, and the lure of her smile and her attention focused so happily on him made Cameron's tension gradually ease, until he was gentled and instructed, just as a good horse is broken and led by a superior horseman. Tamed, Cameron assumed the lead, and they became as one dancer. Having caught the eye of the musicians, the couple soon seemed to dominate the floor, moving beautifully together, intimately, and Cameron loathed to let Honey Radcliffe go when the musicians finally paused.

"I suppose we must sit down," he said, holding her in his arms.

"Unless we want to make an embarrassing spectacle of ourselves," Honey said.

"We've already done that, at least I did at first, stumbling after you."

"But now that you're accomplished, I shall insist we do this often, while we can. I don't suppose there are many places to waltz on the trail to Santa Fe."

Cameron laughed. "None."

"I'm afraid I must ask you to take me to my cabin now, Mr. Wolfe."

Cameron nodded regretfully.

"However, perhaps we could enjoy a short promenade. I believe the air would be good for us both," Honey said, all at once feeling the effects of the quantity of wine and brandy she had consumed.

Although the night air on deck was pleasant, Honey was glad for her lamb's wool cape and happy to lean on Cameron's arm and be pulled close to his side. She felt no impulse to pull away. At peace and a trifle drowsy, she leaned her head against Cameron's shoulder. Conscious of a strong desire not to part with him, she allowed him to walk past her cabin without a murmur of protest.

When he brought her into the barely lit alcove of a stairwell and pulled her against him in an easy yet inescapable embrace, Cameron tensed, waiting for Honey's response. When she yielded softly, he smiled the barest of smiles, then kissed her in a manner that spoke clearly of a hungry impatience.

Honey responded with a degree of feeling that was by now familiar, yet it still astonished her. Unleashed within her was a kindred driving passion that seemed to burn within her soul. As his strong arms encircled her more tightly, and he pressed her against him, she felt herself on fire, and seemed again to lose all sense of time and place. All need she had ever felt to defend herself against him vanished.

When Cameron finally let Honey go, her gloved hand trembled as she grappled with a tiny purse for her key. When she extracted it, Cameron took the key, led her to her door, and unlatched it. Then, lifting her into his arms, he carried Honey over the threshold. Surprised, she laughed and nuzzled him, then sought his mouth with hers. Parting her lips invitingly, she coaxed him with her tongue. He tasted deliciously of dark, rich brandy and peaches and cream.

When Cameron lowered her gently to the floor, Honey felt the need to hold on to something solid and, as he lit the lamp, reached for the back of a chair to steady herself. She felt her heart pound and the room begin to sway.

Cameron softened the lamplight to a faint glow and latched both the outside door and the one leading to Shahar and Nollie's adjoining cabin. Quite ready to fall on the bed with Honey and pursue passion vigorously with her, he thought better of it, suspecting she was hardly a woman one could spring on and have a good wrestle with the first time. He would have to restrain himself; it would be difficult.

When he turned to face Honey, his desire was so evident even in the tenderness of his expression that she felt overwhelmed by shyness and experienced her first hesitation of the evening. She realized that Cameron expected her to be a knowledgeable married woman, and certainly, from her usual responses to him, he had no reason to doubt that she well knew and welcomed the obligations of a wife.

Abruptly, Honey turned her back to Cameron. He perhaps would think her modest, she thought, but in truth, in spite of undeniable and lingering desire, she was afraid. Although on other occasions she had been very bold and had been on the verge of bringing this man who was not her husband to her bed and allowing him to take her maidenhead, Honey could not even begin to broach the subject of her status as a virgin.

In danger of suddenly being overcome by diffidence, Honey was startled to have Cameron come up behind her and slip his arms around her tightly. He bent to kiss the back of her neck, nibbling at the wispy curls that had escaped from her exquisitely dressed hair. "I've longed to do this," he breathed against her ear, and lightly nipped kisses along her shoulder, then turned her to face him. "And you, Mrs. Radcliffe, have wanted me at least as long as I have wanted you."

Honey blushed crimson, lowering her chin and lashes to avoid his gaze. But Cameron would not have it and raised her face so that she was forced to look him in the eye. "You deny it?" he demanded.

"No," Honey answered directly, as if she possessed more courage than she did.

He smiled, her frankness having made her even more appealing. Cameron despised the coquettishly evasive manners of many women he had known and hoped Honey would be direct—and demanding—when he finally bedded her. She was the type of woman raised to be passionless, a trait urged on white eyes women that baffled Cameron. He believed both men and women to be naturally endowed with passions and thought white eyes incredibly stupid to train their women otherwise. For a moment, when she had turned her back to him, Cameron had sensed a recurring timidity on Honey's part, and with conscious restraint he now leaned to take slow possession of her mouth, then gained entry with his tongue until she yielded to his probing and answered with exploring kisses of her own.

Her hands at first lay almost defensively upon his arms, as if at any moment she might push him away. But as she thawed beneath his kisses, her hands moved to his chest, to the fabric of his coat, to pull him closer.

Suddenly Cameron's kisses grew urgent, and he began to undress her, though he did not hurry unduly. Calmly he untied the great knotted bow of the sash at her waist, and patiently undid the exasperating tiny velvet-covered buttons down the back of her gown.

With his help, Honey slowly exposed herself to Cameron, exciting him even more with her beauty. He sensed her eagerness and her reserve—a modesty, a sweetness. She was a widow—a woman acquainted with a man—yet he was stricken by her air of apparent innocence and responded with tenderness.

If he had been less intoxicated by her, Cameron might have held back, but as Honey stood before him now, coaxing him with her inviting beauty, naked except for an incredibly soft lawn camisole and pantalettes, he was no man to resist her. Her round, ample breasts summoned his hands, and soon the camisole lay discarded upon the floor with the rest of her feminine trappings. He pulled off his coat and rapidly unbuttoned his shirt and would have made swift work of the rest of his few and, mercifully, uncomplicated garments but for Honey's intervention.

With her assistance, then, more slowly than he intended, Cameron revealed to Honey his magnificent body. She interrupted his disrobing to stroke his chest, to run her fingers over the furred plane of hard articulated muscle as, many times, she had longed to do.

He endured her petting only briefly and pulled her against him, bringing her breasts into firm contact with his bare flesh. Her arms went around his neck, and her nipples grew unbearably taut. Flesh on flesh, their kisses were no longer tentative or seeking but possessive, hot and driven.

Cameron's hands went down Honey's slim back to her silk-covered buttocks and pinned her hard against him. His body long tense with readiness, he moved against her forcefully. Then he eased his hands beneath the fabric of her pantalettes, and his fingers forward into warm crisp curls.

Honey clung to Cameron hungrily as he coaxed her legs apart. She was wet and almost as eager as he was, his invasion inside her with one, then two exciting fingers left her avid for more vigorous caresses. Gentle at first, then demanding, he prepared her, transforming all doubt into breathless desire. Cameron then carried Honey to bed and put her down on cool sheets. As she lay waiting, he stood before her confidently and pulled off his few remaining clothes.

Honey forced herself to fix her gaze on Cameron's eyes and recognized in them a feral if adoring gleam. In the few seconds it took for him to disrobe, Honey's emotions tangled hopelessly, the intoxicating eagerness she had felt evaporating into air. Her desire had not waned—only her courage.

Still a virgin, untouched, she suddenly perceived the lusty man before her not as a lover who dropped his thrilling kisses on her neck and shoulders and seized her against him in a way that sent delicious sensations to her core but as someone she knew not at all. Honey trembled to realize Cameron believed her to be a knowledgeable married woman, prepared to entertain the joys of experience.

In his heightened state of excitement, not the least aware of any shift in Honey's mood, Cameron took her into his arms. Quickly his mouth went to her breasts; he expected Honey to surrender joyfully.

Instead, between them there began a confusing struggle, an undulating dance that pitted her conflicting desires against his passion and his force of will. She stiffened with the shock of his mouth on a suddenly tender breast and put her hands into his hair with every intention of forcing him away. But intense pleasure registered within her, and she lay back and pressed him to her, soon begging him not to favor one breast over the other.

When he raised his mouth to hers and moved fully onto her, his tongue darted into the warm recesses of her mouth, strangely confusing her focus of attention. He made her crave his every kiss and eager for his total possession. Yet when Cameron sought to pull off Honey's pantalettes, again she came alert. She succeeded only in slowing him down, with Cameron not even aware of their tug of war.

Naked, Honey felt his heat against her sudden chill, but as his kisses grew harder and more impassioned, she began to ache for him with body and soul; he appealed to her in the most natural and primitive way. She inhaled his scent, was captured by the seductive murmurs of his voice, seemed to drown in the sea of blueness of his eyes. Her senses keenly aroused, her defenses mislaid, no part of her still wished to battle on. Honey knew his urgency and inexorably fell into that space reserved for lovers between dreams and reality.

Her hands sailed smoothly over Cameron, lingering here and

there in places that quite obviously pleased him, until he captured a hand and brought it to his large, straining member. He closed her fingers tightly around him, showing her exactly how vigorous to be. Abruptly then, Cameron lowered himself forcefully between her legs and thrust deeply into her.

At his invasion, Honey cried out and tears came to her eyes; only with enormous effort did Cameron still himself. "I've hurt you . . ."

"Yes. No," she stammered, with no words to express the mingling of pain and pleasure, even joy, at his invasion. She could only pull his mouth to hers again and with the motion of her body urge him to resume.

This time he began more gently, building on sensation and emotion until she came to a new level of excitement and raised her voice in fierce cries of seeking and ecstasy.

Honey urged him on, bearing Cameron's full weight as if he were as light as air, glad to have him deep inside her, wanting him even nearer than he was. When he could no longer restrain himself from climax, she felt him come, the sound of joy in his voice echoing within her. She closed her eyes then and seemed to whirl away from earth, only to be flung back, seized finally by the glorious responses of her own body and the rapture of his embrace.

Moments later, breathless, panting, they smiled into each other's eyes, then laughed gently for the fierce pleasure of their union. But Honey's euphoria quickly turned to tears that slipped silently from her eyes and down her temples. She held her breath to try to stop them and, failing, sobbed aloud, revealing herself. "I'm sorry," she cried and, embarrassed, tried to turn away.

Cameron tried to comfort her. "What's wrong?"

Honey shook her head. "Nothing. It's that . . . I . . . it was . . ." She faltered. "Wonderful."

She felt an utter fool, her tears an excess of feeling, an expression of her joy at being touched for the first time. And more —for his tenderness. She never imagined that the coupling of man and woman could be so splendid.

"I've dreamed of you for a long time," Cameron confided. "I'm sorry if I hurt you."

"You haven't, I give you my word."

Inclined not to believe her, Cameron tried to remember the exact progression of their lovemaking, questioning how he might have caused her pain. He lifted himself from her and rolled to one side, sweeping her lovely body with his concerned gaze. Immediately he had his answer: A smear of blood between her legs and a bright stain upon the sheet told him all there was to know.

His expression hardened. "Why didn't you tell me, Mrs. Radcliffe?" he demanded. "A man has a right to know he beds a virgin."

Cameron's rights in the matter had never crossed Honey's mind.

"I would not have touched you."

"Then I'm glad you didn't know."

Cameron stared at Honey. Soft and alluring, she was everything he had dreamed; vastly different from himself, still she held the promise of love that so far had eluded him. He took Honey's hand and kissed the open palm. "It's more than I deserve."

"No," she whispered, and drew him down with her again.

PART TWO

Love

Love is the fulfilling of the law.
Romans 13:10

CHAPTER SEVENTEEN

To marry a man was one thing, to love him another. Honey Greer had married Nathan Radcliffe. She was in love with Cameron Wolfe.

When she was very young, Honey did not question the fact that she would marry and from an early age knew that her family's opinion about a suitable husband would influence any choice she made. Any thought to the contrary was unconsciously accepted by her as the wicked rebellion it was; divergent opinion was anathema in her circle of society. No young woman could expect to be a lady if she seriously pursued marriage to a man who did not receive her family's nod of approval.

Under this code, Honey had never voiced any doubts about Nathan Radcliffe or even consciously entertained them. She grew up expecting to marry the heir to the Radcliffe Plantation. Everyone agreed Nathan was eminently suitable for her. He had everything a young woman could desire: a dashing appearance, a virile essence, gracious public manners, education and social position, personal wealth. Honey Greer believed she loved Nathan and was definitely disposed enough toward him to submit herself to a lifetime as his wife.

Now, in the midst of her intense affair with Cameron Wolfe, suddenly Honey's view was dramatically altered. At her betrothal to Nathan Radcliffe, had she been aware of a greater range of sentiment beyond the rapture of poetry and the romantic musings of friends that she had dismissed as foolishness, and feeling as she did about Nathan, willing but essentially unstirred, Honey never would have consented to spend the whole of her life with him. Marriage, she believed strongly, was the commitment of a lifetime.

Honey's memories of Nathan were charged with sadness and regret; his loss was a bitter one overlaid by all the losses of the war. She at one time had thought she loved Nathan. Certainly the people around her believed she did.

"Nathan, Nathan," Honey murmured, eyes bright with unshed tears. In the four years of war, Honey had never seen Nathan dressed in anything but his flattering uniform, the stark gray of the fabric accentuating his tawny complexion, blond hair, and blue-gray eyes. But when she thought of him now, Honey preferred to see Nathan as he had been in the years before the war, before lines of fatigue had crossed his forehead and worry had dulled the color of his eyes, before the burdens of command had checked his humor, before a calculating and cool side to his nature had surfaced. As she preferred to remember him, Nathan had been amusing, adoring, sure. In the end Honey had married him almost without thinking, as the natural outcome of the long years she had expected to wed him, as an act of hope for the future. Carried away by the nearly hysterical celebration of both the advent of 1865 and, as it turned out, the last successful defense of Fort Fisher, Honey Greer and Nathan Radcliffe had consented to wed before a small throng of supporters, soldiers, and officers of the Confederacy.

On Christmas Day, 1864, Fort Fisher at the port of Wilmington, the South's only remaining stronghold on the Confederate coastline and its foremost link to the outside world, had once again been defended successfully against attack by the U.S. Navy. It had been a battle worth celebrating. At that date any victory for the Confederacy would have been cause for wild celebration, but Wilmington was in the unique position of having provisions to supply a party on a grand scale. Cargoes of recently arrived blockade runners provided barrels of Nassau hams; crates of French champagne; flour, butter, and sugar for bread and pastries; and many other vital supplies for a grand fete.

Governor Zeb Vance had come all the way from Raleigh by steamer, and on written invitation from Colonel Lamb, the commander of Fort Fisher, plus a coaxing note from Nathan, Honey also went to Wilmington, escaping for a moment her personal conviction that the South was more than ever doomed to defeat.

In the midst of merrymaking, when their host at Tarrington House proposed that Nathan and Honey begin the new year on a happy note and marry on New Year's Day, the couple, caught up in the jubilation and unable to resist their long-suppressed desire to marry, consented. "Your uniting before us shall symbolize your faith in the future, as well as be a significant boost to our sometimes flagging faith," their host, an Englishman, had said.

The circumstances of the suggested wedding were exceedingly wild compared with the usual aristocratic decorum of such an occasion in the Greer and Radcliffe families, but the port of Wilmington was scoured for the correct official, and a marriage bond was obtained. At last the wedding, which had several times been postponed for periods of mourning, would take place. On January 1, 1865, dressed in a satin gown of creamy pale pink, surprised by her nervousness, Honey waited for the ceremony that would make her Nathan Radcliffe's bride.

Shahar, who had accompanied Honey to Wilmington, was far from pleased about the couple's decision. Indignant, she said, "It won't do. A lady doesn't marry in haste. Dr. Greer would be furious."

"It will be legal," Honey retorted, cross with Shahar for trying to put a damper on the festivities.

"Mr. Nathan's mama will be in a fury, and, child, you don't want to start married life with Mrs. Radcliffe's nose outa joint."

It was true. "I can't back out now," Honey insisted.

"You could."

"Shahar . . ."

"Don't marry Mr. Nathan," Shahar had pleaded with a clear note of urgency. "He'll bring you nothing but grief."

Astonished, truly unable to believe her ears, Honey stared at Shahar. In all the years she and Nathan had planned to be wed, Shahar had never said one word against their hopes. "You can't mean it."

"I do, sincerely."

As if Shahar's advice had made her weak in the knees, Honey sat down on a chair and supported herself on its arms. She shook her head in bewilderment. "Why wait till now to speak?"

"Your papa made me promise to hold my tongue."

"When did that ever stop you?"

Shahar gave Honey a slight smile. "You make it sound as if I was an unruly sort."

"As long as I've known you, you took unprecedented license —but don't you change the subject! Why are you advising me not to marry?"

"I say nothing of the kind. Only not to marry Nathan Radcliffe."

"Based on one of your hallucinations, I suppose."

"I see many things."

"Kindly spare me the details," Honey snapped, "and advice based on heathen superstition."

"Marrying Mr. Nathan will have an evil end."

"Shahar!" Honey covered her ears and closed her eyes. "Not another word!"

If it had been anyone other than Shahar, her speaking out the way she had would have been cause for whipping. Honey Greer did not lack the power to order such a beating; only the depth and intensity of their relationship made such an action unthinkable.

Quickly, Honey had become obsessed with other details in order to take her mind as far away as possible from Shahar's upsetting pronouncement. She fretted over the suitability of the gown she wore, especially the daring neckline. The remaining lines of the gown were youthfully bouffant, suggesting purity and innocence, and the dress was a favorite of Nathan's; therefore, after much deliberation, Honey reluctantly decided the gown would do.

She then occupied herself considering her lack of jewelry. In her few dreams of a wedding, Honey had always seen herself suitably jeweled. With the dress that now would be her wedding gown, she usually wore a multistrand choker of pearls with a diamond catch, but all that she wore this day was a diamond-edged heart-shaped locket Nathan had given her at their engagement almost five years before. To alleviate the stark simplicity she added a ribbon of cream-colored lace threaded with pale pink satin, tied at her throat in a small, graceful bow.

Little by little Honey had been forced to sell her jewelry to survive the war. All she had left was Nathan's locket, which she had sworn never to remove, a vow that had become entangled with her dream of marrying Nathan and the possibility of losing him to war as she had lost so many other loved ones. Contrary to her usual nature, Honey now wore the locket under the veil of superstition and preferred to starve, she said, rather than be forced to give it up.

Such a test had not been necessary, and if the level of celebration and the bounty of the feasts of the last few days were any prediction, it seemed unlikely she would have to. Wilmington was not Vicksburg. In these last few days, if one could overlook the multitude of gray Confederate uniforms and the evidence that some officers were still recovering from their injuries, at times the war seemed very far away, an event almost remote in time. Honey and Nathan had even been promised they might slip away together for a few days after the wedding.

There was nothing she could do about her lack of jewelry, and she began to fidget, first tugging at the bodice of her gown in the hope that she could cover more of her curving breasts. Then she fussed with her hair, with the wide sash at her waist, with the loops of the bow at her throat. Slimmer than was fashionable and as tall as most men, still Honey was unquestionably beautiful. Graceful, she displayed an abundance of shimmering, sunflecked, dark blond hair that fell to her waist when loose but that she often wore up in braided coils. On some the style looked severe, but on Honey Greer the twists of braids sat on her head like a golden crown. This day, her wedding day, the crown was one of curls.

Honey radiated health, seducing most observers with a heartwarming smile. But she first captured the attention of all with her golden-brown eyes, and in them most mortal men were lost. Even an impromptu wedding with a gown drawn from a traveling trunk found Honey ravishing the eye.

Finally, Honey admitted there was nothing more she could do to be ready, yet she remained disturbingly ill at ease. The interminable wait for the justice to arrive gave her an unwanted opportunity to reflect on the step she was about to take, especially with Shahar's ill-timed advice now ringing in her ears. To Honey, reflection on one's fate was a useless occupation. There were far too many events over which one had no influence or control.

Beside herself with nerves, Honey had sat on the bed and reached for the open Bible that lay on the table. She thumbed through the pages, reading verses she knew well, but soon her mind wandered back to Shahar's prophecy. Honey glared at the now silent Shahar, who sat across from her in a small rocking chair, seemingly composed.

It surprised Honey greatly that Shahar had not revealed her opinions about Nathan years earlier. Honey had always sensed a rigid reserve in Shahar's behavior toward Nathan, but never the hostility Honey heard now in her unsettling prediction. Feeling miserable and dejected, she breathed a deep sigh.

What if by magic or providential decree she suddenly had control of her life? Honey wondered. What exactly would she do?

Marry Lieutenant Colonel Nathan Radcliffe?

Honey dropped the Bible back onto the bedside table with a disrespectful thud, then for several long moments stared at her gloved hands folded primly in her lap.

Would I marry Nathan?

"No," she whispered.

If she were absolutely free to chose, Honey knew, she would *not* marry Nathan. Perhaps she would defy all social expectation and *never* marry at all.

Perhaps.

At the very best, Honey knew she would go to whatever lengths necessary to be a physician.

However, because she was not in charge of fate, marrying Nathan seemed a wise decision, Honey concluded. Nathan Radcliffe was a sound choice for a husband, for all the many reasons her father had instilled in her. There was no question that she would marry him, no question that she would ignore Shahar's superstitious nonsense. In fact, through the many personal traumas of the war they had shared, she and Nathan now were closer than they had ever been.

That decided, Honey expected her mood to be restored to one of confidence. Yet she remained in a state of distress.

Are all brides this nervous? Honey had wondered. *And more troubling, why have I always been relieved when there were good reasons to postpone our wedding?* she had questioned herself honestly.

Honey shivered, but not with cold.

"Is the bride ready?" Zeb Vance called through the door.

Honey jumped from the bed, relieved to open the door and escape her thoughts. Shahar followed, attempting to brush the wrinkles from the skirt of Honey's gown.

The governor of North Carolina, long a friend of the Greer family, would give the bride away. Governor Vance smiled on Honey and offered his arm. "My, Mistress Greer, you make an enchanting bride."

"Thank you, Governor," she said, then immediately turned back to Shahar and hugged her. "Give me your blessing."

Shahar struggled with her conscience. "And if I don't?"

"I'll marry him anyway."

Shahar had smiled and kissed Honey on the cheek. "Child, I dearly love you, but you're a grief to us all with your willfulness."

"I know." Honey pressed one last hug on Shahar, then took the governor's arm and walked down the long hallway to stand above the wide, curving staircase where, composed, she stood regally, her turbulent emotions hidden.

Waiting to descend, Zeb Vance looked thoughtfully at Honey. "Truly, my dear, you are the most beautiful bride I've ever seen," he whispered reverently above strains of *Lohengrin* played on a piano in the salon below.

Honey held tightly to Zeb Vance's arm as they descended the long staircase, where Nathan and about a hundred others waited in silence.

Nathan smiled as he received his bride. He took her soft gloved hand in his and raised it to press a kiss against the palm. "At last," he whispered. "Soon you will be truly mine forever."

A wave of shyness swept over Honey, and she did not smile.

Then, after the words of promise had been repeated, Nathan Radcliffe and Honey Greer became man and wife, *until death do ye part*. The stanza rang in Honey's ears when, as Mrs. Nathan Radcliffe, she turned to face the many witnesses clad in cold, gray military dress. Her mind eased a little when she began to dance with those Confederate officers and others who desired a dance with the lieutenant colonel's bride.

The young commander of Fort Fisher, Colonel Lamb, was the first to toast them with frothy champagne, but not much later he drew them aside, his cheerful expression gone. "I'm sorry to have to do this," he said, carefully avoiding Honey's gaze, "but I'm forced to renege, Colonel, on my promise of time for a brief wedding trip."

"Sir?" Nathan waited for his orders.

"Word has arrived that we must return to the garrison at once."

Alarmed, Honey gripped Nathan's arm.

"My apologies, Mrs. Radcliffe," the colonel said.

Honey could not hold back a rush of tears, and so she turned her face away.

The colonel nodded to Nathan and left the couple alone.

Nathan pulled Honey into his arms. "Hush now," he whispered firmly.

"How can you be called away so soon!"

Nathan smiled rakishly. "Don't for a minute believe I'd leave you a virgin by choice."

Honey blushed scarlet but convinced herself that only several glasses of French champagne had loosened Nathan's tongue.

"I promise I'll return to remedy your unfortunate state as soon as possible."

Honey ignored Nathan's leer, and her eyes filled with tears. "I'm sorry. The excitement of the last few days has caught up with me," she said, hoping to excuse her response, not wanting

Nathan to take his leave with her bawling like a spoiled child.

Nathan pulled his new wife roughly against him. "I love you, Honey. I shall long for you while we're apart, as always—more, now that you're mine."

Honey held Nathan close and would have stayed in his arms longer, but Governor Vance came to their side.

"I shall see Mrs. Radcliffe home, Colonel," he promised Nathan as he escorted the couple to the door. He gave Honey his arm when it came time for Nathan to depart.

In stoic silence, Honey watched her husband take his leave with Colonel Lamb and the other officers. She at once pardoned Nathan for imbibing too much champagne, her benevolence serving to assuage her guilty conscience over the treacherous thoughts that had filled her head before the ceremony. In daring to think of not marrying Nathan, Honey felt disloyal. His bravery alone entitled him to finer sentiments. He had showed courage in standing for the cause in which he believed. Nathan Radcliffe was a superior man, and she, she knew, was an ingrate, fortunate beyond her due to have him marry her. Far too many women in these days of war did not have so fair a choice. Her wish to be a doctor, she reminded herself, came from the selfish side of her nature and reflected her vanity—her wish to be the center of attention, to be admired—as her father had sometimes suggested when the debate over her future came up.

Watching Nathan go, Honey reaffirmed to herself that it was his duty to stand with his regiment in defense of Fort Fisher regardless of the outcome. That North Carolina must be defended against the assault of Union troops was not an issue for argument, but already Honey's losses to the cause of freedom, as it was called by Southern patriots, had been enormous. Dear God, they were enormous! A father and three brothers, a fortune in impressed goods, confiscated land, and slaves.

If she were to lose Nathan too . . .

Had she had a premonition then? Honey questioned as she lay comfortably ensconced in her warm bed aboard the *Lady Mildred*. Had some inborn foreknowledge been the true cause of her turmoil on her wedding day?

As she recalled the night she had just spent with her lover, Honey was both saddened and grateful that she had not known Cameron Wolfe before the time when he had actually come into her life. Being pure and passionless, as was urged, had always been difficult for Honey, yet from their first meeting Cameron

Wolfe had seemed too naturally exciting, even dangerous, for intimate regard. Honey ached to think that had she known him earlier, he would have been forbidden to her, for clearly he was not a worthy suitor. Although in this age a woman was supposedly free to love a man of her choosing, it was a concept that was often an illusion.

Honey could well imagine her father's attitude regarding Cameron Wolfe, *"A cowboy? A former roustabout?"* At a minimum, Phillip Greer would have considered his daughter deranged, as she herself not too many weeks ago had judged Shahar, whose perception of Cameron as her soul mate had offended Honey deeply.

Honey had dearly loved and admired her father, but the idea that she might have passed through life without loving Cameron was pure agony. In the week they had been lovers, Honey had known a sweetness of existence she had never dreamed of.

Previously, she had come to respect the physical body, to wonder at its many parts and variety of remarkable functions, to accept the limitations it imposed. That it might be a vehicle of union that verged on spiritual ecstasy never occurred to her until she had been transformed by love. It was a sentiment Honey knew could easily be judged overwrought, yet there was no denying she felt an unutterable joy with her lover.

Had she known Nathan in the way she now knew Cameron, would she have felt the same emotion?

No! Honey insisted vehemently. For it was not simply a matter of becoming acquainted with the carnal side of human nature. In all the years of familiarity with Nathan, there had been a feeling of reserve, an almost conscious desire to be separate, while the pull toward Cameron Wolfe in retrospect seemed to involve an immediate drive toward union.

Honey smiled at how much a contradiction this seemed in view of her reservations about Cameron before she had met him and, after she met him, her worry about putting herself into his even temporary custody. Had she truly felt Cameron draw her spirit to him from the start? And who could give cold intellect credence over what she now enjoyed with him? Undeniably, she now felt a powerful and mysterious pull toward him, which, she insisted, was not merely a function of the glands. Suddenly Shahar's sentiments began to make sense.

Honey stretched out beneath the covers of the bed; the place beside her where, until moments ago, Cameron had lain all night was still warm. Part of Honey's heart wished Cameron had chosen to stay with her until he normally would rise. She appreciated his concern for her reputation, even though, rather than forgo Cameron's embrace, she gladly would have tossed respectability into the river.

As it was, censure came from a surprising source. Nollie, her lifelong friend and accomplice in many sometimes naughty childhood deeds, was suddenly acting more the castigating mother consumed by a passion of her own, a passionate dislike for Cameron Wolfe.

Surprising them in bed one morning when Cameron had both overslept and failed to bolt the door that separated Nollie and Shahar's room from Honey's, Nollie was outraged. "Have you lost your mind?" she later demanded of Honey, shocked by Honey's lack of virtue. "I'm surely speechless."

Honey made no reply.

"You're behaving no better than a harlot, Honey Radcliffe. He'll never marry you. And if he would, you shouldn't consider marrying him. He's not your kind. He's as common as dirt, for pity's sake. I just can't believe my eyes. And you raised so proper. Tell me I didn't see him under your blankets and you all in a tangle with him!"

"You didn't see any such thing," Honey forced herself to say lightly.

"Lady, you lie! Your daddy's positively turning in his grave!"

Honey glared at Nollie. "For someone 'speechless,' you've found plenty to say."

"Well, someone needs to, when you've so obviously lost all good sense."

"Nollie, *please*! Hold your tongue!"

"I'll hold my tongue when you hold your skirts down like you ought to!" Nollie drew herself up into a more dignified pose. "I suppose I haven't any right to carry on. I'm no better than a slave to you."

Honey gave Nollie a look of contempt. "That's even more outrageous than my taking up with Mr. Wolfe."

"And a *wolf* he is. You're shaming Colonel Radcliffe's memory."

Afraid she might strike Nollie, Honey turned away. Her voice was low and icy. "Colonel Radcliffe's memory has nothing to do with my feelings for Mr. Wolfe."

"When I mention your husband's name, don't you see how

outlandish it is for you to take up with that . . . that cowboy? You never sniffed around Colonel Radcliffe like you do *him*!"

Beet-red, Honey faced Nollie again. "You'd best understand, Nollie Daniels," she said slowly, "I don't want to hear one more word from you about Mr. Wolfe. I'm sorry that you feel so strongly against him."

"I don't hate the man, I only—"

"Regardless, I think you'd better not say another word. In fact, your opinion on the subject is of no concern to me." It was untrue, but Honey managed to convey the sentiment as truth to Nollie. "I shall love whom I please."

For a long minute more Nollie and Honey stared at each other, the heat of their emotions burning between them. Then, hurriedly, Nollie gathered up Honey's laundry and fled from the cabin.

For the remainder of the *Lady Mildred*'s journey, whose course after entering the Mississippi was now set for Saint Louis, Nollie often voiced her opinion but tried to avoid heated argument with Honey, the air between the two women was growing more electric with tension each passing day.

CHAPTER EIGHTEEN

Honey smiled down at Cameron, communicating her love with a gaze, a caress, a soft, random kiss. She manipulated his senses masterfully, playing with him as a cat does a treasured captive: one moment obsessed, then feigning total indifference the next. So able was she to torment him and to give satisfaction that at times he found it hard to believe Honey had not devoted a lifetime to the occupation of gratifying a man's desires.

When he said as much, Honey laughed. "You inspire me."

He abandoned all thought of her as a passionless female, nevertheless, she thought herself a somnambulist before she loved Cameron, for although she had always seemed alert to everything about her, she in fact had been asleep. In his embrace, Honey discovered what it meant to be alive. Surely her previous self had been only partly conscious, she mused, for at his touch her senses became incredibly more keen; at times she was almost too intensely aware of the sensations he roused. "Please," she would cry, "I can't go on."

Patient when he needed to be, Cameron would coax Honey to a level of ecstasy so filled with rapture that she could think of little but lying with him. She gladly would have spent the entire trip from Louisville, Kentucky, to Saint Louis, Missouri, a voyage of fourteen days, locked in Cameron's embrace.

"I shall throw away my key to the cabin—and keep you prisoner here with me," she threatened.

"As long as you have food sent in. A man needs fortifying for what's on your mind." He relished Honey's enthusiasm for lovemaking and to his delight found it unnecessary to avoid the strength and heat of his passion. He discovered her to be easily aroused and often as hungry as he was.

But sequestered as Honey had proposed, they would not have danced the early evenings away as they became accustomed to doing after the long day of separation. It was a time of mutual joy, a prelude to lovemaking. While dancing, they grew close and, very gradually, covertly intimate. So subtle were they, no one suspected they were beginning what would culminate in hours of passion. It was while they were dancing that Cameron first told Honey in words how he felt about her. "I love you," he whispered, pulling her especially close.

"I love you also," she answered, radiant.

When they were together they seemed to float above the world around them. The music, ordinary and unusual sounds, and the voices of others seemed far in the distance. They were fully aware only of each other.

Even on the evening they entertained the other members of the Greerfield party at dinner in the first-class dining salon, Honey might have been alone at the table with her lover for all she observed. The evening was lively and Honey gracious with goodwill toward all but apparently was distracted. She smiled, but her thoughts were elsewhere, not on the conversation, which ran to the experiences on the trail thus far and their expectations for the future. The men recounted tales of hair-raising mishaps, careful to point out that their examples were unusual. Gazing at her lover, Honey heard it all as if in a dream. Thoughts of danger escaped her. How could she be in danger with Cameron by her side? Even Ruth's murmured retelling of Cameron's handling of the men who had abducted Honey seemed not to faze her.

"I call them executions, don't you, Mrs. Radcliffe?"

"They were hardly upstanding citizens," was Honey's only remark.

Truly, Honey knew, from the facts of who they each were and where they came from, she and Cameron were, as Nollie protested, incompatible, yet theirs was no simple infatuation or a relationship for the purpose of satisfying unduly aroused animal instincts. Although before she fell in love with Cameron, Honey had believed there was nothing especially stirring about the male body, Cameron's fascinated her. She longed to touch him. He was perfect in her sight, unmarred even by the scars that he carried and that she caressed. She beheld him as he was. She often lay next to Cameron and marveled at how pleasurable a sight his body was to her, her hands roaming slowly over him, enjoying the varying textures she found—rough and smooth, leather and satin.

For a man used to commanding others, Cameron gave himself over to Honey with remarkable ease. Honey was available to Cameron, and he to her, on a level neither one remembered or had known; all knowledge and memory of others had evaporated. They were like children, innocent, playful, or serious according to the dictates of mood. In the time they spent on the two rivers, sailing between shores where few persons, even for a moment, would have condoned their liaison, Honey and Cameron lived only for the pleasure and love of the other.

Adoring him, Honey would caress Cameron as he voiced murmurs that raised her own desire, until the spiral of emotion brought them together as one body and one soul. Honey sensed she belonged to Cameron, as if she had been created for him, not merely for his carnal pleasure but as an essential part of his being; she now held firm the belief that the rigid sense of time the world around them argued as indisputable fact was inaccurate. She held Cameron in her arms and knew she had loved him before. She did not again experience the strange dreamlike state she had that last night in Greerfield, but she had other vivid dreams, much like the one that had awakened later that same night.

Sometimes Honey would wake crying and, clinging to Cameron, be inconsolable and oddly inarticulate. Then she would cry herself back to sleep and wake in the morning with no clear memory but with a despondence and physical pain on her left side and in her abdomen that threatened to make her bedridden at least for the day. The reality of Cameron's absence from her bed only made her feel worse.

On these occasions Nollie never overlooked the opportunity to point out how Honey's lover was affecting her adversely. "Well, if such suffering amounts to love, I'll be glad never to be acquainted with the disease."

Contrary to Nollie's intent, such jibes and the inability to resist sparring with Nollie served to bring Honey slowly from her dark moods. "I think you envy me, even if I sometimes give the impression of being forlorn."

"'Give the impression'?" Nollie harrumphed. "You're plain addled if you don't know how down in the mouth that man makes you."

"Oh, but you don't know the other half of it," Honey purred.

"And I don't care to, you hear."

"I wouldn't think of it." Honey smiled and stretched languidly, her nakedness barely concealed by bedcovers that were half-torn from the foot of the bed. "Are you aiming to be a spinster, Nollie?"

"You know I am."

"Then you shall miss the very best reason for being alive."

"Lord, you surely got it bad."

Honey rose from the bed, totally naked, her long twists of golden curls falling around her shoulders like a cape of glimmering silk. "No, I have it quite good. There isn't a woman alive who wouldn't want to know the rapture I feel with the man you feel so beneath your contempt."

"You're speaking little better than a harlot, Honey Radcliffe. You'd never have talked that way about Colonel Radcliffe."

Startled by Nollie's accuracy, Honey inhaled slowly, not in any attempt to control her anger at Nollie for mentioning Nathan but in reaction to her own knowledge of how close she had come to living a life without love or passion for the man she had married. "I hope, Nollie, someday you'll have reason to speak aloud of your joy with a man."

"The day I do, you have my permission to cut out my tongue."

Honey laughed deliberately, concealing a mounting rage at Nollie's relentless disapproval. She expected her friend to be happy for her. "Nollie, you're incorrigible."

"Better than being disgusting."

Honey laughed this time with genuine amusement at Nollie's

obvious outrage but soon had real reason to be furious with her.

Lovingly, Honey coaxed Cameron to stay with her longer each morning, until it became the rule for them to wake late, entwined in each other's arms and legs. Then they began to take breakfast together in her cabin.

To preserve their privacy, Honey asked Shahar to serve the food from trays brought to the cabin, but Nollie begged her mother to allow her to perform the service. "You shouldn't tax your arm that way with those heavy trays," she said.

Shahar's wound, sustained on the road to Panther Pass, had healed decently but sometimes gave her considerable pain, so, with Honey's approval, she had been glad to let Nollie serve breakfast. On the evening before Shahar had burned her hand ironing out the wrinkles in the gown Honey had chosen to wear that night, so Nollie's assistance became necessary.

Nollie smiled to herself as she dressed that morning. What a delicious opportunity, impossible to resist!

In the galley, Nollie ordered two large trays loaded with coddled eggs, beef hash, bacon, buckwheat pancakes, apple fritters, orange custard, sliced peaches, blueberries, butter, maple syrup, coffee, and cream. She carried one heavy tray and a steward another to Honey's cabin door. At Nollie's insistence, the steward laid his tray on the floor outside the door and disappeared.

Balancing her tray carefully, Nollie knocked on Honey's door. "Breakfas', Miz Radcliffe, fo' ya an' yo' gennamin fran wha' spant the night," she announced loudly, hardly able to control her glee, smiling too broadly at a couple who walked by in the passageway. "I hopes I's na 'rupting anythang."

By the time the door was flung open by a furiously red-faced Honey Radcliffe, Nollie had composed herself. She continued loud and clear. "Mornin', Miz Honey." Nollie dropped a quick curtsy. "Lordy, wha' be takin' ya so long? My po' a'ms 'bout ta come 'hinged wi' this here loada food. Good thang my mammy ain't be waitin' here while yo twos gets yoseffs decent, or her arms bust off fo' shur," Nollie said as she waltzed into the cabin with her tray, seeming to be oblivious to Honey's murderous glare. "Please ta leaves the door open, cuz theys one mo' tray for me ta brang in. Guess I musta 'rupted y'all. But ya tol' me ha'f pas' nine, an' I 'spected y'all ta be ready. I knows ya don't likes yo' eggs cold. Yo' coffee neither." People in adjacent cabins and across the hall would have had to be deaf or unconscious not to hear Nollie's announcements.

Honey slammed the door shut when Nollie brought the second tray inside the cabin, but Nollie continued to rattle on as though she were completely innocent of malicious behavior.

"Now jus' take no time 'tall ta set the table," Nollie said as she unrolled a damask linen cloth and laid the silver for the small round table Honey and Cameron would use for breakfast.

"Nollie Daniels, why are you carrying on like a fool and talking like a field nigger?" Honey demanded under her breath.

Nollie ignored her and turned to acknowledge Cameron. "Good mornin', sir. Mmmmmm, don't it shur look like ya oughta had a mite more sleepin' in? Not mentionin' some nourishin' up afta the trouble Miz Honey's put ya ta durin' the pas' night."

For the moment Honey was struck dumb.

"Nows y'all settle into yo' seats, whiles I be sarvin' up some this invig'ratin' breakfas'," she said, certain she had observed amusement in Cameron's eyes.

Honey found her tongue. "If you're planning to continue this absurd farce, you can leave at once," she said, again under her breath.

"An' leaves y'all to sarves yo'sefs? No, ma'am, Miz Honey. I cou'n't do that. Cou'n't even thinks 'bout it hardly. Gave my mammy my word that I's goin' stan' fo' her." Nollie laid a plate for Cameron with eggs, hash, and bacon, with side dishes of apple fritters, custard, peaches, and blueberries. She also served him steaming buttered buckwheat pancakes and maple syrup.

"Now, I knows, Miz Honey, 'spite ya bein' up ha'f the night entatainin' yo' man fran here, ya don' eats ver' much ta mornin'." Nollie gave Honey coddled eggs, apple fritters, bacon, fruit, and custard. She poured ice water and coffee for both and laid out a pitcher of cream. Then she stepped to the side as if waiting to assist them.

"You may go now, Nollie," Honey ordered. She had never been so angry. How dare Nollie embarrass her pretending to be an ignorant darky? Honey was afraid that if Nollie objected to leaving, she would start screaming and only embarrass herself more.

"Better I stay on, Miz Honey," Nollie said in a worried voice. "I jus' hates ta thanka yo' goin' wi'out propa sarvis."

Honey couldn't believe her ears. "I'm afraid, Nollie, that I won't be able to eat a thing until you leave us alone," she said as civilly as she could.

Nollie feigned concern. "Ya got the stomachaches, I bet, Miz

Honey. Lordy, tha's a shame." Before Honey could protest, Nollie removed all but the bowl of orange custard from Honey's place. "This custud's almos' as good as sick custud," she said to Honey's astonishment. "Good thang Mista Cam'ron's feelin' jus' fine. Look at him dig in. I's not much su'prised, though. Yo' been keepin' all hours, not ever havin' a good night's rest. I knows 'cause I hears you rollin' round on them squeaky bedsprangs, and a-talkin' and chucklin' an' havin' yo'seffs the goodest time."

As she stood up, Honey tipped over her chair. "Get out of my sight, Nollie Daniels, before you regret ever having taken your first breath!"

"Oh, Miz Honey, yo' surely won't beat me in front yo' night's guest?"

"Not if you immediately remove your ungrateful black body from my sight, I won't."

Nollie smiled like she was half-witted. "Oh, thanky, ma'am. Yo' too good to me. Thank ya," she said, judiciously backing out the cabin door. Shutting it gently, she all but skipped down the passageway to her own cabin, Cameron's deep, rollicking laughter drowning out her own.

CHAPTER NINETEEN

Unable to hide her mirth, Nollie faced her mother with an infectious smile that quickly changed to laughter and descended into giggles, then tears. For several minutes Nollie carried on, laughing and crying and hiccupping until she threw herself down on the bed she shared with Shahar and pulled a feather pillow tightly against her chest.

Shahar was silent until Nollie lay peacefully. "All right, now, child, you've some explaining to do."

At first Nollie did not answer, but finally she said, "Miz Radcliffe'll tells you a' earful. Ya jus' has ta waits till she call."

Extremely uneasy with Nollie's bad talk but holding her tongue, Shahar managed to refrain from probing. "I hope I don't have reason to regret your filling my shoes."

Her back to Shahar, Nollie answered with more silence.

Nollie lay clutching her pillow, seeking the comfort she knew would not come from any other source, until she heard her mother gather her own breakfast tray and go out the door. Then Nollie immediately turned onto her back and stared at the white ceiling. She tried to collect the thoughts that, without order or logic, filled her with dangerous emotions. The image of Honey Radcliffe made Nollie's heart nearly burst with anger. She had, she felt, every reason to hate the woman. But as the moments passed, Nollie's feelings softened toward her lifelong friend.

Nollie remembered herself and Honey as children and recalled how dear Honey Greer had been to her, as familiar as the reflection in the looking glass. At night, when they should already have been fast asleep, they would steal into each other's rooms, a feat they managed almost every night. Because they did not want to be overly harsh in punishing the little girls, this was one ritual the adults—her mother and Dr. Greer—had given up hope of ever stopping.

The two girls were fiercely intimate allies, although sometimes they were rivals. With each other, they ignored the issues of color and caste and lived in a world with separate codes defined by them alone. They were sisters, each a devotee of the other.

At first, when her hair was cropped as short as a boy's against her head, Nollie did not understand. When long, hers was not the usual head of fuzzy black curls but straight, with lovely waves, like her friend Honey's, only a different color. Shorn, shamed, Nollie begged her mother to let her hair grow out once more so that she could wear one long braid down her back again, just like she and Honey both had done for as long as either girl could remember.

But the point of cutting Nollie's hair, which neither girl knew at the time, had been to ensure that Nollie and anyone who saw her knew who she was—the daughter of a slave. Thus leveled, the inquiring eye might be drawn away entirely from the beauty of the light-skinned negro child, the curious mind stilled from questions of paternity.

Shahar, of course, was unmovable, and thereafter Nollie covered her head with a scarf in the timeless way of a bondswoman. The first thing she did after learning President Lincoln had emancipated the slaves was refuse to let her mother cut her hair. "Over my dead body," Nollie declared, and as soon as length allowed, began to wear her hair uncovered, first in imitation of Honey, then, sufficiently satisfied to have regained what she had lost, in row after row of slender braids, the ends sealed with tiny coils of brilliantly colored ribbon.

As for her paternity, Nollie, the unusually outspoken daughter, early on learned not to make those kinds of inquiries of her mother. Lin-Davey, a man at a distant plantation, was her father. That Nollie hardly knew the man was explained away by the fact of slavery. Because of Shahar's responsibilities, it was also easily explained why her mother's bed, which was next to her very own, was often empty: Mammy was up later at night and earlier in the morning than the child; therefore, Nollie simply did not observe her mother's comings and goings. Such explanations satisfied Nollie only for a while, although they did serve to silence her.

A slave, Nollie grew up having less, expecting less, but not wanting less from life than her friend Honey Greer. That she had few clothes and toys and, increasingly, as the years of childhood passed, privileges was not lost on Nollie. She understood the situation but did not accept it as her due. Unlike her mother, the wish for freedom burned within Nollie. Like the ash-covered embers from last night's fire, her dream of freedom only needed stirring.

Nollie dreamed of living well, of beautiful rooms, of beautiful clothes, of beautiful horses and carriages, of dancing with handsome men—negro and white—of elegant occasions and plentiful food. Of happiness, of outshining Honey or, at least, of being her equal.

Did that explain why she had taken such immense pleasure in bad talking Honey this morning? Nollie wondered. Now that Honey was no better than a strutting cowboy's whore.

Why, then, did she also feel tremendous outrage over Honey's affair with Cameron Wolfe? Why wasn't she delighted with Honey's long fall from her pedestal?

Could it be possible, as Honey had suggested, that she was jealous? That she wanted Cameron's attention for herself?

"Never!" Nollie insisted aloud.

First of all, Nollie recounted to herself, *if Mrs. Radcliffe cared to recall anything at all about life before she leapt bare-bosomed into that man's bed, she would remember I gave my oath in blood never to marry.* That vow had been given a long time ago, Nollie admitted, and later she had amended her position to allow the possibility of a little romance: She would consider an extravagant courtship, but *only* a courtship. Something chivalrous. Certainly she would never lower herself to accept a *cowboy* as an admirer, no matter how handsome he was.

Or virile.

Or, truthfully, intriguing.

Nollie continued in silent enumeration of Honey's sins. It irked her greatly that Honey Radcliffe, who was supposedly a lady of considerable delicacy, would dare to try to charm a man more suitable to, say . . . herself.

Given the great scarcity of men who had survived the war, Honey Radcliffe had no right to infringe on the population of men whom a woman of a little less delicacy might allow to court her. "If she were interested, that is," Nollie said, affirming to herself that she was not at present interested in the serious attention of any man.

I don't deny the man is attractive in his way. If he were to look at her the way he looked at Honey, Nollie admitted she would be tempted. Those piercing blue eyes would catch any breathing woman's heart, "for a time." She perhaps could see herself in a brief dalliance with Mr. Wolfe. "But I'd never act as if I'd married him!" she swore aloud.

If Nollie were being absolutely honest with herself now, she would have to confess that she had hoped that during the journey west Honey and she might grow as close as they once had been. Before Honey had begun to work with Dr. Greer and Nollie had been given ever-increasing responsibilities in the kitchen, long before the war tore apart everyone's life, before Honey had gone away to school—before Honey Greer was courted formally by Nathan Radcliffe.

When Nathan Radcliffe was woven into the fabric of Honey's daily life, truly everything had changed. Nollie's mind recalled the exact moment, and she was able to see herself clearly as she had been, readily concealed behind blossom-heavy azalea bushes scattered along the long Greerfield Plantation drive, spying on Honey Greer and her promised suitor, Nathan Radcliffe.

As Nollie kept her subjects in sight, she perspired profusely, more from the damp heat of her excitement than from the exertion of trotting surreptitiously from bush to bush. Acutely aware that beautiful Honey Greer probably would never again find herself in circumstances to suffer such unladylike sudations, Nollie was filled with both disgust and flagrant envy. To her distress,

Honey seemed every day more commited to fulfilling Dr. Greer's ambition to be the perfect gentlewoman, preface, of course, to becoming Nathan Radcliffe's perfect wife.

Although no official betrothal had been announced yet, the Radcliffe and Greer families had already come to an understanding about their children. Nathan Radcliffe, while senior to Honey by five years and heir to the Radcliffe fortune, seemed content with the arrangement. He would be a decided prize as a husband, Nollie knew, while Nathan would be the recipient of a splendid, beautiful bride. The time allowed before the engagement would give Honey a chance to grow only more desirable—and Nathan time to sow wild oats.

Nollie had watched Honey play at being seductive in her newest silk gown, an airy confection in shades of lavender, pink, and blue. Slowly, she twirled a matching parasol with a lavender fringe as it balanced charmingly on one fair, partially exposed shoulder, long, dark golden curls cascading obediently along the other.

How could she? Nollie had fumed silently, feeling betrayed. Yet she could not tear herself away; a lifetime of taking mental note of Honey's every move was fixed irrevocably within her. In Nollie's experience, Honey's behavior with Nathan Radcliffe was something new to Honey, yet she seemed to be performing very adequately from the look on his face. At moments he seemed fairly to devour his young bride-to-be and, judging from his ready smile, was also often amused by her.

Nollie was certain she herself would never behave in such a coy manner. Certainly she would never overtly seek the attentions of a man, which could only lead to things she did not care even to imagine. Until this moment, contrary to accumulating evidence, she had insisted on believing that Honey Greer was still of the same firm virtuous opinion. Nollie feared only more distressing revelations of a similar nature lay before her in the future. Already she felt the weight of them pressed heavily against her back.

At a noise behind her, Nollie stopped her speculations and abruptly straightened her posture. She turned to find Billy Greer about to grab her at the waist. "Spying on Sister, I see," he announced rather loudly.

"Shhhh," Nollie hissed, used to Honey's protection.

"See something you desire, Nollie?" Billy laughed. "He's taken, and it'll be years yet before he's available to you, I think."

He offered her his arm. "On the other hand, there are many others willing to pursue your favor. Myself, for one. All others shall have to stand in line."

Eager to escape the possibility of Honey's overhearing them, Nollie allowed Billy to escort her away from the long, curving drive deeper into the thicket of shady trees and wild azaleas where, with Honey, they often had roamed together. Only three years older than Honey, Billy often had been the girls' companion in freer times. Nollie pretended to ignore Billy's suggestive remarks. When safely out of earshot, she removed her hand from Billy's arm.

"After all the time we've spent together, you should show me favor," Billy pursued.

"I've no intention of showing favor to anyone."

"There will come a time, Nollie."

"Never."

"What makes you think you can avoid your duty?"

"Mammy says I might."

Billy laughed and pulled the ribbon holding back Nollie's dark curls, fashioned as Honey usually wore her own hair. "Something Mammy never succeeded doing herself. Or are you as innocent as Sister pretends to be?" He tossed the bright silk ribbon over a high branch, well out of Nollie's reach.

Outraged, Nollie came to an abrupt halt and struck Billy on the arm as hard as she could with her fist. "Mammy is a virtuous woman," she cried, the need to defend her mother outweighing the value of the precious ribbon. "You've no right to say anything to the contrary. Dr. Greer wouldn't have her under his roof if it wasn't so. What puts it in your head to be so mean?" She swung to strike Billy again.

He caught her arm and twisted it easily behind her. She screamed shrilly, but he pulled her hard against him. A head taller than Nollie, Billy glared down at her menacingly. "Honey's been far too familiar with you, and I not nearly enough."

Nollie's gray eyes widened with her sense of danger. "I'll tell, Billy Greer, I'll tell. You've no right."

"I've every right. You might wear Honey's cast-off dresses, but you're just a nigra. I can do anything I want with you."

"Your daddy'll skin you!"

Billy laughed derisively and pushed Nollie down with him on the damp ground.

"You'll ruin my dress," Nollie protested, as if that were the only thing at risk.

Billy laughed louder. "It's not your dress, it's Honey's, and she's a room full of dresses she can give you," he said, and took her mouth for a hurtful kiss. "But if you just cooperate, girl, we won't mess the dress too much."

Nollie struggled violently and managed to scream loudly for several seconds before Billy succeeded in covering her mouth with his hand. "Damn it! Know your place! You want on-lookers?"

Determined not to be an easy victim, Nollie did all she could to save herself. She had never fully believed Shahar's warnings that this could be her fate, especially not with Billy, in the past her friend, at times seeming almost a brother. Yet now he seemed possessed of the madness that she had been cautioned sometimes overcame white men with negro women. "I'm just fourteen!" she screamed as she rolled helplessly with Billy while he tugged and ripped her clothes.

"High time," Billy grunted as he pressed her down beneath him, having successfully raised her skirts and torn her drawers. "Shoulda whelped at least one baby by now." He struggled with his own clothes and kept Nollie constrained.

"What are you doing?" Honey shrieked, running toward them, although she knew well what Billy was about. "You can't treat Nollie that way!" she commanded, and rushed at Billy with her folded parasol, using it as if it were a lance. First she aimed for his ribs, succeeding in forcing him to roll away from Nollie, then began to batter him as if she were holding a club.

She had triumphed at first with the element of surprise, but neither girl, or both together, no matter how enraged, was a match for Billy. Slender, muscular, and unusually strong, he very quickly had both girls on the ground. Except for the fierce seriousness of the moment, it might have been years earlier and the three engaged in rough and tumble play.

Close behind Honey, Nathan Radcliffe and Shahar arrived, Nathan swiftly pulling Billy to his feet, Shahar helping up the girls.

"How dare you! How dare you!" Honey spat, but for Shahar's restraint again leaping on her youngest brother. "Nollie's not just anyone, she's family almost! You mistreat her, you mistreat *me*. You're base, vile, disgusting trash!"

"I'll buy her from you, if you insist," Billy answered calmly, squaring his shoulders with a relaxed motion and relieving himself easily of Nathan's grip.

"Father'd *never* agree," Honey said, still hot with fury. "Nollie's mine, and you can't have her! Ever!"

Billy gave Nathan a knowing look. "You're to have your hands full with my sister as a wife. I don't envy you," he said with clear despair for Nathan's fate.

Nathan held Billy's gaze a moment, then turned and held out his hand to Honey. "No real harm done, it seems," he said, unruffled, and gallantly began to brush off the clumps of mud clinging tenaciously here and there to Honey's dress. Billy took the moment to saunter away. He began to whistle idly.

Humiliated by her brother's conduct and feeling chagrin for her own wild if understandable defense of Nollie, at first Honey was speechless, but she then turned away from Nathan's ministrations and embraced Nollie. She had seen the terror in Nollie's eyes. "I am shamed beyond words for Billy's actions, " she said, then turned to Shahar. "You must tell my father about this, Mammy. You can be sure I shall speak to him myself." She saw the ribbon Billy had pulled from Nollie's curls hanging above them. "I should have scratched his eyes out!" Honey said, then, remembering what she had been about before this ugly incident, turned back to Nathan, at once hating to consider her appearance, blushing as her gaze met Nathan's.

As she was led away by Nathan, Honey did not see the look on Shahar's narrow face, but Nollie did. Bewildered by the fire there, she protested. "I didn't do nothing wrong, Mammy!"

"You've been watching her too close for too long. Time's come for you to keep more to yourself. Miss Honey can walk with Mr. Nathan and make calf eyes at him, but you can't do any such thing, especially with a white man."

"But I . . ."

Towering over Nollie, Shahar shook her roughly by the shoulders for several seconds, effectively silencing her. "I knew all along in my heart it was foolish to let you get too close to that child. Yet it was natural to love her and let her love you. But you best not mistake yourself for a white lady. Nobody else will." The contrast of Shahar's dark skin with her daughter's lighter shade was never more striking. "The law's against crossbreedin' for wrong reasons, and you, girl, have the most to lose. More important, nothing to gain."

"I don't want a man—ever," Nollie whispered, genuinely frightened by Billy's attack.

Half-smiling, Shahar had scoffed. "You're young yet. If you don't forget this day, you'll likely overlook it some day. And likely will continue to want whatever Miss Honey has." She let go of Nollie.

Nollie shifted from one foot to the other and pulled herself erect. "I've sense enough not to fool with Mr. Nathan, even if I wanted him, which I don't," she answered firmly.

Shahar stared at her daughter, full of apprehension, her demeanor suddenly sad. "I dreamed it would be different for you and her—that somehow *everything* might be different. All I've been is a fool."

Nollie put her arm around her mother and snuggled against her lovingly. "It will be, Mammy. I know it will be."

Shahar embraced her child. "I pray for once your vision's clearer than mine."

Although Shahar never said a word to her, Nollie reflected, from the beginning she had sensed her mother's antipathy for Nathan Radcliffe. It was something Nollie had never understood, for as far as Nollie could tell, in spite of her own avowed disapproval of marriage, Nathan Radcliffe would have been an excellent husband for Honey Greer. As far as Nollie knew, Honey had never threatened to be a spinster, which Nollie more than once had suggested she do.

Nathan Radcliffe had come from a family of good reputation and wealth. He was admired by everyone in the Greer family and had a striking and desirable appearance, which, before their marriage, Nollie was in a better position to know than Honey, having on more than one occasion observed him nearly naked.

It seemed to Nollie that the postponement of Honey's wedding for long periods of mourning had been reasonable only once or twice. At the third delay, when Nollie pointed out to Shahar that other Southern ladies managed to get themselves to the altar in spite of the regular appearance of death in their families, Shahar forbade Nollie to make any such remark to Honey.

But Nollie did not fail to notice that in spite of her grieving the death of the latest family member, Honey's mood seemed to be elevated a notch whenever the wedding was postponed. As a result, Nollie felt uncharitable and guilty when Honey took to her bed at Colonel Radcliffe's death. Still, she could not help but wonder if there was more to Honey's indisposition than simple grief.

Glum and not as certain as she had been of her motivations for performing for Honey and Cameron the way she had this morning, Nollie got up from the bed. She pulled off the scarf she had worn to play the role of slave and ran her fingers through her shoulder-length black satin hair. She had not braided the shining cascade of curls since she had come aboard the *Lady Mildred*, and now she massaged her scalp to try to ease away the tension that overtook her, certain there would be a penalty to pay for her performance this morning.

But she had no regrets. Given another opportunity, Nollie knew she would do just as she had done. Honey's wrath might be formidable, but her aggravation, her chagrin in front of Cameron Wolfe, would make any chastisement easy to bear. Triumph was sweet, if fleeting.

Furthermore, Nollie thought, smiling at herself in the mirror, she would not for the world deny herself the pleasure of the other tricks she already had up her sleeve.

CHAPTER TWENTY

In the face of Cameron's thorough teasing about the degree of her fury at Nollie, Honey had restrained her impulse to vent her rage at Nollie with Shahar. Not one day passed, however, before Honey regretted her decision.

That night, just as she and Cameron were carried away by passion, they heard the tinkling of a bell coming from somewhere underneath the bed. With each thrust and reply, it sounded. On hearing the bell, Cameron smiled broadly, knowing exactly who was to blame. But Honey found nothing amusing about the musical accompaniment to their lovemaking.

"How dare she?" Honey demanded, livid and thoroughly distracted. She wriggled out from under Cameron and, kneeling on the floor, raised the mattress flounce. Furious, she peered carefully into the dark skeleton of the bedsprings, but in the dim lamplight there was nothing to see. "Where did she hide it?"

"Come back here," Cameron urged, patting the mattress with his hand, "and we'll listen more carefully this time."

Honey sat back on her heels and glanced at him skeptically. "How can you think this outrage amusing?" Honey wanted to shake Nollie until her teeth rattled. "It's as though she's spying on us. I wouldn't be surprised if next she drilled a hole in the wall and watched!"

Cameron laughed at Honey's irritation. "A good whipping is what she needs."

"Don't tempt me."

"Shall I beat her for you?"

The tone of his last remark sounded almost serious and sobered Honey instantly. "Slavery made brutes of us all at times," she said, "but I never had Nollie whipped, and never would."

To the accompaniment of the bell, Cameron sat up and put his legs over the edge of the bed. Before she could dive in search of the bell again, he brought Honey between his legs and held her tightly in his embrace. "She probably thinks you're too much a lady for the likes of me."

"Nollie can be damned," Honey snapped back, regaining her anger.

Cameron smiled. "Then let's give her something to listen to."

Honey laughed and, considering the degree of her rage, was persuaded rather easily to focus only on the sweet sounds of their lovemaking. At first she listened to the irregular rhythm of their breathing and their sighs, then easily drifted with Cameron into a world of their own making, indifferent to any sensations but those which led them to ecstasy. She heard and felt only his kisses and the sounds of his pleasure with her.

That she could if she chose easily bring him to orgasm intrigued her; that he could do the same for her stunned her utterly. Just now, Cameron was toying with her fragile nerve endings in delicious ways, and in his loving hands she slipped into what could only be called a dream, full of wonderful sensation, joyful, near delirium.

In the short time he had known her, Cameron had learned a great deal about her, certainly more than he knew or ever cared to know about any other woman, more than Honey had ever known about herself. He knew the very places in her beautiful flesh that responded to light touch and those which were more responsive to slightly more pressure. He delighted in his discoveries and in her appreciation, which she expressed with thrilling sighs. Each fresh pleasure made the familiar new for him.

It was heaven for Honey to have her body coupled with his, to have his warmth and the fullness of his embrace surround her in bliss. Sometimes, fleetingly, images from another time filled her head, and although Honey usually stayed with the present moment, she often felt a connection with Cameron that transcended the usual sense of time.

"Eternal time," she whispered dreamily, floating slowly back to earth, the last note of the bell subsiding. They savored their pleasure as long as possible in the quiet, and astride him, her fingers laced in his thick brown hair, Honey cradled Cameron's head. She gazed lovingly down at him, at a softness, an openness in his countenance she saw only when he made love to her. "I love you," she said, and bent forward to bestow her lips on his. "Sometimes I feel I have always loved you."

Cameron knew the feeling well and smiled, bringing Honey down to snuggle with him, her head against his shoulder. He held her tightly. He sometimes felt as if Honey had been the first and only woman he had ever loved.

Reasonably, he knew that he had loved his Apache wife— loved her enough that, grieved and shaken when she and their baby had died, he had been driven from the existence he had adopted as truly as if he had been born Apache.

But my heart, my soul, is with this woman, Cameron realized as he gazed into Honey Radcliffe's beautiful face. And then he slept the profound sleep of one who is at last at peace with his memories.

CHAPTER TWENTY-ONE

Half-dressed, with a silk wrapper carelessly thrown over her nakedness, Honey burst into Shahar and Nollie's room through the common door. "Where's Nollie?" she demanded.

"Why, she's just gone out on deck for some air," Shahar said, looking up from mending the hem of one of Nollie's petticoats.

"This is the last straw!" Honey said, gesturing in the direction of her cabin, where Shahar could see the bedding ripped from the mattress.

Shahar immediately suspected Nollie of playing some trick. She had sensed that the air between the two young women was hot and disturbed since Nollie had taken her place that morning at breakfast, although Honey had yet to complain about Nollie's conduct.

"It's probably a good thing she isn't here." Honey spoke in a low, intense voice, but her feelings were unmistakable. She closed the door behind her, preventing Cameron from overhearing more. "Truly. I'd like nothing better than to wring Nollie's neck. She's been playing jokes on us. To embarrass me in front of Mr. Wolfe. First, she played the idiot darky at breakfast, pointedly letting us know she knew exactly what kind of affair we were conducting.

"'Po' Mista Woof. That nasty woman's keepin' ya 'wake all hours of ta night? Eats up, now, an' gits yo' stenth up sum.'

"I'm going to tear the black hair out of her ungrateful head!"

Shahar disapproved of Nollie's behavior, yet she could not suppress a smile. "You mustn't be so hard on Olivia. Unless you've told her, she has no understanding who Mr. Cameron is. Neither of you girls was raised for loving a man outside of marriage."

"That in no way mollifies me," Honey snapped back. "If she's jealous, you can tell her Mr. Wolfe is not interested in courting a bad-talking slave or anyone who thinks a bell tied to the bed-springs is the least amusing."

Shahar laughed out loud.

"I want her to stop. Tonight we found the sheet not tucked at the foot of the bed but brought up and folded over the blanket as if everything was done properly."

"Perhaps enough is enough."

"Indeed!"

Shahar put her mending aside. "I'll fix the bed for you."

"Don't bother yourself. I've made thousands of beds. I can make my own. Just 'fix' Nollie. Or else I will." Honey opened, then slammed the door between the cabins.

Shahar heard Honey complaining of Nollie as she made the bed. She also heard, indistinctly, Cameron's replies. Eventually, Shahar guessed, he had soothed Honey's temper, for soon she heard little but silence and occasionally the creaking of bed-springs.

When Nollie returned to their cabin, Shahar greeted her with a nod and noticed that as her daughter sat on the bed and let down her hair, she seemed to be straining her ears in the direction of Honey's cabin. "Listen to those bedsprings. They do sing out. Mrs. Radcliffe's not alone, you know—*again*," Nollie announced.

Shahar nodded.

"I *used* to think you'd drown me in the Cape Fear if ever I thought of behaving that way. I told Honey she's no better than a Yankee whore, but she paid me no mind. You raised us both far better than she's doing. Why're you so easy on her now?"

"Mr. Cameron is someone from the past Honey can't turn away from."

"Then she at least ought to marry him before bouncing up and down. Her daddy's turned upside down in his grave this minute. Not to say Colonel Radcliffe. *He* must positively be whirling in his grave."

"It's not time for marrying yet."

"No preacher man. No weddin'. No kissin'. That's what I remember."

"I'm grateful to hear it."

"So your advice was just for me, not her . . . nor, I guess, for following by you."

For some moments Shahar stared silently at Nollie. She knew that one day Nollie would question her relationship with Phillip Greer. Maybe this was that day. There was too much that was unspoken, too much difference in the way she had raised the two girls.

Within her circle, Honey had been protected from abuse and ruin by a number of restraints, among them careful chaperoning and common morality, which Nollie had not been protected by. A female slave—white man's property—especially a light-skinned beauty like Nollie, was in jeopardy from a very early age. Fortunately, Nollie had heeded the restrictions Shahar had inculcated in her from the cradle. Nollie's sauciness, which easily might be construed as compelling or seductive, was confined to her mother and her young mistress. Shahar was grateful that to the world at large Nollie was retiring and obedient, for a certain class of white man liked nothing better than to teach a negro wench a lesson.

Owing to Shahar's relentless instruction, Nollie believed the worst thing that could happen to a negro woman was to be subjected to her master's lust. Nollie translated her mother's cautions into a fear of white men in general. Her later disdain for all intimate contact with men may have grown from these very seeds, Shahar concluded. But even that fate would prove better for Nollie than to suffer the way Shahar had. Nollie's father, Phillip Greer, was one white man in a million. "Men's mostly dogs," Shahar had long ago heard an old slave woman observe. By her strict discipline of Nollie regarding men, Shahar believed she could spare her precious daughter much agony.

"Don't you envy Honey. She has a painful row to hoe."

"Envy her? Why would I envy her?"

"She's always had much that you've wanted yourself."

"Not Mr. Wolfe. I promise."

A shiver of fear ran through Shahar as the image of Nollie with a white man she recognized suddenly flashed before her eyes. "Don't you ever go forgetting that Dr. Greer was not a commonplace white man," she admonished.

"I'm not likely to," Nollie answered firmly. "Tell me, Mammy, why'd you never marry again after my daddy died?"

The question startled Shahar. "Was no need to. Your . . . Dr. Greer . . ." she stuttered. "I was no particular use as a breeder woman."

"Why'd he treat you so good?"

"Get more from a fed slave than a starved one, I suppose."

Nollie spent a few moments in speculation. She watched Shahar closely. "I remember your mourning Lin-Davey, but when Dr. Greer passed, you were laid up for days."

"For many long years he was my master—a rare and decent man."

"Dr. Greer was my daddy, wasn't he?"

There it was, the question Shahar had waited all these years to hear. Still, she had no answer.

"That's why you cut my hair, why my skin is as light as coffee and cream. And why, sometimes, when I hurry past a mirror, my mind plays tricks and I think I catch a glimpse of Honey's face."

Slowly Shahar nodded confirmation, and after a short silence, Nollie demanded, "Haven't you something to say?"

"No good could ever come from you knowin'. I thought it best to keep the truth to myself."

"I'm to tell the truth, but you're not?" Nollie demanded, bitterly.

"The truth might've put ideas in your head had no good reason to be there."

"Might make me an uppity negress, you mean?"

Shahar sighed. "You had the best we could give you, considering."

"Considering I was the massa's spoil."

Shahar hid her humiliation and anger. "You can't deny Dr. Greer treated you like a father for a very long while. You got far better than most, Nollie."

"I shoulda been told who my daddy was!" Nollie cried. "I had a right to know!"

"Slaves have no rights, Nollie. Knowing would have only been pain to you—watchin' Honey and knowin' you two sisters, and you always having less. Would that have made you happy?"

"Does Honey know?"

"Not unless she guessed and didn't say nothing, and that isn't likely."

"Mammy, you said *never no white man*. How could you? How could you let me be born?" The outrage in Nollie's voice pierced through Shahar.

"Dr. Greer—your daddy—was a fine man. Maybe you can't understand this yet, but I wanted *his* baby. I loved him. You can be proud to have his blood in your veins."

"You loved him—if he loved you, how could he just use you, never saying a word all these years? I'm older than Honey, you know?"

"Wasn't easy for us."

"Wasn't easy! Wasn't easy?" Nollie cried, and dissolved into tears. "Is my white daddy the cause of you telling me over and over not to go messin' with white men? If he was such a decent, fine man, how come I'm to keep my hands off?"

"White men mostly don't call on a negro lady for reasons of love. Save your virtue for a good man the same color as you."

"Like you did," Nollie challenged.

"Maybe you'll understand more when you come to love someone yourself."

"Never! For me no man—white, black, or blue! I don't want any part of them," Nollie announced as she threw herself on the bed and pulled the pillows over her head. She cried until she was exhausted, then at last fell asleep.

CHAPTER TWENTY-TWO

Obsessed as she was, within her scope of vision Honey could see little besides Cameron Wolfe. However, Nollie, who seemed to have no better purpose in life than to annoy and embarrass her, was a prominent distraction. She seemed almost to be possessed. If not possession, Honey wondered, what could account for Nollie's malice?

Although Honey had accused Nollie of being jealous of her favor with Cameron, Honey truly doubted that desire for Cameron was the cause of Nollie's mean-spirited pranks. After all, it was not so long ago that she would have said that if ever there was a born spinster, Nollie fit the bill. On numerous occasions Nollie had taken great pains to end all matchmaking on her behalf. She had said plainly that Honey was a fool to agree to marriage.

But spinsterhood had held no appeal for Honey; in her opinion, it was more a prison for a woman than marriage. Married, she would have had children and a fair amount of freedom to circulate in the larger world.

Perhaps Nollie, too, was having serious second thoughts about living her life as a chaste unmarried woman. Maybe Nollie was just as vulnerable to Cameron's appeal as she herself had been. Certainly, Honey mused, at a loss to explain the precise ingredients of Cameron's allure, she'd found his appeal to be irresistible. Nollie could hardly be blamed for being susceptible.

To be utterly frank, Honey admitted, in her attraction to Cameron Wolfe she'd faced the feral side of human nature intimately for the first time. Suddenly she possessed a ruthless desire to keep her lover solely for herself.

"Beautiful Nollie" was how Honey had thought of her friend as a child. Skin the color of coffee and cream, with shining smoky gray eyes and long coils of jet-black curls. So unlike herself yet in so many ways a true reflection, and easily, in spite of Shahar's proscriptions, a likely rival for any man's affections.

But Nollie Daniels is a slave—or was.

A querulous voice in Honey's head instantly retorted, *What difference does that make to a man*?

Judging from the large numbers of mulatto children, it meant nothing to many white men. Slavery was a convenience to the slave master. Why would it not be a means to procure a woman? If the bondage of human beings could be defended as ordained by God, the institution could be used for all manner of purposes besides profit, including whoredom. Slavery, Honey now believed, had been a curse upon the South.

Men like her father, who, convinced that states had the right to secede from the Union, had supported the Confederacy in the name of honor, duty, and patriotism, in fact had fought to uphold the institution of slavery. Dr. Greer believed slavery an institution that would eventually pass from the land but was dependent on the slave economy for profits that allowed him and his family to live in a grand style. He believed strongly that he had a reciprocal and almost paternal obligation to his slaves and therefore provided decently for them. But in spite of this philosophy, as an absentee master of three plantations, abuses did occur that could never fully be undone. Over the years Dr. Greer had come to question the morality of the institution.

To view the negro people as lesser creatures than white men was not something Dr. Greer could do reasonably. He was a doctor, after all, and if nothing else knew black men suffered no less than white men with the same wound or affliction. He knew too many good negro men and women and, at the same time, whites who were no better than the most degraded slave. He also knew men who mistreated their negroes for no better reason than that they could do so without fear of punishment. Before the war Dr. Greer had believed that the South sooner or later would have to abolish the system of slavery, an event that would have come at no little expense. But surely, Honey reflected, the cost would have been a million times less than the recent long and hideous war.

Honey had grown up thinking slavery ordained by God, believing that Shahar and Nollie were a cut above the rest. She understood both were slaves, and at times she put on airs, testing her power as the young mistress. But for long years, without question, female authority in the Greer household had rested with Shahar. For the most part, Honey literally did not see the color of their skins but looked beneath that tissue-thin layer of flesh and saw instead with what lay inside their hearts.

When very young, if she thought about slavery at all, Honey did not think of Shahar or Nollie. Slaves worked her father's plantations. She never dreamed his intent to provide decently for the men and women he owned might be ignored in his absence. Carefully exposed and chaperoned, she was insulated from the awful reality of slaves who were not treated well. Only when she began to help her father as a nurse did Honey have the opportunity to see a little of the life of other slaves. To withstand the tragedies that Dr. Greer was unable to save her from, Honey judged any mistreatment or neglect as aberrations of the slave system, convinced that the ignorant or abusive master would reap what he sowed. She believed in justice. That slavery itself was unjust did not occur to her until much later, and her ability to do anything significant about slavery seemed even more remote. Thus Honey had put all her energies into trying to persuade her father to allow her to become a doctor.

Now, as she pondered her relationship with Nollie, she supposed that Nollie's recent behavior might only be evidence of the rage and loathing for white people that was rumored to lurk in all black people's hearts. Even before abolition became a real possibility, fear of reprisal by slaves had haunted slave masters and other Southerners, while at the same time the rage of black men and women was deemed incomprehensible.

How dare Nollie be angry with me! I am not to blame. I did not injure her—or anyone. I am innocent.

But the sins of the fathers, Honey knew, are visited upon the children. What Nollie now expressed with pranks might be her way of showing the white woman something of the anger, the rancor, the bitterness that had festered in her heart over the years. Assuming this was true, Honey was indignant. *How can she hold me responsible? I'm her friend. Almost her sister.*

Honey preferred to reject these last suppositions out of hand. But then, the thought of jealousy being the cause of Nollie's antics rested no better in her mind. Honey's thoughts now swirled in disarray. Hot tears of anguish for herself and for her friend—for their apparently lost love—fell rapidly behind them.

CHAPTER TWENTY-THREE

When Cameron would wake enough to realize he was lying in Honey's bed, the sensation of peace that washed over him was one he had never known before—a curious result, he thought, of the most intense passion for a woman he had ever experienced. The idea that this luminescent being could love him seemed inconceivable; more than anything else in his life, Cameron wanted Honey's oath of love to be truth.

He was not a man to spend much time in reflection, but Honey Radcliffe stirred him to consider what lay for them beyond their stolen nights of passion. He loved her deeply, but soon this time of traveling on the river and their denial of the larger world around them would end.

At the next port, reluctantly or not, they would be forced to pry themselves from each other's arms and it would be some time before they might indulge themselves in the rapture most of the world would regard as gratification of simple animal lust. The next port was Saint Louis, where Trevor Jefferson had agreed to arrange for certain provisions for the balance of the trip west and leave additional monies for expenses. As he had said in his final letter to Cameron before he had left Richmond, "I feel certain the extra funds will be not only handy but necessary. By the time you arrive in Saint Louis, you will surely be convinced that my darling niece requires the best accommodations. I, perhaps, should have arranged for her passage by clipper ship, but loathing water conveyance myself, I saw no reason to inflict such a journey on one of such delicate disposition."

It was apparent to Cameron that Honey had found neither the occasion nor the necessity to disabuse Trevor of the notion of her fragile nature as she often had with him.

Cameron had intended never to set foot in the city of Saint Louis again but now had no choice. His memories of Saint Louis were bitter gall—as intensely painful as his experience with Honey was pleasurable. Even his good memories of the city were tainted. He dreaded bringing Honey into Saint Louis, fearing she somehow would be contaminated—poisoned by the city's air.

Just as one might be infected in an epidemic of dreaded yellow fever, Cameron believed the sentiment of others who once had loved him might corrupt the love Honey vowed for him and cause her to turn against him. In Saint Louis Honey might see him in a new, more revealing light and with a fresh eye; all the love that now poured from her and flowed over him like a soothing balm might evaporate.

How could Honey continue to love him, Cameron wondered to himself, when even his family could not? He knew all too well that truth could destroy love.

So overwhelming was his fear, Cameron failed to reason that Honey most likely would never learn what the family knew of him unless he dared to reveal the truth to her.

As a rule Cameron Wolfe was not controlled by fear, but in this case he was its victim. His dread of losing Honey impaired him in a way that drove him to be distant.

Honey sensed the change in him immediately.

Suddenly Cameron was unavailable to Honey, as if a door had been closed and the lock turned. Where once they had sailed in unison, each now traveled alone. She caressed him and sensed for the first time that he no longer felt her touch. They were not intimate in the way they had been; their wellspring had dried up.

Finally, one morning when Cameron had left her, Honey could not bear her depression in silence any longer. She cried bitterly, and her tears brought Nollie to her side.

Over and above her disapproval for the affair Honey was conducting, Nollie, sensing that Honey's tears stemmed from deep within her, felt only sympathy for her friend—her sister. This morning Nollie intended no recriminations, but Honey did not give her a chance to prove that such was the case. "Leave me alone!" Honey cried when she realized Nollie was sitting beside her. "I won't listen to anything you have to say."

Vexed by Honey's tone, Nollie immediately forgot her empathy. "If you don't shut off your tears, your face will swell up like a head of lettuce."

"Get out!" Honey screamed before pulling a pillow over her head.

"Disposition like a rattlesnake this morning," Nollie snapped as Shahar entered from their cabin.

Shahar gave Nollie a little shove through the doorway. "You should know better than to provoke a rattlesnake," she said, and shut the door behind her daughter and sat next to Honey on the bed. "What's all this hollerin'?"

"I didn't mean to wake anyone."

"You always did when you got to crying."

"Just let me wallow in misery a while."

"Wallowing's bad."

Honey turned to face Shahar and wiped her eyes with the hem of the sheet. "It's worse than learning of someone's death."

"What's worse?"

"When someone dies, there's no choice but to accept the loss. But when someone living leaves you and you still love him, it's much harder to accept." Honey sat up and used the handkerchief Shahar handed her. "I don't suppose I'm making any sense."

"No, you're not."

After a long silence Honey said, "He's stopped loving me." Tears welled in her eyes again. "So much for your vision of our destiny together, Shahar," she sniffed. "Cameron Wolfe's not properly informed. And when I was half believing, I sometimes felt deeply connected with him, as if our souls..." Honey blushed. "That's your fault, you know, for filling my head with absurdities."

"What's this talk of him leaving you?" Shahar countered, ignoring Honey's jibe.

Honey shook her head. "He didn't say, 'I don't love you anymore,' but I feel it, as if he'd used a knife and cut away his love from me."

"You should have more faith."

"More faith? How can you say that? Henceforth I shall trust only in what I feel in my gut!"

Shahar smiled down at Honey. "You must trust more than your gut, Honey Greer. Remember all you've shared with him past and present, and trust him to prize what he has known with you."

Honey stared at the older woman. "You're too trusting, Shahar."

"And you, Honey Greer, are like your daddy sometimes said —too smart for your own good. Too many brains gets you into trouble."

"I've been relying on my heart, not my brain, in the last weeks, and look where I am."

Shahar smiled at Honey and tucked the covers around her. "I'll leave you alone to stew some more. But I'll be back in a while with some breakfast."

Honey did her best to be calm. Finished with sleep and, she hoped, done with tears, she summoned anger as a defense against her unhappy frame of mind. But anger did little to soothe her as she lay waiting for the day to dawn. Cameron Wolfe had introduced her to a new range of emotions—from the elevated heights of ecstasy to the lowest form of despair. To think that one man alone could draw such range of emotions from her defied Honey's vision of herself as a rational being and disturbed her greatly.

If she could be so emotional, she reasoned, perhaps she was too emotional to be suited to the necessarily intellectual practice of medicine. Perhaps her female mind *would* overrule her intellect when it mattered the most. If she had never met Cameron Wolfe, never loved him, not made love to him, she would never have questioned her suitability to be a physician. Now the question nagged her.

For now that she loved Cameron Wolfe, she was changed. She was *forever* a very different woman.

CHAPTER TWENTY-FOUR

The *Lady Mildred* docked in Saint Louis in the late afternoon of a sultry day. "Nearsa hundred degrees t'day, ma'am," the porter informed Honey as he loaded her baggage into a carriage. "The veranda at the Janus's shady, so's it won't seem so terrible," he predicted.

Later, feeling the heat more than she usually did, Honey doubted that assessment. Irritable in general, she realized everything was likely to annoy her and anticipated being dissatisfied with Saint Louis in total: the heat, the food, the well-regarded Hotel Janus. Cameron, who had been seeing to the loading and transport of their wagon and the details of provisioning their party, did not escort her to the city's most elegant hostelry. Honey, Shahar, and Nollie arrived at the august hotel by themselves.

The party planned to be in Saint Louis for a week at most and for less time if at all possible. As many provisions for the trail as could be obtained would be arranged in Saint Louis and carried to

Independence, the official starting point of the Santa Fe Trail.

Set apart from the rest of the Greerfield party, who located themselves in tents on the outskirts of the city with the duty of keeping an eye on the wagons, horses, and various property to be transported, Honey felt abandoned. Comfort from Shahar and Nollie did not exist for her, although Shahar did at least offer.

Cameron's absence, his obvious preoccupation whenever he was near, brought Honey to a state of nervous distraction, but she pretended otherwise. Gay and seductive, she sometimes called attention to herself among the other patrons of the hotel, and if they had resided at the hotel any longer than they did, introductions would have been finagled by several male admirers.

With careful planning, on the second night of their stay in Saint Louis, Honey managed to lure Cameron into the hotel's ballroom after dinner. She was irresistible as he held her in his arms, and while he danced with her it seemed as though nothing had changed between them.

He looked into her golden eyes and imagined he saw how truly and deeply she loved him, and for the moment he believed nothing could ever change such emotion. But the echo of the nearly forgotten Apache taboo regarding gold rattled in his brain: To disturb and raise gold from the body of Mother Earth was a sacrilege, an abomination to Ussen, God the Creator. "Beware of fool's gold," Cameron whispered aloud without being aware.

"I'm sorry, what did you say?" Honey said as his whispers drew her out of a dreamy state.

"I shouldn't waste the night dancing. There's still much to do. I expect we'll be ready to leave the day after tomorrow."

"So soon?" Honey pleaded, fearing once they were on the trail, Cameron would grow even more distant.

"Yes, so soon."

He seemed to smile at her, she thought, detecting the faintest light shining in his eyes while tears glistened in hers. "Are you so anxious for us to go?"

He answered her coolly, factually. "We must get as far from here as fast as possible. The longer we delay, the less grass and water ahead of us."

"Yes, of course." Their brief idyll on the river had become ancient, irrelevant history.

When the music ended, Honey allowed Cameron to lead her from the dance floor and upstairs to her door. Although they were alone in an inside corridor, he bade her good night with the barest hint of intimacy as he raised her gloved hand to his lips and pressed a kiss to her open palm. "I'll see you at noon tomorrow for supper," he said, and taking the key from her purse, began to unlock the door.

Before he finished, Shahar opened the door for them. When Honey passed through the doorway, Cameron remained outside. "Good night," he said quickly, and turned away.

Honey's face betrayed her shock, but eyeing Shahar, she tried to compose herself. Only later, as Shahar helped unlace her corset, did Honey complain. "All that I feared is true, and you, Shahar Daniels, couldn't have been more wrong about Mr. Wolfe. If we were ever lovers in another lifetime, we're surely jinxed in this one."

"Perhaps what needs to be resolved between you two will not be resolved in this lifetime, either."

Honey squeezed her hands into fists. "By the eternal, Shahar, I wish you'd never filled my head with this rot about souls passing from one life to another. You had me half believing you. To think that I even invited you to call on your ghosts. What an utter fool I am—I deserve all this misery."

Her corset undone, Honey rushed away from Shahar and pulled her nightgown hastily over her head, her long coils of hair becoming tangled in several buttons on the back of the gown. Angry at Shahar, she tried to undo the damage by herself but, unable to see, made the muddle worse. She tried to pull the gown back over her head, to her regret. "Please help me," she finally begged.

Shahar coaxed Honey to sit down and patiently extricated her hair from the buttons, then supervised Honey as she put on the gown successfully. With this accomplished, Honey sat on the edge of her bed again. "I can't even put my own nightgown on without assistance!" she groused. "I've made an awful mess of far more than my hair!" Honey clenched her teeth together tightly, hoping to hold back tears that begged for release. "Risking what I have, daring what I've done, it's only justice I ought to face my sins. But I'd certainly prefer not to crumble like a lovesick schoolgirl." Honey's voice caught on the tears that had begun to slide down from her watery eyes. "I feel so helpless," she sobbed.

After a few moments of indulgence, Honey stiffened her posture and resolve. "I absolutely refuse to put any more faith in your hocus-pocus, Shahar Daniels, no matter how much I want it to be true. And I don't care to hear another word from you about my destiny. Or Mr. Wolfe's."

"I understand your pain, child, but—"

Honey covered her ears. "No buts!" she cried. "I won't listen. And no more predictions! Promise!"

When Shahar nodded, Honey lowered her hands. "Now give me a hug along with your oath," Honey insisted, hugging Shahar tightly, "or else I won't be able to sleep."

"I promise," Shahar said reluctantly.

"Oh Lord, Shahar, but it's going to be a long journey to California."

Much longer than you think, Shahar reflected silently.

Honey had spent the long hot day visiting a few of the many shops in Saint Louis and after the emotional evening expected to fall asleep immediately. Instead, discontented, after more than an hour she still lay wide awake. She stared about her, memorizing the dark shapes of furniture in her private sleeping room, and wished that tonight at least she was sharing a room with Shahar and Nollie, who were, she imagined, now fast asleep in their own room across the parlor from hers.

The night was warm and the windows open as Honey pushed the sheet from her body and sat up. There was not even the hint of a breeze; the heavy air portended rain. Miserable, she sat up and poured a glass of water from the pitcher on the bedside table. The water was tepid and unrefreshing.

Honey got up then, not bothering to cover her shoulders with even a light shawl, and from the sitting room, through airily draped French doors, escaped onto a small balcony that overlooked the carefully tended formal garden at the rear of the hotel. After several minutes Honey gave up the notion of it being cooler outside but, certain that sleep would continue to evade her, sat down on a comfortable rocking chair just outside on the balcony.

Out of boredom, she began to count the windows of the rooms in the wing adjacent to her section of the hotel, seeking Cameron's window, and discovered a light on in his room. From time to time the shadow of a man's figure appeared to pace across the room, back and forth before the windows. His apparent agitation aggravated her own restlessness and made the night's atmosphere even more oppressive. Sensing Cameron's unbearable tension, she hastily retreated to her own suite of rooms, then, hesitating for only a few moments, deserted them.

Honey had slipped her arms through the sleeves of her silk wrapper and tied its broad sash tightly about her waist. Swiftly, she had twisted and pinned up her hair, then hurried out her door in the direction of Cameron's room. Barefoot, a wraith in the corridor, she scurried silently lest she be observed. When the corridor turned sharply into Cameron's wing, Honey slowed her pace. This long hallway seemed darker than her own, and her heart thudded violently inside her chest.

Suddenly, toward the end of the passageway, a door opened and a woman entered the corridor and began to move in Honey's direction. Frozen in place, certain the door that had been opened was Cameron's, Honey wished to flee the humiliation of seeing another woman depart her lover's room. But she also was obsessed with seeing her rival face to face.

The woman, dressed in refined street clothes, walked with a determined gait and had an air of respectability that belied her unescorted presence in a man's room this late at night. Dressed as Honey was, guilty as she herself was of the indiscretion of loving a man she was not married to, Honey smiled to herself at this instantaneous judgment and placed herself directly in the path of the advancing woman. When the woman corrected her stride to avoid colliding with Honey, Honey again deliberately moved to impede the woman's progress. Forced to stop in her tracks or bump into Honey, the woman, who was perhaps a decade older than Honey, halted abruptly. She said nothing but, disconcerted, stared at Honey as curiously as Honey stared at her. Honey realized that she herself—a woman in her nightclothes in the hallway of a hotel—was a surprising sight.

When Honey finally stepped aside, the woman resumed her motion and swiftly disappeared around the corner into the other wing, leaving Honey staring after her.

Honey stood motionless for many minutes, all kinds of explanations for the woman's presence in Cameron's room passing swiftly through her brain until, from behind, she heard another door open. She whirled around in time to see Cameron exit his darkened room.

He proceeded toward her at a hurried pace, but when he saw her, he abruptly slowed down. When he stood but a few inches away, Cameron stared down at Honey, unsmiling. In the dim light he scrutinized her with a cold gaze, touching her face and lifting it close to his. Then he gathered her into his arms and, crushing her against him, kissed her deeply.

From his response it was obvious this was not a man who had just spent himself in the arms of another woman, yet the unknown woman's recent presence nagged at the edges of Honey's consciousness even while she began to lose herself in Cameron's hungry embrace. Yet when he lifted her into his arms and carried her swiftly to his bed, Honey made not one note of protest.

He lit a lamp, stripped away his clothes, and pulled her down with him onto the mattress, then turned and covered her with his body. "Tell me you love me," he urged. "I want to hear you say it."

Honey laughed with pleasure and drew Cameron's mouth to hers. She kissed him passionately. "With all my heart, I love you," she whispered, and kissed him again and again. "How can you doubt me?"

"I want to believe you."

Honey grew pensive. "Perhaps I am the one who should have doubts. Didn't I just now see a woman leaving your room?"

"She's no one to concern you."

Honey almost laughed at his response. "You're more silent, less revealing, than any man I've ever known."

"I'm different than any man you've ever known."

"I should say! But the woman I saw . . . she's very beautiful. Can you have tired of me so soon?"

It was Cameron's turn to laugh, which he did with thorough amusement at Honey's petulant yet anxious tone. "How could I ever tire of you? I'm the one to worry."

He sounded worried in earnest, and Honey responded from the depth of her heart and soul. "I shall never stop loving you," she murmured as she held him close in her embrace. *"Never.* I promise."

CHAPTER TWENTY-FIVE

Vowing to avoid his uncle's store, the largest of its kind in Saint Louis, Cameron had managed to acquire all the necessary equipment and provisions without once entering Wolfe and Steinhart's Emporium, a store that specialized in the best hardware and goods necessary for housekeeping in town or on the road west.

For more than twenty-five years William Wolfe had profited from the urge of the American people to explore westward and fill the continent with new settlements in spite of the many hardships. He had outfitted and often underwritten numerous merchant caravans, most of which traversed the Santa Fe Trail. Gold rushes in California, Kansas, and other places west of the Mississippi and the dauntless urge of Americans to migrate west had made William a fortune, with losses to the hazards of the trail being far outweighed by gains.

For eight of those twenty-five years, Cameron's father, Joseph, William's youngest brother, had ridden with or led those caravans. Later, Joseph had ventured onto the familiar southern route with his young family, and all but Cameron had lost their lives. Now, more than a wide gulf of miles, more than a mere expanse of searing desert and empty prairie separated Cameron from his Saint Louis family, and the distance between Cameron and his uncle seemed insurmountable. Cameron had little hope of reconciliation, sometimes even doubting he had the courage to confront William Wolfe again. Despite promises to the contrary, Cameron reasoned that the ignorance and fear that had nourished William's earlier hostility still existed. He had no wish or need to be reminded how easily love could be extinguished.

However, Cameron's decision to avoid his family had been undermined by pleas from William's daughter, Katherine, who by coincidence had recognized her cousin Cameron in the Saint Louis streets. "I was compelled to follow you to your lodgings," she had said, and later in the evening went alone to his room, where she had related her understanding of her father's current sentiments and her desire for Cameron and her father to be reconciled.

"I feel my father deeply regrets the attitude that caused you to leave us again," Katherine said. "And I'm certain only his pride kept him from searching for you. Pardon an old man his pride. Now there is no time left to simply wait for his pride to wear away—Dr. Wixon predicted some months ago that Father had no more than a year remaining. Already he has begun to waste away before our eyes."

Katherine's blue eyes glistened with tears. She pulled a delicate lace handkerchief from a small velvet purse and dabbed at her lashes. When she regained her composure, she went on. "When you returned to us from the Apache, I was guilty of holding my opinions to myself, which I've done far too many years.

It was my habit to be silent when I should not have been. Especially with regard to you, I regret holding my tongue. How I did not stand by you is inexcusable, I know. The family should have overlooked your life among the savages, and you left us so soon —before the benefit of time could overcome our narrow minds."

Katherine paused as if she expected some reaction from Cameron, but he was silent and gave no sign of his reaction to her outpouring of sentiment. She appeared calm, if a little baffled by his unresponsiveness, and soon continued. "Dear Cameron, I'm certain, if you were to go to Father now, the outcome would be very different this time. And I'm here to plead with you to give him the opportunity to set straight the wrong done to you. I'm hoping you'll find it in your heart to give a sick man an opportunity to clear his conscience before death takes him."

Katherine's sympathetic response to him on his first return to Saint Louis disposed Cameron to believe her now. Approaching middle age, Katherine was still very beautiful, and he was not entirely immune to her tearful pleas. He knew she had been too much under her father's influence to stand up for him in the past; in fact, he knew Katherine had not married the man she loved and had turned away her suitor even before he had asked William for her hand because she knew he did not meet William Wolfe's approval.

Cameron appreciated Katherine's humility in coming to him now and reasoned she would know her father's sentiments. Although he did not agree at once to go to William, Katherine's plea gnawed relentlessly at him. After their rejection, Cameron had turned his back on his white family, he thought forever. Deep within himself he harbored a bitterness toward them for their cruelty, yet a part of him yearned for reconciliation.

From Katherine, Cameron learned that William still went to the emporium very early every day it was open for business. Although impaired by pain, which seemed to increase daily, Katherine said, William still spent the majority of the day in his office above the store. Few of his associates or employees knew of the severity of his illness, although they should have been alert to the wasting away of his robust figure before their eyes.

After Katherine had left him and after the buoying effects of hours spent making love to Honey Radcliffe, Cameron had reflected for some time on William Wolfe. Of anyone in the family, Cameron had expected William to grasp the difficulties he had surmounted as a captive white child among the Apache. His survival had been nothing less than miraculous. William's rejection, based on the belief that Cameron was irredeemable, had proved almost unbearable for the proud warrior.

Yes, he was different. Yes, he was changed. But he was also worthy of their acceptance, of their praise and their rejoicing at his return.

Could illness and the imminent approach of death cause William to accept him? Cameron wondered.

His gut told him it was unlikely, yet . . .

Yet Katherine was firm in her conviction that her father had undergone a change of heart. Cameron wanted to trust her, and the morning after Katherine's visit he went to Wolfe and Steinhart's Emporium the hour it opened, eager to prove his cousin's appraisal right and his own instincts wrong.

Looking prosperous and civilized, Cameron was quickly shown to William's upstairs office at the back of the store. Startled by his uncle's white hair and by how diminished he was, Cameron had to force himself to rely on his habit of stoicism to conceal his shock. The man looked twenty years older, not the mere seven that had elapsed since Cameron last had seen him. He was withered and pale, and there was an air of death about him. William Wolfe could have been a man in the latter stages of starvation, a condition Cameron had seen his fill of in the southwestern desert.

William did not rise to greet him, nor did his expression convey any pleasure in seeing his nephew again. "I'd hoped never to set eyes on you again," he said finally. "What do you want?"

Impending death had not made William more diplomatic or softened his sentiments, but Cameron chose to keep his temper in hand in spite of this new humiliation. "This is the first time I've been back to Saint Louis—"

"Which did not require you to call on me," William interrupted. He stared at Cameron with the cool blue eyes of the Wolfe family. "Unless there is something the emporium can provide you—in which case, one of my clerks can assist you. You appear prosperous enough. You've given up your penchant for looking like a savage." With this observation, William seemed to take a sudden interest in his nephew. "Indeed, you look quite reformed." His voice betrayed his surprise.

"Something you didn't believe possible." Although well past

childhood, Cameron felt no older than the nine-year-old who had once been his uncle's favorite, and that nine-year-old still wished for his uncle's approbation.

"You gave me no hope of your redemption. Justifiably, the Wolfe family could not embrace a dirty savage."

Cameron swallowed his uneasiness. "Katherine tells me you aren't well."

"That is no concern of yours."

"She believed you wished to see me again."

"My daughter erred in that assumption," William said, dismissing the intelligent and warmhearted child within the man as if he had never existed. William stared at Cameron, the perfect image of his father when that man was young. A strong-willed man, Joseph had wanted to go west some years before he did. Unreasonable confidence had allowed him to travel the Cimarron Cut-off on the Santa Fe Trail alone with his family. Cameron was cast of much the same metal, and it was William's opinion that nine years with the Apache had ruined him forever.

Cameron's jaw was tight, and he was unaware that his hands were balled into fists at his sides. Cameron bit back the kind of apology he had learned to make in civilized society in such awkward circumstances. "Sorry to have interrupted" did not come close to what he wanted to say to William Wolfe. But concealing and keeping a firm control over his emotions, more an Apache response to insult than a white one, Cameron simply turned away from William.

As he put his hand on the door, Katherine opened it and entered her father's office. She was smiling. "Isn't it wonderful to see Cameron again?" she said to her father. Only then did she see the disdainful expression on her father's face. Her smile vanished.

She threw her arms around her cousin then and hugged him fiercely. "But Father," she pleaded, "this is a precious chance to make amends. How can you reject him again?" Katherine turned to her father. "All that he asks of you is that you accept him. Look at him, Father!" she demanded. She turned and touched Cameron's cheek. "Anyone can see Cameron is a man to be admired. There's no wickedness in the mouth, nor deceit in his brow, or cruelty in his eyes."

"Katherine! This is uncalled for."

Gently, Cameron took Katherine's hand in his. "You were wrong, and I was foolish," he said quietly.

Tears streamed from Katherine's eyes. "Forgive me, please, for having put you through this a second time."

Cameron nodded and, leaving his uncle's store, swore to put the Wolfe family behind him again—this time forever.

CHAPTER TWENTY-SIX

Cameron had disappeared. He did not show up at the hotel for dinner, although the night before he had promised to dine with Honey. A messenger sent to the area on the outskirts of town where Ruth Blocher and the men were encamped with the provisioned wagons brought her news that no one in the party had seen him all day. Surely, if they were to leave Saint Louis tomorrow as he had suggested they would, Honey reasoned, he should have been in touch with them sometime during the day.

By ten at night Honey finally gave up the notion that they would be on the road to Independence the following morning. Beside herself with worry, she thought of the night they had just spent together and how unlike himself he had seemed. She ached for him and her memory of his need for reassurance, his need to feel certain of her affection. She wondered how he could doubt the love she had given so freely.

Perhaps Saint Louis had gotten the best of Cameron too, Honey thought to herself as she suffered another night of miserable heat. If only it would rain and break the stretch of oppressive weather! She had said good night to Shahar and Nollie and turned out the lamps in the sitting room, then lingered a final moment at the windows of the French doors. She looked again in the direction of Cameron's room. Still there was no light.

Perhaps he's gone to see the woman I saw in the corridor last night.

Honey's stomach tightened in misery. Tears filled her eyes. She knew so very little about Cameron Wolfe, she admitted. Beyond Trevor's evaluation of him, she had relied on her instincts as a woman, which, with her lack of worldly experience, she realized now, she had no reason to trust.

How easily she responded to him! And how wild her responses! It was as if society and morality did not exist.

She had fulfilled all his desires eagerly, granting whatever he wished. He excited her in ways she found shocking, provoking a nature within her that until his advent had been sleeping unawares. Often they came together like animals in urgent heat, and other times they were so far above that brutal plain that it seemed a level of ecstasy reserved for the gods. In his arms, she could have cried her love for him to the whole world from his balcony, only he had restrained her with more lovemaking. Surely she and Cameron Wolfe were bound together by something more enticing than passion. Otherwise, their union was beyond all reason.

Engrossed by her thoughts, Honey did not hear the key turn in the lock; as if by magic, all at once Cameron stood before her in the darkness. For an instant she wondered if she was hallucinating, but when Cameron embraced her fiercely, a deep sigh of relief escaping him as he pressed her near, she knew this was no simple fantasy.

Cameron began to make love to Honey with an urgency in his touch, an unfamiliar violence that sent a shiver of excitement down her spine. The day of anxious waiting made her responses especially passionate and allowed her to ignore an alarming sense she had of his need to possess her with or without her consent.

When he broke their embrace and lifted Honey into his arms to carry her to bed, the impassioned man who held her seemed a stranger in the guise of the man she knew. Honey's excitement escalated into fear as Cameron suddenly stripped away his clothes and all but ripped away hers, then fell upon her with demanding kisses and caresses, his touch exceeding impatient lust, as though he wished to inflict more pain than pleasure.

Instinctively, Honey resisted him, struggling as she lay beneath him, murmuring protests at his bruising mouth and hands. But her voice yielded only unintelligible sounds and even to her own ears seemed more to coax than to rebuke. When he entered her, she was ready to receive him and, losing control, matched his frantic rhythm, rocking with him in that timeless motion, striving for completion. As she lay under Cameron's full weight afterward, breathless and angry, Honey tried to push him away.

"Let me go!" she cried in nothing more than a hoarse whisper, and attempted to lift him from her.

His breathing still labored, he raised himself above her slightly and gazed down at her, then bent to kiss her. "I planned to spend all night making love to you. I want more—*much* more."

"You hurt me just now."

"I felt your pleasure, then mine." Clearly, he thought her protest absurd.

"How can you take pleasure in my pain?"

"Pain? Is that what it was? I heard you—Shahar and Nollie probably heard you—enjoy yourself."

"I'll have bruises to show you tomorrow."

Not taking her seriously, Cameron laughed. "I'll be glad to see them," he said as he began to caress her again.

"No." Honey tried again to push him away.

Cameron ignored her. Perhaps he had been too vigorous, but he had brought her ecstasy, he reasoned, her responses leading him swiftly to his own. Now fully aroused again, he entered her ungently.

Honey began to cry.

Stunned and annoyed, Cameron withdrew.

Honey pulled away from him gratefully. "Don't ever touch me that way again."

"What the hell does that mean?"

Fearful of his dark look and tone, Honey reacted defensively, her voice sharp and uncaring. "Think whatever you will."

"Are you saying you don't love me?"

Honey didn't answer him, and a deep silence descended between the lovers.

Suddenly self-conscious, Honey pulled up the blanket to cover her nakedness and moved as far from Cameron as possible in the bed. Her gaze swept the length of his muscular body, even now not immune to its beauty or its power to attract her. Appalled by the ease of her arousal, in anger and shame, Honey judged Cameron harshly, and herself as well. Certainly, on occasion he was nothing more elevated than a rutting beast—and, to her chagrin, she confessed she was also. He summoned in her passions that both reduced her to kinship with the lesser creatures of the earth and glorified her very existence.

While she silently remonstrated with herself for the level to which she had descended with him, Cameron rose from the bed and dressed. Fully clothed, he turned briefly to face Honey again, his look unfathomable; then, without another word, he left her to stare after him, leaving the door into the sitting room standing ajar. Honey listened as he exited the suite and heard him pull the door to quietly, the sound of its closing reverberating in her soul.

CHAPTER TWENTY-SEVEN

Cameron had intended the small caravan from North Carolina to leave Saint Louis the next day. "Shahar has taken ill," Honey explained when he arrived at her door early in the morning to inform her of the departure time later that day. Appearing calm, as though nothing unpleasant had happened between them, she let him into the suite.

"How bad is she?" Cameron looked to both Honey and Nollie for an answer.

"I imagine we can leave tomorrow, if you don't expect the drive to be very arduous," Honey said coolly.

Nollie nodded in agreement, but her expression told him she was concealing something.

Cameron hid his considerable irritation well. "Then we'll leave at dawn tomorrow."

"I'll send word if my judgment of her condition turns out to be too optimistic." Honey's tone was cool.

Cameron's jaw tensed. "If I don't hear anything, I'll send a wagon for you ladies in the morning."

Honey showed Cameron to the door and immediately turned to Nollie. "How could she!" Honey said in a low, furious voice. "She knows we need to be on the road."

"Don't shout at me. I'm not to blame."

"I'm *not* blaming you," Honey said impatiently. "But this isn't the time or place for your mother to be communing with the Spirits, for heaven's sake."

"Just remember who started all this messing with Spirits," Nollie snapped.

"I'm trying to forget."

"You weren't happy to let sleepin' dogs lay. You just had to stir up the pot, didn't you?"

Honey glared at Nollie. "I'm well enough aware of my sins."

Nollie's face held a smirk that disappeared with irritating slowness.

"There's only one thing to do as I see it, and that's encourage your mother to regain her equilibrium *at once*."

"Just what do you have in mind? A pail of cold water?"

"Get thee behind me, Satan," Honey replied earnestly as she crossed the sitting room to Shahar's door, which she opened with a flourish. After entering the room, she went to the windows and drew open the drapes, filling the room with bright sunlight. "Shahar, Shahar," she called in a loud voice.

Shahar lay utterly still and, as Honey expected, appeared not to breathe.

"Shahar!" Honey called loudly again. She touched her shoulder and shook her gently, then more roughly.

Nollie stood in the doorway. "You trying to wake the dead? It's never been done before."

Honey felt instantly rabid. "You don't know that for certain."

"No, I don't, but mightn't you be hurting her, doing like that?" Nollie demanded.

"If I thought I'd be doing harm, I'd not do it." Honey pulled the covers off Shahar's body.

"Of course. Beggin' yo' pa'don, ma'am. I knows tha's how ya conduct yo'self in *all* mattas, Miz Radcliffe."

"Are we talking, Nollie, about your mother's health or my morals?" Honey countered, the color raising in her cheeks with the level of her ire.

Challenged, Nollie backed down. "I'm first concerned about Mammy."

Honey turned her gaze back on Shahar. "So am I," she promised. "You've chosen a very inconvenient time and place this time, Shahar, and it's a time to wake up. I know you can hear me. I've had all the prophecies and insights I can tolerate. Damnation, Shahar, if nothing else, we can't afford a delay. Time is of the essence when you're journeying west."

"You're wasting your breath, Honey."

"Probably." Honey sighed and, after several minutes more of staring at Shahar's silent form, pulled the covers under her chin again and drew the drapes closed. Then she and Nollie left the room.

Shahar was undisturbed. She had not heard Honey's pleas. Even if she had, she would have ignored them, for troubled as she was with Cameron's disturbed aura since their arrival in Saint Louis, the excursion, although disruptive of their travel, was completely voluntary on Shahar's part.

The motherly heart of Shahar Daniels had read Cameron Wolfe's distress and yearned to ease him. In his presence, she had every reason to trust him, she felt, and sensed that unlike most white men, he did not inherently fear the Spirits. She believed there would be a time to speak to him of the past and the future.

She sought the Spirits now for better understanding of this man who she knew would greatly influence her life and others, yet in her "travels" she saw not Cameron but light-colored sand turned red with blood and, nearby, a bulbous, fist-sized pulsating object filled with blood. Her eyes burned from dark clouds of smoke; her ears were assaulted by a terrifying roar many times louder than the wind.

When she awakened from this dream, Shahar felt drained of energy from her travels, more so than was the rule. She had learned nothing to cause her to bound from bed and announce the future; however, she had no doubt at all that those who followed Cameron Wolfe would find a trail of blood.

CHAPTER TWENTY-EIGHT

Led by Cameron, the party of four wagons finally departed from Saint Louis for Independence late in the afternoon of the following day. Silent, Honey hoped to avoid Cameron's gaze, unaware that he was also assiduously avoiding hers.

Cameron prepared the group for the leg to Independence. "We've got to connect with Dillingham's caravan. We'll push hard to make up time. Road's flat; river crossings shouldn't be much trouble. This isn't a picnic," he said, mostly for the women's benefit.

"We'll head for Defiance, then follow the Missouri till Boonville, then cut south of the river due west to Independence. No more than four days. That means dawn to dark."

Originally Cameron had planned to drive Honey's wagon, but

instead he asked Timothy Watts to assist her. Cameron drove Shahar and Nollie's team, while Roarke Murray rode with his sister, Ruth. That left Wilton Ramsey in charge of the fourth and last wagon. Nollie enjoyed the obvious tension between Cameron and Honey. Ruth Blocher also noticed with interest that there was something amiss. "Not as easy to consort with common folk on shore where everybody's lookin'," she remarked to Nollie. "Guess Miz La-Di-Da finally realized he was no gentleman— guess she had to see him with his clothes off first." In response Nollie only glared at Mrs. Blocher. It was one thing for Nollie to criticize Honey but quite another for an outsider to speak against her.

In the provisioning of the party, expense had not been the utmost consideration. Cameron had sought the best-quality goods, then deliberated and negotiated their prices. He had sold the party's original wagon for a handsome profit and purchased four Conestoga wagons, then paid a premium for the best mules available to pull them. Since they would lose animals on the trail, he bought several extra. The string of saddle horses already in the party's possession was a bonus to the party. In addition, Cameron purchased two cows to provide milk and butter—and meat, if the need arose. An extra man was hired to manage this collection of animals as far as Independence.

For a constant supply of fresh eggs, ten hens were obtained and loaded in tiers of baskets at the end of one wagon. In addition, there were several barrels of flour, dried beans, salt, vinegar, sugar, coffee, fresh apples, potatoes, and fresh vegetables, as well as dried and pickled vegetables and fruit, cornmeal, hams and slabs of bacon, sour pickles to prevent scurvy, and many other staples. The meals might be monotonous, even supplemented by fresh game acquired on the trail—antelope, hare, prairie chicken, and buffalo—but the party would not starve along the way, as those who made the trip poorly provisioned often did. Tools and a variety of materials to repair the wagons were included in the inventory, for the full trip would not be without several incidents requiring carpentry or other types of repair. It was an axiom of the road, however, that even with careful planning and provisioning, there would be incidents for which they were not adequately prepared.

"Be rainin' by the time we get set up for the night," Timothy guessed aloud to Honey just before the party began to move onto the road. "That'll maybe give us a change a weather. See how the mules're nerved up."

The teams of four did seem unduly restless, and the air was thick and charged with electricity, but Honey was not certain that her sense of the weather had much to do with reality or that, with her emotions being in such a sorry state, she only imagined there was going to be an impressive downpour.

Everyone was excited to be on the road once more—everyone but Shahar, who was alert enough to travel but decidely dull of spirit. There was no luster in her eye or any smile. She was unusually quiet.

Nollie made up for her mother's silence. "Lord have mercy," she said from inside the wagon, and rolled her eyes heavenward as Honey settled in the seat next to where Cameron would be driving his team of mules. "You be bringin' scandal down on us fo' shur, Miz Ra'cliffe." She clicked her tongue in disapproval for Honey's choice of garments for the road.

"You'll grow accustomed to the sight," Honey insisted.

"I don't think so. Lordy! Mmmmm, no, ma'am. I don't think so. If yo' papa could see ya, he give ya d' switchin' of yo' life."

"You know he only once raised a hand to me—and because of you."

"Wear boys' clothes and you be treated like a boy instead of a lady." Nollie shook her head at Honey's outfit of a man's heavy denim pants, flannel shirt with the sleeves shockingly rolled to her elbows, boots, and broad-brimmed felt hat tied under her chin. The pants, cut to fit a man's figure, rode well below her narrow waist, and she had been forced to roll cuffs on the long legs.

"It makes good sense, at least some of the time," Honey argued. "I decided on this costume well before we arrived in Saint Louis."

"No lady dresses that way."

"If you want to talk like a common field hand, I guess I'm free to dress as I please," Honey declared. "However, I didn't come to argue, I've only come to make certain Shahar is comfortable."

"Mammy's just fine. But it's good she doesn't just yet get an eyeful of your getup, or likely she'll be going off again."

"She just better not!" Honey declared as she stepped down from the wagon.

Cameron caught sight of her then, his jaw dropping at her

costume, but in her presence he acted as if it were normal. "Time to get moving," he said coolly.

Honey would ride horseback the first day and declined a side-saddle. "You'll regret it," Cameron tried to warn her, uncomfortably conscious of the pull of cotton flannel across her uncorseted breasts.

"I shall manage, thank you," she said, and because no one else was in earshot, added boldly, "No fear of rupturing my maidenhead."

Cameron was momentarily at a loss for words. Wearing men's clothes seemed to have a definite emboldening effect on Honey. He was amused, but he gave not the least hint of a smile and seemed to Honey only to glower.

When she turned her back on him, his gaze drifted to the tight denim that covered her curving hips, and fixed on the natural sway of her gait as she sauntered away from him. Cameron's face colored with excitement and his pulse raced. Stirred by desire, he had to force himself to turn away and concentrate on the business of getting the wagons underway.

With Cameron in the lead, everything went smoothly as the party traveled that first day. The road to Independence was flat, well worn, and filled with other travelers. Honey frequently cantered ahead of the wagons, enjoying the relative freedom without fear of becoming lost. When the storm Timothy Watts had earlier predicted came up, the party was forced to stop early for the night.

Hastily, they encamped near a rare grove of trees next to the Missouri River. A meal of sliced jerked beef, bread, and hot coffee sufficed. The men accommodated themselves for the night within their assigned wagons after a tent was pitched for the women. They slept on cots to keep as dry as possible.

With the onslaught of the storm, excitement turned to edginess. As Honey listened to the sound of rain on the roof of the tent, she found herself expecting its collapse at any moment in the especially heavy downpour. She wondered how much sleep anyone could get. Of course, because against all well-meaning advice she had insisted on using a man's saddle, Honey realized she deserved to lie awake, her aching lower back and thighs a just reminder of how unladylike her stubborn choice had been.

With more reason than most to lie awake, Honey imagined Cameron, cosseted in Shahar and Nollie's wagon, sleeping soundly. In spite of her lingering outrage for his rough use of her two nights before, in the first rain-soaked night on the road Honey could not delude herself into thinking she did not miss the pure comfort of Cameron's warm embrace. Although she felt she had had no choice but to make it clear she would not tolerate abuse, she yearned for him. From every sign it also seemed clear that Cameron intended neither to abuse nor to enjoy her intimate embrace ever again.

Intensely proud, Cameron was not the kind of man to easily apologize, and Honey feared that once more she would have to learn to sleep—and be—very much alone. She also knew that like the road west, the task would not be easy.

CHAPTER TWENTY-NINE

Saddle sore and unwilling to risk getting drenched in the steady drizzle of rain, Honey retreated to the dry enclosure of her Conestoga wagon the next day. Unable to sleep much the night before, she dozed and read most of the morning. When she awoke, the party had stopped for a small meal shortly after noon, "nooning it," they called it on the trail.

Not truly refreshed, Honey nevertheless climbed down from the wagon eager for at least a drink of water. She wore a dress and did not expect to receive any comment about her appearance, but as she took a plate of bread, cheese, and fruit from Nollie, Ruth found an excuse to remark on Honey's choice of apparel.

"I can see we're to be having a guessing game. Every day we're out, we're to be wondering what Mrs. Radcliffe'll be wearing."

"Only if you've nothing else to occupy your mind," Honey answered as she seated herself in a chair at the camp table.

"I'm thinking we'll have more to think on than Mrs. Radcliffe's getups," Roarke Murray chided his sister. "Today it's mud."

Indeed, although the sky had cleared of any evidence of rain, the mud made traveling a very slow proposition. The party had made pitiful progress during the morning. Cameron, who seemed to Honey to be scowling at her personally, frowned only at the progress of their small wagon train.

Delayed by Shahar and now by rain, Cameron worried that they would not arrive in Independence in time to meet a merchant's caravan he had arranged to join. The party needed to get to Independence no later than the tenth of June, and at the rate they now were traveling, chances were only fair that they would make that deadline. Under leader Avery Dillingham's charge, the merchant caravan would afford Cameron's party the safety of additional numbers and needed assistance in the event of mishap or danger. Avery's reputation for being a skilled operator of merchant trains was well deserved. He let little slow him down and once had gone from Indepedence to Santa Fe in twenty days. That time was short of miraculous and impossible with the addition of inexperienced travelers to the caravan.

The four women in Cameron's party would certainly slow Avery down—but not much, if only because Avery Dillingham would drive on regardless. He had agreed to take on Cameron's party, including four females, because of his knowledge of and experience with Cameron. If the women slowed anyone down, it would not be Avery Dillingham.

With Shahar nearly recovered, Nollie joined Honey in her wagon that afternoon, and the two women shelled peas and pared potatoes and carrots for the evening meal. Nollie seemed relaxed and disposed to be friendly. Honey wondered if her change in temper had anything to do with the obvious chill in the air between Cameron and herself.

"What on earth put it in your head to get up in a man's clothes?" Nollie laughed. "You sure know how to turn heads. I thought Mr. Wolfe's heart was going to stop. You sashayed off, and he turned beet-red."

"Must have been the heat."

Nollie laughed again. "Maybe his blood was hot. Wasn't the weather."

Honey was secretly pleased to know that she had had such a stimulating effect on Cameron but sad to consider that perhaps his feelings for her did not transcend the purely physical.

Truthfully, Honey admitted to herself, she had enjoyed the discovery of the sexual side of her nature immensely, but surely not just *any* man could have awakened that side of her. In all the years she had been courted by Nathan, he had hardly begun to stir the fires that a few weeks with Cameron had ignited.

Honey touched Nathan's diamond-edged locket, which she nearly always wore around her neck. Its engraved inscription read "Mine Forever." Why she continued to wear it after Cameron had come to occupy her heart so fully, she could not explain. *Forever*, Honey mused, had been a period of very short duration.

And so was your affair with Mr. Wolfe.

Honey forced back tears as she rinsed the scrapings from a potato in one kettle and set it to soak in another.

"I notice Mr. Wolfe's been keeping his distance since we set foot on land," Nollie observed, "and the climate's almost frosty now that we're on the road again. Guess he only gets romantic on the water—like some get queasy." Nollie eyed Honey for any sign of a response. "I still find it startling, you taking up with him—a *cowboy*, for pity's sake. Barely a notch above a field hand. Lord, he barely got the dust washed off before he was under your quilt."

Feeling she deserved to be reprimanded, Honey bit back a sharp reply.

"And won't the man you marry next be in for something of a surprise—thinking you a good and virtuous Southern lady."

Honey could refrain from a retort no longer. "He should rejoice. I'm better than I was."

"That's not everyone's opinion."

"*Everyone* be damned," Honey snapped.

"You're *not* better than before. A lady doesn't say such things."

"When you come right down to it, Nollie, a *lady* hardly *says* anything at all! Nor does a *lady* do much that's especially useful. The only thing a lady is, is useless."

"Well! That's long been *my* opinion."

Nollie and Honey stared at each other until Honey smiled, and soon the two were laughing, then giggling foolishly.

"You do regret taking up with Mr. Wolfe, don't you?" Nollie dared when they had finally collected themselves. "You ought to say so out loud, or else you could get to pining after him when you ought to be nothing but ashamed of yourself."

Honey stiffened. "I've *no* intention of pining after Mr. Wolfe. But I've even *less* inclination for wallowing in shame."

"I can't believe you're so proud."

"I'm hardly proud."

"Oh, yes, you are. You should hear yourself. You're not even a little bit sorry."

Truthfully, I'm not. But proud? "You should be a preacher, Nollie."

"Females aren't preachers."

"Or much of anything else—unless it needs to be scrubbed, pared, and chopped." Honey glowered as she tossed another potato into Nollie's lap. "Just remember, Nollie Daniels, silence is next to godliness."

"That's cleanliness."

"Not in your case, Nollie. Not in your case."

CHAPTER THIRTY

The party from Greerfield arrived in Independence by the deadline of the tenth of June. While Cameron went to locate Avery Dillingham, Honey, Nollie, and Shahar rushed to add to the company's supply of fresh food before dusk, when the stores closed for the night. The town and roads were crowded with wagons and people with the same intention as the group from North Carolina: to go west. The routes to the promised land had only just begun to be active again since the war. The major debarking point these days was not Independence but Westport, some nine miles west, but there was bustle enough in Independence to suit Honey. By nightfall Cameron's wagons were stationed next to those of the merchant's caravan and prepared to depart at dawn the next day. The evening meal was taken at Noland's Hotel in a private dining saloon, still the largest in town, though no one would spend the night in the hotel. Tents would not be pitched, but everyone would sleep in the wagon camp, the women in their wagons, the men in bedrolls nearby on the ground.

Avery Dillingham joined the North Carolina party at dinner at Noland's, where Nollie and Shahar served dinner from trays brought to the private dining room from the kitchen, then joined the table. "I wondered, when I saw them, how you was going to get around having your nigras at our table this time," Ruth said to Honey just as they sat down. "Those two surely don't behave, and you don't treat them, like any nigras I've ever known."

"You can't already have forgotten the events of the late war, Mrs. Blocher. If you'll recall, Nollie and Shahar are free."

"There's free and there's free," Ruth huffed. "I don't see livin' with them like they was as good as we are. The Yankees might've won the war, but that'll never make white and nigra equal."

Honey turned pointedly away from Ruth and fastened her attention on Avery Dillingham, who was bald to just above his ears and wore his remaining bushy white hair to his shoulders. An abundant quantity of bristling black eyebrows above inquisitive brown eyes made the bald crown less noticeable, and an impressive black and gray mustache framed a wide smile, showing off his large but perfect teeth.

He found it impossible to keep his eyes off Honey and directed his remarks to her more often than not. "Raised in Virginia myself," he informed Honey in particular. "But did a fair amount of huntin' and trappin' in your territory. Never got as far as Cape Fear, though.

"Couple of my men on this trip are brothers from South Carolina. Both veterans of the recent squabble. I understand you're a widow woman. My sincerest sympathies, ma'am."

He barely stopped talking long enough to eat his dinner, which, Honey assumed, must have had something to do with Avery Dillingham's gaunt appearance. Over six feet tall by several inches, he looked somewhat emaciated, but he certainly did not lack the energy to talk at great length. The other men in Cameron's party were already acquainted with the loquacious Dillingham; inherently more taciturn, they were comfortable to dine without much talk.

"Yes, I know your esteemed uncle, ma'am. Trevor Jefferson is known wide. He'll put you up grand. Maybe not quite what you're used to, but comfortable."

By the time dinner was finished, Honey felt exhausted by Avery's chatter.

"Now there's a man who could hold his own on sewing day." Shahar laughed. "Wears a body out just listening."

Honey nodded as she took Shahar's arm and they walked back to the wagon camp. "Hardly a lullaby, but it will suffice," she said, unable to stifle a yawn but awake enough to ask the questions she had been saving for an appropriate moment. "Tell me, Shahar, what did your Spirits have to say this time?"

"Wasn't any conversation."

"What, then?"

"Signs."

"Well, go on, before I expire with curiosity."

"Some things are best kept private."

"Usually I have to stop you from giving me too many details!" Honey interpreted Shahar's silence to mean the Spirits had rendered some sort of negative judgment about her relationship with Cameron. "They probably didn't tell you anything I don't already know."

Shahar did not rise to Honey's bait and changed the subject. "You comfortable enough in your wagon to get all the way cross country?"

"Surprisingly. The bed is a trifle narrow, but as I won't be sharing it, I imagine I'll manage just fine. How about you and Nollie?"

"Almost luxurious from what I expected," Shahar answered.

From all exterior appearances Cameron had purchased standard Conestoga wagons, but the interiors were unusual in detail. Each wagon had a false floor, and underneath, cupboards had been built for the storage of items infrequently in use. The wagons' heavy canvas covers were lined with soft green cloth, and many pockets had been sewn in for keeping small items conveniently. A cast iron stove had been installed at the end of Nollie and Shahar's wagon, which made it possible to keep a fire going and even keep a pot of something simmering, if the pot was lashed down and the firewood doors were locked.

The organized nature of the wagon pleased Honey, but her bed—two feather mattresses unrolled onto the lid of a narrow wooden trunk—left something to be desired. All manner of items were stored inside the trunk, including most of Honey's clothes. Honey's bed was uncomfortable and lonely but, especially weary after laying out clothes for the next day, she fell asleep at once. She slept soundly and several hours after turning in was not aware as someone pulled aside the front curtain and stepped into the wagon.

Well after moonrise, the intruder let enough moonlight into the wagon to illuminate Honey in repose. She stirred and sighed and turned away but did not wake. Her visitor stood watch for almost an hour, then departed, taking with him a delicate lace-edged handkerchief embroidered with the initials *HJG* that Honey had laid out earlier.

Up before daylight, Honey discovered that she had forgotten to lay out a clean handkerchief, which made it necessary to dig into her trunk. Usually this would have seemed a minor matter, but on this first day of travel with Avery's caravan the oversight greatly annoyed her.

Cameron had made a point of telling the women especially that although Avery Dillingham might seem in no hurry at dinner, on the trail he was a driven man, far different from the chatterbox at the hotel. In relating this, Cameron had gazed fixedly at Honey, and she had no intention of making a slow start, especially the first morning.

She rode in the driver's box with Timothy Watts until they stopped at noon. They had moved at a good pace, with a steady wind keeping the dust from the road stirred up around the seventy Conestogas, only four of which were Cameron's responsibility. Dillingham used both oxen and mules to carry his heavily laden wagons and boasted he was prepared to handle almost any emergency on the two-mile train. He had a fair-sized remuda of extra animals and three large dogs that he claimed hated Indians. "One whiff and they're showin' their fangs. Better sentries never lived," he claimed.

"Been on the road twenty years and I know what to expect—a lot of trouble before I count my profit." Although he had a wife and children in Saint Louis, he spent most of every year on the road between Missouri and Mexico. "They'll bury me somewhere between Independence and Chihuahua—not soon, I hope."

Breakfast before daylight had been a nourishing but quick affair. By one o'clock everyone was ready for the largest meal of the day—ham, an array of fresh vegetables, cornbread and fruit preserves, coffee or tea—and they were back on the road again in three hours. They made excellent time, traveling twenty miles the first day, and set up camp by nightfall at the edge of the last thick woods they would find before entering the wide grassy plains.

The second day's journey was slower and covered only fifteen miles, as far as Lone Elm camp, a mere thirty-five miles from Independence, which set Avery Dillingham to loud grumbling and made his men forget the presence of the women. The language used by the drivers shocked the women and forced Nollie to cover her ears.

"You can't go all the way to California like that," Cameron teased her, lifting her hands from her ears.

"I may have to," she answered in a huff.

They were forced to stop for repairs when one of Dillingham's ox-driven wagons turned over on the descent of a small bank; while repair was under way, a rattlesnake set the remuda into a scurry, requiring a full halt of the wagon train to round them up. The delay had come annoyingly early in the trip. Later on, such an occasion provided an opportunity to rest the draft animals, but this early it only meant irritation. But by morning the wagon train was on the trail again as if nothing had happened.

At Lone Elm camp, aside from that one tree, there was not another piece of wood or even a shrub, but fortunately there was ample grass and water for the animals and for refilling stores. Cameron had provided each member of his party with a five gallon India rubber water bottle, which was kept filled with water for the stretches of road where fresh water would be impossible to find.

The following day Honey decided to ride horseback rather than sit in the wagon and again choosing to wear her unladylike costume, caught many a man's eye. For the most part she kept pace alongside Nollie and Shahar's wagon, seeming to keep company with Shahar, who sat next to Cameron.

Because of the great quantities of dust from the road, most of the men wore false eyes, and Honey was forced to wear the only fashionable hat she had brought with her. When she tied and tucked its heavy veil into the neck of her shirt, even Cameron smiled at her.

"I know I look peculiar," she said, "but better this than to have my skin peeled off." As usual, she wore thin leather gloves to protect her hands and, as a result, was encased in some sort of covering head to toe.

In Kansas now, when the wind was not gusting, the morning air was cool and bracing, and the array of wildflowers across the prairie flatland as far as the eye could see was breathtaking. When they stopped at noon, Honey let the other women fuss with the preparation of food while she collected armfuls of a wonderful variety of flowers.

When she threatened to wander off almost out of sight in the head-high grass, Cameron went after her. "Watch for snakes and holes. There's rabbit and snake holes to catch your foot in. And marshy spots that can swallow a whole wagon without a trace."

"I've learned to be wary of serpents, Mr. Wolfe, and now that you're here, you can rescue me if you feel I'm in any danger," she said, and casually handed him an enormous armful of wildflowers before continuing on. Only after she had gone several yards ahead of him did he follow in her wake.

"I think Nollie and Shahar . . . and Mrs. Blocher too . . . would appreciate some flowers. Since you've joined me, I can bring each of them a big bouquet." She gathered more flowers, then turned an easy smile on Cameron. "I could spend the rest of the day picking flowers, couldn't you?"

"I never thought to do such a thing," he answered, surprised that anyone would consider such a possibility.

Honey gave Cameron a long, speculative look. "No. Of course not." She paused to break the stems of three delicate flowers and pushed them through the empty buttonhole at the open neck of his shirt. "Even so, you should have a decoration," she said. Then she twisted a handful of flowers to make a wreath and rested it on the brim of Cameron's hat. She gazed at him—at the darkness of his skin shaded from the sun, at the contrast of his apparent vigor with the delicate crown of flowers he now wore.

He smiled with engaging warmth. "I must look almost as foolish as you do."

For a moment Honey was able to forget her anger, wanting to lean against him, to feel the strength of his muscular arms, to be pressed near. She wished he would feel her warmth toward him now and be seduced.

Cameron watched Honey as closely as she watched him and sorely wished he could trust the look of desire in her golden eyes. But he keenly remembered how clearly she had communicated her distaste for him only a few nights ago. If he were to touch her, to pull away the veil of her hat and hold her against him, he felt certain she would recoil. Not wanting to feel the sting of Honey's rejection again, Cameron kept his distance. This time he would remember that a man like himself should admire a lovely woman like Honey Radcliffe from a polite distance.

Finally, Honey retrieved the bouquet she had laid down and turned away from Cameron. "Only a few more," she promised as she began to gather more flowers, color rushing to her cheeks and unshed tears stinging her eyes. Honey gritted her teeth as she rushed away from Cameron, all but yanking the flowers she gathered from their roots, under her breath vowing that Cameron Wolfe would live to see hell freeze over before she let him know how deeply his indifference had wounded her pride.

CHAPTER THIRTY-ONE

On the seemingly endless prairie, the amount of grass and water varied and wood grew scarce; cottonwood trees found near the banks of rivers and streams were useless for campfires. Fortunately, both Avery Dillingham and Cameron had been prudent enough to see that their wagons carried a good supply of wood. A few live coals were always kept in the grate of Nollie's stove, even when the thermometer rose above a hundred degrees.

For safety's sake, the women grew used to climbing down whenever the wagons encountered a hill of any degree of incline. "A wagon can turn over and splinter just like that," Avery Dillingham had announced, snapping his fingers, "just when you don't expect. The draft animals and passengers could be injured or killed in such an accident." On days when the going was especially slow, Honey walked alongside the wagon, and on many such occasions she was joined by Nollie, if not Shahar.

Hoping to make better time wherever they could, they expected to be on the Santa Fe Trail for perhaps sixty days. While there seemed an endless number of things to keep Nollie and Shahar occupied, such as mending, bread making, and other food preparation, Honey grew bored and on the fourth day on the trail began a diary of the journey.

First she made notes from her recollection of the journey to Saint Louis from Greerfield. In her memory that portion of the trip had seemed more eventful and trying than the current undertaking. She now wondered at her initial worries about traveling on the frontier but acknowledged to herself that the relative calm might only be a lull before the storm.

In noting details, Honey consulted with Shahar and Nollie and stringently omitted all reference to her feelings regarding Cameron. Anticipation of events, she knew, could sharpen one's sensibilities and by comparison make the actual occasion pale. She thought that perhaps her recall of the intensity of the earlier leg of their expedition had more to do with her heightened emotions involving Cameron than did the reality of the events. She described only the details of the voyage down the Ohio and up the Mississippi rivers that she would want someone else, even a stranger, to read and made no mention of the journey her heart and soul had made. Similarly, Saint Louis and Independence were logged and accounted for by descriptions of time and place and routine events.

On the Santa Fe Trail the camps and places where they stopped for midday meals or were stalled for one reason or another were carefully noted and described. She even explained the passing of One Hundred Ten Mile Creek, which was in fact 95 miles from Independence but 110 miles from Franklin, Missouri, the original starting point of the Santa Fe Trail. In addition, Honey pressed wildflowers, nothing where the flowers came from in relation to their camp.

She had hoped such occupations would distract her thoughts from Cameron, but she ached for him in spite of her efforts to keep busy. She forbade herself to dream at night, with little success. Countless wild roses like those from the plains wound through her tangled dreams and became lavender, sage, and thyme; her lover was sometimes Cameron, sometimes not, but familiar nonetheless.

Then one day, completely unbidden, Nollie apprised Honey of her personal observations regarding Cameron. From the animation of Nollie's expression and the interest in her eyes, Honey knew Nollie had fallen under his spell. A flare of sharp anger rose in Honey's breast, and any desire she had to caution Nollie was overshadowed by the need to castigate her, much as Nollie had done with her. She did not suspect the depths of Nollie's rancor, and, face burning, she bit her tongue and listened as Nollie chattered on and on.

Finally, Honey said, "I don't care to hear the minute details of your infatuation. In fact, don't you dare mention that man's name in my presence ever again."

Nollie smiled to herself. In spite of Honey's stoic silences, Nollie knew very well she had been rubbing salt into open wounds. But now that Honey had begged for relief, Nollie rejoiced. "So you *are* sorry to have taken up with him?"

Honey's face flushed a deeper pink, but for reasons she could not explain, she was unable to say the words Nollie longed to hear. Instead, tears filled Honey's eyes and she fled the campfire.

The night air was cool, and Honey raised her shawl around her shoulders, covering herself tightly in warm wool. It was clear and bright, and an enormous moon that seemed about to tumble onto the darkened prairie ballooned above the earth. The farther from camp she strolled, the closer to the stars Honey felt. One had only to walk a little more, it seemed, to come to the edge of the world.

After walking for several minutes, Honey stopped to gaze back at the campfires. They were not just one large camp but four, and other wagons from other trains were camped nearby. Lights from a hundred campfires dotted the dark landscape.

Yet how vulnerable in the dark the little groups of humanity on the vast sea of prairie grass seemed. She viewed those distant campfires and wondered how anyone had the courage to venture onto that possibly dangerous sea of grass. Yet men and women were called by a variety of reasons and driven to risk everything, leaving the safety of known habitats, to satisfy their curiosity about what lay beyond the familiar.

While she understood the desire to remain behind, Honey also felt the urge to forge into the dangerous unknown—just as she had been compelled to respond to the pull she had felt toward Cameron Wolfe, a man as mysterious as what lay beyond the ocean of prairie.

She watched him even when she vowed not to. Her eyes sought him among all others. Her ears strained to hear his voice. Although they were joined with another larger caravan, the party from Greerfield remained intact and, she reasoned, it was hard to avoid him.

Honey covered her hair with her shawl and sat down. Hidden in the grass, she felt alone but safe. She did not want to go back to camp—where Cameron was—and watch Nollie or Ruth Blocher flutter around him. But why wouldn't they be attracted to him? If he could draw her to him, why would other women not also be drawn toward him?

Cameron carried within him an urgent vitality that communicated life not only to her but to everyone. He seemed to offer a promise that if one drew close, one would be endowed with some of his vitality.

Thinking of that electricity, Honey shivered in the damp grass and, looking up, was startled to find Cameron standing above her. His back was to the moon, which cast him against an unreal landscape. Honey felt suddenly weak, the draw she was so keenly aware of as distinctly physical as if he had put his hands on her and pulled her against him.

"Are you trying to get yourself lost?" Cameron demanded, but softly.

"I'm not lost."

"Maybe not, but I'm relieved to find you."

"Perhaps I should return to camp," she said, and started to rise from the grass.

Cameron held out his hand. Honey refused it.

On her feet, very close to him, she shivered, drawn to the heat of his body as if he were fire. If he called her name, if he reached out for her again, Honey realized she would be helpless to resist.

But Cameron only stared at Honey with a gaze so cold that it made the bracing night air seem warm. Then he took Honey's hand roughly in his and led her back to camp as he might do with a wayward child. He hurried, his long stride not in the least accommodating her lesser one. He took her directly to her wagon and waited while she climbed aboard. "Don't ever leave camp alone again," he said. "It only begs for trouble."

Honey felt chastised and more lonely than ever. But what should she expect, she wondered, as she lit her small lamp. Hadn't she been responsible for the end to their affair?

Honey sat down on her trunk and lifted her journal, thumbing through the several pages she had already filled with her graceful script. In its usual perfection, her penmanship displayed her calculated thoughts; it had been drawn in pencil lest she should need to change an entry at some future date. Tonight, however, in pen and ink, Honey would for the first time record her thoughts and more important, her feelings about Cameron Wolfe, conscious that this entry in the journal, unlike the others, was indelible.

16th of June 1865, Friday

Cameron Wolfe came to me in the midst of my Grief for a Husband I had not fully known. I was grieving also for other Loved Ones and for a Habit of Life swept away by War. From the moment he arrived, his Presence troubled and Challenged me. Without his Knowing, I presume, Cameron Wolfe made me Aware I was a Survivor of that terrible, long conflict. Until he came to Greerfield I could all but Feel the damp Earth cover me. But he made me realize that I had not Followed my loved ones to the Grave. He made me want to Live.

Immediately I Sensed he is a man very Unlike others. He has a Reserve about him I would not classify as a Coldness of nature—perhaps it is a Dignity—that other men do not naturally Possess by reason of mere Wealth or Station. This Quality in the Man spoke to me and Forced me to be acutely aware of him, although by Reason of rank alone, he is a person Unsuited to my notice.

I am Accustomed to deference. Apparently, he is Accustomed to Elevating few others above himself. I sensed at once he regarded himself at least my Equal, if not my Better. I am Curious that he should be so Innocent of the customs of Society. He is a Proud man—Not to say Vain.

When I say he is Reserved in Character, I do not intend to imply that he Lacks for Vitality. He is the Most Vital of men. As never before, he Forced me to Know not only that I am Alive, but made me almost unbearably aware that I am a creature of This World. To gaze at him is to sense his Spirit, to Apprehend on a Mysterious level the Lord's Purpose in creating Man and Woman.

While I think it safe to say he Pursued me, he did not Possess me against my Will. In a manner of speaking I truly was seduced, yet I chose to be Liberated of all Constraints. Freely I Joined him. In this, I was his Willing accomplice.

No one Prepared me for the Discoveries I made. No One. And it is yet Impossible for me to record the nature of my Experience. It may be I shall Never find the right Words.

We were as One. Now we are Estranged. I dare not hope, yet Tonight, on this almost limitless Prairie, he said he Feared I might be lost. Truly, I am more Desperately Lost than I would be if I were alone and Adrift on this sea of grass.

I, too, am Proud, but I pray there is a Common Ground where Cameron Wolfe and I may come Together once again.

H.G.R.

CHAPTER THIRTY-TWO

Since every day on the trail deducted from his profit, Avery Dillingham was in the habit of pressing the caravan hard. But foolhardy speed and dangerous procedures—taxing animals unwisely with excessive loads, too lengthy drives in one day, or failing to let passengers out to walk as the wagon descended a slope in the road—might cost him more money in the end. Avery insisted on exercising reasonable caution as he shepherded freight trains along the Santa Fe Trail. Nevertheless, accidents happened, as when Honey's wagon, in which she was napping in the heat of the day, failed to negotiate a seemingly insignificant slope in the road.

As he followed the other wagons, noting the ease of their decline, Timothy Watts did not see any need to rouse Honey from her nap, especially as she had "taken pale." He advanced her wagon, carefully applying the brake, but halfway down the slope one mule stumbled into its mate and caused the Conestoga to roll, then pitch forward as the animal tried to regain its foothold. The wagon then flipped over, throwing Timothy headfirst into the dirt. He somersaulted out of the fall but for a moment was stunned. He stared at the overturned wagon until Shahar's screaming suddenly brought him back to his senses. He remembered his passenger then and got to his feet, but Cameron reached Honey's wagon first.

As other men hurried to unhitch the frantic, braying mules, Cameron, heart pounding, searched for Honey in the wreckage, where nothing had escaped violent rearrangement. Buried under it all, Honey Radcliffe lay frighteningly silent.

It took several men to lift the wagon so that Cameron could crawl into the wrecked interior; the stays used to support the wagon cover were broken into small sections now suitable only for kindling. Calling her name, Cameron clawed swiftly through the disorder to reach Honey and pulled her as carefully as he could from the wreckage.

Lifting her into his arms, Cameron then carried Honey to the shady side of Shahar's wagon and gently laid her on a blanket Nollie had put down. He kneeled by Honey's seemingly lifeless form, his usually unreadable emotions plainly seen.

Nollie was in tears, but Shahar forced herself to be composed. "At least she's breathing easy," she said, and pulled a handkerchief from her pocket to blow her nose. "How could this have happened?" she demanded accusingly of no one in particular.

Just then a dozen men with Avery Dillingham in charge succeeded in righting Honey's wagon. Avery hurried to Honey's side. "Damnation, man," he yelled as he stooped down next to Honey. He rubbed a thumb over a lump the size of a small egg that had raised itself on Honey's forehead. Then he stood up. "It doesn't look good, but you just can't bet on these kinda things. Damn fool let her ride out the ridge ought to be horsewhipped."

Then, more calmly, he said, "Well, Wolfe, let's have a closer look at the wagon. It might not be as bad as it looks, and we need to get rolling again. Can't waste time."

It was hard for Cameron to turn away, but finally he did as Avery suggested. Nollie covered Honey with a quilt, and Shahar propped her head on a pillow. As they knelt anxiously beside her, Shahar bathed Honey's face with water. "Oh, for some ice," she said to Nollie as she applied a cool compress to the lump on Honey's head.

Nollie washed several abrasions on Honey's legs and hands. "She's going to look a sight. What will we do if she dies, Mammy? What will we do?"

"Don't say such things," Shahar snapped at Nollie, and just as though she did not want to miss a good argument, Honey stirred and opened her eyes.

"Did I split my head open?" Honey moaned.

An enormous smile spread across Nollie's face. "You nearly did!" she said.

Honey winced as she touched the lump on her forehead. She glared at Nollie. "You needn't sound so jolly."

Nollie laughed. "If I am, it's because you're alive, you brat."

"You two sound not a day over seven years old," Shahar scolded. "Must be the bump on the head in your case, Honey. But I don't know about you," she said to Nollie with a scowl.

"What happened? I last remember lying down for a nap."

"The wagon rolled going over in a gully that Mr. Wolfe said was nothing much."

Honey raised herself up far enough to lean back on her elbows. She raised her legs slowly, one at a time. "I don't think any bones are broken."

"Now that's a blessing."

"Help me up, please."

"Maybe you should rest awhile longer," Shahar said cautiously. "It'll be awhile before Mr. Avery puts us on the road again. Your wagon's in splinters."

"Oh, no," Honey said, and started to rise, but clutched her head and leaned back again.

"You stay put. Mr. Cameron's looking after things. If they can be put right, he'll see to it."

Honey nodded.

Shahar was very concerned by how pale and pinched Honey's face looked. "You in any pain?" she wondered.

"Just some of my muscles protesting their jarring."

As it was late in the afternoon, camp was set up for the night.
Shahar had a rocker taken from her wagon and set by the campfire when Honey asked to sit up. "You maybe ought to go lie
down in my wagon."

Honey declined, preferring to sit by the fire. "I'm a little
chilled," she said. "The fire will warm me up." She refused dinner but asked for some tea and was drinking a cup when Timothy
Watts came up to her.

"Glad to see you alert, ma'am. Terribly sorry about what happened." He looked down at his boots. "Looks like your wagon'll
be on the road in the morning, though. Need to replace two
wheels and a tongue and ribs—but anyways, it's doable."

"That's good news. And it wasn't your fault, Mr. Watts, I
know that."

"Thank you, ma'am," he said, and backed away as he saw
Cameron approach.

Shahar handed Honey a cold compress for the lump on her
forehead, then shooed Nollie and Ruth from the fire so that
Honey and Cameron might be alone. Cameron did not like
Honey's look, and for the first time in a long while he realized
how fragile she was. "You scared us all," he said.

"I'll be sore and lame for a while, but I'll be all right."

"You'll have to sleep in another wagon at least for tonight."

"So I hear."

"We'll have it rolling by morning." he promised. "Mind if I sit
with you while I eat something?"

Honey started to rise and serve Cameron some dinner from the
pot on the fire, but as she stood up, she began to black out.
Cameron caught her as she fell. "Something's wrong," she said
as he lifted her into his arms. "Something's awfully wrong."

She felt cold in his arms, and he could feel her terrible tension
as she resisted a sudden stroke of pain. Cameron hurried with her
into Shahar's wagon and put her down on a bunk.

"What you been holding back, Honey Greer?" Shahar demanded.

"Terrible . . . pain."

"Protesting muscles, my foot."

"Hoping it'd go away," she said between clenched teeth.

"Bones, back? What?"

"Insides. Oh, Shahar!" Honey cried, doubling over.

Shahar gave Honey her hand to hold tightly. "Fine doctor
you'd make," she said gently.

Shahar stood up. "Time for you to get back to fixin' that wagon so's it can go on the road when we do," Shahar said to Cameron. When it was obvious Cameron was rooted to the floorboards, Shahar waved at him. "Shoo," she said, and tried to push him gently out. She pulled the drape aside. "I'll look after her good—if you care," she whispered.

"Care? I love her, you know."

"She shouldn't be the last to know."

"She sent me away."

Shahar was pensive. "This one will die also."

"What?"

"You had a baby once that died?"

Clearly, Cameron was startled. "Yes . . ."

"This one's dead also," she repeated.

"No!" He tried to push past Shahar and go to Honey again, but Shahar stood in his way.

"It's already happened. But this time your woman will be spared." Frozen in place, Cameron stared at Shahar. "I see many things. Sometimes not nearly enough, but I do know, Mr. Cameron, you can't fix anything here just now. I do see you fixing the wagon," Shahar urged.

Cameron looked into Shahar's eyes, truly seeing her for the first time. "You a witch?"

Shahar shook her head and laughed. "You know better—a dark-color angel, maybe. We'll talk about it later. Now go! One of my own babies needs tending."

Reluctantly, Cameron did as Shahar advised.

In the morning, Honey was still writhing in pain as Cameron conferred with Shahar outside her wagon. "The wagon's fixed, and Avery will stop for nothing short of fire or flood. I don't advise staying behind unless it means her life to roll."

"The motion won't do her any good, but I guess you can put us on the road."

The look on Cameron's face was one of immense relief. "She'll be all right, then?"

"I told you so last night. It's a mishap, but she'll get over it."

Cameron climbed into the driver's box. "I'll be driving this wagon today."

"I'm not sure Mrs. Radcliffe will be pleased to hear it. Just now your name's mud with this trouble you caused," Shahar cautioned him.

"Then don't tell her."

The man knows how to handle Honey. Shahar smiled to herself as she went to sit next to her.

Honey felt considerably worse with the rolling, frequently jarring motion of the wagon. By the time the party stopped shortly after noon for dinner she was half wishing she were dead but was finally able to sleep with the wagon stopped.

"She's sleeping soundly now," Shahar informed Cameron as he helped her, then Nollie to the ground.

"Let me sit with her," he said, then vanished behind the drape before Shahar could protest. He knelt silently beside Honey's sleeping form. Her hair disheveled, her face strained, not fully relaxed even in sleep, she looked very pale. The odor of blood assailed him.

He wondered how Shahar knew about the death of his wife and his child. She could not have guessed, and there was no way she could know. Clairvoyants were known among the Apache. Perhaps Shahar, too, had the power.

Cameron lifted a few soft strands of Honey's curls to caress. It was torture to be reminded his love alone could not protect her from pain such as this.

Then Honey opened her eyes and for several moments gazed at Cameron in silence, at last seeming at ease. She smiled and turned on her side to face him. She reached for Cameron's hand and pressed it against her cheek, then kissed his open palm.

"I love you," he said. "I have always loved you."

"As I have always loved you," she whispered, and, holding to him tightly, slowly drifted back to sleep.

CHAPTER THIRTY-THREE

During the following week Cameron continued to drive Shahar's wagon while Honey convalesced. When the road required that she leave the wagon, Cameron carried her in his arms while one of the other men took charge of getting the wagon to safety. Yet, he sat by her bedside only once and with each day grew increasingly silent. To Shahar, he seemed to brood, as did Honey, whom she frequently found in tears.

At the end of a week Honey was able to come forward and ride most of the day in the driver's box with Cameron. He was polite, and so was she. They might have been two strangers. Taciturn by nature, Mr. Watts had been verbose compared with Cameron. After two days of relative silence, Honey again retreated to her narrow bed.

One day when they stopped for a very late midday meal and Honey did not appear, Shahar went to her bedside. "What ails you now, Mrs. Radcliffe?"

"I can't bear his silence. I might as well be dead."

"I think it's time you got on your feet and took some exercise. You're not bleeding. Get out and walk alongside the wagon after you have something to eat."

Honey agreed but ate very little at dinner and then returned to bed.

Shahar shook her head as she rode next to Cameron. "I'm worried," she confided. "Yet I suppose it's good she's able to sleep."

Cameron said nothing.

"Your silence doesn't help, you know," Shahar asserted, but she only received more silence in response.

Later, however, Cameron drew out Shahar. "How'd you come up with the idea I had a woman and baby that died? There's folks'd say you're a witch if you told them such things."

"It's the truth, though—about the woman and baby?"

Cameron nodded. "What else do you know?"

"I see you and Mrs. Radcliffe together again."

"I doubt she sees the same. When she's on her feet and gets her temper back, she won't want anything more to do with me. You see how quiet she is riding next to me. Before we left Saint Louis she made it plain she wanted no part of me."

"You're a man of much intuition, Mr. Wolfe. Have you no sense of who she is?"

"I don't follow you."

"Tell me what you believe happens when we die."

"I don't dwell on it."

"Have you never felt something unusual about Mrs. Radcliffe?"

Unusual? To say the least! Cameron thought, but it was difficult to put his feelings about Honey into words.

"Maybe I should say 'special,' Mr. Wolfe. Is Mrs. Radcliffe not someone special to you?"

A man's thoughts about a woman were a very private matter, not as a rule discussed. Yet, his curiousity aroused, Cameron ventured to speak. "Mrs. Radcliffe is no ordinary woman—having nothing to do with her being beautiful or a lady. Or my loving her. When we're together, time is nothing, it's as though we've been together always. I can't think of living without her."

Shahar nodded. "You are meant to be together now and forever, and you must trust this sense you have about Mrs. Radcliffe, because your path with her won't be easy."

Cameron smiled. "Doesn't take a witch to figure that out."

Although exhausted when he crawled into his bedroll later that night, Cameron had trouble getting to sleep. He wondered over Shahar's strange words of encouragement. In spite of Honey's words of reassurance when she was most ill, it seemed to Cameron she now was pulling away from him again. Honey had only been delirious with pain when she spoke lovingly to him, he reasoned. From her frosty distance with him now, she obviously had forgotten, or maybe now regretted her words.

Shahar said to trust his sense of Honey as meant for him. But instead, Cameron lay awake considering how to survive without Honey's love. Cameron knew more than a few men who did not have women who loved them without a set price or for longer than the time it took to collect that fee. It was not unusual for a man to be alone or to know that no one loved him. It was much more difficult to live, Cameron realized, when a man knew his life could be otherwise.

CHAPTER THIRTY-FOUR

A deluge of rain and a severe wind came up suddenly, causing the tents to come down more rapidly than they had been set up. Drenched, men hastily retreated to their wagons for protection. The storm had swirled into camp at dusk and, with nature's fireworks lighting up the sky, promised to rage all night.

Once again living in her own wagon, Honey feared for a time that the Conestoga might blow over; her recent brush with death, from which she still bore bruises, only magnified her worry. The storm seemed to have the fury of a rampaging hurricane, and as the rocking of her wagon worsened, Honey pulled her shawl over her head and burrowed under her quilts.

Exhausted, she managed to doze off, but when a particularly furious gust of wind suddenly blew open the drape covering the front entry, Honey was forced to emerge from her cocoon. Trembling with cold and fright, she struggled to resecure the fastening ties, terrified that at any moment the wagon would roll over. Just as she was about to succeed with the awkward ties, the heavy canvas drape was torn from her hands by Cameron. Lightning again lit up the darkness, and Honey jumped back, but before Cameron could tie down the curtain again, she was doused by rain.

"You all right?" he shouted over the noise of wind and rain and thunder. Soaked to the skin, Cameron dripped small rivulets of water on everything around him.

"So far," Honey said, and lit the lantern. "And I was dry at least until you burst in." Without pausing to consider exactly what she was doing, Honey began to undo Cameron's water-soaked outer coat. "Have you been out in the storm all night? You could catch your death, you know." She did not see the surprise on Cameron's face, but with his help, he was soon half-naked.

Honey took a quilt from her bed, wrapped it around his shoulders, then nudged him to sit down. She pulled off his boots, then took charge of the quilt, holding it while he stood up and struggled out of his wet Levi's.

"Your skin's cold, I can feel it. How can you not be shivering even a little?" Honey wondered in amazement at his obvious indifference to the elements.

"I've lived on the prairie a long time. A little rain is nothing," he said, his answer drowned out by a deafening clap of thunder that seemed to come simultaneously with a bright flash of lightning. Honey jumped at the sudden overwhelming noise and light and threw her arms tightly around Cameron, who received her with open arms. "It feels as if the world is about to be washed away." She snuggled gratefully against Cameron as if he could protect her from all threats.

Cameron brought the blanket around Honey also and pulled her against himself, the sudden affect on his senses of holding her so close causing him to shudder.

"Cold?"

"Not at all," he said smiling, aching to kiss and caress her.

Aroused, yearning, Honey wanted to respond to his obvious desire but cautioned, "It's too soon after my . . . mishap for us . . ." She saw in Cameron's face a mixture of understanding and misery. "But please, if you would . . . could stay with me . . . this storm . . . I need you. I've missed you."

"I love you."

"I know," she said. "And I love you." She kissed him tenderly.

Now quite unaware of the terrifying storm that continued to broil around them, Honey leaned joyfully against Cameron. "No matter what happens, we'll always be one," he promised as he cradled her against himself.

When they lay down together in her bed, a feeling of contentment she had never known before flooded over her. She lay with her head on Cameron's shoulder, and, nestled comfortably, they tried to sleep.

Their thoughts drifted separately. Cameron reflected pensively on his obsession with the woman he held in his arms. If he were a man obsessed by sex, he knew it would be impossible not to be affected by Honey Radcliffe. But he loved her for more than the enormous pleasure her woman's body gave him, and there was more to his obsession—if that was what it amounted to—than the need to gratify himself physically. Honey Radcliffe was far too complex and fascinating a lady to be worshiped for her sensuality alone.

Deeply content with Honey in his arms, Cameron fell asleep easily and for a long while slumbered in a dreamless void. When he began to dream, he confronted a mixture of memory and desire. People from the past whom he had loved tugged strongly at his emotions, and his feelings were strong enough to make him murmur and stir restlessly. The landscape of his dreams varied, and so did time, yet always present in his vision was Honey—perfect and beautiful. In his vision she did not look exactly as she did now, but he recognized her all the same, his passion for her constant, yet at times his heart filled with almost unbearable grief.

Images of her naked, making love to him, then the next instant broken and bruised on some unknown forest floor drove Cameron to cry out in anguish in his sleep.

Next she stood before him in somber dress, veiled in mourning. He saw beneath that sheer covering, saw her pain and confusion. Then he dreamed of a wall of fire rising and separating him from her. He called to her frantically, then suddenly was aware that he was asleep. "I am only dreaming," he cried within his dream, then put his hand into the fire and was not burned.

"Come here. Stand next to me," he urged Honey in the nightmare.

Honey shook her head.

"You must!" he cried. "I can't move."

Obviously terrified, Honey began to move forward into the fire. "I can't move," he shouted, then watched with horror as Honey was consumed by grasping fingers of orange flame.

"I am only dreaming!" he cried frantically, jolted awake and gasping for air.

Honey, too, had fallen asleep, but his jostling disturbed her. "Shhhh," she whispered sleepily, and tried to hold him still. "You're only dreaming." She brushed her lips against his heaving chest.

Cameron's heart beat wildly, the feeling of panic not behind him yet. He rolled over and brought Honey beneath him. "Shahar—what has Shahar said about me?"

"Mmmmmm."

"What does that mean?"

"It means go back to sleep."

"You were in my dream."

"I love you," she said and pulled his mouth to hers.

He pulled away. "I must start a fire to take away the danger."

"But it's pouring rain?" she muttered as he started to rise.

He lay down again. "You were always with me."

"Yes," she said.

"You're not listening."

"Mmmmmm," she answered. "Have you never dreamed before?"

"Dreams of ghosts are warning."

"Ghosts?" He had her full attention now.

"The dead."

"Sometimes you say the oddest things." She yawned. "Still, I love you. Now, go back to sleep."

"Shahar says we've been together always."

"Yes, I know."

"You're in my blood."

"I fear you're in mine, too—like a fever." If ever a woman loved a man completely, irrevocably, that was how, Honey believed, she loved Cameron. In loving him, she perceived beyond passion, felt their souls merge as one.

"Apaches would say you and I are as married as people get," Cameron said, interrupting Honey's reverie. "Apaches believe love and spirit, not words, unite a man and a woman. They make no vows but invite friends to celebrate their union with a feast." Cameron raised Honey above him so he could see her face. "You are my woman, Honey Radcliffe, and nothing in earth or heaven can ever change that."

Honey basked in her precious lover's adoration. "Nothing ever will, I promise," she vowed, and touched by his sentiment did not even pause to wonder at his odd allusion to the ferocious Apache, whose land they were about to enter.

CHAPTER THIRTY-FIVE

The caravan, a monstrous snake whose movement caused the sky to rain dust back on the land, pressed on. Every footfall brought the travelers closer to the Little Jornada, a waterless sixty-mile expanse of searing desert that at best was a three-day journey that not even the most experienced freighter welcomed. As they approached the Jornada, Avery Dillingham's men took special care to see that the stock was adequately watered and fed and extra water stored. While draft animals grazed, men used sickles to cut grass, which they bundled and stored for passage through the grassless desert.

Those in the parties responsible for feeding the hungry were in a frenzy to bake bread and lay up food for the dry camps in the miles ahead. Game—antelope, rabbit, deer—that had been plentiful would be unavailable. On the Jornada, only what remained of the jerked meat supply would find its way to the table. They would journey at night, when it would be cooler.

As they approached the desert, the increase in temperature each day warned them the Little Jornada was close. Chances to bathe and wash clothes loomed as precious opportunities. At this point the Cimarron River was not as clear as it had been or as alkaline.

Since the recent War between the States, the Santa Fe Trail

had been all but deserted by white caravans; much of the southwest territory had been depopulated by white men, who feared reprisals from natives who knew that the United States Army posts and forts were no longer manned. In their absence, indians presumed the prophecies of their wise men, or shamans, had been fulfilled, believing God had banished the white man from the world as promised. Unfortunately for the indian, the war only meant, as Cameron told Honey, that white men were too busy killing each other to be bothered with indians.

Now that the war was over and white men and women were beginning to return to the territory, the menace of the Apache in particular was at the back of the mind of every white traveler. However, without word of specific incidents of bloodletting, anxiety about "the hostiles" was to some degree allayed. Bathers like Honey Radcliffe went into streams more concerned with water snakes than with the prospect of indian attack.

"Why do you remind me of serpents at a time like this?" Honey said, shivering in spite of the water's warmth. After nooning it, the party had lingered in camp to avoid unnecessary physical exertion by men and animals at the peak of the day's heat, and Cameron had found a secluded bend of the river for Honey to bathe in while he kept watch.

"You just keep your eyes open," he warned, unconcerned by Honey's aggravated tone. He loved to gaze on her as she bathed, especially the moments when she lost the sense of his presence and relaxed her modesty. Now she waded hip-deep and unselfconsciously floated on her back. Her guard down, Honey seemed ethereal, bewitchingly graceful even as she washed her hair and tempting body in the lulling warm water.

Cameron had begun to tantalize her with stories of hot springs in the country in which they would travel beyond the Jornada. He had promised her country like she had never seen before, filled with strange plants and animals and, from all appearances, as dry as a bone. Yet those as intimate with the territory as Cameron could lead her to imposing cliffs and canyons where one could find water hot enough to soak away the misery of cramped trail-weary muscles—and maybe also endanger her morals by making her a willing victim of seduction.

"With you as my guide, I warrant I'll be in grave danger." She had enjoyed his assurance that she would be, and as she soaked in the murky waters of the Cimarron, she could only imagine the clear heated pools in Apache country. "Won't it be dangerous?"

she had wondered. "The savages . . ." She had faltered, not wanting to speak aloud of what terrified her most about the journey west. She had tried to exact Cameron's promise that they would be safe, changing the subject entirely when it became obvious he could give no such oath.

When Honey stepped onto dry ground, a chill passed over her as the air, warm as it was, struck her wet skin. Quickly she seized the linen towels she had laid on the rocks next to the shallow bank where Cameron kept watch, coiling one towel around her hair and into a turban; a second was thrown about her shoulders. Abruptly the image of a young woman bathing in a cold forest stream crossed Honey's mind. She shivered violently.

Cameron held a last towel for Honey, and she stepped gingerly into his embrace. She stared pensively at him while he smiled adoringly at her. Honey tried to evade what was obviously on his mind. "We've not been terribly discreet," she began, "and by now the entire train knows of our liaison."

"Don't let it keep you awake nights."

"*You* keep me awake nights." She let him kiss her lightly. "I've begun to receive very speculative glances from some of the freighters."

"I'll talk to Avery."

"That isn't necessary."

"Maybe you should say something to Shahar."

"Shahar? I'm afraid she knows all about us. Perhaps more than we do—surely you don't think she'd say anything to anyone. I can assure you she wouldn't."

"You didn't tell me Shahar was a mind reader. What's she told you about us?"

Honey blushed. "She believes—it's so fantastic, I'm embarrassed to say." She scrutinized Cameron's face. "Promise you won't laugh when I tell you."

"No," he said, and tried to kiss her again.

Honey resisted.

"What does Shahar say?"

"Do you think we might have shared a life together in another lifetime?"

"Is that what Shahar says?"

Honey nodded.

"I only know you're my woman—and always have been."

Cameron's grip on Honey suddenly intensified; growing impatient, he bent to seize her lips with his again.

Still she refused him. "But how can it be, for goodness sake, that I've been your lover *always* when in fact I was another man's wife? How can we reasonably overlook that fact?"

Cameron shrugged. "*In fact*, you never were."

Honey lowered her head and her gaze. "No, I never was Nathan's wife, and never would have been." She raised her eyes. "Oh, he'd have claimed me, eventually. We were so well matched—our union planned from the cradle, our future together, truthfully, nothing but the vulgar breeding of prize stock." Honey tried to remove herself from Cameron's embrace but succeeded only in turning her back to him.

As he held her fiercely against himself, she felt like crying and had to suck in her breath to prevent her tears from spilling, suddenly too shy to confess what was in her heart—*I could never love Nathan or anyone the way I love you*—the passion behind her sentiment overpowering her ability to speak forthrightly. "I seem to remember you from another lifetime," she whispered. "I have strange dreams I can't explain."

"I hope you're not as frightened by your dreams as I am of mine."

Startled, Honey laughed and turned to face him, "I take no comfort, sir, in the notion that you can be made to feel afraid. My Uncle Trevor sent you to protect me; you're not permitted to be frightened—ever."

Cameron smiled. "I'm *afraid* I love you," he confessed. "I always have and always will."

"With all my heart, I want to believe you," Honey answered, and in his sure embrace finally yielded with sweet acquiescence to his desire.

CHAPTER THIRTY-SIX

Shamelessly fascinated, Nollie watched the scene unfold before her. When she came upon Honey and Cameron, he so intent on the figure of his lover bathing, Nollie pivoted on her heel. But instead of hastening back to camp, she found a secure hiding place among the cottonwoods where she could watch them unobserved. Horrified by coming upon such a private scene, any decent lady would turn away, Nollie told herself, yet here she stood as if she were firmly rooted in the ground.

Nollie felt the electricity between the couple suffuse itself directly through the air and engulf her in its charge. Tantalized and mesmerized as Honey was, the breath in Nollie's lungs caught just as her friend's did. At last Nollie understood the fire that compelled Honey to the flame.

Only after Honey was fully clothed again did Nollie dare to wander to the water's edge. "It's almost too warm." Honey advised her.

"It's hardly worth getting wet for when all you do is rub off dry dirt with thin mud," Nollie said, disgusted, unable to look either Cameron or Honey in the eye.

"I'll keep watch," Honey offered.

"No need."

Quick to tease, Cameron said, "Want me to stand by instead?"

"No, sir, Mr. Wolfe."

Honey laughed. "If you aren't back at camp in half an hour, I'll send Cameron to rescue you. Don't forget the wedding."

"It's the only reason I'm bathing in *this* water, I tell you," Nollie answered.

Honey hurried back to camp with Cameron. She laughed at how ridiculous she was to be excited about the evening ahead, but the prospect of a wedding was the most entertainment they had had in nearly four weeks on the trail. It was a momentous occasion for Honey each time Cameron pointed out a named juncture in the road—the Arkansas River crossing, Ash Creek, Pawnee Fork, or Cow Creek—but not worthy of celebration for anyone save herself. Tonight, however, Ruth Blocher would marry Wilton Ramsey, providing an excuse for gaiety even among the hard-boiled freighters. A feast of sorts was anticipated; there would even be cake. "Don't expect much in the way of fancy, but wedding cakes just the same," Avery promised.

As Honey opened her trunk and removed a very wrinkled peach-colored silk taffeta gown Cameron had warned her against packing, she tried not to dwell on other wedding celebrations, memories sufficiently clear to make her mouth water: delicious tender layered cake and frothy French champagne drunk from long-stemmed thin crystal goblets.

Honey frowned at her gown and its low, square neckline, with its panel of intricate smocking dotted with tiny nests of baby pearls that would daringly help raise her curving breasts for everyone's attention. Yet the dress's rumpled condition would hardly qualify her as a fetching example of womanhood. *It will be dark, and no one will notice*, Honey assured herself, but was not comforted, reminded of how far she had fallen. Even a year ago it would have been unthinkable for her to appear in public dressed as she would be tonight.

"Never look back," Honey offered aloud to console and fortify herself.

From the trunk, Honey also removed petticoats and a corset and, because there would be dancing to the accompaniment of a fiddle, harmonica, and Spanish guitar, satin dancing slippers. In spite of Cameron's denials, there would be an occasion for dancing on the trail! Honey rubbed the shiny satin slippers with a handkerchief to bring out the shine, smiling as she recalled with tenderness the nights she and Cameron had danced aboard the *Lady Mildred* and how, as she so keenly remembered, she had fallen in love with him on that first night when he had held her in his arms and submitted to her instruction. If nothing else, she loved him then for his willingness to please her, for surrendering for the moment his commanding stature, for being man enough to let her for a time assume the lead.

Certainly Nathan had not been that sort, Honey reflected. Intuitively, Shahar had realized Honey and Nathan would have been a doomed pair shackled together in matrimony, as helpless in their union as slaves bound together in a coffle.

Honey shuddered and raised her hands to cover her face. She wondered if it was truly evil to be grateful not to have to live out her life with a husband who would surely have made her miserable.

Honey admitted how devoutly she now wanted to believe as Shahar did—that fate commanded that she be with Cameron, that it indeed was God's plan for her to fall in love with him. If not, there could be no condoning their sinful affair. Honey sighed and reached for her journal. She did not need to dress for the wedding yet and wanted to put a few of her troubling thoughts down in an organized fashion.

Feelings and wishes, Honey knew, did not necessarily bear resemblance to fact. But could matters of faith ever be proven?

Of late, much of what the world held to be true and real had been threatened. Men of letters as well as armies sometimes succeeded in turning the known world upside down. Honey smiled broadly. Perhaps one day the notion of one lifetime succeeding another would be a popular philosophy and Shahar Daniels would be recognized as a venerable philosopher! But more likely, Honey knew, Shahar's fame would be linked to sorcery and witchcraft, and Shahar portrayed as a black seeress able to render her followers trembling and praying for salvation—just as Honey herself had sometimes been tempted to do.

30th of June, 1865, Friday

I suppose if God is a stern, leather-skinned, angry Old Man residing in the clouds with plump Cherubs at his beck and call, as some envision, then all that Shahar believes True is, likewise, Possible. I confess she has an Uncanny habit of prognosticating things that are, on occasion, Believable. She swears to have seen Cameron Wolfe in her mind before he set foot in Greerfield. If I believe her Not to be a Liar and trust her in all other matters, why wouldn't I believe this statement about Cameron Wolfe? What purpose would she have to Lie to me?

She vows she is Privy to certain knowledge, knowledge which Serves to substantiate my Dreams. Whether my Dreams are a result of her suggesting certain things, or whether they are Real is, it would seem, Unknowable. Yet, I Feel more strongly than I have Ever felt about anything I can Recall that this Man—this "Unsuitable Cowboy," as Nollie calls him—is closer to my Heart than my own Soul. Surely, it is not Lust only that compels me to him. But what the Reason for his Presence in my life is, I am not yet aware. Even if my Dreams be True, I have not an inkling why we have come Together in this Life-time.

Shahar insists Life is the Great Mystery. If that be true, why would Dreams unfold the past to us? Why would anyone be privy to the knowledge that Shahar claims she is?

And why would I give all I Possess to know if she is mad or not?

I have, in spite of a glorious Reconciliation with my lover, a great sense of Foreboding about which I have not consulted with Shahar. He believes this Sense is only some primitive Wisdom warning me we are about to travel a waterless tract of Desert. He says, when one often Journeys in this Land, one has a knowledge of such things. Perhaps it is an instinct that the lesser Beasts are created with and give not a thought to. Oddly, he believes in the significance of dreams

*—and would have built a fire in a driving rain, but I succeeded in
distracting him. I think it better not to be aware of pending Danger—
or remember anything of a Distant past!*

H. G. R.

CHAPTER THIRTY-SEVEN

To one side of a campfire, Ruth and Wilton Ramsey stood solemnly before the members of the caravan. Ruth wore a pale blue
dress and carried a bouquet of wild grasses and prairie roses
that had been collected a wide distance from camp by thoughtful
freighters. As the couple exchanged vows, there was hardly
a sound from those assembled, but as Wilton Ramsey kissed
the bride, deafening whoops of approval fanned across the
prairie, and soon the night rang with music, loud voices, and
clapping.

Everyone danced, men with men, others solo, and of course
the four women of the party, besieged by endless eager partners.
Honey wanted to relive a few moments of dancing with Cameron, and a few moments was all she had the opportunity to
enjoy. The men who stood in line and danced with her were
gravely polite, which amused Honey, for she had reluctantly
grown tolerant of their ordinarily rough-hewn ways. A queen,
she decided, could not have received more admiration and respect.

Nollie, too, was showered with attention and before the end of
the evening had received two proposals of marriage. "It must be
catching," she remarked to Cameron in something of a huff. But
she secretly considered one proposal tempting, not because of
any particular appeal of the man involved but to escape her fears
of what loomed ominously ahead of her if she continued on to
California with her mother and Honey.

"Tell me about California, Mr. Wolfe," Nollie prompted when
he drew her into the fray of dancers. "Maybe I should've stayed
behind at Greerfield."

"I expect Mr. Jefferson won't have any objection to your being in Mrs. Radcliffe's employ."

"I'm free, and I might do something different. It's the 'something' that's perplexing."

"There's no end of need for a lady who can cook. Maybe someone'll stake you for a house so you can take in boarders. Always a boomtown springing up somewhere, and hungry men to follow. In San Francisco there's hotels and restaurants. Sacramento, too. If you'd rather do laundry—"

"I'd rather not."

Cameron smiled and pulled Nollie closer. He spoke conspiratorily. "Miss Daniels, I'm afraid you might not know how to survive in the white eyes world, so I give you a little free advice. Above all, you've got to be ready to take advantage of the moment, do whatever needs doing, love money first, and be sure to charge a large enough fare to make a good profit."

"I believe every word," Nollie answered.

"Does Mrs. Radcliffe know you're thinking about leaving her?"

"No, and you mustn't say a word. Please."

Cameron looked down gently on Nollie. He'd thought she and Honey had arrived at friendly terms early on the trail. Again the resemblance of the two women struck him. He wondered if either recognized the other for who she was. "I'll keep your secret."

Nollie relaxed noticeably and was soon dancing in someone else's arms. As she danced away, Cameron went to Honey's partner and cut in. "You're limping."

She laughed. "Only slightly."

When it was time for the cake to be cut, the bride did the honors, offering the first piece to her husband with a kiss, then serving generous slices to the crowd. When it was Honey's turn, Ruth whispered, "This might be a good night to persuade Mr. Wolfe to make things between you . . . you know . . . more proper. People are talking. Preacher Dillingham's in a marrying mood."

"I'm not," Honey said coolly, barely able to keep her jaw from dropping. Livid, she turned away and all but dropped her slice of cake into the hand of the startled freighter beside her.

Honey hurried to escape to her wagon, but the music started up again and an unsuspecting freighter caught her by the hand and pulled her with him into a circle of dancers. At first Honey resisted, but her partner, fully enjoying the festivities and slightly under the influence of strong whiskey, was oblivious. Intending no injury, more used to persuading mules and oxen than leading a woman in dance, he gripped Honey fiercely and waltzed whole-heartedly. More amused than angered by her inability to shake off her partner, Honey finally gave in and, laughing, did the best she could not to incur permanent injury to her feet, which, foolishly, she had optimistically shod in satin slippers.

When the evening was over, she was exhausted, as was nearly everyone else. "I'm going to need a week's rest before I go another step," Nollie protested.

"Not likely on Mr. Avery's schedule," Shahar said.

Escorting Honey, Cameron offered Nollie his other arm. "Camp breaks at daybreak, no matter what condition you're in."

"I don't think some of these folks'll dry out till they get across that Jornada desert you've been telling us about," Nollie observed wryly, which set Cameron to laughing as if he wouldn't stop and Nollie and Honey to giggling uproariously at him.

Following them, Shahar shook her head. "Who's helping who, I want to know," she wondered aloud as, like drunkards themselves, arm in arm, Honey, Cameron, and Nollie staggered to their wagons.

CHAPTER THIRTY-EIGHT

Of the three black freighters in the caravan, Nollie favored Bobs Carney. Of medium height and darker than Nollie, Bobs let his direct gaze settle on her whenever he was in Nollie's presence, which reduced her to extreme self-consciousness and hot-faced silence. From the fact that no one, not even Shahar, made any comment on the man's forward behavior, Nollie began to imagine Bobs had singled her out. However, his proposal the night of Ruth and Wilton Ramsey's wedding gave him away.

Now in the wagon she shared with her mother, wound in a cocoon of blankets, Nollie entertained the notion of becoming Bobs Carney's wife. She assumed that if they married, Bobs would continue to drive for Avery Dillingham, and the idea that he would be long on the trail made his offer especially appealing. The security of marriage yet, with her husband gone a lot of the time, considerable independence seemed to Nollie an almost ideal arrangement.

Since he at all times maintained a respectable appearance and claimed three saddle horses of his own, Nollie knew that Bobs Carney was somewhat better off than the average freighter, with a habit of putting his wages to a more useful purpose than whiskey and women. Even at the wedding celebration she did not see him sharing the ubiquitous bottle of whiskey, a favorable sign in Nollie's opinion. She was, however, totally unprepared to have Bobs promise her a house of her very own.

"Got no house now, but I can get one jus' for you if you be my wife. Maybe a farm."

Nollie had laughed aloud. "You expect me to plow and sow the fields?"

"My wife won't be no field nigra," Bobs replied stiffly.

Suitably impressed, Nollie had smiled in response; however, as she now contemplated the obligations a wife could not expect to avoid, she found the offer much less agreeable. Bobs Carney was probably a decent sort, but only on exceedingly rare occasions did she sincerely feel any interest in romance.

She could conjure vivid fantasies of herself adorned with glittering jewels and dressed in stylish gowns of luminous fabrics. She could see herself dancing in the arms of an admiring man with other handsome suitors waiting impatiently to shower her with heartfelt compliments. She heard the whispered words of adoration for her light coloring, the perfection of her figure, which gloriously enhanced the dressmaker's art, the temptation of her long graceful curls that begged for the stroke of a man's reverent hand. But her imagination did not extend beyond this limited vision, for Nollie loathed the possibility of being the object of more than a man's sincere appreciation of her beauty, of providing more than pleasure for his eyes. While the legitimacy of marriage appealed to her, the idea of matrimony itself did not. Purposefully, Nollie had always closed the door firmly on the idea of marriage. In the light of reality, she thought just before she welcomed sleep, escaping the present circumstances in the arms of a man was less desirable than the uncertainties of life in California.

In the wagon next to Nollie's lay Honey, with equally disturbing thoughts that, with the comforting sound of Cameron's deep even breathing gently filling the air, she only now had time to contemplate. Although she had been distracted by dancing and the general gaiety of the night, Honey had not succeeded in dismissing Ruth's pointed suggestion from her mind.

She rationalized that the new Mrs. Ramsey would probably never lose the uncanny ability to needle her and admitted the woman had successfully pricked her skin again. Honey insisted it mattered not at all that her affair with Cameron was undoubtedly common knowledge among Avery Dillingham's men. The opinions of such rabble, Honey argued, could hardly be of significance.

What did matter was the sincerity and depth of Cameron's affection and, she realized, the unmistakable sense of the depth of their connection with each other. The longer they were together, the more certain Honey felt that her dreams and "lapses of sanity" were not that at all but memory of a kind not subject to polite mention, hidden away much as other topics of delicacy were avoided among persons of any refinement.

Of course, among well-bred individuals, Honey would have to face the fact of her illicit affair. Cameron had obliquely referred to marriage, but, she noted with a certain fresh uneasiness, he never actually had asked her to marry him. Advising her that Apache couples celebrated their union with their savage friends did not constitute an offer of marriage.

Suddenly uncomfortable in Cameron's embrace, Honey squirmed on the narrow mattress they shared. Her back to him, she lay with her head on his shoulder as he hugged her tightly and, instead of freeing her, only shifted his position and brought her even closer against him. Unwilling to pull away from an embrace she had recently yearned for with all her heart, Honey stilled her squirming, comfortable in body if not in spirit.

She would be furious, Honey acknowledged, if she thought Cameron did not intend to marry her, but she confessed with utmost surprise that she was not certain she would marry him! At this revelation Honey knew she ought to be writhing with shame. Instead she smiled, her admission a restating of a familiar desire: to be more than a woman at some man's disposal, more than a wife and the mother of namesakes and heirs. Perhaps in a more primitive setting, such as California would be, Honey daydreamed she might be allowed more than a life as a glorified concubine. Perhaps she might have an opportunity to put her knowledge of medicine to use.

Honey sighed, disheartened. Such an event was unlikely ever to come about, she realized as she listened to her lover's deep breathing. Honey reflected on Cameron's presence and her deepening affection for him. Truthfully, she would gladly marry this particular man who slumbered now beside her and be at peace.

Shortly, her mind at ease, Honey slept soundly, but an hour later, in the silent depth of night, it was Cameron's turn to lie awake and restless, alert to every cricket chirp and breath of wind. Cameron smiled as he listened to the night sounds. Now that he lived as a white eyes, his senses were dull compared with what they had been when he had lived as an Apache. Earlier in the night he had been dead to the world, enjoying the sleep of spent lovers and drunkards—a combination of sleeping potions a true native of the land could ill afford.

Cameron felt uneasy, not troubled by any sense of danger but rather by the disquiet of his soul that invariably occurred whenever he approached Apache territory, disturbed by the appeal of his keenest memories of a country still free from true conquest by the white man. In the land of the Apache, the indian still retained the upper hand, knowing intimately every feature of the earth— plain, arroyo, canyon, rock, and mountain. The indian knew how to find water where there appeared to be none, and pathways up sheer cliffs without apparent footholds. He could disappear mysteriously into the landscape and outdistance his pursuers with that knowledge.

If the Apache were ever to be conquered, Cameron believed privately, it would come only as a result of the relentless numbers of white eyes who were moving westward to claim the indian territories for themselves. The War between the States had stemmed the ardent flow of whites for a while, but as Avery Dillingham's caravan testified, that period had merely been a respite from the flood of eager settlers. Soon appalling numbers of white eyes would begin again to lay claim to Apache country.

Even before the war, land designated by treaty for the indian had been encroached on by ever-greedy whites. All the indian had to do was agree to settle down on a piece of land and it became an inherently desirable tract of land for white eyes. White eyes called for peace, but when it was granted, they failed to keep it. After Cameron had left the Apache in a relatively peaceful period in the territory, the great Cheis had come in under a flag of truce only to be set on by the very men with whom he had treated. On that occasion Cheis had barely escaped with his life; the warriors who had come in with him were less fortunate. The territory's military commander had ordered the extermination of all "hostiles," which to the white eyes mind meant every last indian—man, woman, or child.

Unaware of any miraculous change in either official policy or white eyes thinking that would allow white eyes to abide peacefully with indians in their midst, eventually, Cameron knew, the Apache would be driven out of the Arizona and New Mexico territories or murdered down to the last soul. Periods of peace to which, for the most part, the Apache had been devoted came to an end because of a small number of indian renegades but more as a result of treacherous white eyes who failed to abide by their agreements with the indians. Apparently the Apache were expected to live on air, because the promised rations had not been provided. No rational man starved himself and his family to death when his neighbor had a fat cow in his pasture. The Apache could overlook their betrayal by white eyes only so long before they abandoned peace. After the murder of the great Apache chief Mangas Coloradas in 1863 by the soldiers with whom he had been invited to treat, Cameron believed the Apache would probably be set forever against white eyes. He now could foresee for the future only an endless cycle of revenge and counterrevenge between white eyes and Apache.

Cameron inhaled the night air deeply into his lungs. He thought of the wild, free life he had lived among the Apache. They were an honorable people whose word meant something. Part of his soul longed to live among the Apache again, but he foresaw for them little but endless pursuit by white eyes who seemed to despise all people of different color, thought, or habit from theirs, intolerant of differences of opinion or religion even among their own race. Ussen had commanded the Apache to live at peace with their neighbors, an impossible goal, Cameron feared, if one's neighbors were white eyes.

He longed to share the treasures of the land they were shortly to enter with the woman who now lay entwined with him. Yet it was a country so foreign to Honey's experience that Cameron believed it likely she would be repulsed and not at all enamored as he was. But to live and not share with her the things that mattered most to him seemed impossible.

Cameron pulled Honey's sleeping form nearer his, savoring the joy of holding her close. Might Honey Radcliffe, he wondered, know him for who he truly was and love him still?

The idea that she might loomed more improbable than the miracle that she could love him at all. Cameron therefore resolved to keep his many secrets strictly to himself.

CHAPTER THIRTY-NINE

His attention was immediately riveted as the graceful creature came into his range of vision at the water's edge. Instantly, he slouched down and froze, blending with the earth, watching for the perfect moment to advance with lightning speed, to spring with lethal precision. Poised for the kill, he blinked his eyes of yellow gold and waited.

In no apparent hurry, his victim was oblivious to danger. She frolicked at the water's edge, then waded deeper and disappeared beneath the water's surface.

Anxiously, the giant cat raised himself for a better view and stared at the telltale swirl of water the creature left behind until, with a furious leap and splash, she rose to the surface again. Despising water except to assuage his thirst, the cat hunkered down again and continued the vigil.

Then the delicate creature of a kind he had often seen dragged several bundles with her into the river, where she was out of normal reach. She began to thrash around in the water, making a noisy, confusing spectacle, and emitted soft calls in repeated refrains, perhaps calling others of her kind to her side. Unobserved, impatient, the juices of hunger boiling in his gut, the cat danced silently in place, chattering in a voice that was unheard by his intended victim.

The quarry, of meat he had eaten before, was near perfection in his eyes. Although more lean than he preferred, this creature would be an easy kill. One precise leap, one carefully aimed seizing of the neck in his life-destroying jaws, and she would be his to relish.

At last she emerged from the water but at once commenced distracting, furious movements with her arms, acting on the items she had played with in the water. Her voice grew louder and more boisterous. The cat did not advance; he did not flee the alarming actions of his prey but assessed the scene anxiously. Angered by the delay and perhaps by the foiling of his scheme, he gave a low growl and swished his weighty tail violently.

With growing alarm, yet fascinated, the cat watched as the creature furiously flapped her arms and flung the items that obsessed her onto the high, almost flat rocks that lined the shore. Nervous but determined to take almost any risk to have her, the cat moved to a still concealed but closer position, unaware at first of the entry of another observer to the scene.

Then, assailed by an unmistakable scent, the cat sensed a sudden trap and, pressed, snarled furiously. Hearing this, his victim froze, death suddenly seeming a breath, a movement away. Distracted as he was by imminent danger to himself, pangs of hunger receded in his consciousness, replaced by the more compelling juices of the instinct for survival.

The intruder knew that the cat sensed his peril, but for the moment, owing to his intended victim's position, the skilled marksman who held the cat in his rifle sight could not fire to kill or even to wound without risking hitting the woman by the happenstance of a miscalculated shot.

Unaware as she was of potential rescue, terror poisoned the woman's veins. Scenes of her short life passed before her eyes, and without thinking she turned and fled back into the water until, waist deep, she moved against the current, believing her escape was upstream.

Then the man moved suddenly closer to the cat and fired. He missed, the shot streaking a hair's breadth from the cat's shoulder. Confused and terrified, the cat sprang in the direction of the water in resolute pursuit of his victim.

Screaming, not hearing the explosion of the rifle in her hurry, the woman lost her balance and splashed frantically in the water, where after but a few lightning-swift strides in her direction, the cat stood adjacent to her at the water's edge. He sprang toward her. Expecting death, she watched the cat leap into the air and sail toward her, fierce yellow eyes gleaming and focused hypnotically on her. The moment seemed fixed in time, as if life had ceased to move relentlessly forward.

Then, in midair, the cat's ascent was interrupted. With a blood-chilling shriek, the animal fell dead in the water inches from the woman, who stared unbelieving into the cat's open eyes. Sobbing, frantic, utterly unnerved, the woman thrashed wildly in

the water, then, without seeing, spent, tried to drag herself to
shore.

Suddenly strong arms sustained her, making certain she did
not fall. Dazed and shivering, she held on to him. Then the rush
of terror subsided, replaced by high excitement. Crying softly,
forgetting who she was, not realizing that she was water-soaked
and dripping, she clung to him. Slowly her shaking eased, and
with her first awareness of the warm blood coursing through her
veins, she repeatedly kissed her rescuer for joy in the knowledge
that she was still alive. Then, unexpectedly, those kisses turned
seeking, carnal, a startling animal passion overtaking returning
reason.

He responded instinctively, giving his own impassioned
kisses, naturally touching her in ways that were gentle yet demanding, seductive, hips thrusting vigorously in primitive appeal. If she had been subject to reason, she would have pulled
away. Instead, enthralled, Nollie was eager only for more of the
caresses that left her breathless and reeling. Moments before,
death had been but seconds away. It now seemed fitting to celebrate survival in the most life-affirming way.

Then, in the midst of passion, just as he was about to make an
irreversible move, Cameron was seized by a rush of awareness.
He backed off and began to button Nollie's dress. "It happened so
fast," he said in apology.

Stunned back to her senses, Nollie nodded with shame, eyes
downcast. She was shocked by her responses—less so by his—
and tears welled in her eyes. *"Don't you dare tell Mrs. Radcliffe
about this!"*

Sober, Cameron stared at Nollie. "Not a word," he swore in a
wry tone. "She'd *never* forgive us—and neither of us wants to
live without her."

"I could do just fine *never* seeing her again," Nollie shot back
angrily as the tears she had managed to suppress began to fall.

Cameron let the remark pass without comment and turned
away to pull the puma's body from the water. Next, he gathered
the laundry Nollie had strewn on rocks to dry and other pieces
still floating in the river. When he returned to Nollie's side, she
was no longer crying. She faced him dry-eyed, almost defiant.

In response, Cameron smiled and ceremoniously presented
Nollie with the wet bundle of laundry, then lifted his rifle from
the ground and, taking a moment to carefully consider the gesture, gently put his arm around Nollie and led her back to camp.

CHAPTER FORTY

Twenty-two days from Independence, the caravan lingered restlessly at the middle crossing of the Arkansas River, waiting with combined dread and eagerness for nightfall. Only then could they commence their journey across the waterless Jornada, which with luck would take only two long nights of effort. The stock was watered and rested, and all preparations were confirmed for the last time. Cameron skinned the puma he had killed and, after all three women disdained the drying of the cat's hide on top of one of their wagons, secured the pelt over the canopy of the fourth wagon. "By the time we get to California, Nollie, you'll want that cat hung over your mantel to remind you of the occasion," Cameron teased.

Nollie answered quickly. "No, sir, never." She wished only to forget the incident that had forced her to confront her mortality. She was, however, less successful in denying the reality of her responses to Cameron Wolfe. She trusted he did not mean to reveal their passionate encounter to Honey. Yet to her great surprise, she was inundated with disturbing images of other, more passionate outcomes to their encounter.

With stunning clarity, Nollie now understood Honey Radcliffe's fascination with the man she herself had always sneered at as a lowly cowhand. Something within Cameron Wolfe had ignited the passion Nollie had been convinced did not flow in her veins. It pleased Nollie outrageously that Cameron had responded to her; he had reciprocated her fire measure for measure. She tingled deliciously at her all too fresh memory, willingly releasing her image of herself as a perpetual virgin.

Cameron had stopped short of dishonoring her, an event that on contemplation truthfully left Nollie irrationally indignant, her heart filled with jealousy for Honey's ability to tempt him beyond the limits of polite restraint. His apparent love for Honey, which had caused him to stop making love to Nollie, was suddenly something she coveted fiercely.

Even so, Nollie smiled with wicked pleasure at the fact that she had sorely tempted Cameron, and now she began to entertain the notion of making the dreary life on the trail more exciting from day to tiring day. The desire of the slave to possess all that the white mistress had again reared its head. It seemed to Nollie she had spent a lifetime wanting what Honey had, and she suddenly became determined as never before to have equal or better.

On Cameron's part, he immediately dismissed the incident, excusing his responses to Nollie with the comforting notion that he had simply reacted naturally to the high excitement of the moment. He was, after all, a man, and Nollie Daniels was a thoroughly appealing female. In spite of this reasoning, a guilty sense that he might readily betray Honey began to nag him and found him brooding more than ordinarily was his nature.

In reflection, he realized nothing in his life, among either his Saint Louis family or the Apache, had prepared Cameron for what now haunted him: a growing conviction, a heartfelt sense that had slowly been revealed to him in dreams that perhaps he had lived before, that he and Honey Radcliffe had been profoundly connected in that past.

The Protestant world Cameron had known as a white child promised eternal life for the chosen; the converted Apache believed in a hereafter for the honorable indian following a life that did not separate the natural and the supernatural. Yet neither society envisioned or promised a succession of lives on earth.

Dreams were important to Apache life, often to be acted upon, yet Apache traditions were not sufficient to explain the vivid, troubling images that came to Cameron unsummoned when he slept. Honey Radcliffe filled these nocturnal visions, sometimes in circumstances that were familiar, other times not, but always she was there. Soon it became clear that these dreams signified both the past and present—perhaps even the future.

If there was a connection of past to present life, in Cameron's mind it followed there would be atonement of one kind or another, a making right of wrong. To betray the affections of a woman as intimately connected to him as Honey Radcliffe was seemed only to beg for retribution, a profound conclusion for a man who as a rule was not given to even mild philosophizing.

Honey Radcliffe had changed the texture and the meaning of his dreams, his life. Ill disposed to trifle with her, therefore, Cameron began to give Honey more than his passionate regard and at the same time, guardedly, something less.

CHAPTER FORTY-ONE

On the Jornada the caravan traveled into the night for twelve hours without stopping, the wagons rolling forward until the daytime heat forced the men to let the beasts of burden rest. At six in the morning the thermometer approached a hundred degrees. After feeding and watering the animals and themselves, all the caravan members availed themselves of sleep.

At first the heat made sleep impossible for Honey, but finally, to escape the more intense heat of the wagon's enclosure, both she and Cameron took bedrolls and slept in the shade of the wagon. Exhausted by the heat alone, Honey was unable to fall immediately to sleep, but at last, feeling light-headed and drugged, she drifted uneasily into the void.

She woke some hours later to find Cameron also awake and propped on an elbow, smiling down at her. "I feel like I had too much whiskey, when I haven't." He ran his fingers through his hair. "Couldn't be more than two o'clock."

Too hot to breathe deeply, Honey rolled languidly on her side to face him. Not close enough to kiss him, she kissed one of her fingers and gently touched his lips. "You look as if you didn't sleep at all."

"I know I slept, because I had another strange dream."

"Of what?"

Cameron gazed at Honey thoughtfully. "If I told you, you'd say the sun's made me *loco*." He reached above his pillow for the canteen of water and offered it to her. "And if I'd not had the dream before, I'd agree with you."

Honey smiled at the irony in Cameron's voice and gratefully drank the warm water he gave her. "Tell me your dream. I promise not to make light of it."

Cameron looked at her speculatively. "Do you dream things over and over?"

"Sometimes."

"Then it means something."

Honey shrugged. "Perhaps."

Preferring not to let Honey look directly into his face and perhaps see him as a fool, before beginning Cameron lay back and stared up at the underside of the wagon bed. "I know it was you and me in my dream, though it wasn't," he began awkwardly. "That is, we weren't as we are now."

Honey's breath caught in her throat.

"We were someplace else and some other time, also." Cameron sighed. "You won't like most of it—"

"Go on," Honey urged impatiently, unable to imagine why he had stalled.

"You were a servant; at least you were dressed poorly in homespun—when you were dressed, that is. The country was rugged, beautiful, with many rivers and streams. Everything was green. I was a soldier in the cavalry with many men in my command. I wore plated armor sometimes, or strange clothing of fine materials, some with pearls stitched on.

"I loved you. You loved me. But because you were a servant and I wasn't, we could only be together in secret. I loved you, but we had words about another woman you thought I loved. When you learned I married the woman..." Cameron paused when his voice seemed suddenly to catch. He rolled on his side to face Honey again and grabbed her arm roughly. "You threw yourself under my soldiers' horses while I watched." His voice was full of pain. "You killed yourself and the baby you were carrying."

Taken by surprise by the intensity of his response as well as by the nature of his dream, Honey stared at Cameron wide-eyed. When she recovered her voice, she said defensively, "It hardly sounds something I would do." She tried to pull away. "It's only a dream, Cameron," she offered more soothingly, wishing to console herself as well.

Cameron recognized the tight grip he held on Honey and let go. "It felt real," he said emphatically. "What's even stranger, I've had the same dream before."

"So have I," Honey whispered.

Cameron took a deep breath in spite of the terrible heat and for several moments gazed fixedly at Honey, not certain he had heard her correctly. Then he lay back again, folding his arms behind his head. He stared without seeing at the wagon above them. "How can we have the same dream?" he finally wondered aloud. "I've heard of seeing the same sign, or hearing the same ghost, but not having the same vision."

Honey had no ready answer for him, and silence gathered between them. The camp was almost perfectly still, the heat seeming to have killed any desire for movement. They lay side by side, separate but unified in a confusion of thoughts. "You know what Shahar would say: We're together again for the purpose of . . . righting wrongs."

"How? How do you atone for killing yourself and our baby now?"

"I don't know," Honey answered with dismay, feeling a strong, clear sense of guilt. "You speak as if you've nothing to right. Surely you weren't completely innocent."

Cameron felt the weight of grief the dream they shared always evoked in him. Uncomfortable, he rolled on his side again and moved so that his body touched hers. He outlined the features of Honey's face with gentle, adoring fingers. "If my punishment is life without you, I will gladly give up this lifetime."

"Only to make the sin of taking your own life the one you must atone for in the next?"

Perplexed, Cameron shook his head slowly. "I only know I love you. I won't give you up for any reason, this life or any other."

"Nor I you," Honey pledged, as blind as he to what lay before them."

CHAPTER FORTY-TWO

Early the next morning the party reached the Cimarron River, and on the first Fourth of July since the end of the war the caravan wildly celebrated more than the end of their trek across the Jornada. Whiskey, which flowed faster than the river beside the campground, appeared early in the day. Cheer was high, and plans for spending time and money in Santa Fe abounded among the freighters. Game was soon caught and prepared for dinner, a feast highlighted by rabbit stew with wild rice and onions, corn bread, and fresh gooseberry pie.

"I hope you've got a good stiff boot on tonight," Nollie said to Honey when someone announced that the fiddler would begin to play just as soon as he finished a second helping of pie.

"A good idea," Honey answered, and hurried to put on her sturdiest pair of boots.

In the meantime Nollie made certain she was standing next to Cameron when the music started. "May I have this dance?" she said before he could find Honey in the crowd of men who also had their eye out for her.

Satan ain't black for no reason, Nollie thought to herself as she smiled up at Cameron with a purposefully innocent expression. *Nor you a man and me a woman.* Nollie wanted to laugh for joy. *White ladies get the good men, but sometimes black girls get them also. Anyways, this'n's more my kind than yours, Miz Honey.* She thought of her mother and Master Phillip Greer. *History is about to repeat itself, Mammy. And ain't nothin' you can do 'bout it.* What a soaring triumph it would be to have Honey's lover fall in love with her.

Nollie wondered what it would be like to have Cameron openly, unlike her mother's relationship with Dr. Greer. But however it worked out, Nollie felt in her bones that she would know the pleasure of having Honey's man right under her nose. Perhaps not now, but one day. The notion gave her a thrill. *This is the devil's doing, surely,* Nollie thought, and this time laughed out loud. She might love Honey sometimes as a sister, but at times the only emotion she felt was closer to hate.

Nollie moved a little closer into Cameron's embrace and, when Cameron adjusted his hold, gave no hint of satisfaction in her countenance. The dance was lively, but at every opportunity in which Nollie ordinarily would have withdrawn politely, she let Cameron touch her with more familiarity than necessary.

She succeeded in making Cameron feel only unusually clumsy, and he was grateful when Bobs Carney came to rescue him—and Nollie. Cameron went directly to claim Honey from another man's arms. "You'd best be wary. I've been stamping on Nollie's feet."

"You're not the only one," Honey offered. "But this time I've my heaviest boots for protection." Honey raised the hem of her skirt to confirm her choice of footwear, then allowed Cameron to pull her close.

He moaned softly in her ear. "My God, you smell good."

"A bath does wonders."

"The fact your perfume isn't whiskey helps." The music slowed a little, and Cameron moved deliberately against Honey as they danced. "Makes a man's blood warm."

"I've had enough heat for a while, thank you. I'm enjoying the cool night air." Light from the campfires made Honey's eyes shine.

"I want to kiss you."

Honey pretended to pull away. "Sir, in front of all these people?"

"Yes. Marry me. Avery could marry us tonight."

Honey stopped dancing. She stared at Cameron.

The noise of the men's voices in the circle surrounding the dancers gradually died down, and soon the fiddler stopped playing. The other women and their partners also grew still, but Honey seemed unaware of anything but Cameron. "No," she whispered as everyone strained to hear her. "I can't." Then, suddenly conscious of her vast audience, she fled from the center of the crowd. A loud murmur rose behind her, but almost immediately the fiddler's music filled the air again, and loud celebration soon followed.

The crowd had closed itself around Cameron, but pushing through it, he was fast on her heels. From behind, in midstride, he caught Honey's arm and pulled her to face him. "What's got into you?" he demanded. "You act as though I insulted you." His pleading turned rancorous as Cameron recalled all the moments from the first when he had felt Honey Radcliffe look down on him as though he were beneath her regard. "You think my proposal an insult?"

"No, no, never." This time Honey pulled Cameron into her arms and hugged him fiercely. Then, so that she could look him directly in the eye, she pushed him gently a few inches away. "It's too soon for me to marry. I'm only just a widow."

Cameron almost laughed. "A grieving widow you're not!" He looked down on Honey harshly. "That's not it."

Honey lowered her head. 'No," she said almost inaudibly, then raised her face again. "It *is* disgraceful to think of marrying this soon, but it's that I'm uneasy . . . uneasy with the idea of our shared dream, for one. And other things I can't explain."

Cameron nodded. "I see."

It was Honey's turn to be upset. "How can you, when I don't?" she demanded petulantly. "Ohhh, why is it so complicated?" She put her head against Cameron's chest and leaned against him. He was unresponsive. "Let's imagine you didn't ask me to marry you."

"I can't do that."

Honey sighed as she lifted her head and stood erect. "I'm going to bed."

"You go right ahead," Cameron said, and turned back to the roaring campfires and more amiable companions.

CHAPTER FORTY-THREE

After two exhausting days on the Jornada, the festivities of the evening were loud and long and equally well lubricated with alcoholic spirits but not quite as jubilant as the occasion of the Ramseys' wedding. Nollie was just as footsore, and Bobs Carney renewed the proposal that she had turned down once already. Nollie declined Bobs's offer for sound reasons, she thought, totally ignoring the reality of having turned her sights on another man: Cameron. She wished to have him with or without the sanctity of marriage, wholly disregarding her very argument against Bobs Carney's suit.

During the evening Nollie did not dance again with Cameron but on more than one occasion caught him looking at her speculatively. In response, she tried her most alluring smiles and poses and glanced suggestively in his direction. Her seductiveness produced no immediate results, but she was willing to be patient, sensing that Cameron was paying her more than her usual due. Patience, she noted, often won out.

At the close of the evening, Avery came forward. "What you all've been waiting for," he shouted, and had the revelers clear a wide space. There was clapping and cheering as he then proceeded to open a large chest of rockets and a small barrel of gunpowder. With the help of three of his men, soon the sky was alight with fiery trails and the air whistling then exploding with sound. When the last rocket expended itself, the party broke up.

By this time Nollie had positioned herself next to Cameron. "Walk me to my wagon, please," she said, and slipped her arm through his before he could respond one way or the other. "The journey's been unremarkable, wouldn't you say, Mr. Wolfe?"

Cameron laughed. "You've a very short memory," he said, well aware of how cozily Nollie had snuggled up to him.

"Well, I meant aside from that nasty cat. You did give us awful dire warnings and made us learn to shoot straight."

"The journey's not over. The best excitement might be coming up."

"I've been hearing some of the men talk of Santa Fe, of its fiestas and fandangos. Can we go to one?"

"Shahar might object."

"You saw, Mammy loves dancing. I hear the women wear bright colors even on their faces."

Cameron nodded. "And wives get won and lost at card games."

"It sounds almost wicked." Nollie's eagerness showed in her smile as they arrived at her wagon.

Shahar was waiting for her in the driver's box. "You best get in to bed, girl," she said sternly to her daughter. "This night's been long enough already." She offered Nollie a hand up. "Good night, Mr. Wolfe. I recommend not waking Mrs. Radcliffe."

"Wouldn't think of it," Cameron muttered, and took his bedroll from Honey's wagon and slept underneath the stars.

"Jeezzzzuss, Gaud, almighty," Avery shouted, and fired several rifle shots into the air. "Fire! Fire!" he screamed. The sleeping caravan sprang to its feet, collectively and instantly sobered. "Thought everything landed in the river," he said of the rockets.

The wind was in their favor, blowing away from camp. But wind direction changed at the whim of the gods, and no one wasted any time putting the caravan back on the road, any reluctance overcome by intimate knowledge of what a full-blown prairie fire could mean. "If the wind holds, it'll burn itself out on the river," Cameron suggested as Honey huddled against him in the driver's box for courage.

"When we arrive in Sacramento, ask me to marry you again," she urged in a half whisper.

In the gathering light of dawn, Cameron smiled down at Honey and knew he loved her more than life itself. "Think I'll let you ask me," he said as he wrapped one arm around her and pulled her close. "And *I* won't say no."

CHAPTER FORTY-FOUR

Originally the plan was for the caravan to rest on the fifth of July; therefore, by daybreak, when they were well away from danger, camp was made where they could linger overnight. "We're more than halfway to Santa Fe. If all goes well," Cameron promised Honey, "we'll be there in less than three weeks' time."

Honey smiled as if that were wonderful news, but she realized that Santa Fe was but half the journey they would make. She was, she realized, hardly a vagabond by nature. She was more than ready to settle in one spot and never move. *I'll never complain again about anything so trivial as bathwater being too tepid or a cushion at my back being not just so.* Trevor's home in Sacramento loomed a palace, a regular bath—even a tepid one —something of a fantasy.

But as the miles rolled by, instead of boredom, Honey began to be fascinated by an at first, almost imperceptible change in Nollie. Within a week, Honey realized her friend was trying to seduce Cameron before her eyes. Nothing bold, but a sweetness of tone, a lingering look, or when there was an occasion, the lengthening of a touch. At first Honey denied this change in her friend's attitude, but she soon realized that only a fool could have kept up that illusion for long. Occasionally Nollie would disappear from view, then Cameron. Then both would reappear, sometimes alone, sometimes together. Coincidence, Honey insisted to herself, and detected nothing guilty or sly about Cameron's behavior at least.

Reassuringly, Cameron appeared invulnerable to the onslaught of Nollie's charms and steadfast in his affection for Honey; therefore, when they at last arrived in Santa Fe, Honey was not the least prepared for Cameron's manifestly friendly response to another woman, an unlikely competitor named Tía Luz.

Santa Fe, unlike what Honey had been led to expect by road-weary freighters, was a dusty, dirty little town of adobe houses and government buildings all badly in need of paint, huddled around a large dusty center plaza. The streets were narrow, the landscape uninvitingly barren, and the climate unreasonably hot. "Frightful. Unkempt," Shahar pronounced.

But with the arrival of the caravan and its thirsty, trail-bored, about-to-be-paid freighters, the gay spirit of the town surfaced immediately. The air filled with the voices of welcoming citizens, Spanish guitars, and gay señoritas—the most massive in size and inelegantly boisterous of whom seemingly intimately acquainted with Cameron.

Dressed in black silk, a black lace mantilla, and fingerless lace gloves, Tía Luz immediately launched into a furious fire of Spanish, mingling her words with wild embraces and kisses to Cameron, who greeted her with similar enthusiasm in Spanish, their laughter unrestrained. Honey was nonplussed, and Nollie was horrified—and for the entire time in Santa Fe both women were extremely out of sorts.

Cameron seemed to know everyone in Santa Fe; the more outrageous, the better acquainted they appeared. Honey camouflaged her surprise well, and because many of the conversations were conducted in Spanish, knew little of the nature of the relationships. Cameron always introduced Honey, and she was treated with utmost deference by all, including Tía Luz.

The wagons whose cargoes were destined for Santa Fe were unloaded rapidly, and as quickly, the dancing and carousing began. With the exception of a good profit, the residents of Santa Fe liked nothing better than an excuse for a fiesta or fandango. Houses and larders were opened, and soon long, groaning tables with all manner of fragrant foods filled the wide verandas along the central square. The hotel, with its wide patio, was graced by the presence of the local women, young and old alike, dressed in their gayest party costumes. The more traditional ladies of Mexican descent dusted their faces with white powder and painted their cheeks and lips vermilion, their hair and throats festooned with colorful beads to match the bright colors of their dresses. For Honey, who was accustomed to more subdued shades and, lately, the black of mourning, the sight was indeed unusual.

But everyone seemed so naturally congenial, it was almost impossible for any of the women of the caravan—even Nollie— to remain aloof; none of the men had even considered remaining at a distance.

"There's a rumor that Tía Luz came to Santa Fe the year after the Spaniards arrived," Cameron explained jocularly when he noticed that an unnatural silence had overcome Honey. "That was in 1650." He smiled broadly, but Honey seemed not at all amused. "She's also the best monte player in the territory. Or Mexico," something Tía Luz demonstrated with regularity during the evenings they were in Santa Fe as she lawfully fleeced many a freighter of his recent earnings. "This I do as a favor to Señor Dillyham. Keeps his *hombres* from retiring before they finish the trip home. As you see, señora, there are many more temptations in this place."

What she alluded to, Honey could not imagine, but she smiled and in response received a broad grin that revealed several of Tía Luz's teeth were missing. The woman then shoved a long black cigar into the most prominent space, puffed energetically, and slapped Cameron heartily on the back. "My favorite *gringo*," she confided to Honey as she fondled his arm. "And he dares to show his face with a beautiful señora in tow. You care nothing if you break *mi corazón*. *¡Tu eres el diablo, Señor Coyote!*"

To Honey's astonishment, genuine tears appeared to fill Tía Luz's eyes, but not for long as another willing monte victim sat down optimistically before her. "*Vete mi amor y bailes con tu reina mientras le quito dinero miserable de esto hijo de puta.*"

To the sound of her laughter, Cameron led Honey away from the monte table. He fed her bits of unusual and deliciously spiced foods and quenched her thirst with champagne. Then he brought her to the dance floor, where they waltzed to violins and sad Spanish guitars.

The unrestrained joviality continued until well past midnight, not a soul seeming to want the gaiety to end. The warmth and openness that pervaded the atmosphere had infected Honey, and she brought Cameron directly to her room at the hotel without imposing any form of subterfuge, as she at least would have ordinarily considered.

In the morning she blamed the champagne for her wanton conduct but admitted, "Truthfully, the good opinion of the people of Santa Fe is of no consequence to me." She moved on top of Cameron and began to kiss him. "While you, my love, have the esteem of nearly *everyone*. You could be mayor or, perhaps, governor of the territory, if you desired."

"All I desire is you." He tried to make her straddle him, but she preferred to tease.

"You say that now, señor, but what of Tía Luz? She fondles you publicly. You keep secrets from me, I'm certain. Do you see *her* in your dreams?"

Cameron laughed loudly. "Perhaps she was one of my soldiers."

"The one whose horse stepped on my face and broke my cheekbones and nose."

Cameron frowned. "I've been witness to many deaths, but none troubles me the way yours does. None." He sounded convincingly distraught.

Honey kissed him gently. "Perhaps it was . . . only a dream," she offered.

"Do you believe that?"

"No," she answered solemnly.

"Neither do I."

CHAPTER FORTY-FIVE

At noon in August, Santa Fe baked in the sun. Everyone who could retreated to the relative cool of adobe houses for at least a brief siesta. Honey chose this time to bathe, cherishing the slight chill she experienced when she stepped out of the tepid bath and the dry desert air quickly evaporated the water from her skin. Cameron sat with her and brought her to bed as soon as she stepped from the tin tub.

"Soon we'll be on the hot dusty trail and forced to forgo these pleasures," he said. They had only lingered in Santa Fe because Ruth Ramsey had taken ill suddenly.

"Perhaps the food?" Nollie had suggested. "It's disagreeable enough." But no one else had become sick.

"Perhaps the oldest ailment known to woman," Shahar remarked.

As Ruth was more ill in the mornings, Honey felt Shahar's suspicions were more than likely correct. "We'll know in a day or two."

Half of the number of Avery Dillingham's wagons, which had been emptied of cargo at the Santa Fe trading post, were now loaded with wool to be hauled back to Leavenworth on the return trip. These wagons, along with one-third of the crew assigned to them, would wait in Santa Fe while the rest of the freighters continued into Chihuahua, Mexico, with the remainder of the caravan's cargo.

Cameron had intended for the North Carolina party to ride with Avery's caravan along the Rio Grande as far south as Fort Seldon, where they would then turn west and head for the Gila River and meander with that waterway across the territories of New Mexico and Arizona into California. When it was clear Ruth Ramsey was not seriously ill but merely pregnant, Cameron continued with this original plan in spite of the considerable discomfort of the patient in her rolling wagon.

"Serves her right," Nollie judged as they jostled along the slow, sandy road.

"Don't be so quick to speak," her mother cautioned. "You might someday be cursed the same way."

"As I never intend to marry, I won't trouble myself to worry," Nollie answered saucily, utterly disregarding her continuing plan to woo Cameron from Honey.

"That's what you say *now*."

"That's what I'll *always* say," Nollie said as she watched out the back of her wagon with a jealous eye on Honey, who sat next to Cameron in the driver's box of their wagon.

"Then *I* needn't worry about you lately watching Mr. Cameron like a hungry cat eyes a fat bird."

Nollie stiffened. "What makes you say so?"

"I've got eyes."

"In the back of your head. Not to forget your third eye." Nollie purposely turned her gaze away from Honey's wagon. "So what's your prophecy?"

Shahar put her mending down in her lap. "I've nothing clear."

"Well, I do. I'm not getting no man's big belly. I see no good reason to bring somebody's brat into the world . . . or if I get myself carried away, I'll come to you for one of your potions you were always mixing up when their daddy found out the Greer boy'd seeded a slave woman. You needn't feel bad. We just be setting another soul free."

Shahar took a deep breath and let it out quickly, letting Nollie's jibes go by her. "Better you use caution in the first place," she urged firmly.

"Don't you go worrying yourself about me."

"Somebody needs to."

But if there was worry in anyone's heart as the North Carolina party continued south toward the border with Mexico on the last leg of the Santa Fe Trail, each one kept it to himself. Those in charge, however, were keenly aware they were in Apache country. The road followed the east bank of the Rio Grande to Albuquerque, a settlement south of the river in a broad river valley surrounded on the east and west by high tablelands and mountains. Honey remembered the name of Albuquerque from the war. Confederate General H. H. Sibley had occupied the town early in the war but had fled after only a brief tenure. Honey saw little to stay for. Off the road one encountered varieties of thorned bushes and cacti, a very inhospitable tract.

South of Albuquerque to Socorro the going was exceedingly slow, the rolling flat road of sand, the heat intense. They started at daybreak and quit about ten in the morning to rest in the high heat of the day, embarking again early in the evening and not stopping until after midnight. It took three days to reach Socorro, a settlement west of the Rio Grande in a flat river valley at the foot of impressive hills. As they journeyed south, they were surrounded both east and west by mountains.

The caravan rested two nights near Socorro, where there was ample food and water for the animals and, in the central marketplace in town, supplies of fresh fruits, vegetables, meat, and eggs and, regrettably, ample supplies of liquor. They stayed over ostensibly to fortify the animals for the forthcoming three-day stretch across the waterless Jornada del Muerto desert, for which the Little Jornada some weeks earlier had been training, but the freighters also fortified themselves for the dry road. "I think they get stinking drunk," Nollie theorized, "so they feel so low and miserable already, they won't notice so much the hard traveling ahead."

Honey thought the idea a novel one. She discovered that her memory of the Little Jornada was insufficient to prepare her for the Jornada del Muerto. In her imagination, hell itself was more pleasant. However, at least traveling at night they were escorted by a luminous full moon that cast an eerily beautiful light over the desert landscape.

Past La Jornada, they were glad to arrive at Fort Seldon, where the party of eight from Greerfield was due to separate from the larger caravan and head west on their own. The numbers of troops at Fort Seldon had recently been increased to deal with the increase in Apache depredations, a fact concealed from the four women who bade good-bye to Avery and his freighters filled with hope and great eagerness for their separate journey.

Cameron and the other men kept their knowledge of recent Apache attacks on wagon trains, ranches, and towns in the region—reputedly Cheis's band—strictly to themselves. They directed the wagons toward the Gila River beneath the Mogollon mountain range and past Ojo Caliente, home to the Apache Chihuahua's band, their every nerve on edge. It was country Cameron Wolfe knew extremely well, for he had lived there, and the deeper they traveled into Apacheria, the keener his memory and senses became.

With the sale of one wagon in Santa Fe, which the party no longer needed for supplies, William Rourke assumed the responsibility of driving Honey's wagon, allowing Cameron to ride horseback well ahead of the small train. In this manner he could scout the region as well as more effectively distance himself emotionally from the other members of the party. With every mile they traveled west, Cameron became more the Apache warrior and less the white eyes.

Cameron knew for a fact that the thievery and depredations the Apache were accused of were frequently the work of Mexican or American miscreants. For every head of stock carried off by the Apache, four were stolen by white thieves. Fortunately, this leg of the journey, which carried them into the Arizona Territory, proved uneventful.

Honey found it difficult to penetrate Cameron's increasingly remote silence. The river of emotion between them, as she thought of it, had narrowed to a trickle, as did the waters of the Gila River they now followed west.

"Have you seen something? Are we in danger?" Honey prodded, wondering whether she ought to worry. His one-syllable replies did not satisfy her. "Have you a fever?" she wondered, putting her hand to his forehead. She had come up behind him as he sat drinking coffee by the campfire. He shrugged her hand away. She began to massage his shoulders and neck. "You're so strained. There's something you're not telling me. You've spotted indians, haven't you?"

"When you see an Apache, it's too late."

"Are we in danger of imminent attack?"

Cameron took Honey's hand from his shoulder and drew her to his side. "No."

Even in their wagon, Cameron managed to keep to himself. While she held him in her arms, Honey sensed he wasn't with her in spirit, her ecstasy diminished by his apparent distraction. Spiraling to the earth alone, tears filled Honey's eyes.

Cameron fell asleep completely unaware.

Late as it was, Honey's imagination ran wild: *He's tired of me; Nollie's caught his eye.* She forced herself to remain calm. She listened to Cameron's regular breathing. Perhaps, in spite of what he said or did not say, he was only worried about the Apache. Honey shivered; her worst fears about the journey west loomed before her in the dark: a picture of a man riding a jet-black stallion, a half-naked, half-human beast with a long feathered headdress flowing down his back, carrying a weighted lance, leapt before her mind's eye.

Honey sat up in bed, jostling Cameron, who woke abruptly. "What is it?"

"Nothing." She could give one-word answers too, she thought as she replied.

"Maybe I should take a bedroll under the wagon if you can't sleep."

"Go."

For a moment Cameron stared at Honey in the dark, then started to rise.

"No. *Please* stay." She held his arm. "I'm afraid."

Cameron pushed the hair that fell against Honey's cheek behind her ear and drew her mouth to his. "The Apache fears nothing. You best face him without fear, also."

"Then they *are* watching us."

"There is nothing that comes into this territory that the Apache doesn't see. They've a head count even on rattlesnakes."

Honey couldn't help but laugh. "But it's not *their* country anymore."

"This has always been Apache land. The Americans took it from the Mexicans. The problem is, it wasn't theirs to surrender."

"That argument won't keep white men out."

"Then they'll continue to pay a heavy price for trespassing."

"You sound as though your sympathies lie with the savages. The Apache are no better than fiends. Why, they murder women and children!"

"There's a bounty for Apache scalps—man, woman, or child. A hundred dollars for adult scalps, fifty for children."

"Dear God," Honey gasped.

Cameron nodded.

"Tell me why you've been so sullen since we left Fort Seldon."

"This is difficult country."

"What you mean to say is, dangerous." Honey shuddered. "I wish now I'd never left home. The scenery is perfectly hideous; even the river is ridiculous. How can you call something that narrows to a trickle a river? Why, it's laughable. As far as I'm concerned, the Apache can have this country *forevermore*."

"I'd love to show you this country. There're places in the mountains that're as close to heaven as you'll find on earth."

"With Apache nearby it couldn't possibly be heaven."

Cameron knew there would be no convincing Honey otherwise. He said nothing else but pulled Honey against him and for the moment eased her fear of marauding indians by holding her close.

CHAPTER FORTY-SIX

Cameron did not completely allay Honey's apprehensions about the Apache. Nevertheless, she and the rest of the party were unprepared for the attack. With soul-piercing ululating cries, bare-chested warriors sprang upon them as if they had materialized from thin air. Cameron's words "When you see an Apache, it's too late" had been prophetic. Their warriors' agility and brutal methods were exceedingly quick and efficiently administered; their reputation as living demons amply justified in Honey's mind.

While they ate breakfast at dawn, a band of five Apache warriors fell on the small wagon train, striking Roarke Murray and Timothy Watts dead with lance and bow and arrow before either man could react. The women ran screaming for their wagons, with Nollie falling injured from a gunshot wound in midstride and, nearby, Shahar struck unconscious by a blow from a war club. Ruth Ramsey died clinging to the wheel rim of her wagon, and her husband, Wilton, of knife wounds near the morning campfire.

Initially owing to her tardy presence in her wagon, only Honey escaped harm. Still dressing, standing in a shawl, chemise, and petticoat, she observed the murder scene in frozen horror. The dark-skinned Apache were of small stature, with straight black hair of such great length that the ends were twisted and looped into the waistbands of the warriors' deerskin breechclouts and kept off the forehead by a band of cloth. On their feet and legs the indians wore high-topped moccasins that reached their knees, and they carried an assortment of weapons they used with consummate skill: guns, knives, lances, war clubs, bows and arrows. With ferocious grace each man moved swiftly, their contorted expressions making them seem vicious gargoyles.

Honey was spellbound by terror and shock and by Cameron's reaction, the only one among their party to truly engage the enemy. He maneuvered as nimbly as the Apache, killing two with knife and gun and wounding another. Then, after several long minutes of violent athletic combat with a third warrior, he collapsed. Only then did Honey move from her petrified stance.

Cameron's body hardly touched the ground before she emerged from her wagon like a banshee, shrieking with tortured grief. Before she reached him, Honey was captured, restrained by the half-naked murdering Apache whom she thought had slain her lover.

With no regard for her own life, Honey continued to struggle to reach Cameron's side. Her aggressor, no taller than she, had at least three times her strength. Despite this, driven by powerful forces suddenly unleashed, Honey forced her captor to yield. She knelt beside Cameron and at first screamed outraged invectives at the indians.

Upon touching Cameron, however, Honey grew silent. She caressed his face, certain he was dead. She lifted his head into her lap and began to sob, yet by training, without thinking, her fingers felt for a pulse and she examined his numerous wounds.

Soon she was soaked with his blood and totally unaware of the three remaining Apache who stood over her or of their arguing. When Honey realized Cameron was not yet dead, she began to speak low and lovingly to him. "Please," she begged, "live. Don't leave me alone with these murderers." Too immersed in caring for him, she could not cry as she pressed the most vicious of several knife wounds to his chest with her hand. As his lifeblood ran from him, Honey felt as if an essence of her own self was flowing with it, and only after what seemed a horribly long time was she able to stem the bleeding.

With nothing to fear from her or anyone, the warriors did not interrupt but left Honey and her patient alone and ransacked the wagons, looking for desired booty with surprising speed and skill born of experience.

Meanwhile, Nollie and then Shahar came to their senses. The gunshot wound to Nollie's thigh had missed the bone and, after bleeding vigorously, had clotted successfully. She pretended to be dead until one of the indians came to her, fearing she was about to be scalped, she gave herself away, screaming loudly the moment the warrior touched her. To her utter surprise, he did not kill her but swiftly bound her hands and feet together. Rendered helpless, she was furious. "Dirty, filthy, stinking pig!" she spat. If he had understood her words, the warrior would have done more than silence her with a slap so powerful that tears came to her eyes, which he followed with a telling gesture of his knife.

More cautious when she revived, Shahar was silent and, swaying dizzily, hurried to Honey's side. "He's not dead. He can't be."

"No. Not yet," Honey said, stifling a sob. "Oh, my God, Shahar, how can I help him here in this hideous wilderness?" She gestured despairingly to the wide plain that spread from the shallow Gila River with its sparsely scattered thorny, faded green shrubs and few miserable-looking trees with hideously twisted limbs and shriveled leaves.

She had ripped several tiers from one of her petticoats for bandages and, stripping away his shirt, swathed the worst of Cameron's wounds. "I suppose these murdering savages won't let any of us live for long," she said before she thought.

"Why haven't they killed us already?" Shahar whispered fearfully.

"You tell me!" Honey answered, silent at the one possibility more terrifying than death to her. All three women thought they knew what it meant to be a female captive of indians. Without giving details, even Cameron had told the women they would be better off dead. "Save a bullet for yourself," Honey remembered fearfully.

When at last she and Shahar looked again to the scene around them, they saw all but one wagon overturned and the remaining wagon piled high with what the indians considered valuable: food, tools, utensils, and weapons. The saddle horses were gathered up, the oxen's throats cut, fire set to all else. In a wild dash, Honey managed to retrieve more petticoats and a dress of hers and put them on. Finally, in full view of the horrified women, the heads of the dead were severed from their bodies and impaled on poles.

Only Honey, who had seen many unspeakable sights on stilled battlegrounds, did not vomit, but she did not escape the conviction held by the two other female survivors that they soon would be forced to endure an even more loathsome fate.

"Oh, Lord in heaven, what do they plan to do with us?" Nollie cried.

One by one, then, the women were approached by the warriors. Expecting the worst, they struggled and were beaten. Nollie, her hands and feet untied, made a brave resistance and, before subdued, suffered a broken nose and two black eyes. Honey, with hardly better luck, sustained a bloody nose and a nasty trail of abrasions along her lower jaw and lip as in her struggle she was dragged facedown in the rocky dirt. The final insult came when she at last was restrained by a warrior, who straddled her obscenely to wrench Nathan's locket violently from her throat, the necklace chain cutting viciously into her tender skin. She screamed and tried to capture the necklace, but the warrior only laughed as he held it out of reach.

Still dizzy, Shahar was no match for her assailant, and soon all three women found themselves seated on saddle horses, hands lashed to saddle horns, feet to stirrups. "I expected much worse," Nollie said to Honey under her breath.

"As did we all," Honey answered.

Next, to their astonishment, from their horses, which were tethered in a line behind the wagon, they saw the Apaches lift Cameron gently into the wagon, then carefully lower him to a thin mattress and cover him with a blanket.

As they followed along behind the wagon, Honey, dazed and already grieving, watched her precious lover and, knowing nothing else to do, poured out her heart in tears and frantic, silent prayer.

CHAPTER FORTY-SEVEN

If not trussed on their horses, the women would have fallen to the ground with fatigue, for they had traveled behind the solitary wagon from just after sunrise until almost dusk. With her beating and the jostling on her horse, Nollie's thigh wound had opened, but eventually it closed again. All three burned with thirst and from direct exposure to the sun. They were half-dead and held no hope at all for Cameron.

As they traveled, the women had watched the blanket that covered him slowly become saturated with blood. Honey had cried bitterly until she felt certain she would never cry again, even if she lived to a ripe old age. Now, numb and silent, she stared at something unseen with no visible expression in her face or eyes.

Finally the indians brought the women, the wagon, and themselves from an open plain to the edge of a region of fantastic rock formations. Instead of turning the direction of their travel, they stopped. The women looked up into the mountain of rocks and at the Apache in wonderment, then at each other with obvious bewilderment.

Only Nollie spoke. "I suppose they expect us to climb this rock pile," she said disgustedly to Honey, her bruised eye closed shut. "Water. Water, *please*," she demanded.

Much to the women's astonishment, the indians appeared to understand and offered each of them a brief turn at an animal skin filled with water.

When it came her turn, Honey gestured in Cameron's direction. "Please, let me see to him." With her hand she patted her own chest. "Wounds. I must look after his wounds." But as one of the savages began to untie Honey, Nollie began to whimper with fear.

"They're not going to let you touch him. They be after you!" Nollie began to squirm and weep.

Honey was none too sure of the indian's intention and, heart pounding, watched him undo her restraints. He handled her roughly then, and terror made her tremble, but he brought her to Cameron without delay.

In anguish, Honey cried softly as she fell to her knees beside him. Cameron seemed almost not to be breathing, and his skin felt cool, but it was not the chill of death. Quickly she ripped more of her petticoat and applied fresh bandages. He had bled significantly, but at the moment there was only slight seepage from his wounds.

Honey reached for another blanket from a pile the indians had seized. As she did, a strong, filthy hand grabbed hers. She looked up into the black eyes of an Apache who seemed more a creature from hell than a human being. She could barely speak, her voice a hoarse whisper as she shoved Cameron's blood-soaked blanket into the indian's face. "This is no good anymore. It won't keep him warm." She shivered for emphasis, not needing to pretend to tremble as she quaked before the beast who had brought Cameron down. Yet she remembered he had also been the man who later seemed to speak in Cameron's favor and apparently saved him from being killed outright or left to die on the trail. When at last the fearsome Apache let go of her hand, Honey quickly covered Cameron with two fresh blankets without further hindrance.

Honey then appealed in pantomime for water, which she received, and bathed Cameron's face and lips, but this did not revive him as she had hoped against hope it might.

All the while she looked after Cameron, the Apaches unloaded the wagon. They spoke very little to each other, obviously companions who had done this sort of thing on numerous other occasions. When it was empty of all but Cameron and his mattress, they removed him to the ground and began to dismantle the wagon.

The women watched curiously as the indians constructed a kind of triangular stretcher, using blankets and lumber from the wagon. When finished, they loaded Cameron with the mattress beneath him on the stretcher and trussed him to it to prevent his sliding off. Shahar and Nollie were then enlisted to bear him as if they were draft animals. Leather thongs were harnessed around their chests so that they could pull him like horses before a plow.

"No," Honey protested loudly. "You've horses," she insisted, gesturing, she thought, clearly. In answer, one of the warriors shoved Honey brutally to the ground, at which Nollie began to scream. This caused her to be slapped viciously several times, which did nothing to improve the condition of her already bruised eyes and broken nose and nearly caused her and her mother to lose their balance. They grabbed at each other to steady themselves, fearing for Cameron's safety. "I'm naming that one Rat Face," Nollie muttered venomously, spitting blood from a badly cut lip and tongue. "Where does this figure in your prophecies, Mammy?"

Shahar did not answer the challenge.

"Shut your mouth, Nollie. Now is not the time," Honey said as she got shakily to her feet. For once Nollie said nothing more.

Another travois fitted with booty was prepared and strapped to Honey. She looked around them slowly. "Where in heaven do you suppose they expect us to go? Surely not up these rocks?"

"Surely not," Shahar echoed.

But after the horses and mules were packed with all the goods in the wagon and the remains of the wagon were set on fire, to the women's astonishment, that was exactly where they were led. Into an unseen passageway, through giant walls of rocks, the women disappeared into a fortress. With daylight waning, they were led into a series of wooded valleys filled with lush vegetation and sliced with streams. As they were led into this heavenly landscape, each woman separately believed she would never live to see the outside world again.

CHAPTER FORTY-EIGHT

The arrival of four strangers and the booty from a raid in the indian encampment occasioned much excitement. The dark-faced Apache gathered around them, with Cameron's presence and, perhaps, the gravity of his disability a cause of apparent concern. Honey, Shahar, and Nollie, lame from the trek, were terrified and viewed every approach by their stern and curious hosts as threatening. Honey covered her panic by trying to persuade her captors to let her examine Cameron again. "Please," she begged, dreading an inability to communicate, "let me look after him." Her approach was met with resistance. Rat Face, as Nollie called him, shoved Honey roughly back into place. Furious, Honey could do nothing but acquiesce for the moment.

When Cameron's crude stretcher was removed to an equally crude shelter made of brush and twigs, Honey attempted to follow. "I must look after him, otherwise he will die." Tears sprang to her eyes and coursed readily down her face. "He may die anyway," she sobbed, "but let me at least try to help him."

Although no one appeared to understand her words, the heartfelt tone of her pleading and perhaps her tears, which were obviously not for herself, conveyed her message. She was allowed to follow Cameron into the fragile-appearing brush structure. She had motioned Shahar and Nollie to come along, but they were restrained. She would have to go alone.

Honey ignored her lover's grim-faced indian attendants and fell to her knees beside him. When she touched Cameron, she forgot everything else, the awful cold of his skin making her own blood icy. Honey was glad for a small fire at the center of the hut, ventilated by a gap at the top of the structure's outer covering. She wished the fire larger but acknowledged that wish dangerous in a house made of straw.

"Orderly, more blankets," Honey demanded as if she were still in a Confederate field hospital, and looked up into the blank eyes of three Apache. Realizing at once where she was and knowing that conditions were far more desperate than they had been in the war, she gestured at the bloody blanket Cameron had worn most of the day. She waved it imploringly. Next, she hugged herself and pretended to shiver violently. "Blanket. Blanket," she said loudly, as if the Apache were hard of hearing, not ignorant of English.

A light appeared in the eyes of one indian, who immediately left and returned moments later with a large but very dirty buffalo hide, which he presented to Honey before gently covering her patient. Honey winced at the soiled, matted condition of the hide but, knowing it was fruitless, did not protest. Soiled or not, the blanket would provide the warmth Cameron urgently needed.

Turning back the hide blanket for the moment, Honey examined Cameron's wounds while an Apache she had not seen before entered the wickiup carrying a basket filled with flat paddle-shaped, thorn-covered leaves. Honey watched with as much curiosity as apprehension while the indian took each leaf and burned off its numerous thorns in the fire, then divided the leaf in half with a knife to completely expose a gelatinous interior, which he then applied directly to Cameron's wounds, repeating this until all the wounds were covered with leaves. Honey then tore more fabric from her petticoats and wrapped this makeshift bandage carefully about Cameron's chest, all the while beseeching God aloud to spare him. "Let this do more good than ill," she prayed.

The other indians in the wickiup watched Honey silently, but amid her ministrations to Cameron, she had only fleetingly been aware of them. Now she looked into their blank countenances, unable to fathom their opinions. "I'll keep vigil," she said as firmly as she dared, and settled into a sitting position next to Cameron, legs crossed, prepared to roost there the night if they would only allow it. She made a cup of her hands and pretended to drink. "Water, please."

The medicine man who had applied the leaves to Cameron's wounds left the shelter and summoned a woman, who brought water for Honey in a large gourd. Unsmiling, the woman poured water into a small clay cup for Honey.

Grateful and nearly desperate from thirst, Honey drank greedily, then proffered the cup for more. She was not refused, but when she asked for a third filling, hoping to bathe the dirt from the abrasions on her face, Rat Face bade the indian woman put the gourd jug down out of Honey's reach, then snarled rather than spoke words that Honey, without much confidence, interpreted to mean that for now she should drink no more. Then she and Cameron were left with only one guard, who stared at her with a dogged expression.

Exhausted, Honey could have fallen asleep sitting upright without much trouble but for the growling in her stomach. For the first time in the long day she felt hungry. She was also worried about Nollie and particularly about Shahar. Honey preferred not to look the indian who watched over her and Cameron in the eye, but hunger drove her to attempt communication. She rubbed her stomach with her hand in a circular motion and then pretended to eat.

Her guardian stared at her, unmoved.

"You've a gift for lively conversation," Honey said with weary disgust. "I suppose we'll starve to death before someone thinks to feed us." She felt like crying but assumed a stoic pose, not daring to stare down her attendant. Her prediction of starvation was avoided when within minutes food was brought to her. "My friends?" she inquired of the woman who brought her food. "What of my friends?"

Honey started to rise, but her guardian put a forceful hand on her shoulder. "I must see to my friends. They were injured this morning also." This time she was allowed to go to the outer opening of the wickiup and look out. She turned in indignation. "How dare you tie them up?" Honey demanded at seeing Nollie and Shahar tethered loosely to a sapling no more than six feet from her door. Their hands were tied behind them, and their feet were bound at the ankles. But worse, they wore a leather collar that was attached to the tree. "They're not cattle," Honey cried, and moved forward, intending to undo them, but was forcefully restrained and brought to sit by the fire with Cameron once again. A clay bowl of gruel and some flat bread were pushed roughly in front of her. That she should mind her own business and eat was clearly the message.

Honey scowled at her jailer. "I hate to think what this could be," she said as she lifted the bowl of warm mush. She sniffed for an aroma, which turned out to be bland, and took a cautious bite of the mild, nut-flavored bread. Quickly she devoured both bread and gruel. "If I weren't half-starved, I'd not be impressed," she said, pushing the empty bowl away from her but grateful nonetheless.

Cameron stirred then, and Honey almost leapt in his direction. She felt his forehead and took one of his hands from beneath the buffalo robe. He was reassuringly warm. "My love," she crooned, and smoothed the hair from his forehead.

"Water," Honey said automatically, and when there was no response left Cameron's side and retrieved the water gourd and cup herself. She poured a small portion of water into the cup and used it to bathe his face. "This will help," she promised him as if they were alone. She left a few drops on his lips and, forgetting her audience, lightly kissed his cheeks, his mouth, his eyes. "You must live," she whispered, and as she never had before, tried consciously to pass her strength and will to live to him. "For me. For us," she cried.

CHAPTER FORTY-NINE

Darkness settled quietly over the valley while Honey sat next to Cameron as he hovered near death, afraid if she closed her eyes, he would die and the indians would steal his body away so that she would never see him again. She was, she thought, too tired to feel any fear of the Apache warrior who stared at her impassively while he sat across the fire from her. He looked to her like the other Apache she had seen, all of whom she judged to be cruel, calculating, and cold. She could not suppress a shiver at the precise coincidence of her earlier imaginings about savages who lived in the region and what she now judged to be true. How Cameron could have spoken even mildly in the defense of such people astonished her.

Her Apache guardian seemed watchful rather than sleepless, the personification of the cunning warrior. That the indians might fear anything from a sorely wounded man, Honey doubted, her curiosity about their having saved him, Shahar, Nollie, and herself enormous. What the savages could want with them, she preferred not to imagine. Perhaps a ransom. But who would ransom them? Trevor was so far away, and . . .

Honey stood and moved to the blanket-covered entrance of the wickiup. Her guardian stood also. He moved toward her but did not impede her as she pushed aside the covering. "Shahar, Nollie?" she called softly, and prayed she would not wake the entire camp and bring the wrath of the savages upon them.

"We're here," Nollie answered in a hoarse whisper. "Are you all right? And Mr. Wolfe?"

When Honey's eyes adjusted to the dark, she rushed to them, knelt down and embraced them both. All three women began to cry.

"We're all right," Nollie whispered, "at least for the moment. The bleeding of my leg has stopped, and they fed us—after they chained us like dogs. Look, they even gave us blankets. This one's yours," she said, holding up Honey's quilt. "I need it, or I'd give it to you."

"Thank God you're safe! Don't worry about me for now—I've a blanket and a fire." Honey wanted to tell them of Cameron's condition but feared articulating the worst. "I'm afraid to leave him any longer than a moment," she cried, yet did not completely break down. "Dear God, what a day! And I'd thought I'd seen all there was of inhumanity."

Calm again, Shahar was all that Honey hoped for. "Don't concern yourself with us. Go back to Mr. Cameron. Lend him your strength. Heal him with your love."

Honey embraced them one last time, then returned to Cameron and, much like a child who is terrified of the dark, tried to force herself to stay awake. Tears came easily to her eyes as, wearier than she remembered ever being, she sat cross-legged and stared at Cameron's still figure. She prayed for strength—for herself and for him—and refused to dwell on anything but his survival or to admit any of the frightening images that nagged at the edges of her mind.

Without her knowing, Honey's eyes closed and she slept. Slowly, she drifted down, pulled physically away from ordinary reality to enter the world of dreams as easily as if she had stepped from one room into another.

First the blurred horror of the Apache attack on the small Greerfield party replayed itself: She saw Cameron struck down and herself flying to his side. Then the scene changed, and they were in North Carolina, where she sat by the bedside while he lay ill with fever. She heard again fragments of his peculiar ramblings in an unknown tongue. Her dream then ricocheted from quiet bedside to the trail's bloody horror, the cadence, rhyme, and tone of the strange language suddenly familiar. She heard the ululating cry that had set her hair on end. Heart pounding, Honey woke from her vision with a start, a distressed cry escaping her throat as she realized Cameron Wolfe spoke Apache!

Honey's impassive guardian did not seem alarmed.

Honey took a deep breath and tried to clear her head, aghast that Cameron would have knowledge of the indian language. With due respect for the upright lance planted menacingly in front of the warrior, Honey stirred cautiously, rising to her knees.

Anxiously, she touched Cameron's face with a cool hand, to find him reassuringly warm. It was a hopeful sign, although she knew he was far from being out of danger. Agonizingly, there was still nothing for her to do but wait.

Honey took one of Cameron's hands from beneath the blankets and pressed kisses into the open palm. "I don't pretend to understand," she whispered of her revelation. "If you should die, my love, I'll wait for you to come to me again," she whispered, her voice catching on tears. This promise gave her comfort and managed to forestall the overwhelming grief that already was gathering within her.

She thought of her father and Shahar and of Shahar's almost unnatural calm following Phillip Greer's death. Shahar had grieved as they all had, but in a markedly reserved fashion, effortlessly preserving the illusion that she and her master had been nothing but slave and owner. Yet a greater demonstration of grief would have been within respectable bounds.

Had Honey not known of her father's deep regard for Shahar or been privy to their apparent affectionate regard for each other, which had seemed wholly natural and proper, she would have questioned Shahar's true feelings for her father. Only in the face of Nathan's death did Honey reproach Shahar for her stoicism. "Is that how you get by death so easily," Honey had charged, "by ignoring it? When Lin-Davey died, you shrugged your shoulders. When my father died, you took to bed dry-eyed while the wailing of other slaves filled the air for days. If I'd not known otherwise, I'd've thought you, at best, indifferent."

Shahar answered with confidence. "Your father and I will meet again. This is but one lifetime, not our last together. And then . . ."

"And then?" Honey prompted.

"One day we shall be united with God forever."

Shahar did not believe in man's descent from lower forms of life but believed the various estates in human form to be punishment enough for failures in a given lifetime. She also varied from traditional Hindu belief by insisting God loved women as well as men: He did not punish a male soul by giving it another life in female form. "There are joys and lessons to be learned which can only be gained as a woman," Shahar persisted.

On her knees, Honey held Cameron's hand in hers and stared

at the man she loved. She wanted with all her heart to believe Shahar's philosophy of hope. This mysterious man she clung to, who in fever spoke a foreign tongue she now suspected was Apache, seemed undeniably a part of her, a part that she could never forget or deny.

Honey held this last declaration as solid truth, but she could also not ignore her other fresh assumption: Cameron's connection to their vicious captors. If in fact he had spoken the Apache language in his fevered slumber, she reasoned he was more than briefly acquainted with the Apache. Surely Cameron's life and their lives had been spared only because at least one warrior had recognized him.

Honey remembered her first impression of Cameron. Certainly he had a savage grace, a way of moving that spoke of the cunning warrior, a fearlessness, the power and daring of a wild animal. She shivered at the images she was suddenly able to conjur—and for a fleeting instant wished for her precious lover's death so that she might be spared firm knowledge of what she now feared as truth.

CHAPTER FIFTY

When Cameron lay near death, as close to the spirit world as a man can come, except for his visions of Honey Radcliffe, the images that floated in his brain were Chiricahua. Many times he dreamed of the owl, which to the Apache is a messenger of the dead and sometimes an omen of death. And even in the midst of dreaming, Cameron knew it was a sign that he soon would die. Perhaps, he would later muse, his Apache dreams had been interspersed with glimpses of the earthbound—of shimmering light-colored hair and the reflection of dark golden eyes—to give his spirit reason to cling tenaciously to life.

Slowly, far into the Arizona Territory under the burning Chiricahua sun, before the color of his white man's skin had deepened several shades, Fierce Enemy, in flight from another kind of grave, emerged once again from the soul of Cameron Wolfe.

But Honey, unaware of this metamorphosis, was joyful only to see recognition fill her lover's eyes. For him, she had breached strict codes of conduct that had ruled her life as a Southern gentlewoman, and now, gazing into Cameron's open eyes, Honey knew there had been for her no other possible course.

She smiled at him, silent as tears coursed down her dirty face. In tatters, bloodied and bruised, her skin parched from the dry air, long curls knotted and in disarray, she nevertheless seemed to shine with a blinding brilliance to the man who still wavered between this world and the next. She knelt beside him and lifted his hand in hers.

A man of ordinary vision and sensibility, cognizant of the blood-encrusted sores around her mouth, anticipating the rough feel of her kiss, would have pulled away abruptly. Yet the kiss infused the man who lay before her with life, and with an effort that seemed to take all his strength, Fierce Enemy drew Honey down next to him. Gently she laid her head on his sound shoulder. With no strength for words but at peace, he lay with her and listened as she told him between sobs of joy how much she loved him. Then he fell asleep.

Only in the morning did Cameron notice the deep abrasions on Honey's neck and gently touch her throat near the still raw edges of her wound. "Your necklace?" he wondered of the bejeweled locket she often wore.

"Stolen," she answered.

"I'll ask for its return."

"There's no use. It was obviously a trophy, and the savage responsible is no longer in camp. I'll never see the locket again." In spite of her resolve, tears welled in Honey's eyes. "As it represented lost love—perhaps its loss is as it should be," she said, but logic gave way to a cascade of tears.

It had been given to her by Nathan to celebrate Saint Valentine's Day and their engagement when she was sixteen, and Honey had sworn to wear the heart-shaped locket forever. "Mine Forever" the locket's engraving said, and inside there were pictures of the hopeful couple.

On the verge of breaking down completely, of shedding tears for something that was better forgotten, fearing that once she started to weep she might never stop, Honey stiffened her resolve. "At least I've not lost you," she said to Cameron, and bent to kiss him. "I have not lost you," she murmured again, and cradled him in her arms.

He was very weak, and the degree of his debility made

Honey tremble at her core. His injuries alone were severe enough
to have killed most men; his loss of blood profound. She credited
his survival to his extraordinary and resilient constitution—and
God's mercy.

But much of the gratitude was due Honey. And in spite of a
sense he had of Honey's confusion about their present circumstances, Cameron felt Honey's abiding love and knew that if it
were a matter of her will alone, he would survive.

Renowned as a daring warrior once, a man of important
Deer Ceremony, Fierce Enemy's desires were of significance to
the Apache band that in the end had rescued him. Nantan
Cheis himself came to Fierce Enemy's wickiup and greeted him
solicitously, regretting his injury and promising all aid and assistance to ensure the warrior's recovery. But the overt tenderness and regard Fierce Enemy showed for the white eyes
woman whom he called to his side was, in the Apache way, a
disturbing sign of weakness. Among the Chiricahua, Honey's
fair striking beauty, graceful strength, and apparent devotion
were worthy of a man's regard, but Fierce Enemy's consideration for Honey seemed excessive, an enigma and an embarrassment to the people.

Mindful of this breach with his brother Apache, Fierce Enemy
felt compelled to obscure from everyone, including Honey, the
extent of his passion for his woman—his wife, as far as the other
Chiricahua knew. Alone with Honey, however, this circumspec-
tion was more difficult. Even as he again surrendered to the
Apache way, Fierce Enemy continued to love Honey Radcliffe
with a frightening intensity.

He was still very weak, and talking at any length exhausted
him; therefore, his explanations to Honey about their circumstances were brief. "We're with the Chiricahua Apache under
Cheis's authority. This valley is Cheis's fortress. I was lucky to
be recognized as Apache and not killed outright for a white
eyes."

"You're not an Apache."

"Yes, I am."

Honey ignored his inflexible statement for the moment. "What
do you mean, 'white eyes'?"

"The white of an indian's eyes is muddy."

"Of course," Honey said of what was obvious but, under duress, overlooked. "I've had plenty of opportunity to notice—having been stared at and doing my share of staring in return. But

why were you spared—if you can call what those monsters did being spared? And why were Shahar, Nollie, and myself not murdered like the rest?"

"I'm told your actions made it obvious that you belonged to me. And as Nollie and Shahar were serving me breakfast when the Apache ambushed, they simply reasoned the two were my slaves."

"But how could the savages know you?"

"The man who spared my life is a friend from long ago. We trained as warriors together."

"He is also the one who tried to murder you," Honey reminded Cameron, and resisted what she cared not to hear.

As Cameron continued over the course of several days to reveal the story of his earlier life with the Apache, Honey simply listened, finding his story of capture, degradation, and conversion from white eyes child to Apache warrior incredible, viewing it as more fable than fact. With rigorous effort she concealed her disgust, mindful of Cameron's precarious health. Finally, she recognized that only a person of extraordinary strength and courage could have survived the ordeals Cameron had, and unlike most white eyes she was unable to begrudge his survival. Honey was struck dumb by his making peace with the Apache for what they had done to his family and to him and thought of Christ on the cross. *"Father forgive them, for they know not what they do."* Was absolution possible for every crime? Moved deeply, she said, "You were so young to have suffered so much."

In hearing his tale, Honey relived the horror of the more recent massacre of half of her own party, people who were of no relation to her. She would carry that memory forever, she knew, and sensed the pain Cameron had suffered on losing his family to violent murder. She also understood his instinct to survive and smiled when he told her his Apache name meant "Fierce Enemy." All at once what had been mysterious about him now seemed clear.

But the more Cameron told her of his life as an Apache warrior living with Chihuahua's band in territory north and east of where they were now, the more Honey felt her blood run cold even in the high heat of day. Reluctantly, she began to look at Cameron with different eyes. She was aghast that he claimed to have at one time been one with the savages, not at all inclined to give up her opinion of the people as no more than dirty, ignorant, vicious monsters.

Nollie and Shahar were equally disturbed. "Surely he's only raving with fever," Nollie protested.

Honey shook her head and sighed. "I pray you're right."

Honey was not amused by the indians' assumption that she was Cameron's wife, nor were Nollie and Shahar pleased to be designated slaves again. However, all three women readily acknowledged the wisdom of continuing the charade, not wishing to risk the unknown.

Nevertheless, in her role as wife, Honey chafed at serving her husband like a slave. "No Southern gentlewoman could ever expect this dreadful life to agree with her," she complained. From daylight until long after dark, while he watched or slept, Honey labored. In spite of her ardent prayers for his rapid recovery, with strength left at day's end only to grumble softly, "I seem to remember the slaves were freed," Honey was immensely grateful for Cameron's continued lethargy when she curled next to him at night.

"Life is hard here," he acknowledged, but insisted stubbornly that Apache women were revered, protected, and loved.

As he lay on his back, feeling ease and only fleeting desire, he hugged Honey to his uninjured side. He kissed the top of her head as she lay against his shoulder but, with a warrior's appropriate responses in mind, swallowed the words of love that so readily welled within him.

Although she was bone-tired, sleep came more slowly to Honey than to Cameron; while in part she was relieved by his inattention in this strange and often terrifying world of the Chiricahua Apache, Honey was troubled by her sense that Cameron's affection had begun to wane. As unnerved as she was by Cameron's unfolding story about his past, her sense of his withdrawal from her came as a devastating blow.

Again Honey thought to beg Shahar to seek her Spirits' advice but believed the risk was too great: One of Shahar's trance states might be interpreted by the indians as death, and Shahar would be buried alive. Honey could never explain the trance condition to the Apache and knew Cameron's health was far too precarious to rely on him for clear interpretation.

On many nights she feared she would wake and find him dead, and she would often force herself to lie awake and listen to the rhythm of his breathing. She tried not to recall the war and her desperation in nursing men with methods that proved insufficient, or the frightful death rate from septic wounds, or the distressing sanitary conditions that by contrast with the primitive indian encampment now seemed almost salubrious.

When she had used up her own petticoats, Honey made bandages from the petticoats off Shahar and Nollie's backs. She boiled water and did her best to keep his wounds clean. Whenever available, Honey applied the strange gelatinous paddle leaves called *nopales* to Cameron's wounds. They seemed not to cause any harm. In fact, the wounds seemed surprisingly wholesome. With some concern but without comment as she ministered to him, Honey even endured the low and, to her ear, unmusical chanting of frightfully masked, half-naked, garishly painted dancers cloaked in garments made of animal skins and feathers. Worst of all were the occasional fits of ululating cries in which some of the shamans engaged. In Honey's view, the rites performed were fearsome and disturbing, but Cameron steadfastly believed in them.

"I believe in your power, and Apache songs also," Fierce Enemy promised his skeptical nurse, but was careful not to disclose that the dancers were mediums for Apache Spirits.

She fed him gruel and sometimes broth, kept him still, and lived in terror of a second hemorrhage, a fatal sloughing of a wounded artery. She waited anxiously for the appearance of "laudable pus" as she bathed Cameron with water and indian soap called *amole*, then dressed his wounds, only to have shortly afterward yet another shaman, full of his own self-importance and chanting at length, dust Cameron's body with pollen and tuck a small twig of lightning-riven wood into the folds of his bandages.

Helpless, Honey stood by glowering as Cameron was induced to drink concoctions unknown in her experience. The indian medicine produced no miraculous results, nor was it a cathartic, as so many white eyes potions were. Cameron said he thought he felt better for the bitter dosings. "At least you've not been poisoned yet." Honey sighed in resignation at his acceptance of Chiricahua rituals and potions and confessed that over all she believed he was recovering slowly.

Then fever set in.

Her worst fears realized, Honey at once expected to relive the agony of watching a man die of his festering wounds. In order not to alarm him, she struggled mightily to hide her grief, but it

was manifested in her face and in the way she held herself erect.
She seemed to shrink, weighted after all with too heavy a burden.
Never one to hold her tongue, at least with Nollie and Shahar,
Honey grew unbearably silent. Then the weather turned ex-
tremely hot, and a remorseless wind blew dust into her eyes and
over everything.

Honey spent the day bathing Cameron with cool water,
worried that before the day was out he would be gone, burned
alive by the heat of fire raging inside him. Sometimes he slept
even as she aided him. Occasionally he would wake and acknowledge her, but his eyes were fever-bright. Or he would
stare beyond her as if he did not see her. Her own vision was
blurred by tears.

In the evening and through the long night that followed, he
whispered to her, mingling Apache words and English.

"I don't understand," she answered, which made him angry.

"Shhhh," she crooned as one might to a fussy child, but he
grew increasingly restless and was rarely lucid.

Honey lost hope.

Shahar came to her side. "I've seen Mr. Cameron will survive, but by extraordinary means."

"Not one of these damnable witch doctors, surely?"

"That I don't know."

"Have you seen any remedies in this alien landscape?"

Shahar was reluctant to say what in fact she had seen.
"Worms, only worms."

Horror filled Honey's face, and tears sprang from her eyes.
"Can't that only be a harbinger of death?" She gritted her teeth,
refusing to break down completely. "I'll not hear of his dying!"
She sent Shahar away.

Honey slept only when Cameron did and, with a start, woke
shortly after sunrise to a dark figure of terrifying ugliness block-
ing the light from the doorway and hovering over both of them.
Masked, the upper body painted black with charcoal and adorned
with various blue and yellow geometric figures, wearing a robe
patchworked with animal skins and a grotesque feathered headdress, a female shaman wobbled over them, chanting incompre-
hensibly.

Honey scrambled to her feet, her terror on waking having
turned to anger. "Get out, witch!" she cried, fully aware she was
required to be silent during a shaman's ceremony but unable to

help herself. "You're more harm than help, more useless than even I am."

From a pouch the shaman withdrew a sharp instrument of bone. Wielding it with apparent malice, she advanced on Honey.

As Honey's gaze riveted on what seemed a dagger, she was seized from behind by the shaman's helper and her arms were twisted behind her. She cried out with abject terror and struggled with her captor but was forced to kneel and be still.

While she glared at Honey, the shaman used a smoldering stick to light the odd pipe Honey had feared was a dagger and then, as Honey watched, blew smoke to the four directions, beginning with the east and concluding to the north. To each cardinal point the shaman next rasped a song and prayed, tapping a buckskin-covered pottery drum with a curved stick. Each song had four stanzas; each prayer, four verses. As she sang, she repeatedly approached and then backed away from her patient.

After a short pause, the shaman began a monologue that Honey supposed was meant to beseech yet another unseen Apache power for instructions. Weary of being on her knees, Honey mentally ticked away the minutes, knowing the ritual could take hours. At least an hour passed before the shaman ran out of steam.

Then there was an almost endless silence until suddenly the masked shaman took a pouch from a basket on the floor and from the pouch drew pollen, which she cast to the four directions and up and down. She bent low and, with two fingers, made a cross of pollen on Cameron's brow. On each shoulder she drew two parallel lines.

Cameron appeared still to be sleeping, but Honey knew that even though his breathing was regular, he was now quite beyond ordinary slumber. Her eyes filled with tears that would have spilled but for the movement of the shaman in her direction. Restrained by her captor from shying away, Honey was forced to lift her face. A rough hand pulled Honey's hair away from her forehead and marked her face with pollen as Cameron's had been marked. With more pollen, the shaman then drew a star in the palm of her own right hand and for many long minutes stared at the figure; then she beseeched her unseen power for assistance.

Next, the shaman took a round piece of abalone shell and an eagle feather from her basket, pressing the shell into Cameron's forehead, where it adhered as though glued. She pushed the feather point into Cameron's breast. His skin remained unbroken, yet the feather stood erect, which meant in the Apache belief that the shaman's cure would work.

Honey sucked in her breath and froze as, suddenly, the shaman drew a knife and, chanting, cut away the bandages from Cameron's chest. From another pouch she produced a dark, foul-smelling ungent, which she smeared on Cameron's already purulent wounds before Honey could react. Quite beyond responding overtly to pain, Cameron made no reaction to the shaman's touching his tender wounds.

Stunned, Honey began to scream "Nooooo!" but was prevented from doing anything but wailing her grief and loudly cursing the shaman, for which she received a vicious blow before being thrown to the dirt floor. Spent from the extremes of emotion and the blow, Honey lay silent. Throughout the ordeal Cameron had lain unconscious; fearing the agony of horribly contaminated wounds, Honey prayed in earnest that he would die without ever coming to his senses.

Not satisfied with Honey's silence, the shaman next ordered her pulled to a sitting position and once more addressed the unseen power. Chanting rhythmically, the shaman drew a circle on the ground with pollen, inscribing within it symbols that had no meaning for Honey.

Next, from her basket, the shaman removed a necklace with seven blue-green beads strung on rawhide, the center bead—fat and vaguely heart-shaped—much larger than the rest. She raised the necklace to the four directions, and Honey realized it was not simply an ornament, as her locket had been, but an amulet. Still chanting, the indian woman threw dried herbs on the low-burning fire and bathed the amulet in the resulting fragrant smoke, then slipped the beads over Cameron's head, chanting another song of repetitious verses, obviously a prayer, and afterward traced footsteps with pollen from where Fierce Enemy lay to the entrance of the wickiup. With one last scattering of pollen to the four directions, the shaman retreated.

From what Cameron had told her, Honey knew the footprints in the dust symbolized the trail of a long life, which the shaman's ceremony was supposed to guarantee. Outraged by the horror of the putrid salve the shaman had rubbed into Cameron's wounds, Honey moved to erase all signs of the heathen rite. "If there are Apache gods with power to save Cameron, I've not seen one!"

she screamed from the entrance of the shelter at the figure of the disappearing shaman. "Your ceremonies are nothing more than evil witchcraft!"

But stricken with fear for Cameron's life, Honey whirled away from the temptation to obliterate the pagan track. Something in her did not dare to tamper with a power that might heal this man she loved to the point of unreason. Instead, Honey knelt at Cameron's side and shed a torrent of hot tears, all the while trying to keep away the flies that were drawn to the shaman's foul and sticky ointment. Out of clean bandages, Honey had nothing with which to dress the wounds. Finally, exhausted, she lay down beside Cameron and for an hour slept fitfully.

Hunger alone should have kept Honey alert, for the shaman's ceremony had taken nearly all day. Yet she lay dreaming, quite ignorant of her body's hunger or thirst. Her dreams were filled with shamans' masks and death, with fierce, murderous savages, faces from the war—her brothers' and her father's, those of the countless wounded who had survived or died, depending on their luck. And Cameron, whose image provoked extremes of joy and sorrow.

Honey sank deeper into sleep and for a time lay dreamless. Later the more recent past filtered into her mind: butchered companions and the face of the vicious savage who had ripped the bejeweled locket from her throat and, she feared, would have stolen more or killed her but for the intervention of his comrades. Sweating, screaming, Honey woke to the dark of night.

In the stillness, Honey's terror abated at a dreadfully slow rate, and in its wake came overwhelming grief. What would happen to her—and to Shahar and Nollie—if Cameron died? The only reason they had been spared a brutal end in the first place had been the Apache's recognition of Cameron as one of their own. If Fierce Enemy should die now. . .

Honey did not dare prophesy the future.

Instead, she cursed the darkness and the Chiricahua. "May you all burn in everlasting hell." The only blessing of the dark, she thought, was the merciful coolness of the air compared with day. The daytime temperature of late summer scorched the blood.

Honey touched Cameron. Unbelievably, he felt merely warm, not fevered, his breathing regular and peaceful. She reached for the water jar and repeatedly, in an almost hypnotic gesture, pressed a cool, wet hand against his skin until she felt his hand on her wrist, his kiss upon her palm. "Cameron," she whispered, and bent nearer to kiss him. "The fever is broken," she told him, but dared not trust that he now would be all right. By the time it was light again, the fever had returned; her reluctance to rejoice sadly justified.

When he slept, Honey secured Nollie's help in fanning flies, then fled the wickiup and ventured to a nearby stream. Waist deep in water, still dressed, she bathed herself, hardly feeling the shock of the ice-cold water in the daytime heat. She reclined in the water and for several minutes floated on her back, alive but on the verge of drowning not with water but from sorrow. Many times Honey had racked her brain for something she might do to save Cameron but had concluded there was nothing else to do, no prayer she had not already offered, no sacrifice she could make, no miracle she could work.

Suddenly Honey rose from the water, possessed. "Worms! Worms!" Dripping, she raced back to camp, shouting, "Meat! I must have meat."

Although at first convinced Honey's mind had slipped a cog, Shahar and Nollie gave up a decent-sized rabbit they were desperate for and watched in disbelief as Honey slit the stomach open and laid it on the ground to spoil. "Have you taken leave of your senses?" Shahar demanded, in a mind to rescue the meat before it was too late. "It's already drawing flies."

"Exactly what I want. Flies and especially maggots— worms!" Honey replied, an answer that gave Shahar and Nollie no confidence at all in her sanity. "Don't you see! Just as you said, Shahar! Worms. They're my only hope. I've nothing else."

To their doubtful stares, Honey sighed impatiently, as if they should have known her purpose. "The putrid salve that damnable witch applied will kill Cameron but for the flies we've been doing our best to shoo away."

Shahar and Nollie stared at each other.

"I can't bear to dress his wounds, and as you've seen, every fly for miles has come by to feast and lay their eggs. I've been frantic; then I remembered hearing of a doctor in the war who ran out of bandages. Your dream, Shahar! Without dressings, gaping wounds lay open to flies, and their *worms*. Miraculously, almost all the men whose wounds *weren't* dressed recovered. Don't you see?" Honey demanded of the disbelieving women. "Maggots cleaned the wounds."

Hand to mouth, Nollie fled.

Shahar looked as though she wished to follow, although she saw the merit in Honey's logic and its connection with her own visions. "I know what I said, but . . . your daddy'd turn in his grave if he knew."

"Better he turn in his than Cameron be laid in one," Honey snapped. "I know I'm right. You'll see," she said, but was not sure at all. The only thing of which she was certain, of which she had seen a good deal, was the damage done to patients by the experimentation of their doctors. There was laudable pus and not so laudable pus. She hoped the maggots knew the difference— which men did not.

"I shall trust heaven," Shahar counseled herself.

"And so shall I," she said. *Now that I remember those precious maggots.*

No reasonable physician would dare do this, Honey admitted to herself, and with her desperate act to save the man she loved, her dream of following her father, of becoming a doctor seemed to finally slip away for good. The next few days were agony for Honey and her patient.

After that, when Cameron's wounds were clean and she had plucked out the last of the maggots, Honey rejoiced at his recovery. Cameron smiled broadly at Honey as she gritted her teeth and stifled a searing reply to his translation of the sha-man's interpretation of his miraculous recovery. "She insists her power convinced the sickness to leave my body."

Honey glared at the shaman as she might have at another woman who had stolen Cameron's affections, her hatred evident. "Damnable witch," she muttered, and thought the woman's claim that Apache medicine alone had saved the Chiricahua warrior Fierce Enemy outrageous. But she bowed to heaven and prayed she would never again have an opportunity to test the efficacy of maggot therapy.

When the indian shaman left the wickiup, Honey tucked the end of a clean, dry bandage into a fold and mustered a smile. "There. Now, I'll be able to sleep nights."

"Thanks only to your maggots?"

"No thanks to that filthy witch doctor!"

"Have you no faith?" he teased. "You don't believe in the power of amulets either, do you?"

"Utter rot," Honey sniffed, washing her hands after clearing away discarded dressings, still furious that Cameron refused to let her throw away the variety of lightning-riven twigs and fragments of shell and filthy bits of cloth that had accumulated.

"You don't believe that if I remove these beads, I risk certain death, do you?"

"Of course not." Honey gave Cameron a worn, annoyed look. "In spite of everything, you're white eyes, not a savage."

"How do you know?"

She was emphatic. "I could not love a savage."

"But you love me." It was a statement, not a question.

"With all my heart."

He did not debate the point he had tried to make but pulled her closer and drew her lips to his. *"Enjuh."* "Good," he said of the kiss, although it was an intimacy abhorrent to the Apache.

For the first time in what to Honey seemed a lifetime, she tasted his hunger for her and was overcome by her own desire. "You're not yet strong enough for lovemaking," she struggled to caution him.

Cameron caught her hand and moved it beneath the blanket below his waist. "Well enough," he insisted, and urged her to confirm the strength of his erection. "I need you."

Honey laughed as he lifted her astride him. "You're more fit than I imagined."

"And very determined."

"Very, I see." He raised her skirt, and Honey lay along the length of him. He sighed at the feel of her flesh against his: the firm belly, the rise of soft curls, the long length of bare legs.

He pulled her mouth to his, showing her with the degree of his passion just how much ground he had gained, his voice revealing how deeply she affected him. His hands were insistent and powerful, his touch and his kisses producing in Honey a responding feverish need.

She surrendered joyfully. At last to touch him in passion and not for any obvious purpose of healing! She kissed his eyes, his cheeks, his mouth. She kissed his throat and pushed the amulet of turquoise aside to kiss his chest above the bandage.

She welcomed his fingers on the buttons of her bodice, his knowing hands and mouth upon her breasts, lingering there and driving her to the brink of ecstasy. Very near completion when he at last thrust into her, she seized and rode him vigorously, their mutual cries of pleasure blending almost into song.

"It seems impossible that I could ever be near you and not feel desire," he said when, replete with satisfaction, they lay side by side.

"A sign that you, indeed, are nearly well." Honey smiled and stared into Cameron's loving eyes. "For a man near death has other matters on his mind."

"Or, maybe, is out of it," Cameron suggested, although for the moment he was content only to savor the simple joy of feasting his eyes on the beauty of Honey's features, the fresh color of her satin skin, her soft hair, and her gold-flecked eyes. If possible, he mused, the fierce Apache sun had made Honey even more beautiful than before. Now the sun-deepened color of her face and throat and the dip of the modest V of the dress she was forced habitually to wear contrasted sharply with her creamy white breasts—and almost concealed the scars caused by the violent wrenching of her locket from her neck.

But Cameron saw the scars, ran a gentle finger along the line where the necklace should have lain, and remembered she had pledged to love Nathan Radcliffe *forever*. "Forever," Cameron whispered. "I will love you forever."

"I love you, too."

"But not forever?"

"I will love you always."

Cameron looked into Honey's trusting golden eyes. "These beads aren't made of gold and diamonds, yet they're even more precious than your locket," he said as he removed the Apache amulet from his neck and lowered it over Honey's head. "Giving this to you, I give you my life and my love forever."

Tears sprang to Honey's eyes; she was aware, though she truly wished not to be, that Cameron believed in the power of the five turquoise stones, the largest of which now nestled perfectly between her breasts. She conceded that the blue-green beads held a primitive beauty of their own—not as dazzling perhaps as the diamond-edged locket she once had worn yet possessing a strange if earthy allure.

Honey lifted the larger heart-shaped turquoise to her lips for a light kiss, then caught her breath and leaned gratefully into Cameron's embrace. Eyes closed, she pressed him to her and, in the stillness that followed, opened her soul for the right words to express her feelings. He was the only man she had ever truly loved, her destiny. But with all that had happened, words of promises did not flow easily from her.

And then they came.

"If there is a forever, my love belongs forever to you," she whispered to the white man who was in vital part Apache. "I accept your amulet . . . and all that it means." And with this pledge, embraced eternity.

PART THREE

Truth

God offers to every mind a choice between
  truth and repose.
Take which you please—you can never
  have both.

Ralph Waldo Emerson

CHAPTER FIFTY-ONE

Honey watched Cameron recover at a steady pace, her joy mingled with apprehension as instead of seeing the virile white man she had known gradually emerge from sickness, she observed an equally virile Apache warrior metamorphize. To her eye, the natural process had been reversed, with the beautiful butterfly becoming a repugnant caterpillar.

Within a short time, Cameron's skin became so dark from exposure to the sun that except for his dark brown hair, it was difficult to distinguish him from the other Apache. He had assumed Apache dress—buckskin breechclout, high-topped, flat-toed moccasins, and shirt—as had she, Nollie, and Shahar, who donned deerskin blouses and skirts and moccasins rather than go nearly naked in their white eyes tatters. It was no point of pride to Shahar and Nollie that they, as Cameron's slaves, were responsible for the fine rendering and decorating of the deerhide clothes they wore. It was backbreaking, finger-cramping labor to scrape the hide clean and work the buckskin to produce garments whose very nature shamed them. "I haven't come halfway round the world to be a slave to an Apache savage," Nollie complained bitterly. "When's he going to take us out of here?"

"Lord only knows," Honey said, still unable to believe he was the savage he sometimes seemed to be.

"Well, if you won't ask him, I will."

"You'd best wait till he's alone and spoken to you first, or else he'll have to beat you to satisfy the savages. If he doesn't, he'll invite their wrath."

"Always some easy way for a master to thrash a slave," Nollie all but snarled.

When she looked to Shahar in appeal, Honey turned an alarming shade of gray. "Oh, Shahar," she whispered. "How could you?" She looked around them, fearful of the indians' notice.

Honey knew better than to touch Shahar, for if she did, Shahar might tumble sideways, still maintaining the erect position she now held. "What are we going to do?" Honey demanded of Nollie in a conspiratorial tone. "Think of something."

Alarmed, Nollie stood up and tried to block Shahar from the wide view of others in nearby campsites. "Best we don't do anything for now. But when the others leave the wickiup, we'll drag her inside."

"What good will that do?"

"At least she'll be out of sight."

"What do we tell Cameron?"

Nollie shook her head. "Tell him she's sick, I guess."

Honey groaned. "I doubt slaves recover their health in the master's quarters."

"Then *you* invent an excuse."

Honey thought a while but then conceded. "I'm fresh out of excuses."

"Say he's fond of dark meat."

Honey felt Nollie's remark beneath contempt. "Why would he want an old hen when he could have tender *poulet*?"

"Experience," Nollie offered as evenly as she could muster, then sighed. "Maybe they won't notice."

"Of course they won't," Honey snapped. "Who'd notice someone sitting as rigid as a statue in the middle of camp? Or haven't you *noticed* that the Apache don't miss a thing?"

"Quick! Get me a blanket."

Honey did as she was told, and Nollie threw it over Shahar, hoping the gesture would be missed. "She'll suffocate under there," Honey whispered as she looked nervously around.

"She doesn't breathe much in that state, remember?"

Honey rolled her eyes to heaven in gratitude and nodded.

"Act like there's nothing unusual going on," Nollie ordered as the blanket covering Cameron's wickiup flapped open and two Apache walked out with Cameron behind them. The two women held their breath and, as casually as possible, shielded Shahar from the warriors, who did not seem to cast a glance in their direction. "So insignificant are we," Nollie muttered under her breath.

"Thank the Lord."

"Let me remind you, this is your fault, Honey."

"My fault?"

"Who dragged up the Spirits in the first place?"

"That was decades ago."

"Not so."

It was nearly dusk, and with his guests departed, Honey and

Nollie caught Cameron's attention. "What're you whispering about? Planning an escape?"

"If only we could," Nollie said.

Cameron ignored her and spoke to Honey. "What're you hiding?"

"Shahar," Honey answered.

"That's army-issue; she can't breathe." Cameron moved to uncover Shahar.

"No," Honey ordered in a low but insistent voice, and prevented him from exposing Shahar. "Just hold aside the door while we carry her inside."

Cameron looked at Honey doubtfully but did as he was bidden. When they unwrapped Shahar, he asked, "She's sick?"

"No."

"Yes."

Cameron raised his eyebrows at the two women. "Make up your minds."

"She's not ill but traveling," Honey said, lowering her eyes, afraid if she went into detail, he'd think her stark raving mad.

"I see," Cameron said as he stared into Shahar's glassy-eyed gaze.

"You do?" Clearly, Honey didn't believe him.

"I think you'd better explain."

Nollie spoke hastily, "Do you believe in ghosts, Mr. Wolfe?"

"Yes," Cameron said slowly, obviously taken aback.

"Well, my mother is convening with ghosts."

Cameron did not care to hear this explanation. The Apache were afraid of very little, but even the mention of ghosts was one of the few things that struck terror in their hearts.

"She is *not* dealing with ghosts," Honey interrupted, trying to keep her voice low, knowing of the Apache aversion.

"Spirits, then."

Honey could tell Cameron liked that description not one notch better. "It's not easy to explain," she said, rubbing her forehead as if a little massage would improve her ability to interpret, "but it's quite safe."

Nollie snickered disdainfully. "*You* say."

"Yes, I say!" Honey shot Nollie a murderous look. "And I can tell Mr. Wolfe what he needs to know without any further help from you. Bring us some food," Honey ordered. "And, remember, wives are within their rights to beat their slaves."

"Easy, Honey, easy," Cameron cautioned, but Nollie strode out of the shelter gladly.

"It's difficult. She loves baiting me," Honey said as she knelt next to Shahar and secured the blanket over the woman's shoulders. "Her temperature drops until you'd think she's dead," she said, looking up at Cameron. "She has strange visions she uses to interpret future events. For instance, before you came to Greerfield, she saw us together in one of her dreams. I thought her mad, but look at us now. She sometimes dreams of remedies. She saw worms before I remembered the maggots."

Cameron relaxed visibly and crouched down next to Honey. "*That* I understand."

"You do?"

"Better than the dreams we've shared." For a few minutes Cameron watched Shahar, then reflected, "Among the people, she'd be a dream shaman."

Honey smiled. "It wouldn't surprise me at all, but please, let's keep her hidden until she comes back to earth."

Cameron readily agreed. "Let her stay the night with us. Tomorrow you and Nollie can build her and Shahar a shelter of their own. You should've done so long ago. They needn't have slept outside this length of time."

Honey nodded, then automatically touched Cameron's forehead and cheek to check for fever. "I find waiting until you're well enough for us to leave this place pure agony," Honey said, taking Cameron's hand. "I thank God you're alive but won't trust my eyes until we've arrived back in civilization." Honey watched as a shadow seemed to cross Cameron's face. "Surely you aren't thinking of staying here?"

Cameron only stared at the small banked fire whose embers Honey would stir later in the evening.

Honey shook her head vehemently. "You can't want to remain," she said with emotion close to panic. She was trembling, and tears she had no control over filled her eyes and ran down her cheeks. "I've fed myself with dreams of leaving here with you. Of going, as we planned, to California, of marrying you." She looked pale even in the dusky light. "You can't mean to stay."

Cameron looked at Honey steadily now, and in his eyes she saw a resolve that frightened her. "I must stay."

"Then you can't make me stay. You wouldn't."

"You're my wife," he said gently. He touched the center stone of the turquoise amulet that Honey always wore. *"Mine forever."*

Honey's pulse throbbed in her temples. She closed her eyes and lowered her head, not wishing to see the face of an Apache or the look of yet another man who insisted he owned her because she loved him.

Her heart ached as she felt it harden against him. She remembered that the name given to the people called Apache had been given by their enemies and meant "enemy." That for his defiance and bravery Cameron should be called Fierce Enemy by the people who had captured him was understood by Honey. That she might come to judge him so as well tortured her. Loving him fiercely and perhaps irrevocably did not change this sudden knowledge.

Holding her tongue was never an instinct with Honey, and dwelling on the thought of being forced to stay with the Apache in their stone fortress made her wild. "Surely Trevor is already searching for us, and the Union cavalry as well."

"Nantan Cheis's stronghold is impregnable by white eyes," Cameron answered tersely.

"Nothing is 'impregnable,'" Honey insisted without internal conviction, for it was certainly true that Cheis's people lived within the stronghold unmolested and with no sign of unease. "Please, take me to Trevor. You'll come to your senses once we leave. They wouldn't stop you, would they? They didn't before, why should they now?" He had told her only that he had left the Apache when he was eighteen, not how or why, an act that by her way of thinking required no explanation.

"They'd not prevent us from leaving," was all Fierce Enemy said in answer.

"Surely I've not heard you correctly," Honey said as he stood to go to the nightly campfire and partake of food and ritual storytelling, a means of passing Apache tradition on to the young and fortifying tradition for the others. There he would also drink *tiswin*, a fermented beverage that in sufficient quantities made one mildly drunk.

"You heard me right," he said firmly, and when she refused to rise and go with him, left her alone with Shahar.

When he had gone, Honey, feeling betrayed, felt her tears turn to racking sobs. Nollie, when she returned, could not console her, although she tried. At Fierce Enemy's command, Nollie brought Honey food, but she could not eat, all hunger from the seemingly interminable day of collecting and grinding acorns, gathering fresh berries and firewood, and the eternal task of scraping deerskin to a suitably malleable state for use gone.

Nollie could not pry from Honey the reason for her near hysteria and finally gave up. "Go ahead, cry yourself blue in the face," she said, her already thin patience evaporating.

By the time Fierce Enemy returned, Honey appeared calm and dry-eyed; by then, the fire in the center of the wickiup had burned down to the last ember. His stomach full, restored by the night's storytelling to a renewed Apache pride, he berated Honey for her negligence, for being a lazy wife. "I should beat you," he growled, but softly, and, mellowing, further subjected Honey to his *tiswin*-loosened tongue. "I'd've lived the rest of my life with the Apache if my wife and baby had lived."

Suddenly Honey's numbed feelings awoke, her ears tuned as they had never been before. For the moment at least, her smoldering anger at being kept captive was set aside by this intriguing information. The notion that Cameron had been married—and might have loved before—ignited jealous fire within her. Mercilessly, Honey felt her heart pulled in two directions: The chance to prove that he could love no other woman more than he loved her struggled with her fervent wish to flee to the white eyes world and imagined safety.

"A good Apache wife never allows the fire to die," he said as he stirred the ashes himself.

"Since you've apparently warmed yourself plenty with Apache swill, I'm surprised you notice."

"And you talk too much. From now on, I'll call you 'Woman Who Talks Too Much.'"

Honey glared at him.

"My Apache wife's name was Welcome Brook. She made you think of a pure, refreshing spring in the desert. Everything about her was beautiful; her face, her voice, her way."

Honey couldn't help herself. "Every squaw I've ever seen desperately needs a bath."

"So do you sometimes—I loved her."

"I'm *thrilled* to hear it. I wouldn't want to think it was a union based merely on lust."

Lost in thought, Fierce Enemy didn't hear Honey's retort, nor did he read the hurt in her eyes, which despite her quick tongue was also obvious.

"We had a baby when she died," he related when he came from his brief reverie. "My son would have been a warrior someday."

"Like his father . . . of course," she said with contempt.

Fierce Enemy looked at Honey as though seeing her for the first time. "Yes," he said, "an Apache warrior just as his father *is*. Maybe, as you white eyes say, a chief like I might've been if I'd stayed where I belonged."

Anger bubbled to the surface of Honey's heart again, but fear of losing Cameron was at its center. With the Apache, her greatest fear had been that she would lose Cameron to death, but now that he was nearly healed, she might still lose him to a world and people whose appeal she could not fathom.

To summon courage, Honey closed her eyes and took several deep, slow breaths. She could not so easily let him go, she realized, and on opening her eyes, emerged a warrior herself. Fearless, resolute, she deliberately chose the only weapon she had to hold him—love.

CHAPTER FIFTY-TWO

Begrudgingly, Honey eventually was forced to admire the resourcefulness of the indians. Within Cheis's forty-acre stronghold she saw no planted crops of any kind or large herds of animals, yet the people thrived. They lived off the land, their diet consisting of a variety of plants, fruits, seeds, nuts, and grasses collected within and without the fortress. The women were responsible for gathering and preparing these foods, and from the start Nollie and Shahar learned the various techniques of harvesting, skills they passed on to Honey as soon as she was able to leave Cameron's side. What was not immediately used was stored or prepared for storage. The men provided game of various kinds—deer, rabbit, prairie dog, and sometimes beef—obtained through raiding or, occasionally, fair barter. While Cameron recuperated, the warrior responsible for his wounds saw to it that he and his women were provided for.

As soon as he could, Cameron began to follow the women on their forages, not to participate, which in the Apache view was unthinkable for a man, but to aid in regaining his strength. "For an Apache, covering fifty miles on foot in a day is not unusual," he said.

Honey looked at Cameron sideways. "Not this week," she said skeptically as she balanced her basket on her head in imitation of the indian women they followed.

"I'll be winning footraces again, sooner than you think."

Honey turned her head slightly to look at Cameron, who still needed to use a walking stick of twisted manzanita. Aware that Apache men loved to compete in footraces, she remembered her first sight of Cameron at Greerfield and could easily imagine him racing against other Apache warriors, giving all he was worth. "This must be where you acquired your passion for gambling also. And I was afraid Tía Luz was the first to corrupt you."

Cameron laughed and then, grimacing, grabbed his left side.

Honey threw her basket down to steady him. "Are you all right?" She was pale with fright.

Cameron nodded. "No laughing yet, I guess," he said as Honey helped him sit down on the ground. He had promised to sew her a new pair of high-topped Apache moccasins with their odd, flat upturned toes while he waited, and he now set to his task. Using a cactus thorn needle and sinew for thread, Cameron would fashion the shoes of prepared deerhide, the hair left on to increase the durability of the soles.

"I'll be close by if you need me," she promised as she went to gather mesquite beans with the other women.

"I'll keep an eye open for mountain lions."

"You do that."

"You'll like roasted cat. The meat's real sweet."

Honey ignored him, her mind rebelling at his suggestion. She had already been forced to eat an appalling list of foods. The Apache were called "gut eaters" for their habit of not gutting game. Thus far, her favorite addition to the assorted grains, nuts, and berries was wood rat. "It'll be a long, cold day in hell," she had said when one was presented to her by another woman. Nollie and Shahar had agreed, but all three women watched in fascination as the gift was buried in coals—fur and all—to later be eaten with relish.

"I know some folks at home ate no better in the war," Nollie speculated. "Still . . ."

"I don't doubt it, but I'm not hungry enough yet," Shahar concluded.

Now, as Honey joined the other women harvesting the warped bean pods that were scattered on the ground in abundance beneath the mesquite trees, she tried not to think about wood rats or mountain lions or worry about Cameron, for the moment glad to help in the gathering of a staple of the Apache diet. She had been exceedingly grateful for the bounty of the finely ground mesquite beans, which Nollie made into gruel and sweetened with wild honey. Cameron had lived on this and other nourishing thin gruels for weeks before gaining enough strength to eat more heartily. While their diet was a far cry from what she was used to and was sometimes unappetizing for its blandness alone, the people as a whole seemed well nourished and strong. "The year's been a good one," Cameron explained, "with enough stored for winter. Lucky for us, it looks to be an easy winter ahead."

"I don't think we'll need to be here that long," Honey said almost offhandedly. "Perhaps you aren't quite well enough to undertake a long journey before winter, but we might get somewhere civilized by then." Cameron did not flatly reject this half-hearted plan, Honey noted happily. She refused to abandon her dream of returning to civilization but decided to bide her time and wait until he had fully recovered his strength before raising the subject again for full discussion. She alluded to her desire occasionally and never forced the issue, having decided restraint was the most intelligent course. Having made that decision, Honey lavished her devotion on Cameron with the clearheaded intention of rendering his recollection of his virtuous Apache wife a less compelling memory and fulfillment of her wishes his first desire.

Shahar's latest trance and her firm refusal to discuss her vision were also on Honey's mind. "Not clear. Not at all clear," Shahar had muttered with disgust on waking. A worried frown that gave Honey more concern than her silences had disturbed Shahar's face for days.

"You're not telling me something," Honey prodded while they culled seeds from dried sunflower heads together. But when Honey wheedled, Shahar still said nothing, until one night when Honey had been awake for hours trying to help Cameron ease the mysteriously recurring pain in his freshly healed wounds with applications of buckskin-wrapped, fire-heated stones. Then Honey woke Shahar and demanded to be enlightened. "Tell me he will be all right," she pleaded as she knelt by Shahar, who remained prone. "Promise me he won't die and leave us stranded with these . . . people."

Not fully alert, Shahar responded without thinking. "He won't die, not here anyway."

Honey gasped and began to cry.

Shahar sat up quickly. "You caught me before I came to my senses. What I meant to say," Shahar said, peevishly, "haven't you ever been too tired to talk sensible?" The dilemma for Shahar was that she could not trust what she had clearly seen. Certain things were impossible even if one did see them, she reasoned. "There was too much smoke, I couldn't see clearly," she said, a truthful response as far as it went.

"Or was it merely you didn't like what you saw?"

"Please, for your sake, go back to bed, Honey Greer." Shahar yawned, hoping to dismiss her inquisitor. "If you've been up all this time with him, you need some rest." She stood and helped Honey up from her knees. "Trust me to tell you anything that comes clear."

Still upset, Honey came very close to accusing Shahar of lying but held her tongue, conscious of the need for discretion with Shahar as well as with Cameron. For an instant Honey even questioned whether her desire for Cameron's recovery was real, which warned her at once that, as Shahar had suggested, she desperately needed sleep.

CHAPTER FIFTY-THREE

The fall rains had been heavy, and winter was close at hand before Honey truly felt secure enough among the Apache to regard them as individuals. Until she was convinced she, Nollie, and Shahar would not be harmed and realized the Apache took the presence of the white eyes women among them for granted, Honey had regarded the Apache only as a terrifying enemy. Then, convinced of her safety, she could view the people more humanely, at last free to interpret a gaze in her direction as something less than treachery and every approach as less than menacing.

When the Apache became more than a blur of dark, hideous faces, Honey realized that aesthetically many were handsome or beautiful, others plain, some ugly, tall, short, fat, thin, broadfaced, or slender. Some were people Honey would have liked to know better; others were of an unpleasant nature.

While they lived very meanly on the land, Honey came to see

that even in their uncivilized state, the Apache were an industrious and ingenious people. Nor could she help but notice that the people genuinely cared for one another, the well-being of every individual in the band of concern to all, love of parents for children, husbands for wives, and wives for husbands truly apparent above an outward reticence.

While Honey did not entirely abandon her concept of the Apache as fierce primitives, she also could not ignore their deeply spiritual nature. Every morning Cheis's morning song, a hymn of praise and gratitude, wafted through the valley. Cameron assured her the Apache never forgot their dependence on God, whom they called Ussen, and individually prayed daily and often; all significant junctures of life were celebrated in tribute to God.

As they prepared to watch the four-day rite celebrating a chaste girl's ascent to womanhood, Honey was astonished to learn from Cameron that it was the people's most sacred ceremony, an accolade that seemed to fly in the face of the endless labor women were required to perform. Still, this claim struck Honey forcefully, for however natural the event was in a girl's life, the first menses was hardly an occasion for public celebration in white society. At first the mere idea that the occasion was celebrated shocked Honey greatly, but on further pondering she found the idea intriguing, even liberating—the sanctification of the ability to produce life a worthy ceremony. It struck her that in a society in which a woman was so honored, a female might not be restricted to being a servant or confined to being an ornament on her husband's arm; she might even be considered fit to be a medicine woman—or doctor—which was the case among the people she had so easily labeled savages.

When Cameron told her that next to Ussen, the most revered deity was White Painted Woman, Honey was certain she had misunderstood. However, later, as she watched the vulgar Clown, another Apache deity impersonated by a painted, nearly naked dancer who pranced and pulled on himself obscenely, Honey concluded the Apache were surely perverse enough to revere a female supernatural. Certainly they were pagans!

Except for the obvious, most Apache humor escaped Honey entirely, but then the people's raucous joviality forced Honey to smile and served to soothe her. In her eyes the Apache were still the enemy, but she saw them now as something human. Finally, if reluctantly, she began to see the people as more complicated than the white eyes' curse of "savage" allowed.

Another factor that rocked Honey's preformed notions about the people centered on the fact that almost from the start the three white eyes women had worked well and easily with the indians. With surprise, they conceded nervously among themselves, as if they must have imagined it, they had felt nearly immediate acceptance. Of course, a distinction between slaves and wife was made, but beyond that classification the three American women did not sense that they were regarded as inferior, which they knew full well would never have been the case had the situation been reversed.

Not that other aspects of the culture did not continue to horrify Honey, among them the general nakedness of the children and the immodest dress of both men and women; the brutal treatment of unfaithful wives, whose noses were sliced off, rendering them disfigured and shamed for life; and the ruthless training of young men, some of whom were mere boys, to become warriors. She watched in horror as male children used actual knives, arrows, lances, and slings with stones against each other in mock battles that for every thrust were true to life. She held her breath as the apprentices dodged the nearly noiseless weapons and raved with fury when one boy lost an eye after failing to dodge a stone fired from a sling. "I suppose his name will be One Eye," she answered hotly when Cameron tried to explain the necessity for taking such risks.

"They won't be storekeepers or blacksmiths when they're grown. They'll be warriors. They learn now, or they won't live long enough to grow old."

Honey glared at Cameron's harsh logic, angered by the justification of savage behavior. She thought of a warrior's purpose, of war and its awful penalties, especially the death of young men. What fools men were, she thought, to seek death and glory in war. "I suppose I should rejoice that this particular boy will be one less enemy for white eyes to engage, while the others will no doubt only grow old enough to murder their allotment of white eyes," she snapped. "And so there will always be war, with no chance for peace between the white man and the red."

"I don't see white eyes laying down their weapons. I also know for certain the last war's not been fought."

Honey knew he was right and, with no purer vision of the future, could only pray. "Allow us to leave here—soon," she begged silently each night before she slept next to Fierce Enemy on the unyielding, cold Apache ground.

CHAPTER FIFTY-FOUR

Ussen, Honey decided, had an Apache sense of humor, for He answered her prayers by putting it into the Apache mind to move south, deep into Mexico, where it was warmer, for the winter. She resolved in the future, therefore, to be more precise in her appeals. From now on she would not be so vague as to ask to "leave soon" but would ask specifically for "safe passage to Sacramento at once."

Having appeased her unhappiness over Cameron's reluctance to leave the Apache with the notion that her lover was not yet fit for such a long journey, she found that the announcement upset her enormously. "I won't set one foot south of here," she stated unequivocally, a reply that fell on deaf ears. "Didn't you tell me the Mexicans hate the Apache even more than the Americans? How absurd to tempt them."

Fierce Enemy's only recourse was to punish his recalcitrant wife, but as he had slaves to pack his possessions, he was able to dodge the issue for a short while.

"You're asking for a beating," Nollie cautioned under her breath. "A man can't have rebellion under his roof."

Honey sat unmoved. "He wouldn't dare."

"You think I want to go? What I want is to keep my flesh on my bones."

"If ever I leave this place, I'll go west or north, not one inch south."

"You'll get lost and die in the desert."

"Better than to live like this forever."

"Only just maybe."

There was no question in Fierce Enemy's mind that Honey would come with them. He simmered with anger, and not until they were ready to begin the trek did he make any move against Honey. By then Nollie and Shahar were beside themselves with

nerves, from the first having been certain of his determination
that Honey would go with them. They had not dared inquire of
his plans, and only at the last minute did he act.

Very calmly then, he entered his wickiup for the last time and
pulled Honey to her feet. When she struggled, one well-placed
fist left her limp in his arms.

When she came to, Honey found herself tied and slung over a
horse's back, facedown. Her jaw felt as though it had been dislo-
cated. "You bastard! You bastard!" she screamed. "Take me off
this beast, at once!"

Fierce Enemy rode ahead of her and then dropped back. "You
spook the horse, he'll run off with you."

"You wouldn't dare," Honey fumed, but softly, not at all certain he wouldn't. "How long must I ride like this?"

"I haven't decided. One, maybe two days. Whatever it takes
to shake out the wrinkles."

Trusting he meant exactly what he had said, Honey knew what
it felt like to truly want to murder someone. "I wish I'd let you
die," she spit.

Cameron wouldn't allow Fierce Enemy to smile.

Cheis's band traveled without stopping until well after nightfall. Only then did Fierce Enemy allow Shahar to give Honey
some water. Otherwise he ignored her until after he had eaten his
fill of food, which in Honey's opinion smelled like ambrosia
from the gods. He gave her bottom a solid whack before she
realized he was standing next to her.

"Damn you!" she snarled, straining at her tethers.

"Time to give the horse a rest," he said as he untied her and
gave her minimal help down. When her legs would not hold her,
he let her fall.

Shahar rushed forward to help Honey, but Fierce Enemy
pushed her away. "She's a lesson to learn," he said gruffly, and
gave the horse to a young boy to look after. "Now's a good time.
I won't have a woman who thinks she's a burro."

Too spent to protest, ill with a mixture of exhaustion and rage,
Honey lay for the night on the ground exactly where she had
fallen. In the morning she woke stiff, to her surprise covered with
a blanket; another was tucked under her head. She sat up slowly.
Awake before anyone else, she glowered in Fierce Enemy's direction, thinking she wanted to kill him. The degradation alone,
she swore, would never be forgotten by her. But when he stood

before her and extended his hand to help her up, she refused the offer for only a moment.

He led her to the edge of the stream they had camped near. "Get in," he ordered.

She looked at him with hatred. "I'm too cold to even consider it. I'm not a warrior, you know."

"I'd hoped you'd learned your lesson," he said, and swiftly picking her up, threw her over one shoulder and strode hip deep before tossing her into the icy water.

"I promise I'll kill you if I ever get a chance," Honey screamed, sputtering as she came up for air.

With one hand he grabbed the crown of her head, pushed her under the water, and held her down. He did this repeatedly, each time asking whether she had had enough and was ready to act like a good Apache wife.

Watching from the edge of the stream, Shahar and Nollie held on to each other. "Is this what you saw and wouldn't tell?" Nollie demanded of her mother, abandoning all thought of ever seducing Cameron.

"I didn't foresee this at all," Shahar muttered, close to despair.

"She's called him by his name all right—Apache bastard." Nollie feared the worst. "If she doesn't kill him, I will!" Just as Nollie pulled away from Shahar, determined to wrestle him to rescue Honey, Fierce Enemy brought Honey, lank as a rag doll, out of the water. "You've killed her. You've killed her," Nollie screamed, and ran forward, swinging at him with her fists.

He shrugged Nollie off with ease, making her fall. "She's not dead yet," he said as he held Honey bent at the waist. Water poured out of her mouth, and almost immediately she began to cough and vomit. Then he laid her gently on the shallow grassy bank while she gasped for air.

Shahar ran for a blanket and threw it over her before he could order, "Leave us alone," to the two women who hovered anxiously. Helpless, they retreated, the sound of Honey's crying and choking torture to their ears.

The fire was gone from her eyes, and Fierce Enemy stroked Honey's back until she was calm. "Now the people will call you Woman Who Learns the Hard Way. I preferred Woman with Gold Eyes."

"Woman Who Loathes You is more precise," she whispered but defiance was absent from her tone.

Fierce Enemy took a deep breath. "Woman Who Tastes Like

Honey was always my name for you." For a moment he seemed
to smile. "You'd be stupid to keep this up," he said gently, then
purposefully edged his voice with cold, sharp steel. "Don't trap
me into flaying you before a crowd." The whip was the greatest
humiliation an Apache might endure.

Honey rolled on her back and looked into his clear blue eyes.
She saw that he meant exactly what he had said and wondered
how she could ever have loved him. "I am your obedient slave,"
she answered.

For several long minutes he stared at her, his thoughts unknowable from his expression. Although furious that she had deliberately acted to humiliate him, he struggled not to pull her against
him and try to comfort her. He saw then that any dream he had had
of her remaining with him and his people was doomed.

When he stood, Fierce Enemy offered Honey his hand. She let
him help her up and then, in deceitful silence, docilely followed
as he led her back to camp.

CHAPTER FIFTY-FIVE

Over the next several weeks that Cheis's band traveled to its
favorite winter camp, Honey was sullen and distant, obedient but
unreachable. Both Shahar and Nollie worried themselves into
similar states. Fierce Enemy seemed not to care at all about the
state of Honey's mind, concerned only that his wife did not defy
him. When they bedded down for the night, at first he left her
strictly alone; then, finding her demeanor a kind of challenge as
well as infuriating, unable to trust himself, he banished her to his
slaves' wickiup.

With each day that passed, he seemed less and less the man
they had known. He now spoke only Apache, even to them,
commanding their actions with words they of necessity grew to
understand.

Fierce Enemy came to be convinced he had been returned
from the brink of death for the purpose of reclaiming his Apache
soul and renew his connection with Ussen and set out to retrieve
the warrior in himself. He honed his skills for war and raiding.
To make his heart strong, he bathed every morning in the ice-cold

stream and hardened himself to endure. He recaptured the skill of running up mountains while holding his breath; he remembered to breathe only through his nose, for a dry mouth in the desert would be deadly.

To renew his claim to Deer Ceremony, Fierce Enemy fasted four days and nights and summoned visions. As a rule, an Apache did not seek a particular Power but was chosen as a host who would use his Power for the good of the people. Fierce Enemy was repossessing Power lost because of disuse. Among the Apache there were ceremonies for nearly every purpose—curing, procuring horses, obtaining love, success in hunting, and myriad others. Fierce Enemy had once possessed Deer Power and now wished only to renew and strengthen his claim on Power bestowed.

His visions were more than ordinary dreams. His spirit returned to the sacred place where Deer Spirit resided, the journey requiring courage, for Deer's mountain abode was guarded by ferocious supernatural animals. To reach this place at all was a death-defying feat over treacherous bridges and terrain, with footholds provided only miraculously at the Power's whim.

But convinced of the purity of Fierce Enemy's quest, the Deer accepted him and granted him Power to make the journey. Through Deer Power, in the hunt Fierce Enemy could realize the deer's consent to be sacrificed for the good of the people. Wearing a deer head blessed by Deer, Fierce Enemy would use his Power to ensure he would find deer to stalk.

Fierce Enemy immediately used his Power to great success. His reputation for Deer Medicine spread, and other men called on him to use his Power, which enlisted the animals' cooperation in the hunt, for their benefit. A few approached him to use Deer Magic to aid them in winning the women of their desires, but having just regained his ceremony, Fierce Enemy refused, not wanting to weaken his power with perhaps more trivial use.

Soon he joined the warriors on raids against the hated Mexicans and was often gone for weeks at a time. When the war party returned, Fierce Enemy celebrated his share of the booty in Apache style with dancing, chanting, and intoxication.

But following one raid, Fierce Enemy did not join in the customary celebration. He felt responsible for the death of the only Apache in the raid and felt it his paramount duty to assist the dead warrior's family. After the widow cut her and her children's hair as the sign of mourning and removed her belongings from her home, she burned all her husband's possessions in their brush wickiup. As soon as the dead warrior was buried in a secret crevice high in the hills, Fast as a Snake and her children moved into Fierce Enemy's wickiup.

He did not trouble himself to explain to Honey or his two slaves that he had not made the woman his wife or that he would only shelter and provide for the dead warrior's family until her brother-in-law returned to camp from another mission.

"Well, what do you make of that?" Nollie huffed. "Not so much as an 'I do, do you?'"

If the arrangement he had made with Fast as a Snake, who was about to deliver her third baby, troubled Honey, she gave no sign.

"When it's born, I hope it keeps him awake nights," Nollie said.

There was no curiosity among the Apache about the terms between Fierce Enemy and Fast as a Snake, but there was a good deal of speculation about the final outcome of Fierce Enemy's relationship with Woman Who Learns the Hard Way. If she continued to be sharp-tongued and contrary, it was judged he would be wise to throw her out of his wickiup permanently, which would pose a great problem to a woman who had no family to whom she could return. She would be unprotected, therefore, and because of her ill temper, there was common agreement among both men and women that Honey would have trouble finding another husband in spite of her comeliness and accomplishments as a woman.

Since their confrontation, Honey simmered with anger. Although she appeared quite normal, even unflappable, and carried out her appointed tasks as necessary, she was not in her right mind. Nollie suspected it; Shahar knew it.

Shahar visualized Honey's affliction as a carbuncle of the heart, a slowly enlarging mass of poisoned blood gradually infecting the whole of Honey's system. Any day, Shahar feared, the dark mass would reach its zenith and burst. She watched Honey anxiously now that Fast as a Snake seemed to have usurped her position in Cameron's wickiup. "Since he tells us nothing, we're not to assume the worst," Shahar urged Honey. "I don't dare go off," she confided to her daughter, "but I sorely need to consult with the Spirits."

For once, Nollie agreed.

Neither did Shahar feel right about conferring with Fierce

Enemy as she would have with Cameron Wolfe on matters that concerned her about Honey. The air about him was hot and disturbed, she sensed. He was not approachable.

I'm shamed I ever coveted his affections, Nollie confessed to herself, and silently heaped her feelings of ill will on him. "Be careful, Mammy, or you'll call down some awful Apache Spirit," Nollie nervously cautioned Shahar as she watched her mother burn wild sage in an abalone shell while she sat by the fire late one night. "You're likely to summon some fierce devil we won't know what to do with," she said, shivering with fright.

"We've our own Apache devil with us already. I need help with him. Before matters get any worse."

"What am I to say when you're out cold? They might just cart you off to the mountains and bury you, you know."

Shahar waved the thought away. "I have to take that chance. He says I'm a dream shaman. Argue that for me."

While Honey slept and Nollie quaked under her blanket, Shahar closed her eyes and meditated. When she opened her eyes, she was gone.

Nollie knew she would not sleep a wink that night, but as dawn poured slowly over their part of the earth, she had to be wakened from a very deep sleep.

"Get up, Nollie," Honey said, shaking her roughly. "Did you know your mother has gone off? You should have told me. Perhaps I could have persuaded her against it. Who knows what kind of humor he's in this morning; he might say she's dead."

Honey's fears coincided with her own, but Nollie denied it. "Why should he? He's provoked with you, not her. Besides, he's called her a dream shaman himself."

Tears rose to Honey's eyes. "We don't know what he'll do anymore."

Nollie pursed her lips, then said accusingly, "I don't think that's it at all." She ventured a guess. "I think you don't know your mind; that's the trouble."

Honey sniffed away her tears and threw back her head. She looked her most arrogant as she narrowed her eyes on Nollie. "What makes you think I don't know my mind?"

Nollie sat up. "I think you're still sweet on him, and mad as a wet hornet you can't make him do what you want."

"I wish he'd tried to drown you like he did me."

"You're blessed he didn't whip you and make you eat guts three times a day for the rest of your life. You humiliated the man in front of his people. What'd you expect him to do?"

Honey slapped Nollie's face and, rising, ran from the wickiup. Fighting tears, she ran as far and as fast as she could from camp before her breath gave out and she broke down. If she were any less sane, she thought, she *would* run away. *But only the Apache know how to survive in this land*, she realized. Only the people knew the secret places where water flowed from deep within the rocks and quickly disappeared mysteriously around a bend; only they knew the hidden valleys in mountain homes where a dozen families, if they chose, could sustain themselves for a lifetime without being found.

It was tempting to think of escape, but in spite of her recent display of stupidity, for which she truly was ashamed, she was not crazy. Yes, she admitted, she was ashamed—for behaving so badly, for forcing Cameron to act against her, for being too proud to ask for his indulgence with her temper. And now, she assumed, the time was past to beg for forgiveness: He had already taken another woman to his side.

She might be forced to live with the Apache for another fifty years, but she could never accept being only one of Cameron's wives. Nor could she escape feeling that she had brought this fate upon herself.

Honey sat on the ground and leaned against a large boulder. When she finally turned and looked back in the direction of the camp, she could see thin spirals of smoke from evening cooking fires beginning to rise into the air. So safe were the people here, there was no need for them to hide, she thought as she rose to go back before someone came after her and she would have the devil himself to pay. "I've provoked you enough."

When she returned to the campground, a number of the people were gathered around Cameron's wickiup, but fortunately, Nollie was the first to see her and hurried to draw her away from camp again. "Fast as a Snake's been trying to have that baby since last night," she whispered as she pulled on Honey's arm. "I'll never understand how they're so silent birthing babies. All I can think is they get 'em out a different way than the rest of us. But this time, something's wrong. The only way I know this is *he* told me himself—*in English*."

Nollie expected a reaction from Honey but, getting none, went on, still hurrying Honey away from camp. "They say someone's witched her. And guess who's been picked for the witch?" Nollie didn't smile. The Apache believed witches put curses on people they disliked, and on their children especially. It therefore followed logically that jealousy might have driven Honey to curse Fast as a Snake in childbirth. "Your being gone didn't win you anybody to defend you. Not even your lover."

Honey took the news seriously. Witches were banished from the band and left to wander in the wilderness alone or burned alive.

"But at least he's worried about you. If Snake Woman dies, he's afraid you'll be punished. Some of them want to kill you now so she'll deliver all right."

Honey paled beneath her suntan.

"He says the baby won't come and she's sometimes bleeding like a stuck pig."

"I don't suppose they'll let me near her."

"Are you mad, girl? They've got medicine men humming around her and flinging pollen every which way. Maybe you ought to stay out here in the brush till it's all over."

"And have them hunt me down? No thank you."

"He said to tell you, by the way, she's not his wife. But I think maybe he believes also you're the witch involved."

Honey pulled away from Nollie's grasp. "Well, if I'm already damned, I won't endanger myself by seeing what, if anything, I can do."

"Don't be stupid; they'll kill you before they'll let you lay a hand on her."

Honey feared Nollie's words were accurate but was solemnly determined. "I must at least try to help her."

CHAPTER FIFTY-SIX

When the small group of men gathered before Fierce Enemy's wickiup caught sight of Honey, they raised a menacing clamor, bringing Fierce Enemy outside. When he saw her, his expression, which he carefully guarded most of the time, changed to one of great relief. With an upraised hand he staved off those who would have advanced on Honey.

"I'm not sure I can protect you," he said. "I hoped Nollie would keep you away."

"She tried. I came back because I may be able to help."

"The ceremony woman wants to kill the baby to save the mother."

Honey was adamant. "That would be impossible if the baby is breech." She tried to move forward, but Fierce Enemy held her back.

"The people believe a hard birth is caused by a witch," he warned.

"So I hear. It's superstitious rot. Surely, *you* don't believe—"

"I'm not sure what I believe anymore."

Not knowing quite how to take his remark, Honey stared at Fierce Enemy a moment before she launched her attack. "Well, let me tell you, then! I am *not* a witch, or *at least* not the witch involved!" Honey's face was quite red from anger. "Now, you think of something appropriate to tell them so I can get inside to see her. Or do you want the woman and her baby to die?"

Cameron stared at Honey for several moments that to Honey seemed a lifetime, then turned to the Apache and spoke several sentences in their tongue.

There ensued a sometimes heated exchange during which Honey waited anxiously. Finally Cameron spoke to her. "They want to search you for a witch's pouch."

"A witch's pouch? I've no witch's pouch, and you know it."

Cameron looked at Honey and said flatly, "I tried to tell them, but they also know we've not been together for some time."

Honey eyed the Apache with a look of fury before she pulled off her skirt and grabbed the fringed hem of her buckskin blouse and pulled the garment over her head. "I've nothing to hide. Not a thing but your precious amulet under here. Satisfied?" she demanded of the cautious Apache. Humiliation seemed to be a requirement of dealing with the people, she thought, her anger raised several degrees for their superstition and their accusations. She turned around so there would be no question that she was holding something behind her back, then put on the blouse and shirt again and stepped toward the shelter.

Again Fierce Enemy barred her. "Not yet. You've not finished the test."

Honey took a deep breath. "And in the meantime, Fast as a Snake can bleed to death. What must I do?"

A woman stepped forward with a gourd cup.

"What's this?"

"Tiswin."

"Tiswin?" She sniffed the beverage and made a sour face. "Good heaven, what's it laced with?"

"If a witch drinks this potion, she dies. An innocent person won't."

"I see," Honey said. She sniffed the brew again, held her breath, and drained the cup. She shuddered at the taste and struggled to hold it down.

Cameron's look now was clearly one of alarm.

"Oh ye of little faith," she gasped at Cameron, then turned her glance on the waiting Apache. "Sorry to disappoint you all, but I'm alive and well." She wondered for how long. "Now that I've passed your tests, I've a bargain to make with you also, Mr. Wolfe. If I'm successful in saving the mother's or the baby's life, you must promise to take me back to civilization."

He wondered if she knew she had him in the palm of her hand, for he did not want the death of the warrior *and* his wife and child on his conscience. "You've my word of honor," Cameron said, and stepped from her path so that Honey could enter his wickiup. "You should've asked Shahar to help you. She's brought many, many babies into the world."

"She's 'traveling.'"

"I'd hoped she'd be back by now."

Fierce Enemy took longer than Honey liked to explain that while she was difficult to live with, she was not a witch but a woman of important medicine in the white eyes' world. He credited her above the indian shamans for the fact that he was alive and well. In spite of his praise, the eyes of the ceremony woman and the Apache midwives showed little trust. "They believe you must bear a child before you can be a medicine woman."

Honey rolled her eyes heavenward. "I suppose a man must bear a child also."

Cameron talked longer and harder until finally the Apache women relented and agreed to accept Honey's help for the sake of their sister, who now could not kneel in the birthing position without being held. Clearly, the woman was on the verge of total exhaustion, perhaps already in shock, with no sign of the baby presenting itself.

There was strong objection to Cameron remaining in the

wickiup. "Women's blood makes a man sick," he explained to her.

"I don't give a damn what they think. I need you to make them understand," Honey insisted, then demanded clean water and *amole* and again stripped off her blouse and scrubbed her arms. "Pray," she said to Cameron as she knelt before the woman in trouble. "Have them help her stand."

Once the woman was standing, Honey slowly inserted her hand into the birth canal. She closed her eyes, her head rested lightly on the mother's swollen belly. Several minutes later, Honey sighed. "There! I've a foot. She's breech, just as I thought. If I can turn the baby slowly into a better position, there's a chance nature will take its course."

Cameron spoke to the indian women, who gave Honey the nod.

It seemed like hours that she was on her knees. By the time the baby was turned, she was drenched in sweat, the poor mother bearing her misery with occasional soft growls of protest. "If nothing else, she'll soon be dead from exhaustion," Honey said to Cameron as he helped her up. She was shaking with fatigue. "Be careful how you touch me. The woman's blood could make you sick."

"Don't be a fool," he said gently, half-smiling, and wrapped a blanket around Honey's shoulders.

Within the hour, a baby girl was delivered, bathed with water, which was warmed in the ceremony woman's mouth first, dusted with pollen for long life, and wrapped in moss; before nightfall, she was sleeping in a cradle made expressly for her.

"Fast as a Snake named her baby Upside Down," Fierce Enemy told Honey later as she lay in her wickiup, doubled over with stomach pain. "And you've been christened Doesn't Give Up."

Honey grimaced with pain. "Perhaps I should have. What was in that drink you gave me?" she demanded, fearing she might die.

"Nothing that will kill you if it hasn't already."

"I wouldn't think of freeing you of your promise!" Honey said as she suddenly fled to the door.

Nollie and Cameron laughed at her plight. "If nothing else," Nollie said, knowing Honey well, "she'll live out of pure spite."

CHAPTER FIFTY-SEVEN

When Shahar revived, she told Nollie, "An Apache baby will bring peace between Honey and Mr. Wolfe. He will promise to do whatever she wants, only he will not fulfill his promise at once."

Nollie was not impressed. "You're too late for that to be a prediction," she said, and filled her mother in on the events she had missed while traveling. "They're already gone."

"You don't mean they've left us behind?"

Nollie shook her head. "They've gone to soak in some pools of hot water and take mud baths. They'll be gone maybe six days. Then he promised we'd be leaving."

Shahar stewed a while on whether the excursion Honey and Cameron now were making was the delay she meant. She had not seen mud baths and hot pools of water. She saw the baby and a cradle; that part of the vision was fulfilled. Then a man appeared —obviously Apache but no one she knew—a hunting club, Fierce Enemy's amulet, a skeleton. Shahar went over and over the signs. She was certain Cameron would indeed fulfill his promise to take Honey away from the Apache, but her premonition held no hope of a lasting truce between them. "It will be a state worse than war."

Shahar ruminated on her vision over a dinner of deer jerky, flat bread, wild onions, and dried *pitahaya* fruit. *Perhaps I am getting too old to see clearly.* "Perhaps the food doesn't agree with me."

"I beg your pardon. I'm doing the best I can with such as we have," Nollie replied tartly. "I dare you to do better."

"The stuff's more suited to mortar than bread," Shahar said quickly, "but that's not what I meant. You've done yourself proud. It's just not nourishing stuff for dreams."

"I couldn't say," Nollie replied, again glad not to be subject to visions.

* * *

Buoyed by Cameron's promise to get back on the trail to California, Honey readily agreed to go away with him to visit the mineral mud baths and hot springs. Privately, even while banished, she had worried about the progress of his healing and for a time had blamed his actions against her on the effect his pain had had on his nerves. Surreptitiously, she had watched to see if he continued to treat himself in her absence and found that while they were separated, he continued to treat his wounds with heat and partook of the sweat lodge often, a therapy that, as a woman, was forbidden her.

He said he felt fully restored to health, yet at times he still suffered great and unexplainable pain in the region of his wounds, which upon examination one would think had healed completely. On consultation, a medicine man who made him promise to haul back as much pale pink clay as he could carry reminded Fierce Enemy of the sacred mud baths and nearby hot springs that were only a few days away from camp. He would be cured there, he believed, and promised Honey they would leave for California as soon as they made a visit to this holy place.

"Certainly the Apache side of you is almost religious, and this is a pilgrimage. Might there be a shrine? I think you mentioned holy water," Honey teased.

"Pain can make you call God's name, if only profanely."

"I remember." There were times in the war she had thought she would never stop hearing the screams of the injured and dying. She heard them even in her dreams. Perhaps she had been right in thinking pain had driven him to extremes of behavior with her, a thought that encouraged her to make allowances for his cruelty.

Honey smiled at Cameron and watched his lips curve into the smile that never failed to tug at her heart, a smile that traveled gently over his face and settled in his blue eyes, and she would be drawn to him in that deliciously familiar way. Easy, so easy, Honey recalled, to be pulled into his arms and borne away.

They traveled for three days, winding through desert and mountain and into low foothills, finally arriving at their destination at dusk the third day. "You mean we've come all this way for this?" she said, gasping. "The smell is unspeakable."

Cameron laughed. The mud pool was rich in minerals, including sulfur. "You can watch if you want, but I'm going in."

Honey watched for a while, then sat on the rim of the natural cauldron and dangled her feet in the ooze. The warmth felt wonderful, she admitted. Finally she joined him. Before the heat sapped all their strength, they climbed out of the pool and let the clay dry on their bodies until it fell away, sometimes needing a little persuasion, leaving their skin soft and their souls rejuvenated.

They took shelter and built a small fire for the night under a shelf of rock that protruded from a monolithic formation above the mud pools. They dined on dried venison and raspberries, walnuts, and bread made from sweet *tornillo* flour. They put their blankets on a bed of dried moss they had brought with them, and steam rising from the mud made their shelter warm; the opportunity to renew their love made it perfect.

With her confession to herself that defying Cameron had been stupid and disgraceful on her part, Honey felt the current of affection for him resume its flow. And when they came together physically, it felt as if life's blood had resumed its flow between them, their connection as mysterious as the spark of life itself.

They spent the following day in the mud and the next two at nearby hot springs. Cameron declared that his pain had eased significantly, while Honey's obsession with the idea of returning to civilization seemed almost to evaporate. "If only we could stay here forever," she declared wistfully, a statement she would later have trouble remembering.

CHAPTER FIFTY-EIGHT

Fierce Enemy and Honey's return to Cheis's camp was preceded briefly by the arrival of a triumphant war party led by the Nantan Gokhlayeh, a man with a ferocious hatred for Mexicans. Among the warriors was Dzaneezi, Fast as a Snake's brother-in-law, who upon sighting Fierce Enemy met him with words of gratitude. While it was tradition for the band to provide whatever was necessary for members in dire need, nevertheless Dzaneezi thanked Fierce Enemy for taking in his brother's widow and her children. He did not blame Fierce Enemy for his brother's death and presented him with a fine Mexican knife that he had just captured in battle. "We drink to success of our war party," Dzaneezi said, pointing to two casks of *jerez*, a rich sherry fortified with brandy that was prized by the Mexicans. "We killed many, won much booty. Look at the steers," he said, pointing to a small remuda the war party had captured. Most would go with Gokhlayeh, but two would go to Dzaneezi for his share. "We were lucky; no warriors were lost, and we reclaimed three Apache women who have been held as slaves by the Mexicans."

Fierce Enemy and Honey arrived several hours after sunset, and each warrior had already been recognized for his accomplishments with dancing and song. A huge bonfire was blazing. The round dancing about to begin; clay drums, wooden flutes, and rasps of sheep's bone were calling the people to dance. For four days and four nights there would also be feasting, drinking, and, between couples, much private revelry.

The war party organized by Gokhlayeh, chief of another Apache band, included warriors from several different Apache bands, among them men Fierce Enemy recognized from Chihuahua's band, which had been his own, including Coyote, whom Fierce Enemy recalled with strong emotion.

Years ago, even before Fierce Enemy had returned to the white eyes world, Coyote had left Chihuahua's camp and pledged his fealty to Gokhlayeh. He had left in bitterness, a bitterness that had reasserted itself the moment he laid eyes on Fierce Enemy. Both men were older now, yet their hatred for each other had not diminished with time and separation. The men did not greet each other and avoided one another.

Honey sensed immediately a change in Fierce Enemy's mood. For no explainable reason that she could observe, he was on edge, wary and distant. They shared in the food and drink, but he refused to participate in the round dancing that would last until dawn.

But on the following night, when the women chose partners, Honey persuaded her lover to dance. Couples faced each other without touching and, to the beat of the music, circled the fire in a sunwise direction, each couple moving close to and then away from the flames. For hours, without interruption, the wheel of dancers spun slowly around and around. With love shining, the fire and music entered their souls and throbbed in their veins; in Honey and Fierce Enemy's vision, all but they burned away.

All else burned away too for a man who watched the night's dancing from outside the circle. The whirling wheel of dancers came by him again and again, yet his eyes saw only Fierce Enemy and his white eyes wife, and as he stared, he silently laid out plans that, if not finished, would not give him rest even in death.

Honey knew only that the man's name was Coyote and had, more than once, found him staring at her. "Am I imagining things, or is that man staring at me?" she had whispered to Nollie, her hands self-consciously going to the figure-eight coil of hair at the nape of her neck.

"You're not dreaming," Nollie replied. "But his name should be 'Jabali.' He looks more a hog than a dog, especially his eyes."

Honey agreed, surprised that he was named after the coyote, a night prowler, an often sinister figure in Apache lore, the character who brought darkness and death to men. When she inquired, Cameron explained. "The Mexicans, who have reason to know, gave him the name because he's a ruthless and cunning warrior. He's one Apache who *always* takes scalps. He'll risk anything to settle a grudge." Scalps from his latest raid dangled from the waist of Coyote's breechclout.

Honey shivered. "I don't like the way he looks at me."

"He hates white eyes almost as much as he hates Mexicans."

"Do you know him well?"

"Well enough. We trained together, completed the four raids to become warriors," he said quietly, and led her away from the man's scrutiny.

During each night of the celebration, the *jerez* was imbibed liberally, the sweet sherry quickly having its powerful effect. Even though she did not care for the drink particularly, Honey had her full share. "It reminds me of civilization," she explained when Fierce Enemy teased her for drinking something she did not especially like. "And as you've given your word, it reminds me that I'll soon be enjoying other things more to my liking."

On the fourth night Coyote approached Honey with a bolt of vibrant blue silk, a gift he offered her if she would dance with him in the last dance of the celebration. Since Coyote was one of the war party's most honored warriors, to decline would have been extremely insulting and would have incurred the wrath of the people, who feared such a slight would bring them bad luck. With a helpless look of appeal in her lover's direction, Honey accepted the fabric and was led to the fire.

With another expression, perhaps a different set to his eyes, Honey thought, one could describe Coyote as handsome, but vacant and cold, his eyes reminded Honey of death. In her opinion,

Coyote had a murderer's gaze. He epitomized the savage
Apache.

His features were aquiline, his head and face small, his broad
forehead clear. Not as tall as Cameron but equally lean and muscular, Coyote had many more scars, a scattering of fresh bruises
from the violence he had encountered in battle apparent on his
naked torso and arms. The apron of his breechclout and his high-
topped moccasins were spattered with blood.

Without touching, men and women danced facing one another
in parallel rows on either side of the fire. Tonight, for Honey, the
dance had no mystical aura surrounding it, as it had the night
before when she had danced with her lover. Terror swelled in her
chest and made her heart quiver as with chant and song the warriors' deeds and victory were recounted over and over again,
fierce ululating cries tearing at her ears like knives. While the
dancers moved rhythmically back and forth, close and apart,
Coyote's eyes never left Honey, his riveted gaze suggesting he
had memorized forever her every feature.

The heat from the bonfire was oppressive; to Honey it seemed
the dance was unending. Soon she lost all track of time, uncertain
whether they had danced for minutes, hours, or days. She was
light of head and body, mesmerized by Coyote's stare, the chanting and singing echoing in her brain, her heartbeat thundering
like a drum in her head. Sweat poured from the dancers; they
were swimmers on fire.

When the dancing was finally over, Fierce Enemy rescued
Honey quickly and lead her away. Alone in their wickiup, he fed
her more sherry diluted with water. This time it tasted like nectar,
as did her lover's passionate kisses.

CHAPTER FIFTY-NINE

In two days' time Cameron intended to take the women back to
civilization. They would carry ample provisions to get across the
mountains and desert to Tucson, mainly dried venison, mesquite
meal, and water carried in woven wicker jugs coated with piñon
pitch. Although it would be a long, rough journey in which at this
time of year they might encounter snow as they came closer to

the American border, Honey, Nollie, and Shahar anticipated the departure eagerly.

Honey had Cameron's promise, which was all she said she needed, but at the back of her mind she wondered whether, when they arrived in Tucson, he would continue to California or return to the indians. While she confessed a slight appreciation of the intimacy the people had with nature and the stark beauty of the harsh simplicity of their lives, never for a serious minute had she ever entertained any real thought of staying among them. Honey realized, however, that for the man she loved the choice was less easy.

In his place, she believed she would never have adapted so well to the indian way of life. Honey thought of herself at nine years of age, the age at which he had been captured, and while she often had been something of a test to her father and Shahar, she had always been thoroughly domesticated. Wild rides on ponies and surreptitious excursions to forbidden places with her brothers and other companions had never had any implication beyond simple naughtiness or deeds done out of pure boredom. With the exception of her long-held desire to be a doctor, she would not have described herself as especially daring. Even in that wish, Honey intended to practice medicine only within the limits of accepted behavior, not undergo any sort of dramatic change in herself. Nor did she dream of altering the profession.

But Cameron had undergone more than a surface metamorphosis, had shed more than his white eyes skin. With the exception of his lighter hair and blue eyes, when he had stripped off white eyes clothes and exchanged them for buckskin, he had become Apache to the soul.

Honey shivered at the thought of their arrival in Tucson. She wanted more than anything for Cameron to disown the Apache once again but was by no means certain he could do so. The only hold Honey had on Cameron was love, but she fully realized he might love her more than life itself and still elect not to live his life as a white eyes.

Paralyzed to think that what she offered would not be enough to lure him, Honey became sullen.

"Thinking makes you too sober," Nollie complained while they packed the baskets and distributed what they could not carry with them among the indians. "I'd expect you to be turning handsprings, not pouting."

Honey forced a smile. "When we arrive in Tucson, I promise

to put on an acrobatic exhibition like they've never seen before."

"I hope all the signs are favorable, Mammy. I'd hate to think of us giving away all this food we slaved to put by and end up staying."

Shahar shook her head. "Must be something in this country; nothing seems clear."

"Must be the Apache Spirits' fault. Probably they ran your spooks off." Nollie could not wait to get away. "This is a thoroughly disgusting place. We aren't leaving here any too soon to suit me. If His-Apache-Self changes his mind about goin', I'll wait till he's asleep and slit his throat myself." She said the last with such pure conviction in her voice that Honey and Shahar stopped what they were doing and stared at her. "You just wait and see. It'll be my pleasure, I can tell you." Neither doubted her.

"You know, of course, you'll be slitting your own throat as well. Ours, also," Honey pointed out.

"I'm glad none of the people speak English," Shahar said, looking around. Their camp was several yards away from any other but next to an often used pathway.

"I'm just giving you a little warning of how I *see* things. No trances for me, thank you. And no more delaying."

Nollie could be counted on to be testy in tense situations, Honey reminded herself. One needn't take her seriously, she believed; there was no room in her own heart to consider that Cameron might renege on his vow.

A few moments later Honey hiked a short distance from camp to pick raspberries that were just coming into perfection. The succulent fruit would be a last treat, a sign, she hoped, of good things to come. With no time to dry them and make them into little cakes, as was usually done, Honey planned to pick enough to have berries for the first few days of their journey.

She set about her task in the full sun, taking to shadier vines under trees when the heat began to bother her. Never fully acclimated to the intense heat of the region, Honey never, even at her worst moments, considered escaping from the indians because any attempt would require a flight through the desert. Without a knowledgeable guide, only a slow hideous death would await her in the desert. If it was death she intended, Honey thought, she would find a far quicker method than drying to dust in the sun.

She arrived in the raspberry patch early but was not alone in her quest. Other women were also busy collecting their share of the harvest, and most, like Honey, now had their lips stained with bright berry juice. After two hours, her baskets were full and she headed alone back to camp, balancing one basket on her head and one on a hip. From time to time Honey stopped for a moment and accomplished the switching of one basket to the opposite hip, which as of yet still required her to stand perfectly still to bring her raised arm down to claim the lower basket, then raise the other before the basket on her head tumbled to the ground. Apache women could accomplish this feat without halting their stride, but so far whenever Honey felt confident enough to try it, there was disaster.

Thinking it might be her last chance, Honey was determined to try one more time. Nollie had succeeded, and so had Shahar. "Why not me?" She laughed, then steadied her gait and her baskets. She waited for a level place in the path and, holding her breath, eased her hand from her head, a ballerina in the middle of the pose.

Without a hitch, Honey quickly switched hands on the hip basket and raised her other arm to steady the basket on her head, only to have the basket fly to the ground. "Oooooh," she shrieked in disgust with herself, and whirled around to stare a large paint horse in the face. Stunned, Honey jumped backward and screamed with fright. The rider, who had toppled her basket from her head, was Coyote, and he now glared down at her viciously.

"You nearly scared me to death!" Honey complained. Her heart leapt in her throat as she bent to collect the spilled fruit. "How can you be here when you left three days ago?" she demanded, although she knew Coyote did not speak English. "Did you get lost?" she wondered sarcastically. The notion struck her as funny, but her laugh was nervous. She had not heard him approach because Apache horses were never shod.

Honey had barely collected a handful of berries before Coyote dismounted, kicked her basket aside, pulled her roughly to her feet, and threw her over his shoulder. She kicked and struggled and swung her fists; she tried to bite him. He seemed not to notice and mounted his spotted horse with her draped and flailing over his shoulder as if she were no burden at all.

"What do you think you're doing?" Honey screamed as Coyote urged his horse to a gallop and headed away from the campground. "I'll be missed. If I'm not back at camp soon, they'll come looking for me. If you recall, they can track spiders in a rainstorm. Cameron will not rest till he finds me." She screamed and kicked and beat on his back with her fists until she was spent.

Her capture made no sense at all to her. Stealing another man's wife was not the habit of the Apache. Surely, if it were, Cameron would have cautioned her. *Surely?* She remembered how uneasy he had been when Gokhlayeh and his war party had been in their camp and cursed herself for not insisting on an explanation. "What do you want of me?" There was no answer, of course, only silence. She imagined the worst.

Honey fought back tears but, faced with imminent death and perhaps rape and torture, lost the battle. *If nothing else*, she thought wildly, *I'll annoy him with tears running down his back*, and proceeded to weep and thrash like the madwoman she was very near to being.

CHAPTER SIXTY

Coyote carried Honey on horseback over his shoulder for hours, finally stopping for a horse and a pack mule he had hidden away earlier. He put Honey on the horse and lashed her hands together. The horse had no saddle, only a blanket. "I hope you intend to ride slowly," she snapped as Coyote gathered her reins in his hand. She gripped the animal's mane tightly. "I don't ride well bareback. I'll fall if you go fast. Of course, you don't understand and don't care."

Honey knew she was beginning to rave, but somehow silence seemed worse. His purpose in stealing her mystified Honey. "You must realize we'd be followed. He won't let you have me." She tried not to cry. "What do you want from me? I've nothing. Nothing at all." The only possibility she could think of was too horrible to speak of or even consider. She fortified herself with what Cameron had told her: An Apache did not take a woman for a wife without her consent, nor did the Apache rape captives. However, from the little Cameron had said about the man, Coyote seemed capable of aberrant behavior; the image of the scalps he had taken in the Mexican raid was hideously clear in her mind. As a rule the Apache did not take scalps.

She chattered on to her unhearing guide. "I'm not a good wife for an Apache. Ask my husband. Actually, I wonder if I'd make any man a good wife. I don't cook or clean or want babies." Then Honey began to wail, both enraged and terrified. Coyote rode ahead as if she were not there.

Finally Honey fell silent, and they continued in silence through canyons and hills and into the foreboding desert. Coyote continued into the night as Honey, exhausted by fright and her overworked emotions, began to nod. Several times she jolted awake, miraculously able to right herself before falling to the ground. Added to her terror was the knowledge that the Apache did not travel at night. The fact that Coyote, like his namesake the night prowler, did increased the man's sinister aura. She begged to stop, but deaf or asleep himself, Coyote did not call a halt until the sun was up and high in the cloudless sky the next day. When he helped her down from her horse, Honey's legs would not hold her. She collapsed and lacked the strength to get up.

Growling an obvious reprimand, Coyote pulled Honey from the ground and dragged her under the shelter of nearby overhanging rocks, where he dropped her. Too fatigued to move, she lay still. The heat was intense even in the shade and made Honey feel drugged. When she was on the verge of falling into a stupor of sleep, Coyote made her sit up and thrust a small piece of jerked deer meat, a potato flour biscuit, and a bag of water into her hands. Limp with weariness, she stared at the food as though she did not know what it was.

Coyote stood over her glowering; when she did not begin to eat, he grabbed her face and pulled it toward his, then shoved a biscuit into her mouth with quietly furious orders to eat. His grip was painful, his menace real. More than anything else, Honey wanted him not to touch her and choked down the dry biscuit without further struggle. Then, wanting only to sleep, she lay down. She passed out rather than fell asleep.

It was night when Honey woke, and she sat up at once as if someone had yanked her into a sitting position. Unrested, stiff, hardly able to move, Honey wondered if she was dreaming. Dazed, she trembled in the cold night air. Although dark, the night was illuminated like day by a moon of astonishing perfection that seemed close enough to earth to touch. When she saw the solid figure of Coyote, Honey knew her nightmare was real.

Coyote offered Honey more water, which she accepted and drank greedily this time. "Where are you taking me? What do you want? Why are you leaving an obvious trail?" she demanded as she noticed he was making no effort to conceal their presence.

As usual, Coyote did not answer but led her away, in much more of a hurry today than before. After dark, they camped again in another rocky area many miles away from the first, just inside the entrance of a cave Honey was reluctant to enter. But she had no choice as her captor dragged her with him, with her crying, "But there might be lions or bears—bears, do you hear me?" She growled madly. "*Oso*," she whimpered as he pushed her to the floor at his feet. "Aren't you afraid of bears like other Apache? Are you at all like other Apache?"

He did not answer but squatted next to her and began building a fire with twigs he had brought with him into the cave. Nervously, Honey continued to interrogate her captor. "You are different, aren't you, Coyote? Not afraid to break taboo, bear or otherwise, not afraid to travel at night when snakes are about," she said, her voice not betraying the terror this knowledge struck in her. "And there's something terrible between you and Cameron. Something you wish to avenge through me. Am I right? Oh, God, I wish you'd tell me if I'm right," she cried.

"You've left a trail for him to follow, which is what you want. And now you're even building a signal fire to let him know exactly where we are. Cunning devil." Her speculation both terrified her and made her furious. "How dare you, how dare you!" she raved. Intent on starting the fire, Coyote ignored her. "Only a coward strikes down women and children to punish a man! You're a slimy, disgusting, slithering snake." With the fire started, Coyote demanded her silence, striking her viciously and causing her teeth to tear into her lower lip.

Shortly, a decent fire was burning in the cave. Then Coyote spent a long time rigging a trap, which, if someone walked into it, would catch and hoist the intruder and cause him to dangle over the fire, just far enough from the flame to roast slowly. Honey's insides contracted with fear. Escape seemed next to impossible.

With a look she conceived as a twisted half smile, Coyote then dragged Honey to her feet. He tugged at the turquoise amulet at her throat, demanding that she give it to him. When she did, he threw it next to the fire where no one could miss it.

Then Coyote pulled a long knife. Honey expected the worst. She screamed and tried to elude him but to no avail. He caught her and threw her down with ease, pinning her with a knee in the back. He grabbed her hair, which was pulled to the back of her head and bound in a large figure eight. She feared he would scalp her. Remarkably, he only cut her hair.

Not quite believing she hadn't been scalped, Honey watched Coyote uncoil the thick mass of her hair and drape it over a rock so that at first glance it seemed to be an actual scalp. He cut her left wrist and let her bleed, smearing her blood on rocks nearby, then stanched the wound with a filthy rag and bound it.

Then Coyote took wood from the fire for a torch and led her farther into the cave. She shook with fear as he forced her ahead of him, one arm twisted behind her back. "What do you want?" she cried over and over again. The cave was cold, rank with a musty smell. She had never been so afraid in her life.

When they rounded a sharp, narrow curve, Honey immediately saw what Coyote wished her to see: two skeletons, apparently mother and child, laid in a natural rock alcove. The child, a small baby, would have been interred atop its mother, but instead, the body disturbed, it lay alongside her. Honey sucked in her breath and violently resisted going an inch nearer the obvious grave, her horror magnified by the knowledge that Apaches *never* visited grave sites for fear of ghosts.

"What in God's name has this to do with me?" Honey begged Coyote. Suddenly verbal, Coyote began speaking furious Apache. Her eyes wide with alarm, her heart pounding, she could understand only a word here and there. Frantic, she watched him kneel beside the grave and used the moment to flee. What fate could be worse than to be held by a madman? she reasoned as she plunged into the dark and tried to retreat the way she had come.

Honey knew she had mere seconds to elude Coyote. She darted for a crevice she could barely see in the dwindling torchlight and forced herself into a wedge just as Cameron had told her Apache sometimes did to escape a pursuer. In terror, imagining snakes and spiders crawling over her, this crevice perhaps her grave, Honey tried not to breathe and prayed Coyote would not see her.

But she heard him, then saw him as he carried the torch and searched for her. When he stood next to her, Honey's heart beat so violently that she expected to be discovered, but he went past. She knew better than to move, and he returned, this time more carefully inspecting the hidden channels between the rocks. When he saw her, Coyote growled like a furious beast and sprang at her, catching her by the hair and dragging her out of the crevice, then fell on her, forcing her to the floor.

Honey struggled and screamed, the echo of her terror ricocheting off the walls of the cave as if the sound were bullets aimed at her ears. Then, suddenly, she was silent, every ounce of her strength reserved for the effort to keep Coyote from raping her. Fear that he might kill her for resisting him did not stop her. She clawed and bit, her every movement an effort to make it more difficult if not impossible for him.

When he succeeded in raising her skirt to a dangerous height and exposed himself, he crushed her beneath him. He held both of her hands helpless above her head in only one of his hands, and he entered her with violence.

She spit in his face.

He only laughed and, obviously enjoying himself, began without haste to rock his body against hers violently. He could afford to be leisurely. There was no need to hurry. Prolonging her torture suited him fine.

Honey struggled not to cry but failed and fervently wished she were dead. She closed her eyes to block out the glowering triumph she saw in Coyote's animal eyes. If he did not kill her, she knew nothing would ever take away the degradation she felt at this moment. As she lay sobbing, it seemed her misery would go on forever; then, suddenly, Coyote was forced free of her body as Fierce Enemy leapt at him, throwing Coyote backward.

Honey rolled away from the men and watched, knowing that whatever had driven Coyote to the madness of taking her hostage would not be settled with fists; their struggle would be a fight to the death. In the flickering torchlight, the two men grappled with each other, their mutual hatred plain even in the dim cave, which now seemed much smaller than it had only moments before. They growled and groaned as they strained in combat. Coyote was naked; Fierce Enemy was stripped to his breechclout. Honey prayed fervently for Fierce Enemy's success. Finally, Fierce Enemy gained the advantage and had only to plunge Coyote's own knife into the man to be victorious. Stunned, terrified, Honey begged for the kill.

In the last moments, both nearly exhausted, the men eyed each other and exchanged words that to Honey's ears seemed furiously fast but surprisingly calm. Then Coyote corrected his stance to stand tall and without a trace of fear in his eyes accepted the death blow, a thrust of the knife to the heart.

This was not the first time Honey had seen a man die but was the first occasion that she as a witness had been so intimately involved. With Coyote's death she felt like an animal sprung from a fatal trap. Jubilation coursed through her veins.

CHAPTER SIXTY-ONE

The moment before death Coyote's look had been one of horrified surprise as, with the man's own knife, Fierce Enemy slashed the man's genitals from his body. Transfixed, unable to believe what she was seeing, Honey did not hear herself screaming. When he dropped the knife and turned to face her, she fainted. He took her in his arms and, taking up the torch, carried Honey back to the fire, where he laid her down gently. He covered her with a blanket and sat beside her until she revived.

As he waited, Fierce Enemy grieved. This was a place of ghosts and death. That he should be here at all was unthinkable to an Apache; he had scrupulously avoided the site all these years. That he should be driven to kill a man who once had been his best friend burdened his soul; the fact that he had come to despise Coyote mattered little in this regard.

Fierce Enemy's mistake with Coyote had been to forgive the man his jealousy. Absolution was a white eyes way, not Apache. An Apache *never* forgives. He would never forget this brutal lesson.

He worried how Honey would handle the shocks she had suffered and knew she might never accept, even if she came to understand what had happened: what had been in his mind and what Coyote had thought he was doing. Perhaps no one who could claim to be sane could successfully live in two worlds at once, when the realities of one world alone were almost more than a person could endure.

Fierce Enemy kept the fire alive while Honey slept on. She seemed so small huddled under the blanket. Sun-touched, her shorn hair much lighter and her skin darker than ever before, she was more beautiful now than when he had first seen her. He loved her, at this moment a feeling that made him feel desperate. He wanted to hold her against him and know her tenderness, to have her console him at this hour at least as much as he would comfort her.

If she would stay with him in the country of his people, he believed someday she would find it possible to understand all that had happened. But with her heart set on leaving, he acknowledged that there would be no keeping her with him here.

Later Honey woke slowly, alert but dazed. At first she lay on her back and for many long minutes silently stared at the sheet of rock that stretched overhead. Strangely calm, she turned her head to regard Fierce Enemy solemnly, then turned away. Nothing he could say, she realized, could ever mitigate the horror of what had happened to her or what she had seen him do, an act of such barbarity that she could not reject it as something imagined, a nightmare. Until now Honey had never considered death a means of escape from life's trials and pain. Now she felt she would have preferred to be murdered than to be forced to live with what she had seen and experienced.

Fierce Enemy honored her silence. When she sat up, she wrapped the blanket around her, drew up her knees, and hugged them tightly. He offered her water and a handful of raspberries. She accepted his offerings but looked at him sadly. "What now?" she whispered.

"When you're ready, we'll go back for Nollie and Shahar."

"I'd rather die in the desert than stay here."

He nodded. "I want to explain."

"I don't want to hear."

"You don't want to understand?"

"There's no earthly way to explain away what I saw."

"What did you see?"

Tears flooded Honey's eyes. Sobbing, she put her head down on her knees. Fierce Enemy tried to take her into his arms. "Nooooooo, don't touch me!" she spat, flinging her arms out to push him away.

He saw pure hatred for him in her eyes and sat back on his haunches to wait out her crying. "What I say will change nothing that happened."

"Then why say it?"

"I *must*, and you'll listen and, I hope, understand." Honey stared at him defiantly, and he felt her rage. "Did he tell you whose bones rest here?" Honey shook her head emphatically, feeling it irrelevant. "They're the remains of my Apache wife and child."

Honey flinched. "I'm sorry," she said reflexively, yet was unable to fathom why it should matter.

"He stole you to punish me for her death." Honey's look was incredulous. He went on. "Coyote blamed me—my white blood." Cameron paused, doubtful that he could ever make Honey understand something so complicated and, to the white eyes mind, irrational. "We both were in love with her, but she accepted me. When she did, Coyote turned against me. When she died giving birth, he believed it was my white blood that killed her: If her husband had been Apache, she would be alive. He could not forgive me.

"He became a renegade among the people, a man you could always count on to be exceptionally cruel. As a rule, Apache don't rape women, if for no other reason for fear of losing their power as warriors. But Coyote often disregarded that taboo."

"What has that to do with me?"

"He did what he did to punish me by hurting you. He'd've tortured and killed you before my eyes if he could to avenge her death."

"His reason makes sense to you?"

Cameron nodded.

"Then *you* are a savage no better than he was," Honey cried. "How can you excuse what he did to me—what he would have done? You're saying you'd accept even his murdering me." Honey put her head down on her knees again and sobbed. He touched her, wanting to comfort her, but she screamed "Don't touch me!" and pushed him away, fire in her eyes. "This, of course, justifies your mutilating his body—no, that's not right—mutilating him while he was still alive." She was nearly hysterical.

"Apache believe a man goes through eternity as he is at death. The man called Coyote will go as he should for his crime against you."

When Fierce Enemy's last statement registered with Honey, she began to laugh, at first softly, then more and more wildly, until she was forced to lie down from weakness, her laughter quickly turning into furious, heartbroken tears.

On the verge of tears himself, Fierce Enemy moved next to Honey and began to massage her back gently, hoping to console her and also himself.

Her body turned rigid under his hand. "Don't touch me," she whispered. "Don't touch me ever again!"

CHAPTER SIXTY-TWO

The journey from Mexico across the desert and into the Arizona Territory was arduous. They faced extremes of drought and heat in the desert and cold in the mountains, where they encountered snow. Cameron had hoped to persuade Honey to wait until the weather to the north was warmer, which would have meant he and the women would stay two months or more with the Apache in Cheis's winter campground. However, after the incident with Coyote, Cameron decided Honey's state of mind was more urgent than the hazards of bad weather.

He would have preferred her to be openly hostile to him rather than sullen, he thought as they traveled; Coyote had been more successful in punishing him than the man had ever dreamed. Beyond the announcement that Coyote was dead, Cameron had said not a word to Nollie or Shahar about the events of Honey's abduction. As far as he knew, Honey had added only that she was certain Coyote had intended to kill her. Cameron left it to her to explain the circumstances further, but she did not.

At Honey's insistence, they stayed in the Apache camp only as long as it took them to pack the necessary provisions for the long trek to Tucson. The journey through Mexico was anxious and strained, the most feasible route bringing them close to the cave where Honey had been raped. In the Apache way, Cameron led as they rode single file through a canyon filled with large rock formations. A fierce wind commenced, blowing sand and debris, scouring the trail, and blinding the travelers. They were forced to stop in their tracks until the howling died down.

Trapped in a flaying cocoon of stinging dust that whirled around them eerily, they dismounted and hunched together for protection under a tent of blankets thrown over their heads. In a huddle nearby, the animals nickered and danced. Here, near the cave where Coyote had died, Honey's nerves, already frayed, began to unravel. Unpleasant as it was, only Honey was adversely affected, succumbing to tears and trembling. Fierce Enemy knew her affliction as ghost sickness.

Coyote's ghost, whose presence was manifested in the howling wind, Fierce Enemy believed, had not yet left the place of death but remained on earth to make trouble for his enemies before descending into the underworld to begin the afterlife. His mutilation, Fierce Enemy feared, would only prolong the ghost's presence. If Honey's recovery was not spontaneous, only an Apache shaman could cure her.

Fierce Enemy did not share his knowledge of Honey's disease with anyone, especially Honey, out of fear of provoking her and causing a more serious case of ghost sickness to emerge. If knowledge would have helped her, he would have spoken without hesitation even at the risk of alienating her from him further.

He relied on Shahar and Nollie to comfort Honey, but they were cramped together and nearly suffocating, and Nollie lost patience almost at once. "I've never seen you carry on like this before; you're usually the tough nut. What's got into you? Just recall you're the one wanted to get going. We could've waited the season out—not that I cared to stay on any more than you did. Trouble is, you don't know your own mind."

As they continued north, Honey seemed to recover. By the time they reached the American border, Honey, if not cured, was at least in much better spirits. "I don't know what you're lettin' up for," Nollie exclaimed. "Remember where we were when we got into trouble the first time? I won't breath easy till we see your fine Uncle Trevor Jefferson sittin' comfortably on his own veranda."

Honey smiled. "I'll feel a whole lot better even in Tucson."

Cameron doubted it, for there was nothing especially commodious about Tucson. "It won't fit your idea of civilization, but I guarantee you a bath and maybe some regular food and a bed," he promised, hoping his influence with Hattie Mullins was still intact.

"As we all look like indians dusted with flour, you're sure we'll be welcome?" Nollie wondered, seeing that their buckskin garments were covered with white alkaline dust. "I'd hate to get so close and get shot."

"Now there's a perfect end to our troubles," Shahar observed, "but I don't foresee it."

"And just how much of this did you foresee?"

"Far too little, as it turns out."

"Don't speak to me of ghosts and spirits," Honey chimed in, "ever again, or I *shall* lose my mind."

"A good rest will fix that," Shahar said.

"A good rest is three or four years."

The closer they came to civilization, the more compelled Shahar felt to her Spirits. Among the Apache, she had perceived herself as barricaded from that source of wisdom, and only occasions of supreme effort had permitted her to tap into their echelon. Now she strongly felt a summons but declined her impulse to travel, if only for the sake of Honey's sanity, which Shahar worried about for the first time in her life. Shahar wanted Honey to feel safe and feared her traipsing off might bring her to ruin.

Shahar could not avoid knowing something awful had happened to Honey while she had been in Coyote's hands. It troubled her that Honey did not confide in her. Her insight seemed to be off. *Maybe I'm ahead of myself*, she thought, vowing a spiritual journey almost as soon as she set foot in Tucson.

From a distance, one could see Tucson, determine it to be a collection of dwellings, and assume it was a town. However, the closer one came, the less likely that description seemed. "They call this a town?" Nollie demanded. "Why, it's nothing but ruins."

Cameron smiled. "That's a fair description." Out of the desert, during some indeterminate age, flanking four sides of a rectangular plaza, there appeared to have fallen a collection of mud houses in various states of decline. A few were whitewashed, or had been in some distant era. Most looked to be crumbling, but there was no way to tell whether this would be accomplished sooner or later. Animals—from chickens to cattle—for the most part roamed freely, their attendant litterings as often as not underfoot. The human habitants looked mainly to be the refuse of the rest of the world.

"We lived better with the Apache," Nollie observed.

The dress of the travelers occasioned many curious glances, but one man and three women did not intimidate anyone. They seemed to have a specific destination in mind, and no one troubled them. When they arrived at Hattie's, which was one of the few perhaps recently whitewashed establishments, she, after recognizing him, welcomed Cameron enthusiastically. "Look what the desert's coughed up and the 'Pache's spared." Without a moment's hesitation for his appalling filth, Hattie hugged him fiercely and seized a kiss full on the mouth. "Not just a sight for sore eyes but a sore sight," she said happily. "It'd been so long since I seen you, I'd gone believin' the tales goin' 'round 'bout you bein' scalped by 'Pache." Reluctantly she turned her attention to Cameron's companions. "These the ladies carried off by those murderin' savages?" Hattie paused to appraise them more carefully. "Never seen such a bunch that could still claim to be this side of the grave."

Honey thought Hattie's description summed it up nicely, but under her liberal coating of grit, she felt her cheeks burn, which she believed to be caused by humiliation over her own filthy condition rather than irritation at Mrs. Mullins's obvious familiarity with Cameron. "I hope you can accommodate us, Mrs. Mullins. For the last hundred miles, Mr. Wolfe has promised me a bath and a bed."

"A bath I can do, but I'm real particular about who shares my bed," she said with a glance at Cameron, then led all of them to her airy bathtubs. "You don't look so prosperous just now. This something I'll be offerin' for trade?"

Cameron gave Hattie a friendly whack on the backside. "Don't worry, we got through with our money but nothing else worth mention."

Hattie laughed. "You're a rare one. Can't wait till you're cleaned up." She saw to it that Cameron was settled in hot water before she took care of the women. "I've only two other tubs. It'll be for you to say who's last to get washed."

The honor went to Nollie. "She sure knows which side the butter's on," Nollie said to Honey when she reappeared after submerging herself entirely in the hot water. Nollie handed soap to Honey. "Not as good as indian soap."

"Better," Honey insisted, too exhausted to keep up any conversation and therefore unable to ignore Hattie's giggles and the smothered shrieks that emanated from Cameron's bath station.

"Maybe it's not Mr. Wolfe but someone a good deal closer," Nollie suggested.

Honey gave her a glance that could have cut glass. "I couldn't care less," she insisted, and leaned against the high back of the tin tub. She rang bathwater from a washcloth and placed it over her dust-irritated eyes. "I intend to sit here until the water turns cold."

"And be entertained. My imagination runs wild."

"On second thought," Honey said, and resumed taking her bath. After a moment she raised her voice considerably. "Oh, Mrs. Mullins," she called in the direction of the woman's voice.

There was an irritated sigh. "Yes, dearie?"

"I'd like a word with you, please."

"Sure, Mrs.," she said, and appeared in Honey's enclosure, wiping water from her hands on her apron. "What you be wantin'?"

"Some clean clothes."

"I take in laundry. But I'm opposed to doing anything has anything to do with indians."

"I wouldn't ask you to do such a thing. Mr. Wolfe has funds for us to acquire new wardrobes, providing, of course, one can acquire such things in this . . . place."

"Sure you can."

"In that case, Mr. Wolfe will make it well worth your while if you would buy us the articles of clothing we need at once. Isn't that right, Mr. Wolfe?" Honey called over the mud wall between them. "I'd consider it an act of Christian charity if you would act on my request at once, so we don't have to wear our indian clothes ever again."

Hattie ducked her head back around the wall dividing Honey and Cameron's tubs to get his consent, then popped back, her hand full of cash. "The water won't have time to cool off before I'm back with your necessaries," she promised, and disappeared on her errand.

CHAPTER SIXTY-THREE

With as much graciousness as was possible for Mrs. Mullins, Honey, Shahar, and Nollie were put up for the night on borrowed pallets in the small three-room adobe house Hattie called home. "Not wishing to cause you embarrassment in front of the ladies," Cameron said as he went to sleep outside. Hattie was not certain whether she had been slighted.

The arrangement lasted three days. By then Cameron had bought a wagon and provisioned it, and the women had acquired more than one change of clothes. Honey, in a shrill mood about her shorn hair and especially her swarthy, sun-darkened skin, bought a black velveteen wide-brimmed hat with outrageous quantities of sheer netting. "From Paris, France, I'm told," she remarked to Hattie.

"Yes, I know. The man's had it for a while. Got to thinkin' he'd never unload it." Hattie appraised its suitability for Honey. "Well, if you can't wear it, nobody could. Whatever happened, Mrs., to your hair?"

"I'm just grateful I didn't lose my scalp along with it."

"You should be. And lucky you weren't made a 'Pache buck's bride."

"Yes, wasn't I fortunate!"

"I was tellin' Mr. Wolfe that your uncle was out here for a while late last year. He offered a high reward for anyone could find you."

"That's comforting information. I'd wondered if our disappearance had ever been noticed."

"Oh, it was noticed, all right. Just nothing anybody was in a position to do about it. The lying 'Pache denied knowing anything, which is strange, because the indians usually like to arrange swaps for white women. They prefer their own, or Mexicans, which is all right with me."

Almost as soon as he had stepped out of the tub, Cameron had telegraphed Trevor in Sacramento to announce their safe return to civilization. The response: "Message received with great joy and thankful prayers. Make all possible haste to Sacramento."

They would be on the road and headed across the Ninety Mile Desert to Fort Yuma in the morning. While Honey, Shahar, and Nollie tried to sleep, Hattie shared a bottle of whiskey with Cameron out in the night air. However, their muted voices and in particular Hattie's laughter made sleep for more than a few minutes at a time impossible for Honey.

Shahar and Nollie had much less trouble. Awakened twice by especially sharp squeals, they covered their heads with their pillows and managed to ignore all further assaults on their rest. Honey, however, lay in distress for what seemed like hours until Hattie came inside and tiptoed to her bedroom. Even then Honey would have sworn she heard more laughter, but eventually she decided she must be hearing things.

She sat up at the next rush of giggles. She supposed Cameron could easily have gone in through Hattie's bedroom window, the idea settling uncomfortably fast in her mind. She thought of confirming her suspicions by simply stepping outside for some air and thereby learning whether Cameron was sleeping under the stars or whether. . . . *What concern is it of mine?* she admonished herself. *What concern, indeed!*

The journey to Fort Yuma was as hot and miserable as any of the preceding desert miles, made more so in Nollie's opinion by Honey's waspish mood. "You tell me why you should care who he beds down with? You're out of love with him, so I thought."

"I care not one whit."

"Then give us a smile." Nollie pinched both of Honey's cheeks. "Gone rain here sure from the looksa yur face."

Even Shahar stewed. "I need to get someplace I can sit awhile and meditate on matters."

"Not as far as I'm concerned," Honey said. "I'm asking Uncle Trevor to put you to hard labor the second we arrive. I don't think you should be given any time off to stir your trouble pot."

"Slavery's done, remember?" Nollie protested.

"Maybe so, but we need to keep your mother occupied and not meddling with Spirits. I don't ever again want to hear 'This the man you been waiting a lifetime for.'"

"I stand by my statement. That much was clear as window glass."

"Well, if he was, I was wasting valuable time, wouldn't you say? Time I'd rather have spent occupied elsewhere, if you please."

"So if I be takin' up with him, you'd give your blessing."

Honey's jaw dropped. When she recovered, she said to Nollie, "You don't need permission from me. As far as I'm concerned, you may take up with the devil himself, if you please." But she gave Nollie a look that was at once both icy and hot. "Mr. Wolfe is part of a past life I intend to forget. As for the future—*mine* doesn't include him."

CHAPTER SIXTY-FOUR

The journey through the center of California to Sacramento began at a ferry crossing on the muddy Colorado River at Fort Yuma. In Los Angeles they abandoned their wagon and horses to board a Concord stagecoach for the final leg of the odyssey, which had taken many more months than expected. "Can we nearly be there?" Nollie wondered as she leaned back into the insufficiently padded seat she shared with her mother and Honey. "It wouldn't surprise me if the earth opened up and swallowed us before we got there."

Honey pinched Nollie. "Don't you even suggest such a thing."

Nollie slapped Honey's hand away. "I guess he couldn't take staring us in the face the rest of the way," she said of Cameron, who was riding topside with the driver.

"It's been a long, hard road for us all," Shahar said. "I say he's gladder than we are it's about to end."

Three other passengers boarded the coach before they were off, companions they would have until they reached San Fernando. After San Fernando, they had the coach to themselves and even had newspapers, which they read avidly. "Well, would you listen to this: 'President Andrew Johnson declares an end to the war in Alabama, Arkansas, Florida, Georgia, Louisiana, Mississippi, *North Carolina*, South Carolina, Tennessee, and Virginia.'" Nollie looked up from the paper. "Has there been another war while we been outa town?"

Honey shook her head slowly. "The world might have ended for all I know." She wondered if she would ever feel anything again, for now she felt nothing. She was numb, rather like some of the war wounded, she thought, whose wounds were not as traumatic as others' yet who seemed to have lost a vital part of themselves. She had often thought when she looked into their eyes that a light had gone out. "This man just needs a little rest. Don't we all," the doctors would say, and send those unfortunate soldiers back to the war. The bed, after all, was needed by someone more critically wounded. "Malingerers" they were sometimes called, but even then Honey had privately questioned that description.

How many had survived? she wondered now. How many had walked out of the hospitals and gone back to the field to fight on? How many had come to a point where death was far easier than living? How close to suicide had those soldiers with the light gone from their eyes come? How easy in war to lay down one's gun and . . .

"Soon as we get to your uncle's, I'm going to fix you a tonic to put some sparkle into your eyes again," Shahar decided. "You're looking miserable."

Nollie laughed. "Uh oh, now you've had it."

"Seems you could use a little something, too."

"Not me. I'm lively as a cat with his tail on fire."

And ready to romp, Shahar figured. The light had not gone out of her daughter's eyes. While Honey sulked, Nollie preened. Shahar sensed trouble. "Soon as we get there, I'm going to ask Mr. Jefferson to put you to work. He's bound to know someone needs a good cook."

"And how about you?"

"I'm going to rest on my laurels a while and look after Mrs. Radcliffe."

"I don't need looking after," Honey objected.

"You wouldn't say so if you'd seen a mirror lately."

"It's my hair," Honey complained. She had abandoned her Parisian *chapeau* for a more modest domestic creation, but as short as it was, her hair sprang into curls that would not stay tucked under the brim. "I shall have to have a wig of some sort for a while, or go into hiding." *Now there's a thought. If only I could!* But as it was April, she could come out of her widow's mourning. Something told her she would be unable to persuade her uncle of any need to be in seclusion. Even when he had been with her in Greerfield shortly after the news of Nathan's death, Trevor had talked of social occasions in California, happy at the thought of having his beautiful niece by his side. The man had been thinking of running for governor even then and, on taking Honey in, would expect her to appear on his arm. He thought lengthy mourning stupid. No doubt her ordeal with the Apache would in Trevor's mind also be best forgotten in the diversion of merriment.

Perhaps I do need a tonic. She doubted she could muster the energy necessary to even consider dressing for a party, not to mention greeting a room full of guests, all of whom she did not know, and worse, having to attempt to carry on a reasonably alert conversation. The mere idea exhausted Honey.

She closed her eyes and rested her head on the back of the seat. The Concord coach, which was as comfortable as could be had, jolted and bumped; the road was riddled with puddles from the recent storm, some of them a far cry from shallow. The problem with closing her eyes was the visage that eventually always slipped into her mind. How she could think of him—much less *want* him—after what he had *done*, what he had *said*—humiliated Honey deeply. In her shame, Honey dealt with only her mind, for her heart was submerged in a pain of the kind that grips one's whole being in suffering. She felt wronged and betrayed by a man who under his white skin was a savage Apache. The man she had loved had died in the desert the day the indians had attacked the small party from Greerfield. She would deny every thought of Cameron, every surging in her blood that affirmed an inviolate connection with him.

The coach lurched and almost turned over. Thrown off balance, with Honey tossed into Nollie's lap, the women started shrieking. Finally, listing considerably, the coach stopped, the air blue with the stage driver's curses. "Pardon me, Mrs.," he said as he came to the door, "but we broke a wheel in one of them danged potholes."

As she climbed down, Cameron took Honey's hand from the driver's and would not let go. "I want you to come with me," he said. "We've some talking to do."

Honey resisted and tugged at his firm grip. "There's nothing more we could possibly have to say to each other."

Cameron was persistent and led her away from the coach to the south, opposite the direction in which they had been traveling, leaving Shahar and Nollie staring after them. "I've had enough of abductions," Honey protested.

As though they were dancing, Cameron whirled her in front of him. "And, I've had enough of your pouting. We've not said more than ten words to each other since that night in the cave."

"I've nothing more to say to you. You as good as lied to me by not telling me about your life with the Apache, a deceitful, dishonorable thing to omit. How like an Apache!"

"What I did out there in the desert, I did as an Apache. I was Apache then. You've no right to judge one man by rules made for another."

"I don't understand you, and I don't want to. I'll never accept what you did, or your reasons for doing it."

"Don't you think, if I could, I'd change what happened to you?"

"Would you?" she spit.

Silent, with a firm grip still on her hand, Cameron looked long and hard at Honey Radcliffe. In her beautiful face he saw fear and misery but arrogance also. He saw that she hated him. If she could believe he would have permitted her to suffer if there had been any way possible for him to prevent it, then he had wasted his breath. She was right; no explanation was necessary.

Reluctantly, Cameron released Honey's hand and left her staring after him, standing alone in the road.

CHAPTER SIXTY-FIVE

Trevor Jefferson used the same powers of persuasion on his niece that he used on the California voting populace, successfully prevailing on Honey to be his hostess on occasions requiring the appearance and grace of a beautiful woman. It would, he argued, keep her mind off the tragedies of the irretrievable past, and it would also serve him magnificently. Apart from the delay caused by the detention of his unfortunate niece by the red devils in the Arizona Territory, Trevor believed his schemes were working rather well. Jerome Pauley had taken a strong bite on the line Trevor had put out for him, and Honey, God bless her, seemed pliable if not yet fully aware of and in agreement with his plan to marry her off to, as it happened, the highest bidder; Trevor's need to reline his pockets in the wake of enormous and unprofitable wartime investments was crucial. He was in debt up to his sideburns, a splendid pauper.

When Honey had finally arrived, Trevor recalled impatiently, he had had to coddle and humor her for some time, during which he had been under a considerable strain, fearing she was not going to cooperate. But patience, he had thankfully been quick to remember—patience with a woman always paid off. Eventually Honey had come through and dazzled them all, including himself. Trevor smiled, then quickly forced himself to be sober. He must not assume anything before his hand was played out and the winnings were collected. He felt not one ounce of guilt in using Honey for his purposes. Women were born to be used; beautiful women, like Honey, were only more useful. It had been useful and romantic for him to feign a lifetime of mourning a lost love to untimely death all these years and a pleasure to keep mistresses. However, but for the appearance of his niece, he was so desperately needy for an immediate improvement in his financial circumstances that he seriously had considered marriage to the sister of one of his wealthy political cronies.

Trevor admitted to having had qualms about sending Cameron Wolfe to North Carolina after his niece, but there was no denying Wolfe had been the best man around for the task of bringing her west. Reasonably, the two should have been oil and water together, yet the man's reputation with the ladies had increased the likelihood of Honey's succumbing to him. In the end, Trevor had gambled that Honey's fresh widowhood would serve to protect her, and apparently the deck had been stacked in favor of that bet. If Honey Radcliffe had a kind word for Cameron Wolfe, Trevor Jefferson had yet to hear it.

It amused Trevor to watch Honey pointedly ignore Cameron Wolfe, which did not for a second seem to deter him. One would think, Trevor figured, that having been scorned for all those months on the trail, the man might give up. Perversely, however, Cameron Wolfe seemed almost amused by her obvious disdain. He baited; she parried by lightening rather than swallowing the hook.

None of this mattered to Trevor. Honey soon would be primarily Jerome Pauley's concern, although Trevor doubted that if Cameron continued, a husband would be as amused as he was with Cameron's laudable efforts to seduce Honey. Twenty years older than Honey, Jerome Pauley would want her uncompromised attention. Trevor wondered just how long and how far Cameron Wolfe would carry this game he seemed determined to win.

If Honey allowed herself to be carried away, she could almost imagine herself in Greerfield before the war, not in Sacramento. Uncle Trevor entertained often and lavishly or was himself entertained, and since shortly after arriving, Honey often as not found herself on his arm. "As a kindness to me," he had implored her. "You can help me fend off the merry widows and mothers with eligible daughters. Not that I want to trap you into a lifetime of saving me from the altar, but for now, until some previous matters are settled, I'd consider it an enormous favor." After a short period of rest, Honey felt she could not politely decline his request. Life became one dinner, soiree, or party after another. Even Shahar and Nollie bustled around her much as they had at home in Greerfield.

Tonight would be for Trevor the most important occasion yet. The selection of the Popular party's candidate for governor was mere days away, and Trevor, who was keen to firm up commitments he believed he already had, argued that many important political decisions were made during lulls in grand entertainments; the enjoyment and pleasure of significant supporters figured in many a successful politician's career. *If that is a fact, then Uncle Trevor will be the Popular party's candidate*, Honey thought.

Weary of these kinds of affairs, bored with the drone of meaningless gossip, Honey hoped that once Trevor was his party's choice, she would be able to retire from her place at his side. If nothing else, she imagined, she then would see less of one man in particular. Honey could then shut out Cameron Wolfe from her life for good, but until she retired from her uncle's social whirl, it seemed Cameron Wolfe could continue to be underfoot, reminding her uncomfortably of her deplorable weaknesses. To Honey's horror, the man on occasion could still provoke in her the basest of desires.

Trevor only once stated his opinion that Honey should think of marrying again, and soon. "Nathan was a man I'd known all of my life," she protested, shocked by the suggestion. In Sacramento she was barely acquainted; it would be some time yet before she would be comfortable thinking of the men she met as possible suitors.

"You're too young and too beautiful to wither in widow's weeds," Trevor had replied almost wistfully.

"I must look younger than I feel," Honey had answered. It made her nervous to think that among the men with whom she danced and dined and whom she tried to amuse, there were some who might consider her eligible.

But Honey admitted privately that she was restless; her life was truly empty. When she paused for a moment in the heady rush to be fitted for a gown or a hat or dressed for this meal or that party, she was bored. She had felt more purpose in life while living with the Apache!

Honey had only to close her eyes to be troubled with visions, which was one reason she consented to stand by Trevor. While awake and occupied thus, she had some hope of escaping thoughts that annoyed her and destroyed her attempt to recuperate after the long ordeal of a journey. But she had not realized how often Cameron Wolfe would be invited or called on by Trevor, whose business affairs frequently involved Cameron. "As you know intimately, he's a good man, one on whom you can always rely," Trevor said in Cameron's praise, which in fairness Honey could hardly deny.

However, the fact of Cameron Wolfe's reliability did not prevent severe irritation when he cut in while Honey was dancing with someone else. "You know, I've never seen the man dance before," Trevor remarked to Honey innocently, on the first occasion.

"Evidently he had a superior teacher," Honey said icily.

"I'll ask him to rescue you more often."

What was worse was how she responded. Sparks might fly from her eyes as Cameron gazed at her, seemingly much amused, but that was not how her body replied to his holding her near. She felt weak; her breathing was shallow, and she had to force herself to appear unaffected. Then she realized she was addicted as one might be to morphine, which gave not only relief from pain but its own kind of pleasure. Convinced she needed only avoid Cameron more regularly, she believed the effect he had on her would wear off eventually.

During the time she and Cameron had lived with the Apache, Honey realized, there had been a void in her dreams of the lives they supposedly had shared. Now she felt herself to have been unduly under Shahar's influence when she had conjured those erotic images of herself and Cameron as lovers from the past— an argument that did nothing to explain Cameron's coincident visions, which Honey conveniently forgot.

Now, as Honey watched Shahar fuss with her short curls, she sighed. "I don't know what I'd do without you." How the woman could coax her shorn hair to look as long and as full as it did astonished her. Tonight she would wear her hair pulled back from her face with a cap of petallike curls crowning the top and back of her head.

"It's not easy. But easier than reading signs."

"If only you could do something about my skin," Honey lamented. Rosewater and avoidance of sunshine had not had the bleaching effect she had hoped they would. Powder gave her a death-mask look, and she refused to use it, declaring she was not out to charm anyone with her beauty anyway. "Reading signs from heaven, by contrast, would be easy, I suppose."

She was surprised by Shahar's comment, for when they reached Sacramento, Honey had been certain Shahar would at once find good reason to consult her Spirits. But as far as either Honey or Nollie knew, Shahar had kept her feet on the ground. "Why haven't you traveled?" Honey probed now.

"I'm just plain worn out travelin'."

Honey smiled but was not fooled. "That surprises me greatly."

"Me, also," Shahar answered, which was not quite true. She had begun to have "insights," as she called them, which was her way of describing the unexplainable things she had begun to see unbidden. She would think she had heard a noise and look up or peer around a corner, and for a split second she would see something her rational mind knew could not possibly be true. "I suppose I'm still settling in," Shahar argued.

"Perhaps," Honey agreed. "Did you know, tonight Uncle Trevor has drummed up a Russian gypsy who'll tell everyone's fortune. I told him he could have called on you instead. Or the two of you might read tea leaves or some such together while the rest of us are at dinner; compare notes."

"Probably an old fake," Shahar grumbled.

"Does that mean you'd care to entertain us with a trance?" Honey laughed. "Now there's an idea with possibilities. The *Alta Californian* would have stupendous headlines: 'Candidate for Governor Has Divine Knowledge of Outcome of Election.' You could attract a following."

"No, thank you. I've trouble enough with souls I'm already familiar with." And with tales she could tell that would put a permanent crimp in Honey's short hair. "I can tell you one thing. You're not finished with Mr. Wolfe as yet."

Honey's lightheartedness vanished. "You don't say," she said flatly. "I'm curious, however, to know why the man ever entered my life—in your opinion, that is. To torment me, perhaps?"

Shahar studied Honey's cold visage in the ornate mirror that hung above the dressing table. She heard all the doubt and bitterness of Honey's tone, felt the hurt that vibrated from her essence.

"You know the reasons better than I."

"I don't have an inkling."

"You must. Perhaps the knowledge you seek is only smothered in pain."

"I shall forget him."

"Forgive, not forget."

"Hell shall freeze over first, I promise."

"He will—"

"No, Shahar! Not another word." Honey glared at Shahar in the mirror. "We've already had and finished this conversation long ago."

"As you know, that attitude changes nothing at all."

"Perhaps not," Honey conceded, afraid any foreknowledge might be more than she could bear.

CHAPTER SIXTY-SIX

Trevor Jefferson's gypsy fortune-teller was but one of the attractions of the evening. At Trevor's request, Cameron Wolfe had persuaded Doria LaLage to come from San Francisco, where the petite, arrestingly beautiful chanteuse was appearing with a troupe of dancers and actors at the Mermaid's Pavilion, a theater in a richly infamous hotel perched on the cliffs above the ocean on the peninsula south of the city. Her public appearances outside the theater were exceedingly rare, but, claiming a "soreness in the glands of my throat," Doria had taken a few days off from the revue to enjoy herself and especially to renew her fond acquaintance with "this adorable American man," as the pale beauty with cascades of curly black hair and dark eyes frequently referred to Cameron.

With her she brought Eugene Harley, her "adorable" piano player and manager, and sang all the songs that had made her the toast of America, the most romantic and naughty of which she sang with her suggestive gaze on Cameron. Most of the other men envied him; the women, if they had not already, thought twice about him. She was sitting like a queen indulging her court in a gown of sheer lilac silk with amethyst stars at her throat and ears, and Honey secretly writhed in the throes of infuriating but nonetheless biting jealousy.

If Doria glittered, Honey shone, at least in Cameron's eyes. In part it amused him to toy with her, but it was much more serious than mere teasing. He had no reasonable hope that Honey would soon recover her senses, yet he felt compelled to put himself in her path; in some inexplicable way his life seemed to depend on having her attention, even when his attentiveness seemed to offend her. Although their relationship at present was in a sorry state, Cameron had no regrets. What he had done, he knew he would do over again regardless of the outrage to Honey's sensibilities.

To sincerely admiring applause, Cameron now gave his arm to Doria LaLage and escorted her from the slightly elevated stage of Trevor Jefferson's salon. "Ah, such magnificent surroundings," she said to Trevor, speaking of his estate, a palace by comparison to all other houses in the California state capital. "I wonder that you are so alone. One would think others would be quick on your toes to outdo you, building better and bigger, which seems the American way." Doria beamed.

"I've hope that there soon will be others. I've merely chosen the course others will take to best me."

"How clever of you," Doria purred.

"Let me introduce my niece," Trevor said, easily escorting the singer to the place where Honey reigned.

"*Enchanté*," Doria said. "I have already heard about you from that adorable man." She nodded in Cameron's direction. When Honey looked up, she found his gaze resting on her. "He told me at one time you wanted to become a *docteur*. Therefore, I pictured a manly woman, not the adorable creature you are. But maybe he thought not to make me *jaloux*. I am so *jaloux* if he even looks at another woman."

"*Je vous assuré, Mlle LaLage, il ne faudra rien d'inquiétude*," Honey promised. You need not worry.

"*Mon dieu, vous parlez français! Je suis très étonné! Ça me plaît beaucoup! Mon cher Cameron ne m'a pas dit.*" You speak French. I am very happy. Cameron did not tell me.

"Mr. Wolfe, Mlle LaLage, I assure you, doesn't know me as well as he pretends."

Doria giggled musically and agreed to allow Trevor to show her his beautiful house. As they departed, Cameron made his way to Honey. "I'm claiming you for this dance, Mrs. Radcliffe." His gaze rested gently on her face as he took a hand Honey did not offer him and led her onto the dance floor.

"Aren't you afraid you'll cause Mlle LaLage *paroxysmes de jalousie*?"

"She thinks I'm in love with her."

"You, of course, have done nothing to persuade her of this?"

Cameron smiled. "Nothing."

"Nothing but be 'adorable.'"

Cameron laughed. "If I didn't know different, I'd think you green-eyed."

"*Au contraire, M. Wolfe*, I am delighted you've found someone *else* to amuse you. You'll now be free to stop tormenting me with your attentions."

With the hand at her waist, Cameron pulled Honey very close to him as they danced. "Tell me you never dream about me. Tell me I'm not in your blood. Swear that you hate me," he whispered as both a dare and a threat.

Honey thought her heart would leap from her breast. Where her body came against his, she throbbed at the connection. "I never...you're not...I..." Honey stammered, precipitously close to tears. "Let me go, please!"

"Never," he swore, then released her.

She fled from the room and would have disappeared up the stairs for the evening, but she met Trevor and Doria coming down. "Oh, I've been given such a marvelous tour. And I met your lovely negress, Shahar. And her daughter, Olivia, also. How odd, the younger one looks so much like you. She could be your sister, Madame Radcliffe. Perhaps having the same *maman* has some way influenced you. They say we all begin to resemble the people we live with. I suppose *colour* does not negate that principle."

Honey could not think of a polite reply and was shocked by Doria's remark, yet she was not offended. Her candor was one of the more disarming things about the songstress, and her luscious accent permitted her to get away with saying things that on anyone else's tongue would have been grandly insulting.

"We are now hurrying to have our fortunes told by *un petite gypsy. Oh, j'adore ces choses, et vous?* I think *votre oncle* must have arranged for her to come just for my entertainment." She patted Trevor's cheek. "One must always keep in touch with the mystical, or one loses one's grasp of *réalité, n'est-ce pas?*"

Honey would never have expressed it in quite that way, she realized, but did not resist as she was taken in hand by the irrepressible Doria, who now ignored Trevor and treated Honey as she might a favorite sister, holding her hand with almost childish excitement and waiting for the gypsy woman.

Cosima, a perfect crone, small, gray, withered, and slightly

stoop-shouldered, swept majestically into Trevor's salon within
the minute. A hush fell over the guests as Cosima's aura filled all
empty space.

"Ooooh, she is something of a showman this one," Doria
whispered to Honey as she squeezed her hand with excitement.
Cosima was dressed in a worn black silk dress under a glossy
purple velvet cape. A fragrance of warm exotic spices wafted
from her with every step. When she turned to face the audience,
she let her silent perusal roam slowly over them. Then she closed
her eyes and raised her hands before her into a wide V. She
breathed deeply while all the others seemed to hold their breath.
She had captivated them without saying a word.

As Honey let her gaze play over Trevor's worldly but attentive
guests, she saw Shahar slip quietly into the room. One seeress
examining another, Honey thought, and wished she had managed
her escape as she had intended before Doria LaLage had sealed
her in her clutches. One witch in the house was more than enough
to suit Honey. *Where are your tarot cards and crystal ball?* she
wondered as Cosima opened her eyes before the audience began
to get restless.

Cosima moved slowly around the room, reaching for one and
then another of Trevor's guests' hands. She examined the palm
briefly, then pressed it against hers thoughtfully and uttered a
prediction that provoked mild laughter, some of it nervous, or
awed sighs of recognition. When she came to a couple near
Honey, Cosima took the woman's hand but made no prediction
until she held the husband's also. "You both have been married
before, but this shall be a long and fruitful union." The woman
blushed; the man barely concealed a smile as Cosima moved on
to Jerome Pauley.

Polished and grand-looking, he peered at the gypsy woman
intently. "You, sir," Cosima began, "are accustomed to having
whatever you wish at all times. But something you now desire
much will be denied you. There will be nothing you can do."

Jerome's expression shifted to one of determination. "We'll
see about that!"

At that moment Nollie entered the room with a large silver
tray laden with crystal glasses filled with sherry and champagne.
Cosima stopped her progress, indicating she should put the tray
down. Nollie looked to Trevor Jefferson nervously; when he nodded his approval, one of the guests took the tray from her hands.

"I see great disturbance. Much anguish and turmoil boiling," Cosima warned.

Instinctively, Nollie looked over her shoulder. "You speaking to me?"

"You love someone forbidden you."

Nollie pulled her hand out of Cosima's. "I don't any such thing! You'll excuse me, please." The onlookers chuckled.

Doria was next. "Soon you will marry a nobleman in exile."

"Oh, how exciting! Tell me his name!"

At last Cosima smiled. "He has more than one. I can tell you this: He is missing the middle finger of his left hand."

"You don't say!" Doria's eyes brightened. "I think I already know this gentleman. I should *never* marry him. Why, he is already married."

"You shall, I am sure of it."

Doria giggled with pleasure.

Cosima was about to take Honey's hand, but Shahar caught Cosima's eye, and she abruptly left Honey still standing with her hand outstretched. Cameron, who was behind her, reached forward and took it, holding the ungloved hand firmly in his. She tried to pull away but could not do so without drawing unwanted attention to herself.

While Honey glared at Cameron, Cosima said to Shahar, "I have become aware of another person in our midst with the gift of sight. You are very troubled by what you see. You are wishing you did not, and think perhaps you have seen wrongly. You may trust heaven, dear friend."

When Cosima returned to Honey, Cameron dropped her hand and moved several feet away from her. Cosima looked at Honey intently. "You harbor very passionate feelings for people in this room. This will bring you much misery, but you will defy everyone to have what you want. A man will die because of you."

Honey did not like what she had heard, but Cosima was not finished. Instead of going on to Trevor, who was standing next to Honey and whose fortune was logically the next to be read, Cosima continued to hold Honey's hand and drew her along with her to stand before a man whom Honey had never seen before; then she turned abruptly and brought Honey face to face with Cameron Wolfe.

Cosima took Cameron's hand with her free one and closed her eyes. Her lips moved as if she were praying. When she opened her eyes she said, "This is your last chance. Your path is very

narrow. You must be careful not to fall into the abyss. Beware of
dead men."

"I always am," Honey all but hissed, and yanked her hand
away.

Trevor came up behind her and laughed. "What about the host
of this amusement?" he asked jovially. "I don't want to be the
only one overlooked."

Cosima held Trevor Jefferson's hand for a long while as she
stared at him. "You are very cunning, sir," she said, then paused.
"I see you will have what you deserve."

"Wonderful news!" He laughed, eager to relieve the tension
that dominated the room. "I shall be governor elect shortly," he
predicted to wild hurrahs and toasts of warm Spanish sherry and
bubbling French champagne.

CHAPTER SIXTY-SEVEN

Shahar was obviously distracted and often muttered under her
breath things she felt and dared not repeat. The old gypsy's confirmation of her interpretations of signs did not give her any peace
of mind. She felt that second sight was a burden she would rather
not have anymore. "I've a mind to lock you up," she warned
Nollie.

"As long as it's in the kitchen, I'm agreed," Nollie said
lightly, used to ignoring predictions she did not like. But she did
like working in Trevor Jefferson's kitchen, albeit for a pitiful
salary, which she squirreled away. Of the three women from
North Carolina, Nollie was the only one who seemed to thrive in
the furiously busy household that seemed to be always filled with
hungry guests. She actually enjoyed the cacophony in the below-
stairs kitchen; not that she understood much of the Chinese or
Spanish spoken by the other staff members, but she was learning
many new recipes and methods that, once shown, she never forgot. "I'll soon get fat on sauces, forced as I am to taste."

She thought the gypsy's pronouncements stupid. "She looked
at me and said to herself, 'This girl's ripe for marrying.' That's
how she came to be talkin' about my being in love. I don't love

any man. Never will. I'm going to make my fortune and spend it on myself."

Honey also openly scorned the gypsy's predictions, but in private they nagged at her. She was uncomfortably aware that as she had looked into the gypsy's black eyes that night, she had wanted and almost expected to hear Cosima say she should forswear outrage and embrace the man who loved her. She reminded herself that beneath the fine evening clothes was a savage. How could she even for a second yearn for the consent of a gypsy to love him?

The idea that she would defy everyone to have what she wanted intrigued her. *Beware of dead men.* Was there anyone who wasn't leery of the dead? She wondered about this prediction in connection to Cameron. Indeed, a dead man had already come between them. Should she ignore the events that had driven her from Cameron? *How can I?* she wondered, the memory of the savagery of what he had done causing her to shiver.

Certainly she felt passionately about some of the people in the salon that night, just as Cosima had said, and indeed, she had endured much misery. But Cosima had spoken of the future. *A man will die because of you* was not a statement of something that had occurred in the past.

Honey did her best to forget the evening. She had a lot to forget, not only the fortune-teller but the shameful desire for Cameron Wolfe that welled within her in spite of her wish to deny these feelings. Doria LaLage's instant affinity for Honey made forgetting even more difficult. While she visited with Cameron Wolfe, Doria called on Honey daily. "You must prevail upon M. Jefferson to carry you with him to our theater. It is very lively and *très amusant*. You should love it. I shall arrange a box. My adorable friend," Doria said, squeezing Cameron's hand, "you, *mon cher*, will escort Madame Radcliffe to *le pavillon* and we shall have such times. Promise me, *s'il te plaît*?" she begged Cameron, who readily agreed. "You have been her chaperone in the country; you can be such again in San Francisco. It is not so much wicked there. You can go on the steamboat from here to there. I shall make Uncle Trevor give me his pledge of honor," she said, and turned her eye on Trevor.

In spite of herself, Honey found it impossible not to be charmed by Doria, who was as much a sprite as anything else. She could understand Cameron's being drawn to her. Everyone was. Why should she be jealous? But when Trevor promised to see that his niece went to San Francisco, Honey wrote to Jerome Pauley and invited him to join the party.

"I shall be delighted," he responded. "And you must consent to stay with me when you come to the city. I won't take no for an answer—no matter what that old crone of a gypsy predicted. I shall not be disappointed in this at least."

Honey laughed when she received Jerome Pauley's reply. She pretended to ignore how Cameron's eyes narrowed with displeasure when she told him of her arrangements and, for the first time in a long time, smiled at him with pleasure.

CHAPTER SIXTY-EIGHT

Mr. Jerome Pauley, widower, banker, owner of sailing ships and waterfront property, builder of railroads, did not fit into Shahar's view of things. She definitely had not foreseen his presence in Honey's life. The man's sudden rise to Honey's attention floored Shahar and provoked sleeplessness. "If you don't get some sleep, you won't be able to go with us to San Francisco," Honey fretted.

"Don't you worry yourself. I wouldn't miss it for anything."

Neither would Honey. She would make it painfully plain to Cameron Wolfe that she had no further interest in him. The kind invitation from Jerome Pauley for an extended stay in San Francisco suited her plans perfectly, even if it did include Mlle La-Lage and her escort, Cameron Wolfe. There would be riding, yachting, and a charity ball to attend. Honey planned to be at her beguiling best, if necessary, everything she had always despised in intelligent women: silly, coquettish, melodramatic. She would charm Jerome Pauley, who she suspected liked his women helpless and fawning and at all times under his thumb, and do her utmost to be the delicate creature Cameron Wolfe had dreaded from the moment they had met. She might, if she performed adequately, be done with Cameron Wolfe once and for all.

"Have you packed smelling salts?" Honey pestered Shahar.

"And gallons of the nauseous perfume you insisted on. You planning on drawing flies? Then there's four fans, three parasols, a trunk of clothes. We're just visiting, not moving in."

Finally Cameron called for Honey and escorted her to the riverboat. "She's not the *Lady Mildred*," he said of the passenger steamer that would carry them from Sacramento to San Francisco. The trip would take all day; they would arrive in time for a late supper with Mlle LaLage after the theater.

"I shall be glad to see Mlle LaLage again. She's very amusing," Honey said as they strolled the steamer's upper deck. She carried a parasol to protect her face from the sun. "Have you told her your experiences with the Apache? She would declare your tales adorable, I'm certain. Of course, I shan't say a word."

"I just might tell her *everything*."

Honey's jaw dropped. "Why are you making this so difficult?" She seated herself on a bench before the side railing. Honey looked directly into Cameron's enticing blue gaze, hoping to impress him with her resolute expression, but had to turn away from his powerful scrutiny.

She watched sea gulls that were unusually far inland and listened to the churning of the side-wheeler's paddle, its rhythm in time with her heartbeat. She closed her eyes, the sound stirring memories of passionate nights spent with the very man she now wished to discourage once and for all. *If we could only go back in time*.

"I haven't changed *my* mind," he said, jarring her. "I love you."

Honey gave an exasperated sigh and opened her eyes. "What will it take to convince you *I don't love you*? Must I marry someone else? Will that convince you?"

"No."

"No? What do you mean, no?" She looked both perplexed and furious. "Shall I order the printers to do up some notices and post them from here to San Francisco? Shall I have to hire ruffians to keep you from darkening my path?" Honey began to laugh. "You've exhausted my patience," she said, then looked at him sternly again. "Answer me, please. What will it take to convince you I do not desire you?"

Cameron's gaze hardened; even the color of his eyes seemed to deepen. "Did you ever love me, Mrs. Radcliffe?"

Honey gave him a despairing, wounded look; she could hardly find the voice to answer him. "How can you dare ask such a question?"

"I must know before I can answer you."

"Yes," she whispered, nearly strangling on the words. "Yes, I loved you. With all my heart and soul. More than honor, more than I have loved anyone—ever, more than life itself." She felt naked, exposed to him and vulnerable; she was shocked at herself for revealing herself so completely.

"You're a damned liar!"

The heat of rage flared in Honey. Color rose in her face, and there was pure astonishment in her expression.

"You never loved me. You're just a steep-priced whore who for some reason, maybe amusement, got generous and gave it away free." His tone was brutal and cold, and Honey flinched as if he had struck her. Cameron watched his ugly words sink in. Anger, bewilderment, and pain alternated in Honey's expression. "You're a whore, Mrs. Radcliffe."

Tears of both rage and pain brimmed in Honey's eyes. She would not have been more surprised if he had beaten her with his fists. She could not answer him, her brain rejecting the idea that he could believe what he had said, although he was utterly convincing. Honey held her jaw tightly clenched. She knew if she even opened her mouth slightly, she would lose control and begin to sob hysterically.

Next Cameron smiled warmly, in an instant all the hate and bitterness apparently gone from him. "You're not a whore, Mrs. Radcliffe. I believe you loved me just as you said: with all your heart and soul. That kind of love doesn't dry up in the desert."

Honey tried to turn away from Cameron as tears sprang from her eyes as if they were falling from a fountain, but he put his arms around her and held her fiercely. At first she resisted, then leaned against him gratefully. "What you say you felt for me—what I feel for you—isn't destroyed even at death."

Devastated, Honey let Cameron comfort her, glad to have someone's arms around her for a moment at least, but when her crying subsided, she pulled away. She looked at him without hatred but did not feel any love for him, either. "Perhaps, as you say, love like I felt for you might not die," she conceded, "but I promise you, there are worse things than denying a lover. Living with a man who is no better than a savage is one of them."

A proud man who had dared to lay his heart and soul open to the woman he loved, Cameron was devastated. If Honey had taken a knife and reopened the wounds in his chest, she could not have injured him more.

CHAPTER SIXTY-NINE

Honey praised God for the whirl of activity that awaited them in San Francisco and the friendship that Doria LaLage showered on her. The world was a vast audience for Doria, and she was on stage every waking moment, filled with boundless gaiety and affection for everyone. Honey doubted that any man could not love the beautiful songstress. She was utterly candid with her friends, and Honey knew that Cameron enjoyed more than Doria's delightful company. That this revelation could sting her now after all that had been said amazed Honey.

"He is adorable, isn't he? Like a god." Doria sighed. "So loving and virile. If you were not once a married woman, this might embarrass you." Embarrassed she was, but ignorant of this, Doria carried on. "We must find a man for you equally good, though I don't think we'll find one. I would marry him, but, alas, he is not the nobleman who misses part of a finger, so I know I must leave him behind when I am ready to go." Doria laughed. "Maybe I will leave this adorable man to you as a parting gift when I am ready. Only for friendship." She stopped to assess Honey's reaction to her offer. "No? Oh, how can you resist him?"

Tongue-tied, Honey did not answer but only shrugged her shoulders in bewilderment.

"It doesn't matter. I think M. Pauley will take you up before I am ready to be so generous. He looks to me like a man who is thinking of marrying again."

Honey suspected the same thing. A man who liked female companionship, he had been married twice and widowed both times. "I married for love twice, women my age. Now I want a young wife who will outlive me," he said when he proposed to Honey. "If you don't love me, I can accept that. Perhaps that's not very romantic, but practical. I know from what Trevor has shared with me, you've endured much and lost almost everything of meaning to you. I'd like to fill your life with all the things that might make you happy. I should like to help you forget all that

has made you unhappy." He smiled warmly at Honey. "I know
you're a lady, but I'm grateful the gods spared you from falling in
love with Mr. Wolfe on that long tour you made together across
country. Not many mortal women can resist him. Now I hope the
gods will bless me twice—and you will say yes to my offer of
marriage."

Honey was not surprised by Jerome's proposal, which came
during a private luncheon they shared while Cameron and Doria
were dining with friends, nor was she surprised to find herself
saying, "I'll give you my answer this evening." She was in a
mood to be practical.

She knew from bitter experience that loving a man with all of
her being did not promise happiness. As she weighed Jerome's
proposal, Honey realized she would never love anyone the way
she loved Cameron. The truth seared her soul.

She sat on a cushioned bench in a bay window of the third-
story room she occupied in Jerome Pauley's house and watched
the traffic of ships in San Francisco Bay. With Jerome Pauley,
Honey's world would be vastly different from anything she had
known before. He suggested they might sail to the Orient on their
honeymoon, in one of his ships, of course. Cameron would not
follow her to the Orient, and she could forget him completely
while she and her new husband sailed to the far exotic shores.

"Before you go, Shahar, I've something to tell you."

"Better hurry with whatever you're going to say if you want
the wrinkles pressed out of this dress for tonight."

"I'm going to marry Mr. Pauley."

For a moment Honey thought Shahar might faint, but she recovered. "I can tell you you're *not*!"

Honey laughed at the woman's response. "Well, I am. Next
month."

"For a fact, I can tell you you're not."

Honey scowled. "We're going to the Orient on our honeymoon. We'll be gone two years."

"I'm not bothering to pack."

Honey raised her hand as if to ward off a lecture. "You
needn't waste any breath telling me the Spirits haven't mentioned
any marriage."

"Not only that, his name hasn't even come up," Shahar insisted.

"I'll try to buy you a new crystal ball in the Orient. It appears

Mr. Wolfe turns out not to be the man I was waiting for," Honey said smugly.

"I'll see about that!"

Honey heard the threat of Shahar doing some traveling of her own. "Don't be galloping off with your Spirits until we get back to Trevor's," Honey cautioned. "A trance would be very hard for me to explain. I don't think Mr. Pauley believes in Spirits."

"That's all right," Shahar said as she went out the door, "they don't believe in him either."

CHAPTER SEVENTY

"From the contributions, they'll be able to say the Hospital for Poor Children was built of solid gold," Jerome Pauley announced to the charity ball guests who filled the ballroom in the south wing of his mansion. Originally the room had been built for his first wife and faced the south so that it would take in maximum sunlight through its wall of windows. The first Mrs. Pauley had died of consumption, having escaped to a sunnier climate too late. The second Mrs. Pauley had died when her buggy turned over on a pier and fell in the bay. She, her driver, and the horse had all perished.

"In addition to this fund-raising success, I would now like to proclaim another, more personal triumph," Jerome said after the cheers and applause at his first announcement had died down. "I have asked a marvelous lady to marry me, and she has agreed." The second clamor exceeded the first. "I present to those of you who do not know her yet my bride to be, Mrs. Nathan Radcliffe, widow of the late Colonel Nathan Radcliffe, CSA, and niece of our next governor, Mr. Trevor Jefferson." Hurrahs went up again as the blushing bride to be was escorted to the marble platform to stand by Jerome at the grand piano.

Honey was quite astonished by her reception. She knew many of the guests, but many she did not, some of whom appeared to be quite unaccustomed to the fine dinner coats they were wearing this evening, but everyone cheered. Trevor came first to congratulate Jerome and hug his niece. Next Doria rushed forward to kiss Honey enthusiastically. "My adorable girl," the songstress chirped, hugging Honey joyfully. When her gaze fell on Cameron, Honey stopped breathing for a moment at the stark look of misery she read in his eyes. She gave him her hand, which he raised to his lips and kissed. "I know you will want to wish me happiness," she said.

"Yes, and more. The peace which I will never know."

Honey smiled gently. "I think I shall never understand you," she whispered before she accepted another guest's good wishes. A wagonload of champagne was poured, and the couple was toasted again and again before the evening came to an end. A dozen musicians with violins and Spanish guitars and someone at the piano played music into the night. A few minutes before midnight, the floor beneath the dancers began to roll. First there was a gentle slide to the west, followed immediately by a sharp jolt to the east. Shrill screams of terror undulated with the earth's movement. When the quake was over, the window side of the ballroom collapsed suddenly, trapping a dozen people under glass and debris. Three huge chandeliers within the ballroom crashed to the floor also.

There was pandemonium. Guests were screaming and running for their lives, knocking people down, stepping on the fallen in their panic. *"Mon dieu! Mon dieu!"* Doria cried as Honey came to her side. "He is bleeding." Doria had been dancing with Jerome when the quake struck. They had been near the south windows.

"It's nothing. Only a small cut." Jerome blotted the blood from the cut above his left eye with a silk handkerchief. "But others, I fear, are badly hurt." He hurried to the ruined side of the room and helped Cameron, Trevor, and other men free the injured from under terrible quantities of shattered glass and lumber.

Since the benefit had been for the Hospital for Poor Children, there were several doctors and medical students from San Francisco Medical College in attendance who provided help for the injured. Honey at once donated her long satin gloves for tourniquets and without a pause for thought stepped out of her petticoats, which were ripped into bandages, not even looking when a murmur went up among the onlookers.

When it was all over, Dr. Harold Case, Jerome's personal physician and friend, smiled at Honey and said, "It seems, Mrs. Radcliffe, you might have done this before."

"More times than I care to recall. I was nearly naked by the end of the war."

Her extremely candid reply startled him, and when she realized what she had said, she blushed furiously and they both began to laugh uproariously, only to be shocked from their amusement by another scream of distress.

"Hurry, hurry, Dr. Case. Come quickly!" It was Doria again. "This time it is truly something terrible!" she cried, pulling the doctor with her to Cameron. "He was rescuing, and a shard of glass cut off his fingers," she sobbed. Without hesitation, Honey brushed past Dr. Case and knelt before Cameron, who was seated on a chair. She examined the injury. "Only part of one finger," she reported. He had lost the middle finger of his left hand at the first joint. Blood soaked the cloth he had held over the stump, but the bleeding was stanched. "That shall have to be sutured." Cameron was ashen in color, and Honey was stark white.

Honey turned Cameron over to Dr. Case but stood by for comfort and held his other hand during the painful suturing. Jerome brought him a dose of laudanum from a bottle he had on hand.

When the stitching was done, Honey shook her head slowly at Cameron. "What am I going to do with you, Mr. Wolfe? You're worse than a schoolboy; you can't seem to keep out of scrapes." She smiled at him, then put her arms around him. A slight murmur went up among a few onlookers. "I think you'll have to marry Mlle LaLage now," she said lightly when she pulled away. She lifted a lock of Cameron's hair from his forehead and pushed it back into place. "You now perfectly fit the description of the man Uncle Trevor's gypsy said she would marry."

"*Mon dieu, c'est vrai!* That is right!" Doria cried. "No," she said a moment later. "I remember now he would be a nobleman with more than one name, *n'est-ce pas*? Oh, bad luck, for I would gladly marry you, *mon cher*, if it was my fate, but for now, M. Pauley, please to escort me away," Doria begged, feeling faint. "I must lie down, I fear. I have no stomach for blood. This is too much for me."

While Jerome drew Mlle LaLage aside, Honey looked into Cameron's eyes inquiringly. "You were once the son of an Apache chief; I suppose that's a nobleman of a kind," she said gently. "And you've more than one name—an Apache one as well as a white one."

"That was in another life. And I am already married—Apache married—to you, for life."

"You can't have it both ways, Mr. Wolfe. You're either

Apache or you aren't," she said, suddenly growing irritated. "As I remember it, Apache men often have more than one wife."

"I am white eyes enough to need only one." Cameron smiled. "Two is considerable trouble."

Honey got to her feet. "I'll see you get laudanum for the pain, but you're already beginning to talk out of your head." She looked down at him coolly. "You must take care of your hand. As you know, the wound has to be cleaned and dressed often. Come to me if you have any problems."

Cameron's thoughts were still focused elsewhere. "Apache cut off the noses of unfaithful wives."

"And what is it they cut off offending men?" Honey wondered, exasperated, and abruptly turned on her heel.

CHAPTER SEVENTY-ONE

The next day, Cameron again refused laudanum when Honey examined his hand. "I recommend it," she urged in spite of her knowledge that an Apache warrior was expected to endure pain without complaint. "You've nothing to prove—especially to me." The severed finger had good color and no sign of infection.

"If it gets to looking bad, I'll just throw on some maggots."

Honey smiled. "I thought of that, too," she said. "I'm hoping it won't come to that."

The quake had been a minor one, causing irregular damage, with the collapse of Jerome Pauley's ballroom one of the more severe results. On the return trip to Sacramento, Honey's party was unusually quiet, but try as he might, Cameron failed to doze in his high-backed seat.

Honey knew he had to be in great pain, with the loss of bone excruciating. It showed in his eyes. Restless, he finally went on deck, and Honey followed him after a while. "Dr. Case gave me some laudanum, just in case you change your mind."

Cameron shook his head. After a long silence he said, "The Apache believe earthquakes are a sign of Ussen's disapproval."

Honey sighed. "It doesn't surprise me."

"I think he must be angry at your plans to marry Mr. Pauley."

"That doesn't concern Him."

Cameron pulled the Apache amulet from a pocket. "Do you remember your pledge to me?"

Honey nodded reluctantly, the instance of passion and love coming clearly to mind. "That promise was made, as you yourself said last night, in another life. It is not relevant now."

"I'll never accept that. I'll never agree; nor does Ussen."

Honey frowned and left him alone on deck.

When they arrived in Sacramento, Cameron accompanied Trevor, Honey, and Shahar back to Trevor's house so that Honey could dress his hand once more before he headed home. Nollie greeted them at the door, obviously shaken.

"You felt the quake, too?" Shahar asked when she saw her.

"I've got bigger news than the earth rattling, but as it is, the ground's about to swallow Mrs. Radcliffe up." Nollie had their attention. "Better sit down, Mrs., I got something to show you." While other servants collected bags of luggage, Nollie urged the foursome into the front parlor. "Just you wait," she insisted when she saw them seated, and hurried from the room, careful to shut the wide double doors behind her.

Honey laughed nervously. "Have you any idea what her surprise is?" she asked Shahar.

Shahar looked at her hands, which she had folded in her lap. Her mouth was drawn tightly closed.

"You'd tell me if you knew, wouldn't you, Shahar?"

Shahar answered with a shrug and waited in silence until the door opened slowly and a man with a cane emerged.

At first Honey sat frozen in place. Her stomach lurched violently. The others gaped; Cameron's pain seemed to vanish even without laudanum. Then, crying wildly, Honey stood and rushed toward the man, who held out his free arm to welcome her. "Nathan, Nathan," Honey called. "Oh, my God, Nathan!" She seemed to be weeping for joy as she flung her arms around him.

"My God, man, what a shock!" Trevor said to Cameron, obviously shaken. He had not seen Nathan since Nathan was a child, but he had seen photographs and recognized him immediately. His appearance would ruin all of his plans, but Trevor moved forward as if he were delighted at Nathan's return and reached for his hand. "Sit down. Sit down and tell us all about it. It's not every day one is resurrected from the dead!"

Honey and Shahar were crying and comforting each other as Nollie brought a large cut-crystal decanter of whiskey and poured everyone a large drink. "Some for your mother and yourself as well on this unusual occasion," Trevor said. When they had their glasses, he raised his. "Here's to your rise, sir, from the dead."

Cameron looked to Honey. Shock and joy seemed to bring high color to her cheeks, he thought, and tossed back his drink in one swallow. Nollie poured him another. "My hand's hurting worse than before," he said.

"Can't say it surprises me," Nollie said under her breath.

To Honey, Nathan looked drawn and pale, and his embrace was almost frail. In many ways he looked different: He wore his light brown hair parted high on the left side, almost in the middle, with a thick fold of hair covering the right side of his forehead. He limped slightly, and even in the cleverly cut gray suit he wore elegantly, she could tell he had lost weight. His blue eyes, once lively, were now somberly set in face; his once full lips had narrowed considerably by the way he now held his mouth.

"Someone should have warned us," Trevor said after introducing Cameron to Nathan and briefly explaining the role he had had in bringing Honey west.

"I did write, once."

"We received nothing," Trevor said, shocked.

"When I was able, I came straightaway. No point in staying in Greerfield; your choice to leave was a good one, my dear." Nathan's gaze rested on Honey's, but there was no warmth in it.

"I'd never have left home if I'd known!" Honey said as she sat beside him on the cut-velvet settee. She reached for the hand nearest her and held it tenderly in both of hers.

"What do you mean you came straightaway?" Trevor inquired. "Mrs. Radcliffe didn't even leave Greerfield until June."

Nathan explained that in the Fort Fisher explosion he had been badly hurt, terribly burned on the right side of his body, with the right pocket of his uniform, in which he carried identification, essentially burned away. Another pocket had held papers that belonged to another man under his command who was already dead, whose family Nathan had intended to notify by letter. In the enormous confusion that had followed the explosion Nathan was misidentified and eventually sent to a field hospital some distance away. "Mad with pain, I at first didn't have the presence of mind to correct anyone when they bothered to addresss me by the other fellow's name. I was very ill for months, sometimes more lucid than others. Morphine, when I could get it, didn't clear my head. When I attempted to correct things, I couldn't get much accomplished very quickly. The Union boys may have won the war, but they were as disorganized as we were."

When Nathan had finally gone home, there was still some question of whether he would recover. "I decided to let things be as they were until I could get out to California."

"You should have sent for me. I should have been with you," Honey said.

Nathan was immediately defensive. "I made the decision as I saw fit," he said firmly.

Honey's smile wavered. "Of course," she answered softly.

As they listened attentively to Nathan's story, Cameron harshly appraised the man Honey had married. Having himself been horribly wounded and at times in ill humor as a result, he made allowances for the severe hardships the man had endured. Nevertheless, Cameron disagreed with almost all the choices Nathan Radcliffe had made and strongly resented the way he spoke to his wife. After the first shock, Nathan Radcliffe's return from the dead made Cameron's pain seem to expand. He felt the pain in every cell of his body. He excused himself to depart for home, which was less than an hour away but now loomed as a vast distance.

Honey followed Cameron out of the parlor. "I can't let you go without seeing your hand," she called from the massive stone porch as he waited for his horse to be brought to him. Lifting her skirts, she hurried down the twenty wide, gently inclined steps to the ground. She led him back into the kitchen. "Sit down while I get some fresh bandages."

"No petticoats this time?"

"Not this time." When she finally settled in a chair next to him and began to undo the dressing, he winced at her touch. "I still have laudanum," she offered. "It's going to hurt for a while."

"Maybe I will take some with me. Whiskey and laudanum should put me out of my pain."

"Just be cautious how you mix it," she said.

"Guess the wedding's off."

"I'd almost forgotten."

"Are you happy to see your husband, Mrs. Radcliffe?"

"Of course. How can you ask?" Honey lifted the final layer of his dressing away as Cameron tried not to flinch. She cleaned the wound with sudsy warm water, rinsed it, and waited while it dried in the air.

"How're you planning to explain your experience?"

Honey looked at Cameron defensively. "I don't intend to explain anything."

"Then you'll play the virgin."

"It's none of your business, Mr. Wolfe, what I plan or don't plan to do with regard to my husband." She felt outraged that he would introduce the subject of sex into their conversation. Her face was furiously red. She wrapped his hand in clean bandages and stood up.

Honey showed Cameron to the front door. "Send for me if you should need me," she said without thinking, then, embarrassed, hurried away.

If I need you? Cameron thought bitterly, certain he would need more than a few doses of laudanum and whiskey to deaden his pain.

CHAPTER SEVENTY-TWO

Nathan Radcliffe rose late every morning. After luncheon, he and Honey would go for a short walk or ride, then he would rest until supper. In the evening he seemed to be at his best.

He had no particular plans. Before the war, a well-bred Southern gentleman managed his plantation and other assets if he had them, but there was no expectation that he would do any sort of menial work. A profession was also disdained among his class of Southerner; Phillip Greer's practice of medicine was barely tolerated in the best circles. Labor of any sort was deemed fit for negroes; it would take more than a decree from Washington to adjust Nathan's thinking on that subject. Used as he was to being supported by family, reliance on Honey's uncle for support of himself and his wife did not give Nathan any pause. Relatives leaned on kin as a general rule in his way of thinking.

Nathan approved of Trevor's flamboyant style. Like Honey, he found it easy in Trevor's domain to imagine that little had changed. He might have altered his place of existence, but for the most part he could exist as if there had been no war. However, there were more than a few impediments to his vision of married life.

When Nathan first beheld Honey again, he hardly recognized

her. Gone was the girl he remembered. She had lost more than her splendid mane in the nearly two years since he had seen her. Before the shock of his reappearance registered in her, he beheld a beautiful, poised, confident woman, sensing immediately that Honey was no longer the malleable ore she once had been. Something had happened to change her, and he knew instinctively that it was not the war but what had happened since that accounted for it. He recognized she was now a woman who knew her own mind, not one to hold her tongue merely because her husband expected it.

On their first night together, Nathan and Honey only lay close in each other's embrace. She, obviously exhausted by the emotion of their reunion, seemed capable of little but tears. Without apology, Nathan explained that he was physically exhausted by his journey west and too tired for anything but holding her near. He fell asleep quickly, a habit he thereafter often seemed to cultivate.

At first the soul of compassion, Honey empathized with Nathan's weakness. In fact, she was greatly relieved to have the burden of beginning their relationship as man and wife postponed, she hoped, until the shock of his reappearance had time to wear off. She pitied Nathan for this dreadful experience and truly was filled with joy that he had survived.

He bore scars from his burns, but clothing and a change in the way he parted his hair usually covered them. A vain man, he admitted the scars horrified him and wore a thin, pale doeskin glove on his right hand at all times to cover the scars. But the worst scars of all from the war were not visible. He suffered most from headaches, which plagued him, striking without warning to blind him with pain that threatened sometimes to drive him mad. At his worst, he thought of doing away with himself to end the depth of his pain. "I apologize for returning to you less a man than I was."

Honey responded with tears. "I'll do whatever I can to relieve you," she promised. The headaches proved beyond her capacity to heal. A tincture of morphine supplied by her friend, Dr. Case, was the only remedy that gave Nathan ease if administered early enough in the course of his headache and in a large enough dose to allow him to sleep. Steady quantities of bourbon, Nathan discovered, also seemed to keep the worst of his headaches at bay.

When weeks went by and still Nathan did not make any attempt to make love to her, Honey was bewildered. At first going to Nathan's bed made her exceedingly uncomfortable. She dreaded his touching her; the idea that he would do more than kiss her paternally was somehow unthinkable. With surprise, she realized, in spite of her insistence to the contrary, in her mind the right to make love to her belonged not to her husband but to Cameron Wolfe. If at times Nathan Radcliffe thought he might lose his mind, so did his wife sometimes question her sanity.

Early, Honey went to Shahar. "Is this what you saw?" she demanded. "Why didn't you tell me? I could've done with a little preparation, you know."

Shahar admitted to seeing Nathan—"plain as day"—which had caused her to question her own sanity. "Resurrection from the dead, you must realize, isn't real common."

Honey found her excuses not very consoling. "Promise me in the future, you'll tell me if there's anything I might like to know."

"Mmmmmmm."

"Mmmmmmm, what?"

"I'll tell if you need to know. This knowing the future isn't always the best."

Honey wondered if Shahar knew the sorry state of her married life. "Have we much of a future, Nathan and I?"

"A full one."

"And children?"

"I don't have an exact count."

"But children?"

"You'll have them, all right." Honey's face seemed to light up. "But for now give the man a chance to get himself drawn together before you start taxing him to make babies."

"I wouldn't think of it." But it worried her that Nathan appeared not to think of it at all.

Worry about their future in general occupied a lot of Honey's time. She knew they could not expect Trevor to support them indefinitely. She was privy to very little regarding Trevor's financial affairs, but from all appearances he had no present worries about money. She was unaware of his financially disastrous contributions to the Confederate cause, nor did she know that his fortune was diminished to the point where he heavily relied on his friends and supporters to cover expenses. Cameron Wolfe, among others, had lent him large sums of money, which he expected to more than repay when he gained the office of governor.

When the day finally came that Nathan expected to make love to Honey, he failed dismally. The lamp burning low, Nathan began as usual by holding her near and then turned to her, seeking, his hands wandering over her curves. "You've no idea, Mrs. Radcliffe, how I've dreamed of this moment," he whispered.

Honey smiled in response but cringed underneath.

He was eager to see her; until now their exposure to each other had been exceedingly chaste. They always dressed and undressed in separate dressing rooms and came to bed fully covered with nightshirt and gown. The one she had on this evening was almost as concealing as any garment she might wear in public: ankle-length, high-throated, long-sleeved, a confection of silk, satin, and lace but all the same modest.

Tiny pearls for buttons ran down the fitted bodice and caused Nathan great difficulty. In no hurry to be exposed to him, Honey let him struggle, wincing inside as he finally opened the front of her gown. He groaned in pleasure at the sight of her breasts and immediately suckled them. Honey closed her eyes in agony, not for any discomfort but for the feeling that he had no right to be at her breast. *It shall come to feel good*—as it had with her lover— she told herself over and over, but for the present, as Nathan obviously gloried in his inch-by-inch discovery of her, Honey writhed invisibly.

If Nathan noticed that Honey lay unmoved before him or cared, he gave her no sign. He made love to her slowly and at length. After what seemed an age, it came to her clearly that if she had been in Cameron's arms, by now she would have been almost wild with eagerness to move forward. If he had not done it already, she would have torn off his nightshirt and, if necessary, taken the lead. But Honey had no desire to do the same with her husband. She was stunned to have Nathan not even attempt to carry the act to the finish and had no words to interrupt the silence that followed his rolling away from her, their union still unconsummated. At that low point, after several long moments of unbearable quiet, all Honey could find the courage to do was move against Nathan's back and put an arm around him for comfort, her way of saying it was all right: There would be other nights.

When Honey heard Nathan's soft, even snoring, she doubted he was even aware.

CHAPTER SEVENTY-THREE

Honey felt there was something terribly wrong with a man who often could not finish making love to his wife. When he did accomplish the feat, the act was so abrupt and devoid of pleasure on her part that in her worst moments she considered it no better than rape. She strived to keep this opinion from her thoughts, believing she had come to this conclusion because of her vastly different experience with Cameron, an experience she would not have had if she had behaved like a respectable woman.

When she pried into their financial affairs, Honey risked further alienation from Nathan. "It is my duty to support us, and yours not to concern yourself with such matters," he told her. Honey knew Nathan had money from the sale of valuable North Carolina watershed land, funds he used to stake himself at poker games with Trevor's associates.

Nathan fell into the habit of playing cards in the late afternoon and early evening, whenever a game was to be had. An accomplished card player and a man of considerable luck, he at first parlayed several hundred dollars into thousands. Trevor laughed and told Honey, "With his kind of luck, your husband should go into politics."

Honey despaired, but Nathan said lightly, "Life is a gamble," and dismissed her concerns when she dared express them. "Don't worry yourself. The gods are obviously on my side." Honey believed the gods to be fickle and so made plans of her own.

Although not quite as raw as the Arizona or New Mexico territories, California was still very much a frontier state filled with men who with considerable effort had done very well for themselves. Many had considerable wealth in the form of land and farms or were engaged in lucrative professions or businesses. Some of these men had aspirations to raise themselves and their families above the level of yeomen. They craved education and cultural refinement. Sometimes their social goals had strings—a desire to improve their financial lot by acquiring the means to rub elbows with a more aristocratic and moneyed sort—but often the desire stemmed only from the wish to have an acquaintance with or mastery of the best of what civilization had to offer. They believed they had earned the right to possess whatever the world could offer, to partake of its riches.

These Californians, Honey believed, had the same aspirations for their children as parents who had sent their daughters to Mrs. Isabel's Boarding School in Columbia, South Carolina, before the war. In addition to subjects an enlightened young woman would be expected to study, such as literature, Honey also believed herself as fit as anyone to impart to properly regulated young ladies knowledge of "Piano, French, Dancing, Tatting, and Embroidery, Deportment and Other Necessary Attributes," which a San Francisco newspaper advertisement announced for such a school in that city. She would dust off her best "passionless" deportment.

Honey approached Trevor with her idea. "You shouldn't worry yourself with money matters. That's rightfully Nathan's concern."

"You don't actually think a life spent playing poker and drinking bourbon an admirable one, do you?" Honey parried bluntly.

"I agree it's a low sort of occupation, not one, I believe, his family intended."

"Nor was it a life my family expected me to share as his wife."

Trevor later pondered Honey's suggestion more seriously. Given the results of the war, many formerly well-to-do Southerners were forced in these times to creatively carve out a lucrative niche for themselves in the world. Well acquainted with Nathan's frequently disabling headaches and profound lack of preparation, not to mention inclination, to support himself in any profession or trade, Trevor believed Honey had found an acceptable and likely alternative. Many a respectable woman faced with financial necessity turned to teaching children the refinements of life. God knew, he would not be able to support them if the gubernatorial election did not go his way. His reasons for urging Honey to come west in the first place had been almost solely based on greed, and Nathan's resurrection had dashed them. Thus Honey's proposal now seemed exceptionally wise.

"I think you might begin to inquire about the availability of a suitable house, one large enough for you to take in your students as boarders."

"I've a perfect house in mind. Now that your friend Mrs.

Langdon has decided to return to New York, I expect she will want to sell her house."

Trevor agreed. "Have you spoken to her about your plans?"

"Not yet."

"Then let me negotiate for you."

"What about Nathan?"

"Let me take care of him."

Honey's plan seemed more appealing when broached by Trevor than it had been coming from his wife. Trevor approached the scheme as a notion with lucrative possibilities. "Just think how fortunate you are to have a wife willing to engage in such an enterprise. Most Southern belles would perish at the thought. Honey, on the other hand, wishes to keep herself occupied. Guess you have Dr. Greer to thank for her more lively inclinations. You can possibly turn yourselves a very nice profit with all the lower crust wanting their daughters to marry better than they deserve."

In these terms, Nathan could recognize the potential of Honey's suggested enterprise. Upon reflection, he realized Honey's avocation would not interfere with the way he spent his time. In fact, he would have less on his mind, be freer to pursue his interests full-time if he wished. "Trevor has agreed to lend us the money for you to establish yourself; therefore, you might search for a house for your school," Nathan announced.

"Mrs. Radcliffe's Academy for Young Ladies."

Nathan nodded. "That has a solid, respectable sound."

"I'll need a piano and certain furnishings if it's to be a boarding school."

"Whatever you want." After all, Trevor had agreed to finance the venture fully, which, Nathan decided, Honey need not know. That way more funds would be available for investment in his personal ventures with gambling. He had lost heavily recently, but not all his money was gone. He only needed to keep at it and his luck would return; his most daring adversary by far was Cameron Wolfe, who played all hands as if he never had anything to lose, although that was rarely the case. He bet high, almost recklessly. Nothing bluffed him; no stakes were too high. Win, lose, or draw, it did not appear to matter. "You're a cunning bastard," Nathan said to him in exasperation after Cameron had cleaned him out.

"If you want to talk cunning, you should play a few hands with the Apache," Cameron suggested around the edges of a fat, aromatic cigar. Without Nathan's knowing, some of Cameron's recklessness was an attempt to help Honey by allowing Nathan to win back some of his money.

Nathan admired Cameron's confidence and, with a sense of the man's vital engagement with life, also envied him. Nathan recognized that here was that rare kind of man who when necessary faced the world head-on in the full force of the wind without fear or regret, daring what he did without being hampered by regard for fate or with any obsession about how others would judge him for winning or losing.

Nathan was unaware that he alone possessed the one asset Cameron Wolfe regarded as beyond price, and his envy of Cameron turned into a personal rivalry heavily tainted with an amorphous resentment, the kind that is easily converted into hatred when men are pitted against each other as adversaries.

CHAPTER SEVENTY-FOUR

The house Honey wanted for her young ladies' academy had been originally built and occupied by a large, prosperous family. "I would have thrilled to have such a school available when my girls were of an age," Mrs. Langdon said when she heard of Honey's plans. "We were forced to send our children east for proper schooling." If anything, Honey's vision of the demand for such an establishment within the Sacramento community was an underassessment. Two days after she placed a small newspaper advertisement, she had her first quota of girls to enroll and, soon after, a waiting list of hopeful attendees whom she hoped to accommodate the following spring. She had visions of requiring and hiring two more teachers to assist her. For now, Shahar and Nollie were her right and left hands.

Nathan Radcliffe successfully concealed from everyone his shame at having been reduced to circumstances that required his wife to earn money to support them, a disgrace that was magnified when his gambling losses reduced him to near penury. At the last minute they had secured the Langdon house out of their own funds, but if he had not been for Honey's income, they would now be penniless and forced to retreat to Trevor's protection again. Even worse in Nathan's view, Honey's new role as head-mistress of the young ladies' academy appeared to give her a sense of independence and a strong feeling of self-worth that allowed her to be more forceful in her relations with him. While never having appeared to crave Nathan's affection, which was an appropriate attitude for a well-bred lady like Honey, tired of rough use, she now dared to discourage him frankly, if gently. Despite the fact that it befitted her class of woman, Nathan was angered by Honey's apparently passionless nature. She countered his advances with a firmness that almost belied detachment. As he was frequently impotent, her denial of his rights when he was in the mood translated into crushing rejection. Unconsciously, Nathan turned a lascivious eye on his wife's students.

But more easily lured and, in fact, more attractive to Nathan than these schoolchildren was a woman who, for as long as Nathan remembered, he assumed one day would be a conquest of his. If only the world had stayed in its original orbit, Nollie Daniels, his young wife's companion and slave, Nathan believed, would have come to him in Greerfield. The notion that the event might occur after all served to pacify Nathan's anger with Honey slightly; the effort required of him to seduce Nollie took all his energies and in the meanwhile kept his mind off Honey's trans-gressions.

Nollie had her own reasons for succumbing to Nathan. She was not satisfied with her lot in Canaan, for as yet the riches she had dreamed of did not flow in her direction; only hard work of a very familiar nature came her way. She realized if she were to go to San Francisco or to one of the boomtowns in Nevada, she might more readily make her fortune, but she had not summoned the courage to venture out on her own yet. She was ripe with disappointment, and her friend Honey Radcliffe was a perfect target for her resentment.

When they first arrived in Sacramento, and after they had slept for days at a stretch and bathed often enough to finally rid themselves of the grit and dust from the trail, it seemed to Nollie that Honey had transformed herself into the most noxious kind of Southern lady she could imagine, the sort she truly had never been before. "Brainless and witless," Nollie described her. "Why, she never behaved so peculiar at home." Shahar had to agree.

Honey seemed not to have an opinion or much of a spine. She agreed with everything anyone said to her, treating servants, Nol-lie especially, not only as if they were property but as if they were beneath her regard. Because she was unaware of Honey's hope that such inane behavior would alienate Cameron, that attitude only served to infuriate Nollie and put a solid wedge between them.

Later, it amused Nollie to have Honey's husband right under Honey's very nose—in Honey's own bed in broad daylight!—while for a change Honey slaved with her nice but, in Nollie's opinion, pathetically rustic young ladies.

The affair with Nathan Radcliffe also fulfilled a strange notion of Nollie's that Nathan's coming to her was, in an odd way, as it should be. Long ago, she too had foreseen the possibility that she might one day be Honey's husband's mistress. Hadn't Honey's own brother suggested it? As Nollie saw it now, the affair fulfilled unwritten law, the black woman having been created for use and abuse. Their union also defied Shahar's strict notion of how her daughter should lead her life. From childhood Nollie had been kept behind her mother's skirts, urged and cautioned never to become the white master's wench, and the path that was forbidden became the inviolable course. That her actions might hurt the two people Nollie loved most in the world glanced off her conscience like a leaf in a windstorm.

"When'd it first come into your head to sweet-talk me into your bed?" Nollie pried, curious.

"Long ago, when you and your mistress were still children, I looked into your beautiful face and fell in love with you."

"Even when you were courting Miss Honey?"

"Even then. I knew you'd bring me more happiness than that pale child could ever imagine. Perhaps I courted her to have you."

Nollie refused to consider her lover a liar; the pleasure of thinking Nathan Radcliffe preferred her to his Southern lady was enormous. The fact that he made rough use of her and at other times treated her either unpleasantly or indifferently was conveniently overlooked.

Publicly, Nollie embarked on a course of action that did not give her as much pleasure as it once might have. "Mr. Wolfe will be calling for me again this afternoon," she announced to Shahar in Honey's presence. He called for her at least once a week to go riding. Sometimes they went to town to shop, where he bought her small gifts—a hat, ribbons, exotic seashells from a warmer clime, a whatnot box carved in ivory from Africa. Cameron turned to Nollie to preserve a precious link to Honey, who, with

Nathan Radcliffe's return, now seemed irrevocably out of his reach; an honorable man, white or Apache, did not tamper with another man's wife. Nollie suggested that her connection to Cameron was romantic though it was not.

If by spiritual means Shahar was privy to the duplicitous nature of her daughter's conduct, she did not let on, but she noticed a marked change in Nollie, who suddenly eschewed frank pronouncements and became secretive and closed, as if she were concocting a devious plot. "He's not yours for the taking," Shahar warned of Cameron. "A white man will always be poison for you."

Nollie laughed at her mother's warning. "As I've my white daddy's blood in my veins, I can't see why a white man is more poison to me than any other."

"You're tampering with things you've no right to."

"I don't want to hear any of your heavenly announcements. Mrs. Radcliffe's says she's done with him. That's good enough for me. You don't think she's intending up to make a fool out of Mr. Nathan, do you?"

Shahar shook her head. "It's not in her. . . . As yet she doesn't know her own mind."

"Well, I'm not going to sit till I go feeble-minded waiting for Honey to come to her senses."

For her part, Honey looked on Nollie's apparent affair with Cameron with blood in her eye, surprised that she could care so intensely that he would turn to Nollie for affection. She felt deeply betrayed by both parties; however, when Nollie approached Honey about her feelings, she concealed her true sentiments. "As far as I'm concerned, you're free to do as you please. Just don't be deceived, Nollie Daniels; in his heart he's a savage."

"Then you won't go so far as Mammy to say I shouldn't take up with a white man."

"It does seem an unnatural affinity, but then, he's less white than Apache," Honey answered, miffed that Nollie should bring up the subject of her affair with Cameron at all.

"Then our blood should mix better than yours and his," Nollie said icily.

"I daresay."

"Maybe that's why when you worked so hard at mixing your blood with his, you had a mishap. Nature wouldn't stand for crossing two different breeds of cat."

Honey felt suddenly trapped in the familiar cycle of childish exchanges in which, over long years, she and Nollie often engaged. "Perhaps."

"Then how do you explain your daddy's my daddy too?"

Honey stared at Nollie, unprepared for that statement. "What makes you even dare think that, Nollie Daniels?"

"Mammy."

Honey's color faded considerably.

"Mammy told me, and she ought to know."

Nollie's slanderous charge made something inside Honey explode. Vague, sometimes confusing memories of Shahar and her father shifted slightly and became clear, but Honey resisted the internal confirmation. "You're a liar, Nollie, and always were!" she cried, her voice rising, shrill and defensive. "Your daddy was Lin-Davey. I know because I met him," she replied with force, as if the intensity of her statement would give it verity.

"Doesn't mean a hill of beans who the husband was!"

"You must've heard Mammy wrong. Your mammy and my daddy were master and slave. Nothing more." She felt hysterical.

"Just think of it, we're sisters, and always have been. Ask Mammy yourself if you don't believe me."

"Dr. Greer deplored the mingling of white and negro. Especially masters using their bondswomen. He'd never . . . he just *never* would. You're a devil to suggest it. I thought you were my friend."

"I'm your *sister*, not your friend."

Honey put her head in her hands, feeling suddenly betrayed by all those who had been dearest to her—her lover, her friend, her father, her beloved Mammy. She tried to trace the roots that had led to such a horrible twist in the conversation. Then she remembered and returned her gaze to Nollie. "You and Mr. Wolfe can go to hell on horseback with my blessing."

Nollie knew better and, greatly pleased by this turn of events, watched Honey make a hurried retreat. She wondered where the tangle of lovers, past and present, would lead.

CHAPTER SEVENTY-FIVE

The first term at Mrs. Radcliffe's Academy for Young Ladies had come to an end. Honey was both exhausted and thrilled to have been so successful with her daring venture. She felt useful and had been almost too busy to worry about the more troubling aspects of her life. Soon the spring term would begin. She had seen her way clear to hire another teacher and had added six more girls to the enrollment. Honey loved the tasks required of her, the children, ages nine through fourteen, eager to have their rough surfaces polished. She came to think of them as the children she and Nathan would probably never have. In very fanciful moments Honey even dreamed of finding some way to entice Nathan to give up his cards, horse races, dog fighting, and cockfighting, on which he seemed to spend most of their money, to oversee a group of young gentlemen in the fall.

By the end of the week a new two-story wing of the house would be finished, including four bedrooms upstairs and one large classroom below. The students from the past term had all gone home for three weeks. With their absence Honey felt as if she had nothing to do, and this morning in the quiet she had chosen to do nothing but lie in bed and sift through her thoughts —a luxury she had not enjoyed in months. On reflection, Honey realized she felt strangely alienated from all of her loved ones, which had been easier to overlook with six young ladies clamoring for her attention.

As her unease with the state of her marriage had increased, Honey had forbidden Shahar to repeat to her any premonitions or messages from the Spirits. With Nathan returned, it hardly mattered if the Spirits were calling for her to favor Cameron. The fact that she was miserable could not be helped by knowing the Spirits were on Cameron's side.

Shahar held her tongue as requested, but it was obviously a strain. Under the circumstances Honey had not had the nerve to bring up the subject of Nollie's paternity, yet she gave it much thought.

Honey forced herself to imagine Shahar and Dr. Greer as

lovers and at first found it impossible. She could not tolerate the idea of the loyalty and trust and genuine affection she remembered between them being tainted by carnal images. Her father felt it grossly immoral of white men to increase their stock of negroes by impregnating their slave women—which, Honey now realized, did not necessarily exclude a genuinely loving relationship between master and slave. Still, such a union violated secular and moral law and did not negate the fact that negroes, no matter how much one loved certain individuals, were an inferior race. Many were no better than animals, with a startling similarity to the savage Apache. Some, such as Shahar and Nollie, reflected good choices in breeding, but could love alone transcend the question of race? It had for her father, if what Nollie claimed were true. The possibility stunned Honey and challenged her deepest convictions. She doubted her good feelings for Cameron could in the end overcome his deep identification with the Apache race.

If what Nollie had said was true, it meant her father and Shahar had conducted their scandalous affair while Margaret Greer had been alive. The thought scalded Honey. Nollie had to be lying! Her father had loved her mother. Her father would never have engaged in an affair while her mother was still living. A decent man would never have done such a despicable thing.

Honey questioned Nollie's motive for wanting to hurt her and wondered what she might have done to offend her this time. She recalled that the subject of Nollie's paternity had come up over Nollie's flirtation or, possibly, affair with Cameron Wolfe. *How like Nollie to try to wound me when she perhaps was feeling guilty about Cameron!* Honey held little hope that whatever had come between her and Nollie would be resolved soon, for there was far too little time as it was and no time for the kind of scene it usually required to resolve issues that stood between her and Nollie.

There was hardly time these days even to converse with her husband, not that she and Nathan had much to say to each other. He was gone from the house a good deal, "handling our affairs," he said. When they were together, there was only one thing he seemed to want from her—his rights as a husband. He made no pretense of affection at other times, and any tenderness he had for her then seemed to be lost in his obsession with *his* arousal and, that accomplished, his ability to complete the sexual act. Not only was it Honey's duty to acquiesce to his desire, it also was her responsibility to arouse him, and any failure experienced hers.

Of course, Nathan knew without a doubt whose fault it was when he did not have a competent erection or when it faded before the desired end, for he was never impotent with his black mistress, only with his wife. A man, he believed, was entitled to have a woman who would provide for him sexually so that he might not tax his wife overly much. He hardly touched her, yet his failures with Honey were so common that he became obsessed with the reasons for her inability to arouse him.

Since Nathan believed negro women came by their sexual powers more naturally than white women, it was reasonable that Nollie would be more exciting than Honey. Recalling that Honey had had no trouble arousing him before they married, he figured there had to be some reason for her failure to arouse him now.

Honey was a well-bred, upright, and moral lady, deemed passionless and spiritually superior to the more lustful male, but in Nathan's view these qualities did not preclude her ability to arouse him sexually. The only valid conclusion for Honey's failure in his judgment did not settle well, but the more he turned it over in his mind, the more logical it seemed: Honey must be reserving the full extent of her charm for a lover.

Nathan knew that before his return Honey had planned to marry a prominent San Francisco gentleman. Might Honey and her suitor have been entangled more deeply than he had imagined? Perhaps there were others, just as Trevor Jefferson had said, equally enamored with his lovely wife. And what about the guide who had brought them across the continent and managed to get them captured by Indians? Honey had said very little about Cameron Wolfe or their experiences. Nollie, of course, would know the answers to all of these questions.

When Nathan spoke to her, Nollie tried to dismiss his queries with facile replies and thought she had succeeded. But he kept after her, for some reason obsessed with the idea that Honey was unfaithful to him. "Judging others by yourself?" she teased as she sat astride him. "Maybe it's just your conscience botherin' you, darlin'." She laughed. "When could she possibly find time for a lover, 'specially one not under her roof? You keep her busy enough, don't you? Or are you wore out after our naps together?"

Nathan scowled at Nollie and rolled over, pulling her under him. "That's none of your business. But a wife's affairs are her husband's business, especially when she's not as attentive as she should be."

"Seems peculiar."

"What seems peculiar?"

"That Mrs. Radcliffe wouldn't be interested, given her past enthusiasms."

Nathan smiled. "I knew she had a lover."

"I don't think she does now."

"Who?"

"Mr. Cameron Wolfe. And she was plenty disgusting. Not caring who knew she was floppin' down with a hired man. On the steamboat on the Ohio, Mammy and I had to listen to all their carryings-on 'cause our beds were pressed up against the adjoining wall. I tried to shame Mrs. Radcliffe with your memory, but she just kept at it.

"When we were with the Apaches, she pretended to be his wife. Then something happened, I don't know what, and so far as I know, it's all over between them. I don't think she wants any part of him now. But he's still sniffin' around. For a while, I thought he was taking a interest in me, but it's your wife he wants."

Nollie looked into Nathan's eyes and did not like what she saw there. "Mrs. Radcliffe thought you were dead."

"I wouldn't even have been cold in my grave before she brought him to her bed!" Nathan snarled.

"Well, don't get too carried away now. Remember, you *weren't* dead." She noticed Nathan seemed not to be listening and was suddenly sorry she had opened her mouth. Furthermore, the telling did not give her the satisfaction she had expected. "Best to forget I said anything. I shouldn't have told you." Nollie started to get out of bed.

Nathan grabbed her arm and pulled her down. "Where do you think you're going?" he demanded, then defended his stand on Honey's behavior. "A man is entitled to know when his wife is unfaithful."

Nollie smirked at the irony of it. "I doubt you'd want me to tell Honey what *you're* up to."

Nathan slapped Nollie's face viciously. "What a man does and what a wife does are two different things! If you say one word to her about us, I'll beat you within an inch of your life—or worse."

Tears welled in Nollie's eyes from his blow. "You've no right to hit me."

He slapped her again and again. "Don't tell me my rights, you little whore." Nathan's excitement and anger fueled another erection, which Nollie, unlike his wife, did not succeed in deflating.

Thereafter, all sexual encounters between Nathan and Nollie were strictly against her will. His curiosity unabated, Nollie fed him with stories—some true, others not. Intimidated by Nathan's continuing threats and actual violence, feeling bitter toward Honey yet ashamed of betraying her sister, Nollie kept silent, the malignancy in her relationship with Honey ready to burst.

CHAPTER SEVENTY-SIX

Seated on horseback, Cameron stared proudly over the acres of wheat that stretched in front of him below the levee. Under an overcast sky, the grain rustled and swayed, seeming to surge like swells of ocean waves in a gentle breeze. The yield of wheat this first year was going to be nothing short of miraculous, but it had taken more than a miracle to transform the waterlogged lowland property along the Sacramento River. It had taken tremendous amounts of thought and backbreaking effort to build a levee to hold back the fickle river, which in summer was often too shallow to support significant water traffic and in the spring washed out farmland near the river. After the levee was built, he had had to drain the land, prepare the soil, and plant.

Now Cameron longed to share his triumph over land and river with someone besides the hired hands and neighbors who had also had fortitude and determination enough to battle the river in its run to the sea. The person Cameron wanted to have by his side at this moment was a woman who, it appeared, would never stand next to him. He continued to dream of her, trusting his love for her but not his luck. Shahar counseled patience, but Cameron began to doubt heaven.

Cameron marveled at the fact that he had ever dared to be a farmer. His white eyes family were merchants, and in the Apache view, farming was suited only for women. At first this doubly negative heritage had limited Cameron's use of his land. An Apache warrior had a lot of experience herding cattle acquired in raids on Mexican or white eyes ranches, and driving cattle and the life of a cowboy was a logical choice for an Apache warrior trying to make a life for himself in the white eyes world. Later it was a natural extension of his Apache experiences for Cameron to become a cattle rancher.

Cameron attained manhood as an indian through recognition as an Apache warrior, husband, and father. It was a life filled with ritual and ceremony. He did not feel connected to the white man's world in any permanent way; the most ceremonial aspect of civilization seemed to him to be the exchange of money. Furthermore, Cameron had been rejected by the white eyes who meant most to him. His own blood kin looked on him with horror, as did almost anyone who learned of his Apache experience. Since his principal identity came from the Apache, in scorning him they rejected his manhood; Honey Radcliffe's rebuff had been the final thrust.

When Cameron's hopes for a life with Honey Radcliffe were crushed, at first he planned to sell his land in the Sacramento Valley and return to the Apache forever. For many days following his return to Sacramento, Cameron sat alone in his house and grieved. He cut his hair as was the Apache custom in mourning. At times he was filled with hatred for Honey. Then he fasted for three days, which was also the Apache way, and beheld a vision that let him rise above grief.

The Apache believe that when a warrior faced death head-on, he rose above death and attracted supernatural power to take back to his people. In his vision Cameron saw himself waging war for Honey Radcliffe even to death and believed time would heal her anger and revulsion. He would remain in California. If necessary, Cameron knew, he would wait forever to have Honey at his side.

When Honey had agreed to marry Jerome Pauley, Cameron had been shaken but knew he would not stop pursuing her simply because she was another man's wife. Honey had been Cameron's wife first and in his mind would be his forever. He trusted that what they had felt for each other was more enduring than lust. However, Nathan Radcliffe's rise from the dead had been a far more serious blow to Cameron's nebulous scheme. When he saw in Honey's face the love she felt for her husband and her utter joy at his return, Cameron questioned his right to pursue the battle.

In less agonized moments, he considered using the Apache Deer Ceremony to lure Honey to him, but before doing so he looked to Nollie for confirmation that Honey was unhappy. "Never been a happier bride," Nollie said, yet whenever he chanced to watch Honey, he did not see that. She always looked away, not in anger or hatred or even modestly but timidly, as if she were hiding something she did not want him to see. At times, Cameron thought himself a fool for this assessment and berated himself severely for seeing only what he wanted to see.

Discouraged but not ready yet to pack up and return to Arizona permanently, Cameron sought an obsession at least as exhausting as his passion for Honey Radcliffe and threw himself into improving his land and experimenting with farming. It was absorbing and new, far more challenging than cows, for Cameron to set to taming all his property that returned to the Sacramento River whenever given the chance. He and his hands moved thousands of yards of soil, building a levee above acreage he intended to farm as soon as it was dry enough to till.

In his spare time, the Apache passion for gambling of any kind stirred in him, and Cameron amused himself playing cards, often with Nathan, hoping to get to know him better, to see if he could discover whether Honey loved the husband who had risen from the grave.

He worried about Nathan's gambling losses. With knowledge about most family fortunes at the end of the war, Cameron wondered how Nathan had come by his apparently inexhaustible fund of money to gamble away. Some of it, Cameron reasoned, had to come from Honey's profits with her school. Although he agreed a wife's earnings belonged to her husband, he did not think much of a man who squandered such money in gambling. He saw little to admire in Nathan Radcliffe but also admitted he probably was the last person on earth to ask for a testimony to the man's character.

If Cameron saw Shahar when he went into town, he always pulled her aside. "She's made fools of us both."

"Not any such thing."

"You can't still believe there's hope?"

"Sometimes we just have to wait longer than we think we're willing to."

Cameron chuckled. "Am I going to live long enough?"

"Surely."

"But you're not promising soon."

"Not as soon as you'd like."

"Then I could go spend two or three years with the Apache and not be missed?"

"I fear Mrs. Radcliffe'd take it badly."

"I may have no choice."

Trevor Jefferson had related Cameron's experience with the Apache to a military acquaintance of his, and Captain Parkins, U.S. Cavalry, stationed in San Francisco, had quickly sought Cameron's advice. Captain Eustace Parkins was, aside from Trevor, the first man Cameron had met who seemed genuinely respectful of his Apache experience.

"You've lived intimately with the Apache. I'd value your opinion on pacifying them on reservations. What're the chances, do you think, that Cochise will ever come in again?"

"The Apache want peace. It's white eyes who don't live up to their word that makes peace impossible. Why should Apache trust white eyes when men such as yourself promise safe conduct under a flag of truce, then murder anyone who comes in under that flag?"

Captain Parkins grunted.

"What chance is there for peace when the advice of good white eyes like Steck is ignored over and over again? Apache alone can't make peace. Unless good range is allotted to the Apache and white eyes feed them as promised for giving up their right to hunt in *their* land, the Apache will have to go where they have always gone to hunt for food. A brand on a cow means nothing to a hungry Apache. I doubt now the people will ever accept being herded into one corner of the territory to live there forever. It's not in the Apache nature to stay in one camp."

"The government is prepared to live up to the promise of rationing whatever is needed."

"If you were Apache, would you trust white eyes?"

Captain Parkins gave Cameron a rueful smile. "Apache are arrogant devils," he said, his tone more admiring than disrespectful.

"They've a right to be."

"I'd like to see you go out and talk to the Apache about coming in. They know you, and from all I've heard, they trust you. Think of it as your doing something for the Apache, not the army. Better they come in peaceful than be dragged in like whipped dogs."

Annoyed by the captain's own arrogance, Cameron said, "What makes you think you can ever bring them in?"

"Sheer numbers. We outnumber them. Eventually we'll win."

Cameron thought that boast over.

"You'd be doing your people a favor."

Maybe, Cameron thought, but said he would think over the captain's request. He would like to see the Apache live in peace with the Americans as they had at first, as they had tried to do many times. He would be glad to be the instrument of an honorable peace. With white eyes, peace loomed more heroic than war.

Cameron looked over his wheat fields of gold. He had time to spare, time to help the Apache make peace with the white eyes. For it would be a long while, if ever, he knew, before he gazed over these fields with Honey Radcliffe held close in his arms.

CHAPTER SEVENTY-SEVEN

Just as he passed through the oak grove on the rear approach to his house, Cameron saw Honey Radcliffe come up the drive. Wearing a black riding habit with its full skirt draped beautifully to one side, she held an elegant pose mounted on Trevor's splendid bay gelding. Cameron had never seen Honey look more breathtaking.

Before she could dismount, Cameron came to assist her. Although he said not a word, his face betrayed his curiosity over her presence as he offered his hand and helped her to the ground. When she held his hand longer than necessary, Cameron lifted the veil of her hat and drew Honey to him, kissing her tenderly. She replied with a sweetness that made his heart constrict in his chest. He could not help himself then and began to kiss Honey again and again, growing more passionate with each kiss.

Honey returned Cameron's passion in kind, and they stood alone in front of the silent house, unable to let go of each other even for a second. They exchanged kisses for several minutes, then Cameron lifted Honey into his arms and carried her into his house. When he put her down, he unpinned her hat and dropped it at their feet and ran his fingers through her short, soft curls. He held her head in his hands and stared at her, his loving gaze caressing her face. He kissed her one more time. "I thought of using Deer Medicine to lure you here."

"But you didn't?"

Cameron smiled. "You've come, haven't you?"

Honey laughed. "Now, thank God, I've something to blame this madness on." Tears sprang to her eyes. "I need you," she whispered.

"I love you," he said.

"I don't know how you could."

"But I do."

Cameron unhooked the cameo brooch at the throat of her jacket, which he unbuttoned and dropped on the floor with her gloves. "Does he take off that glove when he makes love to you?"

"He doesn't make love to me."

Nothing she could have said would have surprised Cameron more. "So you came to me."

Honey nodded.

Cameron knew he wanted Honey—her reasons for wanting him hardly mattered, he thought as she deftly undid and removed his sheepskin coat and the flannel shirt underneath. While she did, as though they were engaged in some restrained ritual dance, he slowly moved them a few feet farther into the dim room.

Honey ran her hands gently over Cameron's lightly furred chest and bent to kiss the vivid line of his scar there. He sucked in his breath and groaned with pleasure. Their slow waltz had brought them to the foot of the stairs. As they began to climb, Honey left her pale silk blouse on the last knob of the handrail. When they reached the bedroom door, they did not enter but nestled in each other's arms again. Cameron laughed. "You wouldn't lead me this far, then change your mind?"

"I don't think I'd dare," she said rather seriously.

"Good!" Cameron said, and carried her straight to his bed. Their boots, her riding skirt, and all but her last sheer cotton petticoat were tossed on the floor, and they reclined together on the mattress that lay directly on top of the floor.

"Someone steal your bedstead?" Honey asked, and laughed. What little furniture there was in the house was starkly simple but beautiful.

Smiling broadly, Cameron pulled her nearer. "I don't like sleeping too high off the ground."

"Then you ought to sleep downstairs."

Cameron laughed. "I didn't come up here to sleep."

"Neither did I," Honey said, and gave her mouth to him and kissed him hungrily.

Cameron drew Honey tightly against him, then moved so that he could easily nip at her breasts and lower. He tugged at her last petticoat then, and Honey obliged him eagerly, pulling the petticoat down so that he might feast on her succulent flesh, whimpering seductively as he descended to her sex, calling out her pleasure in soft whispers.

When she drew him to her mouth again, her hands went to the fly of his Levi's and quickly exposed him, fully erect. She did not touch him but slowly let her kisses descend from the curve of his ear to his dimpled jaw, to his nipples, then to his ribs. She was diligent and thorough, finding places he barely remembered as tender to such loving caresses; there was hardly a place on his body that did not lure her—or succumb as he moaned with need.

Kisses to the corded, prominent veins in his muscular arms and hands made him weak with desire, but when she held his heavy testicles in her hand, he protested the pleasure and brought her swiftly beneath him. He paused to look at her for only a moment before filling her and thrusting into her deeply again and again. She gasped, her hands firm on his hard-muscled buttocks, wanting him as fiercely as he wanted her. When suddenly he came explosively, Honey savored his special stirring inside her, then made the final ascent and joined him in rapture, the deep sound of his satisfied voice blending with her own softly shrill one.

Afterward, they held to each other tightly, her soft cheek on his chest. Only after a long pleasurable silence did Cameron ask her, "Does he sleep in your bed?"

"Yes."

"But you said he doesn't make love to you. What'd they do, shoot his balls off?"

Honey gave Cameron a poke in the ribs, then said seriously, "What he does is not inspired by love. I was afraid I couldn't feel anything ever again."

Cameron pulled Honey closer. "Now you know different," he whispered.

"Now I know."

CHAPTER SEVENTY-EIGHT

Nathan stewed for days over Nollie's revelations about the affair between his wife and Cameron Wolfe. He asked her to repeat her tales and probed for more detail. She invented episodes to avoid boredom and told him of her mother's role in provoking the couple's affair. "Relations with a man who was a long-lost love from another lifetime would be justified, wouldn't you think? Who are you to me, I wonder?"

Incensed, Nathan thought of the years Mammy Shahar must have spent filling Honey's head with wild tales of sexual abandon. Shahar, who was known to have enslaved her master through the use of her race's naturally promiscuous allure, had spent a good part of her lifetime corrupting Honey Greer. What could he expect of a wife subject to such tutelage but a woman whose nature was wanton and deceptive?

Nathan compared Nollie's reports with his own experiences with Honey and found her responses to him remarkable for their lack of passion. From the beginning Honey had accepted his attentions with nothing more inspiring than resignation to wifely duty, which in his innocence, Nathan realized, he had attributed to her fine Southern breeding. Now he perceived her as no better than a lying, cheating whore.

If he were to believe Nollie, whom he had no reason to doubt, Honey had been a smoldering vixen with her lover. She had flaunted her affair on the riverboat and while they were with the merchant caravan. She and her lover had even lived as *man and wife* when they were held captive by savages. Honey had been pregnant with this man's child, the mere idea of which made Nathan livid. Honey's grossly immoral conduct became an obsession with Nathan that interfered with his occupations and pleasures.

One afternoon Nathan left his gaming—a horse race that had gone badly for him—early. He expected to find Honey at home sifting through her account books and notes for the upcoming term but instead found the house empty. A note from Honey—addressed not to himself but to Shahar!—informed him his wife had impulsively gone riding and would be gone the entire afternoon. "Do not expect me at any particular hour," the note said. It was an announcement that left Nathan feeling even more out of sorts than he was, for Honey would be riding a mount that was owned by Trevor, giving emphasis to the obvious fact that as her husband Nathan still could not provide adequately for his wife.

Nathan thought to assuage his agitation for an afternoon with Nollie, but she was nowhere to be found. Instead, he found himself in his wife's small study, rummaging through her papers. Nathan recalled Honey saying the indians had destroyed everything but what they considered useful, so he knew there was probably no memorabilia from her affair with Cameron Wolfe in Honey's possession, just as he knew the locket he had given her had been stolen by the thieving Apache. Still Nathan thumbed through Honey's papers, a task he found surprisingly fascinating.

Nathan found Honey's papers to be very organized and her thinking to be unusually superior for a woman, reflecting an almost masculine intelligence. He had always felt Honey had uncommon sense but had never considered intellect of much importance in a woman. Nathan did not want a simpleton for a wife, but as a woman provided little more than companionship and childbearing in marriage, she was not required to have much more brain capacity than a twelve-year-old child. Given the startling frequency of women dying in childbed, Nathan concluded he might have fared better with Honey Greer if he had married her at that tender age. Such an arrangement perhaps would have precluded his now being a cuckold!

Nathan admitted he had fallen short of his responsibility to Honey in the matter of turning her thoughts to her wifely duties. He had not devoted himself with enough diligence to his duty to see that she became pregnant and had permitted her far too much freedom, allowing her to occupy herself not with proper female occupations but letting her found and run Mrs. Radcliffe's Academy for Young Ladies, which, distressfully, had turned out to be more and more an economic necessity.

In thinking it over now, Nathan decided to dedicate himself to making Honey pregnant; if nothing else, he thought maliciously, it would give her ample opportunity to hone her skills as a vixen with him. She was still beautiful, and he would see to it a little more energetically that she lose her fine young figure. Several pregnancies, one after the other, would probably render her less attractive to a sporting man. Matronly corpulence would go a long way toward spoiling her chances of cuckolding him ever again.

But Nathan did not limit his thinking to the future and contemplated how he might avenge himself. How much of an assault to his honor did a man have to endure before he sought redress? Nathan wondered as he picked up a slim volume bound in red leather from Honey's desk, which on perusal he found to be a diary of Honey's remembrances of her trip west.

Nathan recalled Honey saying she intended to put her memories down before they became too hazy to recall vividly, and as he scanned the diary he found it to be just that, a vivid recollection of the trip from North Carolina to Sacramento. Nathan searched for passages remarking on the tempestuous affair Nollie had told him about but found nothing of interest. Every reference to Cameron Wolfe was scrupulously void of emotion. Honey remarked on their guide's general appearance, his perceptions and plans for the journey, his aptitudes, and his feats along the way, but there was nothing about her feelings or her amorous involvement with the man. It never occurred to Nathan that Nollie might have invented the tales she had repeated.

Disappointed, he tossed the red volume carelessly onto Honey's desk. In ill humor, he then further scoured the drawers of Honey's desk and turned up another book, this time a blue leather volume that, with its prominent gold lock, appeared at once to be more promising than the first. Would an honorable wife find the need to hide her musings under lock and key?

With no key in sight, Nathan tried without success to pry the small lock with the tip of a fountain pen, then hurried to Honey's dressing room and wildly searched her bureau, opening drawers and pulling out the contents, turning over a box of hairpins, rifling her jewelry box, all in search of a key. Left with no alternative, he severed the leather binding with a penknife. If the volume contained what he expected, Honey would have no reason to wonder who had destroyed her fine journal.

Nathan sat down on Honey's side of the bed and read avidly. The contents did not disappoint him, as the pages were filled with his wife's most intimate thoughts. Although they were undated, it appeared the notes were recent yet had been written over a period of time and not in one sitting. She wrote of her lover, her passion, her sensations, and revelations. She mentioned her dreams,

which she interpreted to possibly reflect a life shared with her
lover in another lifetime. She spoke of shared dreams. Obviously,
at one time Honey had adored Cameron Wolfe. But she also
wrote of the experiences that had driven her away from him.

Nathan was fascinated with Honey's vivid tale of her time
with the Apache, which had not been as colorfully accounted for
in the first diary. Here she spoke of her terror for her lover above
her own, the agony of the possible severance of their affair
through death—which she dared to describe as far more wrenching than the loss of her husband. She compared her passion for
Cameron with her affection for the man she had married and left
no doubt about whom she preferred. Nathan was devastated; his
wife was a harlot. Nollie had spoken plain truth—perhaps eu-
phemistically. Nathan Radcliffe believed he could never again
hold his head up in public with a wife as debased as Honey was.

The final stroke was the ending section.

*Perhaps we have all wished to have the Power to turn back Time. With
Nathan's return, I've been granted that wish in part, but with unfortunate outcome, for I see too clearly the Folly of my past acquiescent
nature. I married a man someone else decided my Perfect match. My
Qualms were dismissed as foolish; my wishes gone around by forcing me
to think Selflessly of others' wishes, the Wishes of those who, it was said,
had only my Best interests at heart. I was so swayed by the arguments of
those Dear to me, when Shahar finally had Courage to speak against my
plans to marry Nathan, I could not listen.*

*Perhaps I allowed her to influence me Unduly in other matters. It may
be that I used her notions about life After life to incite and excuse my
actions concerning Cameron Wolfe. Be that as it may, I now bring
Experience to my marriage that alters my perception of the purpose of
Marriage itself. I have borne my husband's callous, wholly self-
interested attitudes in silence because I can think of no means to
Change him. There seems in him no willingness to consider that he do
other than he Already does. Nothing I have ever known about him
suggests he would Alter his behavior to suit me. He is of the solid
opinion that whatever he decides is Right. I wonder how he managed
in the army to comply with orders of a Contrary nature to his opinions, if such an Event occurred.*

*I have been Miserable in my husband's bed. The terror I experienced
with the savage Coyote made that incident the worst I ever hope to
endure, but my experiences with Nathan are Not much elevated in
nature than rape. I think—if only I were more eager for him to touch
me. I try to be more receptive, more agreeable and welcoming, but at*

the Center of my Soul I find myself crying out—"No! Don't touch me. You've no right. I do not love you. I never shall." I tell myself, one need not love one's husband in any romantic sense to make a sound and productive marriage, surely Passion the least thing of importance in a relationship that endures a Lifetime.

I think of my lover and try to Remember how little we had in common but Passion. Yet there was also a respect between us, a high degree of Regard for each other, and a simple affection that went beyond what transpired between us in bed. He Valued me. And I him. He valued my opinion, not that we always Agreed. He actually seemed to think I was entitled to an opinion. A rare man, indeed. A far better one than my husband. A man I should admit I love still and shall forever, only if God Himself were to ask me.

As for passion, I shall not sleep in the same bed with Nathan for the rest of my life, especially if I have the Long life I intend. Better Nathan find someone more agreeable than I am to Entertain his needs and desires. If he should want to Divorce me, I shouldn't argue, and if not, I suppose I shall be obliged to have a few babies, but if this does not come about in a Reasonable time, I shall not submit myself to him forever.

With regard to passion, I have had many occasions to wonder if there is now something changed in my abilities to respond to lovemaking. It is said a woman who is treated as I have been is Never the same. Perhaps I shall never enjoy the sensations I once did. Yet I can remember almost too clearly my Emotions with my lover. At odd moments, I have considered calling on him and have reason to think he might be Receptive.

H.G.R.

Nathan considered where he might find Honey today. Might this hiatus in the academy's schedule not be a perfect occasion for Honey to pay a call on her lover? Nathan wondered as he rose from the bed with fire in his soul and a matter of honor to settle with his wife's lover.

CHAPTER SEVENTY-NINE

Honey had almost forgotten the immense pleasure of lying with her lover after making love. A quiet tenderness, a separate but not lonely peace settled over them as they lay embracing each other after making love a second time. She felt drowsy and longed for the luxury of sleeping away the rest of the afternoon nestled in Cameron's arms. She was half-dressed and Cameron was asleep when she heard the approach of a rider.

Honey hurried downstairs to collect the rest of her clothes, first her blouse from the stair, then her jacket and hat. She stood before a mirror over a small table and adjusted her cameo, then her hat, which required pinning. Suddenly Honey froze in place, her hands in midair, as behind her she saw Nathan's face, his look of cold fury reflected clearly. "You're so brazen, you don't even bother to close the doors behind you," he spat.

Honey whirled around to face him, the color in her cheeks drained away. As she did, Nathan struck her with his open hand with force enough to knock her against the table and knock her hat from her head. Then Nathan grabbed for Honey, but she eluded him. He tried again and caused her to stagger backward. She tried to steady herself but, losing her balance, caused the gilt-framed mirror to crash to the floor, its shattering making an explosive noise.

By the time there was silence again, Cameron was downstairs, gun in hand, with only his pants and Apache moccasins on. Honey sprang in his direction. Cameron caught her in his arms.

"You, sir, owe me satisfaction on the field of honor for taking my wife to your bed!" Nathan growled. "It appears she's no better than a whore, but she's mine, *forever*, or have you forgotten, Mrs. Radcliffe?"

"No, please! I'm not worth your murdering each other."

"Of course you're not. But I've my pride, if little else. Your lover has assaulted me through you. You can't protect a man from his folly, my dear. When his stupidity comes to light, he must bear the consequences. My folly was marrying you. His," Nathan said, pointing angrily at Cameron, "was being seduced."

Honey turned back to Cameron. "Please, if you love me, refuse the challenge."

Cameron looked down at Honey and could not miss the agony in her eyes, but he believed Nathan had every right to protest, to demand satisfaction. In Nathan's place he would do the same. Not to do so would be unnatural, unmanly. His gaze on Honey, Cameron said firmly, "I accept your challenge."

Honey put her head in her hands.

"Excellent. Your choice of weapons, time, place, and distance."

"Pistols. Three shots. Twenty paces. Nine in the morning, day after tomorrow," Cameron announced without hesitation. No point in delay. "As for your claims on Mrs. Radcliffe, in the Apache way she's as much my wife as yours. And I am the wronged man." Smiling at Honey, Cameron lifted her face and lightly touched the tip of her nose with a finger.

Remembering the minimum Apache punishment for infidelity was mutilation of the woman's nose, Honey pushed Cameron's hand away with a frown. "Why is it men must always soothe their pride violently, usually to a woman's misery?"

Neither man answered her.

"Even when you thought me dead, you didn't marry—you only lived with him like the whore you are. And I've no doubt there will be other men."

"Why do you want her, then?" Cameron demanded, glad he soon would have the opportunity to punish Nathan for abusing Honey so readily. "I object to your calling the lady a whore."

"The truth will out, but until I'm done with her, she's mine, which anyone who dares touch her will come to know." His position made clear, Nathan ordered, "Come with me, Mrs. Radcliffe," and to Cameron, "I shall send word of my second and expect you to do the same."

"I'll not leave with you," Honey insisted, and Nathan, having thrown down the gauntlet, satisfied, left without her.

"How could you?" Honey demanded when he had gone. "He's so much less a man than you are. You've nothing to prove. When I learned dueling is not legal here, I thought, 'At last, a sane country!' But I neglected to remember how vain men are. Please," she begged, "if only for my sake, don't go through with it."

Cameron pulled Honey against him protectively. "Are you afraid of him?"

"No." Her tone was not convincing.

"You needn't go back to him."

"I've appearances to think of. He's my husband. He's suffered enormously. I don't know what I was thinking to have come here at all!"

Cameron smiled down at Honey. "Deer Medicine, remember?"

"Oh, yes." Honey sighed, glad to be in Cameron's strong arms, her face against his bare chest. She kissed him. "If he should kill you . . ." Her voice caught on tears.

"He won't," Cameron promised. "But there are some things a

man must do, even if his woman begs him not to. When we made love just now, we gave your husband the right to call me."

"If you should kill him, I could not live with myself. We could never be together."

"Then either way I lose."

"Yes. Either way *we* lose."

CHAPTER EIGHTY

Word spread quickly about the duel, which would be held in a grove on Trevor's property. Several witnesses, including a few women, had gathered by seven o'clock in the morning, and it appeared that no one had bothered to notify the legal authorities. Why would anyone want to spoil what promised to be a real show? The dishonored husband, the lady in question, the lover, all of whom were well known, would be the subject of gossip for months following, whatever the outcome. Already Honey realized that the notoriety alone would be her undoing.

Trevor was to be Nathan's second; one of Cameron's cowboy hands, his; Dr. Case, the attending surgeon. The morning was damp, and the trees dripped with dew, the silence in the grove broken only by the sound of spattering dewdrops on leaf litter on the ground. Sitting in a closed carriage off to the sidelines, huddled in a heavy coat trimmed with lynx fur, Honey shivered and knew she would never be warm again if Nathan killed Cameron. But she also despaired of injury to her husband, for she could not foresee any future for herself and her lover with Nathan's death on the so-called field of honor. How could they start a life together launched with Nathan's blood?

Seated next to her, Shahar insisted she had foreseen this event in the smoke she had dreamed about. "Seeing the misty day and knowing they choose guns, I know now where the smoke comes from." She would not discuss the outcome of the duel, whether she knew it or not. Nollie, too, was at the scene, though she appeared to have suffered a great shock. She was extremely nervous and terribly sober. Shahar frowned at her daughter as she squirmed and fidgeted. She did not believe the story Nathan had told of learning of the affair between Cameron and his wife by discovering and reading Honey's diary. "He had to have a reason to look out for it," Shahar had insisted.

"No matter now," Honey had answered.

The women waited, each suffering her own bitter thoughts until Nollie said hotly, "Genteel murder is all this business is. What Mr. Nathan'd ought to do is cut Mr. Wolfe to keep it from happening again. That'd put the word out."

"You imply that an affair is likely to be a repeatable offense on my part," Honey shot back.

"Chicken's out of the henhouse now. And you and Mr. Nathan don't seem compatible enough to patch this up any time soon. I heard you telling him not to touch you. Just think, last night might've been the last time you ever have with your husband, and you turned him down flat."

Honey looked away from Nollie but couldn't avoid wondering what had brought them back to sniping at each other. Her curiosity waned as Cameron rode onto the field.

Honey's heart lurched; she felt her whole being incline to him. The last thirty-six hours had been desperate ones in which she had written him a long letter she had not had the courage to send.

Honey signaled her uncle. "Please take this message to Mr. Wolfe."

Trevor refused. "I'm surprised you'd ask. After all, I'm your husband's second. And if you care at all for Cameron, you won't clutter the man's mind at a moment like this."

"Whose side are you on?" Nollie queried insolently. Trevor gave her a look that should have wilted her, but Nollie glared right back.

Honey tucked her letter back into the pocket of her cloak as Trevor joined Cameron's second to finally mark the field, then toss a coin for the right to choose sides and give the signal. Trevor won and selected the east side of the field for Nathan, which meant Cameron would face into the sun.

Nearby stood Nathan, who at the moment carefully studied Honey and thought over his position for the last time. He hoped to get through the duel before the pain in his head overwhelmed him.

From Nathan's view, without the redress of dueling he would not be able to live with the shame of his cuckolding or with the knowledge that his wife preferred another man to him. It was humiliating enough to know Honey was a passionate woman and not as demure as he had thought. But the worst of it was to realize that the woman he had married and had known since childhood, whose bloodline and breeding were beyond question, actually preferred a man as common as dirt, a man who preferred the company of savages to that of civilized men. The idea caused Nathan's physical pain to intensify, as if Honey's association with such an inferior man also contaminated him. Nathan thought Honey the perfect example of the easily corruptible female and the reason decent men insisted women be sheltered from the more shocking elements of life. No doubt the war and Honey's experiences as a nurse had been responsible for her ultimate downfall.

Nathan did not worry about the outcome of the duel. He knew he might be outmatched, but he was an excellent marksman and counted on his morally superior position as the wronged husband to see him through to a just conclusion. He would face his rival without flinching and mete out the punishment due him. He would aim for Cameron Wolfe's heart.

The seconds loaded the guns for three rounds as Nathan approached his wife's carriage. "You do wish me luck, don't you, my dear?" He had one of his blinding headaches, which the usual treatment had failed to eliminate; he thought he might be willing to die to put an end to it.

Honey smelled bourbon on Nathan's breath. "You can still call this off, which you must if you've been drinking. I've prayed that one of you would come to your senses. I give you my word never to see him again."

"It's too late now," Nathan answered almost casually.

Honey bit back tears as Nathan walked away.

"He talks as though he's the only one that's not a sinner," Shahar said, with a heavy heart in spite of her long-held dislike for the man.

"The self-righteous are always sure of themselves," Nollie said.

After stripping to their shirtsleeves, the duelists examined their pistols, then entered the field of honor where it was marked at the center. They stood left side to left side, facing opposite directions. When they finished pacing, they were to face each other and, pistols rising or dropping, at Trevor's signal, fire between the count of one, two, and three until three rounds were fired. If no one was killed or pinked after the third round, Nathan might consider his honor satisfied or demand more rounds until someone was wounded or killed.

It was enormously tense; there was utter silence in the grove except for the crunching of leaves on the floor of the field as the two men paced off the agreed twenty paces. With Nollie and Shahar, Honey, afraid to breathe, stood outside the carriage, her hands clenched in fists, her gaze steadfastly on Cameron. She prayed neither man would be killed or badly injured.

Cameron was confident of his skill as a marksman. At this range, twenty paces, he would have no difficulty shooting his opponent fatally. What he had come to doubt was the wisdom of killing Nathan. He knew Honey would never come to him if Nathan died on the field of honor, although in challenging Cameron, Nathan had consented to end his life there. "I could not live with myself or with you," she had said firmly of the possibility of Nathan's death.

Cameron knew Honey had not intended for Nathan to discover them, yet now he was not confident of her reasons for coming to him. "I need you," she had said, *not* "I love you." The need to know if she could respond to a lover as she had, he knew, was not the same as her loving him still. He was troubled also by the fact that Honey had refused to accept communication from him or speak to him in person since the challenge. He now had larger doubts than ever about any future with Honey Radcliffe.

Cameron knew he could not decide what exactly to do until the moment arrived, but that moment came sooner than it should have. Before they had walked twenty paces, Nathan whirled precipitately and fired twice. The crowd gasped in shock at Nathan's violation of the most basic ethic of dueling. Obviously, he was not the gentleman he pretended to be.

Nathan fired wildly, missing Cameron completely with the first round but grazing Cameron's left shoulder with the second, the pinking obvious from the immediate show of blood on Cameron's white shirt. Even Cameron was shocked at Nathan's disgraceful breach of honor. "I protest! I protest!" Cameron's second shouted, and stepped onto the field. A roar from the crowd indicated their agreement.

Nathan faced Cameron squarely with his gun lowered to his side, barrel down, as if to say to Cameron, "You've two shots coming."

Everyone froze as Cameron raised his pistol and took careful aim, then slowly raised the gun over his head and fired two shots into the air.

Nathan stared at Cameron with a look of pure hatred. He did

not wish to be spared, a greater shame in his view than an unfaithful wife or his own dishonor on the field.

Nathan Radcliffe then turned and walked calmly from the field toward his wife. When he was two feet from Honey, he stopped, placed the barrel of the gun in his mouth, aimed up, and fired, showering his wife, Nollie, and Shahar with bloody fragments of his brain.

CHAPTER EIGHTY-ONE

For several weeks after the duel Dr. Case came often to see Honey and prescribed strong sleeping powders. Honey slept without dreams, only to waken to the fresh horror of clear memory. She dreaded a lifetime of living with her recollections—of Nathan's last look and the agony of his death. She wondered how long after Nathan pulled the trigger she had stopped screaming. From her hoarse voice, which lasted for days afterward, Honey knew she must have carried on for quite a while. The guilt she felt would torment her to the grave.

The notoriety of the duel alone prevented Honey from reopening the young ladies' academy for the new term even if she had been sufficiently recovered from grief to conduct the new session. Newspapers throughout the state were full of the details of the duel, the scandal kept alive for weeks by commentary of one sort or another, the most popular argument concerning dueling as a means of settling disputes. All the reports Honey had seen of the tragedy were full of misinformation, but none enhanced the reputation of anyone involved, especially the headmistress, who was portrayed by all as a scarlet woman. Within a week she had received notes of withdrawal from the families of all but one of her students.

Trevor took Honey in the morning of the duel. He saw to it that her house was closed, and within a month he sold the property with her consent. She hardly remembered Nathan's funeral, except for the crowd of spectators. Many friends and acquaintances sent condolences to the widow, but many others did not. Her reputation ruined, she feared the scandal would also hurt Trevor politically, although he declared that almost any fame was better than none. Aside from the inconvenience associated with looking after his niece's affairs, he almost seemed to enjoy the public notice.

With the unwelcome opportunity to think and rethink what had led her to the awful situation in which she now found herself, Honey regretted everything and knew she alone was largely to blame for all that had happened. She wondered how she would live with herself for setting into motion the events that had led her husband to suicide. Trevor called suicide a death without honor. "The man disgraced himself."

Perhaps that was so, Honey conceded, tears spilling like raindrops in a sudden storm. It was a burden to even have to consider the possibility. However, one thing she knew for certain—if her position with regard to Cameron Wolfe had been difficult before the duel, it was now impossible.

When she had gone to Cameron that fateful day, Honey had not yet admitted to herself that she still loved him. Cautiously, not wishing to hurt him purposely, Honey had told Cameron only that she needed him—needed to prove that after everything that had happened to her, she was capable of feeling anything with anyone.

In surrendering herself to him that day, Honey had surrendered all barriers, ones that would have remained erect with Nathan even if they lived together forever. With Cameron, who seemed to love her in spite of her faults—her hatefulness, her pettiness, her contrary opinions—Honey was free to be herself, while with Nathan, she was loved not for herself but for the perfect Southern womanhood she was thought to embody.

Honey had once told Cameron she could never forgive his savagery, and while on the surface sparing Nathan appeared to be an heroic act, in the end it turned out to be as brutal as his actions against Coyote.

Would Cameron have fired into the air, however, Honey asked herself now, if she had not sworn they could never be together if Nathan should die in the duel? Had she been the savage to suggest it?

It had been savage of Nathan to take his life in the manner he had. Perhaps, Honey reflected, the savage abides in the heart of every person. Perhaps, we are all capable of savage acts given the right moment in time.

As things stood now, Honey could not look at Cameron Wolfe or even think of him without in her mind's eye seeing Nathan with the gun in his mouth, without being overwhelmed with sorrow and guilt. Could there be any greater impediment to the joy of being with her lover than such a memory? She was convinced that the only fair price for her transgressions was a life without love.

As time passed, Honey began to consider a future for herself and when she had been a widow for six months, Trevor hinted she should consider venturing into the world again. She contemplated returning to North Carolina but decided that in the surroundings where Nathan had been very much a part of her life, she would fare much worse emotionally than she did in California. The idea of another trip across the continent terminated any such plan.

Tonight Dr. Case and two medical students, who had come to Sacramento to inquire about opening a small practice together when they matriculated from the San Francisco Medical College, would dine with Trevor and Honey. In the months following Nathan's suicide, Dr. Case had become Honey's close friend. She gravitated to him naturally. They had like minds; almost any topic he brought up interested her, especially anything to do with medicine. Although she had abandoned any notion of becoming a doctor, the subject still fascinated her.

She dined with Dr. Case often, for he came to look in on her frequently. At first she suspected him of being a friendly spy for Jerome Pauley, which he admitted freely when she dared to inquire. It flattered her that Jerome would be solicitous of her health but saddened her that he would not come forward himself. She was, she knew, a pariah socially.

Maybe, as Trevor insisted, it was time for her at least to see people at home, she thought, and allowed Shahar to pull from her wardrobe a modest dress of black silk, which, with its high collar, would cover her from chin to toe.

Nathan's ghastly death had effectively silenced Shahar in Honey's presence, but Honey knew it had not altered the woman's inner visions.

It was true Shahar did not yet have the heart to urge Honey to look forward. In fact, for the first time ever, Shahar looked on Honey's health as particularly fragile.

Shahar did not spare Nollie, however, and lit into her daughter even on the day the duel took place, although well out of Honey's earshot. "You set this all in motion, I know for a fact. You'll regret till your dying day."

"Can't help fate, Mammy."

"You just keep in mind your own fate is involved in this also."

"I'll keep on just as I have, whatever happens."

Shahar gave a scoffing laugh. "Life will never be the same for you, or any of us."

"Don't you get tired of saying the same old predictions?"

"You'll be leavin' us soon."

"Is that so? Where I be goin'?"

"To the high hills." Shahar stood back and contemplated her daughter coldly. Had she made a mistake bringing this child into the world?

"So what else do you see? Should I best pack up, or can it wait?"

"I been contemplating what a grave with black flowers growing out of it means."

"Never heard of black flowers."

"You'll understand what it means soon enough. You're a shame to me, daughter."

Nollie glared at her mother. "Just livin' out your visions is all I'm doin'. Somebody's got to. Miz Honey ain't been makin' you out much of anything but a false prophet."

Shahar's dreams lay heavy on her heart. The signs were terrible: a grave deep enough for three, a daughter lost forever, another nearly so, cords severed and then knotted with others, death and ruin everywhere, the appearance of a man she knew by heart but did not recognize. Shahar moved cautiously among her yet to be realized visions and prayed for courage.

CHAPTER EIGHTY-TWO

Both medical students seated at Trevor's table were familiar with Mrs. Radcliffe's story from lurid newspaper accounts and equally vivid gossip. If anything, in person she was more beautiful than rumor had it. Slender as a wisp of wind, with her hair pulled back severely from her face, drawn into a heavy chignon at the back of her head, her skin without a blemish and her coloring boasting vibrant health, she took the younger men's breath away. Although they tried not to, they stared at her, especially when she listened to Dr. Case and her golden gaze was lively with intelligence; at other times they were fascinated with her dark reserve.

With the medical students present, Honey was reluctant to enter the conversation, but Dr. Case drew her into the discussion. "Tell me, Dr. Case, are there any women attending lectures at the college?"

Dr. Case cleared his throat. "Only one, a Mary Bennet, and she creates a flurry of dissent."

"Has she distinguished herself?" Trevor wondered with a knowing glance in Honey's direction.

"Not as yet, but she is as well educated as most of the men."

"Has she disgraced herself, then?"

"Not at all. She seems uncommonly adapted to the subject," Dr. Case replied, but Honey heard his reluctance to admit it. "In view of the rudeness and strife to which she is sometimes subjected, perhaps she *has* distinguished herself. Many of the faculty as well as the students seem to go out of their way to attempt to discourage her."

Honey noticed the color rising in the face of one of the medical students. "Dr. Gleason, you seem to have an opinion to express. Please don't let my presence prevent you from speaking freely. I'm sure we'd like to hear anything you might have to say."

Dr. Gleason's color darkened even further with Honey's interest. "The thought of that woman makes the humors rise. She's a disgrace to her sex. No woman of decency would consider medicine. She wastes the valuable time of our professors and takes a man's place. There are also certain peculiarly female functions, which I decline to discuss here, that impair a woman's mental and physical performance."

"Yes, I've heard that point of view voiced before," Honey acknowledged. Menstruation was a disease that weakened minds and sapped energy.

"A woman's intellect is not the same as a man's, of course."

Honey knew that Dr. Gleason meant *all* women were of limited intellectual capacity. Women were impulsive and irrational, with passive minds and weak bodies, dependent, excitable, even hysterical. "But I thought I heard Dr. Case say this female student was holding her own. Might she be superior to ordinary women?"

"I hardly think so. Even if she manages to finish her lectures and hospital trials, she will no doubt marry and have children, which will destroy her mind for useful occupation."

It was Honey's turn to have her color rise. She seethed at the common prejudice against her sex, although she would have been surprised to hear anything else. "Did you know that among other people, women are doctors along with men, and revered equally? And these women heal as effectively as men."

"What 'people' would that be?"

"I know it is true of the Apache. There may be others. And I believe in Africa—"

Dr. Gleason laughed. "Niggers and indians? My dear lady, you mean to say savages. You can't call their practitioners doctors," he scoffed.

"Perhaps if you'd been with me in the late war, you might not be willing to mock the savages out of hand." Honey could hardly believe that remark had come from her own lips and was galled to have Trevor rescue her by adroitly changing the topic.

Honey left the men shortly afterward, with Dr. Gleason's arguments still nettling her. The idea of the inferiority of women was hardly a new concept to her, but it rankled nonetheless. It was obvious some men were not equal to medicine: Some were; surely *some* women were, also. She for one! Honey was discouraged by Dr. Case's hesitant praise for the one lone, harassed female student, who, Honey imagined, must be extraordinarily brave to every day face the glares and jibes of men who despised her. It must be a little like living among people who would just as soon see you dead as look at you. Honey did not envy the woman her monumental task; her heinous crime, after all, was only a want of certain body parts.

In her room, Honey sat on the edge of her bed and brushed her hair furiously, which at long last was past shoulder length. She pulled the mass of her hair back from her face and caught the ends, pulling them forward to examine them. As thick as her hair was, the strands flared out in a shape resembling a bushy mustache.

Honey stood up and advanced toward the mirror above her dressing table. She held the mustache under her nose, then under her chin. She smiled as if she were mad, tossed her hair over her shoulders, and threw a dressing gown over her nightgown. She took up a small lamp then and hurried downstairs into Trevor's study, where she began immediately to write to Mlle Doria LaLage.

My Dearest Doria,

*I've a matter of some Urgency to discuss with you, and would con-
sider it a great Favor to me if you would consent to Meet with me
some afternoon next week. Perhaps, we might take Luncheon at Maison Verte, say at two P.M., if you would Care to meet me there.
Perhaps on Thursday. I await your Reply.*

With sincere regard,

(Mrs.) H. Radcliffe.

CHAPTER EIGHTY-THREE

Within relatively few hours Cameron Wolfe went from a mood of
rejoicing to one of extreme depression. One moment he held in
his arms the woman he had despaired of ever loving again, and in
the next he saw her slip away from him forever. Over the years
he had seen many men die violent deaths, but the horror of
Nathan Radcliffe's suicide, he believed, would remain in his
memory for a lifetime. Like Trevor, Cameron considered taking
one's life a death without honor, unthinkable for a warrior unless
one could no longer be of use to one's people, a public suicide
the act of a man of especially low rank, one who would destroy
those about him as well as himself. Cameron knew Honey Radcliffe's suffering would be much greater than his own, which
added to his sorrow.

That afterward she had refused to see him and, through Trevor, demanded he not present himself at the funeral devastated
Cameron, a request that, of course, he honored. She returned his
letters unopened and denied him when he called on her. Cordially
but formally, Trevor Jefferson had informed Cameron that Mrs.
Radcliffe wished to convey that she would never receive him.
Hurt and bitter, Cameron mourned Honey Radcliffe a second
time. Would killing Nathan have been a better choice? He felt
betrayed.

A month later, the anticipated call came for Cameron to return
to Arizona. The word he had was that the Apache had applied for
peace. Cameron would go to Santa Fe and discuss the U.S. gov-

ernment's latest treaty plans for pacification of the Apache, then approach his people to convey those arrangements. Cameron knew it was a perilous mission and might well be a move made too late. Revenge and counterrevenge was a deeply instilled way of life among the Apache.

While the Apache had first looked on Americans as allies against the despised Mexicans, men whose greed outstripped their honor betrayed the indian, setting in motion acts of revenge by one side and then the other, which, Cameron believed, might continue until doomsday unless Apache and white eyes mutually declared a truce and lived up to it honorably. The greatest risk to peace, however, lay with the white eyes.

The government's record of treachery and its failure to meet the requirements of previous treaties had given the Apache every right to distrust any appeal he brought them. A certain few on either side would not trust him or would wish to see the disputes and bloodshed continue for their own reasons.

But Cameron agreed with Captain Parkins that without a shadow of a doubt there were almost countless numbers of white eyes in contrast with a finite number of Apache. The fact that Apache and white eyes had at times in the past shared a peaceful existence perhaps augured for a peaceful future. Cameron felt he owed it to the people to try to gain such a future for them. But in returning to the Apache, Cameron realized he might be drawn to remain with his people. Only the experience would tell.

It was a convenient time for Cameron to return to the Arizona Territory. This was the time of year to buy yearlings there and bring them to California. Also, the debate about whether to arrest someone for the illegal duel in which Nathan Radcliffe had died had heated up again. Cameron had a feeling the authorities were not considering arresting the beautiful widow!

But also at the back of his mind was a nagging worry that Honey might destroy herself. He remembered the dream he and Honey had shared, and since the duel he had experienced the same dream at least a half dozen times. The image of Honey dying in his arms had awakened him each time, leaving him drenched in a terrified sweat. Cameron wondered if Honey might be despondent enough to kill herself in this lifetime. From even casual reports of her frame of mind, it seemed a real possibility. But if Honey had her mind set on such a thing, what could he do to prevent it? She refused all his attempts at communication.

Might pursuing the matter be enough to set in motion what he dreaded?

Cameron growled with disgust, not for the first time feeling himself a fish out of water, the dilemma of being too white eyes to live with indians and too indian to live among white eyes again boiling to the surface. Torn between two worlds, wanting to leave, wanting to stay, Cameron felt the familiar battle that always warred within him. If he stayed in Sacramento, at least he would be near Honey, which had to be, he realized, a form of self-torture.

If he were of one world or the other, his choices would be clearer. Still, as a different breed, yet a man, Cameron wanted what all men wanted: a place to live—to thrive—and a woman with whom to fulfill his destiny. Regrettably, the woman he recognized as his was neither a different breed nor now of a mind to join him in either world or be reconciled between. Once, perhaps . . .

Cameron believed the most serious mistakes in his life had occurred whenever he violated the Apache prohibition concerning forgiveness. Apache never forgave an enemy or a wrong. Forgiving his Saint Louis family had only led to further rejection. Forgiving Coyote the man's mad jealousy and hatred had merely postponed the inevitable. That one act of forgiveness had allowed great harm to come to Honey Radcliffe, which in turn had brought Cameron even more painful rejection. And surely, forgiving Honey had led to disaster. Perhaps he should never have forgiven the Apache for their murder of his family. . . .

Didn't all experience suggest the Apache would be fools to forgive the white eyes' past transgressions against the people and embark on a course of trust? What was he doing going to his people to suggest they accept the white eyes' treaties? Was his yearning for the people to be safe in their own land a symptom of madness brought on by his straddled position between the white and indian worlds?

But in every situation that had come to his mind, Cameron wondered, would failure to forgive have brought better results? Miserable and torn by conflicting emotions on subjects that haunted him, Cameron felt almost like a madman.

Yet Cameron could not avoid the feeling deep in his gut that mutual forgiveness between Apache and white eyes was the only peaceful solution possible. To forgive did not mean to condone either party's past behavior, but it might be the only means of salvaging the future. Likewise, unless he could forgive Honey's rejection of him and she in turn could forgive him his transgressions, Cameron knew he would never have a future with Honey Radcliffe—the only woman with whom he felt an undeniable spiritual bond, a bond as deep as the one he felt with the Deer, whose Medicine he claimed.

The Apache claimed never to forgive, yet Cameron realized now that their acceptance of him as one of their own was a result of forgiveness: The Apache had forgiven him his white blood. Forgiveness was the Apache way, after all.

After Nathan's death, Nollie found she did not need sleeping powders, but her dreams were grotesque and disturbing. She would never forgive her lover's hideous act, which she saw as an atrocity committed as much against Honey as against himself. Nollie felt enormous hatred for Nathan and no pity. And to her surprise, she felt great sympathy for Honey. She felt Nathan had subjected her to more misery than she deserved. Perhaps Shahar had been right about white men after all . . .

Weeks passed, and Nollie spent many hours bathing before she felt herself rid of the blood and brain matter that had spattered her face and clothes at the duel. She had insisted that her clothing be burned with the things Honey collected for a kind of funeral pyre. When Honey burned everything that belonged to Nathan, Nollie wondered whether Honey was consciously observing the Apache tradition of burning the dead one's belongings, but for once she said nothing.

Honey, Nollie believed, did not know of her relationship with Nathan, which, in a state of shock herself, Nollie dwelled on painfully. She realized she had used Nathan as much as he had used her. It was not a love affair; there had been no affection. She had wanted only to make Honey suffer, to hurt her, yet Nollie had shuddered guiltily at moments when it seemed Honey might learn of her and Nathan's betrayal. Now, with his death, Nollie grieved for herself, for Nathan, for Honey, for pain and horror more massive than had ever been intended. And Nollie would have reason never to forget—more than all the others involved.

Until Trevor sent Cameron away, he sent letters to Honey daily and occasionally called. He also sought out Nollie for information when he could catch her. Some men were fools for sure and good, Nollie thought, but did not hesitate to go to Cameron when it was expedient.

The opportunity to present herself at Cameron's door came when Nollie learned of his plans to return to Arizona. "I hear you're leaving us," she said when he invited her in.

Cameron nodded. "Day after tomorrow, early," he said, then smiled. "Don't tell me you'd like to go with me."

"Not on your life. But I did wonder if you'd think of having me put up here in the house while you're gone. I could keep the house ready for your return, and whatever you'd like me to do." Cameron eyed Nollie sternly, and she hurried on. "You can't know how bad things are—Mrs. Radcliffe looks like death herself; everybody's miserable. Even Mr. Jefferson's in a stew."

"What do Shahar and Honey say about your plan?"

"I don't need my mother's permission, and Mrs. Radcliffe doesn't own me."

"There's something you're not telling me."

Nollie's face flushed deep with color. "I'm going to have a baby. The daddy's Nathan Radcliffe."

Cameron glowered at Nollie, clearly disgusted. He was also surprised, for at first glance she seemed as slender as ever. What a fine thing for a woman in mourning to have to face: betrayal by friend and husband. "Does Honey know?"

Nollie shook her head. "No one knows. I've been starving myself and taking pains with my posture. You'd be amazed what you can hide under an apron."

Cameron felt rage at Nollie but reasoned that if he took Nollie in, he might at least spare Honey the embarrassing proof of her betrayal. "I'll tell my men you'll be staying here."

Nollie grabbed Cameron's hand and pressed it with gratitude. "You won't regret it," she promised.

"I hope not."

Nollie took a deep breath. "There's just one other thing."

"What's that?"

"Do you still love Mrs. Radcliffe?"

Cameron prided himself on presenting his unknowable Apache countenance, but Nollie's direct and unexpected question struck a nerve. A flash of misery crossed his face, and then a darkness that frightened Nollie. "Do you?"

It was a question neither would answer aloud.

* * *

Nollie told Shahar of her departure, saying Cameron had asked her to look after things while he was away. "They won't miss me in the kitchen. Certainly Honey won't know I'm gone."

"Not right away." Shahar knew and was not especially shocked by Nollie's fleeing the troubled household.

Tall and slender, Nollie concealed her pregnancy under long aprons and let-out waistlines. She arranged with Cameron for a hired hand named Darr to get any supplies she needed. Nollie offered to cook for his men, an offer they readily accepted, gladly agreeing to pay her a nice wage.

"I've no way of knowing how long I'll be gone. Six months, maybe longer. What will you do?" Cameron asked Nollie when she arrived on his doorstep, bag in hand.

"I'll tell Shahar eventually. She'll help me." Nollie did not tell Cameron that she had earlier implied the two of them might be involved in an affair and that by giving her refuge, the assumption might be that he was responsible for her condition, a notion for the time being she intended neither to encourage nor to discourage.

Sins of the mothers, Nollie reflected. She had done the forbidden. Had the act of forbidding itself sealed her fate? The fact she was bringing yet another bastard child into the world weighed heavily on Nollie, who had seriously considered killing her baby before it was born with remedies Shahar could easily provide her. The sin of her union with a white man and another woman's husband was nothing to the sin of bearing an illegitimate child. Of all Nollie's burdens, illegitimacy was the heaviest. Nothing she might ever accomplish could ever compensate for the fact that she was a bastard, a fact that could never be erased from her slate of attributes. She might be beautiful, wealthy, sought after, brilliant —but first, last, and always a bastard. Nothing she did in life would ever alter that one fact. It was difficult enough to be a negro slave; to be a bastard on top of that seemed insurmountable. Even white people could not hold themselves up proudly under that condition.

Yet for all her yearning for legitimacy, for all her anger at Honey and rebellion against Shahar, all her bitter feelings for Nathan, Nollie could not destroy the life within her. More than ever since she realized she was pregnant, Nollie was burdened with wide swings of emotion. One minute she hated those dearest to her, the next felt her love for them. She had no notion of what she would do when delivered of a son or daughter, but she would deal with that later. Life, she maintained even at her most tumultuous moments, was to be welcomed and used to the fullest.

Perhaps, Nollie acknowledged, she was her mother's daughter after all.

CHAPTER EIGHTY-FOUR

Still in mourning, Honey wore black, a most becoming color but not as dramatic as the shades of lavender and blue Mlle LaLage had on. But both women were breathtakingly beautiful and attracted many stares at the grand eatery, Maison Verte, on the main street of San Francisco, where they dined on hot sherried mushroom creme, hearts of palm salad, and baby squab braised in honey and cognac, served with a pineapple and mango sauce. Both women declined dessert but had tea.

"Now you must confess your reasons for calling for me," Doria said after their tea had been poured in cups of wafer-thin English china.

Honey lowered her already soft voice. "I can think of no one else who can help me. I need your advice about a very confidential matter."

Doria squirmed slightly in her chair and inclined her body toward Honey so that she might hear what she imagined would be delicious gossip. "I would be pleased to help you, *ma cherie*." Then she frowned. "I do hope it is not something to punish M. Wolfe. He has suffered *terrible*. I could not console him. And so he has left me—gone to help the indians—Apache—what a wonderful name, so strong and sensual on the tongue. *N'est-ce pas?*"

Honey nodded. "I don't blame Mr. Wolfe for . . . anything. What I need from you has nothing to do with him. What I want is for you to make a man of me."

Doria stared at Honey for several moments as if she had not heard her request correctly. Just when Honey was on the verge of repeating herself, Doria began to giggle, then gave way to rollicking laughter. *"Vous êtes une folle."* Then she grew suddenly sober. *"Mon Dieu, pourquoi?"*

Honey's face was bright red as all eyes in the restaurant were on her giggling guest. "I merely want to *look* like a man, not be one," Honey whispered. "You are a singer, an actress. You're well acquainted with disguises and the trickery of making one appear to be what one is not. I reasoned if anyone could, you could make me look like a man."

Doria narrowed her eyes in careful speculation. She gave an exasperated sigh. "It would be *très difficile*. You are too much a woman—so delicate, oh my, so naturally sensual." Doria stared at Honey. "It will not be easy. When must you be a man?"

"Soon. In October. You must make me invisible. No one must discover me. *No one*."

"Tell me all."

"I must pose as a man so that I can study at the college of medicine."

Doria nodded her head. "I am not surprised. M. Wolfe has told me all about you. How you saved his life. He believes in you. He told me you should be a doctor. Yes, *ma cherie*, I shall help you. First you must get fat—fat as a mama pig. *"Garçon,"* Doria cried. "Bring us the tray of pastries. We shall have one of each."

Two months after their luncheon, and with many extra pounds added to her frame, Honey accompanied Trevor, Doria, and Shahar to the city to find suitable living quarters for Trevor's nephew, H. Radcliffe Greer, who was enrolled at the college of medicine beginning with the fall term in October. Near the school they found a combination of small rooms upstairs in a widow's house. "For seven dollars a week this should be very adequate," Honey told Trevor. "I . . . that is, Mr. Greer shall take his meals with Mrs. Pratt, which will make matters much more convenient." Mrs. Pratt seemed congenial if a trifle odd. In a large, sunny front parlor, she had a large collection of cactus and succulents more appropriate to the desert of Arizona than to the northern California clime, but Honey felt she would feel right at home. For once money was not one of Honey's worries. She had money from the sale of the academy property and would soon receive a small settlement from Nathan's estate.

"I'd feel a whole lot better," Shahar said, "if I could be looking after Mr. Greer."

"He's a grown man now, Mammy," Trevor said.

"Sir, he still needs lots of looking after, I assure you."

After securing the rooms, Honey went for her final wardrobe

fitting at the theater. Doria was joined in the conspiracy by two of
the company of actors, Peter Smythe and Derek James, who were
especially clever with costumes. In preparation for her role,
Honey had been forced to lose her modesty and had gotten so she
could strip to her chemise and pantalettes in a matter of seconds
without a semblance of embarrassment.

She stood that way now, and Peter helped her into a well-pad-
ded vest that bound and flattened her breasts, broadened her
shoulders, enlarged her waistline to match her hips, made her
derriere insignificant, and expanded her abdomen. "You are fortunate there's always a chill wind here, my dear," Peter observed,
"or you'd suffocate." There was also whalebone support to make
her posture more erect and accentuate the width of her shoulders.

Next she donned trousers, shirt, collar, cravat, vest, and coat.
Doria cooed, clapping her hands. "You are a fine, well-fed specimen. No bosoms to give you away and a manly girth." She patted
Honey's backside. Men's shoes with a clever design added an
inch to her height and made her gait more masculine. In her new
wardrobe, in spite of its confinement, she found an enhanced
freedom of movement and range of motion. Women, Honey realized better than ever before, were nearly paralyzed by their ad-
diction to fashion.

Doria appraised their handiwork. "I must confess, *ma cherie*,
until I spoke with Mlle Bennet I did not consider this a truly possible
course. But since she tells me other women have been driven to this
length, and to success, I feel with our abundant artistry and God's
smile, you, Honey, shall be a great success, also! I thought your
hands might give you away, but in your disguise and manicured as a
man's you do not have the hands of a woman, only the delicate
hands of a surgeon. Now for your face whiskers."

What to do about Honey's bare face had posed the most difficult problem, and Derek had produced many mustaches before he
was satisfied, settling on a short bristly one made from whiskers
from his own beard, since his coloring was fair and a good match
for Honey's. "A new one will have to be made every so often.
But that will be the easy part," he promised, tugging at his own
whiskers. "Now, the trick to having it stay on is the white of a
raw egg." He set a cup of what looked to be some sort of glue on
Doria's dressing table. "Every day a fresh mix, or you'll likely
lose your disguise in the soup."

Honey nodded her understanding of his caution, but her look
was grim as Derek carefully applied the lifelike mustache to her

upper lip. When he was satisfied, Honey peered in the mirror and gasped. Little by little she was looking more like a man. Lambchops were added in front of her ears and upper jawline. She would further coarsen her skin, which was no longer the pale perfection it had been before the interlude with the Apache, with regular doses of sun to enhance applications of dark powder to areas of her face where a beard would grow.

"Such fine feathers," Doria pronounced. "Now the most painful, Mme Radcliffe."

"M. Greer, Mlle LaLage," Honey said.

"*Mais oui,*" Doria answered. She sent Peter and Derek out of her dressing room. "They will be busy with finishing your wardrobe for a while, while you go to the barber."

Another of the troupe came into the dressing room. "*M. Coiffeur, M. Greer.*"

Honey's eyes brimmed with tears as the barber took a razor and comb from a small satchel. Her long hair, which had taken many months to grow to an acceptable length after Coyote's near scalping, was about to be sacrificed for the elaborate charade.

Doria tried to console Honey. "A wig would never do, *ma cherie.*"

"Yes, I agree," Honey said. The barber used a strop to sharpen his razor, and it seemed an age before he poised the instrument over Honey's head. She closed her eyes; the process was painless but difficult to endure. When he had finished, Honey opened her eyes to a horror not quite as bad as the one Coyote had committed but close enough to force tears from her eyes.

"One must be patient," Doria advised as she applied a snowy-white, pleasantly scented pomatum to Honey's shorn hair and rubbed it in until the hair had a glossy sheen. Then Doria made a part at the back of Honey's head and brushed the crown portion forward. A small froth of curls fell on her forehead, which Doria swept to either side, leaving a second part above Honey's left eye. Doria smiled with delight. "You are a young man of much intelligence, which I can tell by your proud forehead."

Honey could hardly believe her eyes. "My brother Clayton," she whispered. Her voice, coached an octave lower, made the mirage seem even more real.

"I have decided to concoct for perfection one more illusion," Doria said as she fairly danced in place.

"And what is that?"

"When I am in this city, you shall come to the theater often.

You shall fall in love with me. You shall become my lover."
Honey's jaw dropped. "I shall give you a reputation *extraordinaire*. You shall became infamous for size and stamina. We shall concoct for you *un grand penis imaginaire*. What do you say? Am I not clever?"

Honey grinned. "Indeed, mademoiselle! *Je t'aime de tout mon coeur*." I love you, Mlle LaLage, with all my heart.

CHAPTER EIGHTY-FIVE

The successful charade Honey conducted gave her enormous satisfaction, which was enhanced even more by success in her medical studies. H. Radcliffe Greer, known informally among some of the students as Cliffe, was an apt pupil and would no doubt survive the three-year course of study, unlike some others. For a novice, Cliffe was exceptionally good at dissection and was declared a natural surgeon. If he continued, he could look forward to being the top graduate in the class. He seemed to take the pressing schedule of eight lectures, five clinics, and four quizzes each week in stride and still manage an active social life. He was reputed to be the belle of San Francisco's lover. Mlle LaLage never descended on the city without announcing her presence and begging for his attentions.

"For such a slight fellow, he's put us to shame at almost everything," his envious friends muttered, some of whom had at first judged the man to be effeminate. His reputation as the escort of one of the city's darlings, the *chanteuse extraordinaire* Mlle Doria LaLage, quickly put that idea to rest.

Because of her practical experience, Honey was familiar with the horrors of disease and deformity and did not suffer the shock that others did. She gained a reputation for being appropriately courageous and coolly detached from the suffering of patients and sailed through the first year of studies. When rumors abounded that a woman might be admitted into their midst, unlike most of his fellows, Cliffe said he welcomed her presence. "Let her prove herself capable of the rigors required and, within the same period, ask her to tap a hydrocele of the testicle, such as I've just performed." This suggestion brought the house down with laughter. H. Radcliffe Greer cherished the irony of the moment and longed to strip away her disguise. "If she's up to it, why not give her a place among us?"

The question brought on the usual roar of debate. "What rational man would consent to put his balls on the table before such an unnatural woman grasping a knife?" the most conservative scoffed. "Then find an irrational patient," Cliffe replied without blinking.

In moments of wild fantasy, Cliffe secretly imagined disrobing on the platform the moment his medical degree was conferred. He thought it would do wonders for the future of women in medicine. Certainly it would not do anything to retard the struggling effort.

Her success aside, Honey grieved over Nollie's pregnancy after learning of it in a note from Trevor. When Honey went to San Francisco, Shahar immediately went to stay with Nollie at Cameron's, and a baby boy was born shortly thereafter. Trevor did not comment on the baby's paternity. "No need to!" Honey hissed as she tore the note into bits and threw the pieces down, scattering them on the floor. There was nothing to assume but the obvious: The father of the baby had taken the mother of his child into his home. "Apache savages don't stand on ceremony," Honey reminded herself aloud.

Hot tears stung her eyes. "What a fool I am!" she cried, feeling she had been stabbed in both the chest and the back. But she was clever enough to perform simple subtraction, and her conclusion was that at the very least, Cameron and Nollie had to have been intimate during the time Honey had gone to him that fateful day.

Although Nollie had in fact pointedly inferred that Cameron had courted her, Honey was reluctant to believe Cameron was able so readily to replace her. She chose to believe that Cameron had pursued Nollie merely to gain information about herself. However, with the news of Thomas's advent, it was plain that more than conversation had been exchanged between her lover and her friend during the months in question.

Honey threw herself onto the bed and wept bitterly to realize she had precipitated Nathan's death for the sake of a faithless lover. And she had been but one of his conquests! Besides Nollie, there was Mrs. Mullins, and Doria, of course. "And Lord knows how many others," she moaned aloud.

When she could cry no more, Honey rolled on her back and stared at the ceiling. In no mood to be charitable toward either Cameron or herself, she explored the painful idea that he and

Nollie had enjoyed each other's embrace even on the long trail west. It was easy to recall occasions of Nollie's seductive glances and gestures toward Cameron. While before Honey had insisted she was being absurdly jealous, she now damned her lover and her friend and saw how all of Nollie's talk of Cameron's coarseness had only been subterfuge. He was nothing but a loathsome devil—and she a simpleton to have been seduced.

Honey knew Shahar was likely to be wrathful to find Olivia (which Nollie now insisted she be called) unmarried and pregnant—by a white man, even one who preferred being a savage. Yet Honey received no word of her anger. In his note, Trevor had said Shahar seemed to take the event in stride.

Honey vowed never to set foot in Cameron Wolfe's house again, but Shahar forced her to put aside her vow when, through Trevor, she cunningly advised Honey that if she wished to see her at Christmas as they planned, she would have to come and stay with her at Cameron's, where she was looking after Thomas and his mother.

At Christmas, dressed as herself, Honey succumbed after a brief visit with Trevor. Entering Cameron's house for the first time since the duel had been waged left Honey with a withering sense of his presence; all past sensations invoked by her memory were promptly denied.

Honey also suppressed her fury at Nollie for her perfidy as best she could, overlooking the fact that she had actually given her blessings to any affair between the two.

However, Honey responded joyfully to Thomas Daniels, a lovely, good-natured soul. The pleasure she felt in cradling the newborn baby's warm, small body close to her heart was inexpressible. The baby was very light in color, with as yet dark gray eyes, and it was easy to imagine that he was hers. The desire for a baby of her own rose up in Honey and brought unwelcome tears to her eyes. *But for fate*, Honey thought.

Olivia and Honey avoided each other as much as possible, but late one night, as Olivia was about to nurse Thomas in the parlor before putting him down for the night, she said, "Bein' a mother's just like bein' a slave again—up before dawn, to bed after midnight." She lifted Thomas from Honey's arms. "He's lighter in color almost than his daddy."

"You scolded me so long and hard, I didn't dream you'd ever allow this to happen."

"You know that man could charm a rattlesnake out of his

rattles, if he had a mind to. Why, he was after me even while we were on the trip across country. Tried to seduce me more than once."

Honey's face flushed a deep red as she defended her ignorance. "That's news to me."

"Kept it to myself."

"Hardly sounds like you—keeping your tongue was never one of your virtues."

"I can be discreet when I want."

"So you're saying the two of you betrayed me on the trail?"

"I don't know that it would do you any charity to know," Olivia said, gleefully baiting Honey, "but yes. And, after you were done with him, I sure couldn't be always turning him down. Mmmmmmm, you know how powerful loving he can be."

Honey pretended to ignore Nollie's lilting, suggestive tone. "Still, I'm shocked you—the avowed perpetual virgin—would get yourself bred without benefit of clergy. On the other hand, I'm not surprised at Cameron's lack of propriety." She despised them both.

"You know how it is—we discovered we were kindred spirits."

Honey burned slowly. The urge to pounce on Nollie and scratch her eyes out steadily mounting, she might have indulged herself but for baby Thomas suckling sweetly at Nollie's breast.

"Mammy saw all the signs."

"What signs were those, Olivia?" Shahar said as she entered the room.

Startled, Nollie jiggled Thomas, who began to fuss. She moved him to the other breast.

"Nollie was merely reminding me Cameron's as faithful as a dog on a bitch's scent."

"How would Olivia know that?"

"I presume she has ample reason to know."

Shahar frowned at her daughter. "Olivia, what're you saying? You're not happy 'less you stir up trouble." Shahar never questioned her knowledge that Nathan Radcliffe was Thomas's father. She had seen the image of black flowers growing from the grave and accepted the fact that it meant a dead man's seed would flower.

"Fact."

"What do you suppose Mr. Cameron's reaction will be when he hears?"

"Hard for him to deny the truth," Nollie insisted.

"Your black hide's going to be hanging right up there over that mantel in no time if you don't speak the truth. Mr. Cameron's going to be in his rights to skin you alive."

"You don't think he and Miz Doria just smile foolishly at each other when she's in town, do you? And what do you suppose he and Miz Mullins was doin' in that tiny closet of a room together in Tucson? Don't you imagine he made a little stopover in Tucson this trip, too? And not just for a bath. The least you can say is the man's generous with hisself. Nothing he did might've took with you, Miz Radcliffe, but it sure did with me."

Her own words ringing in Nollie's accusations, Honey stood up and began to pace the floor.

"Long as you're up, walk this baby," Nollie implored, offering Thomas to Honey. "This baby should've been yours. At least the man loved you."

With clear second thoughts Honey took Thomas into her arms and walked back and forth across the room, patting his back and waiting for him to calm down. "You could've refused Cameron —I thought Mammy's protection might serve you, even if it didn't save me," Honey said when she had calmed down.

Nollie sighed. "I guess I always knew, even when we were just girls, that someday I'd be your man's mistress. When he came to me, I felt like it was a dream almost." There was silence from all parties for a long while. "I didn't love him, you know. Didn't even like him."

Honey glared hatefully at Nollie. "How could you foresee all this when we were children? We hardly knew what purpose God had for making male and female. And don't tell me you've second sight, Nollie Daniels!"

Nollie shook her head. "Didn't take second sight. Even Billy said someday I'd be Nathan's woman."

Honey stopped in her tracks, horror plain in her face. "Nathan! My God, Nathan is this baby's father!" she cried recognizing the depth of Nollie's betrayal. "And *you*—you were the source—*you* told Nathan about Cameron. Why he didn't learn about us from my diaries at all, but from you!" Honey's fury, coupled with Thomas's gassy discomfort, caused him to begin screaming.

Nollie was indifferent to Thomas' misery; Honey's attentions were inadequate.

Shahar took the baby as Honey turned on Nollie. "For once in your miserable life, Olivia Daniels, tell me the truth—not how you'd like it to be, but the truth—and you'll have the pleasure of knowing that whatever the truth is, it will punish me." As she waited for Nollie to respond, Honey was certain Nollie was gloating over her obvious agony.

"What difference does it make who the father is?"

"It matters, I tell you!"

Nollie smiled slowly, glad to have the upper hand at last. She wondered which name would give Honey the greatest suffering, the weight of her hatred pushing down all love she held for her sister. "Takes your pick. I had both of them, nearly at the same time. Either could be this light-skin baby's daddy.

"But, that Mr. Cameron—now there's a man. Still, don't you go thinking your gentleman husband wouldn't stoop to no nigger. You're just plain stupid if you do. Especially when you refused him his rights like he tol' me you did. I took pity on the man. Wounded and all."

"You black bitch!" Honey screamed, and in spite of her humiliation began to weep wildly. For a time Shahar and Olivia wondered if she would ever stop, but finally Honey ceased crying. "If he weren't already dead, I'd kill Nathan myself."

Certain as she was of Thomas's paternity, Shahar hoped Olivia would recant her lies, but as she watched her daughter now, Olivia's satisfaction was vividly clear. Shahar realized that Olivia would never retract a word. She could not sit idly by while Olivia twisted the knife in Honey's heart. "Mr. Cameron's not Thomas's daddy. I know it for a fact."

"You don't know any such thing!" Olivia insisted.

"As Nollie says, the man might be a trifle generous with himself, but . . ."

"But nothin'! You weren't there to know, were you, Mammy? That day he killed that wildcat, he climbed all over me. We made love on the bank, and then in the river. And it *wasn't* the first time—or the last. Ever notice the times we both were gone from camp? I promise your eyes'd fallen out of your head if you'd ever come acrost us!" Nollie boasted.

Honey rushed at Nollie and slapped her face. Nollie slapped back. Honey screamed and grabbed two handfuls of Nollie's hair; Nollie responded in kind. "You deserve to mold in the grave next to my precious husband, united with him in death!" Honey screamed as they struggled, each determined to damage the other.

"I'm no worse than you, Miz La-Ti-Da. You're nothing but a

whore and the whole world knows it thanks to your own loving husband!"

Honey swang at Nollie with a fist and bloodied her nose. Screaming, believing her nose broken, Nollie tried to escape more blows but Honey clung fast to her hair with one hand and with the other grabbed Nollie's sleeve, ripping it from the bodice.

After putting Thomas down still screaming, Shahar forced herself bodily between the combatants. "Ladies! Stop this ugliness! You're both past my patience!" She grabbed each woman by the arm, by the force of her will persuading Honey to release the death grip she held on Nollie's hair. "Sit down and cool yourselves down."

They sat across the room from each other and Shahar picked up Thomas again and settled him down before launching her own attack. "Don't take special sight to know you're lying, Olivia Daniels. You had poison green envy for Honey startin' the day she was born and takin' mother's milk outa your mouth. You learned your manners, but hateful blood has always run in your veins with the good, and runs to this day."

Shahar turned to Honey. "If I didn't know better, I'd think you both a couple of Jezebels fightin' over a paying customer." Honey looked away from Shahar's fierce gaze. "Look at me, Mrs. Radcliffe, and tell me what you think a grave with black flowers growin' out of it means?" Shahar questioned. "Doesn't take much speculatin' to know who Thomas's daddy is when that be your dream."

Honey looked at Nollie with pure hatred.

Olivia's ferocious look faded with her mother's retelling of her vision. She stood and ran for the outside door but Honey was at her side before she could open it. "Don't you try to run away and leave *me* with this baby. Whoever the father, this isn't *my* baby!" She grabbed Nollie's arm firmly.

Olivia struggled. "Shouldn't be my baby either!" she cried as Honey dragged her into the center of the room again. "I only wish Mr. Cameron was the daddy! He knows what it means to be a half-breed. But as I see it, you're Nathan Radcliffe's wife and Thomas his son, and it's *your* responsibility to raise him up. None of this ugliness is his fault. What he doesn't need is to grow up feeling he doesn't belong to nobody. Thomas is light-skin enough to be passed off as yours, and seeing Mrs. Radcliffe's disappeared from most people's view, when you reappear, you can reappear with a son. Nobody'll be the wiser. No one'll ever know he's not your and Nathan's son."

"Nobody blind, that is," Honey scoffed. "Where do you fit into this wonderful scheme?"

"I've plans."

"No doubt! And you thought you just might put them in motion this very night." Honey gestured at the front door.

Nollie ignored Honey's sarcasm. "And another thing, Mrs. Radcliffe. If you let Mr. Cameron get away, you're a bigger fool than I realized. You ought to hightail it to Tucson and find him and fall on your knees and beg for all you're worth for him to take you back!"

"I don't think you're anyone to be giving me advice about men, Nollie Daniels."

Frowning, with Thomas on her shoulder sound asleep, Shahar raised a finger in front of her lips hoping to silence the women. She laid Thomas down in his basket, then gave the basket to Nollie and pointed her daughter in the direction of her room.

"Why don't you talk some sense into her, Mammy, while there's a chance?" Honey protested to Shahar as Nollie disappeared. "She's *your* daughter. Do something or sure as I'm standing here she'll run off and leave that brat behind. She seduced Nathan—and probably Cameron also. She caused all this agony. And if she possibly can, she'll pawn off the result of her treachery on me! And believe me, I won't quit my studies to take care of Nollie and Nathan's spawn."

"This circumstance isn't Nollie's doing entirely."

"It most certainly is! You heard her. Why do you defend her?"

"This is one time I'm not taking your side over Olivia's. I'm not takin' either side. A beautiful baby's come into the world and it's not for you and Olivia to scrap over his little body, tossing him back and forth like a hot potato. Oftentimes, Olivia's heedless and you hardheaded, but if either of you makes this child suffer, you'll have no kindness from me, Honey Greer."

"It's her fault Nathan is dead. If it wasn't for Nollie, he would never have learned about Cameron."

"There's more than one way for Mr. Nathan to learn about Mr. Cameron. You forget your diary."

"He had no reason to search for one unless Nollie put him on the scent."

"You don't know that Nollie's to blame. It was no secret to

others in Mr. Dillingham's service about you and Mr. Cameron. Any of those men might have come here. The papers reported Mr. Nathan's resurrection. It's possible word was passed. Good gossip doesn't die on the wind. Men's worse gossips than women."

"It sounds very much to me as though you're taking your daughter's side in this," Honey said angrily then rushed from the room. Forced to retreat in the darkness into Cameron's room, she lay still in his bed, where disembodied spirits seemed to swirl around her. Someone, probably Shahar, Honey imagined, had united mattress and bedstead. She felt suspended in air as if she were lying in a hammock that in her mind's eye swung over a precipice.

Olivia's claim that Cameron had been the lover responsible for Thomas had caused Honey to feel betrayed in ways that seemed to splinter her emotions—hatred, rage, and jealousy among them. When Nollie had named Nathan, the cruel irony of his infidelity had pushed Honey beyond reason.

Outraged by Nollie's demand that she raise Nathan's son, Honey believed the recent birth might have affected Nollie's mind deleteriously. Nollie was mad to suggest such a thing. Thomas would only remind Honey of the awful events she hoped to put behind her forever. She should hate him, not love him.

Yet there was a kind of twisted logic to what Nollie had asked. Twenty-seven years old now, Honey was childless, with no plans to marry—ever. Certainly not before she was finished with her medical studies and she had been cured permanently, she imagined, of romantic affairs. The question was not whether she wanted a child or whether Thomas could be passed off as Nathan's son but whether she could overlook Thomas's connection to the horror of Nathan's death and all the misery that went with it.

Honey could not yet answer those questions; weary, weighted down, plagued with memories and hot tears, she finally found solace in sleep.

The woman lay dead in her lover's arms, a dark shadow rising into the air and surrounding them, then turning to light. Had the shadow been in the dream before? Honey wondered within the dream.

She dreamed then that the Apache warrior Fierce Enemy, lance in hand, rode toward her, his Apache cry echoing within her. Suddenly she realized he would not stop but would ride her down. She could stop him only with the right words—if only she could find them. . . . "I shall never forgive you," she cried.

"Apache never forgive," he called in answer. "Ahagahe!" he screamed, and crushed her beneath his horse's hooves.

CHAPTER EIGHTY-SIX

Some months later, soon after receiving a letter from Cameron announcing his return to California, Nollie secretly packed and left Sacramento, leaving Thomas behind for Shahar to look after. Nollie left a note for her mother saying she would write and a second note for Honey, addressed to H. Radcliffe Greer.

I didn't love Mr. Nathan. He didn't love me. But that doesn't give you the right to have a hard heart for Tommy. He's innocent. I'm leaving him with Shahar. I plan to make my way without Mammy, or you, or anyone from the past. I don't believe what Mammy says. I don't intend to drag the past with me.

You're a fool, Honey Radcliffe, and you always were. You think because you're a lady, you're free to do what you please. Here you had a good and decent man like Mr. Cameron. Yet for reasons not even Mammy can understand, you put him off to try to be a man yourself by being a doctor. I'm telling you, it's unnatural. You should have listened to what our daddy Dr. Greer tried to tell you time and again. Being a doctor is not a fit occupation for a female.

Some weeks later, before Cameron arrived in the area, Honey received a second letter, this one forwarded by Shahar through Trevor.

Dear Mammy,

Cooking for silver miners here in Nevada. I'm doing better than the prospectors are. Not rich yet but salting away good money. Living in a house the size of a coffin, and as yet cooking outdoors, but soon I'll have a true boardinghouse. Watch. I'll be back and supporting us all in grand style some day. Maybe before Mrs. Radcliffe turns up.

Anything was possible where Nollie was concerned. Honey confessed she did not know which made her most furious: the idea of her husband's infidelity or the idea of her lover's affair with her *sister*.

Before returning to school, Honey had forced herself to confront Shahar about the subject of Nollie's paternity.

"It's easy not to see what you don't want to," Shahar had answered. "Easy to sit back and say you saw no such thing. Like with Olivia and Mr. Nathan right under your nose.

"That's exactly how white men could make slaves of black. It was convenient to believe we black people weren't at all like you folks—not human, but put on earth by God for you to look after and use as you willed. Every day that went by, it got easier and more profitable. Soon almost everybody believed it. Then, when something like what happened between Dr. Greer and me came up, people just looked the other way or even looked head-on and didn't see a thing.

"In some sense, ignoring was the best thing to do. We loved each other all those years in peace. Lord knows what would have happened if we'd spoken up. Something of a bloodbath. Your daddy even talked of going north, but we both knew it was only a dream. But sometime. Next time, maybe."

Outraged, having expected a denial from Shahar, Honey demanded, "How can you be sure he really loved you and didn't merely use you?"

"A woman knows. As you know Mr. Cameron's love for you is more than lust."

Nearly irrational at Shahar's confession, Honey lashed out wildly at her. "It must have killed my mother to know about you and my father, ill as she was. You as good as murdered her!" Those were the last words she said to Shahar before returning to San Francisco.

Weighed down by care in her masquerade as a man, unable to shed a woman's tears, Honey felt as if some of life's blood had spilled from her, leaving in its place a red fluid of rage. Contemplating all she had recently uncovered, she became alternately hurt, bitter, angry, and confused. On the one hand, how could she blame her father for loving Shahar when she herself had loved Mammy more deeply than she remembered loving her own mother? Yet both were forbidden affections for which Honey could not escape shame. The idea that she and her father could love a black woman to the depth they did enormously offended

Honey's sense of propriety. In a sense she, her father, and Shahar had all betrayed Margaret Greer.

It was one thing for a man to mingle his white blood with black and quite another to proclaim love in the act. Such a claim was inconceivable in a society that denied the humanity of all persons who were not white.

Suddenly the superiority of white blood seemed brilliantly obvious to Honey. Now, after her long years of devotion to them, she felt deeply estranged from Shahar and Nollie, perhaps forever. Mammy's ultimatum that unless she accepted Nollie and Nathan's bastard, she need not ever again darken Mammy's door suited Honey just fine, especially as that door appeared to be Cameron's. Nollie seemed not the least ashamed of having stolen Nathan away from her, nor did Shahar seem outraged. But what could one expect from the woman who had stolen Honey's father from under her mother's nose, or from her daughter?

Even her greatest difficulty with Cameron before Nathan's death, Honey realized now, in essence had centered on the issue of race. She viewed Cameron's wish to be Apache as a statement of his preference for indians over white men. Honey winced with shame. How she could ever have loved a man who, given a choice, would choose to be a member of an inferior race? With this insight, Honey dismissed her lingering questions about Cameron's fidelity as inconsequential.

Honey felt utterly alone in the world now, unable to trust anyone. Those she had loved most dearly in the world had betrayed her most cruelly. She would never forgive any of them their treacheries. They were without honor, less human than decent people. Blood will tell, Honey realized bitterly. In the future, she resolved, she would keep strictly to her own kind.

Immersed in her medical studies again, Honey found her concentration lagging. Fearful she was about to prove the familiar refrain of the inferiority of a woman's mind, she at last overpowered her emotions, reasserting above everything her dedication to becoming a doctor.

When Dr. Mary Bennet, the female doctor who had precipitated Honey's medical career, presented herself at the college for a consultation, Cliffe made a point of seizing an opportunity to converse with her. Dr. Bennet and her patient had come from Los Angeles to consult with Dr. Case on a disfiguring growth on the patient's face that, unchecked, would blind him. Honey's interest was not in the patient but in the indelicate female doctor.

Dr. Radcliffe Greer saw to it that he was selected to give Dr. Bennet a tour of the surgery ward and afterward invited her to take luncheon with him at the Imperial Hotel. "I'm astonished to find you to appear quite unremarkable. One hears outrageous things about a female who wants to study medicine. It is a rather unnatural calling."

Used to this, Dr. Bennet smiled at Dr. Greer and refrained from speaking as if she were dealing with a simpleton. "Not everyone couches their doubts in such polite phrases, Dr. Greer. Among other things, I've been accused of insanity and witchcraft." She looked steadily at Cliffe, seeming to see beneath his disguise. "But we both know the worry over female intelligence and the protests of delicacy are utter stupidity."

Cliffe's color rose. Undaunted, he queried, "Have you no wish to pursue more feminine interests?"

"I haven't renounced my status as a female. I've not retired from the world at all. In fact, I shall marry soon after I return to Los Angeles."

"But you won't continue with medicine, surely? And then, you'll have used a position in medicine a man would have more justly claimed." On this subject, Cliffe used the outraged and injured tone of his male colleagues that he had often heard.

"I've no intention whatever of closing my practice."

"Then you must intend not to raise a family."

"Only if the good Lord denies me."

"Surely you're aware of what childbearing does to the female brain."

Dr. Bennet sighed. "I don't subscribe to the notion that the female mind is inferior to the male. If I come through the experience intact, my brain will also."

Cliffe scrutinized Dr. Bennet. In his opinion, she seemed a very natural creature of modest good looks and confident bearing. In ordinary circumstances, she would not attract attention as the freakish female creature to which her medical letters automatically qualified her. "Unnatural, indeed," Cliffe muttered under his breath.

"Quite the contrary, Dr. Greer. How is it unnatural to want to aid the sick with the best knowledge available? How is it better to nurse the sick with inadequate training?"

Cliffe smiled. "I agree entirely, Dr. Bennet. Entirely. But do I hear you say you will be satisfied only to nurse the sick?"

"Will you, Dr. Greer?"

"No. Never."

"Neither will I."

Honey returned to the college more confident, refusing to clutter her mind with anything but the pursuit of her degree, a strategy that worked wonderfully well until a certain distraction reentered her life.

In the months he spent among the Apache until shortly before he returned, no one, not even Doria, heard from Cameron, not that Honey cared, she told herself. At times she thought herself half-mad, especially when fatigue and a few light drags of opium smoke provided by "her lover" left her in a particular fog. For appearance's sake, Honey at times spent nights with Doria La-Lage in the singer's suite in a hotel near the theater. Honey learned to kiss Doria full on the mouth and touch her with less than polite familiarity when in public for maximum effect on rumor. Doria made Cliffe's reputation as an excellent lover widely known. However, the greatest test to Honey's performance as an actress came when Cameron returned to California and arrived unannounced at Doria's door.

When Cameron returned to Sacramento and saw Shahar spooning goat's milk into baby Thomas, he instantly assumed the worst about Nollie. Shahar's sad demeanor only reinforced his conclusion that Nollie had not survived childbirth. He was surprised to learn otherwise. "But where is she, then?"

"She's up and gone off, leaving this sweet outraged baby behind for Mammy to keep up with the awful hours babies keep, and no mother's milk. Heaven knows where she'll end up." Fatigue and worry brought tears to Shahar's eyes. With Nollie's desertion, Thomas had not adjusted well to instant weaning. Cow's milk soured his stomach, and he cared very little for goat's milk.

Used to Shahar's rock-steady approach, Cameron was alarmed. "Honey must be up in arms."

Shahar gave a snort of disgust. "She's no better than Olivia. She's run off as well. I'm feeling there's some bad blood somewhere in both those girls."

"Run off? Where?"

"She in San Francisco. You'll have to ask your fancy French lady; she knows her whereabouts better than I."

Puzzled and concerned about Shahar's state of mind, Cameron

instantly decided to make the trip to San Francisco. "Have you tried to get a wet nurse?"

"Nobody's willing to suckle a half-breed."

Cameron's look changed to one of cold fury. "I'll find someone," he swore, which he finally did in a riverfront shanty, a young half-Negro, half-Indian woman with a year-old infant, whom he sent to Shahar. Then Cameron went directly to Doria LaLage to inquire of Mrs. Radcliffe's whereabouts. He considered many scenarios, the one he liked least concerning Jerome Pauley, the man Honey had consented to marry before Nathan's return. Perhaps Jerome had won Honey's attention again.

At the theater, Cameron first encountered Doria's pianist, Eugene Harley. "At the present time, Miss Doria is quite taken with a new gentleman," he warned. "This new man's created quite a stir," he said, and added a number of tantalizing rumors to his report. "They're together now, as a matter of fact." When Cameron started to leave, Eugene called after him. "I wouldn't disturb them. You might interrupt . . ."

Cameron stalked off to Doria's hotel suite, not surprised by Doria's infidelity but irked greatly by the notion that he would not immediately be admitted into her intimate embrace. He was somewhat chagrined by Eugene's ribald accounting of Doria's newest lover. "To cast your eye on him, he's an insignificant little fellow, but from all I hear of Miss Doria's bliss, he's unseen assets of heroic proportion." Cameron had hoped to benefit from Doria's abundant affection, which he had missed in the last months, but more important at the moment was his need to find Honey and try to effect a reconciliation between her and Shahar. He wondered at his intricate web of involvement with the three women from Greerfield and how simple his life had been before he met them!

As he stood before Doria's suite, Cameron did not relish intruding on his notorious rival, but he squared his shoulders and rapped determinedly on the door. When Doria answered, wearing an open, sheer peignoir over a revealing pale lavender satin nightgown, she threw herself into Cameron's arms and kissed him passionately. *"Mon cher! Mon cher!"* she cooed. "I am so joyful to see you, but . . . I am now entertaining someone."

Her passionate embrace stirred Cameron. "I've heard from Eugene you've replaced me," he said, trying not to sound jealous, "but I came for news of Mrs. Radcliffe. Shahar said if any-one, you'd know her whereabouts."

Doria smiled. "First, I have someone to meet you," she trilled, and pulled him with her down the corridor to her sitting room, where she introduced her current pet. "Cliffe, my love, I wish you to know M. Cameron Wolfe. I believe I have mentioned him to you."

In white eyes clothes but retaining the long Apache hair and headband, Cameron appeared very handsome and virile, and Honey was deeply affected. Cameron, whom Doria had seated in such a way that light from a wall of windows interfered with his examination of the competition, was nevertheless startled by the womanish creature Doria introduced. How she could be as enamored of this character as was claimed was quite beyond him and a blow to his ego. Then, shifting his position for a better view, Cameron realized it was Honey Radcliffe who sat across from him; he was immediately struck by her melancholy.

"So you see, as of the moment I am busy. But perhaps, my darling, you will stay for this evening's performance. We might all dine together afterward. Would not that be fun, Cliffe?" Doria beamed.

Honey could barely manage a simple reply, but Cameron declined the invitation and went his way, leaving Honey drenched in sweat. "I'm sure he knows."

Doria giggled. "Don't be foolish. Right now the man is doubting his masculinity if such a little fellow as you can challenge him. He said he had heard I had not been faithful to him. He did *not* sound happy. I think Eugene gave him the most outrageous details, for Cameron was red in the face when he came to my door. You won't be angry if I am not faithful to you with him? He is like a god," Doria purred.

Tongue-tied, Honey could not seem to give a coherent answer. "I . . . well . . . I . . . Yes . . . No."

"Ah ha. So you see you are still in love with M. Cameron."

"How absurd!" Honey huffed.

Doria shrugged her shoulders and laughed in her distinctly musical way. "Yes, you are, my dearest dear. You are still mad for him."

Honey stood up. "I'm no such thing. My God, Doria, I've told you most of what happened between us. Only a fool would love a man who brings her so much agony."

"Perhaps. But the heart of a wise man forgives many things a fool cannot."

"There are far too many things between us for me to forgive."

"Which, for the soul alone," Doria said, "makes forgiveness all the more necessary."

CHAPTER EIGHTY-SEVEN

When Cameron returned to Sacramento, he confronted Shahar gently. "You sent me all the way to Frisco without a word of warning. You do know what she's up to. I can't think of her doing something so peculiar as this without your knowing."

Shahar rocked baby Thomas, patting his back soundly to encourage a burp. "I knew you had to see with your own eyes."

"I'm surprised she sat sit still for having her hair cut! Eugene filled me with coarse gossip and sent me to Mlle LaLage as jealous as a polecat. The lady's having a mighty high time with her hoax."

"Did you let on?"

Cameron sat down opposite Shahar. "The truth is I didn't get a good look at first, and as soon as I realized what was going on, I thought to myself they'd let me in on the joke if they wanted to."

"She's posing as a man so's to go to medical college. A female can't get in."

Cameron shook his head. "She's the damnedest female I've ever known. The world ought just as well get used to her having her way. She's going to have it one way or another," he observed. "But she looked sad. Almost frail." There was obvious worry in his voice. "What's going on between you two? You don't like her being a doctor?"

"I know she'll have her way on that, but she's turned in on herself, on me and Olivia, this baby, and, of course, you."

"I'm used to it."

"She feels we all betrayed her."

"You talked to your Spirits?"

"I don't need to. Living day to day's provided me with plenty to ponder. Just have to keep my eyes open." Shahar sighed.

"There's a few other things you ought to know."

"What's that?"

"For one, Olivia said at first you were this sweet baby's daddy, which didn't go over so good with Mrs. Radcliffe."

Cameron's dark skin flushed with color. "You're saying Honey believed her?"

Shahar nodded.

"How could she think that?" he demanded irately. "If I was bedding the whole countryside, I sure wouldn't've considered spilling my guts on the dueling field for her sake!"

"She's confused."

"Can't you talk some sense into her?"

Shahar shook her head. "For the first time in her life, I can't reach her. Realizing Nathan and Olivia had been together was a great blow. She thinks *none* of us loves her anymore, that we all betrayed her. And with good reason with Olivia. She said some pretty hateful things. Honey wonders whether any of us are worth loving." A silence hovered between Shahar and Cameron that Thomas interrupted from time to time with cheerful gurgles.

"So what do you see for us now? Not a lot, I guess."

"I quit. You must see your own way."

"As if anything were clear," Cameron muttered wearily. "Yet some things are," he admitted. "For one, I've no place with the Apache unless I'm willing to die with them. They're eager for a 'good peace and no lie,' which doesn't exist. White eyes offer bad land no one can survive on and death by starvation. Apache would rather die on their feet—wild and free, not rounded up and abandoned to die. Who can blame them?"

He told Shahar of his journey to Santa Fe and the peace the government was prepared to offer, which in conscience he could not take before his people. "There was nothing in the treaty that hadn't been offered before; the territory offered to Apache is fit for rattlesnakes and not much else. These white eyes don't even pretend to love their enemy."

Instead, Cameron had returned to the indians without an empty offer of peace. "Apache name themselves *indeh*—the dead—and white eyes *indah*—the living. They foresee their destruction."

"And what do you choose?"

"Isn't there room in the world for all of us?" Cameron wondered. "Or is there room only for greedy white eyes?"

"Remains to be seen."

"I'm back to decide once and for all where I belong. I've laid out a good life here. Only. . ." Cameron's voice trailed off as he became lost in thoughts of Honey Radcliffe. After a lengthy silence he said, "My dreams're still filled with Honey Radcliffe. I can't forget her."

Shahar shook her head slowly. "She'll be harder than a rabbit to run down, but with my own eyes I've seen Apache do it."

"Especially a hungry one."

"Beware of your hide. She'll bite and kick," Shahar said, looking at Cameron with affection.

"What'd I want with a woman who wants to be a man?"

"That part's an act."

"I wish you could say that of her sentiments for me," Cameron said, closing the conversation, and for the first time gladly accepted from Shahar the baby who, but for his mother's slip of the tongue, might have been his son.

CHAPTER EIGHTY-EIGHT

The purest use of Apache Deer Ceremony was in the hunt. The hunter with Deer Power used his ritual to seek the animal's consent in its capture and for the use of its meat and hide. But when Love Magic was the purpose, the hunter's quarry was a lover he wished to obtain through the assistance of the supernatural.

When Fierce Enemy and Honey had been with the Apache, he had strived to regain Deer Medicine, which he had lost in the years he had lived among white eyes. A warrior did not dare imitate a ceremony, for without Power a ceremony could be dangerous. Alone, Fierce Enemy fasted and meditated and recovered the blessing of Power. Now, when he returned to civilization a third time, along with the turquoise amulet he wore concealed beneath his white eyes clothes, Fierce Enemy kept his medicine pouch on a rawhide thong around his neck. Where before he had refused to use Deer Ceremony for Love Magic, Cameron thanked Ussen for allowing him to reclaim the Power of Deer Medicine.

Divine intervention, he knew, might be his only hope to bring Honey Radcliffe to his side.

Using Deer Ceremony for Love Magic often ensured obtaining the object of one's desire but little else. The most important question to be asked before performing ceremony was, Would possession of the loved one desired be enough?

Greed played very little part in either Fierce Enemy or Cameron Wolfe's life, but contemplating possession of the sole object of his desire, he acknowledged the possibility that Apache spirits had had a less complex creature than Honey Radcliffe in mind when they offered man the Power of Deer Ceremony for Love Magic. She was a woman who had not been happy living a severely simple existence. She longed for the luxury of mattresses, bathtubs, tables and chairs, food cooked with sauces and consumed with the aid of a knife and fork. She was not a woman one would expect to live on love alone.

Cameron also needed to believe in Shahar's power and in the favor of heaven in which she put her faith. Although somewhat different in expression, her belief also acknowledged the spirit in all things that sustained him. Both accepted the existence of Power beyond mortal man's, which, with faith, a man might summon for help. A man could not live without faith, Cameron believed, and with that conviction, he dared to use his Deer Medicine for Love Magic.

The choice made, late one afternoon Cameron disappeared into the nearby hills and shed his white eyes clothes, once more becoming a dark-skinned Apache. In deerskin breechclout, shirt, and moccasins with sacred turquoise dust wrapped in the folds, his long hair held from his face with an Apache turban, he immersed himself in ceremony and reached out to the world of spirits. From nightfall until dawn, in rhythm with the universe, his vision clear, his purpose pure, his sacrifice willing, Fierce Enemy danced and sang ceremony, his chants and motion freeing him to bind his soul with life more magical than the earthbound.

Apache do not grovel on their knees before Ussen or before lesser spirits. Therefore, the warrior Fierce Enemy raised his face and outstretched arms to the eastern horizon and embraced his Power. His upraised arms tingled with energy as Deer Power flowed to him. Slowly he turned in place, moving sunwise, repeating the motion four times; then he began his song:

Upon this earth
On which we live,
Ussen has Power.
This Power is mine
For the good of my people.

I call on Deer Power
Only Ussen can grant me
For success in the hunt.
I beseech the Deer
Surrender his life
For the good of my people.

I thank Ussen for Power
Only Ussen can grant me.
I call on Deer Power
For success in the hunt
And the good of my people.

I call on Deer Power
Only Ussen can grant me
This once for myself.
I call on Deer Power
For use in Love Magic.

I call on Deer Power
Only Ussen can grant me.
Bring my love to my side.
If need be, I
Forfeit all else.

Upon this earth
On which we live
Ussen has Power.
This Power is mine
For the good of my people.

I see as one from a height
Sees in every direction.
Love Magic I use
As the hunter does
Bow and arrow.

My beloved is mine
Through the strength of Love Magic

> *Granted by Ussen this once,*
> *For between a man and woman*
> *Love is Sacred to Ussen.*
>
> *I hold in my arms*
> *My beloved, who comes*
> *Through the strength of Love Magic*
> *Granted by Ussen*
> *For the good of my people.*

All through the night, Fierce Enemy communed with his Power. Not until daylight, after a prayer to the morning, did the Apache hunter assume his white eyes skin, trusting heaven to deliver Honey Radcliffe, willing to accept her even in disguise as H. Radcliffe Greer.

After the performance of Love Magic, the Apache expectation was for the object of love to hasten to the arms of the eager lover. However, in the white eyes world, Cameron Wolfe expected there might be some delay in the fulfillment of the ritual. He had to allow, he believed, for the difficulty of his case.

When he received Mlle LaLage's invitation to San Francisco, Cameron accepted, not the least surprised at the theater to hear Doria say in greeting, "Something came over me, *mon cher.* I had to see you. I thought I should expire without seeing your adorable face for the many months I shall be gone." Holding their hands between them, Doria snuggled against Cameron and sought his kiss. "I do not forget the prophecy. I believe when I return I shall be a married lady. And I know, if you are the brave man I am certain you are, you shall wed also. For her sake, then, we shall only have to be friends."

Then, lightheartedly, Doria pulled away. "You are so tardy, I am forced to rush away. I must be on stage in but twenty minutes." Already made up, she tossed her wrapper onto an upholstered chair in her dressing room. She stood temptingly beautiful in her corset and many tiers of petticoats. She banged on the wall of her dressing room, her means of summoning her dresser. "You should meet me in my suite afterward. There we can dine together and say our farewells." With her theatrical face on and without her gown, Doria looked very much like a china bisque doll someone had forgotten to dress. She gave Cameron a key attached to a short silk rope with a tassel at the end. "You shall have only a little wait. I have left a delicious tidbit to enjoy in my absence."

Cameron let Doria shower him with kisses before she showed him the door and admitted her dresser. Cameron loved Doria in a very sentimental way that did not touch his love for Honey. He questioned neither her summons nor her plan but trusted his fate to be in other hands.

CHAPTER EIGHTY-NINE

H. Radcliffe Greer's second year of medical studies appeared to be launched with as much success as the first. During the break between the first and second academic years, feeling she had nowhere to go, Honey had remained in the city to work in the hospital attached to the medical college under the preceptorship of Dr. Case. She had spent those four months in the obstetrics ward, where she developed a notable rapport with patients yet avoided sentimentality. She was careful not to mix sympathy with science, which it was feared a woman physician would by nature do.

In her successful disguise, Honey worked harder than most students to earn her medical degree and put most of her fellows to shame. They tried mightily to keep abreast of her. Within the masquerade, she became in many ways an entirely different person from the woman hidden beneath the fabric of men's clothes. Like the man she pretended to be, it was surprisingly convenient to deny the heart beating within her. Free from tender feelings and attendant pain, H. Radcliffe Greer buried Honey Radcliffe, perhaps forever.

The only true respite she had from medicine was on Tuesday evenings, when, as part of the charade, Cliffe spent the night with Doria LaLage in her hotel suite. On occasion they dined publicly to fuel the gossips who thought that afterward they had escaped for a torrid night of lovemaking. As often as not, Honey and Doria would play a hand or two of canasta before both retired for a much needed night's sleep. Tonight would be the last time they could see each other for at least a year. Soon Cliffe's reputation would have to thrive on past rumors alone.

Thank God it's only a fantasy, Honey thought, fatigued beyond the usual, having been called out of bed the night before for an emergency and then required to carry on her regular schedule the following day.

When she let herself into Doria's suite, Honey realized she had arrived early enough to manage almost a two-hour nap, which would do wonders for her performance as the city's most illustrious lover. At least she would not fall asleep at dinner with the first glass of champagne, something Honey knew she could do easily.

She pulled down the counterpane and hurriedly disrobed, always glad to be free of the weighty padding that provided Cliffe with his substantial male physique, including the necessary well-formed appendages to help his trousers hang more naturally, on which Doria had embroidered the imprint of pink lips. Then, minus her false whiskers, Honey leaned over the washbasin and soaped her face. Hearing a key turn in the lock, naked except for her chemise, she darted behind the wooden dressing screen. Certain it must be Doria, she peeked through a carved eye in the border of the screen and started to speak. When she saw Cameron Wolfe, the words froze in her mouth.

Horrified, Honey watched him casually glance around the suite, inspecting her discarded disguise, a broad smile on his face. "All right, Mrs. Radcliffe, you can show yourself. I won't give you away," he said, looking directly at the screen.

After several moments of silence, Honey said, "Please hand me the large towel next to the washbasin."

When Cameron laid the towel over the top of the screen, Honey grabbed it and wound it around herself tightly, then moved from behind the enclosure to challenge him. "What right do you have to barge in here?" she demanded.

He dangled Doria's key in front of her. "Mlle LaLage invited me."

Despite her efforts to put on weight with conscientious overeating, under her padding Honey remained slender, and with soap on her face and her hair mannishly cropped, she looked like a delicate waif. Cameron was not immune to her enormous appeal, and it was equally difficult for Honey not to see the look in his eyes.

She turned her back to him and rinsed her face, then gratefully hid her red face in a second towel, where she thought she would gladly remain as long as Cameron was present. In self-defense,

Honey focused on Doria's betrayal, feeling nothing but rage at her for daring to send Cameron to the suite. "Doria the matchmaker," Honey spit when she turned to face Cameron again. "She thinks it nothing to forgive and forget. Well, her brain must be located somewhat lower than mine," she said, which only amused Cameron. She answered his grin coldly. "I'd like you to leave. Truly, we've nothing to say to each other."

Unwittingly, Cameron's usually impassive countenance revealed the disappointment and sadness her last words had caused him. His feelings passed as a current between them, striking Honey sharply. All at once she stood with tears welling in her eyes, with no will to resist him. "There's far too much for us to overcome," she insisted stubbornly, and when he took her into his arms, she persisted. "Don't you understand? Don't you see? There's too much to ever get beyond," she said, but held on to him fiercely. "Go away! Please, just go away!" she cried, yet tightened her grip.

Cameron stared down at Honey, bemused by her conflicting demands, but with her face inclined to his, there was only one thing to do. He kissed her, and she responded, accepting his mouth hungrily. It was as if she were drowning and, miraculously, he had thrown her a line. At first, she clung to him fervently, but when her urgency exceeded his, she gladly assumed the lead.

When his clothes impeded them, Honey nearly ripped the buttons off his shirt, went for his belt, and then unbuttoned his fly. At the same time the towel she wore simply fell away, and the chemise was tossed off lightly.

Exposed and yearning, Cameron immediately caused her to mount him and helped her ride vigorously, with completion hardly coming soon enough for either of them. Breathless afterward, their smiles expressing the radiant joy of angels or madmen, they clung to each other laughing.

The bed beckoned them, and after Cameron rid himself of his clothes, they refreshed themselves together in its cool comfort, later overcoming the chill of late October with the heat of their passion. "I hope Doria won't be wanting the room tonight."

"If she knows what's good for her," Honey said, feigning seriousness as he gathered her into his arms again, "she'll leave town sooner than she planned."

"I've a bone to pick with you, by the way."

"What's that?" Honey wondered in total innocence.

"How could you think I was Thomas's father?"

"Well . . . I—"

"Worse, how could you think Nollie and I were together on the road?"

"She said . . . and, well, she *is* rather pretty."

"She's more than pretty, but am I a dog chasing after every female in heat that struts by?"

"I don't think that! But—"

"But what?"

Honey couldn't look Cameron in the eye. "Mrs. Mullins. And Doria."

"Another woman never enters my mind when I have you. Even when you turn your back on me, it's you I want. I love you. You can't know how much."

Gladly, Honey let Cameron hold her tightly, her mind vacant of every thought but that of pleasing him. Any notion of his being an inferior man escaped her. Truly, she had never met a man to surpass him. She kissed him again and again, and soon they were enveloped in the safe cocoon of their lovemaking. Only in the dawn did they sleep, and after a few hours they woke together and nestled quietly. "I won't go if you send me away," Cameron said.

"But what of my charade? I've taken such great pains to acquire my reputation as a ladies' man, how would I explain you dogging my heels?"

"I don't care what you say."

Honey shook her head and giggled. "You'd look truly pitiful in a dress." She pressed herself against him happily, refusing to consider the depth of their dilemma. "We'll think of something. Perhaps Doria and I shall have a falling out. Mmmmmm, or perhaps we'll enjoy a *ménage à trois*."

"A what?"

"An affair with three lovers."

"We've had that. It didn't work."

Honey instantly sobered and sat up in bed. "No, it didn't. In spite of Shahar's prophecies, nothing ever goes well for us."

Cameron sat up next to her and put his arm around her. "I should've kept my mouth shut."

"I was only making light of the subject, not truly considering such an arrangement."

"To have you, I'll do anything."

Honey smiled at Cameron. "I love you," she said. "You must

know that. Only I don't see how we can be together now. Later, perhaps, when I've finished at the college."

Cameron realized that he was dealing with a lady of unusual determination and thought better of the ultimatum his heart longed to speak. "That's a long time to go without having a woman."

"For your information, it's an *equally* long time to do without a man. Surely we'll think of something in the meantime, don't you imagine?"

Cameron pulled Honey down with him. "If my brains were between my legs, I'd have an answer already."

"I'm perfectly satisfied with what's between your legs—and mine."

The lovers were sleeping soundly again when the earthquake struck shortly before eight in the morning. However, instead of bolting from bed at the accompanying roar, as was her instinct, Honey was thrown to the floor by the first jolt. As the bed swiveled one way, she flew in the other and, on the way down, bloodied her nose on a small table that for some inexplicable reason did not move with the rest of the furniture. Cameron fared better, at least able to put his feet on the floor at will, but was nearly as unnerved as she was. He had been sleeping very close to her on her side of the bed and was able to help Honey up before the second quake came.

Greater in magnitude than the first, the second quake tipped over the suite's porcelain stove, spilling its fiery contents onto the carpet. Cameron had lit the stove at dawn and restocked it within the last hour. The stunned lovers watched disbelievingly as fire spread across the carpet to the hem of heavy velvet drapes, then to the sheer gauze panels that seconds before had covered the framed window glass. As they saw the flames slither across windows and walls, Honey grabbed a wrapper of Doria's that lay draped over a chair by the bed; Cameron picked up his pants, and they tried to beat out flames, she with a comforter from the bed, he with undamaged draperies torn from the windows.

At the sight of her men's clothes, intricate padding and all, being consumed by fire, Honey suddenly began shrieking and singed her arm trying to rescue them.

Cameron rushed to her. "We've got to get out of here." He put his hand on her waist.

She pulled away. "I can't go without my . . . clothes."

"They're on fire, and so will you be if we don't get going." Cameron grabbed Honey more firmly this time and dragged her with him. She at once came to her senses and did not resist.

On the third floor, the large suite Doria occupied was purposely isolated from the rest of the hotel in a labyrinth of rooms, an arrangement perfect for privacy but not the least suited for escaping from a fire. Honey and Cameron rushed for the closer of two staircases, with alarming amounts of smoke beginning to billow through the last doorway ahead of them.

There was no turning back as jumping flames licked at their heels, the hotel's wooden structure tinder-dry at the end of the typically rainless summer and fall seasons. Reaching the center stairway, Honey and Cameron found it on fire, the hysterical screams of other guests forming a blood-chilling background to their flight. Leaping ahead of the flames and smoke behind them, hardly able to see in the hot haze they had entered, Honey and Cameron held to each other desperately. Honey knew that as long as she lived, she would never forget the icy fear she had at the idea of being separated from Cameron amid the torrid heat of that fire, only to have the staircase give way and feel her hand being wrenched from his.

Honey landed on her feet in a crouched position, thinking both ankles were broken, then fell on her side, the breath forced from her lungs. As she fought for air, Cameron, who had landed nearby, dragged her down a second stairway to the hotel lobby and onto the street. Dazed, Honey held on to him and struggled for air.

As they held each other, a third violent quake struck, sending the burning building into collapse and the able fleeing further into the broad, open street. When they turned to look back again, the hotel, with its collapsed roof and floors, now appeared triangular in shape as opposed to the rectangle it once had been. The recent war came immediately to Honey's mind; the scene was much like a battlefield after an engagement, with a multitude of wounded lying about. She knew what to do and stooped quickly to her work, while Cameron joined efforts to rescue others who were trapped not only in the hotel but in surrounding structures, now mostly burning.

Honey worked for hours, but still the injured appeared. "The earth just opened up," a dazed man said after she had set his arm and used his shirt for a sling. Perhaps it had, and why not? Honey thought bitterly, her pale blue satin wrapper bloodied and dirty. She realized then that it had been a long while since she had last seen her lover. Periodically, Cameron had appeared at her side to rub her aching shoulders and hands. She needed him now.

There were ambulances in the streets to carry off the worst of the injured to hospitals. The able-bodied were fighting fires, the bells of fire wagons clanging all over the city for hours. The worst of it was the wailing of children, Honey thought, wanting to cry out herself. She wondered where Doria might be and how she had fared and thought about Thomas and Shahar and whether they had felt the quake inland.

Automatically then, Honey moved to the next injured person in the line of patients, which Good Samaritans kept adding to, when one of the injured down the line caught her eye. A wail of agony escaped from Honey as she rushed to his side. Almost incapable of rational thought, she fell to her knees. Cameron was insensible, a bloody gash across his forehead.

There was no apparent fracture of the skull behind the wound, but the features of his face were contracted, and blood was hemorrhaging slowly from his left ear. His pulse was barely perceptible, and he was frightfully cold, with the pupils of his eyes dilated. His breathing was slow and labored. Concussion of the brain was the only conclusion Honey could come to as she wept and prayed that the concussion was simple. She forced herself to remember he had survived worse.

Cameron also had several minor burns on his hands and arms and a more serious burn that arched across his left cheekbone. With effort, Honey marshaled her churning mind and emotions. "I'm a doctor," she said aloud as if to remind herself, but fatigued, distraught, to some degree in a state of shock herself, she found it difficult to stop her tears.

"Halt!" Honey cried after men bearing an empty stretcher. "Take this man to the Medical College Hospital," she demanded. "I'm going with you. I'm needed there. I'm a doctor."

"We're going to Saint Francis's first," the man obviously in charge said as they placed Cameron in a wagon along with others, most of whom were moaning with the misery of their injuries. "If as you say you're a doctor, ma'am, you're welcome to come along."

Honey covered Cameron carefully with a none too clean blan-

ket, with a shudder calling to mind another time he had been
injured, then joined the men on the seat of the horse-drawn ambulance.

"You don't look like no doctor. We ain't seen no lady doctor
before."

"Well, I promise you, you're looking at one now," Honey said
in response to his long glance at her satin covering. "Can't you
go a little faster?"

"No, ma'am."

When the other patients were unloaded at Saint Francis Hospital, Honey went to ride with Cameron in the back of the ambulance. His hand with part of one finger missing had slipped from
beneath the blanket, and she drew it to her cheek, then pressed it
with a gentle kiss. Tears came easily to her eyes. "Don't die," she
whispered. "Please, Lord, don't let him die." Honey felt as if the
end of the world had come. "I love you, Cameron. Hear me and
know," she said as she pushed his thick, dark hair off his forehead and examined the gash there more carefully. The area of
injury was beginning to swell, but there was no apparent depression of the skull. Still, she worried, he might have a fissure
fracture of the vault.

Honey stared at Cameron and thought how loving him always
seemed to bring as much pain as pleasure to both of them and
wondered what lesson might be learned from that fact. "Shahar,
Shahar," she whispered, and wept freely.

In the months since she and Cameron had been together,
Honey had endured pain that at times seemed almost physical in
nature. There were so many things she fervently wished she
could do or say differently. Yet Honey believed there had to be
some purpose for events occurring the way they had, if only for
the knowledge gained from them.

She thought of the dream she and Cameron had shared on the
trek across the continent, a period that now seemed more than a
lifetime ago. The events of the dream's lifetime now seemed
reversed: Where once he had held her dying in his arms, she
perhaps held him now. Where he had learned a bitter lesson then,
she learned one now. In the dream, he learned too late he loved
her dearly. Could all she had dreamed of him be true? Honey
called up a vision of herself with him from that time long ago that
now felt as real as the present.

Too confused, too emotional now, Honey could not think past caring for Cameron and helping him heal, tortured to realize once again that there was precious little she could do to make him whole.

CHAPTER NINETY

Cameron was received at the Medical College Hospital with far less uproar than the woman who accompanied him. Dr. Case's jaw dropped when he saw Honey Radcliffe with her shorn hair and scanty dress. His expression was quickly replaced by a deep frown. "This is too much to absorb in an already eventful day," he said.

"You won't deny me looking after this one patient at least."

"I thought Mr. Greer was related to you, which explained the great resemblance. I don't care to be duped."

"You must understand my outrage for being denied a place merely because I am female."

"Yes," Dr. Case said, "I certainly do, which, however, doesn't excuse your fraud." Dr. Case spent a moment in serious consideration. He knew of Honey's extensive nursing experience in the war and her assistance to her father in his practice. He recognized H. Radcliffe Greer's superior abilities. "At present, we've many more patients than usual to occupy us. We should be glad of your assistance. As for after this emergency, your standing will have to be reviewed."

"Thank you," Honey said with no humility.

"You realize this calls your honor into serious question."

"You surely don't expect me to apologize for not having a penis?" she asked in sweet tones, and left Dr. Case gaping after her as she hurried down the corridor after Cameron.

Honey lost no time attending to Cameron. She elevated his head on a pillow and quickly cleaned and treated his burns with carron oil, consisting of equal parts lime water and linseed oil, which she applied with cotton lint. She worried most about the severe burn on his left cheekbone, certain that carron oil would not be adequate. She bathed his forehead, washing away the dried blood, applied calamine ointment, and dressed the gash.

There was no telling the outcome. The possibilities almost numberless, some of them fatal; her gravest concern intracranial inflammation. However, for the sake of her sanity, Honey chose to foresee a positive outcome for Cameron, concluding she had done all that was humanly possible for him. After seeing he was covered, Honey went to look after other patients but kept Cameron under careful surveillance.

At the end of the long day there seemed no change in Cameron's condition, and finally Honey went home to bathe and change and eat for the first time since noon the day before. She found only slight damage to Mrs. Pratt's property, mainly broken dishes, windows, and a number of the odd china pots—chamber, soup, and vegetable tureens—containing the desert succulents that had rattled off windowsills. Mrs. Pratt seemed to have weathered the upset very well; however, she succumbed to shock on seeing her lodger's change of sex. She remembered Honey from the day she had rented her rooms for H. Radcliffe Greer. "I thought Mr. Greer a bit on the womanly side and looking like your cousin, which was you, of course. What would a lady like you want with doctoring?"

"There seems to be an endless want of doctors, even female doctors."

"And what do they have t' say at the college about yer sudden change about? Will ya keep on?" Frugal, Mrs. Pratt had to consider whether to advertise for her rooms.

"I intend to stay put. They'll have a fight on their hands if they try to evict me."

Mrs. Pratt smiled. Whatever the sex, this boarder paid regular rent. "Before I forget, a letter arrived for you last night."

Honey recognized Doria's script as she tore open the note sealed with wax.

My Darling Honey,

I have played M. Cupid—I trust you are not too awfully angry. By the time you receive this note, I shall be already sailing to Europe, having boarded my ship while, I hope, you and M. Wolfe were engaged in reconcile. I love you both. I shall call on you when I return, you can be certain.

In love and friendship. Think of me as I will you, my darlings.

Doria Marie Thérèse LaLage

"Oh, Doria." If Doria only knew how tragically her attempt to reunite the lovers had evolved, she would be devastated.

"You get yourself presentable, and I'll get something for you to eat," Mrs. Pratt urged when Honey looked up from Doria's note. "Then I've some more doctoring of my own to do," she said of her plants, which had spilled to the floor. "Can't keep these ones in the house no more." She had a sizable aloe garden on the south bank below the house where she would add the casualties from the morning's earthquake.

Honey had already begun climbing the stairs to her rooms, when suddenly she turned around. "Mrs. Pratt, please may I have one of your orphan plants?"

The widow was obviously surprised. "What you be wanting one for?"

"Have you ever made medicinal use of any of these plants?"

"Indeed I have. All the time. When I get a scald or burn in the kitchen, I dab a bit of the sap on."

"And?"

"Heals up wondrous well."

"That's what I'm counting on."

Mrs. Pratt was prepared to give Honey whatever plant she chose. "Which one you want?"

"I don't think it matters, but perhaps the least injured," Honey answered as Mrs. Pratt turned over a large specimen with several foot-long spongy fronds.

"Help yourself."

"I surely will."

Honey hurried through her bathing and dressing. With no woman's clothing, she donned a pair of pants and a shirt of her disguise and, without padding, relied on suspenders to save her from total disgrace. She sent a message to advise Shahar of Cameron's condition and ask her to send her some suitable clothing to the city, then devoured a breakfast prepared by Mrs. Pratt and returned to the hospital to find no change in her dearest patient's condition.

All Honey could do about the concussion was wait, but she sliced one of Mrs. Pratt's aloe fronds down the center and applied a strip of the cool, gelatinous inner surface of the leaf directly to the burn on Cameron's left cheekbone and held it in place with a bandage that covered his left eye.

More than twelve hours had elapsed since the earthquake, and still the injured were arriving at hospitals. During lulls Honey sat by Cameron's cot. Shortly before dawn, as she sat wide awake, Cameron stirred restlessly, which she took as a very good sign that he might soon regain consciousness. Later, when Honey woke from a catnap, Cameron's eyes were open and his gaze was trained on her.

She smiled and bent to him. "Hello," she whispered. "I've been waiting for you." His mouth was too dry for him to talk, and so she gave him a few sips of water. "You've a concussion and a few burns. Do you recall what happened?"

Verly slowly Cameron appeared to shrug his shoulders and then closed his eyes.

"How do you feel?"

He opened his eyes again and brought a hand to his bandaged eye.

"The eye isn't injured, but I had to cover it when I bandaged a burn on your cheek," she explained.

"Head hurts."

"I can imagine." Cameron was warm, another encouraging sign. His forehead was swollen, and there had been bleeding into his eyelids, not unexpected symptoms in an injury of the kind he had suffered. Honey took his hand to lend him comfort.

He did not recall the incident that had injured him but remembered performing Deer Magic to bring Honey to his side.

"I love you," Honey whispered. "Do you remember last night?"

Cameron turned his head slowly in denial.

"After the duel, I simply couldn't face you. I felt so responsible." She kissed his hand, then his mouth. "But we'll start over now. I'm not certain how, but I promise we will. In fact, we began again last night—which it's rather ungallant of you to forget," she said lightly.

Cameron did not reply, his lack of response knifing through Honey. Tears came quickly to her eyes. "You must rest now," she whispered when she could control her speech. "I'll be near."

Weak, Cameron closed his eyes, losing consciousness again, the last image in his mind Honey's beautiful face framed by her strangely bobbed hair.

When Dr. Case returned to the ward, he inquired about her use of aloe. "The Apache use it with much success. It won't do any harm." Irrationally, Honey wished an Apache shaman would dance into the ward—anyone—anything to ensure Cameron's recovery. She felt nearly as desperate as she had in the Apache camp when for all she knew Cameron lay dying.

Shortly he became semiconscious and restless; surely, Honey told herself, these were all favorable signs. From time to time he muttered phrases she recognized as Apache, which chilled her blood thoroughly. When he was conscious again, Honey fed him custard and beef tea and milk, which he protested. "I'm the doctor. You must trust me." Afterward, his nose began bleeding, though not profusely. "This isn't unusual," she consoled him—and herself.

Later Cameron experienced another lapse of consciousness, and when he awoke he could not speak. Beside herself, Honey concealed her alarm as in the following days he appeared to be slowly recovering all capacities but speech.

Each time Honey examined the burn on Cameron's cheekbone where the aloe had been applied, she found the wound clean and responding beautifully to the beneficent gel. She suspended use of carron oil and used the aloe exclusively on all his burns.

Except for his aphasia, Cameron was mending fast. His appetite improved daily, and his need for simple nutritious food—custard, beef tea, milk, and the like—diminished. "You're to be discharged tomorrow," Honey promised after six days. "I'm taking you to Shahar. When I return here, she'll look after you. She may even have a physic or two to cure you." Honey knew Cameron might never regain the ability to speak. But if love and tenderness had any influence over health, Honey felt certain he would recover in time. She said nothing about the strain in her relationship with Shahar but had no hesitation in asking the woman to look after Cameron.

Honey went about her usual rounds, and when she returned to Cameron's bedside, she found him fully dressed in the clothes she had brought for him to wear when he would be discharged the next day. "Want to . . . leave . . . now," he said hoarsely.

Startled, Honey stammered, "How about tomorrow?"

"Now," he said. "Come . . . go . . . with me."

With tears in her eyes, Honey put her arms around him. "Just try to stop me."

They took a steamer as far as they could up the Sacramento River in the season of low water, then hired a man with a carriage to take them to his home, where Honey expected Shahar to be preparing for their arrival the next day. For Cameron the journey was physically taxing, and for Honey it was depressingly silent.

He said nothing and seemed lost in deep thought.

Cameron's profound silence worried her. She realized his speech might never be fully recovered, but the link of head injury to instances of dementia troubled Honey the most. Perhaps, she admitted willingly, in this particular case she knew a little too much for her own good.

Shahar welcomed them, fed them, then shuffled the couple off to bed. They slept in the same room where he had made love to her that fateful day before the duel. Lying with her in his arms, Cameron fell immediately to sleep, his slumber restless. Strangely silent all day, he now muttered indistinguishable words, reminding Honey of the first time she had tended him when he was ill.

That time in North Carolina now seemed decades behind her, and still the future was unfathomable. Honey knew only that she wanted never to be separated from Cameron again. If necessary, she would give up her ambition to be a doctor once and for all, but she would never live without Cameron.

Honey lay with Cameron for an hour, unable to sleep, then finally went downstairs looking for brandy.

Downstairs, she found Shahar still up, rocking Thomas. He had just closed his eyes, and Shahar continued to hum her lullaby. With Honey's arrival, she invented new verses. "What you be doing, downstairs with me? Belong in that bed, next to your man."

Honey tried to imitate the familiar rhythm but could not. "Can't sleep; need brandy."

Shahar pointed toward the kitchen. "There's no brandy. Only mescal. Bring me some, too," she whispered.

Honey was disappointed not to find brandy but poured the mescal into teacups, returned to Shahar, and sat down. Thomas was obviously asleep now; still Shahar continued rocking. Honey made a disagreeable face after taking a sip from her cup. "This has to be poison. How can you drink it?"

"He brought quite a supply with him from his trip back to the Apache. It eases all kinds of pains."

"And pain in this life is in abundance." Honey sighed. "His silence these last days made me think of the time among the Apache when he and I weren't speaking," she confessed. "You don't know the hell it's been for me to sit by him helpless again. I would do anything to have him be himself."

Shahar smiled. "Just give him time."

"Have you seen an encouraging sign?"

Shahar shook her head. "No sign. I just know it."

Honey closed her eyes. "I wish I had your faith. Everything between us is always so complicated. Nothing ever comes easily."

"'Cept for your love for him."

"That least of all. How I've resisted him!"

"Was always useless, you recall. No way ever you could turn your back on him forever."

Honey smiled sleepily. "No way on earth."

Perhaps it was the mescal, Shahar thought, but she sensed a familiar intimacy between Honey and herself and ventured some advice. "Something needs mentioning—something that's maybe got by you in all of your struggles with Mr. Cameron." Shahar paused for Honey's acknowledgment.

"It's certainly possible," Honey said wearily, "what with ambushes, indian raids, duels, and earthquakes." She resisted the tenderness she felt flowing to her from Shahar.

"No matter if you believe or don't believe in living before this life and knowing Mr. Cameron before, you still must do the right thing in this life. God's given you chances not everyone gets, and if you've signs and visions and do nothing with them, you're worse than a fool."

Mentally, Honey revised her notion of Shahar's goodwill. Obviously, she was trying to couch her words without gentleness.

"If you refuse to do what's right, you'll never have any peace in this life or any other. You got to make peace with those around you now.

"You can't act like all this happening with Mr. Cameron is my fault and tell yourself you been swayed by your old mad mammy. Something in you, Honey Greer, responded to Mr. Cameron in spite of anything I said or didn't say. You don't always have to have a sign from heaven to know the right thing. Sign or no sign, you got to learn from life as it comes, and use good sense, and not pretend you don't know right from wrong.

"No matter what the past has been for you and Mr. Cameron, none of it means a thing unless you act rightly here and now. You're free to choose how you settle with Mr. Cameron. And however you choose, settle all blame on yourself."

Honey sat in the silence for several moments when Shahar

finished, then said, "I assumed the choices concerning Cameron might be easy now."

"Maybe they will be," Shahar said doubtfully. "Remember you have a choice."

When she returned to bed, Honey tried not to mull over Shahar's advice and vowed to remember she would have a choice. With Cameron, however, the choices were never easy. "In this lifetime, anyway," she muttered before she finally went to sleep.

In the morning, Cameron was reassuringly passionate, seeming not to have lost any of his powers in that regard. He spent most of the following day sleeping, but Honey, not used to being idle, was beside herself. Shahar fussed with her hair. "Not much to do till it gets grown. Maybe without pomade some of the old curl will come back."

Honey despaired. "I'll take it as a sign from heaven I'm not to dwell on my physical appearance."

Later in the day she went riding, and when she returned found Cameron in the stable loading pack horses with provisions. Startled, she said, "What's all this?"

He helped her dismount. She moved readily into his arms and kissed him passionately before he could answer her question. "I'm going into the mountains for a few days," he explained when they came apart. "I want you to come with me."

She thought it a crazy idea. "You're barely on your feet. A trip like that would be unnecessarily taxing."

"I'm fine."

Honey eyed Cameron uneasily. "But why go? It's late in the season and cold."

"Ghost season isn't full on us yet."

With his use of the Apache words for winter, Honey's heart fell, suspicion clearly seen in her eyes.

"We've time before we're forced south with the sun."

"South?"

She stared at him disbelievingly as he nodded.

Honey turned her back on Cameron. Tears filled her eyes. "No! Never!" she cried.

"A wife follows her husband wherever he must go."

"We're *not* married!"

"We're as married as Apache can be."

Silent, Honey lowered her head.

"Tell me, Honey, do you love me?"

She whirled to face Cameron. "Yes! More than anyone! More than anything! How many times must I say it?"

"You don't love *me*. No, you only love me if I deny I'm Apache. You love me only if I am white eyes!

"But white men live worse than savages, without Power, without Ussen. Why do you think there're so many earthquakes here? Because Ussen is angry for the way white eyes live." He spoke with conviction, with a passion he rarely showed.

"I'm not afraid of dying. But I am afraid of living without Power, among people who have no faith. I'm only half a man in the white eyes world. When I am indian, I am whole."

Honey stared at Cameron. Did she even know him—this man who insisted he was more Apache than white eyes? Did, as he said, she only love the part of him that was civilized, that made him fit in? What did he mean he was only half a man in the white eyes world? There was never a more vital man than Cameron!

But for Cameron, something more than his manhood was at stake. "White eyes live without Power, without Ussen." Honey thought the Apache approach to God primitive, but now as she gazed at Cameron, she felt her appraisal had been too limited. And Cameron's plea, his feeling of not belonging, a desire for a richer life.

"You said you believed Deer Power brought us together before the earthquake. Perhaps Ussen is angry. Perhaps He wants you to leave me behind."

"Never. Love between a man and a woman is sacred to Ussen."

Honey could not damn Cameron for wanting to live in a world made more comprehensible by Ussen's presence. Neither could she believe as he did in spirits in every living thing, in the whistling of wind and the hooting of owls as the cries of ghosts, in sickness visited on man by spirits. *How much of myself do I have to give up to prove my love?* Was she not allowed to ask anything of him in return?

When she flatly refused to follow him and he disappeared from her life, what would she do then? Go on about her life, continue with medical school? Become a doctor—that indelicate breed of female—to find solace as she had before in endless work? Would she forget him as she once had hoped and never had succeeded in doing? Could she forbid herself to dream of him as he was now, or in those dreams of other lifetimes, which continued to plague her?

"I will never be the white gentleman you want me to be!"

"And I shall *never* be the Apache squaw you want me to be!"

They stared at each other, a mixture of repulsion and desire in each of them colliding violently, creating a seemingly insurmountable breach between them. Cameron turned away from her and bent to collect a large buckskin bundle. "I'll be leaving at dawn."

"I'll remove my things from your room so you can at least sleep in your own bed tonight."

"I've no need for a bed."

"How absurd of me to forget! A bed is too civilized. Then I'll have my things and sleep there *alone*. I require a bed!" Honey all but ran away from Cameron into the house, tears streaming from her eyes. She told herself she was only furious, not truly brokenhearted. Inside the house Honey encountered Shahar and immediately burst into sobs.

Shahar opened her arms. "The two of you still banging your heads together?"

Sobbing, Honey nodded and slipped gratefully into Shahar's comforting arms. Shahar led her to the high-backed settle and sat next to her and held Honey's hand while she raged over Cameron's decisions and charges. "How could he? How dare he? How could he imagine I'd ever go with him? I can't go with him!" Honey knew it was useless to rave, but couldn't help herself. "I feared all along his silence was more than losing his voice. I thought he was brooding, but, obviously, he's gone mad. How could he think we should return to the Apache."

"The man is part Apache and always will be."

"He doesn't have to be!" Honey felt her rage with Shahar come to the surface again.

"Face the truth, Honey Radcliffe," Shahar demanded. "The man is who he is. If you love him, you have to accept that truth."

"No! Never!"

"Oh, yes, if you love him."

"I *do* love him!" Honey cried, "but I could *never* go back to the Apache."

"If you truly love him, you could."

"I *do* and I *can't*."

"You think you'll ever find a man you love more?"

"Never!"

Shahar contemplated what she would say. She had lost one

daughter. Dared she risk losing another? "Only last night you told me you would do anything to see Cameron be himself again. He has told you what will heal him."

"If *he* loved *me*, he wouldn't ask me to make such a sacrifice. How can he think in a thousand years I would go back to the Apache?"

Shahar shrugged her shoulders. "You have to decide your own fate with Mr. Cameron, Honey Radcliffe, but I tell you this is a debt from the past—and now it's time to pay. This is your last chance. You alone must look in your heart and choose. That's what the preacher man's talkin' about when he says 'free will.'" Shahar let her words sink in. "You think Mr. Cameron's asking a lot of you?" Shahar challenged. "Think what your father asked of me—to be his slave, to be the mother of his child, mother to *all* his children—and to never have my due and honor beside him as his wife."

At mention of Shahar's relationship with her father, Honey recoiled, her old anger with Shahar surfacing. She pulled her hand from Shahar's.

Shahar noted Honey's withdrawal yet continued. "I could've refused your father. I could've run off. I could've done many things—not had Nollie, like I didn't have my other master's babies. But I made my choice." Shahar knew that she had no right to interfere, that the final choice was Honey's alone. "Just remember, child, however you decide, there'll be a price. If you follow Mr. Cameron, once and for all, Honey Radcliffe, you'll have to give up the notion of who you think you are. You can never even think of being a high and mighty lady again. Or being a doctor. Realize you follow him, you may loose your life. As he sees it, there's likely no peace for the Apache."

"You've got all the answers!" Honey said hotly.

"No. Only you have the answer."

"You don't mean to tell me you won't stand by your prophecy that Cameron and I belong together!"

"The decision has to be yours, child."

"Why have we come together at all? Surely you can tell me that."

Shahar shook her head slowly in refusal.

"My God, Shahar, do you—or does he—*truly* understand what he's asking of me? There's too much to forgive!"

Shahar stifled an urge to smile. "That so?" she parried. "If you want forgiveness, you must learn to forgive. But, I grant you, it's easier to stew in your poisonous juices than to forgive. Nathan forgave no one. Nollie, too. If she had, she'd have some feeling for this chil' she left behind. Maybe you'll destroy yourself, too. You're free to, Mrs. Radcliffe, if that's what you truly want."

Honey was silent.

"Think what I forgave to love your daddy: I had to forgive him being white. Apaches are angels next to white men. Think on what I had to forgive to love you. I had to forgive you being white—not to mention your being another woman's chil'—my rival's baby!"

"How does one forgive someone for the color of their skin?"

"Indeed, Honey Radcliffe, how does one?" Shahar mocked gently.

Honey sighed, depression gathering over her. "Race isn't something one chooses," she observed, but instantly thought of an exception. "No one but Cameron Wolfe, that is."

"You think you're a good white Christian lady, but all that Bible reading all those years musta gone by you."

"Just what do you mean by that?"

"I heard the old negro preacher say once, 'The only way you goin' get to heaven is forgive, forgive, forgive!' 'Course, he meant slaves ought to excuse their masters. But never mind that. What the man said is true. Jesus said . . . 'if ye forgive not men their trespasses, neither will your Father forgive your trespasses.' He didn't have a message if it wasn't forgive and forgive again."

Honey frowned.

"Ain't you got nobody to forgive? I know you got angry, hateful places inside you."

"I'm not certain I can," Honey declared and turned her face away from Shahar's.

Shahar shrugged. "What'd I say about having a choice? It's everybody's right to sit and boil in his own poison. Maybe that's what Hell is—with the Devil standin' over, stirrin' the pot." Shahar took Honey's face in her hands and forced her to look her in the eye. "There's something else needs bringing up. I know you have trouble hearing me talk of your daddy and me bein' together. You think you can make your heart hard against me now that you know? You think you can hate me for loving your daddy and him for loving me?"

"I was more mother than your flesh and blood mammy! You're my chil', not hers! Look me in the eye, Honey Radcliffe, and tell me you hate me 'cause your daddy loved me more than his wife!"

The truth made Honey almost blind with rage. Her eyes filled up with tears. "Yes! I . . . hate you! I surely hate you for that!"

Shocked, Shahar felt suddenly unsure of her ground, also angry herself. Then she recognized Honey's response for what it was: the pain of the wounded child within the woman. "Just like you *hate* Mr. Cameron and *love* him at the same time."

Honey began to sob. "To think I brought this all on myself!" Honey declared. "Begging you call your Spirits. I opened Pandora's box."

"To close the lid back again, you'll have to finish what was started long ago, Honey Radcliffe. And don't pretend not to know what I mean."

"I don't know!"

To Honey's look of pain and confusion, Shahar said, "Start where it hurts most."

Honey found no comfort alone in Cameron's room. His presence lingered there and Shahar's words hammered like needles into her brain, those angry, hateful places inside Honey a full boil. How accurately she had gauged the final issue between herself and Cameron! It was not in her heart at all to forgive him or anyone! "I'm not the woman you are, Shahar! I'm not as good as you," Honey cried aloud, half mocking.

Yet even as she silently continued to rail against Cameron, a wave of pure love for him washed over Honey. Truly, she felt more surely connected with him than with any other human being, and at this recurring sense of the deep bond between them, acknowledged the essential wisdom of the Apache marriage custom, which did not require an exchange of vows between lovers as white eyes tradition did. A couple, she realized, were either united in spirit or not. No lengthy ceremony, no thousands of repeated words could unite lovers if they were not already joined in spirit.

At once perfectly at ease with that notion, Honey confessed the depth of her love for Cameron. *Perhaps*, she mused, she could go with him—follow him wherever it was that he must go, even to the Apache.

She remembered their estrangement while they had lived among the Apache. It had eaten into her soul to be alienated from him, and how bitterly she regretted having defied him. The months with her husband and the more recent time without Cameron in San Francisco had been sheer torment. She had only survived by turning her heart to stone. The most important thing was for them to be together. Surely, love of the intensity she and Cameron shared should overcome all difficulties.

But a moment later the euphoria that accompanied Honey's rush of optimism dissipated as Honey came face to face with the reality of the perhaps unbridgable gulf between them: she hated the Apache one and all.

Utterly disheartened and confused, Honey puzzled over the dilemma of loving Cameron and yet being unable to submit to his desire to return to his people.

Was it reasonable or sane, Honey reflected, to anticipate absolute unanimity of thought and feeling between a couple? Was it not possible to love someone and disagree? Honey knew well enough it was expected that a wife bow to her husband in all matters of dispute, the Bible raised as the final authority on the subject. But Honey knew she was no saint, and knew no man she had yet encountered with whom she could agree on every subject. Unquestioned agreement might be possible for the witless among the female sex, but not for a woman cursed to possess more than half a brain. That she and Cameron might never see eye to eye on more than a half dozen things in a lifetime seemed essential truth to Honey Radcliffe. But as she gazed at him from the window as he singled out another packhorse in the corral outside the barn, Honey also viewed it as essential truth that finally refusing Cameron Wolfe would be to refuse her own heart and soul. If Cameron would only feel whole living among the Apache, Honey knew she would only feel whole if she stood beside him.

Think of what it means a voice in her head screamed as she hurried down the stairs and to the barn. *The savages; the mean existence! You'll never be a white woman again. You'll die Apache!*

Apache or white eyes, I am only a woman, her heart answered as she hurried to Cameron. When he turned to face her, Honey rushed into his arms. "I love you. I don't want to live without you," she said. "Take me with you!"

At first she felt some reluctance in his embrace, but as he bent to kiss her and his kiss deepened, she was reassured. "In the morning, we'll go together into the mountains—that is, if you don't change your mind by then."

"I promise I will *never* change my mind!"

"I'll sing ceremony. We'll wait for a sign." Cameron smiled a
Honey, his love and desire for her as keen and deep as it had eve·
been. He believed her when she said she loved him, but h·
doubted that as lovers they were wise.

CHAPTER NINETY-ONE

At dawn the next day, Cameron and Honey were mounted o·
horseback trailing three pack animals, headed for the mountain·
east of Sacramento. As she followed him, Honey refused t·
contemplate any misgivings that tried to enter her mind. Sh·
thought only of how much she loved Cameron, and, truthfully
how purged she had felt when she surrendered to his love. Th·
bond between them was not of this world, she realized.

When she wondered aloud at the purpose of their excursio·
into the mountains, he had said only he had ceremony to per·
form. Honey assumed she would grow used to his need for cere·
mony as she had grown somewhat used to Shahar's calling on he·
Spirits but doubted she would ever be drawn into that world·
which seemed so alien. She believed in God, but in an oddl·
impersonal way, subject to religious ritual only very perfunctor·
ily. She knew the Apaches' Ussen required involvement in
much deeper vein.

After two days of travel, Cameron's silence finally depresse·
her. He refused to be drawn into conversation even the few time·
they had stopped to refresh themselves. When they bedded dow·
for the night, she muttered, "You didn't tell me you'd taken
vow of silence. Even if you did, I didn't."

The afternoon of the next day, when they arrived where Ca·
meron intended, Honey helped build a wickiup, bending slende·
saplings to construct the round Apache shelter, lacing the sap·
lings with brush, which they then covered completely, usin·
hides they had brought with them except for a hole left in th·
center of the wickiup for a cooking fire that would also provid·

them with needed heat. Late in November seemed an odd time for an Apache to make camp in the mountains, however low and barren of snow the mountains were.

While Honey laid a fire in the wickiup and, according to Cameron's advice, set a pail of water to heat, he cleared a large place near the shelter of brush. He piled dry wood and leaves in the center of the clearing for a bonfire, which he did not yet light.

Honey supposed they would eat soon, for they had not eaten since early morning. Instead, just as night fell, Cameron brought two buckskin bundles into the wickiup and on their bedroll laid out a beautifully beaded Apache skirt with small, round tin bangles sewn into the hem, which when they tapped against each other made a delicate bell sound. There was also a long-sleeved, long-waisted fringed blouse and long-legged moccasins for Honey, and for Cameron a warrior's breechclout, fringed shirt, moccasins, and a deerhide skullcap with long streamers of eagle feathers, which when worn would stretch to the ground at the back of the head.

Without a word, Cameron began to undress her and himself. When both were naked, he used the warm water heated on the fire to bathe her with suds from soap made from the yucca root, including her hair. Then he invited her to do the same for him. Unbearably excited, Honey wanted and expected Cameron to make love to her, an opportunity which he had had, but did not take during their time on the trail. She drew him into her arousing embrace and kissed him, but he withdrew gently and handed her the Apache skirt. Reluctantly, Honey dressed in the splendid indian garb and watched as Cameron did the same.

When they were both dressed, Cameron removed the amulet he once had given her from his own neck and put it over her head. "Again this is yours—now it's your wedding ring."

Honey shivered, but was not truly cold.

He then poured mescal in two large brass cups, which they drank as they sat next to the fire. Honey swallowed her portion nervously. He poured her more. "Since we have been together, there's been no one but you in my heart. I think of us as married —Apache married." Honey smiled at the almost simple innocence of this notion. "You know Apache marriage doesn't include any saying of vows."

Honey nodded.

"Our promises to each other should be enough. But you're so white eyes, I feel you need something more to seal us together as man and wife."

Honey smiled. Warm with mescal, she felt the approach of giddiness. "You see through me," she said, touched by his sentiment. "I'm not yet a pagan, but I've the feeling I soon shall be."

Beneath his white eyes clothes Cameron had worn a medicine pouch, which he had kept on when he bathed and changed into Apache garb. Now he took the pouch from around his neck. Inside was the sacred golden tule pollen Apache used for ceremony, and with it Cameron marked Honey's forehead with an inverted V and both her cheekbones with parallel lines. He did the same to himself, and poured more mescal, which they drank slowly.

Next he rolled tobacco in an oak leaf, lit the cigarette, and blew smoke into the wickiup, first to the east and then to all other directions sunwise. He covered Honey's head with smoke, then led her to the clearing he had made earlier, and lit the bonfire, which flamed readily and brilliantly. He added large pieces of wood until their camp blazed with firelight and almost too much heat. More than a campfire, it was a sacred blaze.

Next Cameron lit two fire sticks, gave them to Honey, and then took up a pottery drum, which he began to beat steadily in time with her pulse, which quickened as did the drumbeat. He faced her, and she stared at him, feeling herself drawn into his eyes, into his soul. Mesmerized, she only faintly heard the ululating Apache cry fill the night air. It filled her head, her heart, her whole being.

Cameron moved in time to the drumbeat, taking gliding steps so that his feet never left the ground. Instinctively, without consciously noting them, Honey followed his motions, and they danced together without touching as heat from the fire dried her shorn hair to a soft cloud of spun gold; he, by contrast, was disturbingly dark. Her beauty dazzled him; indeed, she personified the pagan goddess.

After a long while, Cameron stopped and withdrew sacred turquoise dust from the folds of his moccasins and threw it onto the fire, then resumed dancing. She continued to follow him.

When later he began to sing, he seemed to be transported to another plane.

Upon this earth
On which we live,
Ussen has Power.
Deer Power He grants me
For the good of my people.

I call on Deer Power,
Which Ussen has given me,
For success in the hunt.
I beseech Deer to
Surrender his life for
The good of my people.

I seek Deer Power
To use as love magic,
To call to my side
The woman I love,
For the good of my people.

I use Love Magic
To claim my beloved,
For love between a man
And a woman is
Sacred to Ussen.

We come together
This lifetime to learn
The meaning of Love:
Sacrifice and forgiveness,
Which is alien to man
But natural to Ussen.

We abide
As Ussen instructs
In peace with
All of our brothers.
We pray for
Strength in life's way.

We give love to each other
For the sake of our people,
For between a man
And a woman Love
Is sacred to Ussen.

Cameron repeated the verses in the same sequence over and over. Honey learned them, and together they danced and sang ceremony, drank and feasted until dawn, when, after throwing pollen onto the fire and greeting the morning in song, Cameron carried Honey into the wickiup and made love to her. Long hours of dancing and singing ceremony did not exhaust but fueled their passion as they came together joyously, fiercely, the light of the small, smokeless fire inside the wickiup casting a mantle of shimmering gold over their beautiful bodies. The sight they had of each other left a dreamlike impression on their senses which only the shuddering depths of ecstasy dispelled.

Afterward there was silence, a stillness in the mountain forest that even Honey, in moments of restlessness, could not violate; she was deafened to everything but the stirrings of her love for Cameron. She gazed on the white eyes Apache whom she believed she was destined to follow to the ends of the earth and knew it mattered not at all what blood flowed to him through the generations, or the color of his skin, hair, or eyes, but only what he was at heart. Formed human, what distinguished him from another was not something readily seen. Cameron had told her Apaches believed Ussen would not recognize an indian if he cut his hair. But Honey believed God was not so easily fooled as men. He saw not our hair, faces, color, or ornamentation but knew our hearts. The man who lay beside her now was more Apache than white eyes, and what mattered was only how his experience transformed him for good or ill and whether, after all, he still had the heart to love her.

As united by love as mortals can be, for three more nights the lovers joyfully repeated their ceremony. When they woke in the early afternoon after the last night of ceremony, Cameron suddenly broke his silence. "I must return to my people."

Honey nodded in solemn understanding.

"But I'll not be taking you with me. You must go back to your people as I must go back to mine."

Stunned and alarmed, Honey remembered the Apache devotion to revenge, and, terrified, wondered if the last nights had only been an elaborate scheme to achieve her final humiliation. Tears streamed from her eyes. "After all this, you'll abandon me?" she cried trying to hold at bay the hysteria she felt rising within her. "Were these nights all a sham? You brought me as your wife before Ussen, or did I imagine it?" Honey stared wildly at Cameron.

"It would be wrong for me to take you, and wrong for you to go. I trust you'd've tried to be Apache, but you're too damned white eyes; you'd never belong."

"I think I've done rather well as a heathen these past nights," she said indignantly in her defense and threw herself against him fiercely. "I love you! Don't leave me. Please," she begged, "take me with you!" The words seemed to come from a stranger's mouth, but she meant every syllable.

"I sang ceremony these last nights as much for myself as for you. I hoped for some miracle, some act of heaven to make you mine finally; forever. You say you love me, and I believe you, but you love some part of me, not the man I am. Something won't let you. Just now you mocked me by calling yourself a heathen. Part of your heart is still against me."

"What do you mean my heart is against you? I love no one on this earth if not you!"

"How can you truly love me when you've endured so much because of me? Because of me you were raped, your husband was shamed and driven to kill himself. And you shamed and shunned because of it. How can you love me with all this in your heart? When I'm Apache and always will be? How long before our joy turns bitter?"

Honey sat before Cameron without expression. He wished fervently that she would make a heated denial. When she said nothing, he continued. "In each song to thank Ussen for morning, I also beseeched Him to send me a sign that I should carry you with me back to my people. But I've had none." Cameron looked at Honey and felt as if his heart would break. "The sign I needed has always been in your eyes—you have never been able to hide your horror at my being Apache. I tried not to see your hatred because I love you. But I see it even now."

"You can't read my heart. You must trust I love you enough to go with you. You can't refuse me!"

Full of sorrow Cameron said, "Your true heart is in your eyes, Honey. You despise the Apache in me and did from the moment I revealed myself to you."

Tears poured down Honey's cheeks. "If you were right, I would *never* agree to go with you!"

"Say 'I love you for being Apache,'" Cameron challenged cold-bloodedly.

Honey tried, but the words seemed to stick in her throat. When it was obvious she had failed, Honey covered her face with her hands.

He pulled her hands away from her face and held them. "I am Apache!" Cameron cried, knowing he must be cruel to make her understand and to sear his own heart against its pain. "I am the savage you fear! When I return to my people, I will kill white eyes who come to kill savages!"

Honey wrenched herself from him and threw herself down on their bed. She wept as if she would never be consoled. Cameron had managed to find all of the weak joints of their union, and rather than shoring up those points, had pulled out all of the pegs. She remembered he once had dragged her into an icy stream and nearly drowned her to make his point. Again Honey felt she was drowning. Again she faced death.

Suddenly Honey rose from her bed and turned and cried out to Cameron. "You want the worst of what lies in my heart?" she spit at him. "Yes! I hate the savage part of you that comprehends Coyote's raping me and, perhaps, murdering me as an act of revenge; that part of the Apache way that makes revenge an obligation of those who survive; the part of you that refuses to be a white man! I hate you for being the instrument of Nathan's death. I didn't love him the way I love you, but . . . oh, God, no one should be driven to do what he did. I hated the notoriety; I felt covered in filth, but I hate you no more than I hate myself."

Once again Honey was overwhelmed by her tears. "Is that what you want to hear? Is that the sign from heaven you had in mind?"

Honey's sobbing knifed through Cameron.

"Isn't this what you want from me—the confession of the darkest secrets of my heart?"

Cameron reached to hold her against him. "I want only for you to understand."

Honey began to scream amid her tears and flung herself down on the bedroll again. Realizing she was hysterical, she tried desperately to pull herself together and after a while was reduced to mere shuddering sobs. She felt his hands begin to stroke her back. At first she bristled at his touch but then relented to their soothing tenderness.

After a long while, he covered her with blankets then left her side to pack for the journey back to Sacramento. He added firewood to the embers in the center of the wickiup for her warmth while he removed and packed the hides that covered the wickiup frame. He ached for what he must do—leave her behind when he returned to the Apache—but he knew he was right. Her outburst admitting her lingering hatred had ripped at his core but proved his deepest instincts correct.

When the last of their things were packed, he knelt beside her. "Time for us to go." He held out a hand to help her up.

Honey took his hand and led Cameron into the clearing where they had sung ceremony over the last four nights. As they stood in the cold bright light of morning, she held both of his hands tightly in hers and spoke calmly, clearly. "Before Ussen, I forgive you for being Apache, for understanding and desiring to live their way. I forgive myself for loving an Apache not a white man— that I may love you completely as you are with no dark places of hatred left in my heart. Before Ussen, I promise my love for you surpasses everything else between us."

Her face full of love, her eyes at last clear of the reservations and fear he had seen in them, Cameron smiled at Honey, pulled her into his arms and kissed her, the healing warmth of the sun touching them for the first time that morning. As they parted and turned together into the light, a doe and her fawn stepped into the clearing a few feet ahead of them and gazed at them without fear or surprise.

Smiling up at him, Honey put her arms around Cameron once more, knowing if he still needed one, the Apache warrior had his sign.

CHAPTER NINETY-TWO

It was unlike Shahar to go back to bed after getting up in the morning, but she had come to trust the wet nurse that Cameron had found to look after Thomas. Lately she had been feeling but avoiding a strong tug to slip away for an audience with her Spirits. However, now before Cameron and Honey returned seemed a good time to indulge her instinct.

The place she traveled to seemed in the throes of a whirlwind.

She saw Cameron and Honey, and demons fighting over them. The wind and the battle raged on but Shahar watched the scene calmly.

Finally the wind died. Cameron held Honey in his arms and in their faces she saw a peace of the soul Shahar rarely saw nor enjoyed herself. She heard their words to each other.

"We'll go home now," he said.

"Home?"

"Home to Sacramento."

"That's not home."

"It's mine. Ours now." Cameron tried to explain. "When a warrior faces death, he is changed, given Power to take to his people to use for their good. Loving you, I am also changed. Your love makes me whole. Knowing you love *me* for who I am, I'm content to stay with you here. We will build our lives between two worlds."

Honey leaned against Cameron and they held each other tightly as she wept for joy this time. Then she raised herself to look at him. "I could go with you if you must," she promised, clear eyed.

Cameron would remember these words of love as long as he lived. "Maybe I'm not white eyes or Apache, but a different breed. And, you, Honey, not just a woman but a healer—a different breed also."

"Yes," Honey answered renewed by the depth of his obvious love, "a healer of men—whatever their color."

EPILOGUE

Sacramento Valley, California
June 1870

Shahar held Lillianne in one arm and helped Thomas climb into the summer swing Cameron had built with his own hands to Shahar's specifications for just this purpose. When she sat next to Thomas, he laid his head in Shahar's lap and put his thumb in his mouth. His face, a lighter color than his mother's, held a serious expression, his eyelids already heavy. Settling comfortably, Shahar took a moment to decide on the correct tempo for rocking the swing. Thus began the nightly ritual at sunset on the nursery porch at Cameron Wolfe and Dr. Greer's home, at least in summertime.

This evening as usual, Cameron rode into the yard just as Shahar came onto the porch with "her babies." Honey came out to greet him, his arrival at this time of day always an occasion of joy for his wife. Against the sky deep with shades of mauve and gray, the sight of him sitting erect and perfect in the saddle recalled the lean, hard-hewn warrior to Honey's mind and made her heart catch. When he dismounted and came to her side, she flung her arms around Cameron in welcome and received his kiss. Then they hurried to settle on the steps near the nursery porch so they would not miss any of the quiet ritual that had lately come to usher in their nights together.

Shahar prepared Thomas and Lillianne for bed, first with a prayer from Psalms, then, nattering, as if idly, in her own melodious patois until she began to sing a lullaby, words to live by.

> "Bless the Lord, O my soul; and all that is within me, bless His holy name. Bless the Lord, O my soul, and forget not all His benefits: Who forgiveth all thine iniquities; Who healeth all thy diseases; Who redeemeth thy life from destruction; Who crowneth thee with loving kindness and tender mercies; Who satisfieth thy mouth with good things; so that thy youth is renewed like the eagle's."

After a silence, Shahar began a soft soliloquy that varied little day to day:

"Babies, be wary of folks don' know a thing they be talkin' 'bout. When th' gossip wonder how come Thomas be so dark, an' his mama an' papa an' baby blue-eyed, you jus' smile an' say, 'We how th' Lord made us: each one a diff'ren' breed.' You say, 'We livin' how Lord Jesus tol' us: "Love one another, as I have loved you." Th' worl' too dang'rous for we not be brothers.'"

When Shahar paused, Tommy would nod sleepily, then turn on his side and strive to keep his eyes at least half-open as she sang her lullaby. On hearing that familiar alto, sometimes the children's mother would put her head on her husband's shoulder to be held tenderly by him, close her eyes, and dream herself a child again.

> *Night be callin',*
> *Stars be fallin';*
> *Babies close they eyes.*
>
> *Souls be nearin',*
> *No need fearin';*
> *Babies close they eyes.*
>
> *Heartbeats hummin',*
> *Dreams be comin';*
> *Babies close they eyes.*
>
> *No use fleein'*
> *What I seein';*
> *Babies close they eyes.*
>
>
> *All the hatin'*
> *Pleasin' Satan;*
> *Babies close they eyes.*
>
> *Shahar seein'*
> *Love be freein';*
> *Babies close they eyes.*

Han's together;
Hearts together;
Babies close they eyes.

World still needin'
Diff'ren' breedin';
Open up our eyes.

Can't be stallin',
Lord be callin';
Open up our eyes.

Love be only
One kine color;
Open up our eyes.

Lord he say,
Love one 'Nother:
Open up our eyes.

We all be
Sister 'n' brother;
Open up our eyes.

But, Lord knows,
Seein's not b'lievin',
If peoples
Close they eyes.

ABOUT THE AUTHOR

JESSIE FORD, her husband, two sons, and a dog live with three cats who appear to believe they are in charge. By the time this book is published, the menagerie will have settled joyfully in a new home in Vista, California.

Ballantine brings you
The Best in Modern Fiction